ACCLAIM FO

"Be prepared to lose sleep!"

int

The Devil's Colony

"I love this!"

—PIERS ANTHONY,
international bestselling author of
A Spell for Chameleon

"J.R. Rain delivers a blend of action and wit that always entertains. Quick with the one-liners, but his characters are fully fleshed out (even the undead ones) and you'll come back again and again."

—SCOTT NICHOLSON,
bestselling author of *Liquid Fear*

"*Dark Horse* is the best book I've read in a long time!"

—GEMMA HALLIDAY,
bestselling author of *Spying in High Heels*

"*Moon Dance* is absolutely brilliant!" —LISA TENZIN-DOLMA,
author of *Understanding the Planetary Myths*

"Powerful stuff!"

—AIDEN JAMES,
bestselling author of *The Vampires' Last Lover*

"*Moon Dance* is a must read. If you like Janet Evanovich's Stephanie Plum, bounty hunter, be prepared to love J.R. Rain's Samantha Moon, vampire private investigator."

—EVE PALUDAN, author of *Letters from David*

"Impossible to put down, J.R. Rain's *Moon Dance* is a fabulous urban fantasy replete with multifarious and unusual characters, a perfectly synchronized plot, vibrant dialogue and sterling witticism all wrapped in a voice that is as beautiful as it is rich and vividly intense as it is relaxed."

—APRIL VINE, author of *The Midnight Rose*

Samantha Moon

The First Four

VAMPIRE FOR HIRE

NOVELS

Plus the Christmas Moon *Novella and a Never-Before-Published Short Story*

J.R. RAIN

BENBELLA BOOKS | DALLAS, TEXAS

First BenBella Books Edition 2012

BenBella Books, Inc.
10300 N. Central Expy., Suite 400
Dallas, TX 75231
www.benbellabooks.com
Send feedback to feedback@benbellabooks.com

Printed in the United States of America
10 9 8 7 6 5 4 3 2 1

Library of Congress Cataloging-in-Publication Data is available for this title.

ISBN 978-1-937856-17-5

Proofreading by James Fraleigh and Cape Cod Compositors, Inc.
Cover design by Sarah Dombrowsky
Cover art by Cliff Nielsen
Text design and composition by E. J. Strongin, Neuwirth & Associates, Inc.
Printed by Berryville

Distributed by Perseus Distribution
www.perseusdistribution.com
To place orders through Perseus Distribution:
Tel: 800-343-4499
Fax: 800-351-5073
E-mail: orderentry@perseusbooks.com

VAMPIRE FOR HIRE SERIES

Moon Dance

Vampire Moon

American Vampire

Moon Child

Christmas Moon

Vampire Dawn

CONTENTS

BOOK 1

Moon Dance

Vampire for Hire #1

DEDICATION

This book is dedicated to mothers everywhere:
Our amazing, selfless, unsung heroes.
Love you, ma.

ACKNOWLEDGMENTS

I would like to thank
Eve Paludan, Liisa Lee (who's so nice she dots her "i's" twice),
and Sandy Johnston for their
generous assistance with this book.

Moon Dance

1.

I was folding laundry in the dark and watching Judge Judy rip this guy a new asshole when the doorbell rang.

I flipped down a pair of Oakley wrap-around sunglasses and, still holding a pair of little Anthony's cotton briefs in one hand, opened the front door.

The light, still painfully bright, poured in from outside. I squinted behind my shades and could just made out the image of a UPS deliveryman.

And, oh, what an image it was.

As my eyes adjusted to the light, a hunky guy with tan legs and beefy arms materialized through the screen door before me. He grinned at me easily, showing off a perfect row of white teeth. Spiky yellow hair protruded from under his brown cap. The guy should have been a model, or at least my new best friend.

"Mrs. Moon?" he asked. His eyes seemed particularly searching and hungry, and I wondered if I had stepped onto the set of a porno movie. Interestingly, a sort of warning bell sounded in my head. Warning bells are tricky to discern, and I automatically assumed this one was telling me to stay away from Mr. Beefy, or risk damaging my already rocky marriage.

"You got her," I said easily, ignoring the warning bells.

"I've got a package here for you."

"You don't say."

"I'll need for you to sign the delivery log." He held up an electronic gizmo-thingy that must have been the aforementioned delivery log.

"I'm sure you do," I said, and opened the screen door and stuck a hand out. He looked at my very pale hand, paused, and then placed the electronic thing-a-majig in it. As I signed it, using a plastic-tipped pen, my signature appeared in the display box as an arthritic mess. The deliveryman watched me intently through the screen door. I don't like to be watched intently. In fact, I prefer to be ignored and forgotten.

"Do you always wear sunglasses indoors?" he asked casually, but I sensed his hidden question: *And what sort of freak are you?*

"Only during the day. I find them redundant at night." I opened the screen door again and exchanged the log doohickey for a small square package. "Thank you," I said. "Have a good day."

He nodded and left, and I watched his cute little buns for a moment longer, and then shut the solid oak door completely. Sweet darkness returned to my home. I pulled up the sunglasses and sat down in a particularly worn dining room chair. Someday I was going to get these things re-upholstered.

The package was heavily taped, but a few deft strokes of my painted red nail took care of all that. I opened the lid and peered inside.

Shining inside was an ancient golden medallion. An intricate Celtic cross was engraved across the face of it, and embedded within the cross, formed by precisely cut rubies, were three red roses.

In the living room, Judge Judy was calmly explaining to the defendant what an idiot he was. Although I agreed, I turned the TV off, deciding that this medallion needed my full concentration.

After all, it was the same medallion worn by my attacker six years earlier.

2.

There was no return address and no note. Other than the medallion, the box was empty. I left the gleaming artifact in the box and shut the lid. Seeing it again brought back some horrible memories. Memories I have been doing my best to forget.

I put the box in a cabinet beneath the china hutch, and then went back to Judge Judy and putting away the laundry. At 3:30 p.m., I lathered my skin with heaping amounts of sun block, donned a wide gardening hat and carefully stepped outside.

The pain, as always, was intense and searing. Hell, I could have been cooking over an open fire pit. Truly, I had no business being out in the sun, but I had my kids to pick up, dammit.

So I hurried from the front steps and crossed the driveway and into the open garage. My dream was to have a home with an attached garage. But, for now, I had to make the daily sprint.

Once in the garage and out of the direct glare of the spring sun, I could breathe again. I could also smell my burning flesh.

Blech!

Luckily, the Ford Windstar minivan was heavily tinted, and so when I backed up and put the thing into drive, I was doing okay again. Granted, not great, but okay.

I picked up my son and daughter from school, got some cheeseburgers from Burger King and headed home. Yes, I know, bad mom, but after doing chores all day, I definitely was not going to cook.

Once at home, the kids went straight to their room and I went straight to the bathroom where I removed my hat and sunglasses, and used a washcloth to remove the extra sunscreen. Hell, I ought to buy stock in Coppertone. Soon the kids were hard at work saving our world from Haloes and had lapsed into a rare and unsettling silence. Perhaps it was the quiet before the storm.

My only appointment for the day was right on time, and since I work from home, I showed him to my office in the back. His name was Kingsley Fulcrum and he sat across from me in a client chair, filling it to capacity. He was tall and broad shouldered and wore his tailored suit well. His thick black hair, speckled with gray, was jauntily disheveled and worn long over his collar. Kingsley was a striking man and would have been the poster boy for dashing rogues if not for the two scars on his face. Then again, maybe poster boys for rogues did have scars on their faces. Anyway, one was on his left cheek and the other was on his forehead, just above his left eye. Both were round and puffy. And both were recent.

He caught me staring at the scars. I looked away, embarrassed. "How can I help you, Mr. Fulcrum?"

"How long have you been a private investigator, Mrs. Moon?" he asked.

"Six years," I said.

"What did you do before that?"

"I was a federal agent."

He didn't say anything, and I could feel his eyes on me. God, I hate when I can feel eyes on me. The silence hung for longer than I was comfortable with and I answered his unspoken question. "I had an accident and was forced to work at home."

"May I ask what kind of accident?"

"No."

He raised his eyebrows and nodded. He might have turned a pale shade of red. "Do you have a list of references?"

"Of course."

I turned to my computer, brought up the reference file and printed him out the list. He took it and scanned the names briefly. "Mayor Hartley?" he asked.

"Yes," I said.

"He hired you?"

"He did. I believe that's the direct line to his personal assistant."

"Can I ask what sort of help you gave the mayor?"

"No."

"I understand. Of course you can't divulge that kind of information."

"How exactly can I help you, Mr. Fulcrum?" I asked again.

"I need you to find someone."

"Who?"

"The man who shot me," he said. "Five times."

3.

The furious sounds of my kids erupting into an argument suddenly came through my closed office door. In particular, Anthony's high-pitched shriek. Sigh. The storm broke.

I gave Kingsley an embarrassed smile. "Could you please hold on?"

"Duty calls," he said, smiling. Nice smile.

I marched through my single story home and into the small bedroom my children shared. Anthony was on top of Tammy. Tammy was holding the remote control away from her body with one hand and fending off her little brother with the other. I came in just in time to witness him sinking his teeth into her hand. She yelped and bopped him over the ear with the remote control. He had just gathered himself to make a full-scale leap onto her back, when I stepped into the room and grabbed each by their collar and separated them. I felt as if I had separated two ravenous wolverines. Anthony's fingers clawed for his sister's throat. I wondered if they realized they were both hovering a few inches off the floor. When they had both calmed down, I set them down on their feet. Their collars were ruined.

"Anthony, we do not bite in this household. Tammy, give me the remote control."

"But Mom," said Anthony, in that shriekingly high-pitched voice that he used to irritate me. "I was watching 'Pokemon' and she turned the channel."

"We each get one half hour after school," Tammy said smugly. "And you were well into my half hour."

"But you were on the phone talking to Richaaard."

"Tammy, give your brother the remote control. He gets to finish his TV show. You lost your dibs by talking to Richaaard." They both laughed. "I have a client in my office. If I hear any more loud voices, you will both be auctioned off on eBay. I could use the extra money."

I left them and headed back to the office. Kingsley was perusing my bookshelves. He looked at me before I had a chance to say anything and raised his eyebrows.

"You have an interest in the occult," he said, fingering a hardback book. "In particular, vampirism."

"Yeah, well, we all need a hobby," I said.

"An interesting hobby, that," he said.

I sat behind my desk. It was time to change the subject. "So you want me to find the man who shot you five times. Anything else?"

He moved away from my book shelves and sat across from me again. He raised a fairly bushy eyebrow. On him, the bushy eyebrow somehow worked.

"Anything else?" he asked, grinning. "No, I think that will be quite enough."

And then it hit me. I thought I recognized the name and face. "You were on the news a few months back," I said suddenly.

He nodded once. "Aye, that was me. Shot five times in the head for all the world to see. Not my proudest moment."

Did he just say aye? I had a strange sense that I had suddenly gone back in time. How far back, I didn't know, but further enough back where men said aye.

"You were ambushed and shot. I can't imagine it would have been anyone's proudest moment. But you survived, and that's all that matters, right?"

"For now," he said. "Next on the list would be to find the man who shot me." He sat forward. "Everything you need is at your disposal. Nothing of mine is off limits. Speak to anyone you need to, although I ask you to be discreet."

"Discretion is sometimes not possible."

"Then I trust you to use your best judgment."

Good answer. He took out a business card and wrote something on the back. "That's my cell number. Please call me if you need anything." He wrote something under his number. "And that's the name and number of the acting homicide detective working my case. His name is Sherbet, and although I found him to be forthcoming and professional, I didn't like his conclusions."

"Which were?"

"He tends to think my attack was nothing but a random shooting."

"And you disagree?"

"Wholeheartedly."

We discussed my retainer and he wrote me a check. The check was bigger than we discussed.

"I don't mean to be rude," said Kingsley as he stood and tucked his expensive fountain pen inside his expensive jacket, "but are you ill?"

I've heard the question a thousand times.

"No, why?" I asked brightly.

"You seem pale."

"Oh, that's my Irish complexion, lad," I said, and winked.

He stared at me a moment longer, and then returned my wink and left.

4.

When Kingsley was gone I punched his name into my web browser.

Dozens of online newspaper articles came up, and from these I garnered that Kingsley was a rather successful defense attorney, known for doing whatever it took to get his clients off the hook, often on seemingly inane technicalities. He was apparently worth his weight in gold.

I thought of his beefy shoulders.

A lot of weight. Muscular weight.

Down girl.

I continued scanning the headlines until I found the one I wanted. It was on a web page for a local L.A. TV station. I clicked on a video link. Thank God for high speed internet. A small media window appeared on my screen, and shortly thereafter I watched a clip that had first appeared on local TV news. The clip had gone national, due to its sensationally horrific visuals.

A reporter appeared first in the screen, a young Hispanic woman looking quite grave. Over her shoulder was a picture of the Fullerton Municipal Courthouse. The next shot was a grainy image from the courthouse security camera itself. In the frame were two men and two women, all dressed impeccably, all looking important. They were crossing in front of the courthouse itself. In football terms, they formed a sort of moving huddle, although I rarely think of things in football terms and understand little of the stupid sport.

I immediately recognized the tall one with the wavy black hair as Kingsley Fulcrum, looking rugged and dashing.

Down girl.

As the group approaches the courthouse steps, a smallish man steps out from behind the trunk of a white birch. Three of the four great defenders pay the man little mind. The one who does, a blond-haired woman with glasses and big hips, looks up and frowns. She probably frowns because the little man is reaching rather menacingly inside his coat pocket. His thick mane of black hair is disheveled, and somehow even his thick mustache looks disheveled, too. The woman, still frowning, turns back to the group.

And what happens next still sends shivers down my spine.

From inside his tweed jacket, the little man removes a short pistol. We now know it's a .22. At the time, no one sees him remove the pistol. The short man, perhaps ten feet away from the group of four, takes careful aim, and fires.

Kingsley's head snaps back. The bullet enters over his left eye.

I lean forward, staring at my computer screen, rapt, suddenly wishing I had a bowl of popcorn, or at least a bag of peanut M&Ms. That is, until I remembered that I can no longer eat either.

Anyway, Kingsley's cohorts immediately scatter like chickens before a hawk. The shorter man even ducks and rolls dramatically as if he's recently seen duty in the Middle East and his military instincts are kicking in.

Kingsley is shot again. This time in the neck, where a small red dot appears above his collar. Blood quickly flows down his shirt. Instead of collapsing, instead of dying after being shot point blank in the head and neck, Kingsley actually turns and looks at the man.

As if the man had simply called his name.

As if the man had not shot him twice.

What transpires next would be comical if it wasn't so heinous. Kingsley proceeds to duck behind a nearby tree. The shooter, intent on killing Kingsley, bypasses going around a park bench and instead jumps over it. Smoothly. Landing squarely on his feet while squeezing off a few more rounds that appear to hit Kingsley in the neck and face. Meanwhile, the big attorney ducks and weaves behind the tree. This goes on for seemingly an eternity, but in reality just a few seconds. A sick game of tag, except Kingsley's getting tagged with real bullets.

And still the attorney does not go down.

Doesn't even collapse.

The shooter seemingly realizes he's wasting his time and dashes away from the tree, disappearing from the screen. No one has come to Kingsley's rescue. The other attorneys are long gone. Kingsley is left to fend for himself, his only protection the tree, which has been torn and shredded by the impacting stray bullets.

Witnesses would later report that the shooter left in a Ford pickup. No one tried to stop him, and I really didn't blame them.

I paused the picture on Kingsley. Blood is frozen on his cheeks and forehead, even on his open, outstretched palms. His face is a picture of confusion and horror and shock. In just twenty-three seconds, his life had been utterly turned upside down. Of course, in those very same twenty-three seconds most people would have died.

But not Kingsley. I wondered why.

5.

I was at the Fullerton police station, sitting across from a homicide detective named Sherbet. It was the late evening, and most of the staff had left for the day.

"You're keeping me from my kid," he said. Sherbet was wearing a long-sleeved shirt folded up at the elbows, revealing heavily muscled forearms covered in dark hair. The dark hair was mixed with a smattering of gray. I thought it looked sexy as hell. His tie was loosened, and he looked irritable, to say the least.

"I apologize," I said. "This was the only time I could make it today."

"I'm glad I can work around your busy schedule, Mrs. Moon. I wouldn't want to inconvenience you in any way."

His office was simple and uncluttered. No pictures on the

wall. Just a desk, a computer, a filing cabinet and some visitor's chairs. His desk had a few picture frames, but they were turned toward him. From my angle, I could only see the price tags.

I gave him my most winning smile. "I certainly appreciate your time, detective." I had on plenty of blush, so that my cheeks appeared human.

The smile worked. He blushed himself. "Yeah, well, let's make this quick. My kid's playing a basketball game tonight, and I wouldn't want to miss him running up and down the court with no clue what the hell is going on around him."

"Sounds like a natural."

"A natural dolt. Wife says I should just leave him alone. The trouble is, if I leave him alone, he tends to want to play Barbies with the neighborhood girls."

"That worries you?" I asked.

"Yeah."

"You think he could turn out gay?"

He shrugged uncomfortably, and said nothing. It was a touchy subject for him, obviously.

"How old is your son?" I asked.

"Eight."

"Perhaps he's a little Casanova. Perhaps he sees the benefits of playing with girls, rather than boys."

"Perhaps," said Sherbet. "For now, he plays basketball."

"Even though he's clueless."

"Where there's a will there's a way."

"Even if it's your will and your way?" I asked.

"For now, it's the only way." He paused, then looked a little confused. He shook his head like a man realizing he had been mumbling out loud. "How the hell did we get on the subject of my kid's sexuality?"

"I forget," I said, shrugging.

He reached over and straightened the folder in front of him. The folder hadn't been crooked, now it was less uncrooked. "Yeah, well, let's get down to business. Here's the file. I made a copy of it for you. It's against procedures to give you a copy, but you check out okay. Hell, you worked for the federal government. And why the hell you've gone private is your own damn business."

I reached for the file, but he placed a big hand on it. "This is just between you and me. I don't normally give police files to private dicks."

"Luckily I'm not your average private dick."

"A dick with no dick," he said.

"Clever, detective," I said.

"Not really."

"No, not really," I admitted. "I just really want the file."

He nodded and lifted his palm, and I promptly stuffed the file into my handbag. "Is there anything you can tell me that's perhaps not in the file?"

He shook his head, but it was just a knee-jerk reaction. In the process of shaking his head, he was actually deep in thought. "It should all be in there." He rubbed the dark stubble at his chin. The dark stubble was also mixed with some gray. "You know, I always suspected the guy doing the shooting was a client of his. I dunno, call it a hunch. But this attorney's been around a while, and he's pissed off a lot of people. Trouble is: who's got the time to go through all of his past files?"

"Not a busy homicide detective," I said, playing along.

"Damn straight," he said.

"Any chance it was just a random shooting?" I asked.

"Sure. Of course. Those happen all the time."

"But you don't think so."

"No," he said.

"Why?" I asked.

The detective was used to this kind of exchange. He worked in a business where if you didn't ask questions, you didn't find answers. If my questions bothered him, he didn't show it, other than he seemed to be impatient to get this show on the road.

"Seemed premeditative. And no robbery attempt. Also seemed to be making a statement, as well."

"By shooting him in the face?"

"And by shooting him outside the courthouse. His place of work. Makes you think it was business related."

I nodded. Good point. I decided not to tell the detective he had a good point. Men tend to think all of their points were good, and they sure as hell didn't need me to boost their already inflated egos.

I'm cynical that way.

He stood from his desk and retrieved a sport jacket from a coat rack. He was a fit man with a cop's build. He also had a cop's mustache. He would have looked better without the mustache, but it wasn't my place to suggest so. Besides, who better to wear a cop mustache than a cop?

"Now it's time to go watch my son screw up the game of basketball," he said.

"Maybe basketball's not his game."

"And playing with girls is?"

"It's not a bad alternative," I said, then added, "You think there's a chance you're reading a little too much into all of this with your son?"

"I'm a cop. I read too much into everything." He paused and locked his office door, which I found oddly amusing and ironic since his office was located in the heart of a police station. "Take you, for instance."

I didn't want to take me for instance. I changed the subject. "I'm sure you're a very good officer. How long have you been on the force?"

He ignored my question. "I wondered why you insisted on meeting me in the evening." As he spoke, he placed his hand lightly at the small of my back and steered me through the row of cluttered desks. His hand was unwavering and firm. "When I asked you on the phone the reason behind the late meeting you had mentioned something about being busy with other clients. But when I called your office later that day to tell you that I was going to be delayed, you picked up the phone immediately." He paused and opened a clear glass door. On the door was etched FPD. "Perhaps you were meeting your clients in the office. Or perhaps you were in-between clients. But when I asked if you had a few minutes you sounded unharried and pleasant. Sure, you said, how can I help you?"

"Well, I pride myself on customer service," I said.

He was behind me, and I didn't see him smile. But I sensed that he had done so. In fact, I knew he had smiled. Call it a side effect.

He said, "Now that I see you, I see you have a skin disorder of some type."

"Why, lieutenant, you certainly know how to make a girl feel warm and fuzzy."

"And that's the other thing. When I shook your hand, it felt anything but warm and fuzzy," he said.

"So what are you getting at?" I asked. We had reached the front offices. We were standing behind the main reception desk. The room was quiet for the time being. Outside the smoky gray doors, I could see Commonwealth Avenue, and across that, Amerige City Park, which sported a nice little league field.

He shrugged and smirked at me. "If I had two guesses, I would say that you were either a vampire, or, like I said, you had a skin condition."

"What does your heart tell you?" I asked.

He studied me closely. Outside, commuters were working their way through downtown Fullerton. Red taillights burned through the smoky glass. Something passed across his gaze. An understanding of some sort. Or perhaps wonder. Something. But then he grinned and his cop mustache rose like a referee signaling a touchdown.

"A skin disease, of course," he said. "You need to stay out of the sun."

"Bingo," I said. "You're a hell of a detective."

And with that I left. Outside, I saw that my hands were shaking. The son-of-a-bitch had me rattled. He was one hell of an intuitive cop.

I hate that.

6.

I was boxing at a sparring club in Fullerton called Jacky's. The club was geared towards women, but there were always a few men hanging around the club. These men often dressed better than the women. I suspected homosexuality. The club gave kickboxing and traditional boxing lessons. I preferred the traditional boxing lessons, and always figured that if the time came in a fight that I had to kick, there was only one place my foot was going.

Crotch City.

I come here three times a week after picking the kids up from school and taking them to their grandmother's home in Brea. Boxing is perhaps one of the most exhausting exercises ever invented, especially when you box in three-minute drills, as I was currently doing, which simulated actual boxing rounds.

My trainer was an Irishman named Jacky. Jacky wore a green bandanna over a full head of graying hair. He was a powerfully built man of medium height, a little fat now, but not soft. He must have been sixty, but looked forty. He was an ex-professional boxer in Ireland, where he had been something of a legend, or that's what he tells me. His crooked nose had been broken countless times, which might or might not have been the result of boxing matches. Maybe he was just clumsy. Amazingly enough, the man rarely sweat, which was something I could not claim. As my personal trainer, his sole responsibility was to hold out his padded palms and to yell at me. He did both well. All with a thick Irish accent.

"C'mon, push yourself. You're dropping your fists, lass!"

Dropping one's fists was a big no-no in Jacky's world, on par with his hatred for anything un-Irish.

So I raised my fists. Again.

During these forty-five minute workouts with Jacky, I hated that little Irish bastard with all my heart.

"You're dropping your hands!" he screamed again.

"Screw you."

"In your dreams, lass. Get them hands up!"

It went on like this for some time. Occasionally the kickboxers would glance over at us. Once I slipped on my own sweat, and Jacky thankfully paused and called for one of his towel boys who hustled over and wiped down the mat.

"You sweat like a man," said Jacky, as we waited. "I like that."

"Oh?" I said, patting myself down with my own towel. "You like the sweat of men?"

He glared at me. "My wife sweats. It's exciting."

"Probably because you don't. She has to make up for the two of you."

"I don't know why I open up to you," he said.

"You call this opening up?" I asked. "Talking about sweat and boffing your wife?"

"Consider yourself privileged," he said.

We went back to boxing. We did two more three-minute rounds. Near the end of the last round, I was having a hell of a time keeping my gloved fists up, and Jacky didn't let me hear the end of it.

When we were done, Jacky leaned his bulk against the taut ropes. He removed the padded gloves from his hands. The gloves were frayed and beaten.

"Second pair of gloves in a month," he said, looking at them with something close to astonishment.

"I'll buy you some more," I said.

"You're a freak," he said. He studied his hands. They were red and appeared to be swelling before our very eyes. "You hit harder than any man I've ever coached or faced. Your hand speed is off the charts. Good Christ, your form and accuracy is perfect."

"Except that I drop my hands."

"Not always," he said sheepishly. "I've got to tell you something so that you think I'm earning my keep."

I reached over and kissed his smooth forehead. "I know," I said.

"You're a freak," he said again, blushing.

"You have no idea."

"I pity any poor bastard who crosses your path."

"So do I."

He held out his hands. "Now, I need to soak these in ice."

"Sorry about that."

"You kidding? It's an honor working with you. I tell everyone about you. No one believes me. I tell them I've got a woman here that could take on their best male contenders. They never believe me."

Around us the sparring gym was a beehive of activity. Both boxing rings were now being used by kickboxers. Women and men were pounding the hell out of the half dozen punching bags, and the rhythmic rattling of the speed bags sounded from everywhere.

"You know I don't like you talking about me, Jacky."

"I know. I know. They don't believe me anyway. You could box professionally with one hand behind your back."

"I don't like attention."

"I know you don't. I'll quit bragging about you."

"Thank you, Jacky."

"The last thing I want is you pissed-off at me."

I box for self-defense. I box for exercise. Sometimes I box because it's nice to have a man care so vehemently whether or not my fists were up.

I kissed his forehead again and walked out.

7.

I drove north along Harbor Boulevard, through downtown Fullerton, and made a left onto Berkeley Street. I parked in the visitor parking in front of the Fullerton Municipal Courthouse, turned off my car, and sat there.

While I sat there, I drank water from a bottle. Water is one of the few drinks my body will accept. That and wine, although the alcohol in wine has no effect on me.

Yeah, I know. Bummer.

My hands were still feeling heavy from the boxing workout. I flexed my fingers. I couldn't help but notice my forearms rippling with taut muscle. I like that. I worked hard for that, and it was something I didn't take for granted.

I sat in the minivan and watched the entrance to the courthouse. There was little activity at this late hour. I wasn't sure what I was hoping to find here but I like to get a look and feel for all aspects of a case. Makes me feel involved and informed.

And, hell, you never know what might turn up.

Two security guards patrolled the front of the building. So where had they been at the time of Kingsley's shooting? Probably patrolling the back of the building.

Behind me was a wooded area; above that were condominiums. A blue jay swooped low over my hood and disappeared into the branches of a pine tree. A squirrel suddenly dashed along the pine tree's limb. The jay appeared again, and dove down after the squirrel.

Can't we all just get along?

When the guards disappeared around a corner, I got out of the van and made my way to the court's main entrance. My legs were still shaky from the workout; my hands heavy and useless, like twin balloons filled with sand.

The courthouses consisted of two massive edifices that faced each other. Between them was a sort of grassy knoll, full of trees and stone benches. The benches were empty. The sun was low in a darkening sky.

I like darkening skies.

Shortly, I found the infamous birch tree. The tree was smallish, barely wide enough to conceal even me, let alone a big man with broad shoulders. As a shield, it was useless, as the additional bullets in Kingsley's head attested. To have relied on it for one's sole protection from a gun-wielding madman was horrifying to contemplate. So I did contemplate it. I felt Kingsley's fear, recalled his desperate attempts to dodge the flying bullets. Comical and horrific. Ghastly and amusing. Like a kid's game of cowboys and Indians gone horribly wrong.

I circled the tree and found four fairly fresh holes in the trunk. The bullets had, of course, been dug out and added to the evidence. Now the holes were nothing more than dark splotches within the white bark. The tree and Kingsley had one thing in common: both were forever scarred by bullets from the same gun.

The attack had been brazen. The fact that the shooter had gotten away clean was probably a fluke. The shooter himself probably expected to get caught, or gunned down himself. But instead he walked away, and disappeared in a truck that no one seemed to remember the license plate of. The shooter was still out there, his job left unfinished. Probably wondering what more he had to do to kill Kingsley.

A hell of a good question.

According to the doctor's reports cited in a supplementary draft within the police report, all bullets had missed vital parts of Kingsley's brain. In fact, the defense attorney's only side effect was a minor loss in creativity. Of course, for a defense attorney, a lack of creativity could prove disastrous.

Someone wanted Kingsley dead, and someone wanted it done outside the courthouse, a place where many criminals had walked free because of Kingsley's ability to manipulate the law. This fact was not lost on me.

Detective Sherbet had only made a cursory investigation into the possibility that the shooting was related to one of Kingsley's current or past cases. Sherbet had not dug very deeply.

It was my job to dig. Which was why I made the big bucks.

I turned and left the way I had come.

8.

"So how often do you, like, feed?" asked Mary Lou.

Mary Lou was my sister. Only recently had she discovered that I was, like, a creature of the night. Although I come from a big family, she was the only one I had confided in, mostly because we were the closest in age and had grown up best friends. We were sitting side-by-side at a brass-topped counter in a bar called Hero's in downtown Fullerton.

I said, "Often. Especially when I see a particular fine sweep of milky white neck. Like yours for instance."

"Ha ha," she said. Mary Lou was drinking a lemon drop martini. I was drinking house Chardonnay. Since I couldn't taste the Chardonnay, why order the good stuff? And Chardonnay rarely had a reaction on my system, and it made me feel normal, sort of, to drink something in public with my sister.

Mary Lou was wearing a blue sweater and jeans. Today was casual day at the insurance office. This was apparently something that was viewed as good. She often talked about casual day; in fact, often days before the actual casual event.

"Seriously, Sam. How often?" she asked again.

I didn't say anything. I swallowed some wine. It tasted like water. My tastebuds were dead, my tongue good for only talking and kissing, and lately not even kissing. I looked over at Mary Lou. She was six years older than me, a little heavier, but then again she ate a normal diet of food.

"Once a day," I said, shrugging. "I get hungry like you. My stomach growls and I get light headed. Typical hunger symptoms."

"But you can only drink blood."

"You mind saying that a little louder?" I said. "I don't think the guy in the booth behind us quite heard."

"Sorry," she said sheepishly.

"We're supposed to keep this quiet, remember?"

"I know."

"You haven't told anyone?" I asked her again.

"No. I swear. You know I won't tell."

"I know."

The bartender came by and looked at my nearly finished glass of wine. I nodded, shrugging. What the hell, might as well spend my well-earned money on something useless, like wine.

"Have you tried eating other food?" asked Mary Lou.

"Yes."

"What happens?" she asked.

"Stomach cramps. Extreme symptoms of food poisoning. I throw it back up within minutes. Not a pretty picture."

"But you can drink wine," she said.

"It's the only thing I've found so far that I can drink," I said. "And sometimes not even that. Needs to be relatively pure."

"So no red wine."

"No red wine," I said.

My sister, with her healthy tan, put her hand on my hand. As she did so, she flinched imperceptively from the cold of my own flesh. She squeezed my fingers. "I'm sorry this happened to you, Sis."

"I am, too," I said.

"Can I ask you some more questions?" she asked.

"Were you just warming me up?"

"Yes and no."

"Fine," I said. "What else you got for me?"

"Does the blood, you know, have to be human blood?"

"Any mammalian blood will do," I said.

"Where do you get the blood?"

"I buy it."

"From where?" she asked.

"I have a contract with a butchery in Norco. I buy it by the month-load. It's in my freezer in the garage."

"The one with the padlock?" she asked. I think her own blood drained from her face.

"Yes," I answered.

"What happens if you don't drink blood?"

"Probably shrivel up and die."

"Do you want to change the subject?" she asked gently.

She knew my moods better than anyone, even my husband. "Please."

Mary Lou grinned. She caught the attention of the bartender and pointed to her martini. He nodded. The bartender was cute, a fact not lost on Mary Lou.

"So what case are you currently working on?" she asked, stealing glances at the man's posterior.

"You done checking out the bartender?"

She reddened. "Yes."

So I told her about my case. She remembered seeing it on TV.

"Any leads yet?" she asked, breathless. Mary Lou tended to think that what I did for a living was more exciting than it actually was. Her drink came but she ignored it.

"No," I said. "Just hunches."

"But your hunches are better than most anyone's."

"Yes," I said. "It's a side effect."

"A good side effect."

I nodded. "Hey, if I have to give up raspberry cheesecakes, I might as well get something out of the deal."

"Like highly attuned hunches."

"That's one of them," I said.

"What else?" she asked.

"I thought we were changing the subject."

"C'mon, I've never known . . . someone like you."

"Don't you mean something?"

"No," she said. "That's not what I mean. You're a good mother, a good wife, and a good sister. You are much more than a thing. So tell me, what are the other side effects?"

"You saying all that just to butter me up?"

"Yes and no," she said, grinning. "So tell me. Now."

I laughed. "Okay, you win. I have enhanced strength and speed."

She nodded. "What else?"

"I seem to be disease and sickness free."

"What about shape-changing?"

"Shape-changing?"

"Yes."

Having my sister ask if I could shape-change struck me as so ridiculous that I burst out laughing. Mary Lou watched me briefly, then caught on because she always catches on. Soon we were both giggling hysterically, and we had the attention of everyone in the bar. I hate having people's attention, but I needed the laugh. Needed it bad.

"No," I said finally, wiping the tears from my eyes. "I can't shape-change. Then again, I've never tried."

"Then maybe you can," she said finally, after catching her own breath.

"Honestly, I've never thought about it. There's just been too much other crap to deal with, and this . . . condition of mine doesn't exactly come with a handbook."

"So you learn as you go," said Mary Lou.

"Yes," I said. "Sort of like The Greatest American Hero."

"Yeah, like him."

We drank some more. My stomach was beginning to hurt. I pushed the wine aside.

"You ever going to tell me what happened to you?" Mary Lou's words were forming slower. The martinis had something to do with that. "How you became, you know, what you are?"

I looked away. "Someday, Mary Lou."

"But not today."

"No," I said. "Not today."

Mary Lou turned in her stool and faced me. Her big, round eyes were glassy. Her nose was more slender than mine, but we resembled each other in every other way. We were sisters through and through.

"So how do you do it?" she asked.

"Do what?"

"Look so normal. Act so normal. Be so normal. Hell, life's hard enough as it is without something like this coming out of left field and knocking you upside your ass. How do you do it?"

"I do it because I have to," I said. "I don't have a choice."

"Because you love your kids."

"Sometimes it's the only reason," I said.

"What about Danny?"

I didn't tell her about Danny. Not yet. I didn't tell her that my husband seemed revolted by the sight of me, that he turned his lips away lately when we kissed, that he seemed to avoid touching me at all costs. I didn't tell her that I was sure he was cheating on me and my marriage was all but over.

"Yeah," I said, looking away. "I do it for Danny, too."

9.

The shower was as hot as I could stand it, which would have been too hot for most people. Some of my sensitivity had left my skin, and as a result I needed hotter and hotter showers. My husband, long ago, gave up taking showers with me. Apparently he had an aversion to the smell of his own cooking flesh.

My muscles were sore and the water helped. I was thirty-seven years old, but I looked twenty-seven, or perhaps even younger. There wasn't a wrinkle on my pallid face. My skin was taut. Usually ice cold, but taut. My muscles were hard, but that could have been because I never stopped working out. After all, there is only so much one can lose of one's self, and so I was determined to maintain some normalcy. Working out reminded me of who I was and what I was trying to be.

My body was still sore from boxing, but the soreness was almost gone. I heal fast nowadays, amazingly fast. Just your average, run-of-the-mill freak show.

I stood with my back to the spray and let my mind go blank. I stood there for God knew how long until an image of Kingsley and his bloody and confused face drifted into my thoughts. It had been such an angry attack. Full of pent-up rage. Kingsley had pissed off someone badly. Very badly. At one point in the shooting, the shooter had actually paused and looked at Kingsley with what had been thunderstruck awe, at least that's how I interpreted the grainy image. The look seemed to say: How many times do I have to shoot you before you die?

I had already soaped up and washed and conditioned my hair. There was nothing left to do, and now I was only wasting water. Sighing, I turned off the shower. Rare heat rose from my skin, a pleasant change for once. My skin was raw and red, and I was in my own little piece of heaven. The kids were with their sitter, and tonight I was going out with my husband. We tried to do that more and more lately. Or, rather, I tried to do that more and more lately. He reluctantly agreed.

Early on, after my transformation, Danny had been a saint. Someone he loved (me) was hurting and confused, and he had come to my rescue like no other.

Together we had devised schemes to let the world know I was different. It was his idea to tell the world I had developed xeroderma pigmentosum, a rare, and usually fatal, skin condition. With xeroderma pigmentosum, even brief exposure to sunlight can cause irreparable damage that could lead to blindness and fatal skin cancers. People eventually accepted this about me—even my own family. Yes, I hated lying, but the way I saw it, I had little choice.

Danny helped me change careers, and helped me set up my home-based private investigation business. He also explained to the kids that mommy would often be sleeping during the day and to not bother me. Finally, he helped set me up with my feed supply with the local butchery.

Danny had been a dream. But that had been then; this was now.

So tonight we were going to dinner. I would order my steak raw and do my best to participate with him. He would avert his eyes, as usual. Not a typical relationship by any means. But a relationship, nonetheless.

I found myself looking forward to tonight. I had recently read a book about how to be a better wife, how to understand your man, how to show your love in the little ways. It's amazing how we all forget what's necessary to keep a loving relationship intact. Well, I was determined to show him my appreciation.

Of course, most marriages didn't deal with the issues I have, but we would make it through, somehow.

I was still dripping and toweling off when the phone rang. I dashed out of the connecting bathroom and into the bedroom and picked up the phone on the bedside table.

"Hello," I said.

"Hi, doll."

"Danny!"

There was a pause, and I knew instinctively that I was going to get bad news. Call it my enhanced intuition, or call it whatever you want.

"I can't make it tonight," he said.

"But Danny. . . ."

"We're backed-up at the office. I have a court case later this week, and we're not ready. I hope you understand."

"Yes," I said. "Of course."

"I love you."

"I love you, too."

"I've got to get going. Don't wait up."

That was our little joke now. Of course, being a creature of the night, all I could do lately was wait up.

He hung up the phone.

10.

It was evening.

I was pacing inside the foyer of my house. The muscles along my neck were tense and stiff. Outside, through the partly open curtain, I could see the upper curve of the setting sun.

I continued to pace. Breathing was always difficult at this time of day. I was making a conscious effort to inhale and exhale, to fill my lungs as completely as I could.

In and out.

Slowly.

Keep calm, Samantha Moon. You'll be all right.

Nevertheless, a sense of panic threatened to overcome me. The source of the panic was the sun. Or, rather, the presence of the sun. Because I did not, and could not, feel fully alive until that son-of-a-bitch disappeared behind the horizon.

I checked the curtain again. The sun was still burning away in all its glory.

Crap! Had the earth stopped in mid-orbit? Was I doomed to feel half-alive for the rest of my life?

Panic. Pure unabated panic.

I breathed.

Deeply.

Consciously.

I leaned against the door frame and closed my eyes, willing myself to relax. I reached up and rubbed my neck muscles. I continued to breathe, continued to fight the panic.

And then, after seemingly an eternity, it happened. A sense of peace and joy began in my solar plexus and spread slowly in a wave of warmth to all my extremities. My mind buzzed with happiness, pure unabated happiness, and with it the unbridled potential of the coming night. It was a natural high. Or perhaps an unnatural high. I opened my eyes and looked out the window. The sun was gone.

As I knew it would be.

The kids were with Mary Lou and her family at Chuck E. Cheese's. I owed Mary Lou big. Danny was working late, preparing for his big court date. So what else was new?

I had not yet realized just how much my life was unraveling. It occurred to me then, as I was driving south along the 57 Freeway, that I might have to give up detecting if Danny was going to continue working so late. In the past, he would be home with the kids. Now, he rarely got home in time to see them off to bed.

The thought of not working horrified me. Like they say, idle hands are the devil's tools. By keeping myself busy, I was able to forget some of what I had become, and to keep the nightmare of my reality at bay.

But something had to give here, and it wasn't going to be Danny. He had made it clear long ago that this was *my* problem.

My windows were down. The spring evening was warm and dry. I couldn't remember the last time we had rain. I liked the rain. Perhaps I liked the rain because I lived in Southern California. Rain here was like the elusive lover who keeps you begging for more. Perhaps if I lived up north I would not like the rain so much. I didn't know. I'd never lived anywhere else.

I took the 22 East and headed toward the city of Orange. At Main Street I exited and drove past the big mall, and turned left onto Parker Avenue and into the parking lot of the biggest building in the area.

I took the elevator to the seventh floor. In the lobby, I was greeted by a pretty brunette receptionist. *Greeted* might have been too generous. Frankly, she didn't look very much like a happy camper. She was a young girl of about twenty-five, with straight brown hair that seemed to shine like silk. My hair once shone like silk; now it hung limply. Her pink sweater knit dress was snug and form-fitting, highlighting unnaturally large breasts. Did nothing for me, but then again, I am not a man. I sensed much animosity coming from her. Waves of it. I think I knew why. She was working late, and I was part of the reason she was working late.

I gave her my most winning smile. Easy on the teeth. The nameplate on her desk read: Sara Benson.

"Hi, Sara. I'm Samantha Moon, here to see Mr. Fulcrum."

"Mr. Fulcrum is waiting for you, Mrs. Moon. I'll show you to his office."

As she did so, I said, "I understand you're going to help me tonight?"

"You understand correctly."

"I would just like to express my gratitude. I'm sure you would rather be anywhere else but here."

"You have no idea," she said, and stopped before a door. "He's in here."

11.

Kingsley occupied a spacious corner suite, filled with lots of dark wood shelving and legal reference books. Had the blinds not been shut he would have had a grand panoramic view of Santa Ana and Orange. Thick stacks of rubberbanded folders were piled everywhere, and in one corner was a discreet wet bar. A bottle of Jack Daniel's was sitting not-so-discreetly on the counter.

"Generally, the Jack Daniel's stays *behind* the bar during office hours," said Kingsley, moving around from behind his desk and shaking my hand, which he might have held a bit longer than protocol required. Then added, "You keep strange hours, Mrs. Moon."

I removed my hand from his grip. "And you heal surprisingly well."

The scar above his eye was almost gone. Indeed, it even appeared to have *moved* a little—to the left, perhaps—but then again Mom always told me I had an overactive imagination. He saw me looking at it and promptly turned his head.

"Touché," he said. "A drink to the freaks?"

"This freak is working. No drinking." Drinking didn't effect me, but he didn't need to know that.

"Do you mind if I have one?"

"You mean *another* one?" I asked. I could it smell it on his breath.

"You are quite the detective," he said.

"Oh yeah, *that* was a hard one."

He grinned and swept past me toward the bar. "Please, make yourself comfortable."

The closest place to make myself comfortable was a client chair that was currently occupied by a giant box. "Would you prefer I sit on a pile of folders or on top of this box?" I asked, perhaps a little snottily.

Behind me, at the bar, Kingsley had started to pour himself another drink. "Forgive me. We've been so busy lately; the place is a mess. Let me get that for you."

"Don't bother," I said, setting the heavy box on the floor.

Now back behind his desk, drink in hand, Kingsley watched me carefully. He took a sip from the highball glass. The bourbon sparkled amber in the half-light. I love half-light. I watched him watching me. Something was up. Finally, he said, "That box is filled with four fifty-pound plates," he said. "Two hundred pounds. And if you throw in the other crap in the box, that's well over two hundred pounds."

"I'm not following," I said, although I suspected I knew what he was getting at.

"It was a test," he said smugly. "And you passed. Or failed. Depending how you look at it."

I said nothing. I couldn't say anything. Instead, I found myself looking at his fading scars. Not too long ago I had stepped on a thick piece of glass; the wound had healed completely in a few hours. Unlike mine, Kingsley's face had a healthy rosy glow. And he had arrived at my home in the middle of the day and had not worn extra protection from the sun. He was not like me, and yet he had survived five bullet shots to the head.

"Well," I said, "I would have been in trouble had it been too much over two hundred pounds."

He pounced. "You only work nights, Mrs. Moon. You wear an exorbitant amount of sunscreen. Your windows, I noticed, were all completely covered. You lift two hundred pounds without a moment's hesitation. Your skin is icy to the touch. And you have the complexion of an avalanche victim."

"Okay, that last one was just mean," I said.

"Sorry, but true."

"So what are you getting at?"

He leaned back and folded his hands over his flat stomach. "You're a vampire, Mrs. Moon."

I laughed. So did he. Mine was a nervous laugh; his not so much. As I gathered my thoughts for a firm rebuttal, I found myself taking a second glance around his office. Behind his desk on the wall, was a beautiful picture of the full moon taken by a high-powered telescopic lens. There was a silver moon globe next to his monitor. Half moon bookends, which, if placed together, would form a full moon. On his desk was a picture of a woman, a very beautiful woman, with a full moon rising over her shoulder.

"You're obsessed with moons," I said.

"Which is why I picked you out of the phone book," he said, grinning. "Couldn't help myself, Mrs. Moon."

We were both silent. I watched him carefully. His mouth was open slightly. He was breathing heavily, his wet tongue pushed up against his incisors. His face looked healthy, vigorous and . . . feral.

"You're a werewolf," I said finally.

He grinned, wolf-like.

12.

Kingsley moved over to the window, pulled aside the blinds, and peered out into the night. With his back to me, I could appreciate the breadth and width of his shoulders.

"Could you imagine in your wildest dream," he said finally, "of ever having this conversation?"

"Never."

"And yet neither one of us has denied the other's accusations."

"Nor have we admitted to them," I added.

We were silent again, and I listened to the faint hum of traffic outside the window. I spied some of the reassuring darkness through the open slats. I was in uncharted territory here, and so I decided to roll with the situation.

"For simplicity's sake," he said, his back still to me, "let's assume we are vampires and werewolves. Where does that leave us?"

"Obviously I must kill you," I said.

"I hope you're kidding."

"I am."

"Good, because I don't die easily," he said. "And certainly not without a fight."

"I just love a good fight," I said.

He ignored me. "So," he said, turning away from the window and crossing his arms across his massive chest. "How do you want to handle this?"

"Handle what?"

He threw back his head and laughed. It was a very animalistic gesture. He could have just as easily been a coyote—or a wolf—howling at the moon. "This new wrinkle in our working relationship," he said.

"As far as I'm concerned you are still my client and I'm still your detective. Nothing has changed."

"Nothing?"

"Other than the fact that you claim to be a werewolf."

"You don't believe me?"

"Mr. Fulcrum, werewolves are fairytales."

"And vampires aren't?"

I laughed. Or tried to. "I'm not a vampire. I just have a *condition*."

"A condition that requires you to stay out of the sun," he said, incredulously. "A condition that requires you to drink blood. A condition that has turned you whiter than a ghost. A condition that has given you superhuman strength."

"I never said it was a *common* condition. I'm still looking into it."

He grinned. "It's called vampirism, my dear, and it's time for you to own it."

"Own it?"

"Isn't that what the kids say these days?" he said.

"Just how old are you, Mr. Fulcrum?"

"Never mind that," he said. "The question on the table is a simple one: Do you believe I'm a werewolf?"

"No," I said.

"Do you believe you are a vampire?" he asked.

I hesitated. "No."

"Fine," he said. "Is your husband cheating on you?"

"Why would you say that?" I asked.

"I assume he is," said Kingsley. "I assume he's terrified of you and he doesn't know what to do about it yet, especially with the kids in the picture."

"Shut up, Kingsley."

"And since you're not denying it, I will also go as far as to assume he's a son-of-a-bitch for abandoning you in the hour of your greatest need."

"Please, shut up."

"I also know something else, Mrs. Moon. He will take the kids from you and there isn't a single goddamn thing you can do about it."

Something came over me, something hot and furious. I flashed out of the client chair and was on Kingsley before he could even uncross his arms. My left hand went straight for his throat, slamming him hard against the wall. Too hard. The back of his head crashed through the drywall. Teeth bared, I looked up into his face—and the asshole was actually grinning at me, with half his head still in the wall. His hair and shoulders were covered in plaster dust.

"Shut the hell up!" I screeched.

"Sure. You got it. Whatever you say."

We stood like that for a long time, my hand clamped over his throat, his head pushed back into the wall.

"Can you set me down now?" he asked in a raspy voice.

"Down?" I said, confused, my voice still raspy in my throat.

"Yeah," he said, pointing. "Down."

I followed his finger and saw that his feet were dangling six inches above the floor. I gasped and dropped him as his head popped out of the wall.

"Sorry," I said sheepishly. "I was mad."

Kingsley rubbed his neck. "Remind me next time not to piss you off," he said, dusting off his shoulders and opening his office door. "Oh, and I'm sorry to inform you, Mrs. Moon, that you are very much a vampire."

Eyes glowing amber, he winked at me and left.

13.

Sara and I spent the next three hours sorting through files and since Sara was a little on the grumpy side, I did what any rational person would do under similar circumstances. I ordered Chinese. When it arrived she perked up a little. Some people needed alcohol to loosen up, apparently Sara needed fried wontons.

We ate at her desk. Or, rather, I *pretended* to eat at her desk. We ate mostly in silence.

Interestingly, according to the pictures on Sara's desk, she seemed to know how to let loose just fine. There were pictures of her in a bikini on some tropical isle, of her hiking along a heavily forested mountain trail, of her viciously spiking a volleyball, of her dressed as a pirate in an office Halloween party, complete with massive gold hoops, eye patch and mustache. In the background was Kingsley dressed as a werewolf. I almost laughed.

"You played volleyball?" I asked.

"Yes, at Pepperdine. I tried out for the Olympics."

"What happened?"

"Almost made the team. Maybe next time."

"Maybe next time," I said. "Is Kingsley a good boss?"

She shrugged. "He's kind enough. Gives big bonuses."

"What more could you want?" I asked cheerily.

She shrugged and turned her attention to her food. I tried another approach. "Do you like your job?"

She shrugged again and I decided to let my attempt at idle conversation drop. Maybe she needed more fried wontons.

While we ate, we worked from a long list of all of Kingsley's closed files from the past six years. Seven hundred and seventy-six in all. Kingsley was a busy boy. From these files, I removed all those Kingsley had personally litigated. Now we were down to three hundred and fifty-three. Still too many to work with. From those, I removed all violent crime; in particular, murder defense cases. Now we were down to twelve files.

I told Sara I would need copies of all twelve files. She promptly rolled her eyes.

While we made copies, Sara decided to open up a little to me. Okay, maybe she hadn't *decided* so much as *gave in* to my constant barrage of questions. Anyway, I gleaned that she had come here to Kingsley's firm straight from college. Initially, she had loved working for her boss, but lately not so much.

"Why?" I asked, hoping for more than just a shrug. I had the Chinese restaurant's number in my pocket should I need an emergency order of fried wontons.

Turns out I didn't need the number. Rather heatedly, Sara told me in detail the story of the rapist who had been freed because Kingsley had discovered evidence of tampering at the crime scene. She finished up with: "Yes, Mr. Fulcrum's a good man. But he's a better defense attorney. And that's the problem."

I was sensing much hostility here. We were standing at the copier, working efficiently together, passing folders back and forth to each other as we copied them. Sara was very pretty and very young. Any man's dream, no doubt. She was taller than me and her breasts appeared fake, but in Southern California that's the norm and not the exception. She, herself, did not seem fake. She seemed genuine and troubled, and I suddenly knew why.

"You dated Kingsley," I said.

She looked up, startled. "Why? Did he say something to you?"

"No. Just a hunch."

She passed me another folder. I removed the brackets and flipped through it, looking for papers of unusual sizes, or POUS's, that would jam the copier. As she spoke, she crossed her arms under her large chest and leaned a hip against the copy machine. "Yeah, we dated for a while. So?"

"So what happened?" I asked.

"Ask *him*. He broke it off."

"Why?"

"You ask a lot of questions," she said.

"It's a compulsion," I said. "I should probably see a shrink about it."

Her eyes brightened a little and she nearly smiled, but then she got a handle on herself and remembered she didn't like me. "He said things were moving *too fast* for him. That he had lost his wife not too long ago and he wasn't ready for something serious."

"When did his wife die?" I asked.

"A few years ago. I don't know." She shrugged. She didn't know, and she clearly didn't care.

"Are you still angry with him?" I asked.

She shrugged and looked away and clammed up the rest of the night. Yeah, I think she was still angry.

We finished copying all twelve files, many of which were nearly a foot thick. Maybe within one I would find a suspect or a clue or *something*. At any rate, the files would give me something to do during the wee hours of the night, especially since I had recently finished Danielle Steel's latest novel, *Love Bites*, about two vampires in love. Cute, and uncannily dead on.

So Sara and I loaded up the files into a box and as I carried the entire thing out to the elevator, the young assistant watched me with open-mouthed admiration. I get that a lot.

"Jesus, you're strong," she said as we stepped into the elevator.

"It's the Pilates," I said. "You should try it."

"I will," she said. "Oh, and I'm supposed to remind you that these files are confidential."

"I'll guard them with my life."

Outside, in the crisp night air, Sara said, "I sure hope you find out who shot Kingsley." She caught the indiscretion and turned beet red, her face glowing brightly under the dull parking lot lamps. "I mean, Mr. Fulcrum."

I smiled at her slip. "I do, too."

She thanked me for the Chinese food, seemed to want to tell me something else, thought better of it, then dashed off to her car. I watched her get in and back out and drive away. Just as I shoved the box into the minivan, the fine hairs at the back of my neck sprang to life. I paused and slowly turned my head. My vision is better at night. Not great, but better. I was alone in the parking lot. Check that; there was an old Mercedes parked in a lot across the street. A man was sitting there, and he was watching me with binoculars.

I slammed the minivan's door and moved purposely through the parking lot, crossed the sidewalk, stepped down the curb and headed across the street.

He waited a second or two, watching me steadily, then reached down and gunned his vehicle to life. His headlights flared to life, and before I was halfway across the street, he reversed his Mercedes and tore recklessly through the parking lot. As he exited at the far end, turning right onto Parker Avenue and disappearing down a side street, I was certain of two things:

One: he had no plates. Two: those weren't binoculars.

They were night-vision goggles.

14.

With the files in my backseat and thoughts of the night-vision goggles on my mind, I called Mary Lou around 10:30 to thank her for watching my kids.

"I'm still watching them," she said sleepily.

"What do you mean?" I asked.

"Danny never showed up," she said.

"Did he at least call?" I asked.

"No."

I was on the 57 Freeway, but instead of getting off at my exit on Yorba Linda Boulevard, I continued on to Mary Lou's house two exits down. Yeah, it's nice to have family close by, especially when you have kids.

"I'm so sorry," I said when she opened the door. "I didn't mean to stick you with the kids all night."

"Not your fault. I love them, anyway. Tell me you at least made some headway on your case."

"Some headway," I admitted. I left out the part about Kingsley being a werewolf but did mention the guy in the parking lot.

"Maybe he was just some creep," said Mary Lou, frowning. "I mean you are, after all, a hot piece of ass."

"Always nice to hear from your sister," I said.

"I say don't let it worry you."

"I won't," I said. "I can take of myself."

"I know," she said. "That's what worries me."

With the kids in the backseat sleeping, I called Danny's office. He wasn't there; I left a voice mail message. Next I called his cell phone and he answered just before it went to voice mail. He sounded out of breath. Something was wrong here and warning bells sounded loud and clear in my head. I did my best to ignore them, although I couldn't ignore the fact that I had suddenly gotten sick to my stomach.

"Where are you?" I asked.

"Working late," he answered huskily.

"You doing push ups?" I said, trying to smile.

"Just ran up a flight of stairs. Bathroom on this floor isn't working."

"You didn't pick up your work phone."

"You know I never pick up after hours."

"You used to," I said.

"Well, honey, that was before I became so goddamn busy. Can I call you later?"

"Even better, why don't you *come home*."

"I'll be home soon."

He clicked off and I was left staring down at my cell phone. If it was possible, he seemed to have been breathing even harder by the end of the conversation.

It was past midnight, and I had worked my way through more than half of the twelve files when Danny finally came home. He stopped by the study and gave me a little wave. He looked tired. His dark hair was slightly disheveled. His tie was off. The muted light revealed the deepening lines around his mouth and eyes. His eyes, once clear blue and gorgeous, were hooded and solemn. His full lips were made for kissing, but not me, not anymore. He was a handsome man, and not a very happy one.

"Sorry about not picking up the kids," he said. He didn't sound very sorry. He didn't sound like he gave a shit at all. "I should have called your sister."

"That's okay. I'll make it up to her," I said. There was lipstick on his earlobe. He probably didn't think to check his earlobe.

He said, "I'm taking a shower, then hitting the hay. Another big day tomorrow."

"I bet."

He stood there a moment longer, leaning against the door frame. He seemed to want to say something. Maybe he wanted to tell me about the lipstick.

Then he slid away, but before he was gone, I caught a hint of something in his eyes. Guilt. Pain. Confusion. It was all there. I didn't think I needed any heightened sixth sense to know that my husband of fourteen and a half years had fallen out of love with me. We all change, I suppose. Some of us more than others.

After he was done showering, I listened to the box springs creak as he eased into bed and I set down my pen and silently cried into my hands.

15.

I was running along Harbor Boulevard at 3:00 a.m. I had finished reading through the files and needed some time to think. Luckily, I had all night to do so. Being a vampire is for me a nightly battle in dealing with loneliness.

I was dressed in full jogging gear, sweats and sweatshirt. No reflective shoes. I had been pulled over once too often by cops who had advised against a woman running so late at night. I wondered if they would give the same advice to a vampire. Anyway, I kept to the shadows, avoiding the cops and everyone else.

I kept up a healthy pace. In fact, my healthy pace was nearly a flat-out sprint. An ungodly pace that I could keep up for hours on end, and sometimes I did. Sure, my muscles hurt afterward, forcing me to soak in my hot tub. But I love the speed.

Harbor Boulevard sped past me. I breathed easily. The air was suffused with mist and dew. My arms pumped rhythmically at my side, adding balance to my churning legs. Harbor was empty of all traffic and life. I made a right down Chapman, headed past the high school and junior college. Streets swept past me. I dodged smoothly around lamp poles, bus benches, and metal box thingies that had something to do with traffic lights. I think. Anyway, there seemed to be a lot of those metal box thingies.

I didn't need water and I didn't need to pause for air. It was an unusual sense of freedom. To run without exhaustion. The city was quiet and silent. The wind passed rapidly over my ears.

I was a physical anomaly. Enhanced beyond all reason. My husband once called me a super hero after seeing an example of my strength and marveling at it.

There was a half moon hanging in the sky. I thought of Kingsley and his obsession with moons. It stood to reason that a werewolf would be obsessed with moons. I ran smoothly past an open-all-night donut shop. The young Asian donut maker looked up, startled, but just missed me. The smell of donuts was inviting, albeit nauseating.

A *werewolf*?

I shook my head and chuckled at the absurdity of it. But there it was, staring me in the face. Or, rather, *he* had stared me in the face. So what was happening around here? Since when was Orange County a haven for the undead? I wondered what else was out there. Surely if there were werewolves and vampires there might be other creatures that went bump in the night, right? Maybe a ghoul or two? Goblins perhaps? Maybe my trainer Jacky was really an old, cantankerous leprechaun.

I smiled.

Thinking of Kingsley warmed my heart. This concerned me. I was a married woman. A married woman should not feel such warmth toward another man, even if the other man was a werewolf.

That is, not if she wanted to stay married. And I really, really wanted to stay married.

Perhaps I felt connected to Kingsley, bonded by our supernatural circumstances. We had much in common. Two outcasts. Two creatures ruled by the night, in one way or another.

A car was coming. I ducked down a side street and moved along a row of old homes. Heavy branches arched overhead. With my enhanced night vision, I deftly avoided irregularities in the sidewalk—cracks and upheavals—places where tree roots had pushed up against the concrete. To my eye, the night was composed of billions and billions of dancing silver particles. These silver particles illuminated the darkness into a sort of surreal molten glow, touching everything.

I turned down another street, then another. Wind howled over my ears. I entered a tougher part of town, running along a residential street called Bear. Bear opens up to a bigger street called Lemon. I didn't give a crap how tough Bear Street was.

Yet another side benefit: *unlimited courage*.

My warning bells sounded, starting first as a low buzz in my ears. The buzzing is always followed by an increase in heart rhythm, a physical pounding in my chest. I knew the feeling well enough to trust it by now, and I immediately began looking for trouble. And as I rounded another corner, there it was.

Three men stepped out of the shadows in front of me. I slowed, then finally stopped. As I did so, four more men stepped out from behind a low-rider truck parked on the street. Next to the house was an empty, dark school yard. As if reading their collective minds, I had a fleeting prognostication of my immediate future: an image of the seven men dragging me into the school yard. Then having their way with me. Then leaving me for dead.

A good thing the future isn't written in stone.

I smiled at them. "Hello, boys."

16.

Four of the seven were Latinos, with the remaining three being Caucasian, Asian, and African-American. A veritable melting pot of gang violence. I studied each face. Most were damp with sweat. Eyes wide with anticipation and sexual energy. Details stood out to me like phosphorescent black and white photos, touched by ghostly silver light. One was terrified, jerking his head this way and that, like a chicken on crack. All of them around the same age—perhaps thirty—save for one who was as old as fifty. A few had bed-head, as if they had been recently roused from a drunken stupor.

I could smell alcohol on their breaths and sweat on their skin. The sweat was pungent and laced with everything from fear and excitement, to hostility and sexual frustration. None of it smelled good. If *mean* had a scent, this would be it.

A smallish Latino stepped forward. A switchblade sprang open at his side, locked into place. For my benefit, he let the faint light of the moon gleam off its polished surface. He was perhaps thirty-five and wore long denim shorts and a plaid shirt. He was surprisingly handsome for a rapist.

"If you scream, I'm going to hurt you." His accent was thick.

"Gee, what a romantic thing to say," I said.

"Shut up, bitch."

I kept my eyes on him. I didn't need to look at the others. I could feel them, *sense* them, smell them. I said, "Now what would your mothers all think of you now? Ganging up on a single woman in the middle of the night. Tsk, tsk. Really, I think you should all be ashamed."

The little Latino looked at me blankly, then said simply: "Get her."

Movement from behind. I turned and punched, extending my arm straight from my body. Jacky would have been proud. My fist caught the guy in the throat. He dropped to the ground, flopping and gagging and holding his neck. Probably hurt like hell. I didn't care.

I surveyed the others, who had all stopped in their tracks. "So what was the plan, boys? You were all going to get a fuck in? The very definition of sloppy seconds—hell, sloppy thirds and fourths and fifths. Then what? Slit my throat? Leave me for dead? Let some school janitor find me stuffed in a Dumpster? You would deny my children their mother for one night of cheap thrills?"

No one said anything. They looked toward their leader, the slick Latino with the switch. Most likely not all of them spoke English.

"I'll give you one chance to run," I said. "Before I kill all of you."

They didn't run. Some continued looking at their leader. Most were looking at the man rolling on the ground, holding his throat. Switchblade was watching me with a mixture of curiosity, lust and hatred.

Then he pounced, slashing the blade up. Had he hit home, I would have been cleaved from groin to throat.

He didn't hit home.

I turned my body and the blade missed. I caught his over-extended arm at the elbow and twisted. The elbow burst at the joint. He dropped the knife. I picked him up by the throat. Screaming and gagging, he swung wildly at me with his good arm, connecting a glancing blow off the side of my head. I simply squeezed harder and his flailing stopped.

His face was turning purple; I liked that.

I raised him high and swung him around so that the others could see. They gaped unbelievingly.

"You may run now," I said.

And they did. Scattering like chickens before the hawk. They disappeared into the night, around hedges and into dark doorways. Two of them just continued running down the middle of the street. All of them were gone, save for one, the fifty-year-old. He was pointing a gun at my head.

"Put my nephew down," he said.

"It's always nice to see gang raping and murdering kept in the family," I said.

I put his nephew down. Sort of. I hurled the kid with all my strength into his uncle. The gun went off, a massive explosion that rattled my senses and stung the hell out of my hyper-sensitive ears.

When the smoke cleared so to speak, the old man was looking down with bewildered horror.

Switchblade was lying sprawled on the concrete sidewalk, blood pumping from a wound in his chest. Spreading fast over the concrete. A black oil slick in the night.

Blood.

Something awakened within me. Something not very nice.

The older man looked from me to Switchblade, then at the gun in his hand. A look of horror crossed his features and tears sprang from his eyes. Then he fled into the shadows with the others, looking back once over his shoulder before disappearing over someone's backyard fence.

I was left alone with Switchblade. His right hand was trying to cover the wound; instead, it just flopped pathetically.

"Well," I said to him, kneeling down, "nice set of friends you have."

And as I squatted next to him, the flopping stopped and he looked at me with dead eyes. I checked for a pulse. There was none.

Aroused by the gunshot, house lights began turning on one by one. I looked down at the body again.

So much blood. . . .

17.

We were alone in an alley behind some apartments.

The early morning sky was still black, save for the faint light from the half moon. I was nestled between a Dumpster and three black bags of trash filled with things foul. A small wind meandered down the alley. The plastic bags rustled. My hair lifted and fell—and so did the hair on the dead guy.

After my runs, I usually feed on cow blood. The cow blood is mixed with all sorts of impurities and foul crap. I often gag. Sort of my own private *Fear Factor* with no fifty-grand reward at the end of the hour.

Before me lay Switchblade, the punk who had no doubt organized the gang bang. I had ferreted him away before anyone could investigate the shooting and now he lay at my feet, dead and broken.

I looked down at his chest, where blood had stained his flannel shirt nearly black.

Blood. . . .

I ripped open his flannel shirt, buttons pinging everywhere. His chest was awash in a sea of caked red. The hole in his chest was a dark moon in a vermilion sky.

His blood would contain alcohol, as he had been drinking. I didn't care. The blood would be pure enough. Straight from the source. The ideal way to feed. Then again, *ideal* was relative. *Ideally* I would be feasting on turkey lasagna.

I dipped my head down, placed my lips over the massive wound in his chest, and drank. . . .

I returned the body to the same house, and left it where it had fallen. I drifted back into the darkness of the school grounds, where I knew in my heart they were going to drag me off to be raped.

It was still early morning, still dark. No one was out on the streets. Curious neighbors had gone back to sleep; there were no police investigating the sound of a gunshot. Apparently gunshots here were a common enough occurrence to not arouse *that* much suspicion.

The attackers themselves were long gone. They were scared shitless, no doubt. One of their own had been shot by one of their own. Each would awaken this morning with a very bad hangover, and pray to God this had all been a very bad dream.

Instead of their prayers being answered, they were going to awaken to find the body. What happened next, I didn't really know or care. I doubted a group of men would even attempt to identify me, lest they reveal the nature of their true intentions the night before.

At any rate, using a half empty can of beer from the nearby Dumpster, I had cleaned the wound of my lip imprints. Let the medical examiner try to figure out why someone had sloshed beer all over the gunshot wound.

As I stood there in the darkness, with a curiously phantasmagoric mist nipping at my ankles, I remembered the taste of his blood again.

God, he had tasted so good. So damn good—and pure. The difference between good chocolate and bad chocolate. The difference between good wine and bad wine. Good blood and bad blood.

All the difference in the world.

I left the school grounds and the neighborhood as a slow wave of purple blossomed along the eastern horizon. I hated the slow wave of purple that blossomed along the eastern horizon. The sun was coming, and I needed to get home ASAP.

Already I could feel my strength ebbing.

Since my belly was full of Switchblade's blood, I did not want to cramp up and so I kept my jog slow and steady. On the way home, as the guilt set in over what I had just done, I held fast to one thought in particular as if it were a buoy in a storm:

I did not kill him; he was already dead. . . .

I did not kill him; he was already dead. . . .

18.

The kids were playing in their room and Danny was working late. Tonight was Open House at the elementary school, and he had promised to make it home on time.

The words "we'll see" had crossed my mind.

I had spent the past two hours helping Anthony with his math homework. Math didn't come easily to him and he fought me the entire time. Vampire or not, I was drained.

All in all, I just couldn't believe the amount of work his third grade teacher assigned each week, and it was all I could do to keep up. Didn't schools realize mothers wanted to spend quality time with their children in the evenings?

So now I was in my office, still grumbling. It was early evening and raining hard. Occasionally the rain, slammed by a gust of wind, splattered against my office window. The first rain in months. The weatherman had been beside himself.

I liked the rain. It touched everything and everyone. Nothing was spared. It made even a freak like me feel connected to the world.

So with the rain pattering against the window and the children playing somewhat contentedly in their room, I eventually worked my way through all of Kingsley's files. Only one looked promising, and it set the alarms off in my head. I've learned to listen to these alarms.

The case was no different than many of Kingsley's other cases. His client, one Hewlett Jackson, was accused of murdering his lover's husband. But thanks to Kingsley's adroit handling of the case, Jackson was freed on a technicality. Turns out the search warrant had expired and thus all evidence gathered had been deemed inadmissible in court. And when the verdict was read, the victim's brother had to be physically restrained. According to the file, the victim's brother had not lunged at the alleged killer; no, he had lunged at *Kingsley*.

There was something to that.

And that's all I had. A distraught man who felt his murdered brother had not been given proper justice. Not much, but it was a start.

I sat back in my chair and stared at the file. The rain was coming down harder, rattling the window. I listened to it, allowed it to fill some of the emptiness in my heart, and found some peace. I checked my watch. Open House was in an hour and still no sign of Danny.

I pushed him out of my thoughts and logged onto the internet; in particular, one of my many investigation databases. There had been no mention of the brother's name in the file, but with a few deft keystrokes I had all the information I needed.

The murder had made the local paper. The article mentioned the surviving family members. Parents were dead, but there had been two surviving siblings. Rick Horton and Janet Maurice. Just as I wrote the two names down, the house phone rang. My heart sank.

I picked it up.

"Hi, dollface."

"Tell me you're on your way home," I said.

There was a pause. He sucked in some air. "Tell the kids I'm sorry."

"No," I said. "You tell them."

"Don't."

I did. I called the kids over and put them on the phone one at a time. When they were gone, I came back on the line.

"You shouldn't drag the children into this, Samantha," he said.

"Drag them into what, pray tell?"

He sighed. When he was done sighing, I heard a voice whisper to him from somewhere. A *female* voice.

"Who's that whispering to you?" I asked.

"Don't wait up."

"Who's that—"

But he disconnected the line.

19.

We were late for Open House.

I had a hell of a time getting the kids ready, and had long ago abandoned any notion of making dinner. We popped into a Burger King drive-thru along the way.

"Tell me what you guys want," I said, speaking over my shoulder. We were third in line at the drive-thru. The kids were wearing some of their best clothes, and I was already worried about stains.

I looked in the rearview mirror. The kids were separated by an invisible line that ran between their two back seats. Crossing the line was grounds for punishment. At the moment, Tammy was hovering on the brink of that line, making faces at Anthony, taunting him, sticking her tongue out, driving him into a seething rage. I almost laughed at the scene, but had to do something.

"Tammy, your tongue just crossed the line. No TV or Game Boy tonight."

Anthony said, "Yes!" Then pointed at his sister. "Ha!"

Tammy squealed. "But, Mom, that's not fair! It was just my tongue!"

"Tongues count. Plus, you know better than to tease your little brother." We moved up in line. "What do you two want to eat?"

Tammy said she didn't want anything. Anthony gave me his usual order: hamburger, plain. I ordered Tammy some chicken fingers.

"I don't want chicken fingers."

"You like chicken fingers."

"But I'm not hungry."

"Then you don't have to eat them, but if you waste them, the money's coming out of your allowance. Anthony, don't tease your sister."

Anthony was doing a little victory dance in the back seat, which rocked the entire minivan. His sister had been successfully punished and he had escaped unscathed. It was a triumphant moment for younger brothers everywhere.

And just when he thought I wasn't looking, just when he thought the coast was clear, he gave his sister the middle finger. Tammy squealed. I burst out laughing. And by the time we left the drive-thru, both of them had lost two days of TV privileges.

And as I pulled out of the Burger King parking lot, Anthony wailed, "There's mustard on my hamburger!"

"Christ," I muttered, and made a U-turn and headed back through the drive-thru.

20.

After Open House, the three of us were sitting together on the couch watching reruns of *Sponge Bob*. Sadly enough, I had seen this episode before. Danny still wasn't home, nor did I really expect him to be any time soon.

Open House had gone well enough. Anthony was passing all his classes, but just barely. His teacher felt he spent too much time trying to be the class clown. Tammy, a few years older, was apparently boy crazy. Although her grades were just about excellent, her teacher complained she was a distraction to the other students; mostly to the male variety.

Apparently, my kids liked attention, and I wondered if I was giving them enough of it at home.

"What's that smell?" I asked.

"Whoever smelt it dealt it," said Anthony, giggling.

"Probably you," said Tammy to her brother. "You're always cutting them."

"So do you!"

"Do not! I'm a girl. Girl's don't cut anything."

"Yeah, right!" shouted Anthony.

"I don't smell anything, Mommy," said Tammy, ignoring her brother.

I proceeded to sniff armpits and feet. As I smelled, they both giggled, and Anthony tried to smell my own feet.

"It's you, Mommy," he shouted, giggling. "Your feet stink!"

"Do not," I said. "Girls' feet don't stink."

"You're not a girl."

"Oh, really?"

"Then what is she, lame brain?" asked Tammy.

"She's a *lady*," said Anthony.

"Thank you, Anthony," I said, hugging his warm body. "Lady is good."

"And ladies have stinky feet," he added.

"Okay, now you just blew it," I said, and tickled the hell out of him. He cowered in the corner of the couch, kicking pillows at me, and then Tammy jumped on my back to defend her little brother and soon we were all on the floor, poking fingers at any and all exposed flesh, a big tickling free-for-all.

Later, as we lay gasping on the floor as Sponge Bob and his infamous square pants completed another fun-filled romp at the bottom of the ocean, Anthony asked, "Mommy, why are you always . . . cold?"

"Mommy is sick," I said. And, in a way, I was *very* sick.

"Are you going to die soon?" he asked.

"No," I said. "Mommy won't die for a very long time."

"Good!" he said.

"But can we catch what you have?" asked Tammy, always the careful one.

"No," I said. "You can't."

I suddenly wrinkled my nose. The smell was back. From my angle on the floor, I could just see under the couch. And there, in all its glory, was one of Anthony's rolled up socks. A very smelly rolled up sock. I used a pencil and pulled it out, where it hung from the tip like radioactive waste.

"Look familiar, Anthony?" I asked.

He mumbled an apology and I told him to throw it in the wash, and as he got up to do so, Tammy and I made farting noises with each step he took.

Bad move.

He turned and threw the sock back at us and we spent the next few minutes playing hot potato with it, laughing until our stomachs hurt.

21.

After my attack six years ago, about the same time I first went online, I made a cyber friend.

I was exploring through the new and interesting world of chatrooms. I landed in a room called *Creatures of the Night*. The room was comical to a degree, for there seemed to be a running script of a vampire appearing in a castle and sucking the life out of its inhabitants. There were many rapid postings, and it was difficult to keep up. Still, one thing was obvious: everyone here loved vampires with all their heart and soul. And many wanted to *be* vampires.

A private message box had next appeared on my screen. Someone named Fang950 was trying to contact me. He said *Hi* and I responded back. Over the course of the next few hours, which flew rapidly by, I found myself opening up to this Fang950. It was exhilarating. I told him everything. Everything. All my deepest secrets. I didn't care if he believed me or not. I didn't know him from squat. But he listened, and he asked questions and he did not judge me. He was the perfect outlet to my angst. And no one knew about him but me. No one. He was all mine.

It was late, and it was still raining. I had gone to the Open House alone. Danny had yet to come home. I had already fed for the night and was sitting in my office in a bit of a stupor. I always felt sluggish after feeding, not to mention bloated and sick to my stomach.

A private message window popped up on my computer screen, followed by the sound of splashing water. It was Fang.

You there, Moon Dance? he wrote, referring to my screen name, the only name he knew me by.

Yes, Fang, what's up?

Nothing new. How about you?

There was never anything new with Fang. He told me little about himself. I knew only that he lived in Missouri and that he was twenty-eight.

So I spent the next few minutes catching him up on my new

case. I left out names of course, but Fang was computer savvy. If he was interested enough he would find out about the story himself.

What does your gut tell you about the file? he asked.

My gut tells me I'm onto something, I answered.

Too bad your gut can't be more specific.

Yes, too bad, I wrote. *But it's helped me solve cases before, though. I've developed quite a reputation here. But I feel like I'm cheating.*

Cheating?

I thought about that a little, then wrote: *Well, other P.I.'s don't have the benefit of a heightened sixth sense, or whatever you want to call it.*

But other P.I.s work in the day, he wrote. *You are handicapped by working nights.*

It's not much of a handicap. I can get around it.

Nonetheless. Remember, you help people. That's the important thing. Whether or not you're cheating doesn't matter. It's the end result, right? Didn't you once say you turn down more cases than you accept?

I wrote, *Yes.*

Which cases do you turn down? he asked.

Cheating spouses mostly.

Which cases do you accept?

The bigger cases. Murder cases. Missing person cases.

How do your clients find you?

Police referrals mostly, I wrote. *If the police can't solve the crime, they will sometimes send the clients my way. I have developed a reputation for finding answers.*

You do good work. You are like a super hero. You help those who have nowhere else to turn for answers. You give them the answers.

There it was again. Super hero.

The rain continued. I heard Danny come in, but he didn't bother to stop by my office in the back of the house. Instead, I heard him head straight into the shower. To shower *her* off him, no doubt.

But sometimes the answers should remain hidden, I wrote a few minutes later, distracted by Danny's appearance.

Sometimes not, wrote Fang. *Either way, your clients have closure.*

I nodded to myself, then wrote, *Closure is a gift.*

He wrote, *Yes. You give them that gift. So you think this distraught brother took a few shots at your client?*

I'm thinking it's likely. I paused in my typing, then added, *Do you believe that I am a vampire, Fang?*

You have asked me this a hundred times, he answered.

And I have conveniently forgotten your answers a hundred times.

Yes, he wrote. *I believe you are a vampire.*

Why do you believe I am a vampire?

Because you told me you are.

And you believe that?

Yes.

I took in some air, then typed: *I sucked the blood from a dead man last night.*

There was a long pause before he wrote: *Did you kill him, Moon Dance?*

No, I didn't. He was already dead, part of a gang that attacked me. He was accidentally shot by someone in his gang. The shot had been intended for me.

OMG, are you okay?!

I loved Fang, whoever the hell he was. I wrote, *Yes, thank you. It was nothing. The bangers didn't know with whom they were dealing.*

Of course they didn't, how could they? So what happened to the dead guy?

I sucked his blood until I couldn't swallow another drop.

There was a long pause. Rain ticked on the window.

How did that make you feel? he asked.

At the time? Refreshed. Whole. Complete. Rejuvenated.

He tasted that good, huh?

Even better, I wrote.

How do you feel now? he asked.

Horrified.

Does it worry you that he tasted so good?

Not really, I wrote. *But I do realize now how much I'm missing. Cow blood is disgusting.*

I bet. Can you still control yourself, Moon Dance?

Yes. I've never lost control of myself. As long as I'm satiated each night on the blood stored in my refrigerator.

What would happen if you ran out of blood?

I don't want to think about it, I wrote. *It's never happened, nor do I plan on it happening.*

Sounds like a plan, he wrote.

I laughed a little and sat back in my chair and drank some water. I typed, *I met a werewolf.*

No shit?

No shit, I wrote.

What's a werewolf like?

I don't really know just yet. Mysterious. Obsessed with the moon.

Stands to reason.

He's a practicing attorney, I wrote. *And a very good one.*

Well, we all need a day gig.

Or a night gig, I added.

Haha. Well, Moon Dance, it's late. Let me know how it goes with the werewolf. When will be the next full moon?

A few days. I already checked.

Have there been any unsolved murders resembling animal attacks? he asked.

Not to my knowledge.

Might want to stay alert for that, he said.

True, I wrote.

Goodnight, Moon Dance.

Goodnight, Fang.

22.

I was driving south on the 57 Freeway when my cell phone rang. It was Kingsley.

"Have you heard the news?" he asked excitedly.

"That you're a werewolf?" I suggested.

"Tsk, tsk, tsk, dear girl. Not over the phone lines. You never know who might be listening."

"Big Brother? Aliens? Homeland Security?"

"Hewlett Jackson's dead."

I blinked. "Your client."

"Now my ex-client."

"Murder?" I asked.

"Yes. Shot."

"Let me guess," I said. "Five times in the head."

"Close. Nine."

"Appears our killer wasn't going to take any chances this time."

"Find him," said Kingsley.

"That's my job," I said.

"You have any leads?"

"One."

"Just one?"

"That's all I need," I said.

"I see," he said. "Well, the police say you're the best. So I trust you."

There was some static, followed by a long pause. Too long.

"You there?" I asked.

"I'm here," he said, then added, "Tomorrow's a full moon, you know."

"I know," I said. "So, can I watch?"

"Watch?" he asked.

"You know, the transformation."

"No," he said. "And you're a sick girl."

"Not sick," I said. "Just were-curious."

He snorted and I could almost see him shaking his great, shaggy head. He said, "So I heard they found a corpse in Fullerton," he said, pausing. "Drained of blood."

"Tsk, tsk, tsk," I said. "Not over the phone. But if it puts you at ease, no, I didn't kill him."

"Good."

More static. More pausing. With some people, gaps in the conversation can feel uncomfortable. With Kingsley, gaps felt natural. Then again, we were immortal. Technically, we could wait forever.

Kingsley un-gapped the conversation. "So where you headed at this late hour?"

"It's early for me, and I'm following up on my one lead."

"Tell me about your lead."

So I did.

When I was finished, Kingsley said, "Yeah, I remember him. Rick Horton. His brother was dead and the only suspect was walking free because of a police screw up."

"Why, Kingsley, if I didn't know you better I would almost say you sound sympathetic."

"I wouldn't go *that* far."

"Tell me about the incident in the court," I said.

"He lunged at me, but it was sort of a half-ass effort. Mostly he called me a stream of obscenities."

"You must be used to them."

"Like they say, sticks and stones," he said. "He didn't seem the type for violence, though."

"Some never do."

"True," he said. "You know where he lives?"

"I've got his address. I still happen to have friends in high places."

"Good, let me know how it goes."

"Have fun tomorrow night," I said. "*Arr Arr Arrrooooo!*"

"Not funny," he said, but laughed anyway.

I disconnected the line, giggling.

23.

I took the 22 East, then headed south on the 55 and exited on Seventeenth Street. Rick Horton lived in an upscale neighborhood in the city of Tustin, about ten miles south of Fullerton. I continued following the Yahoo driving directions until I pulled up in front of a two-story Gothic revival. A house fit for a vampire.

From its triangular arches, to its cast-iron roof crestings, from its diamond-patterned slate shingles, to its multiple stacked chimneys, the Horton house was as creepy and menacing and haunted-looking as any house in Orange County. It was set well back from the road on a corner lot, surrounded by a massive ivy-covered brick and mortar fence. The fence was topped with the kind of iron spikes that would have made Vlad the Impaler proud. The entire house was composed of a sort of squared building stone.

I used the call box by the front gate. A man answered. I gave him my name and told him I was a private investigator and that I would like to speak to Rick Horton. There was a moment of silence, then the gate clicked open. I pushed it open all the way and followed a red brick path through a neat St. Augustine lawn. All in all, this brooding and romantic Victorian-era home seemed a little out of place in Tustin, California.

Just as I stepped up onto the entry porch, the door swung open. A small man with wire-rim glasses leaned through the open door. "Please come in," he said. "I'm Rick Horton."

I did and found myself in the main hall. To my right was a curving stairway. The ceiling was vaulted and there were many lit candles. The house was probably dark as hell during the day, perfect for a slumbering vampire.

I followed the little man through an arched doorway and into a drawing room. I've only been in a few formal drawing rooms, and, unlike the name suggests, there wasn't a single drawing in the place. Instead, it was covered in landscape oils. I was asked to sit on a dusty Chippendale camelback sofa, which I did. The sofa faced a three-sided bay window with diamond-pane glass. The window overlooked the front lawn and a marble fountain. The fountain was of a mermaid spouting water. She easily had double-D breasts, which were probably a distinct disadvantage for real mermaids. Just outside the window three classic fluted Doric columns supported a wide veranda.

He sat opposite me in a leather chair-and-a-half, which was perfect for cuddling. I wasn't in the cuddling mood. Rick Horton wore single gold studs in each ear. He seemed about twenty years too old to be wearing single gold studs. Call me old-fashioned. He was dressed in green-plaid pajamas, with matching top and bottom. He had the air of a recluse. Maybe he was a famous author or something.

"Do you have a license I can see?" he asked. As he spoke, he looked a bit confused and out of sorts, blinking rapidly as if I were shining a high-powered light into his eyes.

I held out my license and he studied it briefly. I hated the picture. I looked deathly ill: face white, hair back, cheeks sallow. I looked like a vampire. The make-up I had been wearing that day seemed to have evaporated with the camera's flash. The picture was also a little blurry, the lines of my face amorphous.

He sat back. "So what can I do for you, Ms. Moon?"

It was actually *Mrs.*, but you choose your battles. "I'm looking into a shooting."

"Oh? Who was shot?"

"My client; shot five times in the face." Horton didn't budge. Not even a facial twitch. "And I think you shot him, Mr. Horton."

That was a conversation killer. Somewhere in the house a grandfather clock ticked away, echoing along the empty hallways, filling the heavy silence.

"You come into my house and accuse me of murder?" he said.

"Attempted murder," I said. "My client did not die, which is how he was able to hire me in the first place."

"Who's your client?"

His attempt at moral outrage was laughable. His heart just didn't seem into it.

"Kingsley Fulcrum," I said.

"Yes, of course, the defense attorney. It was on the news. Watched him hide behind a tree. It was very amusing. I wished he had died. But I didn't shoot him."

I analyzed his every word and mannerism on both a conscious and subconscious level. I waited for that psychic-something to kick in, that extra-sensory perception that gives me my edge over mere mortals, that clarity of truth that tells me on an intuitive level that *he's our man*. Frustratingly, I got nothing; just the fuzziness of uncertainty. His words had the ring of truth. And yet he still felt dirty to me. There was something wrong here.

"Did you hire someone to shoot Kingsley?" I asked.

"Maybe I should have an attorney present."

"I'm not a cop."

"Maybe you're wired."

"I'm not wired." Weird, but not wired.

He shrugged and sat back. "I can't express to you how happy I was to see that son-of-a-bitch get what he deserved. Trust me, if I had shot him I would be proud to say I had. But, alas, I cannot claim credit for what I didn't do."

"Did you hire someone to kill him, Mr. Horton?"

"If I had, would I tell you?"

"Most likely not, but never hurts to ask. Sometimes a reaction to a question speaks volumes." More than he realized.

"Fine. To answer your question: I did not hire someone to kill Kingsley Fulcrum."

"Where were you on the day he was shot?"

"What day was it?"

I told him.

"I was here, as usual. My father left me a sizable inheritance. I don't work. Mostly I read and watch TV. I'm not what you would call a go-getter."

"You have no alibi?"

"None."

"Do you own a .22 pistol?"

He jerked his head up. *Bingo.* "I think this interview is over, Ms. Moon. I did not shoot Mr. Fulcrum. If the police wish to question me further, then they can do so in the presence of my attorney. Good night."

I stood to leave, then paused. "Hewlett Jackson was found dead today, shot nine times in the head."

Horton inhaled and the faintest glimmer of a smile touched his lips. The look on his face was one of profound relief. "Like I said, the police can interview me with my attorney present."

I found my way out of the creepy old house. I love creepy old houses. Must be the vampire in me.

24.

You there, Fang?

I'm here, Moon Dance.

I visited a suspect tonight, I wrote. When I instant message, I tend to get right to the point.

The one you thought might be the shooter?

Yeah, that one, but now I'm not so sure he was the shooter.

Fang paused, then wrote: *Doesn't feel right?*

I'm not sure.

You're getting mixed signals.

Yes, I wrote. Fang was damn intuitive himself, and often very accurate in his assessments of my situations. I loved that about him. *But he feels dirty, though.*

Well, maybe he's connected somehow.

Maybe. When I mentioned the gun, I got the reaction I was looking for.

There you go. Maybe his gun was used, but he wasn't the killer.

Maybe.

There was a much longer pause. Typically, Fang and I chatted through the internet as fast as two people would talk. Perhaps even faster.

I have a woman here, he wrote. *She wants my attention.*

I grinned, then wrote: *Have fun.*

I plan to. Talk to you soon.

It was time for my feeding.

I checked on my children; both were sound asleep. I even looked in on Danny. He once slept only in boxers. Now he sleeps in full sweats and a tee-shirt. His explanation was simple: He didn't like brushing up against my cold flesh.

Screw my cold flesh. I never asked for this.

I walked quietly through the dark house. I didn't bother with the lights because a) I didn't need them and b) I didn't want to disturb the others. Danny recently commented that the thought of me wandering through the house at night creeped him out. Yeah, he said *creeped.* My own husband.

Screw him, too.

In the kitchen, I paused before the pantry. After a moment's hesitation, I opened the cupboard and reached for what I knew would be there: a box of Hostess Ding Dongs. I opened the box flap. Inside, two rows of silver disks flashed back at me. There was something very beautiful about the simplicity of the paper-thin tinfoil wrappings.

As I removed three of them, saliva filled my mouth. My heart began to race.

I sat at the kitchen table and unwrapped the first Ding Dong, wadding the foil wrapping tightly into a little silver ball. Before me, the chocolate puck gleamed dully in the moonlight. My stomach churned, seemed to turn in on itself, roiling like an ocean wave.

The first bite was small and exploratory. Christ, the chocolate tasted so damn good I could have had an orgasm. Maybe I did. Rich and complex and probably fake, the cocoa flavor lingered long after the first bite had been swallowed.

There was no turning back now.

I quickly ate the first Ding Dong and tore into the second. When

I finished it, the third. Finally, I sat back in the wooden chair and felt like a royal glutton. Granted, most of my tastebuds were gone, but chocolate somehow made it through loud and clear.

Outside, through an opening in the curtained window over the sink, the sky was awash with moonlight. Tomorrow was a full moon. Tonight it was almost there, but not quite. I wondered if the almost-but-not-quite full moon had any affect on Kingsley. Maybe a few extra whiskers here and there. Teeth and nails a bit longer than usual.

I giggled about that and considered calling and teasing him, but it was two in the morning. Life is lonely at two in the morning.

My stomach gurgled.

Here it comes, I thought.

I wondered again how long Kingsley had been a werewolf. I also realized he never really admitted to being one. Perhaps he was some variant of a werewolf. Perhaps a were-something else. Maybe a were-kitty.

I shifted in the chair to ease the pain growing in my stomach. Some serious cramping was setting in.

How old was he? Where was he from?

I suddenly lurched forward, gasping. I heaved myself out of the chair and over to the kitchen sink. I turned on the faucet just as the Ding Dongs came up with a vengeance, gushing north along my esophagus with alarming ferocity.

When done, I wiped my mouth and sat on the kitchen floor. I checked my watch. I had kept the Ding Dongs down for all of ninety-three seconds.

I wanted to cry.

25.

I don't sleep in a coffin.

I sleep in my bed, under the covers, with the blinds drawn. I go to bed the moment the kids head off to school, and wake up a couple of hours before they get out. Ideally, I could sleep through the entire cycle of the day, but I'm a mom with kids and *ideally* is out the window.

My sleep is deep and usually dreamless. It's also rejuvenating in ways that I can't fully comprehend. Prior to closing my eyes, usually minutes after my children have left for the day, I am nearly catatonic with fatigue. So much so that I sometimes wonder if I am dying—or perhaps nearly dead—and the deep sleep itself revives me, rejuvenates me, rebuilds me in supernatural ways that I will never understand.

And the moment my head hits the pillow I'm out cold. That is, until my alarm goes off at its loudest setting. I awaken grudgingly and exhausted, fully aware that I should still be sleeping, and that I should never, *ever* be seeing the light of day. Nevertheless, I do get up. I do face the light of day, and I keep trying to be the best mom I can.

My sleep is usually dreamless. But not always. Sometimes I dream that I am a great bird. I fly slowly, deliberately, my powerful wings outstretched, flapping slowly. I never seem to be in a hurry.

Sometimes I dream of my kids, that I infect them with my sickness and they become like me: Hungry for blood, shunned by society, living a secret life of fear and confusion and pain. I usually wake up crying.

Today, I did not wake up crying. Today, I woke up with a smile on my face. Yes, I was still exhausted and could have used a few more hours of sleep, but nonetheless I woke up with a happy heart.

Today, I dreamed of a man. A great hulking creature of a man with the broadest shoulders I'd ever seen and a mane of hair as thick as any wild animal. A man whose eyes glowed amber under the moonlight and whose grin was more wolf than human. In the dream, Kingsley had been stalking me in the deep dark woods. Sometimes he was half-man, and sometimes he was all wolf. The biggest wolf I'd ever seen.

In the dream, I was hiding from him, but it was a game, and I had no fear of the man-wolf. I was hiding behind the trunk of a massive pine tree as he searched the forest for me.

We seemed to do this forever, playing, and I had a sense that we *could* do this forever, if we so desired. That nothing could stop us. Ever. Finally, I stepped out from behind the tree and just stood there on the wooded path. Kingsley, the man, came to me, hunger in his amber eyes. I had forgotten about such hunger. Pushed it aside. I had assumed such a look would be forever lost to me, replaced only by Danny's disgust and horror.

But not with Kingsley. He *hungered* for me.

More important: He *accepted* me.

Then he was upon me, pouncing, taking me up in his great arms and lowering his face to mine. And as he did so, something flashed out of the corner of my eye. The golden amulet, the same one worn by my attacker years ago. I tried to ask Kingsley about the amulet but he lowered his face to mine and took me completely and wholly to a place I had never thought I would go again.

And that's when I awoke, smiling.

Wow.

A minute later when I had regained my senses, I got out of bed and, averting my eyes from the light sneaking in through the blinds, made my way into the living room. There, under the china hutch, I found the box and opened it. Inside was the medallion with the three ruby roses.

I reached in and turned it over. There was blood on it. A tiny speckle that I had missed.

Why had Kingsley refused to discuss the medallion in my dream? Then again, how could he have even known about the medallion?

Then again, I reminded myself, it was just a dream.

Better yet, why are you dreaming of another man? You are a married woman. Dreams like that could lead to trouble.

A lot of trouble.

I returned the medallion to the box, closed the lid, and smiled again.

It had been, after all, a hell of a dream.

26.

Before I became a full-time creature of the night, I was a federal agent for the Department of Housing and Urban Development, or HUD. Although its acronym was not as sexy-sounding as the FBI, my ex-partner and I busted our fair share of bad guys; in particular, real estate scam artists and loan swindlers and those who preyed on the poor.

Anyway, Chad Helling and I had been partners for just over two years when I had been forced to quit and find a night job. He understood. Or, rather, he understood the *given* reason.

He and I were still close, and through him I used the federal government's resources for all they were worth. In exchange, I did some pro bono investigating work for him.

Chad answered his cell on the third ring. "Hey, sunshine."

"Sunshine?" I asked.

"Sorry. Poor choice of words. What's up?"

"I need some help," I said.

"What else is new?"

I ignored that. "The name's Rick Horton out of Tustin. I need to know if he has a twenty-two-caliber pistol registered to his name."

"Anything else?"

"No, that's it."

"You got it, Sunshine."

"Asshole," I said, but he had already hung up.

It was late evening. I tried Kingsley at his office number, but was not surprised to discover that Kingsley had called in sick since this was the night of the full moon. I tried his home number. It was answered immediately.

"Tonight's the big night," I said. "Arooo!"

"Who's this?" asked a stuffy voice.

Whoops!

"I'm, uh, Samantha Moon. May I speak to Kingsley?"

A pause on the other end. I thought I heard a noise from somewhere in the background. Perhaps my imagination was playing tricks on me, but, son-of-a-bitch, I thought I had heard the howl of a dog.

Or a wolf.

"Master Kingsley is . . . indisposed at this time. I'll tell him you rang."

Master Kingsley?

"Please do," I said, trying to match the upper crust voice. I think I warbled perhaps a little too long on *do*. The line was disconnected, and not by me.

Almost immediately my cell vibrated in my hand. I looked at the face-plate. It was my ex-partner.

"Yup, a twenty-two-caliber pistol is registered to one Rick Horton," said Special Agent Chad Helling. "If you knew that why did you need me?"

"I didn't know that," I said. "I surmised."

"That was a hell of a surmise. We could use someone like you at HUD. Too bad you keep such strange hours."

"Thanks, Chad. I owe you one."

"Or two; I've lost track."

27.

It was 6:30 p.m., and the kids were playing at a neighbor's house.

I was in my study going over my notes and reviewing the internet video feed of Kingsley's shooting. Despite myself I laughed as I watched Kingsley ducking and dodging the bullets. Although immortal, each shot must have hurt like hell, and, at the time, the bullets had done serious enough damage to render him almost useless.

I paused on the clearest image of the shooter, which was still pretty grainy. Unfortunately, due to the poor quality of the image, it was impossible to tell if the shooter had been Rick Horton. Whoever it had been was wearing a generic warm-up jacket and a red ball cap. Seemed obvious to me that the shooter was wearing a fake mustache, too, but I couldn't be sure. It just seemed too prominent, and in one frame it even stuck out at an odd angle, as if the glue had come undone. This, too, was noted in the police file.

I now knew Horton owned a .22, and a .22 was used in the crime. Where did that get me? Not much, but at least it was a start.

I felt uneasy, unrested, *undead*.

Shrugging my shoulders, which at this time of the day suddenly seemed twice as heavy, I absently rubbed—or sought—an ache in my neck that seemed always to move just beyond my fingertips. Like trying to catch a fish with your bare hands. Since my attack, since my change, my body ached in places and in ways I had never thought possible.

Maybe this is what it feels like to be dead.

I next found an article on the internet about the murder of Hewlett Jackson, Kingsley's one-time client who had taken nine shots to the face. And, not being a werewolf, he promptly died. Hewlett's body had been found in a parking lot, still inside his car, shot outside a seedy bar I was unfortunately familiar with. There had been no robbery, just a blatant killing.

Interestingly, no one yet had made the connection between Jackson's murder and Kingsley's attack.

Maybe I was barking up the wrong tree.

Did werewolves bark?

I sat back in my chair and stared up at the painted ceiling. The cobwebs in one corner of the room were swaying gently, though I felt no breeze. I should probably clean those someday. The sun was due to set in a few minutes. Its lingering presence in the sky was the reason behind my current uneasiness and shortness of breath and general foul temperament.

I used to worship the sun. Now it was my enemy.

Or, like Superman, my kryptonite.

I drummed my short fingers on the desk. My nails were thick and somewhat pointed. The nails themselves were impossible to cut. They shaped themselves and seemed to hold steady at that length.

I wondered again if Horton had hired a killer.

But that didn't feel right. No hitman worth his salt would have made such a blatant and dangerous attempt in broad daylight. In front of video cameras. In front of a goddamn courthouse. No. The shooter was making a point; most important, the shooter had not cared about getting caught. I was sure of that. Oh, he cared just enough to wear some silly disguise, but I truly felt in my heart that the shooter had not expected to actually escape.

But the shooter had escaped.

There was a knock on my front door. I swung my feet around and stood. My legs were a little shaky. The shakiness was due to the lingering presence of the sun. I moved slowly through the house, to the front door.

And standing there in my doorway was Detective Sherbet of the Fullerton Police Department. He was holding a bag of donuts.

28.

We sat in the living room.

I was in my grandmother's rocking chair and he was on the sofa across from me. The sun was still minutes from setting, and I felt vulnerable. My mind was firing at a slower rate. My body was sluggish. In fact, I felt mortal. I forced myself to focus on the detective sitting before me.

Sherbet held out the bag of donuts. "Place on Orangethorpe makes them fresh this time every day."

I glanced inside the open bag and my stomach turned. "You are perpetuating the stereotype of policemen and donuts," I said.

"Hell, I *am* the reason for that stereotype." He chuckled to himself. "Lord knows how many of these I've eaten. Can't be too bad for you. I'm sixty-seven and still going strong."

I looked away when he took a healthy bite into his donut.

"You don't look too well, Mrs. Moon. Is it too early in the day for you? I tried coming when the sun set, you know, with your skin condition and all. Now what sort of condition do you have?"

I told him.

"Yeah, right, that one," he said. "Well, I looked into it."

"Really?"

"Oh, I'm not trying to snoop on you, Mrs. Moon, I assure you. I just love learning new things. Always been that way."

I nodded; he was snooping on me.

He continued, "Anyway, apparently it's a very rare condition. Usually shows up first in children, not so much in adults. . . ." He let his voice trail off.

"Well, I'm a late bloomer. Always been that way." I wasn't feeling too chatty. Warning bells were sounding in my head—only my head felt too dull to sort through them. "What can I do for you, detective?"

"Oh, just wondering how your case is coming along. Actually, *our* case is coming along." He chuckled again.

"Our case is moving along fine," I said.

"Any leads?"

"Not yet." I'm always hesitant to share any information with cops. At least, not until I'm ready. When I needed Sherbet, I'd come to him. Not the other way around.

He finished the donut and licked his fingers; he fished around in the bag—which must have gotten his fingers sticky all over again—and removed a cinnamon cake. He seemed pleased with his selection and promptly took a healthy bite.

I was sucking air carefully. My lungs felt somehow smaller. I was having a hell of a hard time getting a decent breath.

His eyes flicked over at me. "You okay, Mrs. Moon?"

"Yes; it's just a little bright for me."

"Your shades are down. We are practically sitting in the dark."

I motioned toward the weak sunlight peeking through a crack in the curtains. "Any sunlight at all can be harmful."

"You have a sensitive condition."

"Very."

"There was a murder in Fullerton a week ago," he said, biting into the cinnamon donut. He wasn't looking at me. "Kid was drained of his blood, or at least most of it. The thing is, the medical examiner doesn't know where the blood went."

"What do you mean?"

"I mean the kid was lying there on the sidewalk, shot to death, and there wasn't an ounce of blood around him—or even in him, for that matter." This time he didn't chuckle.

"Maybe he, you know, bled elsewhere."

"Maybe." Sherbet took another sizable bite. Cinnamon drifted down, glittering in the angled sunlight coming in through the blinds. "No one knows who shot him. No one heard anything. So I keep at it. You know, just doing my job. I find out that the victim is a known banger, has a long rap sheet, name of Gilberto. I talk to Gilberto's friends, discover they had a party the night of his murder. But that's all I get from them. I figure the victim must have been shot after their little party." He paused. "And then we find this."

The detective licked his fingers and reached inside his Members Only jacket and pulled out a photograph of a hand gun. "Kids found it in the bushes a few streets down the road. We test the gun, discover it's the same gun that did the banger. We also lift some prints from it. Turns out the prints belong to Gilberto's uncle. Guy's name is Elias. So I shake down Elias the other night, and he says he shot the gun in self-defense."

Detective Sherbet peered inside the donut bag carefully. The room was still and quiet. Sherbet's face was half-hidden in shadows. The bag crinkled as his hand groped for the next donut. "So I push Elias some more, really come down on him. Believe it or not, I can be a real hardass if I want to be."

Actually, I believed it.

He continued. "And he tells me the whole story. I follow up on the story with the others who were there that night. The story checks out." He paused and studied me carefully. The whites of his eyes shone brightly in the dark. "The story goes like this. They were partying. A woman shows up. Jogging, believe it or not, in the dead of night. Anyway, I get a teenage punk to admit that they were going to gang rape her. But things go wrong, horribly wrong."

I said nothing.

"Turns out they cornered a tigress." He chuckled softly and went to town on a chocolate old-fashioned. He worked his way along the outer rim of the donut. "She showed them hell. A real G.I. Jane."

I almost laughed. I wasn't quite sure what that meant, but it sounded funny.

He continued. "She apparently picks this Gilberto scumbag up by the throat. A two hundred and fifty pound man. Picks him up with one hand. And that's when the story gets a little fuzzy. At some point around that time a gun goes off, and Gilberto takes a bullet in the chest. The others flee like the scattering rats they are. One of them, hiding in the bushes, watches the woman carry off Gilberto's corpse into the dead of night."

We were silent. I could almost hear his tired digestive system going to work on the donuts.

"Hell of a campfire story, if you ask me," he said. He wadded up the paper bag. "What do you think about all of that?"

"Hard to believe."

He chuckled. "Exactly. Group of guys out having fun, drunk and fist-fighting and things turn ugly and a gun goes off, and one of them turns up dead. Happens all the time. Sometimes the group will even put their heads together and come up with a wild story."

He held the wadded-up donut bag in both hands. He rested his chin on top of his hands and stared at me. "But I have never heard of a story more wild than this."

I continued saying nothing.

"You ever jog alone at night, Mrs. Moon?"

"Yes."

We sat quietly. "Now, as far as I can tell, this girl committed no crime. She was acting in self-defense, and I can guarantee you she taught these boys a lesson. I've never seen a group of men so fucking spooked in my life. Still, I would kind of like to know what she did with that body. I mean it went missing for a few hours, then reappeared later that morning. Minus a lot of blood. You have any thoughts on that, Mrs. Moon?"

"No, I'm sorry."

He stood up and gave me his card. "Well, thanks for chatting with an old man. I expect to see more of you."

"Lucky you."

He stepped over to the front door. "Oh, and Mrs. Moon . . . were you jogging that night?"

"Which night was that?"

He told me.

"Yes," I said.

"And you didn't see anything?"

"Nothing that would help you, detective."

"Great, thank you."

He shook my hand, holding it carefully in both of his. His hands were so very warm. He nodded once and then left my home.

So very warm. . . .

29.

I drove slowly past the massive Gothic home, peering through the wrought iron fortification. The house was dark and still. I continued by the brooding structure, parked around the corner and killed the minivan's engine.

Other than a handful of trash cans mixed between some parked cars, the street was empty, as it should be at 2:00 a.m., the vampire's hour.

Whatever that means.

A small wind scuttled a red Carl's Jr. hamburger wrapper along the gutter. Hamburgers are not on my short list of acceptable foods, although raw hamburger meat has been known to sometimes—sometimes—stay down. Where it went, of course, I had no idea.

New topic.

The brick fence that ran along the east side of Horton's home was almost entirely covered in ivy. Streetlamps were few and far between, and none on this particular corner. Better for me.

I stepped out of the minivan and into the cool night air. The darkness was comforting. Perhaps I needed the darkness more than it needed me, but I liked to think that I enriched and added flavor to the night. I liked to believe I gave the night some purpose, a sort of symbiotic relationship.

It was 2:00 a.m., the vampire's hour, and I was feeling good.

I approached the vine-covered wall and did a cursory look around. No one was out. The street was empty. The wall before me was ten feet high and topped with iron spikes. Spikes, stakes, ice picks, railroad spikes, of course, all made me nervous. Hell, I've been known to shudder at the sight of a toothpick.

With a small crowbar tucked into a loop on my jeans, I paused briefly beneath the brick fence and then jumped. High. Soaring through the air.

I landed on top and grabbed hold of an iron spike in each hand. Early on in my vampirism, I discovered I could dunk a basketball. Basketball rims were typically about ten feet high. The kids at the local park had been impressed beyond words. So was I. We had, of course, been playing at night.

Careful of the iron spikes, I squatted there on top of the wall like an oversized—albeit cute—frog. In true amphibian-like fashion, I jumped over the spikes and landed smoothly on the far side of the wall, hands flat on the cement.

I dashed around to the back of the house, and promptly pulled up short, coming face to face, or face to muzzle, with two startled Doberman pinschers. Both were huge and beautiful, sleek and powerful. Both blended perfectly with the night.

Their surprise at seeing me turned quickly to fear. No doubt they caught a whiff of me. Whimpering, they turned and dashed off. Had they owned tails, those would have been tucked between their hind legs; as it were, their round nubs shuddered like frightened little moles poking up through the dark earth. The dogs disappeared within some thick shrubbery near a tool shed.

I had that effect on dogs, and animals in general, who seem to sort of see right through my human disguise. I guess they didn't like what they saw. Too bad. I love dogs.

Horton's house might have an alarm. Hell, in Southern California many lesser homes had some form of security. Although I suspected the Dobermans were the extent of the backyard security, I wasn't taking any chances with the downstairs French doors. Instead, I focused on the second floor balcony with its sliding glass door, leading, by my reckoning, to a guest bedroom.

I reached up, gripped the edge of the balcony's wooden floor. In one fluid motion, I pulled myself up and over the railing and landed squarely in the center of the balcony, which shuddered slightly. Next, I used the pry bar to jimmy open the sliding glass door's lock. Luckily, nothing broke. This time. I was getting better at this.

I stepped into the house.

30.

It was indeed the guest room.

The bed, however, was currently empty of guests. A massive Peruvian tapestry hung behind the bed, evoking a simple scene of village life. Moonlight shone through the open drapes, splashing silver over everything. I loved moonlight. Sunlight was overrated.

The air was musky. Newly-stirred dust motes drifted into the moonbeams. Being a trained investigator, I surmised this room hadn't been used in quite some time.

I stepped through the room and into a dark hallway. Well, dark for others, that is. For me, the hallway crackled with molten streams of quicksilver energy, turning everything into distinct shades of gray. Better than any flashlight.

The hallway segued into a wooden railing. Beyond, was a view of the downstairs living room.

And that's when I met the Cat From Hell.

It was sitting on the railing in perfect repose, forepaws together, tail swishing, ears back, its reflective yellow eyes bright spheres of hate. It growled from deep within its chest cavity; we stared at each other for about twenty seconds, just two creatures of the night crossing paths.

Apparently, it wasn't feeling the same sort of kinship.

Like an umbrella, its fur sprang open. Pop. Then it *screeched* bloody hell, and in one quick movement, slashed me across my face. It leaped from the railing, darted down the hallway, hung a right and disappeared down a flight of stairs.

I touched my cheek. The little shit. The wound was already scabbing. I knew within minutes it would be gone altogether.

Still. The little shit.

I waited motionless, certain someone would come to investigate the devil cat. But no one came.

I continued on, and at end of the hall I peeked into an open door. There, sleeping as peaceful as can be, was Rick Horton. From the doorway, I studied his massive room and noted the various antique furnishings, especially the massive, ornate mirror. The room itself was immaculate; everything in its place. Because of that, it was the last place I would have wanted to sleep. A bedroom needed to be lived in.

Rick Horton slept on an undraped four-poster bed. Instead, coats, sweaters and slacks hung neatly from hangers along the horizontal canopy board, perhaps an extension of his closet. Beneath the bed was a cardboard box. The box was slightly askew and not in accordance with the rigorous precision of the room, as if it had been recently shoved under the bed.

I walked quietly to his bedside. Little did Horton realize that an honest-to-God vampire was leaning over him in his sleep, peering down at the smooth slope of his pale neck, where a fat artery pulsed invitingly. I could easily overpower him, tear open the flesh and start drinking. It would be so easy, and warm blood tasted . . . *so . . . goddamn . . . good.*

I sighed and turned my attention to the box, sliding it silently from beneath the bed. Horton never stirred, although I wondered if his sub-conscious was somehow aware of me. Perhaps at this very moment he was fleeing a beautiful vampire in his dreams. Okay, maybe not beautiful, but certainly damn cute with a curvy little body. I wondered fleetingly if the vampire in his dreams catches him. If so, what does she do with him?

I exited the room and made my way back through the long hallway and found a cavernous study. I didn't risk turning on the light. Instead, I pulled open the curtains and allowed for some moonlight, and sat down in a brass-studded executive chair behind a black lacquer desk. I opened the box.

Inside were folders and papers. I removed the first folder, flipped it open and was greeted almost immediately with my own agency's business card stapled to a sheet of paper. Written on the paper was my physical description. I was pleased to say that I was referred to as being *thin* and *pretty*. There was more. A meticulously written recap of our conversation. Most disturbing was a description of my minivan and my license plate number. He had watched me leave.

The second file was much thicker. Inside was a vast array of facts and photographs of Hewlett Jackson, Kingsley's now-murdered client. Hewlett was a young black man, good-looking. There were some pictures of him coming and going from a residence, pictures of him leaving in a white Ford Mustang, of him sitting in a park with a female companion, and of him drinking late at night with friends at an outdoor restaurant. Careful notes were made of times and places of Hewlett's movements and activities.

One particular time and place was circled in red ink. Most interesting was that it was the exact time and place Hewlett was found murdered.

The last file contained similar information on Kingsley Fulcrum. I read the entire file with much interest, then closed the box, exited the study and returned the whole shebang back under Horton's bed. I even made sure the box was slightly askew.

I stared down at the man who had lost his brother within this last year. I felt pity for him. But Rick Horton had decided to take justice into his own hands. And that's where my pity ended.

And, according to his notes, I was next on his list.

I could kill him now and never worry that he might make an unwanted appearance with my children present. But I do not kill people, especially people defenseless in their sleep. Better to let the law handle this.

I slipped away into the night.

31.

It was early afternoon, and I felt like crap, and I would continue to feel like crap until the sun disappeared in a few hours. We were at Hero's again, where very few people knew our names, but at least the bartender remembered our drinks.

"A glass of Chardonnay and a martini?" he asked, giving us a warm smile. He had cute dimples around his mouth. Thick lips, too. Thick, juicy lips.

"You bet," Mary Lou said, beaming. He winked and moved down the bar to pour our drinks, and Mary Lou continued smiling at his back, or perhaps at his backside. "Isn't he just amazing? What a memory!"

"Down girl. It's his job to remember," I said. "He does well to remember."

He returned with our drinks. Mary Lou handed him her credit card, although she probably would have preferred to slip it inside the waistband of his Jockey shorts. She sipped carefully from her glass and finally looked over at me. "So what's the latest news with your case?"

"Are you done undressing our bartender with your eyes?"

"Not yet. Wait. Okay, now I am."

"You're a married woman, with kids," I said.

"I know. Your point?"

"Married women shouldn't be undressing bartenders with their eyes."

"Show me that in the rule book."

"There is no rule book."

She looked at me. "Exactly. Now tell me about your case."

I gave her an update, and to her credit she forgot about the bartender and his buns and focused on me.

"Well, Horton's obviously your guy. What a fucking creep." She shuddered slightly.

"Do you talk this way around your kids?"

"No, just you. I let it all out around you."

"Lucky me," I said.

"And you were next on his list?" she asked.

"You know, to silence the pesky private eye."

"You are kind of pesky, aren't you?"

"The peskier the better."

"So what're you going to do?" she asked.

I sipped some wine. I tasted nothing, literally, but at least I didn't double over with stomach cramps. Sipping from the wine glass gave me some semblance of normalcy. "I'm going to have a talk with Detective Sherbet this evening."

"But what can he do?" asked my sister. "He can't just barge in there and arrest the guy without probable cause."

"You've been watching too much TV, but you're right. Not without a search warrant. And one needs evidence to obtain a search warrant."

"So breaking into this guy's house and finding evidence hidden under his bed won't fly with a judge, right?"

"Right," I said.

"So what will you do?" she asked.

"The detective and I will figure something out."

"Will you tell this detective about your break-in?"

"Yeah, probably."

"Will he like it?"

"Probably not."

We were silent, and I decided now was the time to tell her

about the attempted rape and the death of the gang banger—and about the sucking of blood. So I did. The story took a few minutes, during which Mary Lou said nothing although I noted she had quickly finished her drink.

"That was very reckless of you," she said when I was done.

"I know."

"And you really drank his blood?"

"Yes."

She was silent. I was silent. The noises of the bar came floating to my ears, the chink of glasses being washed in the sink, the sound of laughter behind me, the snapping opening of the cash register drawer.

"What if this somehow causes you to lose control, Samantha?"

"I love my kids too much to lose control."

"Then you took a foolish chance by drinking that man's blood."

"Yes, I did. But the situation had gotten quickly out of control. Before I knew it, I was holding a corpse."

"You should not be jogging so late."

I drank my wine. Sometimes Mary Lou was impossible to talk to.

"When is there a better time? I'm a goddamn vampire."

"The early evening."

"In the early evening I have the kids and work."

"Then why do you need to jog at all?"

"Because it helps me stay sane."

We were alone at this end of the counter. As we spoke, my eyes constantly scanned the crowd, making sure we had no eavesdroppers. "I walk a fine line, Mary Lou. Everything around me is threatening to crumble away. Something like exercise is within my control. I need control right now."

"Maybe you need help."

We had gone through this before. "There's no one to help me."

"Maybe you need to speak to a therapist, someone, anyone."

"You think this is in my head?"

"No. It's real. I know that."

"The moment I tell a therapist that I'm a vampire, they'll lock me up and take away my kids. Is that what you want?"

She didn't answer immediately.

"Is that what you want, Mary Lou?"

"No, it's not what I want, but I also think your kids are not living a very healthy and normal life." She sighed and reached out and held my hand. "You are a good mother, I know that. I know your kids mean everything to you, but I think they are in an unhealthy environment."

"I see it as a *different* environment," I said, then studied her concerned face. "Wait. Do you worry for their safety?"

She said nothing.

"Do you worry that I will have a craving and drink from my own children?"

Nothing.

"You do, don't you?"

She sucked in some air. "No, of course not. But if you keep behaving recklessly you might, you know, someday lose sight of who you are. Sam, you've fought for so long to keep things together. I don't want to see your life crumble around you just because you found the taste of one man's blood particularly good."

I studied her and she looked away. I suddenly had an insight. "You've been talking to Danny, haven't you?"

She reddened. "Yes. He called me the other night to apologize for not picking up the kids. He's worried about the kids."

"Oh, really? And he shows this by coming home at midnight?"

She shrugged. "He worries that you will have a negative influence on their lives. I told him that was ridiculous. No mother loves her kids more than you."

We were silent. It was just before dusk, and I was irritable and cranky and tired. I wanted to sleep.

"He's screwing someone else," I said.

"You know for sure?"

"No. But I'm going to find out."

"I'm sorry, Sam."

"So am I. But it was bound to happen, right? Who wants to be married to a freak?"

"You're not a freak," she said, and then cracked a smile. "Well, okay, maybe a little freaky."

I laughed. She reached out and took my hand. I reveled in the warmth.

She said, "So what are you going to do, Sam?"

"Follow him," I said. "I am, after all, an ace detective."

32.

The sun had just set, and I was in Detective Sherbet's office. I felt good. Most important, I felt cognizant and lucid.

I sat in the visitor's chair in front of his desk and noticed for the first time that Sherbet was a handsome man. His arms were heavily muscled and tan, with dark hair circling his forearms. I didn't usually go for arm hair on men, but on Sherbet it seemed fitting and a little exciting. He seemed like a man's man, powerful and virile. No wonder it galled him to think his kid might be gay.

"So how did the basketball game go the other day?" I asked.

There was a greasy bag of donuts sitting on top of a very full trash can. The scent of donut oil was foul, and slightly upsetting to my stomach. I fought through it.

"Kid was horrible. He actually took a shot at the wrong basket. Hell, he almost even made it. I nearly cheered. The coach benched him after that."

"Did your boy have fun?"

"No. He was miserable."

"Did you have fun?"

"No. I was embarrassed."

"So what are you going to do? Keep forcing him to play?"

"You sound like my wife."

"Your wife sounds like she might be the only reasonable parent in your household."

"I don't know what I'm going to do with that kid."

"Just love him."

"I do."

Our section of the police station was empty and quiet. The detective had his hands clasped over his rotund belly. Although his stomach could have been flatter, the roundness sort of added to his manhood, pronouncing him as a real man who wasn't afraid to eat.

"You're looking at my fat belly," he said.

"I would call it rotund," I said.

"Rotund? Are you trying to get on my good side?"

"Maybe."

He rubbed a hand over the curving sweep of his belly, then played with one of the clear plastic buttons. His face turned somber. "Samantha, I know you were assaulted six years ago, here in Fullerton. It's in your record. You were found in Hillcrest Park, half-dead. Your throat torn open. Although there was little blood at the scene, you had almost bled to death. At first it was believed that you might have been attacked by an animal, a dog or coyote. But later you told investigators that it had been a man. He was never found."

"Detective, I don't want to talk about—"

"Now, I understand you might not want to talk about it, but there's something strange going on here in my town, my backyard, so to speak. My beat. I would appreciate if maybe someday you could help me understand."

"Someday," I said. "Just not today."

"Okay, fine. On to item number two. What do you have on the Fulcrum case?"

Relieved to be talking about anything else, I told him everything I knew about Horton. When I got to the part about breaking and entering Horton's home, I said, "Are you going to arrest me?"

"Not yet. Keep going."

"Horton had files on Hewlett Jackson and Kingsley Fulcrum, not to mention a new file on me. In these files are detailed information on Jackson's and Fulcrum's movements. A date and time was circled on Jackson. In fact, it was the exact date and time he was murdered."

Detective Sherbet's eyes widened a little. For Sherbet, this was the next best thing to him jumping up and down and yelling *yippee!* "Then he's our man."

"Yes, I think so."

"You think so? Hell, he had everything but the smoking gun. And he might still have that, as well, once we serve a search warrant."

"He just doesn't feel right."

"Is that your gut talking?"

"Yes."

"Well, my gut says he's our man."

"How are you going to convince a judge to issue a warrant?"

He sat back, laced his fingers behind his thick head of salt and pepper hair. "Good question. Any ideas?"

"You're the homicide detective."

He thought about that. "How about a trash run?"

"As in dig through his trash?" I said.

"Sure. It's public domain. We find something incriminating we can convince a judge to issue a warrant."

I blinked. "We?"

"Yes, I'm not going to dig through his trash alone."

"The trash went out last night," I said. "I saw the barrels."

"It's settled then. Next Thursday we go out to Horton's place and dig through his trash."

"Sounds like a date."

"Let's just hope we find something."

"Oh, I'm sure we'll find something," I said. "Let's just hope we find the *right* something."

33.

The kids were in karate class together, so I used the opportunity to work-out at Jacky's. It was late evening, and the sun had set. I was feeling strong and healthy. At the moment, Jacky was taping my fists. We were both silent. I think he sensed I was in one of my moods. Occasionally, he would look up into my face, then quickly avert his eyes.

"I'm not going to bite you, Jacky."

"You think I'm afraid of you?" he asked. "Well, I am."

I rubbed his shining head with my already-taped right hand.

In fact, I was having a hard time letting go of my conversation with Mary Lou. I was trying to comprehend the fact that she had been secretly speaking to Danny. Discussing what an unfit mother I was.

"Whatever's eating at you," said Jacky, "take it out on the punching bag. That's my motto."

And so I did. Pummeling the thing until I was dripping sweat.

We worked in three minute drills, with Jacky screaming at me to keep my hands up. I would finish each round in a flurry of punches, rapid-fire body shots to the punching bag. During one of these flurries, I caught Jacky's expression as he steadied the punching bag. It was one of profound pain. The punches were reverberating through the bag and into him. The Irishman was taking a beating, but he seemed to love it.

At the end of the sixth round I dropped my hands to my side. The gloves felt like bags of cement. Jacky staggered away to get some water.

I leaned my forehead against the punching bag. I was still thinking about Danny. It seemed to me that he was building a case against me. Of course, building a case against me couldn't be easier. Hell, in my current condition, even I knew I was an unfit mother. But I was doing my best and I loved my kids with all my heart. You could never replace that. Ever.

At the far end of the gym, I noticed a tall boxer working out with one of Jacky's long-time trainers. The boxer was young and blond and very muscular. His punches were rapid and precision-like. His muscles stood out on his hot skin.

Jacky came back, holding a little Dixie cup full of water. The cup was shaking in his hands.

"I've been meaning to talk to you about those Dixie cups," I said. "We pay good money to join your gym, and the best you can give us are these paper thimbles in return?"

"Ah, lass, you pay for the atmosphere."

I nodded toward the young, hotshot boxer. "Who's that?"

"That's Desmond Beacon. A boxing champion in the Marines, went undefeated. He's turning pro."

"I want to box him."

Jacky's eyes brightened briefly—perhaps with excitement—and then he came back down to earth and shook his head. "Look, kid, I know I built your hopes up and all that, but that ain't going to happen. Maybe we could arrange a fight with another broad."

"Broad?" I said. "Maybe I should box *you*." I looked again at the ex-Marine. "I want to fight *him*."

"No, lass. I'm sorry."

"So he kicks my ass. At least it'll give me something else to think about."

Jacky looked at me and sighed. "Your day that shitty, huh?"

I thought of Danny cheating—or possibly cheating—and I thought of possibly losing my kids. "Yeah," I said. "Hell of a shitty day."

He sighed again and said, "Hold on." He went over to the Wonder Kid and his trainer, spoke briefly, pointed at yours truly. Desmond Beacon shook his head, said something, and they all laughed. All of them, that is, except Jacky. He got into the tall Marine's face. By got into his face, I mean, Jacky looked up from the man's chest. I had no doubt that Jacky could have taken the Marine in his day. But his day was long past him. They stared each other down for another ten seconds and then the Marine turned away, dismissing Jacky with a contemptuous smirk.

"What was that all about?" I asked when Jacky had hobbled back.

"Fucking prick," said Jacky. "I have a mind to kick his ass."

"What did he say?"

"Doesn't matter."

"He doesn't want to fight me?"

"Doesn't matter."

"It's because I'm a woman."

"He said something about that," said Jacky, looking back at the Marine, who had gone back to shadow boxing. "Actually, he said something about doing something else to you, but I ain't gonna repeat it to you."

"Is that when you stuck up for me?"

"The kid's disrespectful. Someone needs to show him a lesson."

"I agree."

"Samantha . . . I get nervous when I see that look in your eye."

But I wasn't listening. I was already marching over to the six-foot-four Desmond Beacon, who was shadow boxing near the ring. When he saw me coming he stopped, nudged his trainer, and grinned. A wolfish sort of grin. When I got to him, I looked him in the eye, smiled sweetly, and promptly kicked him square in the balls.

Hope he's wearing a cup.

His eyes bulged and a look of confusion swept across his face and then he dropped to a knee, groaning and turning red.

Guess not.

His little trainer shrieked like a monkey. He grabbed my shoulder and tried flinging me around, but I don't fling easily and he lost his balance. Instead, he settled for getting in my face. "What the hell are you doing, Missy? Are you out of your goddamn mind?"

"Just maybe," I said. I pushed the trainer aside and looked down at the boxer kneeling before me. I felt like a queen. "Will you fight me now?"

Desmond Beacon looked up. His face had gone from red to green.

"You bet your ass," he croaked.

34.

Jacky and I were in a corner of the ring.

The little Irishman was doing some last minute adjustments to my headgear. The headgear felt big and clunky. I didn't think I needed it, but having it on seemed to make the others happy. The Marine, in the opposite corner, was also wearing headgear. I assumed he, too, felt the gear was unnecessary.

I stared down at Jacky's bald head as he now worked on my gloves. From this angle I could just make out some old boxing scars above his brow. Many, many old boxing scars. There was a wicked little gleam in Jacky's eye whenever he looked up at me; he was breathing hard and fast, face red with excitement.

"Remember what I always tell you," he said, "keep your gloves up."

"Keep them up? Or down? I get confused."

But Jacky wasn't listening. In fact, he had this sort of dreamy look on his face. Perhaps he had regressed back to the backroom fighting halls of 1950s Belfast, when he was a young prize fighter with something to prove. His fighting days were long gone and I had a feeling I was his outlet, but that was okay. I wanted to fight. I wanted an honest-to-God slugfest. Sometimes you just need to beat the crap out of something.

"Focus on your jabs, doll."

"Don't call me doll, and I'll focus on whatever I want. This isn't a real fight. I'm just going to beat the crap out of him and then pick up my kids."

Jacky pushed me away and held me at arm's length. "Don't get too cocky, kid. You're strong as hell, and to be honest, a little freaky, but this guy knows the fundamentals. I'm not sure you realize what the hell you've gotten yourself into."

"We'll see."

Jacky held up a white towel. "I'm throwing this in if things turn ugly."

"For me or him?"

"Either."

"Ding ding," said Jacky.

Desmond Beacon stood nearly a foot taller than me. In the center of the ring we touched gloves. Now that the pain was gone from his groin, he didn't look so eager to fight a woman—especially now that we had a few female onlookers.

So, to get him back into the spirit of things, I hit him with a quick jab that landed on his chin and snapped his head back. When his head settled back into place, there was a suitable look of irritation in his eyes.

Behind me, Jacky screamed, "Yes, yes!"

Desmond now bounced on his toes and worked his neck, and suddenly flicked his glove out at me much quicker than I was prepared for. I tried to dodge right, but there was no escaping it. His glove hit me square in the jaw and I staggered backwards and promptly landed on my ass, skidding to a halt near the ropes.

"Sammy, you okay?" Jacky's worried, ruddy face peered down at me through the lowest rung of rope.

I got up. "I'm fine."

"I don't like this, Sammy. He's too good."

"Don't call me Sammy."

"Then what the hell do you want me to call you?"

"Just Sam."

We touched gloves again. Desmond wasn't smiling. In fact, he didn't seem to be enjoying any of this. I think he was hoping I would've gone away by now. We circled each other. I was wary of his hand speed. His face was expressionless, although his cheeks were pinched together because of the headgear. He kept his gloves up like a good boy. His fist shot out again, another jab. I blocked it with my own glove, but the force of the punch knocked my own glove back into my forehead. Luckily the headgear is thickest at the forehead. He jabbed again. I blocked it and side-stepped. He was waiting for me to side-step. His next punch rung my bell, and I staggered backward again.

I caught a glimpse of Jacky. Or, rather, *two* Jackys. The old Irishman looked stricken. His interest in seeing a real fight had long ago dissipated. He was holding the white towel up. I shook my head at him, and he reluctantly lowered it.

Back in the ring, Desmond looked a little surprised to see me still on my feet. We circled each other some more. It seemed apparent to me that the Marine and his manager, and perhaps even Jacky, had agreed that I would only receive jabs. Harmless enough, and not too brutal. Wouldn't bode well for Jacky's female clientèle to watch a woman get pulverized by a semi-professional male boxer.

Now even more people were watching. A small crowd of mostly women were standing around the sparring ring, all dripping sweat, their workouts finished or abandoned. They were talking amongst themselves and watching me closely. I didn't like close scrutiny, but I needed to pound something, and the Marine was the biggest thing in the gym.

I focused entirely on the Marine. Sweat dripped steadily down his cheeks and into his headgear. The muscles in his right shoulder flexed and I took a step back just as his lightning-fast jab swished through the air. *Focus on the shoulder.* The deltoid muscles flinched again and I moved back again and avoided the next punch as well. We circled, and he stopped bouncing on his feet and lowered his hands. The moment he lowered his hands, I delivered a combination of left jab and overhead right. Both landed. I am quick when I want to be and strong when I want to be, and I wanted to be both now. The punches staggered him backward and he landed against the ropes. A chorus of cheers erupted from the milling crowd of sweating women. The Marine pushed himself off the ropes and approached me, fists raised. He was looking at the crowd of women out of the corner of his eye. He didn't know what to do. He was in a hell of spot. He didn't want to hurt a woman, yet here was a woman in front of him who was hurting him. I decided to make that decision for him, and came at him like a bull. I faked a left jab and then came hard over his gloves with a straight right that hit him square on the nose. His knees buckled. I hit him again. He gathered himself and quit looking at the crowd. Good. Now he danced around the ring like he meant it. Good. He lifted his gloves and delivered a powerful combination that I used my gloves and arms to absorb. His punches hurt. He was throwing them hard. He didn't give a damn who was watching him now or how bad this might have looked. He was tired of some woman taking potshots at him.

Except I wasn't *some woman*.

Even with the sun still out in the late afternoon sky, my reflexes were better than average. But only slightly better. I still felt weak and sluggish—and that damn sun couldn't set fast enough.

The Marine suddenly threw a wild punch that veered off my shoulder and I used that opening to deliver a rocking uppercut. I caught him under the chin and his head snapped up. He might have even lifted off the mat. Either way, he landed hard on his back. The crowd went wild. Alright, maybe not wild, but definitely a few cheers. The Marine got up and we touched gloves in the middle of the ring again. His eyes seemed a little unsteady. The big boy had taken a few hard blows to the head from a very healthy vampire. He raised his fists, did a little boxing dance, and sort of refocused himself.

And came out swinging.

Holy crap! Hell hath no fury like a man embarrassed by a woman. His punches were powerful and numerous; some landed, but most missed entirely. I soon found myself backed up against the ropes. Spit and sweat and blood flung from the Marine. His arms were a blur of punches. I heard gasps behind me. Surely this looked horrible to Jacky's female clientèle: a woman being beaten to a pulp by a hulking Marine. I'm sure Jacky was about to throw in the towel, when it happened.

I didn't see it happen, granted.

But I *felt* it.

The late afternoon sun had finally set, and I felt alive.

So damn alive.

I slipped under his onslaught and backed into a corner. He was about to follow me in but must have seen something in my eyes and paused. He should have kept pausing. Instead, he charged ahead. As he came at me, I timed my punch perfectly. A hard right to the jaw.

Too hard.

Never had I hit something so squarely and so hard. I floored him. No. I lifted him off his feet and over the surrounding ropes. He landed in a heap on the padded floor. Women screamed and rushed over to him. I saw Jacky run over to the Marine, too. He looked at me, horror on his face.

What had I done?

I stood dumbly in the center of the ring as the Marine lay on his back, unmoving.

35.

I almost killed a man today.

Tell me about it.

So I wrote it up for Fang. As usual, he read like a demon on crack, and posted his reply almost instantly.

The Marine might be re-thinking his boxing career.

I suddenly felt indignant, perhaps to mask my guilt. *Good. He was a pig, and boxing's certainly no way to make a living. Getting your brains beaten to a pulp day in and day out.*

I see, so by knocking him out of the ring, you actually did a service to him.

Yes. He could think of it as career counseling.

Through the school of hard knocks.

Haha.

I think you are trying to assuage your guilt, Moon Dance, to justify your actions.

Okay, fine. I feel horrible! You happy?

No. At least you can admit your guilt.

He didn't deserve what I did to him.

Probably not. Then again, he sounded like he might have needed to be taught a lesson. Did you really kick him in the balls?

Argh! I'm horrible!

Yes, wrote Fang. *You were today.*

You don't let me off easy, do you?

Do you want me to let you off easy?

No, I wrote, thinking about it. *I want you to always be dead honest with me. It's why I keep you around.*

Gee, thanks. So what happened to the Marine?

They took him away in an ambulance. The paramedic said it looked like a concussion. I sent him flowers and a card apologizing.

Perhaps you should find other outlets for your anger, wrote Fang.

Perhaps.

You might have to be a little more, um, discreet with your gifts. You don't want to keep attracting unwanted attention.

I think you're right. I paused. *But why call it a gift, Fang?*

It's how you choose to view it, Moon Dance. You could focus on either the negative or the positive. As in all of life.

Thank you, Tony Robbins.

No, I'm not Tony Robbins but I'm certainly as tall.

Really? What else do you look like? I wrote, eager for more information.

As usual, he ignored any personal questions. *Let's take a look at these gifts of yours. You have enhanced strength, night vision, speed and endurance. Not to mention the ability to shape-change.*

Whoa! I wrote, sitting back. *No one's ever said anything about shape-changing.*

You've never shape-changed, Moon Dance?

Ever recall me mentioning turning into a bat?

There was a long pause, then he wrote: *Most texts, resources and personal accounts are unanimous about this. You should be able to shape-change. Into what exactly, is open to debate.*

I found myself laughing at my computer desk. *Well, if your resources can tell me* how *to shape-change, then I'll give it a shot.*

I'll look into it. Maybe you should look into it, too.

How?

Another pause: *Maybe you need to look into yourself.*

The doorbell rang. The babysitter was here.

Goodnight, Fang.

Goodnight, Moon Dance.

36.

It was late and I was restless.

Earlier in the day, I'd dreamed of Kingsley again, and now I couldn't get the big son-of-a-bitch out of my thoughts. In my dream, we were in the woods again, but this time we weren't playing a game. This time he had captured me early on and I was on my back. I distinctly remembered the pine needles poking into my bare back and the sound of small animals scurrying away in the woods. Scurrying away in *fear*. Kingsley was in his half man/half wolf mode, dark shaggy hair hanging from his huge shoulders, down his long arms. A tuft of it sticking up along the ridge of his spine like a hairy stegosaurus. He was on all fours and he was above me. I was pinned beneath him, distinctly aware that he was far too strong for me to push off. I was submitting to him. Body and soul.

In my dream, he was still wearing the medallion, hanging freely from his thick neck, suspended just inches above my face. Whenever I opened my mouth to ask about the medallion, he simply shook his great head and I knew I was not to discuss it, and so I didn't, although I wanted to. Badly.

Then he lowered his face to mine, a face that was still magnificently human and handsome, although in bad need of a shave. His breath was hot on my neck, my ears, through my hair. He was touching me with his lips or tongue, I didn't know which, nor did I care. I only knew I had not felt this good in a long, long time.

Then the alarm went off, and I could have cried.

A hell of a dream, I thought. *I think you might like the big guy.*

Ya think?

The question was: What did I do about it? I didn't know. Even though I knew in my heart my marriage was over, I still felt guilty for having feelings for another man.

You shouldn't. Your husband is long gone. You can't keep living like this, and nor can he.

But the moment I quit living like this—the moment my husband and I officially separated—would be the moment my kids are taken away from me, and I can't have that.

I can't have that.

So quit thinking about Kingsley.

Easier said than done.

It was late, and I was restless and I couldn't for the life of me keep Kingsley out of my thoughts. Damn him. What right did he have kissing a lonely and hurting woman? What right did he have of putting me through this?

I nearly laughed. It had, of course, been just a dream.

37.

"You home?" I asked.

"Of course I'm home," said Kingsley, "it's two-thirty in the goddamn morning."

"Don't sound so dramatic."

"Dramatic? If anything I sound tired."

"I'm coming over. Where do you live?"

There was a long pause. I wondered if Kingsley had fallen back to sleep. Then a thought occurred to me, maybe he had a woman with him. If so, I didn't care. I wanted to talk, and not with a mortal. Either way, last night had been the full moon, so tonight Kingsley should be his old self.

"Okay," he said, and gave me directions. "Oh, and remind me when you get here that there's something I need to talk to you about."

"That makes two of us."

Kingsley lived in Yorba Linda, just a few cities over. At a quarter to three, I drove east down Bastanchury Boulevard. The night was still and quiet. To my left were empty rolling hills. Beyond was the county dump, well hidden from curious eyes and sensitive noses.

Here on Bastanchury were some of the best properties Orange County had to offer. Beautiful homes slightly removed from the hustle and bustle of the county.

I turned left into a long driveway, drove through a tangle of shrubbery along a crushed seashell drive. The seashell drive, reflecting the near full moon, was as bright as a yellow brick road to my eyes. The driveway continued for perhaps an eighth of a mile, until it curved before a massive estate house.

I parked in front of the portico, and briefly admired the huge structure. It was a Colonial revival, complete with two flanker structures on either end. Nearly the entire facade was covered in dark clapboard, and the windows were enclosed with paneled shutters. All in all, a fitting home for a werewolf.

Shortly after I rang the bell, a porch light turned on and a very tall and dour man appeared at the door, who looked down at me from a hawkish nose. He was frowning. Probably wasn't in his job description to be receiving guests at 3:00 a.m. There was something disjointed and odd about the man. It took me a second to realize what it was. One ear was clearly larger than the other.

"This way," he said. "Master Kingsley is waiting in the conservatory."

"With Professor Plum and the candlestick?" I asked.

Big Ear was not amused.

38.

Kingsley was lounging on a leather sofa with a drink in hand.

He looked like hell: scruffy beard, hair in disarray, serious bags under his eyes.

"Um, you look good," I said.

"Like hell I do."

"Just what I was thinking."

The conservatory was octagon-shaped and faced the expansive backyard which spread out into the hills beyond like a vast estate. Through the French window, I could make out an alabaster fountain gurgling away, depicting a naked nymph blowing water through her cupped hands. The sculptor went a little crazy with her breasts. Men and breasts. Sheesh.

"Would you like a drink?" Kingsley asked.

"Sure. I'll have whatever you're having."

Kingsley motioned to his butler. A moment later, a drink appeared before me.

"Thank you, Jeeves," I said.

Kingsley grinned. "His name is Franklin."

"Franklin the butler?"

"Yes."

"Doesn't have quite the same ring."

"No, it doesn't," Kingsley said, "but he's a good butler, and can pour a hell of a drink."

"It's true," said Franklin. "I almost never spill." His enunciation was clear and precise with a slightly lilting accent that could have been English. When he spoke, his face appeared completely still, as if the muscles were inert, or deactivated. I couldn't help but notice an ugly scar that ran along his chin and extended back to his hairline, as if Franklin had at one time or another lost his entire head.

Kingsley said, "Thank you, Franklin. That will be all. Sorry to rouse you out of your sleep in the dead of night."

"I am made to serve."

"And you do it so well. Off you go. Good night."

Franklin the Butler nodded and left. Curious, I watched him go. His strides were long and loping, as if his legs were disproportionate to his body.

"Franklin is an interesting fellow," I said when he was gone.

"You don't know the half of it."

"Must have survived a hell of an accident, scarred like that."

"Yeah, something like that."

"Where did you find him?"

"He was recommended by a friend."

I sipped the alcohol. It had no flavor at all, and no effect. The ice rattled in the tumbler.

"What do you know of vampire shape-shifting?" I asked suddenly.

Kingsley blinked, then thought about it. "Not a whole hell of a lot, I'm afraid. Why?"

"It's been coming up lately."

"I see."

"So, *can* vampires turn into, you know, *things*?"

He laughed, "They can indeed turn into . . . *things*."

My heart slammed in my chest. "What sort of things?" I asked.

"You really don't know, do you?"

"Would I be asking if I did?"

"And you've never tried shape-changing?"

"I wouldn't know where to begin."

"You could always try jumping off a tree branch and see what happens."

"And think like a fruit bat?"

"Is that the gay bat?"

"You're not helping."

"That's just it. I don't know how to help. My own transformation sort of takes place uninvitingly."

"I understand. So back to the question: What sort of things can vampires turn into?"

"Vampires turn into . . . something big and black." He paused and grimaced as if he had just bitten into something sour. "Something ugly and hideous. Something with massive leathery wings. A sort of hybrid between man and bat."

"You've seen one?"

He hesitated. "Yes."

"And?"

"And that's all I know."

"Who was the vampire?"

"I'd rather not discuss it right now."

"Why?"

He inhaled. His handsome face was mostly hidden in shadows, although that posed little problems for me. I could see the fine lines of his nose and jaw.

"Because he killed my wife."

I breathed. "I'm sorry, Kingsley."

"Hey, it's in the past."

"I ask too many questions. It's the investigator in me. I don't know how to turn it off sometimes."

"You didn't know."

I wanted to ask him more about his wife. Why was she killed? Was she a werewolf, too? If not, then how did they make their marriage work? How long had they been married? And kids? Moreover, who was this vampire? But I held my tongue, which was something I didn't do well. Therefore, I found myself thinking of flying around the city of Fullerton like a super-sized bat out of hell. The image was too crazy. I mean, I'm a mother of two. I went to a PTA meeting last week. I washed twelve loads of laundry over the weekend. Real people don't turn into giant bats, right?

"So basically," I said after a suitable time, "I turn into a monster."

He eased off the sofa and headed to the bar. He poured himself another drink.

"You're not the only one," he said. "Once a month Franklin keeps me locked up in a special room where I won't hurt myself or others." He swirled the contents of his glass. Some of the contents splashed over the rim. He didn't seem to notice or care. "Only monsters need to be locked up."

"But you have taken measures to control the monster within you. In my book, that makes you very much *not* a monster."

"By practicing safe-transformation?" he asked.

I laughed. "Precisely."

As he sat, I noticed a particularly thick tuft of hair at the back of his hand. The hair hadn't been there a few days before. I slipped out of my chair and to his side. I took his hand in my own and ran my fingers through the fur.

"Just what are you doing?" he asked. He didn't move. I could feel his pulse in his wrist. His pulse was quickening. I pulled on the fur.

"It's real," I said.

"Of course it's real."

"You really *are* a werewolf."

"Yes."

"Can I call you Wolfy?"

"No."

A glint of amber reflected in his irises. I could have been looking into the eyes of a wolf staring back at me from the deep shadows of a dark forest.

The forest. My dream. His hot breath. His hotter lips.

I looked away. God, his stare was hypnotic. No wonder he won so many court cases. What juror could resist those eyes? I noticed then that the couch had a light sprinkling of what appeared to be dog hair. The hair was now on my clothing.

"You're shedding," I said.

"Yes, I tend to do that."

"How old are you Kingsley?"

"You will not be denied tonight, will you, Samantha?"

I shrugged. "Perhaps by understanding more about you, I can understand more about me, about who I am and where I'm going."

"Fine," he said. "I'm seventy-nine."

"Is that in dog years?"

"I'm going to bed," he said.

"Wait. What did you need to talk to me about?"

He nodded solemnly. "There's someone looking for you, Samantha."

"Who?"

"A vampire hunter."

"A . . . what?"

"A vampire hunter, and he wants you dead."

I choked on my drink. "Why?"

"Because you're a vampire and killing vampires is what he does."

"How does he kill vampires?"

"A crossbow, I think. Apparently arrow bolts have the same effect on vampires as stakes."

"When did you find this out?"

"Tonight."

"How did you find out?"

"I'm privy to such information. Through associates. From others like me."

"Werewolves."

"Yes."

I thought about that, and then told him about the man from the other night with the night-vision goggles. Kingsley shrugged.

"It could have been him. Perhaps he's been following you."

"No one's been following me."

"How do you know?"

"I watch for tails. It's a habit of mine."

"A good habit," he agreed.

"Speaking of tails—"

"I'm going to bed," he said again.

"Wait. What do you propose I do about this vampire hunter?" I asked.

"Kill or be killed. That's where I come in. Let me help you get rid of this guy."

"No," I said. "I'm a big girl and this is my problem."

"He's a trained killer."

"And I've been trained to protect myself."

He didn't like it, but said no more. We sat together on the couch, our shoulders touching.

"Why are you with him, Samantha?"

I knew who he was talking about. Danny. "It's none of your business why."

"Yes," he said, "it is."

"How so?"

"Because I think I'm falling in love with you."

39.

It was late.

The kids were with my sister, and I was alone in a parking lot, hidden behind some bushes and beneath an overhanging willow. The digital clock on the car radio read 11:22 p.m. Too late for an attorney and his secretary to be working cases.

The engine was off, and the windows were cracked open. Even vampires need to breathe. Actually, I wondered about that. I held my breath, timing myself. A minute passed. Two minutes. Three. Four. Five. I let out my breath. Well, hell. You learn something new every day.

Just what dark voodoo was keeping me alive then? Didn't my brain and blood need oxygen, too? Maybe I just didn't need as much, and the only reason I seemed to breathe on a regular basis was that my autonomic nervous system didn't know enough to shut off. I felt my heart. It was beating, very slowly. I timed the beating. Ten beats a minute. Ah, hell. I should be dead a hundred times over.

But I wasn't. I was very much alive. But how, dammit?

Maybe it was better not to think about it.

I was alive. Perhaps I should have died six years ago, but I didn't. Something kept me alive, and for that I was thankful. Now, not only could I watch my kids grow up but I would probably outlive my grandchildren and their children's children.

Jesus.

I ask again: What the hell kind of dark magic is keeping me alive?

Danny's firm is a small firm. He owned it with a partner, where it occupied the entire second floor of a very plain professional building. Danny specialized in auto accidents. A classic ambulance chaser. He made good money at it, but sold his soul.

I used to give him crap about it long ago, until I realized he actually enjoyed the work. He enjoyed sticking it to the insurance companies. Now he enjoyed sticking it to his secretary.

The night was cool. Trees above me swished gently. The partial moon appeared and disappeared through a smattering of clouds.

There seemed to be a hint of light coming from one of the building's upstairs windows, but it was difficult to tell as the blinds were shut. I sipped from a water bottle. The water was lukewarm. I discovered that I liked lukewarm water, which was a refreshing change from the nightly dosage of chilled hemoglobin.

I thought of the vampire hunter. For the past few days I had been watching my tail, and was confident no one was following me.

Staking out anyone—even your husband—can be boring work. I held up my hand and studied it. My skin was white, almost translucent. Purple veins crisscrossed the back of my hand. My nails were thick and hard. Like my hair, they tended to grow slowly. I touched the center of my palm with my left index finger. The sensation sent a slight shiver up my right arm. Flesh and bone. I was three dimensional. I could feel. I could laugh. I could love my kids.

So why couldn't I die? And what gave me my unnatural strength?

I turned the rearview mirror my direction.

There was nothing in the mirror. Nothing at all, save for an image of the driver's seat headrest. My clothing moved as if occupied by the Invisible Woman. Fairly disconcerting. It was as if the mirror refused to acknowledge my existence. I turned it away in disgust.

"Well, I'm here, dammit," I said to the mirror. "Whether you like it or not."

Or perhaps I was saying this to Danny. Or the world.

So a creature called a vampire had attacked me one night. It tainted my blood with his. Because of that taint I was forever and irrevocably changed.

It had to do with the blood. I thought of blood now. It was the lifesource. Without it, we die. Well, without a lot of other stuff we die, too. Without your head you die. Without your heart you die.

How could something in my blood change me *forever*?

Blood connected everything, flowed through everything. Blood infused throughout the entire body.

The blood, I realized, was the key. My blood, my tainted blood, was keeping my body unnaturally alive—and would, apparently, keep it unnaturally alive for all eternity.

My God, I thought.

And then I wondered: Was I still a child of God? Or was I rendered into something evil?

I didn't feel evil.

The street was quiet, but not empty. Across the street, the door to my husband's building opened. Two figures emerged. One of them was my husband and the other was a woman. I didn't recognize the woman. He had mentioned acquiring a new secretary a few months back. I hadn't met her. This girl was tall and angular, with straight, blond hair. She wore a very tight white skirt.

They walked together into the adjoining parking lot. He led her to a little red convertible with its top down. At her door my husband put his arms around her waist and gave her a very long, and very deep kiss. They held that position for well over a half a minute. Then she disentangled herself from him, got in the car and drove away. He watched her leave, then turned toward me, and I held my breath. For one brief second I thought he might have been looking at me. Then he turned away, reached for his keys in his pocket, got into his Escalade and left. To drive home to his wife and kids.

Numb, I stayed where I was, the engine off. I was surprised to discover that my hand had unconsciously reached inside my jacket for a gun that wasn't there.

40.

Danny and I were lying in bed together.

He was under the covers and I was on top of them. As usual. He was naked and I was completely clothed. As usual. Heat from his recently-showered body emanated from his skin. He had removed the scent of her. What a guy. In the dark, I could see his pale shoulders clearly. I could also see that he was looking away from me, eyes open and staring up.

I rolled from my side onto my back, staring up at the ceiling along with him. The ceiling crackled and swirled with the secret particles of light that only I could see.

"I saw you with her tonight," I said.

"I know."

"You haven't kissed me like that in a long time."

He said nothing. The particles of light seemed to react to the tension around us, swirling faster, agitated.

I said, "You knew I was there and you kissed her in front of me anyway?"

"I saw you immediately when we stepped outside."

"So you gave her a particularly long kiss."

"Yes."

"Why even bother coming home?"

"My kids are here."

My voice started shaking, and I could not hide the fear and the hate. I wanted to rise up and pound his goddamn chest, make him hurt as much as he was hurting me.

"Do you love her?"

"I think so. Yes."

"Do you love me?"

"I don't know. I used to." He paused. "I do not think I can love what you have become. I've tried. I honestly tried. But. . . ."

"I repulse you."

"Yes," he said. "You sicken me and scare the hell out of me, and when I touch you it's all I can do to not gag."

"Words every wife wants to hear."

"I'm sorry, Sam. I really am. I'm sorry that you were attacked.

I'm sorry it has come to this. But a marriage is between a man and a woman."

"I am not a woman?"

"I don't know what the hell you are. A fucking vampire, I suppose. And what is that?"

"I'm still the same person."

"No, you're not. You drink blood in the garage like a ghoul. I have nightmares about you. I dream that you attack me in the middle of the night, that you attack our children—that you just lose it and slaughter us all."

I was crying now. Sobbing and crying and completely out of control. This was my worst fear, and it had come to pass. The love of my life was leaving me, and I didn't blame him for one second.

He ignored my crying. In fact, he turned his back to me.

And then I lost it. Just lost it.

In a blink of an eye I was on top of him. Both hands snaked down around his throat, faster than any cobra, faster than he could defend himself. I pinned him to the bed. "You fucking take my kids and I will kill you, you son-of-a-bitch. Do you understand? I will hunt you down and kill you and tear you into fucking shreds."

My voice was hysterical, shrieking, piercing. I saw my hands around his muscular neck—my narrow, pale, strong hands. His own were struggling with mine, trying desperately to pry me loose, but no luck. I didn't know if he was getting any air, and I suddenly didn't care. He kicked and convulsed, and still I strangled him, still I cursed and screamed at him. Now my arms shook with the effort. One more second, one more pound of pressure per square inch, and I would have killed him, and I would have enjoyed it. At least, in that moment.

Then I released my hold and he rolled off the bed, falling, coughing and gagging and spitting up. His body wrenched with the effort to breathe.

My heart was racing. "Don't you ever take my kids away, Danny," I whispered. "Ever."

41.

Danny was sitting up against the headboard, his knees drawn up against his chest. A sort of guy version of the fetal position. He was watching me with wary eyes. Who would blame him?

Although the room was dark, I could see the red welts around his neck. He had regained his breath and I had calmed considerably. The fury that overcame me had nothing to do with the vampire in me, and everything to do with the mother in me.

"I have given strict instruction to my attorney to release sealed information concerning your . . . *disease*," he said. His voice was ragged and torn, as if he were speaking through a very old microphone. Or a very damaged throat. "That is, should anything suspicious happen to me."

"What do you mean?" I was sitting on the edge of the bed. A sick realization came over me. Danny, despite my threats of bodily harm, would have the upper hand in this situation.

"I've completely detailed everything about your vampirism. Everything. From your attack six years ago to your account with the butchery in Norco."

"No one will believe it. They'll think you're crazy."

"Maybe, maybe not."

"What does that mean, Danny?"

"I've included in the packet two additional items. A video of me holding a mirror up to you while you slept, and a vial of your own tainted blood."

"Are you insane?" I asked.

"Maybe. But I want the kids, and I want them safe, and I want you to stay away and keep your filthy hands off me—and them."

We were silent again as I absorbed all of this. I was stuck. Whether or not anyone believed his story or bothered to test the vial of blood was debatable, but one I could not chance. I had known early on that I could never, ever risk being exposed.

"What about the kids?" I asked.

He took a deep breath and drew his knees up higher. "I'm taking the kids, Samantha."

I needed a clear mind for this. He was leaving, that much

I understood, that much I could try to deal with. But to take the kids. . . .

When I spoke again, I was the voice of reason and calm. "Danny, baby, listen to me. We've lived like this for six years. I've given them nothing but love. I would never harm anyone, not a living soul, especially not my kids. They need their mother."

He snorted. "After what just happened? My God, Sam, I thought you were going to kill me."

"I was furious, Danny. You've been cheating on me. Hell, you practically flaunted it in my face. Any woman—any mother—would have reacted the same way." I paused. He rubbed his neck and winced. "They need their mother, Danny."

"I agree, which is why I will allow you to see them every other weekend. Supervised." He inhaled deeply, raggedly. He knew what he was doing to me, he knew he was killing me, but he continued on. "Don't fight me on this either, Sam. Don't make me expose you for the monster that you are, because I will. I will do it to save the kids."

"Danny, please."

"I'm sorry. I truly am. You never deserved this to happen to you, and you never asked for it. Neither did I. Neither did the kids. But I am determined to keep them safe. I stuck it out this long, Sam. I did it for the kids. I think they're both old enough now to understand that mommy and daddy's relationship isn't so good anymore."

In a flash of rare compassion, he reached out and took my hand. I noticed he didn't recoil in horror, or hold it limply. He held it firmly and compassionately. "This is for the best, Sam. Now you can live . . . your life, however you need to live it. You don't have to worry about picking the kids up from school anymore, or about going to parent/teacher conferences, or about staying up with the kids during the day if one is sick. You can be free to be who you are, to be *what* you are, whatever that is. . . ."

He kept talking, but I wasn't sure if I was listening. I could only think of my children growing up without their mother. I could only think of not seeing their faces every day. Worse, I realized there was nothing I could do short of kidnapping them, and I would never do that because what kind of life would that be? Danny continued talking, extolling the virtues of being on my own, unhindered by the kids and the daily grind of being a mother; he continued stroking my hand, and I knew that my kids were lost to me. Every other weekend seemed an eternity. Suddenly, the daily grind of being a mother never looked better, and every time I tried to state my case the words failed me, because, in my heart, I knew he was right.

I am a monster. I am unnatural. They deserve better.

Bullshit. I'm their mother.

No matter what.

I had always known this day was coming. I had fought against it so hard. I had tried to do everything right and it still wasn't enough.

"If I promise not to fight you, if I promise to give you the kids to raise with whomever you choose, can I ask you one favor?"

He said nothing. Lying next to me, I could almost see him biting his lower lip, as he always did when in deep thought. This hesitation coming from a man who once proposed to me in a hot air balloon even though he had been terrified of heights.

"Please, Danny, just one favor."

"Maybe."

"That I see them every weekend, unsupervised."

He thought about it long and hard. He let out a long stream of breath. "Okay, Sam, every weekend. But I'm afraid I must insist the meeting be supervised."

"Thank you, Danny," I said quietly, my voice full of emotion and pain, unrecognizable even to my own ears. "When will the three of you be leaving?"

And the moment I uttered those words, I realized my mistake. They weren't going anywhere.

"*We* are not leaving, Sam. *You* are leaving, and I want you out by tomorrow night."

42.

In the late evening, I was standing on the ninth floor balcony of the Embassy Suites Hotel in Brea.

It had been a rough day. My sister had come over to help me move, although there wasn't really much to move. Mostly she was there for moral support. Danny was there, too, but he wasn't there for moral support. Instead, he watched over me like a prison warden.

Since it was my last day with the children, I had let them stay home from school. Earlier, I tried explaining to them why mommy was going away. I told them it wasn't their fault, that mommy and daddy could not live together anymore, that mommy and daddy still loved each other but not in that special way. They both cried. So did I.

At the hotel, Mary Lou helped me unpack, even the packets of chilled blood, which we stored in the suite's mini-refrigerator. I caught her studying one of the packets. Her face, I noted, had turned white. To her credit, she didn't say anything about the blood, and I silently thanked her for that.

We sat together on my bed and she rubbed my neck and shoulders and gently stroked my hair. Her touch, her warmth, her compassion gave me strength. She didn't think I should be alone and wanted to stay the night with me. I thanked her and told her I wanted to be alone. She didn't like it, but relented, and when she was gone I found myself alone—really alone—for the first time in years.

The suite had a small balcony with two canvas folding chairs and a circular table. I opened the sliding glass door and stepped out onto the balcony, and was immediately blasted by cold wind. The city was so breathtakingly beautiful from up here. Twinkling lights spread in all directions, as far as the eye could see.

In one swift motion, I pulled myself up onto the balcony's wall and hung my feet hung over the ledge. I kicked my feet absently like a kid hanging from a swing.

Cars sped by on the little street that separated the hotel from the nearby mall. Its various parking lots were jammed with cars. Malls and Orange County sort of went hand-in-hand.

I was hungry and, at the same time, sick to my stomach. Sometimes those two went hand-in-hand, as well.

Wind pulled and tugged at me, moaning softly over my ears. It was just after 8:00 p.m. It had been a hell of a shitty day, and I hadn't slept a wink.

The attack six years ago had cost me so much. It had cost me my job, my sunny days, my home, my husband, my kids, and my life.

I watched people entering and leaving the big mall, eager to spend their hard earned money at over-priced stores. Even from nine stories up, I could make out details of clothing and facial expressions. Most appeared to be in relatively good moods. Just living the American dream. Nothing better than spending an evening at the mall with the family. Shopping for nice things in nice stores with nice-looking kids. One person, returning a JCPenney bag, didn't look so happy.

Like a hawk watching field mice, I watched it all from above, sitting on the ledge, feeling increasingly separated from the human race.

I stood suddenly, pulling my feet up, balancing easily on the wide ledge. The wind seemed to pick up, but not enough to threaten to knock me off.

I looked down at the narrow street below, at the bustling mall, the streaming cars, the distant city lights. Sounds and smells came at me, too. The occasional, echoing honk of a car horn in an enclosed parking garage. The murmur of voices. The murmur of children's voices.

I took a deep, worthless, shuddering breath.

I had nothing to lose, really. My kids had been torn from my life. Hell, my *life* had been torn from my life.

The ground was far, far below. Nine stories up looks like a hundred and fifty stories up, especially if you are thinking of jumping. And I was thinking of jumping.

I closed my eyes, then leaped off the balcony.

43.

Time seemed to slow.

I arched up and out into the night and stretched my arms to either side. I lifted my face to the stars and felt the wind in my hair and experienced a profound and uncommon silence, as if all noise in the world had suddenly been muted. Slowly, I tilted down into a natural dive.

And then I plummeted.

Only then was I aware that perhaps I should have ditched the clothing. I didn't want to be a bat trapped in a cardigan sweater.

By all rights I should die in the next few moments. No one should be able to survive such a fall, perhaps not even a vampire.

A flash of yellow light erupted in my head. And within that light was an image of something black. Something with wings. Something large and alien and frightening.

And then the image disappeared.

The world began to accelerate. The floors to the hotel swept past me. Some of the curtained windows were open. One man dressed only in his tighty-whities turned suddenly, as if he had seen something in his peripheral vision. He had—a falling woman. But I had swept past him before he could complete his full turn.

The image of the winged creature reappeared, but this time taking on greater detail. It was vaguely humanoid with great leathery wings. I felt an immediate and powerful affinity for the creature.

A sliver of sidewalk, once only a silver thread from high above, now rapidly grew into a very real sidewalk. A very real *cement* sidewalk. Picking up speed, I passed a few more floors. Unfortunately for me, the hotel was running out of floors.

I spasmed suddenly.

The ground rose rapidly to greet me.

I had only seconds.

My clothing burst from my body. A huge set of thickly-membraned wings flapped from my arms and legs like a failed parachute.

The ground was upon me.

I changed position, altered my body.

The flapping skin, stretching from my wrists to somewhere around my mid-thigh, caught the wind and snapped taut. My arms shuddered and I held them firm and veered over the sidewalk with just a few feet to spare. I swept up, instinctively knowing just what I had to do.

My right hip slammed into a No Parking sign.

I lost control, tumbled through the air. And as if some ancient memory of flight had been reborn within me, I somehow regained control and righted myself, and flew low and fast over the mall parking lot, skimming over the roofs of a few dozen gleaming SUVs. I lifted my head and gained some altitude, and very quickly I was above the mall.

I was flying.

Flying.

Born from an innate knowledge I didn't comprehend or question, I skillfully flapped my wings and propelled myself up into the night sky.

44.

I was dreaming, of course.

I had to be. I mean, this really couldn't be happening to me, right?

Any minute now I was going to wake up and discover that I wasn't flying five hundred feet above the city of Brea. That I was back in my hotel room, alone, and miserable.

Dream or no dream, I might as well enjoy the ride.

A blast of wind hit me. I lost control and fumbled through the air. I panicked, until my on-board navigational system kicked in again and I adjusted my wings and lowered my shoulder and smoothed out the ride.

As I flew, and as my panicked breathing returned to normal, I looked over to my right arm. Make that *wing*. The arm appendage was thin and black and deeply corrugated with hard muscle. A thick membrane of leathery skin was attached to my wrist and ran down below my waist.

Below was Randolph Street. I followed it for a few minutes before lowering my right arm, raising my left, and making an arcing turn to starboard. The ability to turn came naturally to me, as if I had been doing this all my life.

Brea was bustling at this hour; it was still early evening, the streets crowded with vehicles. I flew over a section called Downtown Brea, alive with hundreds of people, all moving purposefully from one shop to another. The sky was cloudless, just a smattering of stars. Against this backdrop, my black skin would have been almost invisible to the human eye. Surprisingly, Southern California was ideal vampire country.

I decided to experiment.

But first I wanted to see what the hell I looked like. I found a suitable office structure made entirely of glass. I swept past the second floor in hopes of seeing my reflection—and was dismayed to see nothing at all. Same old story.

I swept back up into the sky, flapping hard, gaining elevation. The motion was already fluid and effortless for me. I continued climbing and suddenly wondered how high I dared to go. Already I was many hundreds of feet above the city.

So I continued up, climbing higher and higher.

The sky darkened. The city lights diminished. The wind and cold increased. I felt I could continue forever, tirelessly, across time and space, to other worlds, other stars, other universes. I felt free and alive and for a first time in a long, long time, I did not curse my fate.

I finally stopped ascending and hovered, stretching my arms out, soaring on the currents of space. Orange County shimmered far below. Far off I could see L.A. and Long Beach. To the south the great black expanse of the Pacific Ocean.

The wind was powerful and relentless. I rocked and absorbed the punishment, battered about like a demon kite. A demon kite with no strings. In this form I knew I could travel the earth. Travel anywhere and everywhere.

I had lost my kids on this day—but gained unlimited freedom. In more ways than one.

I tucked in my wings, the membranes collapsing in upon themselves like twin Geisha fans. I rocketed down like a bloodsucking meteorite. The city lights rapidly approached. Adrenalin rushed through my blood stream. I found myself screaming with delight; or, rather, *screeching* with delight. Wind pummeled me. I shook and vibrated and kept my eyes barely above a squint. Natural folds along my cheekbones and brow ridges did wonders to keep my vision clear.

Downtown Brea came back into view, seemingly rising up to meet me. The details of the busy street came rapidly into view, and only at the last possible second did I pull up, lifting my head and opening my arms. The sheer gravitational force on me should have been enough to rip my leathery wings from my arms, but they didn't rip. Instead, they performed wonderfully and I swept down the middle of the crowded street, barely above the roofs of the many SUVs and minivans.

People saw me. Many people. They pointed and turned and

spilled their drinks and ice creams. But I was already gone, turning hard to port and disappearing down a side street.

The side street led back to the hotel, where I carefully settled on my balcony. At least, what I hoped was my balcony. I was breathing hard. Apparently, I did need oxygen.

My arms were still long, slender and black. The flying membranes, attached to each side of my body, hung behind me like twin capes. As I stood there on my balcony, wondering what the hell I was supposed to do next, a vague image of me as a human appeared in my mind.

I opened my eyes and looked at my arms. They were aglow with pink flesh. I looked down and was not surprised to see that I was entirely naked.

I was back.

45.

I flew tonight.

I was typing on my laptop, one of the few possessions, outside of clothing and make-up, that I had brought with me. The hotel provided wireless connections, which was one of the reasons I had picked it. That, and because it had nine floors. Somewhere, in the back of my mind, I was planning on making my leap, and the taller the hotel the better.

You did!? came Fang's immediate response.

Yes!

You figured this out on your own?

Yes.

But how?

I told him the sequence of events leading up to my decision to leap from my balcony. Or, rather, my *impulse* to leap from the balcony.

I am sorry about your marriage, Moon Dance. Maybe someday you can marry me. I promise to be accepting.

I'm not in the mood for jokes, Fang.

No joke.

Then I'm not in the mood to be propositioned.

Sorry. He paused, then typed: *What was it like, flying?*

Heavenly. Rapturous. Nothing like it in the world. I will definitely be doing that again.

What exactly did you turn into?

Something scary. Something nightmarish.

But you were still you, right? You could think, feel?

Yes, I never left. It was still me, just in the skin of something horrific.

Describe it.

I did, as best as I could. I told Fang that there was really very little of me I could see, other than the image I had in my mind. The image was scary enough.

What am I? I asked him when I was through.

You are a vampire, Moon Dance.

But am I even one of God's creatures? Am I something evil? Am I even truly alive?

Do you feel alive?

Yes.

Do you feel evil?

I thought about that. *I feel like such an aberration, a mistake. Something forgotten. Something to be ignored. Something to fear.*

Moon Dance?

Yes?

We all feel that way. You are just different. He paused. *Do you believe in a Creator?*

I paused, then wrote: *I don't know. I believe in something.*

Well, do you think that Something has suddenly decided to ignore you because you were attacked and changed into something different against your own free will?

I don't know, Fang.

There was a long pause. *I don't. I don't think a god of creation has suddenly decided to ignore you, Moon Dance. I think, in fact, you have been granted a rare opportunity to do things some people have never thought possible, to express yourself in ways that many people will never, ever experience. You could choose to see this as an opportunity or as a curse. Do you choose to see the good or the bad?*

So there is good in me?

More good than most.

So I have not been forgotten?

Who could forget you, Moon Dance?

Thank you, Fang. Thank you for always being here for me.

Always. And Moon Dance?

Yes?

Take care of yourself. There are people out there who love you. A long pause. I waited. *And I am one of them.*

Thank you, Fang, that means a lot. Goodnight.

Goodnight, Moon Dance.

46.

On a Thursday night just a little past 9:30 p.m., Detective Sherbet picked me up outside the Embassy Suites. A light rain had been falling and I hadn't bothered with an umbrella.

"Trash night," he said when I slid in next to him. Sherbet was driving a big Ford truck with tinted windows. "Hey, you're all wet."

"I enjoy the rain."

"So enjoy the rain with an umbrella. You're getting my leather seats all wet."

"Get over it. It's just a truck."

"It's not just a truck. It's my baby."

"There's more to life than trucks."

"Someone in a bad mood?" he asked.

"Yes."

He grinned and pulled out into traffic. The truck had a throaty roar. The detective, I quickly discovered, drove like a madman. He pulled into traffic with reckless abandon, confident that his truck could survive any impact. I found his driving exciting. Maybe I was a closet adrenalin junkie.

"So do you have termites or something?" he asked after a cacophony of horns had subsided behind us.

"Excuse me?"

"Is that why I'm picking you up at a hotel in Brea? Does your house have termites?"

"Oh," I said. "Sure."

"Speaking of Brea, did you hear about the flying creature last night?"

"No."

"Police call centers got swamped last night. About a hundred calls in total. Apparently something dropped out of the sky and swooped down the middle of Downtown Brea."

"Maybe it was a bird," I said distractedly. I didn't feel like talking. I was missing my children, and could not fight the horrible feeling that they were forever lost to me.

"This was no bird." He chuckled and made a right onto State College Boulevard. A minute later we were waiting at a stoplight to turn left onto Imperial. Through the side window I noticed a few teenage boys gawking at the truck.

"The boys love your truck," I said.

"They should. It's bitchen."

I laughed, despite myself.

Sherbet continued, "Witnesses say it was black and massive and flying almighty fast."

"What happened to it?"

"Made a right onto Brea Boulevard and was gone."

"Did it at least use its turn signal?"

The light turned green. He gunned the truck as if he were in a drag race. He looked over at me and smiled. "You don't seem to believe any of this."

"No," I said. "Do you?"

"Hard to say. A hundred witnesses is a lot of witnesses."

"Mass hallucination?" I suggested.

"Maybe," he said. "Or maybe they really saw something."

Sherbet pulled behind a long line of cars waiting for the freeway on-ramp. I had the distinct—and exciting—feeling that Sherbet would have preferred to go *over* the cars.

"You hungry?" he asked suddenly.

"No."

"You sure? You look like you could eat."

"I'm sure."

He pulled out of the line of cars, hung a suicidal turn back onto Imperial Boulevard, and headed into a nearby Wendy's drive-thru.

"That was frightening," I said.

"Then why are you smiling?" he asked.

"I guess I like frightening," I said.

He ordered his food and pulled up in line. He said, "The wife tonight made a German dish called *machanka*. She thinks I like it. I haven't had the heart to tell her that I quit liking it fifteen years ago."

"You must love her."

"With all my heart," he said.

"Lucky her," I said.

"Lucky *me*."

He got his food. Two bacon burgers, an order of fries, and a king-sized Coke.

"That'll kill you," I said.

"True," he said. "But on the flip side: no more *machanka*."

Shoving fries into his mouth, he recklessly made a left into a break in traffic that was virtually nonexistent. He looked at me and grinned around the fries.

I grinned, too.

Soon, we were heading south on the 57 Freeway.

47.

It was after 10:00 p.m. when we parked on a street that ran perpendicular with Horton's massive Gothic revival.

A thin sheet of rain obscured the street. We sat in the cab of his truck with the engine and wipers off. Moving wipers attracted attention, as did an idling car. So we ate in the cold and wet. The house before us was massive and brooding. Its towering gables spiked the night sky. Hawthorne would have been pleased. The truck's tinted glass made the world darker than it really was. I liked darker.

After a moment, Sherbet shook his head. "Who could live in something like that?" Sherbet shuddered. "Like something in a fucking Dracula movie."

"I like it," I said.

"Why does that not surprise me?"

"What does that mean?" I asked.

"Nothing. Just being a wise guy."

Sherbet was still sipping on his king-sized Coke. Occasionally some of the sips turned into loud slurps. The remnants of his greasy meal were wadded into a greasy ball and shoved into the greasy bag. The strong smell of burgers and fries suffused the interior of the truck cab. My hungry stomach was doing somersaults.

Easy, girl.

"That your stomach growling?" he asked.

"I don't know. Haven't noticed."

He shook his head and slurped his Coke. The street was mostly empty. Occasionally a big car would splash past, and since tomorrow was trash day, most of the residents already had their trash cans out by the curb. Rick Horton's trash cans were nowhere to be found.

"Maybe he forgot tomorrow was trash day," said Sherbet.

"Maybe."

"Maybe he's one of those procrastinators who runs out just as the trash truck pulls up, dragging their trashcans behind them, beseeching the truck driver to wait."

"Beseeching?" I said.

"It's a word."

"Just not a word you often hear from a cop with a dollop of ketchup on his chin."

He hastily swiped at the dollop, but missed some of it. He licked his finger. "You have good eyes," he said.

"And you have bad aim." I used one of the napkins to clean his chin.

The rain picked up a little. The drops were now big enough to splatter. Overhead, the weeping willows wept, bent and shuddering under the weight of the rain.

"I could use some coffee," the detective said. "No telling when this guy is coming out with his trash."

So we got some coffee at a nearby Burger King. Or, rather, Sherbet did. He bought me a bottled water.

"You're a cheap date," he commented as he mercifully decided—at the last possible second—that an incoming bus was too close to dash in front of.

"And you're the reason fast food establishments stay in business."

"On second thought," he said. "I would never date someone as grouchy as you."

"It's been a bad week."

"Wanna talk about it?"

"No."

He didn't push it. We pulled back up in front of Horton's Gothic revival. Nothing much changed. Horton still hadn't taken out his trash, which was, at least tonight, the object of our interest.

So we waited some more. Investigators are trained to wait. We're supposed to be good at it. Waiting sucks. The interior of the truck was filled with the soothing sound of rain ticking on glass and sheet metal. I sipped some water. Sherbet was holding his coffee with both hands. Steam rose into his face. A light film of sweat collected on his upper lip. The coffee smelled heavenly. Coffee was not on my list. Rivulets of rain cascaded down the windshield. The shining street lamps, as seen through the splattered windshield, were living prisms of light. I watched the hypnotic light show.

"What's it like working for the feds?" Sherbet suddenly asked.

"Safe, secure. Often boring, punctuated with the occasional thrill. My days were endlessly fascinating. I loved my job."

"Do you miss it?"

"Hard to say. I miss the camaraderie of my partners. My job now is a lonely one. When I get the chance to work with someone else I often take it."

"Even with an old dog like me?"

I looked at him. The truck was mostly silent. I heard him breathing calmly through his nose. Could smell his aftershave. He smelled like a guy should smell. Moving shadows from the rain dribbling down the windshield reached his face. The man seemed to like me, but he was suspicious of me. Or perhaps just curious. As a homicide investigator, he had his own highly-attuned intuition, which worried me because I was obviously causing it to jangle off the hook. But I had committed no crime, other than draining a corpse of blood, which I didn't think was a crime, although I'd never perused the penal code for such an article.

"Sure," I said. "Even an old dog like you."

"How reassuring."

Through Horton's wrought iron fence I saw a figure struggling with something bulky. The fence swung open and Horton appeared in a yellow slicker, struggling to wheel a single green trash can. The can appeared awkward to maneuver. Or perhaps Horton was just clumsy. As he deposited the can near the curb, his foot slipped out from under him, sending him straight to his back. I voted for clumsy.

Sherbet shook his head. "Smooth," he said.

48.

"Let's wait a few minutes," said Sherbet after Horton had dashed inside. Horton ran like a girl.

"Doesn't look like much of a killer," I said.

"No," said Sherbet. "They never do."

The rain came down harder, pummeling the truck, scourging what appeared to be a custom paint job. Sherbet seemed to wince with each drop.

"Aren't you a little too old to be into cars?" I asked.

"You can never be too old."

"I think you're too old."

"Yeah, well how old are you?"

"I'd rather not say. Not to mention you've looked at my police record and already know."

"Thirty-seven, if I recall," he said. "A very young thirty-seven. Hell, you don't even have a wrinkle."

"I'm sure it will catch up to me someday," I said, and then thought: *or not*. But I played along. "And before I know it, I'll look into the mirror one day and find a road atlas staring back at me."

He snorted. "Welcome to my world."

We waited some more. The rain continued to pound. Some of the water collected and sluiced along the windshield in shimmering silver streaks. Sherbet and I were warm and secure in our own little microcosm of leather, plastic, wood, and empty Wendy's bags. Here in this mini-world, I was the vampire queen, and Sherbet was my noble knight. Or perhaps my blood slave, from whom I fed.

"Your name always reminds me of ice cream," I said. "I like your name."

"I hate it."

"Why?"

"Reminds me of ice cream."

A light in Horton's upstairs window turned off. The house was dark and silent. So was the street.

"You stay here while I procure the target's trash," Sherbet said. "We're going to have to adhere to some protocol if we hope to get a search warrant out of this."

"Lot of fancy words to basically say you'll be the one getting wet."

"Oh, shut up," he said.

I grinned. "Procure away, kind sir."

"Okay," he said, pulling on his hood. "Here goes."

He threw open his door and dashed off through the rain. His nylon jacket was drenched within seconds. He moved surprisingly well for an older guy. He reached Horton's trash can, pulled open the lid, and removed two very full plastic bags. I was suddenly very much not looking forward to digging through those. He shut the lid, grabbed a bag in each hand, and hustled back to the truck. He deposited both in the bed of his truck.

"You're dripping on the leather," I said when he slid into the driver's seat.

"I know," he said, starting the truck. "It saddens the heart."

49.

We drove until we found an empty parking garage adjacent to an ophthalmologist college. The lights inside the garage were on full force and a white security pick-up truck was parked just inside the entrance.

We pulled up beside the truck. The guard was out cold, wrapped in his jacket, hugging himself for warmth, the windows cracked for air. Sherbet rolled down his window. The sound of thumping rain was louder and more intense with the window down. The guard still hadn't moved.

"Hey," said Sherbet.

The man bolted upright, accidentally slamming his hand against the steering wheel. The horn went off and he jumped again, now hitting his head on the cab's ceiling.

Sherbet turned to me. "Night of Ten Thousand Fools."

"An Arabian farce."

The detective leaned out the window, producing his badge from his jacket pocket. "Detective Sherbet, Fullerton PD. We need to, um, commandeer your garage for a few minutes."

"Of course, detective." The guard's voice was slightly high-pitched. He was fortyish and much too small to be taken seriously as a guard. His neck was also freakishly long. "It's the rain, you know. Knocks me out every time. My bosses found out I was sleeping again, they'd fire me." He looked sheepish.

"Don't worry about it, pal," said Sherbet. "I won't tell if you don't."

He brightened, his job secure. "Is there maybe something I can do for you? You know, maybe help you out?"

"Sure," said Sherbet. "Guard this entrance with your life. No one comes in."

"You got it, detective!"

Sherbet rolled up his window and we eased into the parking structure and out of the rain.

"Commandeer the garage?" I said.

"Sounds important."

I looked back. The guard had positioned his truck before the garage's entrance. "Good of you to give him something to do," I said. "But what happens if someone wants to come in?"

"Then they'll have to deal with Flamingo Neck."

I snorted. "Flamingo Neck? Thought he looked more like a stork."

"Whatever." Sherbet pulled into a slot. "You ready to dig in?"

"As ready as ever."

The covered garage was mostly empty, save for a few desolate vehicles. These vehicles had the look of semi-permanence. Sherbet handed me a pair of latex gloves.

The bags were sodden. One of them stank of rotten dairy. I gave that one to the detective.

"Thanks," he said.

"I'm a lady," I said. "Ladies don't dig through smelly trash."

"They do when they're on my shift."

"Yeah, well, luckily I don't work for you."

"Luckily."

With legs crossed, I hunkered down on a parking rebar. I untied the my bag and was immediately greeted with what must have been last night's chicken teriyaki. My stomach growled noisily. My stomach seemed to have missed the memo about my new diet. My new *blood* diet.

No chicken teriyaki for you, my friend. Ever.

I removed the big stuff first. An empty gallon of milk that, because it was sealed, had bloated to half again its normal size. Boxes of cereal, an empty jar of peanut butter, many cardboard cases of beer. Someone liked beer. A smattering of plastic Coca-Cola bottles. I sorted through it all, leaving a careful pile to my left.

At the bottom nook was a batch of papers which proved to be torn mail, the majority of which were credit card applications. Smart man. Debt, bad.

"Nothing over here," I said.

I looked over at the detective who was squatting down on one knee. His hands were smeared with gelatinous muck. He looked a little green, and for a homicide detective, that's saying a lot.

"More of the same," he said. "Nothing."

Beyond, the security guard was pacing in the rain before his truck. Occasionally he stole glances at us.

"Same time next week?" Sherbet asked.

"Yes," I said. "More fun."

"And Mrs. Moon?" he said, looking down at his rancid ichor-covered latex gloves. "Next time *you* get the smelly bag."

50.

Sherbet dropped me off at the hotel and suggested that I take a shower because I smelled like trash. I told him thanks. At the hotel lobby, the doorman greeted me with a small bow. I could get used to that. Then he crinkled his nose. Maybe I did need to take a shower.

Conscious of my stench, I took the elevator to the ninth floor and inserted my keycard into the lock and pushed the door open and my warning bells went off instantly.

Someone was inside.

Movement down the hall. I turned my body, narrowing it as a target, just as an arrow bolt struck me in the shoulder, slamming me hard into the open door, which in turn slammed shut. I ducked and peered through the darkness and there, standing near my open balcony, was a man. A good-looking man. Tall and slender. Silhouetted in shadows. But I could see into shadows. His spiky blond hair looked like a frayed tennis ball. He was staring at me down the length of a cocked crossbow.

I knew him. It was the UPS man.

He didn't say anything, didn't move. Simply stood there with his crossbow trained, sweat gleaming on his forehead. His hands were unwavering. A flask of clear liquid was at his hip. There was a cross around his neck and a strand of garlic. He adjusted his sights imperceptibly, and I realized he was searching for a clear shot at my heart. I was determined not to give him that clear shot. I looked at him from over my shoulder.

"Who are you?" I asked.

"You don't need to know."

"Then why are you doing this?" My breath came in short gasps. I needed to do something about the shaft in my shoulder, but I didn't dare take my eyes off the man. The strand of garlic was bullcrap. Hell, I cooked with garlic all the time. But the water on his hip—holy water, no doubt—was troubling. I hadn't dared experiment with holy water.

"It's nothing personal," he said.

"The bolt in my shoulder makes it personal."

"It was meant for your heart."

Behind me I heard voices. Someone was getting off the elevator. The voices were mixed with drunken laughter.

Although I hadn't taken my eyes off the hunter, I had unwittingly shifted my weight to the sound of the voices. Apparently I had exposed my heart. He saw the opening he was looking for, and fired.

I heard the *twang* and *snap* of the bolt leaping from the crossbow. I saw it coming, too. Clearly. Rotating slightly in the air. My world slowed down. Much as it had when I leaped off the balcony.

As it rotated, its metal tip gleaming off of light unseen, my hand was coming up. And just before it buried itself into my heart, I caught the damn thing in the air, snagging it just inches from my chest.

The hunter gaped at me in disbelief, then flung himself backward through the open French doors and vaulted the railing. I pushed away from the doorway, stumbled through the suite and out onto the balcony. It was still raining. I peered down over the ledge and saw a man rappelling down the facade of the building. The rope was attached to the roof above. He dropped down into some foundation brush and unhooked himself. He looked up at me briefly and then dashed off. I watched him disappear around the corner of the hotel.

Back in my suite, out of the rain, I gripped the fletched end of the arrow shaft and winced. *Okay, this is going to hurt.* I inhaled deeply and pulled slowly. The pain was unbearable. I gasped and stumbled into the bathroom. The mirror revealed empty clothing, animated clothing, a miracle of special effects. An arrow protruded from the blouse's shoulder area. A thick wash of blood was spreading down from the shoulder. The sight of the bloodied disembodied clothing was surreal.

I closed my eyes, continued pulling. White flashes appeared behind my eyelids. I pulled harder, screaming now. I looked down once and saw that the metal tip was almost out. I also saw that it was bringing with it a lot of meat from my arm.

Tears streamed from my eyes and I heard myself whimpering and still I continued to pull, and finally the bolt came free, followed immediately by a great eruption of blood.

It was then that I fainted.

51.

Sometime during the night I awoke in the bathroom to find myself in a pool of my own blood. I was cold and not very shocked to see that the wound in my shoulder had healed completely. I stumbled into the bedroom and collapsed into bed.

I slept through the day and awoke at dusk. I felt like hell, groggy, disoriented. I had to remind myself where I was. I bolted upright. Shit! I had forgotten to pick up the kids!

I was just about to hop out of bed until I remembered it

wasn't my job to do so anymore. Danny's mother picked them up now. I slumped back into bed, immediately depressed.

My daytime obligations had vanished. Perhaps that was a good thing in away, since I did not operate well during the daylight hours. And, for the first time since the kids had been taken away from me, I felt—which was immediately accompanied by a lot of guilt—a sense of freedom. No kids to pick up. No dinners to cook, no husband to attend to or worry about.

Freedom and guilt, in just that order.

I stretched languidly on the bed, reveling in the surprisingly soft mattress. Why had I not noticed how soft the mattress was? A moment passed, and then another, and then my heart sank.

I had no children to pick up from school and no one to cook for! I missed my kids—but not my husband. Knowing I repulsed him helped sever my emotional ties to him. Yes, I missed the good times with Danny. But I wouldn't miss these past few years.

But I would see my children this weekend. It sucked, but there was nothing I could do about it now, although I vowed to get them back.

Somehow.

For now, though, there was nothing to do but lie here and hurt—and wait for true night to fall. The drapes were thick and heavy and kept out most of the setting sun. My window dressings at home were, in fact, the same heavy curtains found in hotels. Early on, right after my attack, I had wanted to board up the windows, but Danny resisted and we compromised with the heavy drapes.

I massaged my shoulder. Although it still ached, there was no evidence of a wound. Another few inches over and I would have been dead. My only saving grace had been a last-second alarm that went off in my head, a warning that told me to *turn dammit.*

I thought of the vampire hunter. I couldn't have him taking potshots at me whenever he damned well felt like it. I had to do something about him, and short of killing him—which was a definite option—I just wasn't sure what yet.

First things first. I needed to figure out how the hell he kept showing up without me spotting him. I always check for tails, a good habit for an investigator to have. So I was certain he wasn't following me.

Of course, there are other ways to keep tabs on people, especially tabs on vehicles. In fact, at HUD, we had employed such techniques. Tracking devices.

As I waited for the sun to set, I turned on the boob tube and flipped through some news channels and a re-run or two until I came across an Angels game. I couldn't recall the last time I watched an Angels game. I loved baseball, especially the leisurely pace of the game. I liked the quiet moments when the pitcher stepped off the mound and gathered his thoughts while the world waited. My father was a minor league pitcher in Rancho Cucamonga. He was good, but not great, which is why he never made it past single-A ball. Still, surrounded by my three older brothers, I learned to love the game at an early age.

The Angels were up 3-2. Tim Salmon had just hit a line-drive single up the middle.

Those childhood memories seemed to belong to someone else. Someone I barely recalled, yet remembered in detail. I was a different person now. The pre-attack Samantha as opposed to the post-attack Samantha were two different people. Hell, two different *species*.

Salmon had a nice butt. So did most baseball players.

I rubbed my shoulder again as I watched the game. So how the hell did it heal so quickly? What caused this to happen? Ancient magic? If so, was this the same magic keeping me alive? Was I even truly alive? Or was I dead and didn't know it?

Bengie Molina, the Angel's catcher, ripped a line drive back to the pitcher. The pitcher doubled-up Salmon at first. End of inning.

Perhaps I was nothing more than a spirit or a ghost who didn't have enough sense to move on. But on to where? I didn't feel dead.

It was the eighth inning, and the Angels brought in their closer, *El Toro*, the bull. Percival was a big man with big legs. He looked like a bull. I liked the way he squinted and curled his tongue. He looked like a gunslinger. Except this gunslinger slung baseballs. He struck out the first batter in four pitches.

Perhaps I was a plague on the earth, an abnormality that needed to be cleansed. Perhaps the world would have been better off if the vampire hunter's arrow had hit home.

More squinting from El Toro. I heard once that Percival needed to wear glasses but he chose not to while pitching, forcing himself to focus solely and completely on the catcher's signals, blocking out all other distractions. On his next pitch, the batter popped out to center field.

Perhaps I didn't need to know what kept me alive. Perhaps my existence was no more a mystery than life itself. Hell, where did any of us come from? That thought comforted me.

Percival struck out the next batter and pumped his fist. It was the bottom of the eighth inning.

I was suddenly content and at peace with myself. I would have ordered room service if fresh plasma was on the menu. Instead, I sipped from a bottle of water and let the day slip into night. And when the sun finally set, when my breathing seemed unrestricted and my body fully alert, I was ready to take on the world.

Oh, and the Angels won.

With all the time on my hands, maybe I'll catch a night game this season.

52.

I first headed over to an auto repair shop in Fullerton.

The young mechanic came out to meet me as I pulled in front of an empty service garage. He wore a light blue workshirt with the name *Rick* stitched on a patch over his chest.

"Sorry, we're closing," said Rick when I rolled down my window.

I pulled out a twenty dollar bill. "All I need for you to do is lift my van."

"Why?"

"I want to have a look underneath."

"*You* want to? Why?"

"Because this is how I spend my Friday nights. Just lift the van for a few minutes, let me have a look underneath, and the twenty is yours."

Rick thought about it, then shrugged. "Hey, whatever you say, lady," he said and took the twenty.

He motioned me forward. I drove into the narrow space, straddling the lift. I got out and Rick manipulated some nearby controls and soon the above-ground lift was chugging into action. The van rose slowly, wheels sagging down. A few minutes later, now at eye level, I thought the minivan looked forlorn and sort of helpless, like a wild horse being airlifted from an overflowing river.

"Okay," Rick said. "Have at it. Just don't hurt yourself. You need a flashlight?"

"No."

"So what are you looking for?" he asked, standing next to me.

"I'll know it when I see it."

The underside of the van was a mess of hoses, encased wires and steel shafts and rods. I walked slowly along the frame until I found it. Held in place by magnets and twisty-ties, the tracking device was about the size and shape of a cell phone.

"What the hell is that?" asked Rick.

"My TV remote," I said. "Been looking everywhere for it."

"No shit?" he said.

"No shit."

53.

It took two nights of waiting before I saw the hunter again.

I had left the minivan parked in an alley behind a Vons grocery store. I knew the hunter would eventually investigate, and to do so he would have to physically enter the alley. A typical ambush, and I'm sure he suspected a trap. If so, he would be right. This *was* a trap.

I sat on top of the grocery store roof, near a huge rotating vent. My great, leathery wings were tucked in behind me. The night was warm, but the breeze cooled things down. My skin was thick and rubbery. My new hide did wonders for keeping me warm, especially in the higher altitudes. I had discovered that I could remain in this form for as long as I wished. This was a good discovery, as it was nice shedding my old skin for this new one. People should try it sometime.

The alley was dark and mostly forgotten. My minivan attracted very little interest, even from hooligans. So that's why when the bum appeared I perked up.

In my new form, my eyesight was razor sharp and eagle-like, an obvious necessity for high-flying predators. (And thinking of myself as a *high-flying predator* was almost too weird to, well, think about.) The bum was pushing a shopping cart filled to overflowing with what appeared to be junk. I immediately recognized the handsome face, the rugged jaw, the striking blue eyes, and the spiky blond hair shooting out from under a dirty and warped Dodger cap.

Nice costume, asshole.

As an added touch, he even dragged his leg a little behind him. The hunter was putting on quite a show, even hunching his shoulders now Quasimodo-like. I couldn't help but smile. At least, I *think* I smiled. It was hard to tell; plus, I wasn't even sure I had lips. At any rate, I *intended* to smile. Anyway, his shopping cart was, in fact, filled to the brim with soda cans. I wondered if he had purchased the cart and cans from a real bum, or collected the cans himself.

Probably just stole it, I thought.

He continued slowly down the alley, his head sweeping from side to side. Unfortunately for him, he never thought to look *up*. About fifty feet from the van, he removed a camouflaged crossbow from inside his tattered jacket. He armed it quickly with a bolt. And then held it out in front of him like a gun.

He approached my van very, very carefully, leaving behind his cart full of cans. He went slowly from window to window, peering inside with a flashlight. I noted he had forgotten to limp.

I stayed put and waited for my opening.

He tried the doors, discovered they were locked, then popped one open with a Slim Jim. He goofed around inside a bit. Reappearing again, frowning. He seemed a bit perplexed. If anything, I had successfully confused the bastard.

The back door to the grocery store suddenly opened, yellow light splashing out into the alley. A kid appeared, hauling a big blue trash can. The hunter, distracted, turned toward the kid.

Now!

I leaped from my perch above.

54.

I tucked in my arms and shot down.

The hunter's back was still to me. Wind thundered in my ears. The ground came up fast. More importantly, the hunter's broad shoulders came up fast.

At the last possible second, I spread my wings wide. The leathery hide snapped open like a parachute. The hunter turned at the sound, swinging his crossbow around, but he was too late. My outstretched talons snatched him up by the shoulders. He cried out, screaming like a school girl. The crossbow tumbled away, skittering over the ground. I beat my wings powerfully, once, twice and finally lifted him off his feet and then slowly up out of the alley. He weighed a lot. More than I was prepared for. My arms and wings were strained to the max.

He struggled, kicking, as his arms were now pinned to his sides. He kicked the air futilely. We rose slowly into the sky together. I looked down in time to see the kid running back into the store. I think he wet himself.

Up we went. I was growing stronger, getting used to the added weight. The air grew colder. The hunter should be warm enough thanks to his homeless costume, which consisted of many layers of clothing.

I looked down just as he looked up. His face had drained of all color. He looked terrified. He should be terrified. A creature from his nightmares had snatched him away and for all he knew I was going to drop him into an active volcano. Not that there were many active volcanoes in Southern California.

Orange County spread before us, its hundreds of thousands of blinking lights evidence that Thomas Edison had certainly been on to something. We flew over Disneyland, which glittered like its own happy constellation. Perhaps park guests would later report seeing a parade float gone amuck.

We reached the beach cities and finally the black ocean itself. Without the city lights, we were plunged into darkness. He stiffened here, and I think he might have whimpered. No doubt he thought I was going to drop him in. I still hadn't ruled it out.

Much later, perhaps assuming he was safe, the hunter relaxed and sagged in my talons. He spoke to me now, his voice rising up to me along with the smell of sea salt and brine, "How is your shoulder, Samantha Moon?"

The sound of my own name startled me. That this flying creature had a name was hard to believe. I didn't bother answering. Even to my own ears my voice was nothing more than a shriek.

He went on, "I suppose you can't speak in your changeling form. That's fine, I'll do all the talking. I know you've had a hell of a shitty week. I saw your children get taken away from you. And probably the last thing you needed was an arrow in your shoulder. So I guess what I'm trying to say is I'm sorry."

Apology accepted, I thought. I was nothing if not forgiving.

I continued at a steady pace, wings flapping smoothly and effortlessly, propelling us over the eternal black ocean. I adjusted endlessly to the varying wind conditions.

"I've never seen a vampire with a family before. You have two beautiful children. At first I thought the family was just a facade. Perhaps you were just courting these mortals for your own nefarious means. A new angle, you know, to acquire blood. So I assumed you were hideous and vile to formulate such a scheme. Until I saw that this was indeed *your* family. The little girl is your spitting image."

He stopped talking, and the silence that followed was filled with the rippling of water over the ocean's surface, and something else, something deep and unfathomable, perhaps the sound of millions upon millions of megatons of water turning and roiling and moving over the face of the earth. The ocean's song, if you will, and it was beautiful and haunting.

The hunter told me about himself. His name was Randolf, and his brother, years ago, had been killed by a vampire. Randolf devoted his life to finding his brother's killer, and in the process to kill every vampire he came across.

Ambitious, I thought. *But problematic for me.*

His search eventually led him to an old vampire living in a mansion in Fullerton. Randolf ambushed him, killing him with a bolt through the heart. In going through the old vampire's papers, Randolf had come across my name.

He had, in effect, found the vampire who had attacked *me*.

Not just found him. Found him and killed him. Saved me a lot of trouble.

Randolf continued, "But he was not my brother's killer. I still have some unfinished business." He paused. "You are not like other vampires, Samantha. May I call you Samantha?"

I nodded; I'm not sure he saw me nod.

"In your hotel room I found packets of cow and pig blood in your refrigerator. You are not a killer. Not like the others."

I glanced down. He was still wearing the dirty Dodger cap. His spiky blond hair trailed over his ears. His face was purple with cold.

I continued steadily out to sea. I found that distinguishing the black water from the black sky was difficult, but my innate compass kept us on a clear course, and my equally innate horizontal balance kept us from plunging into the ocean. I thought of the old joke: *I just flew in from Chicago, and boy are my arms tired. . . .*

But my energy seemed limitless, even hauling a full grown man. Still, I didn't want to fly too far out to sea; I needed to provide for enough time to safely return before the sun's ascent.

In the far distance, on the surface of the ocean, I spied the twinkling of lights. I altered course and headed toward the lights. Randolf snorted from below. I suspected he had been dozing. A hell of a rude awakening for him, no doubt, hanging from the claws of a flying beast.

The lights turned out to be a ship. In fact, it was a cruise ship.

"You're taking me to the ship," he said.

Smart boy.

"I get the hint," he said, laughing. "You want me to stay away. And thank you for not killing me."

There was a lot of activity on the deck of the cruise ship, so I circled the control tower, and set the hunter on the roof of the cabin. Whether anyone saw a black shape descend from the sky remained to be seen.

Randolf scrambled to his feet, no worse for wear. As I hovered above, as he held down his baseball cap against the downdraft of my wings, his astonishing blue eyes caught the starlight.

He really was kind of hunky—even to a creature of the night.

He called up to me, "Have a safe flight home, Samantha Moon. Oh, and any idea where I'm headed?"

I had no idea.

I circled once and headed back home.

55.

Kingsley looked far more robust and pink than when I had last seen him.

We were at Mulberry Street Cafe in downtown Fullerton, sitting next to the window. It was raining again and the sidewalk was mostly empty of pedestrians. The rain had a trickle-down effect, if you will. Mulberry's was quieter than normal.

Kingsley was wearing a long black duster, and leather Sole gloves, which he removed upon sitting. His dark slacks were darker where the rain had permeated. His face had a rosy red hue and his hair was perfectly combed. He was clean shaven and smelled of good cologne. He was everything a man should be. Gone were the tufts of hair along the back of his hand.

Pablo the headwaiter knew me well. He looked slyly at Kingsley, perhaps recalling that my husband was usually the man sitting across from me. The waiter was discreet enough not to say anything. He took our drink orders and slipped away.

"I'm impressed," said Kingsley, glancing out the window. "Whenever I come here they seat me in the back of beyond."

"They happen to like me here."

"Pretty girls get all the breaks."

"You think I'm pretty?"

"Yeah," said Kingsley. "I do."

"Even for a vampire?"

"Even for a vampire."

Our drinks came. Chardonnay for me and bourbon and water for the counselor. Kingsley ordered shrimp tortellini and I had the usual. Steak, rare.

"You can eat steak?" he asked.

"No," I said. "But I can suck the blood out of the carcass."

"Should make for an interesting show."

"Yes, well, it's the only way I can participate in the human dining experience."

"Well, you're not missing much," said Kingsley. "Food nowadays is entirely processed, fattening and just plain horrible for you."

"Does it still taste good?"

"Wonderful."

"Asshole."

He laughed. I drank some of my wine. Kingsley, no doubt due to his massive size, often garnered curious glances from both men and women. I think, perhaps, he was the strongest-looking man I had ever seen.

"Are we human, Kingsley?" I asked suddenly.

He had been raising his glass to his lips. It stopped about halfway. "Yes," he said, then raised it all the way and took a sip. He added, "But are we mortals? No."

"Then what makes us *immortal*? Why don't we die like everyone else? What keeps us alive?"

"I don't know."

"Surely you must have a theory."

He sighed. "Just a working hypothesis."

"Let's have it."

"I think it's safe to say that you and I hover on the brink of the natural and the supernatural. So therefore both natural and unnatural laws apply simultaneously. I believe we are both human . . . and perhaps something greater."

"Sounds lofty."

"Do you suspect we're something *less*?" he asked.

I thought about that. "No. We are certainly not less."

The waiter came by and dropped off some bread. I didn't touch it, but Kingsley dug in. "You mind?" he asked.

"Knock yourself out," I said. "So what are we, then? Some supernatural evolutionary hybrid?"

He shrugged. "Your guess is as good as mine."

"Maybe we are super humans."

"Maybe."

"But during the day I certainly don't feel super. I feel horrible."

"Because our bodies are still governed by some physical laws, along with . . . other laws. Mystical laws perhaps, laws unstudied and unknown to modern science." He looked at me and shrugged. "Who put these laws into place is anyone's guess. But they're there nonetheless. For instance, one such law dictates I will turn into a wolf every full moon cycle; another dictates you drink only blood."

Kingsley spread liberal amounts of honey butter over his bread. He seemed particularly ravenous. Maybe it was the animal in him.

"Perhaps we are the result of a powerful curse," I suggested.

"Perhaps."

"That makes sense to me, to some degree."

He shrugged. "I'm not sure anyone really knows."

I suspected someone out there *might* know something. Be it vampire, werewolf or something else, something greater perhaps.

I said, "The curse angle could be why holy water debilitates a vampire."

He shrugged. "Sure."

"So to sum up," I said. "We are both natural and supernatural, abiding by laws known only to our kinds."

"And even much of that is open to speculation. For all I know you are part of one long, drug-induced dream I'm still having in the sixties."

Our food came. Kingsley watched me cut a slice of meat from the raw steak, swirl the slice in the splatter of blood, raise the dripping piece to my lips, and suck it dry.

"Sort of sexy," he said. "In a ghoulish way."

I shook my head, then told him about my adventures with the vampire hunter.

He slapped his knee when I was finished. "A Carnival cruise ship?"

"Yes, headed for Hawaii, I think."

"Then let's hope he stays there."

"Yeah," I said. "Let's hope, although he was kind of cute."

"Oh, God."

I reached down into my purse and pulled out the medallion. It was wrapped in a white handkerchief. I unwrapped it for him.

"What's that?" Kingsley asked.

"It was worn by my attacker six years ago."

"Your attacker?"

"The vampire who rendered me into what I am now."

"How did you get it?"

I told him about the vampire hunter, his dead brother, and the UPS package. When I was finished, Kingsley motioned toward the medallion. "Do you mind?"

"Knock yourself out."

He picked it up carefully, turned it over in his hand. The gold and ruby roses reflected brightly even in the muted light.

"So why did he give you this?" asked Kingsley.

"I think he was sort of feeling me out, seeing what he was up against. To him, the medallion had no meaning."

"And to you it does?"

I told Kingsley about my dreams. I left out the part where he ravaged me in the woods.

"Those are just dreams, Samantha," he said, studying the heavy piece, turning it over in his big hands. "I've never seen this before."

"But could you look into it for me?" I asked.

"I'll see what I can do," he said. "Do you mind if I take it?"

"Go ahead."

He pocketed the medallion. We continued eating. Outside, a couple sharing an umbrella stopped and examined the menu in the window. She looked at him and nodded. He shrugged. They stepped inside. Compromising at its best.

"Sometimes I think God has forgotten about me," I said.

"I know the feeling."

"That, in fact, I have somehow stumbled upon the loophole of life."

"Loophole?"

"Like you being a defense attorney," I said. "You look for an ambiguity in the law, an omission of some sort, something that allows you to evade compliance."

He nodded, "And being a creature of the night is the ambiguity of life?"

"Yeah. I'm the omission."

"Well, that's certainly one way of looking at it."

"What's another way?"

"To make the most of the life we're given," he said. "To see life—even for the undead—as a great gift. Imagine the possibilities,

Samantha? Imagine the good you can do? Life is precious. Even for those who exist in loopholes."

I nodded, thinking of Fang. "Someone told me something like that recently."

"It's good advice," said Kingsley. "In fact, it's good advice for everyone."

"So we are like everyone?"

"No," he said, reaching across the table and taking my hand. His was so damn warm . . . mine must have felt like a cold, wet, limp noodle in his own. Self-conscious, I almost pulled my hand away, but he held it even tighter, and that warmed my cold, bitter heart.

He said, "No, Sam. We are *not* like everyone else. I'm a wolf in sheep's clothing, and you're a blood-sucking fiend. Granted, a very *cute*, blood-sucking fiend."

56.

On a Wednesday night I broke back into Rick Horton's Gothic revival.

I found the same box under the same bed. The file on me now contained a photograph of my home and a picture of me getting into my van. The picture was taken with a telephoto lens from a great distance away. I studied the picture closely; I so rarely saw myself these days. My face was, of course, blurry, but my body looked strong and hard. A diet of blood will do that to you. The picture was taken during the day, and I could see the sunscreen gleaming off my lathered cheeks. My hair was hidden in a wide straw hat. I had probably been on my way to pick up the kids from school.

In another file, the same one I had seen the first time I broke in, I found a computer printout that chronicled in excruciating detail a day in the life of Hewlett Jackson, Kingsley's now-murdered client. The paper had notes written in the margins. One of the handwritten notes said: "Not at work. No access." Another note said: "Not in front of his children."

Yeah, this would do nicely.

I pocketed it and returned the box under the bed. In the backyard, with his ferocious guard dogs cowering in the bushes, I wadded up the note in my gloved hands and carefully stuffed it in an empty cereal box in Horton's trash can.

Tomorrow was trash day.

The next night, Sherbet and I were in the same parking structure being guarded by the same rent-a-cop. The same two vehicles were in the same two parking slots. The only difference tonight was that there was no rain.

I extracted the wadded up piece of incriminating evidence from the cereal box and made a big show of it.

Sherbet took the crinkled paper from my hand and studied it closely. He then squinted at me sideways, studying *me* closely, suspicious as hell. I innocently showed him the cereal box where I had found the note. Finally, after some internal debate, a slow smile spread over his face.

"I think we've got our man," he said.

"I do, too."

"And you had nothing to do with this note?"

"I have no idea what you're talking about, detective."

"Let's go," he said. And go we did.

57.

I was leaving the hotel suite to see my children for the first time in a week when my cell phone rang. It was Sherbet.

"You did good work, Mrs. Moon."

"What do you mean?"

"Based on the evidence in the trash can a judge granted us a search warrant. We went through the house yesterday and today we arrested Rick Horton. We found enough incriminating evidence to convict two men for murder."

"I'm not sure that analogy makes sense."

"It doesn't have to. You know what I mean." He paused. "You are a hell of a detective."

"That's what they tell me."

"So why don't you sound happy?" he asked.

"I am very happy. One less killer walking our streets."

We were silent. Sherbet took in some air. "You don't think we got the right guy, do you?"

"I was hired to find out who shot Kingsley Fulcrum," I said. "Did you get Horton's phone records?"

"Of course."

"Could you fax them to me."

"Why?"

"Just humor me."

There was a long pause. Static crackled over the phone line. Finally, I heard him sigh deeply. "Where do I fax them?"

I gave him the number to the courtesy fax machine at the hotel's business center.

"How many months back do you want?" he asked.

"Four months."

"You don't have to do this," he said. "The case is closed."

"I know," I said. "But this detective never sleeps."

"Well, not at night, at least. And Mrs. Moon?"

"Yes?"

"Someday we're going to discuss the eyewitnesses that claim to have seen a man rappel down from your balcony."

"Sure."

"And we're definitely going to discuss the kid who worked at Vons who reported seeing a winged creature carry off a man."

"Sure."

"I don't have any idea what the fuck is going on, but we will talk again."

"I understand," I said. "And detective?"

"Yes?"

"You might have a better idea than you think."

He paused, then hung up.

58.

It was the first time I had been back to my home in over a week.

The house itself sat at the end of a cul-de-sac, with a chain link fence around the front yard. Early on I had hated that ugly chain link fence and wanted it torn down. Danny argued against it stating it might prove useful. He was right. The fence kept my young children away from the street, corralled puppies and kittens, bikes, and loose balls, and was perfect for stringing Christmas lights along. It was also used as a sort of giant pegboard. We attached posters, artwork, and ribbons to it. Advertised their lemonade stands and the birth of any puppies or kittens. I missed that damn fence.

Last year, Danny made us get rid of our dog and cat. The kids were traumatized for months. I think Danny secretly feared I would kill our family pets and feed from them, although he never admitted his concerns to me.

Anyway, now the fence was bare and there were no children playing in the yard. No balls, and certainly no puppies or kittens. Danny's Escalade was parked dead center in the driveway. Usually he parked to the far left half to give my minivan room on the right. He didn't have to worry about that now.

I parked on the street, headed up to the house. The sun was still out and I felt weak as hell, but that wouldn't stop me.

Danny yanked open the door as soon as I reached the cement porch. He stared down at me gravely. He couldn't have seemed less happy to see me. He was as handsome as ever, but that was lost on me now. I only saw his fear and disgust.

"I only have a few minutes, Samantha. These meetings are terribly inconvenient for me."

"Then leave," I said.

"I can't do that."

"Why?"

He stepped in front of me. "For the protection of my children, that's why."

I pushed him aside and entered my house. "Where are they?"

"In their room. You have only a few minutes, Sam. The babysitter will be arriving and I am leaving on my date."

I tried to ignore his hurtful words. Mostly, I tried to keep calm and my voice from shaking. "We had agreed on two hours, Danny."

"Things change, Sam," he said dismissively, and I caught the undercurrent of his words. Things change . . . and so do humans. Into vampires.

He led the way forward and rapped on the children's door. "Kids," he said stiffly. Danny never had a way with our kids. They were always treated like junior assistants, interns or paralegals. "Your mother is here. Come along."

The bedroom door burst open. Little Anthony, with his mess of black curls, flung himself into my arms. Tammy followed a half second later. Their combined weight nearly toppled me over. Squatting, I held their squirming bodies in my arms. Anthony pulled away and I saw that he was still clutching his Game Boy. Neither hell nor high water would separate him from his Game Boy.

"When are you coming back, Mommy?" Anthony asked.

Before I could answer, Danny stepped in. "I told you, son, that your mother is not coming back. That she is sick and she needs to stay away."

I almost dropped the kids in my haste to stand and confront Danny. "Sick? You told them I was sick?"

He pulled me away into a corner of the living room, out of range of the children. "You are sick, Samantha. Very sick. And if I had my way I would report you and have you committed—for your safety and the safety of everyone around you."

"Danny," I said carefully. "I am not sick. I am a person like you. I have a problem that I am dealing with. The problem does not control me. I control it."

"Look, whatever. It's easier for the children to accept that you are sick. I'm going to have to demand that you play along with this, Sam."

I stared at him some more, then headed back to the kids. The three of us sat together on the edge of Tammy's bed while they both chattered in unison. They wanted assurance that I would not die, and I guaranteed them that I would never, ever die. Danny rolled his eyes; I ignored him.

And much too soon, I was back in my minivan driving away, crying.

59.

My sister came by my hotel suite, bearing with her a bottle of Merlot.

Now we were sitting on my bed, legs tucked under us, sipping from our glasses. Mary Lou was on her second glass and already buzzed. I was nowhere near being buzzed. In fact, my last buzz had been when I sucked the blood out of the gang banger.

"So your case is over?" said Mary Lou.

"Yes, I suppose."

"You suppose?" she asked. "It was in the paper. The police found their man. Your name wasn't mentioned of course. Although that hunky detective had his mug on the front page. Sherbert or something."

"Sherbet," I corrected. "And he is kind of hunky, huh?"

She shrugged. "In a grizzly bear sort of way."

"Sometimes that's the best way."

"Sometimes," she said. "So why do you *suppose*?"

"I think we got the wrong guy."

"The detective seems to think you got the *right* guy."

"We're missing something, I'm not sure what."

"Tell me about it?," she said, topping off her glass. "Walk me through it, maybe I can help you."

"Perhaps you could have helped before you started on your third glass."

"You know I'm very lucid when I drink. Give me a shot. Lay it on me."

And so I did. Everything, from working through the files with Kingsley's secretary, Sara, to the multiple break-ins and the subsequent arrest.

"Other than the fact I don't agree with you tampering with evidence," said Mary Lou, "I don't see any holes here. Horton had the evidence, the files. He had the motive, and he even had a similar weapon registered to him."

"I have no doubt he killed Kingsley's client," I said.

"You just don't think he was the shooter who attacked your attorney."

"No," I said. "I don't."

"Why?"

"For one, they don't look alike."

"He was wearing a disguise," said Mary Lou, over-enunciating her words, as she always did when she drank. "Anyone who's seen the video knows that was a fake mustache."

"Horton was clumsy," I said. "Sherbet and I watched Horton struggle with a trash can, and then slip and fall on his ass. He was as athletic as a warthog."

"I don't understand."

"The killer was athletic. Damn athletic. At one point in the video, he leaps smoothly over a bench—"

"And shoots him," said Mary Lou. "Yeah, I remember that. I re-watched the video after you took this case. That stood out. Wow, you're good, sis."

I shrugged. "Still don't know who he is."

"Maybe it's not a *he*," said Mary Lou.

Something perked up within me. "What do you mean?"

"What about his sister? Didn't you mention Horton had a sister?"

I nodded. "She lives in Washington state and is currently recuperating from a broken ankle she suffered a month ago. She was in no condition to shoot and jump over a bench."

"How do you know this?" she asked.

"I'm not considered a super sleuth for nothing."

"Do you think Horton was working alone?"

"I don't know," I said. My gut told me no, but I didn't say anything.

"You going to drink that?" asked Mary Lou, motioning for my glass. I gave it to her. She poured the contents of mine into what was left of hers. "And, since I know you like the back of my hand, you won't rest easy until you find the shooter."

"No," I said, "I won't."

"Perhaps you won't have to wait long, especially if he has an accomplice."

"What do you mean?"

"You were third on the hit list. Perhaps the accomplice will find you."

"Perhaps," I said. "And for the record, I *never* rest easy."

60.

An hour after Mary Lou left the hotel phone rang.

I had been staring down at the lights of Brea, lost in my own thoughts, when the phone rang, startling me. I nearly jumped out of my pale, cold skin at the sound of the ringing phone. I answered it.

"Hello?"

"Mrs. Moon?"

"Yes."

"It's the front desk. We have a fax waiting for you in the lobby."

"Thank you. I'll be down in a minute."

With the fax in hand and back in my hotel room, I hunkered down in one of the straight-back chairs and started reading. The cover letter was printed in tight, unwavering letters. Very cop-like. No surprise since the fax was from Sherbet. In his cover letter, he reminded me that the information contained within was confidential. He also reminded me that the case was closed, that he was looking to retire soon, and the last thing he needed was for me to make his life more difficult. He signed his name with an awkward happy face: The eyes were off-set and the mouth was just a long ghoulish gash, a sort of perversion of the Wal-Mart happy face. I wondered if this was Sherbet's first happy face. Ever.

The rest of the fax consisted of Rick Horton's phone records spanning the last four months. Riveting reading to be sure, so I settled in with a packet of chilled hemoglobin. I flipped through the records methodically, because I am nothing if not methodical. Anyone with eternity on their side damn well better be methodical. I read each number. I looked at dates and times and locations. Most of it was meaningless, of course, but some information began to emerge. First, Rick Horton was obsessed with his sister. A half dozen calls were made to his sister in Washington state each day. Second, Horton had made a handful of calls to Kingsley's office. In fact, eighteen calls in all. Prank calls? Or had Kingsley been in personal contact with Horton?

Next, I searched for key dates and key times and was not really surprised to discover that an hour or so before both

Kingsley's shooting and the Hewlett Jackson murder a telephone call had been placed to the same unknown number. It was a local number.

I dialed the number from my hotel phone, which should be untraceable. I waited, discovered that my heartbeat had increased. I was calling the true killer, I was sure of it. In fact, I felt more than sure. I just *knew*.

The line picked up.

A generic voice mail message. I hung up. Maybe I should have left a nasty little message. Then again, I didn't want to scare the killer away, as ironic as that sounds.

Instead, I flipped open my address book and called my ex-partner, Chad Helling. He didn't answer. Typical. I left Chad a voice mail message asking for a trace on the cell number. Once done, I stepped back to the window, pulled aside the curtain, and continued staring down at the city.

61.

An hour later, still at the window, my cell rang.

The name that popped up on the LCD screen said it was Sara Benson, Kingsley's receptionist. "Mr. Kingsley Fulcrum requests a meeting tonight at the Downtown Grill in Fullerton at ten thirty."

"Oh, really?" I said, rolling my eyes. "And why doesn't Mr. Kingsley Fulcrum call me himself?" I emphasized *Kingsley Fulcrum*. I mean, who has their secretary set up dates for them? Not only was I falling for a werewolf, I was falling for a werewolf with a massive ego.

"He's in a meeting at the moment."

I checked my watch. Geez, defense attorneys kept weird hours. *Talk about the pot calling the kettle black.*

"Fine," I said. "Tell Kingsley I'll be there."

"I'm sure he will be pleased."

More than likely this was a business meeting, but since this was Friday night, who knows, maybe Kingsley had something more on his mind.

As I was getting dressed for what might or might not be a date, my cell rang again.

"Funny how you only call when you need something," said the deep voice immediately. It was Chad.

"Would you prefer I called if I didn't need something?"

"Would be a pleasant change."

"I'll think about it."

"How's that skin disease working out for you?" he asked.

"Very well, thanks for asking."

"Anytime," he said. "You want the name and address for that cell number?"

"Would be nice," I said, very aware that the name he was about to give me could very well be the shooter.

He gave me the name and address. I used the hotel stationery and pen. By the time I finished writing, my hand was shaking.

I clicked off and stared at the name.

62.

I parked in the half full parking lot. Ever the optimist.

I was wearing flats, which slapped loudly on the swath of cobblestones that led up to the rear entrance of the restaurant. The night was clear and inviting, and I had a sudden surge of hope, and love of life. I felt that all was right in the world, or would be, and for the first time I actually believed it. Hell, I almost felt sorry for people who were not vampires, who did not get to experience this side of the night. I was lonely, sure, but that could always change. Loneliness is not permanent.

The cobblestone path ended in a short alley. The alley was kept immaculately clean, for it provided convenient access to the many shops and restaurants. At the moment, the alley was empty and dark. The lights were out. Or broken. I was willing to bet broken. I had long ago lost my fear of dark alleys. My footfalls reverberated off the high walls of the surrounding businesses. I passed behind the back entrance to a used bookstore, a comic book shop, a stationery store and a pet store. The Downtown Grill was the only establishment open at this hour. Music pumped from the restaurant's open door. Fire escapes crowded the air space above the alley like oversized cobwebs.

Sitting on the fire escape was a woman. Pointing a gun at me.

There was a flash, followed immediately by a muffled shot. Something exploded in my chest and I staggered backward. I kept my balance and looked down. Dark blood trickled from a hole in my dress. Next came two more muffled shots—and the impact of two more bullets turned me almost completely around. The bullets had been neatly placed in my stomach. Some good shooting. My red dress was ruined.

The woman walked casually down the fire escape. I saw that there was a silencer on the gun. No one would have heard the muffled shots, especially above the din of music pumping from the restaurant. The fire escape creaked under her weight.

From out of the shadows emerged Sara Benson, Kingsley's receptionist. She paused in the alley and held the gun in both hands like a pro. Her hair was pulled back tightly, revealing every inch of her beautiful face. Her eyes were wide and lustful, and tonight she appeared particularly radiant. Her shapely legs were spaced evenly at shoulder width. A good shooting stance. Any attorney should be so lucky to have such a beautiful receptionist.

Except this receptionist had gone over the edge.

"How could you help that animal, Mrs. Moon?" she said. Her voice was even, and calculating, as if her words had been planned well in advance. I could hear again the undercurrent of rage and hatred, and now I understood fully who that anger was directed toward.

I assumed she was talking about Kingsley. "He's not an animal," I said. Actually, technically, she might have had a point there.

She paused, no doubt surprised that I was still speaking. Her surprise quickly turned into an indignant, self-righteous rant. "Not an animal? Murderers have been set free, rapists have been let loose. The man has no conscience. He's manipulative and horrible."

"He's just doing his job."

"He does it too well."

"Perhaps. But that's neither for you nor I to decide. There are safeguards put into place in the law to protect the innocent.

He upholds these safeguards. Not everyone in prison belongs in prison."

She shook her head, and continued moving closer. I could see tears streaming down her face. Why the hell was *she* getting so emotional? Wasn't *I* the one getting shot here?

"I love him," she said. "There is something so different about him, and I wanted to be part of that. I would have done anything for him. I gave him everything in my heart, but still he left me. And now he has you."

"Let me guess. If you can't have him, then no one can?"

She cocked her head and fired her weapon again. My head snapped back. Blood poured down the bridge of my nose. I'll give her this much: she was a hell of a shot. Which didn't surprise me much, since she was also a hell of an athlete.

And able to leap small park benches in a single bound.

For a brief second, my vision doubled and then even trebled, then everything righted itself once again. Three seconds later the bullet in my head emerged and dropped into my open palm.

Let's see Copperfield do *that*.

Sara stared at me in dumbfounded shock.

From the opposite end of the alley, coming up from the Commonwealth Avenue entrance, another figure appeared. A very large and burly figure. He was standing in a small pool of light from the alley opening.

"Stop!" shouted Detective Sherbet. "Drop your weapon. Now!"

But Sara didn't drop her weapon. Instead, she swung her arm around with the gun.

I jumped forward. "Sara, don't!"

Too late. She didn't get all the way around. Three gunshots exploded from Sherbet's end of the alley. His shots weren't muffled by a silencer. The echoes cracked and thundered down the narrow corridor, assaulting the eardrums.

Sara pirouetted like a ballerina, spinning on one heel. Her gun flung off in one direction and her shoe in the other. And as the sound of Sherbet's pistol still reverberated in the alley, Sara's last dance was over and she collapsed.

Sherbet dashed over to us. He was out of breath and looking quite pale. As he reached down for Sara he called for backup and an ambulance.

Then he looked up at me for the first time.

"You okay, Sam—" And then he stopped short. "Sweet Jesus. You've been shot."

"Really? I hadn't noticed."

"The ambulance is on its way."

"Won't be necessary."

He was silent for a long time. In the distance, I heard the coming sirens.

"We will definitely be talking, Samantha."

"I expect so, Detective."

63.

Rain drizzled outside Kingsley's open French windows.

Water gurgled forth from the fountain with the breasts. Kingsley and I were sitting together on his leather couch. Our shoulders touched. There seemed to be a sort of kinetic energy between us. A sexual energy. At least, there was a sexual energy in *me*.

"Tell me how you figured out Sara was the shooter," he said.

"Three things. First, Horton was in constant contact with her, especially in the hours prior to each shooting. Second, she contacted me from her cell number, claiming she was calling from work, which I found odd. Third, I recalled the picture on her desk, the one taken at the office Halloween party. She went as a pirate."

Kingsley smacked his forehead with his palm. "The mustache. Good Lord, I've seen that picture a hundred times."

"It's the spitting image of your shooter."

"But why didn't you suspect her earlier? I thought you had some sort of ESP thing going on?"

"I do. But it's not an exact science. I sensed a lot of anger from Sara, but I assumed that anger was directed at her failed relationship with you."

"Granted most of my relationships have been failures since the death of my wife, but how did you know about Sara and me?"

"I'm an ace detective, remember?"

"Yes, but—"

"She hinted at it."

"Okay, yeah, we dated. We hit it off initially, but things didn't quite take."

"Ya think?"

We drank some more wine. Our shoulders continued touching.

"Speaking of dating," I said. "Danny's secretary dumped him."

"Is that why you can't wipe that smile off your face?"

"It's one of the reasons," I said. "Not to mention Horton has admitted Sara approached him with a proposal to kill you and your client. He provided the gun and surveillance. She did the shooting."

"Then why attack me in broad daylight, in front of so many witnesses?"

"That was calculated. The shooting was scheduled between security shifts; her getaway truck was parked nearby, the plates removed. Horton was waiting a few blocks away, where they swapped cars. The truck was then concealed in a parking garage." I paused and sipped from my Chardonnay. Even vampires get dry mouths. "Now, with Sara dead and the game up, Horton confessed to everything. He will stand trial as an accessory to murder and attempted murder."

We were silent. Kingsley reached over and gently took my hand. His hand was comforting. And damn big. The rain picked up a little and *plinked* against the French windows.

"You did good work," said Kingsley. "You were worth every penny."

"Of which you still owe me a few."

"When I get my new secretary I'll have her write you a check." He took my wine glass and walked over to his bar and filled me up. From the bar, he said, "I did some research on the medallion."

I perked up. "And?"

"The medallion is rumored to be connected to a way of reversing the effects of vampirism."

"Reversing?" I said, "I don't understand."

"The medallion," he said, "can *reverse* vampirism."

"You mean—"

"You would be mortal again, Sam. That is, if we're talking about the same medallion, which, by the way, is highly coveted, so you might want to keep this on the down low."

My head was swimming with the possibilities. To be human again. To be *normal* again. To have my kids again.

I looked over at Kingsley and there was real pain on his face. He was hurting.

"What's wrong?" I asked.

"Isn't it obvious?" he asked.

"You think that if I choose to be mortal . . ." my voice trailed off.

"I would lose you," he said, finishing. "And I wouldn't blame you for one second."

I stood and came to him, this beautiful, massive man who made me feel alive again, who made me feel sexy again, who made me feel human again, even when I was at my lowest. I sat down in his huge, warm lap and put my arms around his huge, warm neck. I leaned in and pressed my lips softly against his.

When I pulled away after a long moment, I said, "And what if I told you I was falling in love with you?"

"Then that would make me the happiest man, or half-man, on earth," he said. "But what about being mortal again?"

"We'll look into that another day."

"Good idea."

And he kissed me deeply, powerfully, his lips and tongue taking me in completely.

It was a hell of a kiss.

64.

Did I catch you at a good time, Fang?

It's always a good time when I hear from you, Moon Dance.

No girls over tonight?

No girls for awhile. So what's new in your world, Moon Dance?

So I told him. I wrote it up quickly in one long, mangled paragraph.

More type-o's than a blood bank, he answered when I had finished. *I think Sara truly loved Kingsley, at least in her own twisted way.*

Loved him and hated him.

And it drove her to a certain madness.

Yes, I wrote, remembering Sara's pirouetting body. Watching her land in a heap as a pool of dark blood spread around her. I had stared deep into that dark pool, and felt a hunger.

Fang wrote: *She thought Kingsley morally reprehensible, which justified her attempt on his life. And she would have succeeded had he not been immortal. You immortals get all the breaks.*

Some of them, I wrote.

Rejection can make you do some crazy things.

Like jump off a hotel balcony, I added.

Yes. But not everyone has wings.

So why no girls for awhile, Fang?

Because I was in love with another woman.

So who's the lucky woman?

There was a long delay. A very long delay. I wrote: *Fang?*

And then on my computer screen appeared a single red rose, followed by the words: *I love you, Moon Dance.*

I stared at my monitor. More words appeared.

I fell in love with you instantly. I know this sounds crazy because I've never met you, but I have fallen in love with the image I have created of you in my mind. There will never be a woman on the face of this earth who can compare to this image. All will fall short.

He stopped writing, and I read his words over and over again. Finally, I wrote my response.

We are both crazy, Fang. You know that, right?

Yes, I know that.

Goodnight, Fang.

Goodnight, Moon Dance.

[THE END]

BOOK 2

Vampire Moon

Vampire for Hire #2

DEDICATION

To Susanna, the bravest girl I know.

ACKNOWLEDGMENTS

To Sandy Johnston (again!) and Eve Paludan
for helping me look a little smarter than I really am,
and to Elaine Babich, always my first reader.

"The moving moon went up to the sky, And nowhere did abide; Softly she was going up, And a star or two beside."

—*Samuel Taylor Coleridge*

"The devil's in the moon for mischief."

—*Lord Byron*

Vampire Moon

1.

I was alone in my hotel room.

The thick curtains were tightly drawn, and I was watching Judge Judy publicly humiliate this loser slumlord when my cell phone vibrated. I absently rooted through a small mound of Kleenexes on the nightstand until I found my cell. I glanced at the faceplate: unknown number. I briefly debated ignoring the call. After all, Judge Judy nearly had this jerk in tears—and I just love it when she reduces jerks to tears—but I figured this might be a job, and I needed the work. After all, this hotel room didn't pay for itself.

I muted Judge Judy's magnificent rant and flipped open the cell. "Moon Agency."

"Is this the Moon Agency?" asked a male voice.

"Would be a hell of a coincidence otherwise."

There was a long pause. On the other end of the line, I could hear the caller breathing deeply, probably through his open mouth. His voice had sounded nasally. If I had to guess, I would guess he had been crying.

"Are you, you know, a detective or something?"

"Or something," I said. "How can I help you?"

He paused again. I sensed I was about to lose him, and I

knew why. He had been expecting a man. Sadly, I was used to this sort of bias in this business. In reality, most women make better detectives. I waited.

"You any good?"

"Good enough to know you have been crying," I said. I looked at the balled up tissues next to my night stand. "And if I had to guess, I would say there's about a half dozen used Kleenexes next to you."

I heard a sound on his end. It was sort of a snort. "You're good."

"It's why I get paid the big bucks. I have a list of references, if you want them."

"Maybe," he said. More wet breathing. I heard a rustling sound, wiping his nose, no doubt. "Look, I just need help. I don't know who else to turn to."

"What kind of help?"

"Better if we don't talk about it over the phone."

"Are you in Orange County?" I asked.

"Yes, Irvine."

"I'll meet you in an hour at The Block in Orange. The world's third largest Starbucks is there."

"No shit?"

"Actually, I was using hyperbole. But it's pretty damn big."

He made another snorting sound over the phone and I could almost hear him grin. "Okay," he said, "I'll meet you at what may or may not be the world's third largest Starbucks."

Whoever he was, I liked him already. I told him to look for the dark-haired girl in the wide-brimmed sunhat.

"Sunhat?"

"I like to look fashionable. My goal is to block out the sun for anyone standing within three feet of me."

He laughed. I noticed his was a hollow laugh. Empty. There was a great sadness in him. And it had to do with someone he had lost. My sixth sense was getting stronger, true, but it didn't take a psychic to figure this one out.

"Well, we all need goals," he said. "I'll look for the dark-haired girl in the wide-brimmed sunhat causing her own solar eclipse."

This time I grinned. "Well, moons and eclipses do go hand-in-hand."

He gave me his name, which was Stuart, and I verified his cell number should he fail to find the world's third largest Starbucks and the giant sunhat shading half of Orange County.

Yes, more hyperbole.

We agreed on a time and hung up. I unmuted the TV just as Judge Judy finished publicly dismembering the slumlord. The verdict: He owed his ex-tenant her full deposit.

Yea, for the little people!

I didn't want to get out of bed. In fact, I didn't want to move. The afternoon wasn't an optimum time for me. By all rights I should have been sound asleep at this hour, but I had long ago gotten used to getting up at this hour and picking the kids up at school.

Except now I had been banned from picking the kids up at school.

The ban went into place two weeks ago. The monster in me was probably grateful to finally get to sleep in until sunset. But the mommy in me was heartbroken.

And the mommy in me won out in the end.

Prior to a few weeks ago, I used to have to set an alarm clock to wake up on time. An alarm clock turned to its loudest setting and placed as near to my ear as possible.

Now I woke up on my own, at 3:00 p.m., every day. Like clockwork.

Up at 3:00 p.m. with nowhere to go.

And that's usually when I started crying. Not a great way to start your day—or night, in my case.

I wallowed in some more self-pity before finally forcing myself out of bed and into the bathroom. Once there, I proceeded to apply copious amounts of the strongest sunscreen on the market to my face and hands.

Once done, I grabbed my purse, keys and sunhat and headed for the door. And while I waited for the elevator, I wondered what my kids were up to. I checked the time on my cell phone. They would be home by now with Danny's mom, who watched them every day. No doubt they were doing homework, or fighting over the TV, or fighting over the video games. Or just fighting. I sighed heavily. I even missed their fights.

I would call them tonight, as I did every night at 7 p.m., which was my nightly phone privilege with them. I would tell them I loved them and missed them. They would tell me the same thing. They would tell me about their day, and I would ask what they did during school, and about the time Anthony would launch into another long-winded tale, Danny, my ex-husband listening on the other end of the line, would jump in and tell me my ten minutes were up and to tell the kids to say goodbye. Once we said goodbye, Danny would abruptly hang the phone up for them.

Click.

And I wouldn't hear from them for another 23 hours and 50 minutes. I used to have twenty minutes with them, and then fifteen. And now ten.

I was going to need more Kleenexes.

2.

I was waiting for Stuart under a wide green awning, sitting as deep in the shade as possible, as the sun was mercifully beginning to set behind the shining dome of the nearby cineplex.

The Block in Orange is a hip and happening outdoor mall that seemed to appeal mostly to groups of fifteen-year-old girls who spent most of their time doubled over with laughter. Looking at the girls, I was reminded of my daughter. These days, she didn't spend much time doubled over in laughter. These days, she seemed to be sinking deeper into a depression.

Nine years old is too young for a depression.

Suddenly depressed myself, I spotted a man coming around a corner, moving determinedly. He scanned the busy Starbucks crowd, spotted me, and then moved my way. Speaking of shiny domes, the man was completely bald and apparently proud of it. As he got closer, I noted his slacks and tee shirt were badly wrinkled. A thin film of sweat glistened off his head. He wore a cell phone clipped at his hip that looked like it was from the late nineties.

"Samantha Moon?" he asked.

"What an amazing guess," I said.

He looked at my hat.

He said, "Not as amazing as you might think. It's hard to miss that thing."

I usually avoid shaking hands. People tend to recoil when they touch my cold flesh. But Stuart held out his and I reluctantly shook it. Although he flinched slightly, he didn't make an issue out of it, which I was grateful for. As we shook, I also got a strong psychic hit from him. Something bad had happened to him. No. Something bad had happened to someone close to him. And recently. I looked at his other hand. He was wearing a wedding band.

Something bad has happened to his wife.

"Would you like a coffee?" I asked. "Since we're at the third largest Starbucks in the world."

He looked around us. His bald head shimmered in the sun.

"You weren't kidding. A place this big, you'd think the coffee was damned good."

"Not just good," I corrected. "This is Starbucks. Their coffee is magical."

"It sure as hell can make five bucks disappear. Seven bucks if you get all that foo-foo crap."

"Foo-foo crap?"

"You know, whipped cream and syrup and something called java chips."

"Oh, the yummy foo-foo crap."

He grinned and sat opposite me. He was a small man and slender. His bald head was oddly appealing to me. It was perfectly proportioned. No deep ridges or odd grooves. The skin was lightly tan and even. I thought I might just be looking at the world's most perfect bald head. I wanted to touch it. Bad.

He pointed to my hat.

"So do you always wear such a big hat?" he asked.

I generally deflect personal questions, especially any questions that relate to my . . . condition.

I said, "It helps with my phone reception."

He looked at me blankly for a second or two, then broke into a smile. "Ah, it looks like a satellite dish, I get it. Funny."

I asked if he wanted some magical coffee and he declined, claiming it was too late in the day to drink coffee. I used that as my excuse, too, although it was only a half-truth. Six years ago, it would have been too late in the day for coffee, but now coffee only made me sick.

"So tell me about your wife," I said. "It's why you're here, isn't it?"

He sat back and crossed his arms over his chest. His eyes narrowed. His pupils shrank.

"Yes, but how did you know about my wife?" he asked.

"Women's intuition."

He studied me some more, then finally shrugged. He sat forward again and rested his small hands loosely on the table in front of him.

"My wife was killed about a month ago."

"I'm sorry to hear that."

"So am I," he said.

He told me about it. She had died in a local plane crash. She, and nine others. The plane had flown into the side of the San Bernardino Mountains not too far from here. No survivors. I recalled reading about it on the internet, but the story had not been followed up on in the news, and I had no idea why the plane crashed or where the investigators were in their investigation. It had been a big story that turned quickly into a non-story. I smelled a cover-up.

I don't think I had ever known anyone who had lost someone in a plane crash. I recalled Stuart's words from a few minutes earlier: *She was killed.* Not: *She was in an accident.*

"I'm sorry," I said again when he was finished.

He nodded. Talking about his wife dying in a plane crash had sombered him. Had I known him a little better, I would have reached out and taken his hand. As it was, all I could offer were some sympathetic noises and the occasional sorry. Both seemed inadequate.

We were silent for a few more seconds and when the time seemed appropriate, I said, "You don't think the crash was an accident."

"No."

"You think someone killed her."

"I *know* someone killed her. She was murdered. And so was everyone else on board."

An elderly couple sat next to us with their books of crossword and Sudoku puzzles. Both sipped quietly from tall cups of coffee.

In Starbucks speak, tall cups were, of course, small cups.

I studied Stuart. I wasn't sure what to think about him. My sixth sense didn't know what to make of him either. He seemed sane enough, although terribly grief-stricken. The grief-stricken part was what worried me. Grief-stricken always trumped sane.

With the elderly couple nearby, Stuart and I automatically lowered our voices and moved a little closer.

I asked, "Why do you think she was murdered?"

"She had received multiple death threats prior to the plane crash, she and everyone else on board."

Okay, sanity was gaining. But I had questions. Serious questions.

"Why would someone threaten your wife's life, and the others on board?"

"They were going to testify in court. She, and five or six other witnesses."

Stuart unconsciously reached for something that wasn't there. As it was, his fingers closed on empty air. I suspected I knew what they were reaching for: something alcoholic and strong. Unfortunately, we were at a Starbucks, and as far as I knew, they didn't serve any whiskeyaccinos. At least not yet.

"At the time of the crash, she was with the other witnesses?"

"Yes," he said. "They were being flown to a safe house at the Marine base in Camp Pendleton. At the time, of course, I hadn't known where the government was flying her to. I do now."

"Who was she going to testify against?"

Stuart looked at me hesitantly. I sensed I knew the source of his hesitancy. He was about to involve me in something extremely dangerous. He wasn't sure if he should. Here I was, a cute gal wearing an urban sombrero, and no doubt he didn't want to put me in harm's way.

"You can tell me," I said. "I'm a helluva secret keeper."

He shook his head.

"Maybe I should just let this go," he said.

"Maybe," I said. "But I'm a big girl."

"These people are extremely dangerous and, as you can see, can strike anywhere."

"You caught the 'big girl' part, right?"

"It's going to take more than being a big girl, Samantha. It's going to take an army, I'm afraid."

"Call me Sam. And there's very little that I fear."

He squinted, studying me, and as he did so his perfect bald head caught some of the setting sun. There's beauty everywhere, I thought, even in baldness.

"You're really not afraid, are you?" he asked.

"Nope."

"You should be."

"I'm afraid of a lot of things, but men with big guns aren't one of them. My kids' math homework, well, that's another story."

He grinned.

"Fine," he said. "But don't say I didn't warn you."

"Duly noted."

He looked at me some more. He didn't know what to do with his empty hand. It opened and closed randomly. No doubt he was used to holding his wife's hand. Now, I suspected, her hand had been replaced by a crystal tumbler of the hard stuff.

"She was going to testify against Jerry Blum."

I nodded. I knew the name, especially since I had once been a federal agent. Jerry Blum had single-handedly built an enormous criminal empire that stretched down into Mexico and as far up as Canada, which was no surprise since he was, of all things, Canadian. These days he worked hard to bring drugs to the streets and schools of Orange County. Six years ago, he had dabbled in home loan scams, which had been my specialty. He had an uncanny knack of distancing himself from anything illegal, and an even more uncanny knack for avoiding prosecution, which is why my department never caught him.

Last I heard, he had been standing trial for a bizarre crime outside a nightclub in Seal Beach, California, where Jerry Blum had uncharacteristically lost his cool and popped someone with a handgun. Yes, witnesses were everywhere.

I asked Stuart about this, and he confirmed that his wife had indeed been one of the witnesses. She had seen the whole thing, along with five others. She had agreed to testify to what she saw, thus putting her life in mortal danger.

I tapped my longish fingernail on the green plastic table. My fingernails tended to come to a point these days, but most people seemed not to notice, and if they did, they didn't say anything about it. Maybe they were scared of the weird woman with pointed fingernails.

I said, "Why do you think Jerry Blum was involved in your wife's plane crash?"

"Because as of today he is a free man. No witnesses, and thus no case. It's been ruled self-defense."

"But we're talking about a *plane crash*, and if the plane was headed to a military base, then we're probably talking about a military aircraft."

"I know I sound crazy, but look at the facts. Jerry Blum has a history of silencing witnesses. This case was no different. Just a little more extravagant. Witnesses silenced, and Blum's a free man."

I continued tapping. People just didn't take down military aircrafts. Even powerful people. But the circumstantial evidence was compelling.

Whoops! I was tapping too hard. Digging a hole in the plastic. Whoops. A vampiric woodpecker.

I asked, "So what have federal investigators determined to be the cause of the crash?"

"No clue," said Stuart. "The investigation is still ongoing. Every agency on earth is involved in it. I've been personally interviewed by the FBI, military investigators and the FAA."

"Why you?"

"No clue," he said again. "But I think it's because they suspect foul play."

I nodded but didn't tap.

Stuart added, "But he killed her, Sam. I know it, and I want you to help me prove it. So what do you say?"

I thought about it. Going after a crime lord was a big deal. I would have to be careful. I didn't want to jeopardize my family or Stuart. Myself I wasn't too worried about.

I nodded and he smiled, relieved. We discussed my retainer fee. We discussed, in fact, a rather sizable retainer fee, since this was going to take a lot of time and energy. He agreed to my price without blinking and I gave him my PayPal address, where he would deposit my money. I told him I would begin once the funds had been confirmed. He understood.

We shook hands again and, once again, he barely flinched at my icy grip. And as he walked away, with the setting sun gleaming off his shining dome, all I wanted to do was run my fingers over his perfect bald head.

I needed to get a life.

3.

A half hour later, I was sitting in a McDonald's parking lot and waiting for 7:00 p.m. to roll around.

I had already concluded that traffic was too heavy for me to get back to my hotel in time to call my kids, and so I decided to wait it out here, just off the freeway, with a view of the golden arches and the smell of French fries heavy in the air.

My stomach growled. I think my stomach had short-term memory loss. French fries were no longer on the menu.

The sun was about to set. For me, that's a good thing. The western sky was ablaze in fiery oranges and reds and yellows, a beautiful reminder of the sheer amount of smog in Southern California.

I checked the clock on the dash: 6:55.

My husband Danny made the rules. We had no official agreement regarding who could see the kids when. It was an arrangement he set up outside of the courts, because in this case he was judge, jury and executioner. A month or so ago he threatened to expose me for who I am, claiming he had evidence, and that if I fought him I would never see the kids again. Danny was proving to be far more ruthless than I ever imagined. Gone was the gentle husband I had known, replaced by something close to a monster of his own.

Not the undead kind. Just the uncaring kind.

For now, as hard as it was not seeing my kids, I played by his rules, biding my time.

I drummed my fingers on the steering wheel. A small wind made its way through my open window, now bringing with it the scent of cooking beef. Maybe some McNuggets, too. I sniffed again. And fries, always the fries.

I looked at my watch. Three minutes to go. If I called early, Danny wouldn't answer. If I called late, then tough shit; 7:10 was my cut-off no matter what time I called. And if I called past 7:10, he wouldn't pick up. Again, shit out of luck. The calling too late thing had only happened once, when I was in a client meeting. I vowed it wouldn't happen again, clients be damned.

Two minutes to go. I treasured every second I had with my kids, and I hated Danny for doing this to me. How could he turn on me like this?

Easy, I thought. *He's afraid of you. And when people are afraid they do evil, hurtful things.*

One minute. I rolled up my window. I wanted to be able to hear my kids. I didn't want some damn Harley coming by and drowning out little Anthony's comically high-pitched voice, or Tammy's too-serious recounting of that day's school lessons.

Thirty seconds. I had my finger over the cell phone's send button, Danny's home number—my *old* home number—already selected from my contact list and ready to go.

Ten seconds. Outside, somewhere beyond the nearby freeway's arching overpass, the sun was beginning to set and I was beginning to feel good. Damn good. In fact, within minutes I was about to feel stronger than I had any right to feel.

And I was about to talk to my kids, too. A smile that I hadn't felt all day touched my lips.

At 7:00 p.m. on the nose, I pushed the *send* button. The phone rang once and Danny picked up immediately.

"The kids aren't here," he said immediately in his customary monotone.

"But—"

"They're with Nancy getting some ice cream."

Nancy was, of course, the home-wrecker. His secretary fling that had become more than a fling. The name of that witch alone nearly sent me into a psychotic rage.

"They're with *her*?"

"Yes. They like her. We all do."

"When will they be back?"

"I don't know, and that's none of your concern."

"So when can I call back?"

"You can call back tomorrow at seven."

"That's bullshit, Danny. This was my time with—"

"Tomorrow," he said, and hung up.

4.

An hour later, I was boxing at a little sparring club in downtown Fullerton, a place called Jacky's. Jacky himself trained me, which was a rare honor these days, as the little Irishman was getting on in years. I think he either had a crush on me, or didn't know what the hell to make of me, since I tended to destroy his boxing equipment.

The sun had set an hour ago and I was at maximum strength. I was also still pissed off at Danny, hurt beyond words, and now the old Irishman was feeling the brunt of it.

He was wearing brand-new punch mitts, which are those little protective pads trainers use to cover their hands. I was leveling punch after punch into his mittened hands, sometimes so rapidly that my hands were a blur even to my eyes.

And I wasn't just punching them, I was hitting them hard. Perhaps too hard.

Jacky was a tough guy, even though he was pushing sixty. He was an ex-professional boxer back in Ireland who had suffered his share of broken noses, and no doubt had broken a few noses himself. I had never known him to show pain or any sign of weakness. And so when he began wincing with each punch, I knew it was time to ease up on the poor guy. He was far too tough and stubborn to lower the gloves himself and ask for a break.

I paused in mid-strike and said, "Let's take a break."

To say that Jacky was relieved would have been an understatement.

Still, he shot back. "Is that all you got, wee girl?" he asked loudly, and, I think, for the benefit of anyone watching, since I sometimes attracted a crowd of curious onlookers, and Jacky had a tough-guy image to uphold.

Of course, I never wanted to attract crowds of onlookers, as I generally avoid bringing attention to myself. But since that incident last month with a Marine boxer, an incident in which I put him in a hospital, well, I had become somewhat of a hero in this mostly women's boxing club.

"Well, I could probably go another round or two," I said lightly to Jacky.

"I'll pretend I didn't hear that," he said.

Jacky shook off the protective gloves. His hands were ruddier than his Irish complexion; his fingers were fat and swollen.

"Sorry about that," I said. "I'm having a bad night."

"I'd hate to get on your bad side."

"Doesn't seem to worry my ex-husband."

"Then I say he's not right in the head. You punch like a hammer." He shook his head in wonder. I often caused this reaction from the old boxer, who hadn't yet figured me out. "Harder than anyone I've ever trained, man or woman."

"Yeah, well, we've all got our talents," I said. "Yours, for example, is having red hair."

"That's not a talent."

"Close enough."

He shook his head and held up his red hands which, if I looked hard enough at them, I could probably see throbbing.

"I need to soak these in ice," he said. "But if I soak these in ice, the women here will think I'm a pussycat."

I leaned over and kissed him on his sweating forehead. The blush that emanated from him was instant, spreading from his balding head, down into his neck.

"But you are a pussycat," I said.

"Well, you're a freak of nature, Sam."

Jacky, of course, didn't realize how freaky I was. In fact, I could count on one hand the number of people who knew how freaky I was.

"You could be a world champion," he said. Now we were making our way over to the big punching bag.

"I'm too old to be a world champion," I said. Jacky was always trying to get me to fight professionally.

He snorted. "You're, what, thirty?"

"Thirty-one, and thank you."

However, Jacky was closer than he thought. I was indeed thirty-seven calendar years old, but I was frozen in a thirty-one-year-old's body.

The age I was when I was attacked.

Granted, if a girl had to pick an age to be immortalized in, well, thirty-one would probably be near the top of her list.

And what happens ten years from now when you're forty-seven but still look thirty-one? Or when your daughter is thirty-one and you still look thirty-one?

I didn't know, but I would cross that bridge when I got there.

Jacky took up his position behind the punching bag. "So what's eating at you anyway, Sam?"

"Everything," I said. I started punching the bag, moving around it as if it were an actual opponent, using the precise body movements Jacky had taught me. Ducking and weaving. Jabs. Hooks. Hard straight shots. Punches that would have broken jaws and teeth and noses. Jacky bared his teeth and absorbed the punches on the other side of the bag like the champion he was, or used to be. I took a small breather. So did Jacky. Sweat poured from my brow.

"Let me guess," said Jacky, gasping slightly, and looking as if he had taken actual physical shots to his own body. "Is it that no-good ex-husband of yours?"

"Good guess."

"Does he realize you could kick his arse from here to Dublin?"

"He realizes that," I said. "And why Dublin?"

"National pride," he said. "So why don't you go kick his fucking arse?"

"Because kicking ass isn't always the answer, Jacky."

"Works for me," he said.

"We'll call that *Plan B*."

"Would be my *Plan A*. A good arse-kicking always clears the air."

I laughed. "I'll keep it in mind."

"Break's over. Hands up."

He leaned back into the bag and I unleashed another furious onslaught. Pretending the bag was my ex-husband was doing wonders for me.

"You're sweating like a pig, Sam," screamed Jacky. "I like that!"

"You like pig sweat?"

He just shook his head and screamed at me to keep my fists

up. I grinned and unleashed a flurry of punches that rocked the bag and nearly sent little Jacky flying, and attracted a small group of women who gathered nearby to watch the freak.

And as I punched and sweated and kept my fists up, I knew that fighting Danny wasn't the answer. Luckily, there were other ways to fight back.

5.

After a long shower and a few phone calls to some friends working in the federal government, I was at El Torito Bar and Grill in Brea—just a hop, skip and a jump from my hotel.

I was wearing jeans and a turtle neck sweater. Not because it was cold outside, but because I looked so damn cute in turtle neck sweaters. The stiff-looking man sitting across from me seemed to think so, too. Special Agent Greg Lomax, lead investigator with the FBI, was in full flirt mode, and it was all I could do to keep him on track. Maybe I shouldn't have looked so cute, after all.

Damn my cuteness.

El Torito is loud and open. The loudness and openness was actually of benefit for anyone having a private conversation, which was probably why Greg had chosen it.

Personally, I found the noise level here a bit overwhelming, but then again, I'm also just a sweet and sensitive woman.

It was either that or my supernaturally acute hearing that quite literally picked up every clattering dish, scraping fork and far ruder sounds best not described. And, of course, picked up the babble of ceaseless conversations. If I wanted to I could generally make out any individual conversation within any room. Handy for a P.I., trust me. Granted, I couldn't hear through walls or anything, but sounds that most people could hear, well, I could just hear that much better.

"Lots of people over at HUD talk very highly of you," he said.

"I gave them the best seven years of my life," I said.

"And then you came down with some sort of, what, rare skin disease or something?"

"Or something," I said.

"Now you work private," he said.

"Yes. A P.I."

"How's that working out?"

"It's good to be my own boss," I said. "Now I give myself weekly pay raises and extra long coffee breaks."

He grinned. "That's cute. Anyway, I was told to tell you what I could. So ask away. If I can't talk about something, or I just don't know the answer, I'll tell you."

We were sitting opposite each other in a far booth in the far corner of the bar. I was sipping some house Zinfandel, and he was drinking a Jack and Coke. White wine and water were about the only two liquids I could consume. Well, that and something else.

Just thinking about that something else immediately turned my stomach.

I said, "So do you think the crash was an accident?"

"You get right to the point," he said. "I like that."

"Must be the investigator in me."

He nodded, drank some more Jack and Coke. "No, this wasn't an accident. We know that much."

"How do you know that?"

He smiled. "We just know."

"Okay. So how did the plane crash?"

"All signs point to sabotage."

"Sabotage how?"

He was debating how much to tell me. I could almost see the wheels working behind his flirtatious eyes. No doubt he was computing the amount of information he could still give me and still not give up any real government secrets, and yet leave me satisfied enough to sleep with him tonight. A complex formula for sure.

Men are better at math than they realize.

He said, "Someone planted a small explosive in the rudder gears. The pilot heard the explosion, reported it immediately, and then reported that he had lost all control of the plane. Ten minutes later the plane crashed into the side of the San Bernardino Mountains."

"And everyone on board was killed?"

"Yes. Instantly."

"Is there any reason to believe that these key witnesses were killed to keep them from testifying?"

"There is every reason to believe that. It's the only motive we have." He drank the rest of his Jack and Coke. "Except there's one problem: Our number one suspect was in jail at the time of the crash."

The waiter came by and dropped off another drink for Greg. Perhaps the waiters here at El Torito Bar and Grill were psychic. Greg picked up his drink and sipped it.

"It would take a lot of pull to sabotage a military plane," I said.

"Not as much as you might think," said Greg. "This was a DC-12, and the contract the government has with them stipulates that the makers of the planes get to use their own mechanics."

"So the mechanic was a civilian."

"Yes."

"Have you found the mechanic?"

"Yeah," he said. "Dead in his apartment in L.A."

"How did he die?"

"Gunshot in the mouth."

"Suicide?"

"We're working on it."

I followed up with this some more, but Greg seemed to have reached the limit of what he was willing to tell me.

Greg motioned to my half-finished drink. "You going to finish that?"

"Probably not."

"You want to head over to my place and, you know, talk some more about what it's like giving yourself raises?"

I said, "When you say 'talk' don't you really mean boff my brains out?"

He grinned and reddened. I reached over and patted his superheated face.

"You'll just have to give yourself a raise tonight," I said, and left him my card. "Call me if you hear anything new."

"But I live right around the cor—"

"Sorry," I said. "But your calculations were off."

I smiled sweetly and left.

6.

We were at the beach, sitting on the wooden deck of a lifeguard tower. The sign on the lifeguard tower said no sitting on the wooden deck.

"We're breaking the law," I said.

Kingsley Fulcrum turned his massive head toward the sign above us. As he did so, some of the moonlight caught his cheek bones and strong nose and got lost somewhere in the shaggy curls that hung on his beefy shoulders.

"We are risking much to be here," he said. "If we get caught, our super secret identities may be discovered."

I said, "Especially if I show up invisible in the mug shot."

Kingsley shook his head.

"You vampires are weird," he said.

"This coming from a guy who howls at every full moon."

He chuckled lightly as a small, cold wind scurried over my bare feet. Before us, the dark ocean stretched black and eternal. Small, frothing whitecaps slapped the shore. In the far distance, twinkling on the curve of the horizon, were the many lights of Catalina Island. Between us and Catalina were the much brighter lights of a dozen or so oil rigs. The beach itself was mostly quiet, although two or three couples were currently smooching on blankets here and there. They probably thought they were mostly hidden under the cover of darkness. They probably hadn't accounted for a vampire with built-in night vision watching them. A gyrating couple, about two hundred feet away up the beach, might have been doing the nasty.

Kingsley turned to me. I always liked the way the bridge of his nose angled straight up to his forehead. Very Roman. And very hot.

He said, "You became a private investigator after you were changed?"

"Yes."

"So that means you took your P.I. photo when you were a vampire."

"Yes."

"So how did you manage that?"

"I wore a lot of make-up that day," I said smugly, proud of myself. I had wondered what to do about the photo, too.

"So the make-up showed up, even though you didn't?"

"Yes, exactly. I even made sure I blinked when the picture was taken."

"Just in case your eye sockets came up empty."

"Exactly."

"You could have worn colored contacts," said Kingsley.

"But then the whites of my eyes would have come up empty," I said.

He nodded. "So you sacrificed your vanity."

"I might look like a major dork in the picture, but at least I look human. Granted, if you look close enough, there is a blank spot somewhere near my throat, where I had missed a patch of skin, but not too many people are looking at my throat."

"No," said Kingsley. "They're looking at the dork with her eyes closed."

I punched him in the arm. The force of my blow knocked him sideways.

"Ouch!" He rubbed his arm and grinned at me, and the light from the half moon touched his square teeth. Kingsley was a successful defense attorney in Orange County. A few months ago, he had hired me to investigate a murder attempt on his life. His case had come at a difficult time in my life. Not only had I just caught my husband cheating, the bastard had the gall to kick me out of my own home.

A very difficult time, to say the least. The wounds were still fresh and I was still hurting.

And I would be for a very long time.

Not the greatest time to start a new romance with a hunky defense attorney with massive shoulders and a tendency to shed.

"There are two people boffing over there," said Kingsley, looking off over his shoulder. "I think one of their names is *Oh, Baby*."

Kingsley's hearing was better than mine, which was saying something.

I grinned and elbowed him. "Will you quit eavesdropping."

He cocked his head to one side, and said, "I was wrong. His name is *Oh, God*."

I elbowed him again, and we sat silently some more. Our legs were touching. His thigh was about twice as wide as mine. We were both wearing jeans and sweaters.

I sensed Kingsley's desire to touch me, to reach out and lay his big hand over my knee. I sensed him forcibly controlling himself.

Down boy.

I was still looking out over the black ocean, which, to my eyes, wasn't so black. The air shimmered with light particles which flashed and streaked across the night sky. I often wondered what these streaking lights were. I didn't know for sure, but I had a working hypothesis. I suspected I was seeing the physical manifestation of energy itself. Perhaps I was being given a behind-the-scenes glimpse of the workings of our world.

Then again, I've been wrong before.

Kingsley was still looking at me, still fighting what he most wanted to do. And what he most wanted to do was ravage me right here and now on this lifeguard pier. But the brute held himself in check. Smart man. After all, I gave him no indication that I wanted to be ravaged.

"Not yet, Kingsley," I said calmly, placing my own hand lightly on his knee. "I'm not ready yet."

He nodded his great, shaggy head, but said nothing. I sensed his built-up energy dissipate in an instant. Hell, I could practically see it zigzagging away from his body, caught up by the lunar wind and merging with the silver spirits surfing the California night skies.

He exhaled and sort of deflated. Poor guy. He had gotten himself all worked up. He rested his own hand lightly on mine, and if my own cold flesh bothered him, he didn't show it.

And while we sat there holding hands, with me soaking in the tremendous warmth of his oversized paw, I told him about my latest case.

When I was finished, he said, "Jerry Blum is a dangerous man."

"I'm a dangerous girl."

From far away, emerging from under the distant Huntington

Beach Pier, was a lone jogger. Even from here, the jogger appeared to be a very big man. The man was easily a hundred yards away.

Kingsley, who had been looking down at my leg, suddenly cocked his head, listening. He then turned and spotted the jogging man. The man, as far as I could tell, wasn't making a sound.

I was intrigued. "You heard him?"

"Yes and no," said Kingsley, still looking over his shoulder at the approaching man. "But I could hear his dog."

I looked again. Sure enough, running along at the man's feet, about the size of a rat on steroids, was something small and furry. A dog, and it looked minuscule next to the running man. I smiled. For some reason, I found it heartwarming to see such a big man running with such a little doggie.

Kingsley said, "So what, exactly, is your client hiring you to do? Does he want you to take down one of the most dangerous criminals on the West Coast?"

"Taking him down will be extra."

"Taking him down will be dangerous for both you and your family, Sam. Remember, this guy doesn't play nice."

"I won't put my family in harm's way," I said. "And besides, who says I play nice, either? I've been known to bite."

"Very funny. But I don't like this, Sam. This isn't your typical P.I. gig. Hell, the FBI still hasn't figured out a way to nail this guy, and you're just one woman."

"But a helluva woman."

"Sure, but why am I more concerned about your safety than you are?" he asked.

"Because you like me a little," I said, blinking daintily.

"I would like you more if you stayed away from this case."

Something small and furry and fat suddenly appeared in the sand beneath our feet. It was the same little dog, now trailing a leash. It was, in fact, a tea cup Pomeranian, and it was about as cute as cute gets. Maybe even cuter. It wagged its tail a mile a minute and turned in a half dozen small circles, creating a little race track in the sand. It never once took its eyes off Kingsley.

"It likes you," I said.

"Go figure."

Kingsley made a small noise in his throat and the little dog abruptly sat in the sand in front of him, staring, panting, wagging.

And from out of the darkness, sweating through a black tee shirt and rippling with more muscle than two or three men put together—that is, if those men weren't Kingsley—was the same tall man we had seen a few minutes earlier. He approached us with a small limp that didn't seem to bother him.

"Kill, Ginger," said the man easily, grinning. Ginger turned in two more circles and sat before Kingsley again. The man reached down and gently patted its little head. "Good girl." He looked up at us. "Were you two at least a little afraid for your lives?"

"Terrified," said Kingsley.

"I might have wet myself a little," I said.

The man stood straight and I might have seen his six-pack through his wet tee shirt. *Hubba, hubba.*

"She doesn't usually come up to strangers," said the man. "In fact, I'm fairly certain she's terrified of her own shadow. Of course, it's a pretty fat shadow. Scares me a little, too."

Kingsley slipped off the wooden platform, landing softly in the sand, too softly for a man his size. Ginger didn't move, although her tail might have started wagging at close to the speed of light. The attorney reached down and scratched the little dog between turgid ears. Ginger, if anything, looked like a star-crossed teenager at a rock concert. Or me at a Stones concert.

"Okay, that's a first," said the man, looking genuinely surprised. "Took me three months before I was anywhere near those ears."

Kingsley, still petting the dog, said, "She probably had a bad experience when she was a pup. If I had to guess, I would say she was beaten and abused before she found her new home. Probably by a man about your size, and so she doesn't like men, but she does like you, even though you run too fast for her little legs, and you don't give her near enough treats." Kingsley gave Ginger a final pat and stood. "Like I said, it's just a guess."

"Good guess. And spot on. She had been abused before my girlfriend rescued her. Of course, there was no rescuing the man who abused her. Let's just say when I was done with him, he had a newfound respect for every living creature."

Kingsley and I grinned. I had no doubt that the man in front of us could have inflicted some serious damage on someone.

He went on, "And if I gave Ginger any more treats I would have to roll her on my runs."

I snickered and Kingsley laughed heartily. He reached out a hand. "I know you from somewhere."

"Not the first time I've heard that," said the man as he scooped up the little dog, who promptly disappeared behind a bulging bicep muscle that had my own eyes bulging.

Kingsley's eyes narrowed. His thinking face. "You used to play football for UCLA."

"Is there any other school?"

The attorney snapped his fingers. "You were on your way to the pros until your broke your leg."

"Don't you just hate when that happens?" said the man lightly. "And you are, of course, Kingsley Fulcrum, famed defense attorney and internet sensation."

Kingsley laughed; so did I. Indeed, a few months ago, someone had tried to kill the attorney outside of a local courthouse. It was a bizarre and humorous incident that had been captured on film and seen around the country, if not the world. *Kingsley, the man who couldn't die.* The world watched as his assailant shot him point-blank five times in the head and neck.

The two men chitchatted for a bit, and I realized, upon closer inspection, that both men were exactly the same height. Although the stranger was muscular and powerful-looking, Kingsley had a beefy savagery to him that no man could match. Even ex-football players.

After all the silly football talk, I soon learned that the tall stranger now worked as a private eye. I perked up. Kingsley mentioned I was one, too, and the man nodded and reached into his sweatpants pocket and pulled out a brass card holder. He opened it, gave me one of his cards.

He said, "You ever need any extra help or muscle, call me. I can provide both."

I looked at the card. Jim Knighthorse. I might have heard the name before, perhaps on some local newscast or something. On his card was a picture of him smiling, really cheesin' it up for the camera. I had a very strong sense that Mr. Knighthorse just might have been in love with himself.

"Helluva picture," he said, winking. "If I do say so myself."

I was right.

7.

It was far too early in the morning for me, but I didn't care.

The sun was high and hot, and I was sitting in my minivan in the parking lot of my children's elementary school near downtown Fullerton, where I had parked under a pathetic jacaranda tree. The tree was mostly bare but offered some shade.

Beggars can't be choosers.

I was huddled in my front seat, away from any direct sunlight, the shades pulled down on both the driver's side and passenger's side windows. My face was caked with the heaviest sunblock available on the market. Thin leather gloves covered my hands, and I was wearing another cute wide-brimmed sunhat, which sometimes made driving difficult. I had many such hats—all purchased in the last six years, of course—and all a necessity to keep me alive.

And what happens if I'm ever exposed to any direct sunlight?

I don't know, and I don't want to find out, either. All I know is that the sun physically hurts me, even when I'm properly protected. I suspect I would wither and die. Probably painfully, too.

So much for being immortal.

Immortality with conditions.

As I huddled in my seat, I thought about those words again: *wither and die.*

You know, I used to lead a normal life. I grew up here in Orange County, was a cheerleader and softball player, went to college in Fullerton, got a master's degree in criminal science, and then went on to work for the federal government. Lots of dreams and ambitions. One of them was to get married and start a family. I did that, and more.

Life was good. Life was fun. Life was easy.

If someone had told me that one day my daily To-Do

List would consist of the words: *1) Buy extra-duty sunblock. 2) Oh, and see if Norco Slaughterhouse will set up a direct billing . . .* well, I would have told them to go back to their Anne Rice novels.

I sat in my minivan, huddled in my seat, buried under my sunhat and sunblock, wary of any beam of sunlight, and shook my head and I kept shaking my head until I found myself crying softly in my hands. Smearing my sunscreen.

Damn.

I may not have known what lived in me, and I may not have known the dark lineage of my blood, but I knew one thing for fucking sure. No one was going to keep me from seeing my kids. Not Danny. And not the sun.

I opened my van door and got out.

8.

I gasped and stumbled.

I reached a gloved hand out and braced myself on the hot fender of my minivan. Heat from the sheet metal immediately permeated the thin glove. Maybe Stephenie Meyer's vampires had it right. Maybe I should move up to Washington State, in the cold and rain, where gray clouds perpetually covered the skies.

Maybe someday. But not now. I had real-life issues to deal with.

I gathered myself together and strode across the quiet parking lot, filled mostly with teachers' and school administrators' cars. I'm sure I must have looked slightly drunk—or perhaps sick—huddled in my clothing, head down, stumbling slightly.

A small wind stirred my thick hair enough to get a few strands stuck in the copious amounts of sunscreen caked on my face. I ignored my hair. I needed to get the hell out of the sun. And fast.

I picked up my pace as another wind brought to me the familiar scents of cafeteria food. Familiar, as in this was exactly what cafeteria food had smelled like back when I was in elementary school.

After crossing the hot parking lot, I stepped up onto a sidewalk and a moment later I was under an eave, gasping.

Sweet, sweet Jesus.

Keeping to the shade and sliding my hand along the stucco wall to keep my balance, I soon found myself in front of the main office door.

Focus, Sam.

I needed to look as calm and normal as possible. School officials didn't take kindly to crazy-looking parents.

My skin felt as if it were on fire. And all I had done was walk across a school parking lot. I wanted to cry.

No crying.

I sucked in some air, held it for a few minutes—yes minutes—and let it out again. My skin felt raw and irritated. I picked hair out of the heavy sunscreen with a shaking hand, adjusted my sunhat, put a smile on my face, and opened the office door.

Just another mom here to see her kids.

A few minutes later, I found myself in the principal's office; apparently, I was in trouble.

Principal West was a pleasant-looking man in his mid-fifties. He was sitting behind his desk with his hands folded in front of him. He wore a white long-sleeved dress shirt with Native American-inspired jade cuff links. As far as I knew, he wasn't Native American.

Principal West had always been kind to me. Early on, just after my attack, he had been quick to work with me. I was given special access to the front of the school when picking up my kids. Basically, I got to park where the buses parked—thus avoiding long lines and sitting in the sun longer than I had to. Good man. I appreciated his kindness.

That kindness had, apparently, come to an end.

"I can't let them see you, Samantha, I'm sorry."

"I don't understand."

"I got a call today from Danny. In fact, I got it just about a half hour ago. Your husband—or ex-husband—says that the two of you have an unwritten agreement that you will not be picking the kids up anymore."

"Yes, but—"

"He also says that you have agreed to supervised visits only. Is this true?"

Principal West was a good man, I knew that, and I could see that this was breaking his heart. I nodded and looked away.

He sighed heavily and pushed away from his desk, crossing his legs. "I can't allow you to see them without Danny being present, Samantha. I'm sorry."

"But I'm their mother."

He studied me for a long time before saying, "Danny also said that you are a potential danger to the kids, and that under no circumstances are you to be alone with them."

I was shaking my head. Tears were running down my face. I couldn't speak.

Principal West went on, "You're very ill, Sam. I can see that. Hell, anyone can see that. How and why you pose a threat to your children, I don't know. And what's going on between you and Danny, I don't know that, either. But I would suggest that before you agree to any more such terms, Sam, that you seek legal counsel first. I have never known you to be a threat. Outside of being sick, I have always thought you were a wonderful mother, but it's not for me to say—"

I lost it right there. I burst into tears and cried harder than I had cried in a long, long time. A handful of secretaries, the receptionist and even the school nurse surrounded me. Principal West watched me from behind his desk, and through my tears, I saw his own tears as well.

He wiped his eyes and got up. He put an arm gently around me and told me how sorry he was, and then escorted me out.

9.

I hate all men, I wrote.

Even me?

Are you a man, Fang?

Yes, but I'm a helluva man.

Despite myself, I laughed. I was in my hotel room sitting in the cushioned hotel chair. I should have been comfortable, but I wasn't; the chair's wooden arms were bothering me. Come to think of it, the chair wasn't that comfortable, either. Maybe I should complain to hotel management.

Or maybe I should just calm down, I thought. Even better, maybe I should get myself an apartment somewhere and decorate it with my *own* chairs.

It was a thought, but something I would think about later.

How do I know you're a helluva man? I wrote. *I've never seen a picture of you.*

You'll have to take my word for it.

The word of a man? Never! :)

Remember: A helluva a man.

So you say.

What's got you so upset tonight, Moon Dance?

Fang was my online confidant. I had met him via an online vampire chatroom years ago, back when chatrooms were all the rage. Nowadays, he and I just chatted through AOL, although we kept our old screen names. His was Fang950, and mine was MoonDance. To date, I had yet to tell him anything too personal, although he has probed repeatedly for more information. Admittedly, I have too. We were both deathly curious about each other, but I had my reasons to not reveal my identity, and, according to him, he did, too. Of course, my reason had been obvious: I admitted to him early on that I was a vampire. To his credit, or, more accurately, a ding to his sanity, he had believed me without reservations.

So I told him about my attempt to see my kids, and how Danny was stymieing me at every turn.

You could always kill him, wrote Fang.

Sometimes I don't know when you're joking.

There was a long pause, and then he wrote, *Of course, I was joking.*

Good. You had me worried.

Still, he wrote. *It would solve all your problems.*

And create a ton more, I wrote, and then quickly added: *I'm not a killer.*

Thus wrote the vampire.

I'm a good *vampire.*

There are some who would say that's an oxymoron.

Why can't I be good, too?

Because it's in your nature to kill and drink blood. Ideally, fresh blood from a fresh kill.

I won't kill anything. I would rather shrivel up and die.

But by not drinking fresh blood you are denying yourself the full powers of your being.

How much more powerful do I need to be? I wrote.

You have no idea.

And how do you know so much about vampires, Fang? You've told me long ago that you are human.

A human with a love for all things vampire.

And why do you love vampires so much, Fang?

I have my reasons.

Will you ever tell me what they are?

Someday.

But not on here.

Exactly, he wrote. *Not on here.*

If not on here, then where? I asked.

That's the million dollar question.

I changed subjects. *So what am I supposed to do about Danny?*

Another long pause. I often wondered what Fang did during these long pauses. Was he going to the bathroom? Answering his cell phone? Sitting back and lacing his fingers behind his head as he thought about what he would write next?

Finally, after perhaps five minutes, his words appeared in the IM box: *Danny has all the leverage.*

I thought about that. Indeed, it had been something that occurred to me earlier, but I wanted to see what Fang had up his sleeve.

Keep going, I wrote.

Maybe it's time for you to take back the leverage.

I agree. Any idea how?

Something will come to you. Hey, how psychic are you these days, Moon Dance?

More than I was a few years ago. Why?

Some psychics use automatic writing for answers.

What's automatic writing?

It's when you sit quietly with a piece of paper and a pen and you ask questions. Sometimes answers come through and your pen just . . . starts writing.

I laughed.

You're kidding.

No, I'm not. It could be a way for you to find answers, Moon Dance.

Answers to what?

Everything.

I thought about that, and a small feeling stirred in my solar plexus.

So how do I do this?

Research it on the internet.

Okay, I will.

Good. And let me know how it goes. 'Night, Moon Dance.

'Night, Fang.

10.

I did research it on the internet.

Normally, I would have scoffed at such nonsense (automatic writing? C'mon!), but my very strange existence alone suggested that I should at least consider it.

And I liked the possibilities. Who wouldn't want spiritual answers, especially someone with my condition?

According to a few sites I checked out on the internet, the process of automatic writing seemed fairly simple. Sit quietly at a table with a pen and paper. Center yourself. Clear your mind. Hold the pen lightly over the paper . . . and see what comes out.

Then again, maybe I didn't want to know what might come out. Maybe I needed to keep whatever was in me bottled up.

With some trepidation, I found a spiral notebook and a pen. I switched off my laptop and slipped it back in its case.

It was just me, the table, a pen, and a pad of paper.

I stared at the pen. When I grew tired of staring at the pen, I cracked my neck and my knuckles. In the hallway outside my door, I heard two voices steadily growing louder as a couple approached in the direction of my door. The couple came and went, and now their voices grew fainter and fainter.

I picked up the pen.

A domed light hung from the ceiling directly above the table. The light flickered briefly. It had never flickered before. I frowned. One of the sites I had read mentioned that when spirits were present, lights flickered.

It did so again, and again. And now the light actually flickered off, and then on. And then off. Over and over it did this.

I sat back, gasping.

"Sweet Jesus," I said.

More flickering. On and off.

Nothing else in my room was flickering. The light near the front door held strong. So did the light coming in under my front door. It was just this light, directly above me.

And then the light went apeshit. On and off so fast that I could have been having an epileptic seizure.

"Stop!" I suddenly shouted. "I get it. I'll do it."

I brought the pen over to the pad of paper, and the flickering stopped. The light blazed on, cheerily, as if nothing had happened at all.

Okay, that settles it, I thought. *I really am going crazy.*

I set the tip of the pen lightly down on the lined paper. I closed my eyes. Centered myself, whatever that meant. I did my best to do what the article on the internet said. Imagine an invisible silver cord stretching down from each ankle all the way to the center of the earth. Then imagine the cord tied tightly to the biggest rocks I could imagine. Then imagine another such cord tied to the end of my spine, attached to another such rock in the center of the earth.

Grounding myself.

I briefly imagined these silver cords stretching down through nine hotel floors, plunging through beds and scaring the hell out of the occupants below me.

I chuckled. *Sorry folks. Just centering myself.*

When I thought I was about as centered as I could be, I realized I didn't know what to do next. Maybe I didn't have to do anything. It was called automatic writing for a reason, right?

I looked at the pen in front of me. The tip rested unmovingly on the empty page. The lights above me had quit flickering. No doubt a power surge of some sort.

Maybe I should quit thinking?

But how does one quit thinking? I didn't know, but I tried to think of nothing, and found myself thinking of everything. This was harder than it looked.

One of the articles said that focusing on breathing was a great way to unclutter thoughts. But what if someone didn't need to breathe? The article wasn't very vampire friendly.

Still, I forced myself to breathe in and out, focusing on the air as it passed over my lips and down the back of my throat. I focused on all the components that were necessary to draw air in and expel it out.

I thought of my children and the image of me strangling Danny came powerfully into my thoughts.

I shook my head and focused on breathing.

In and out. Over my lips and down my throat. Filling my lungs, and then being expelled again.

And that's when I noticed something very, very interesting. I noticed a slight twitching in my forearms.

I opened my eyes.

The twitching had turned into something more than twitching. My arm was spasming. The feeling wasn't uncomfortable, though. Almost as if I were receiving a gentle massage that somehow was stimulating my muscles. A gentle shock therapy.

I watched my arm curiously.

Interestingly, with each jerk of my muscles, the point of the pen moved as well, making small little squiggly lines on the page. Meaningless lines. Nothing more than chicken scratches.

My arm quit jerking, and I had a very, very strange sense that something had settled into it, somehow. Something had melded with my arm.

The chicken scratches stopped. Everything stopped.

There was a pause.

And then my arm tingled again and my muscles sort of jerked to life and I watched, utterly fascinated, as the pen in front of me, held by own hand, began making weird circles.

Circle after circle after circle. Big circles. Little circles. Tight, hard circles. Loose, light circles. Sloppy circles, perfect circles.

Quickly, the circles filled the entire page. When there wasn't much room left at all, my hand grew quiet.

Using my other hand, I tore out the page out, revealing a fresh one beneath.

My arm jerked immediately, tingling, and the pen wrote again, but this time not with circles.

This time words appeared. Two words, to be exact.

Hello, Samantha.

11.

I stared at the two words.

Had I written them? Was I deluding myself into thinking that something beyond me was writing?

At that moment, as those questions formed in my mind, the gentle shocking sensation rippled through my forearm again and the pen began moving. Three words appeared.

Does it matter?

The script was flowing. Easy to read. Big, roundish letters. Completely filling the space between the light-blue lines of the writing paper.

"You can read my mind?" I said aloud.

My hand jerked to life, and words scrawled across the page.

Thoughts are real, Samantha. More real than people realize.

I watched in amazement as the words appeared before me. I had the sense that if I wanted to stop writing, that I could. I wasn't being forced to write. I was allowing something to write through me. If I wanted this to stop it would.

"Who are you?" I asked. My heart, which averaged about five beats a minute, had increased in tempo. It was now thumping away at maybe ten beats a minute.

There was only a slight pause, and then my hand felt compelled to write the words: *I am someone very close to you.*

"Should I be afraid?"

You should be whatever you want. But let me ask you: Do you feel afraid?

"No."

Then trust how you feel.

I took in some air, and held it for a few minutes, staring down at the pad of paper. I exhaled the air almost as an afterthought.

"This is weird," I said.

It is whatever you want it to be. It could be weird. Or it could be wildly wonderful.

Half the page was now full. My hand also moved down to the next line on its own, prompted by the gentle electrical stimulation of my arm muscles.

A weird, otherworldly sensation, for sure.

"So you are someone close to me," I said, and suddenly felt damn foolish for talking to my hand and a piece of paper. "But that doesn't tell me *who* you are."

There was a pause, and I had a strong sense that whoever I was talking to was considering how much to tell me.

For now, let's just say I am a friend. A very close friend.

"Most of my friends don't speak to me through a pen and paper," I said. "They use email or text messaging."

Words are words, are they not? Think of this as spiritual instant messaging. A SIM.

Despite myself, I laughed. Now I was certain I was going crazy.

I looked down at the printed words. The fresher ones were still wet and gleaming blue under the overhead light. The printing was not my own. It was big and flowing. My own handwriting style tended to be tight and slanted.

Finally, I said, "I don't understand what's happening here."

Do you have to understand everything, Samantha? Perhaps some things are best taken on faith. Perhaps it's a good thing to have a little mystery in the world. After all, you're a little mysterious yourself, aren't you?

I nodded but said nothing. I was suddenly having a hard time formulating words—or even thinking for that matter. I was also feeling strangely emotional. Something powerful and wonderful was going on here and I was having a hard time grasping it.

Then let's take a break, Samantha. It's okay. We made our introductions, and that's a good start.

"But you didn't tell me your name," I blurted out.

A slight pause, a tingle, and the following words appeared:

Sephora. And I'm always here. Waiting.

12.

At 7:00 p.m., and still a little freaked about the automatic writing, I called my kids.

Danny picked up immediately.

"I heard about the stunt you pulled today, Sam," he said.

In the background, I heard a female voice say quietly, "What a bitch." The female probably didn't know that I could hear her. The female was now on my shit list. And if it was the female I was thinking it was—his home-wrecking secretary—then she was already on my shit list. So this put her name twice on my shit list. I don't know much about much, but being on a vampire's shit list *twice* probably wasn't a good idea.

Danny didn't bother to shush the woman or even acknowledge she had spoken. Instead, he said, "That was a very stupid thing to do, Sam."

"I just want to see my kids, Danny."

"You do get to see them, every Saturday night," he said, breathing hard. Danny had a temper. A bad temper. He never hit me, which was wise of him, because even back when I wasn't a vampire I could still kick his ass. You don't smack around a highly trained federal agent with a gun in her shoulder holster. And then he added, "But not anymore."

"What do you mean *not anymore*?" I asked.

"It means you're no longer permitted to see the kids, Sam. How can I trust you anymore after that stunt you pulled today?"

This coming from the man who had been cheating on me for months.

"Stunt? Seeing my kids is a stunt?"

"We had an agreement and you broke it, and now I have an obligation to protect *my* children."

"And they need protection from me?"

There was no hesitation. "Yes, of course. You're a monster."

I heard little Anthony say something in the background. He asked if he could talk to me on the phone. The female in the room shushed him nastily. Anthony whimpered and I nearly crushed my cell phone in my hand.

"Don't take away my Saturdays, Danny."

"I didn't take them away, Sam. You did."

I forced myself to keep calm. "When can I see them again, Danny?"

"I don't know. I'll think about it."

"I'm seeing them this Saturday."

"If you come here, Sam, then everything goes public. All the evidence. All the proof. The pathetic life that you now have will be over. And then you will never, ever see your kids. So don't fuck with me, Sam."

"I could always kill you, Danny."

"Aw, the true monster comes out. You kill me and you still lose the kids. Besides, I'm not afraid of you."

He had something up his sleeve. I wasn't sure what it was, but I suspected it was a weapon of some sort. A vampire hunting weapon, no doubt. Maybe something similar to what the vampire hunter had used on me last month. The hunter who came to kill me with a crossbow and silver-tipped arrow, and ended up on a one-way cruise ship to Hawaii. Long story.

I looked at my watch. It was well past the ten minutes he allotted me each night. "Can I please speak to my children now?"

"Sorry, Sam. Your time for tonight is up." And he hung up.

13.

Fresh off my infuriating phone call with Danny, I soon found myself sitting outside Rembrandt's in Brea. I was drinking a glass of white wine. The woman sitting across from me was drinking a lemonade. Yes, a lemonade. Her name was Monica Collins and she was a mess.

We were sitting under a string of white lights next to a sort of makeshift fence that separated us from the heavily trafficked path to the 24-Hour Fitness behind us. While we drank, a steady parade of physically active types, all wearing tight black shorts, tank tops or tee shirts, streamed past our table and looked down at us gluttons with scorn. Most carried a gym bag of some sort, a water bottle, and a towel. Half had white speaker cords hanging from their ears. There was a sameness to their diversity.

This wine was hurting my stomach and so I mostly ignored it. White wine, water and blood were the only items I could safely consume without vomiting within minutes. Wine, however, rarely settled well, but I put up with it, especially when meeting new clients. I doubted a glass of chilled hemoglobin would make them feel very comfortable.

Monica was on her second glass of lemonade. Correction, third. She raised her hand and signaled the waiter over, who promptly responded, filling her glass again with a pitcher of the sweet stuff. She looked relieved.

Monica was a bit of a mystery to me. She was a full grown woman who acted as if she was precisely fourteen years old. She had to be around thirty, certainly, but you would never guess it by the way she popped her gum, swung her legs in her seat, giggled, and drank lemonade as if it was going out of style. Her giggling was a nervous habit, I noticed, not because she actually thought anything was funny. There was also something screwy about her right eye. It didn't track with the left eye, as if it had a sort of minor delay to it. It also seemed to focus somewhere over my shoulder, as if at an imaginary pet parrot.

She had been telling me in graphic detail the many incidents in which her husband of twelve years (now ex-husband) had beaten the unholy shit out of her. I didn't say much as she spoke. Mostly I watched her . . . and the steady procession of humanity coming and going to the gym.

Monica spoke in a small, child-like voice. She spoke without passion and without inflection. There was no weight to her voice. No strength. Often she spoke with her head and eyes down. She had suffered great abuse, perhaps for most of her life. Women who were abused as children often found themselves in abusive relationships as adults. No surprise there.

She stopped talking when she reached the bottom of the lemonade. She next proceeded to slurp up the remnants loudly. People looked at her, and then at me. I shrugged. Monica didn't seem to care that people were looking at her, and if she didn't care, why the hell should I?

When she was done slurping, she asked me if she could go to the bathroom.

Yes, *asked* me.

I told her that, uh, sure, that would be fine. She smiled brightly, popped her gum, and left. A few minutes later she returned . . . and promptly ordered another lemonade.

She went on. After she had left her husband, he had made it his life's purpose to kill her. She got a restraining order. Apparently he didn't think much of restraining orders. His first attempt to kill her occurred when she was living alone in an apartment in Anaheim.

As she paused to fish out a strawberry, I tried to wrap my brain around the thought of Monica living on her own, doing big girl things, doing adult things, and couldn't. Although thirty-something, she clearly seemed stunted and unprepared for adult life. I reflected on this as she continued her story.

He was waiting for her in her kitchen. After throwing her around a bit, he had proceeded to beat her into a bloody mess with a pipe wrench, cracking her head open, and leaving her for dead.

Except she didn't die. Doctors rebuilt her, using steel plates and pins and screws. Today she still suffered from trauma-induced seizures and had lost the use of her right eye. That explained the eye. It was, in fact, blind.

After the attack, her husband had been caught within hours. But something strange happened on the way to prison. His attorney, who had apparently been damn good, had somehow gotten him out of jail within a few weeks, convincing a judge that her ex was no longer a threat to Monica.

Her ex-husband attacked again that night.

Still recovering from the first attack, Monica had been staying with her parents when her ex-husband broke into their home, this time wielding a hammer. I was beginning to suspect someone had given the man a gift card to Home Depot. I kept my suspicions to myself.

Anyway, her ex went on to kill her father and to permanently cripple her mother. And if not for the family Rottweiler, Monica would have been dead, too. Yes, the dog survived.

Monica grew silent. In the parking lot in front of us, an older white Cadillac drove slowly by. The windows were tinted. The Caddy seemed to slow as it went by. She played with the straw. I told her I was sorry about her father. She nodded and kept playing with the straw. I waited. There was more to the story. There was a reason, after all, why she had called me this evening.

She pushed her glass aside. Apparently, she had reached her lemonade limit.

She said, "He was caught trying to hire someone to kill me."

"Who caught him?"

"The people at the prison."

"Prison officials?"

"Yes, them. But he wasn't, you know, successful." Nervous giggles.

I said, "You're scared."

She nodded; tears welled up in her eyes. "Why does he want to hurt me so much? Hasn't he done enough?"

"I'm sorry," I said.

"He's horrible," she said. "He's so mean."

As she spoke her voice grew tinier and her lower lip shook. Her hands were shaking, too, and my heart went out to this little girl in a woman's body. Why anyone would want to hurt such a harmless person, I had no clue. Maybe there was more to the story, but I doubted it. I think her assessment was right. He was just mean. Damn mean.

She spoke again, "So I talked to Detective Sherbet. He is so nice to me. He always helps me. I love him." She smiled at the thought of the good detective, a man I had grown quite fond of myself. "He told me to see you. That you were tougher than you looked, but I don't understand what he means. He said you would protect me."

I said, "In the state of California, a private investigator's license also doubles as a bodyguard license."

"So you are a bodyguard, too?" I heard awe in her voice. She smiled brightly. Tears still gleamed wetly in her eyes.

"I am," I said, perhaps a little more boastful than I had intended.

She clapped. "Do you carry a gun?"

"When I need to."

She continued smiling, but then grew somber. She looked at me closely with her good eye, not so closely with her bad eye. "I don't have money to pay you. I haven't been able to work at the bakery since he hurt me, but maybe my momma can help pay you. Detective Sherbet said that you know what the right thing to do is, but I don't know what he's talking about."

I smiled and shook my head and reached out and took her hand, feeling its warmth despite its clamminess. She flinched slightly at my own icy touch. I held her gaze, and she held mine as best as she could.

I said, "Don't worry about money, sweetie. I won't let anything happen to you, ever. You're safe now. I promise."

And that's when she started crying.

14.

We were in my hotel suite.

Monica was walking around my spartan room as if it were more interesting than it really was. I sensed some of her anxiety departing. In the least, she was giggling less, which I considered a good thing.

Finally she sat on the corner of the bed, near where I was sitting in the surprisingly comfortable desk chair. My laptop was next to me, closed. Somewhere, in there, was Fang. I wondered what he was doing tonight. I wondered what he did every night. I found myself wondering a lot about him.

And what about Kingsley? I wondered about him, too, but he was a little easier to wonder about, since I knew where he lived and I knew he had the hots for me.

On the round table near me was the pad of paper that contained my conversation with . . . something. At least, the beginning of a conversation.

"You really live here?" asked Monica.

"For now, yes."

"And your husband just kicked you out?"

"Something like that."

She shook her head and smiled some more, but it was a nervous smile. I sensed her about to giggle, but she somehow held it in check.

"I had the opposite problem," she said.

"As in, he never wanted you to leave."

"Yes, exactly." And now she did giggle. Sigh. As she sat there on the corner of the bed, her dangling feet didn't quite touch the carpeted floor. She was so small and cute. And innocent. And sweet. And clueless. In the wrong hands, in the wrong relationship, I could see a brute of a man thinking she was his. A trophy. A little trophy. Something to possess and own. In the right hands, she would have been protected and loved and cherished.

She had found herself in the wrong hands.

Monica asked, "So why did he kick you out, if you don't mind me asking."

"I mind," I said.

She giggled, turned red, and looked away. "I'm so sorry."

I reached out and touched her knee. I had to be gentle with this one. Her social savvy wasn't quite up to par, either.

"It's okay," I said. "It's just a very fresh wound that I don't want to talk about right now. You did nothing wrong."

She nodded vigorously. I patted her knee. She looked at me, nodded again, then looked down. She was so unsure of herself. So lost. So helpless. How could anyone hurt this girl? God, I already hated her ex-husband with a fucking passion.

"Sam, can I ask you a question?"

I smiled. "Sure, sweetie."

"Can I, you know, ask how you're going to protect me?" Nervous giggle. "Is that okay to ask?"

"It's okay," I said, patting her knee reassuring, much as I would my own daughter. And the thought of my daughter—and the possibility of not seeing her or Anthony this Saturday night—nearly brought me to tears. I took a deep breath, steadied myself, and said, "You are either going to be with me, or with someone I trust. You will always be protected."

Her eyes narrowed suspiciously. She pursed her lips. "Who are your friends?"

"Good men. Honorable men. I trust them with my life. They will protect you when I'm not around."

"Why would you not be around?"

"Sometimes I have . . . business to attend to."

She nodded. She understood business. "And one of your friends is coming over now?"

"Yes," I said.

"Because you are going out?"

"Right. I have work to do."

"And I can't come?" She sounded like a child asking her mother if she could go grocery shopping with her.

"Not this time," I said.

"Okay." Petulant. She didn't like the idea of me leaving her so soon. I didn't either, but what I had to do tonight she had no business seeing or being a part of.

"Chad is a good man," I said. "You will like him."

She nodded again. "Will you be back tonight?"

"Yes."

She smiled and kicked her feet out again. She was wearing white shorts. Her legs were thin and tan. They were also criss-crossed with scars. I didn't ask her about the scars, but I suspected she had been beaten badly with a belt.

"So how long will you protect me?"

"As long as it takes," I said. Mercifully, she had no children and, apparently, was on extended leave at her baking job, which I discovered was a donut shop. No wonder why Detective Sherbet liked her so much.

There was a knock on my hotel door. Three rapid knocks, a pause, and then a fourth. It was Chad, using the coded knock we had been trained to use.

"That's my ex-partner," I said. I sat forward and patted her knee again. "You're in good hands, I promise."

She smiled and popped her gum. "I believe you," she said.

15.

I was sitting with Stuart Young three floors up on his balcony, overlooking a sliver of Balboa Beach. Stuart didn't quite have a water view from his balcony, but what I could see gleamed brightly under the waxing crescent moon.

Stuart offered me some wine, but my stomach was still upset from the wine I had earlier. I accepted some water instead, and now we sat together overlooking a mostly quiet street. The street ran between more condos. The condos all looked the same. Row after row, street after street, of identical condos. How I found

Stuart's condo was still a mystery, especially with my dismal sense of direction.

But I knew the answer. I sensed his building, and I sensed his apartment. My psychic abilities were gathering strength.

Anyway, Stuart looked like he had recently been crying. No surprise there. He also didn't seem to care that he looked like he had been crying and made no apologies for it. His eyes were red and swollen. His nose was red and swollen. A light film of sweat coated his perfect bald head. The sweat could have been from the alcohol, since the weather is always perfect. Which is why, water view or no water view, this condo probably cost a small fortune.

Stuart was drinking light beer that he had poured into a frosted glass. Beer was the one thing I didn't miss. Blech. Give me wine any day.

"How you holding up?" I asked.

"Couldn't be worse," he said, and actually smiled.

I sipped my water and leaned slightly to the right to get a better view of the tiny sliver of ocean.

"If you look hard enough, you'll find it," said Stuart. "Believe it or not, I paid for that tiny speck of ocean you can see. Probably cost me another fifty grand."

"It's a nice speck," I said.

He chuckled and drank his beer. He seemed to be enjoying it. Go figure.

"I have it on good word," I said without looking at him, "that, unofficially, your wife's plane was sabotaged."

He stopped drinking.

I went on, "And if it was sabotaged, which appears likely, then that means your wife, along with everyone else on board, was murdered."

He sat back, stared down into his frosted mug. He didn't have much of a reaction. Then again, I wasn't telling him anything he didn't already know or suspect.

I continued, "We all know who stood to benefit from that plane going down. Jerry Blum has not only escaped prosecution, he is now a free man. With no witnesses and no case, all charges have been dropped against him."

Stuart nodded; his jawline rippled slightly.

"The plane crash investigation is still ongoing," I said after a few minutes. "The investigation could take years. Even if the authorities do find out who took it down, or sabotaged it, I suspect there will be very little evidence linking the attack to Jerry Blum."

He set his frosted glass down on the dusty, round glass table that sat between us, and turned and looked at me.

Stuart said, "And even if evidence is found indicating Jerry Blum was responsible for my wife's crash, who's to say that the next batch of witnesses won't be killed as well."

"It's a sick Catch-22," I said.

"This could go on forever."

I nodded.

"I may never see justice," he added. "Ever."

"There is still a chance they could find damning evidence linking Jerry Blum to the downed aircraft," I said.

"Or not," said Stuart.

I nodded. "Or not."

"More than likely he's going to get off, again, and meanwhile my wife. . . ." Stuart's voice trailed off and he suddenly broke down, sobbing hard into his hands. I reached over and patted his shoulder and made sympathetic noises. He continued crying, and I continued patting.

When he finally got control of himself, he said, "I have something I want you to listen to."

16.

Stuart got up and went through the sliding glass door. He came back a moment later holding a Blackberry phone. He sat next to me again and pushed a few buttons on the phone. A moment later, the phone was ringing loudly on speaker mode. An electronic voice answered and asked Stuart if he wanted to listen to his voice mail. Stuart pressed a button. I assumed his answer was yes. The voice then asked if Stuart wanted to listen to his archive. He pressed another button, and he held the phone out between us, face up, above the round table and above his beer.

"Stu!" came a woman's frantic voice. "Stu, listen to me. Something very, very bad is happening. Oh, God! Stu, the plane is having problems. Serious problems. I heard an explosion. It happened right outside my window. On the wing. It blew up. I can see it now. Flapping, burning, on fire. This isn't happening, this isn't happening. Oh, God, Stu!" The voice stopped. From somewhere nearby, I heard a woman screaming in the background. A horrible, gut-wrenching scream. "Stu, sweet Jesus, the plane is going to crash. Everyone knows it. The pilot can't get . . . can't get control of it." Another pause. A voice crackled loudly over a speaker. It was the pilot. He was telling everyone to sit in their seats, to buckle up, to remain calm. And then he told them to prepare for a crash landing. "Jesus, Stu. Jesus, Jesus, Jesus. Oh, good Christ. I wish I was talking to you, baby. I need you so bad. I need your voice. Baby, I'm so scared. So scared. This isn't happening." Someone screamed bloody murder in the background. "I heard your voice, Stu. I heard it when I got your voice mail. At least I heard it one last—one more time. I love your voice, baby. I love you, baby. I love you so much. I'm going to die now." Someone spoke to her rapidly, hysterically, but the woman on the phone didn't respond. "Everyone's losing it, Stu. Everyone's freaking. Stu, the explosion. Something blew this plane up. Something blew the wing up. It's Jerry Blum, Stu. I know it. He did this, baby. Somehow. Somehow he got to us all. The motherfucker. Oh, God. . . ." and now she broke down in sobs, briefly regained her composure, and into the phone, "I love you, baby. Forever."

And the line went dead.

Stuart didn't bother wiping the tears that ran down his cheeks. He stared silently down at his cell phone, which still rested in his open hand. His hand was shaking. Finally, reluctantly, he used his thumb and pressed another button, and pocketed the Blackberry carefully in his light jacket.

He said, "I forwarded my wife's message to another voice mail account I have, and then forwarded the call to the FBI. They asked me to delete the original, which I did. I never told them that I still have a copy of it. Hell, I have a few copies of it, saved in various formats. How dare they ask me to delete my wife's last message to me. The motherfuckers."

We sat quietly for a long time, and I heard his wife's panicked voice over and over again. My heart broke for her. My heart broke for him. My heart, quite frankly, broke to pieces.

"I'm so sorry," I finally said.

He nodded absently and stared off toward the beach and the muted sounds of crashing waves. I doubted Stuart's mortal ears could hear the waves. Probably a good thing, since hearing the sounds of crashing waves would have doubled the value of the condo. Just over the tiled rooftop of the condo across the street, two seagulls swooped down, their alabaster bodies clear as day to my eyes. As they flashed through the night sky, an ectoplasmic trail of crackling energy followed them like the burning tails of comets. The night was alive to my eyes. The night was alive to my ears, too.

Stuart said, "And even if the FBI eventually found the evidence to convict Jerry Blum, he still may never face punishment."

I nodded.

He shook his head. "It's . . . the worst feeling in the world, knowing that this motherfucker killed her, knowing that he let her burn to death." Stuart took deep breaths. "He's a fucking animal and I hate him. You know, fuck the trial. Fuck the evidence. Fuck everything. All I want is ten minutes alone with the motherfucker. Just me and him. Ten minutes."

His wishful thinking got me to thinking.

Stuart went on, "But we can't touch him. No one can touch him. Not the police, not the FBI, not the courts. No one."

"I can touch him," I said, surprised as hell that the words came out of my mouth. I really hadn't thought this through. Not in the slightest.

Stuart snapped his head around. "What did you say?"

I plowed forward, what the hell. "I said I can touch him."

Stuart squinted at me.

"What exactly does that mean, Sam?"

"It means I can hand-deliver you Jerry Blum."

"I'm not following."

It was a crazy idea. Too crazy. But Stuart was hurting and furious and frustrated, and there wasn't a damn thing he could do. Unless. . . .

I said, "Do you really want to face Jerry Blum alone, the man who killed your wife?"

"More than life itself."

"Then what would you say if I told you that I could bring you Jerry Blum?"

"I would say you're crazy."

"Yes, maybe a little."

"But you don't sound crazy."

"Good to know."

But my crazy idea had sparked something in him. In the very least, it had given him something to take his mind off his pain. He turned in his seat and faced me.

"How could you do this?" he asked.

"I have contacts," I said vaguely.

"And your contacts can get you Jerry Blum?"

"Yes," I said. "Sooner or later."

"And I would face him?"

I nodded. "Alone."

"Man against man?"

"*Mano y mano*," I said, which, I think, meant *man and man*, but what the hell did I know?

Stuart said, "What about all his bodyguards, his shooters, his hired killers?"

I shook my head. "It would just be the two of you. Alone."

"And would anyone else know about this?"

"Just me, you, and Jerry Blum."

Something very close to a smile touched the corners of Stuart's mouth, but then he shook his head and the smile was gone. "As much as I would like to believe you, Sam, I have to face the fact that this is nothing more than a fantasy—"

"I can get him," I said, cutting him off. "Give me two weeks."

Stuart stared at me long and hard, then finally he nodded and grinned. He looked good when he grinned; it made his perfect bald head look even more perfect.

"Okay, I believe you," he said. "Why I believe you, I don't know, but I do."

We both sat back in our patio chairs and I listened to the wind and the waves and the sounds of someone in the condo below us making a late night dinner. Shortly, the smell of bacon wafted up. God, I used to love breakfast for dinner.

Stuart rolled his head in my direction. "And what if I kill him?"

"Everybody's got to die sooner or later," I said.

"You're a tough woman."

"Getting tougher by the minute," I said.

17.

It was midnight, and I was sitting in my minivan with my laptop near the Ritz Carlton in Laguna Niguel. No, I don't normally hang out at the Ritz Carlton, but this was as good a place as any for what I was about to do.

Orange County's only five-star hotel sat high on a bluff, which, if you asked me, looked exactly like a cliff. Anyway, I was parked in the guest parking lot in the far corner of the far lot. I doubted I had attracted much attention. Just a small woman in a big van.

A small woman who was about to get very naked.

My windows were cracked open and far below the steep cliff—I was going with *cliff*—was the pleasant sound of the surf crashing along what I knew were mostly smooth, sandy beaches.

I briefly thought about what I had gotten myself into, and the further away I was from Stuart and his heartbreak, the more I realized how crazy my idea had been.

Think about it, Sam: You promised to deliver one of the West Coast's most notorious gangsters to a mild-mannered widower—for a one-on-one smackdown.

Yeah, I've had better ideas.

Of course, as things presently stood, Stuart would never see justice. Or, if he did, it might be years before Blum was locked behind bars again, and that's if the feds could pin anything on him, which I seriously doubted. After all, Blum had been in prison awaiting trial when the plane went down.

A hell of an alibi.

And so what do you do, Sam? You offer to deliver a murderer to a man who's only outstanding physical attribute was perhaps the world's most perfectly bald head?

Stuart was a slight man, to say the least. Jerry Blum would no doubt kill the grieving widower with his bare hands. In fact, Blum had probably done exactly that throughout his career in crime.

And that's if you managed to somehow even get to Blum.

It's good business to under-promise and over-deliver. Well, in this case, I had over-promised . . . and might just very well deliver a murderer.

Great.

I shook my head. I've had better plans.

Jerry Blum needed to go down. One way or another. Having Stuart face the gangster was probably not my best idea, but it was the best I could come up with at the time. For now, I would let the details of the showdown percolate for a few days and see what else I could come up with.

I drummed my long fingers on the steering wheel. I might be a smidgen over five feet, but God blessed me with extraordinarily long fingers. Was it wrong to really love your own fingers?

Of course, now my fingers and thumbs were capped by very strong-looking nails. Not claws, per se, just ten very thick, and slightly pointed nails. Okay, fine. They were claws. I had fucking claws.

Sometimes I hate my life.

Earlier, I had made a few phone calls to my contacts and I had gotten the address to Jerry Blum's lavish Newport Beach fortress. The gangster lived on a massive estate overlooking the ocean. In fact, it was a tiny island just off shore, but not too far offshore. A bridge connected the island.

Now, with my laptop glowing next to me, I used Google's satellite feature and studied the lay of the land from above, memorizing the various features of the island. There weren't many. The sprawling home spanned the entire north end of the island from side to side, leaving only a few acres of trees along the southern tip. For me, the trees were a good thing.

Birds get lost in trees.

But do giant vampire bats?

Once I had the images locked in my brain, I powered down the laptop and scanned the area. All was quiet in this remote section of the Ritz Carlton parking lot. I quickly stripped out of my jeans and blouse and everything in-between. It was the in-between stuff that left me feeling especially vulnerable. And although I had been sitting in my seat for nearly a half hour, the vinyl was still cold to the touch, probably because *I* was cold to the touch, since my body heat had gone the way of the dodo bird.

Just as I got down to the bare minimum, a family of four pulled up in an SUV that was big enough to lay siege to Idaho with. I crouched low in my seat, willing myself invisible. A few minutes later, the family piled out and headed up to the hotel, and when they had disappeared from view, I cautiously stepped out of my minivan.

Naked as the day I was born.

I quickly padded across the smooth concrete, stepped over a guard rail, and worked my way through some scrubby bushes until I was standing at the edge of a very steep cliff indeed. Whoever calls these "bluffs" can bite my ass.

Up here, staring down, the ground looked impossibly far. A faint line of foaming waves crashed rhythmically against the polished beaches. I could see two people walking near the surf, holding hands. And if they should happen to look up, they might see something very, very bizarre. Something that would no doubt give them nightmares for the rest of their lives.

Then let's hope for their sake they don't look up.

I took a deep breath, filled my lungs with oxygen I really didn't need, closed my eyes, and leaped off the cliff.

18.

I jumped up and out as far away from the cliff as I could.

For one brief second I was majestically airborne, face raised to the heavens, just your everyday naked soccer mom doing a swan dive off the Ritz Carlton cliffs.

The night air was alive with crackling streaks of light, flashes of energy and zigzagging flares of secret lightning. At least secret to mortal eyes.

I hovered like this briefly, suspended in mid-air, looking out over the black ocean. . . .

And then I dropped like a rock—head first, arms held out to either side. An inverted cross.

The wind thundered over me. The face of the cliff swept past me in a blur—hundreds upon hundreds of multicolored layers of strata speeding by in a blink.

I closed my eyes, and the moment I did, a single flame appeared at the forefront of my mind, in the spot most people call the *third eye*. The flame grew rapidly, burning impossibly bright, filling my thoughts completely, consuming my mind. And within that flame, a vague, dark image appeared. A hideous, ghastly image.

I continued to fall. Wind continued rushing over my ears, whipped my long hair behind me like a black and tattered cape. The sounds of the crashing waves grew rapidly closer. Too close. Soon, very soon, I was going to crash-land at the bottom of the cliff, splattered across the piles of massive boulders.

Would I die? I didn't know. I also didn't want to find out.

The shadowy image took on more shape, its grotesque lines sharpening. I felt an immediate and powerful pull toward the beastly image.

The image grew rapidly, consuming the flame. Ah, but it wasn't growing, was it?

No. Indeed, I was rushing toward it.

Faster and faster.

And then we were one, the beast and I.

I gasped and opened my eyes and contorted my body as great, leathery wings blossomed beneath my arms. The thick membranes instantly snapped taut like a parachute. The gravitational force on them alone should have ripped them from my body.

But they didn't rip; indeed, they held strong. My arms held strong, too.

I slowed considerably, but not enough. The boulders were still rapidly approaching, the wind screaming over my ears, blasting my face. I instinctively adjusted the angle of my arms—and now I was swooping instead of falling.

And shortly after that, I was *flying*.

I swept above the boulders, just missing them, and now I was gliding over the smooth shore, flashing over the heads of the couple walking hand in hand.

They both turned to look, but I was already gone. Just a great, black winged mystery against the starless night sky.

I flapped my great wings again and gained altitude, and I kept flapping until I was high above the dark ocean.

19.

I flapped my wings again and rose another couple hundred feet. I had about ten miles to go to get to Newport Beach. Would have taken me about twenty minutes along the winding Pacific Coast Highway. But as the crow flies, only a few minutes tops.

Or as the "giant vampire bat" flies.

I soon found myself in a fairly warm jetstream that hurled me along with little effort on my part. Far below, as I followed the curving sweep of the black coast, an array of lights shone from some of the biggest homes Orange County had to offer.

Six years ago, just after dusk, I had been out jogging along a wooded path in Hillcrest Park in Fullerton. The wooded path was one of the few such paths in Fullerton. Probably not the best time to be jogging in the woods (or what passed as woods in Orange County), but I was a highly trained federal investigator and I was packing heat.

I never saw it coming. Hell, I never even heard it coming.

One moment I was running, alert for weirdos and tree roots (in that order), and the next I found myself hurling through the air, and slamming hard against a tree trunk.

Close to blacking out, I sensed something moving swiftly behind me. I tried to reach for my gun in the fanny pack, but something was on me, something strong and terrifying.

Before my vision rapidly filled with black, I was aware of two things: One, that I was going to die tonight. And, two, the beautiful gold and ruby medallion that hung from my attacker's neck.

The wind swept over my perfectly aerodynamic body. A foghorn sounded from somewhere. I was unaware that the beaches of Southern California had foghorns, or even fog for that matter.

I banked slightly to starboard by lowering my right arm and lifting my left. A seagull was flying just beneath me. It didn't seem to notice me, and together we continued slightly northeast, following the coast.

I had been partly correct, of course. In a way I had died that night.

Died and reborn.

And the medallion, through a series of unusual events that I'm still not quite sure what to make of, later came into my possession. As recently as six weeks ago, in fact.

Vampires and medallions are such a cliché, I thought, as I slowly began my descent. As I did so, I recognized the glittering Newport Bay and its equally glittering pier.

Then again, maybe the vampire who attacked me invented the cliché.

Hell, maybe he was the reason for it.

Two joggers had found me in the woods. I learned later that the joggers had initially reported me as dead.

I awoke the next morning at St. Jude's Hospital in Fullerton, surrounded by friends and family and police investigators. Federal investigators, too, since these were my colleagues.

There had been a single ghastly wound on my neck. Whatever had attacked me had violently torn open my neck and nearly removed my trapezius muscle.

I should have been dead.

There was no sign of sexual assault. Nothing had been stolen. Even my gun was still in my fanny pack. I was also shockingly low on blood. The only explanation that seemed to fit was that I had been attacked by a coyote, which are fairly common in those parts of northern Orange County. The loss of blood was unusual, since there had been no large quantities of it found at the scene. Again, that was attributed to the coyotes, which could have easily lapped up my hemoglobin.

And since when did coyotes prefer sucking blood to eating raw meat?

They didn't, but there was no other explanation. Yes, I reported seeing the medallion. I reported being thrown against a tree, too. These reports were largely dismissed. Sure, my detective friends joked lightheartedly about being attacked by a vampire, but the jokes were forgotten as soon as they were made.

The attack made the local papers, and there was a witch hunt on the local coyote population. Many were regrettably killed.

My neck and shoulder had required hundreds of stitches. Doctors had spent hours on it. They were expecting serious issues with infection, and I was placed in a rigid neck brace. Two days later they released me.

And that's when things started getting weird.

The morning after I was released, I noticed two things: the incessant itching under my bandages had stopped, and I was experiencing no pain in my neck at all.

With Danny watching cartoons with little Anthony, then only two years old, and Tammy at school, I went into the bathroom and shut the door and took my first look under the bandages.

And what I saw was the beginning of my new life.

I was healed. I was impossibly healed. I was *supernaturally* healed.

I had been sitting on the edge of the bathtub with the bathroom door locked, when Danny knocked on the door and asked if everything was okay, and I said yes. But I wasn't okay. Something was wrong, horribly wrong.

He paused just outside the door, where I could clearly hear him breathing as if he was standing next to me. How could I hear him breathing from behind the door? And did I just hear him scratch himself? When he finally walked away, shuffling down the carpeted floor, I heard every step. Clearly. As if he been walking on hardwood floors.

Confused and alarmed, I crawled into the empty bathtub and hugged my knees tightly.

And later that day, as I nervously hid my healed wound from Danny—and alternately wondered why I was feeling a very strong need to stay away from direct sunlight—I also had my first craving for the red stuff.

What the hell was happening to me?

20.

From the sky, Jerry Blum's estate was easily one of the biggest for miles around. And in Newport Beach, that's saying something.

His estate was, in fact, an island all to itself, an island that was accessible via bridge from Balboa Island.

An island within an island. Cool beans.

Balboa Island wasn't a real island, though. It was just a long peninsula filled with inordinately large homes and hip bars and restaurants. I suppose calling it *Balboa Long Peninsula* just didn't quite have the same ring to it.

Still, those living on *Balboa Island* were living a lie.

Just sayin'.

Not so with Jerry Blum. He really did live on an island—an island all to himself, complete with a private bridge that arched from near the southern point of Balboa Island.

A handful of small planes buzzed around me, some beneath and some above. I doubted I was being picked up on any radar. A creature who didn't have a reflection, probably didn't return radar signals, either. And if a giant bat-like blip did show up on their radars, then that would certainly give the air traffic controllers something to chew on.

That, and nightmares.

I swept lower, tucking my arms in a little, angling down toward Jerry Blum's private island. Wind blasted me as I raced through the sky. A thin, protective film covered my eyes. Vampiric goggles.

Whoever had created this thing that I sometimes turn into had done a bang-up job. Someone, somewhere had put some serious thought into this thing.

Who that person was, I didn't know. Why I was created, I didn't know. From where this dark flying creature came from, I didn't know.

But I knew I wanted answers.

Someday, I thought.

For now, it was time to go to work.

Hey, even giant vampire bats have to make a living.

I found a large tree on the grounds and settled upon a thickish branch. From here, I had a good view of the rear and east side of the house.

Sometimes I wondered if I had really died that night six years ago. Maybe this was death. Maybe death was living out a nightmarish fantasy that couldn't possibly be real. Maybe death was full of wonder and fantasy.

The thick branch creaked under my considerable weight. How considerable? I didn't know, but if I had to guess, I would say that I weighed over five hundred pounds.

Big girl.

The massive estate was quiet, although men in shorts and Hawaiian shirts routinely walked the grounds. A high wall encircled the property, and barbed wire ran along the top of the wall. There were security cameras everywhere, but I didn't worry about security cameras. Two big Lincolns sat to either side of the main gate. No doubt men with guns sat in those cars. Beyond the backyard fence was the bay, and beyond that was Newport Beach itself. Wooden stairs led down from the backyard to a boat house and private pier. A sixty-foot yacht was anchored next to the boat house. The yacht looked empty, although there were a few lights on inside it here and there.

I sat unmovingly on the branch for a few more hours. My great, muscular legs never once went to sleep or needed adjusting. I suspected I could have sat perched like that all night. Or until the sun came up or until the branch snapped off. Whichever came first.

But Jerry Blum's house was quiet tonight. No doubt he was off somewhere honing his racketeering and murder skills. Perfecting the fine art of gangstering.

I'll be back, I thought, and leaped off the branch and shot into the air.

21.

I swooped around my minivan once, twice, waiting for a security guard to move on. When he finally did, I landed softly atop the rocky cliff nearby, tucking in my wings. As usual, my wings' thick, leathery membranes hung limply, this time in the dirt. And if I wasn't careful, I could step on my wings, which I had done before and it wasn't the most graceful thing to witness. A vampire stumbling on her own wings didn't exactly grace the covers of supernatural romance novels the world over.

With the salt-infused wind hammering me atop the cliff, the flame in my mind's eye appeared again. But this time a horrific creature wasn't standing in the flame. (Unless, of course, you asked my ex-husband.) No, instead, a naked woman was standing in the flame.

A cute little curvy woman with long black hair.

It was one of the few times I actually got to see myself without heavy make-up on. Granted, it was a smallish image of myself, and perhaps only an avatar of myself, but it was me and I always loved looking at it.

And I didn't look half bad. Personally, I think Danny is crazy. Think about it, he could have had a young-looking wife for the rest of his life, a wife who never aged. Granted every decade or so we would probably have to move and make completely new friends, and he would have to put up with my cold flesh, and the fact that I drink blood, but still. . . .

Okay, maybe I wasn't such a great prize, but I still think it's his loss.

The asshole.

And as I gazed on that image of myself, as I stood on the edge of the cliff like a living gargoyle from hell, something occurred to me, something that had been bothering me for the past month or so.

Amazingly, I still cared for Danny.

Yes, the man had made my life an absolute living nightmare. Remember, until recently we had been trying to make things work. And if he hadn't cheated on me, I would still be with him. I had planned to be with Danny for the rest of my life.

Well, the rest of *his* life.

But he had turned into his own kind of monster, which is more than ironic, and even though he began to openly cheat on me, and even though he hurt me more than I had ever been hurt in my life, I still had feelings for the bastard.

Yes, I understood why he did what he did. I get it. I'm a freak.

He wanted out. But did he have to be such an asshole about things? Couldn't he have treated me with compassion and love? Did he have to act like such a douchebag all the time? Did I want to hurt him often?

The answer, of course, was yes to everything.

I sat quietly on the cliff edge, surveying the beach below. There was no one behind me, or anywhere around me for that matter. My hearing in this form was phenomenal.

Danny was the father of my children. As much as it pained me to admit it, I knew he was doing the best he could given the circumstances. How many fathers would have taken their kids from something like me? Probably many of them. How many husbands would have sought a warm body elsewhere? Probably many of them.

Yes, it would have taken an extraordinary man to get through this with me.

Danny wasn't him.

In my mind's eye, I studied the woman in the flame. She stood there passively, naked as the day she was born, watching me in return. I loved that woman. I loved her with all my heart. Life had dealt her a shitty hand, but she, too, was doing the best she could.

A moment later, I was moving toward the woman in the flame. She grew rapidly bigger, taking on much more detail. And then she was rushing at me, too, and a moment later I found myself standing on the edge of the cliff, naked, cold and crying, and staring down into the churning dark depths below, where the surf pounded rocks into sand.

22.

"I think I'm in love with her," said Chad.

It was nearly four in the morning, and we were standing just inside my hotel doorway. It had been a hell of a long night for Chad. Apparently, though, he had loved every minute of it.

"Thanks, Chad. I owe you."

"I'm not joking," he said. Chad was a tall guy, easily six-foot-three. Maybe taller. When you barely scrape five-foot-three, just about anyone looks tall as hell. Except for Tom Cruise, of course. Chad added, "There's something about her."

"She's vulnerable and cute," I said. "And you're a man. It's a simple equation."

We were whispering since Monica was asleep on my bed. We were also whispering because it was four in the morning and we were in a hotel and we weren't assholes.

He glanced over at her sleeping form. I glanced too. Mostly under the comforter, she looked tiny and child-like. Just a little bump in a big bed. Say that five times in a row.

He said, "Sure, but there's something else." He stopped talking. Chad, I knew, wasn't used to expressing his emotions; he needed prodding, like most men. Well, those men not named Fang.

So I prodded. "You feel an overwhelming need to protect her, to help her, to save her."

Chad looked at me funny. "That's pretty much it, yeah. How did you know?"

"Because I had the same reaction," I said.

He nodded and looked back at her sleeping form. "How could anyone do that to her?"

"There are bastards out there," I said.

Chad didn't say anything at first. When Chad and I were partners we didn't talk much, but we always had a comfortable silence. When he spoke, his words weren't empty. They were full of a lot of forethought.

"I would kill him," he said. "If he ever came within a mile of her."

"That sounds like love to me," I said. "And just think, I was only gone for six hours."

"And we talked nearly the whole time."

"You mean she talked and you listened."

Chad grinned, but kept looking at her sleeping form. "Something like that."

"Get out of here and get some sleep, you love-struck puppy dog," I said. "Before you propose to her in her sleep."

"I guess I am being a little ridiculous, huh?"

I shrugged.

"This has never happened to me before," he said.

"Welcome to love-at-first-sight," I said. "Now go on."

He nodded and told me to call him anytime I needed help. I said I would and practically shooed him out of my hotel room. As I locked the door behind him, I resisted the urge to look out the peephole to see if my ex-partner was hugging and kissing the door.

With Monica sleeping nearby, I did some more work on my laptop. In particular, I got the visiting hours to Chino State Prison. On a whim, mostly because the bastard was on my mind, I headed over to my ex-husband's law firm's website. Danny was your typical ambulance chaser. He screwed insurance companies . . . and anyone else, for that matter.

I broadened my search on Danny Moon, chaser of ambulances extraordinaire. His name was all over the net, usually in association with some case or another, usually a case that actually went to court. You see, Danny *didn't* like to go to court. Danny was a lazy SOB, and his firm did all they could to keep cases *out* of court. But sometimes the negotiations went bad and cases actually did go to court. When they did, Danny and his firm actually had to do real legal work. Which generally made him grumpy as hell to be around.

Poor baby.

I next went to his Facebook page. I generally don't go on Facebook. It's not like I have a lot of new pictures to post, right? Anyway, I do keep an account because my daughter has one and I like to see what she's doing. Besides, Farmville is a hoot.

No, Danny and I are not friends on Facebook; apparently, divorcing someone is also grounds for dropping them as Facebook buddies. So I guess you could say I've been defaced.

Anyway, Danny kept his pictures public. Maybe he didn't know the intricacies of Facebook privacy, or maybe he didn't care.

He should have cared.

Although his pictures were very professional, everything a respectable attorney's pictures should be, there was one very *un*professional picture. Apparently Danny had been tagged at a party. And not just any party. A party at a strip joint in Riverside. And not just any party at a stripjoint, but a *Grand Opening* party.

Now, what was a respectable attorney doing at the grand opening of a cheesy strip club in Riverside?

I didn't know, but I was going to find out.

23.

It was almost sunrise and I was feeling my energy fading.

I had already warned Monica of my "condition." That is, she thought I had a rare skin disease that kept me out of the sun, which, of course, necessitated me keeping odd hours. She promised she would let me sleep during the days, and that she would not leave the hotel room on her own. I told her to wake me if she needed anything, but that I didn't awaken easily; she would have to give me one hell of a good shove, or two. I told her she could do just about anything she wanted, other than leave the suite, open the curtains, or answer the door.

She agreed to my terms, and for her sake, I hope she honors them.

My body was shutting down. Quickly. I felt vulnerable and weak and easy to subdue. But even at my weakest, I still couldn't be killed, unless someone drove a stake through my heart.

And why would anyone want to do that to such a sweet little thing?

Vampires might be immortal, but we sure as hell felt human about this time; that is, just before sunrise. (And, no, I didn't sleep in a coffin. Just give me a bed, darkness, and some peace and quiet.)

When I shut down, I do so in waves. The first, a draining of energy, always hits me about a half hour before sunrise. And ten minutes before the sun comes up, the second wave hits.

This is always a rough wave. I am stuck between exhaustion and sleep. I usually lay down at this time, because within minutes I can be out cold. But when the third wave hits, I absolutely have to lie down and sleep. I am out of options.

For now I was in the middle of the second wave. The sun was minutes from rising and my body was exhausted. And that's when my IM window popped up on my laptop.

Are you up, Moon Dance?

Yes, but not for long.

First or second wave? asked Fang.

Second wave. Almost third.

So I have only a few minutes.

Yes.

I like knowing that I'm sometimes the last person you think about before going to sleep.

You've said that before.

When I was in the second wave, I was often short and to the point and didn't feel very flirty. I felt exhausted. I felt as close to dead as a person could feel.

I also like knowing that you might dream of me.

I rarely dream, Fang. And besides, what am I supposed to dream about? Words that appear in a pop-up window?

There was a long pause. Almost too long. I felt myself going catatonic. If Fang didn't say something soon, it was going to take all my last energy to shut the computer down and crawl over to the couch in the pseudo-living room.

Then perhaps we should meet someday, Moon Dance.

Now it was my turn to pause. I sat back, and as I did so, I had the peculiar sense that something wanted to leave my body. What that something was, I wasn't sure. A part of me. Perhaps my soul, if I still had one. Within seconds I would be out cold.

Through a narrow gap in the curtain, I could see the sky lightening with the coming of the sun.

Are you being serious, Fang?

Yes.

I drummed my fingers on the wooden desk. My brain was fuzzy, thoughts scattered.

Did you say meet? I asked.

Yes. Now, sleep, Moon Dance. Goodnight, even though it's morning.

Goodnight and good morning, Fang.

24.

"You're sure you're okay?" I asked Monica for the tenth time.

She nodded but looked a little overwhelmed. I didn't blame her. We were at Chino State Prison in Ontario, California, sitting in a stark waiting room with a few other people. I had made special arrangements with the warden for a late evening visit.

Both he and the inmate agreed. Being an ex-federal agent has its advantages.

The plain waiting room was smaller than I thought it would be. We sat in plastic bucket seats that were covered with gang graffiti. Took some balls to carve gang graffiti in a prison waiting room.

Monica looked lost and fragile, and I wondered again at my logic for bringing her here. Chad was busy tonight and I had had no one else to turn to. As I was contemplating calling the private investigator Kingsley and I had met at the beach, brainstorming out loud, Monica had volunteered to come with me, telling me she would be fine. "After all," she had said, "I'm just going to be in the waiting room, right? I won't be seeing him."

I reached out now and held her hand, forgetting for a moment that my own was ice cold. She flinched at the touch, but then gripped my hand back tightly.

"Sorry," I said. "My hands get cold."

"So do mine. Don't worry about it." She squeezed my hand again, tighter, and looked at me. "So what are you going to say to him?"

"I'm going to convince him to leave you alone."

She nodded and looked down. I didn't want to mention that maybe her ex-husband's next attempt to find someone to hurt her might slip past prison officials. Although all his calls were monitored, there is more than one way to smuggle information out of a prison.

"How are you going to convince him?" she asked.

"I don't know," I admitted. "I'm going to kind of feel my way through it."

"He'll want to kill you, too, you know."

"I'm not worried about him."

She kept holding my hand. Hers, I noticed, was shaking. I shouldn't have brought her—

But maybe this was a good thing for her. Maybe on some level, she was facing her fears.

Just then the heavy main door into the prison opened and a young, serious-looking guy wearing a correctional uniform stepped into the room.

"Samantha Moon?" he asked.

I gave Monica's hand a final squeeze before I released it. "I'll be back," I said.

25.

Ira Lang was shown through a heavy metal door.

Monica's ex-husband was a medium-sized man in his mid-forties. He was wearing an orange prison jumpsuit, and not very well, either. The clothing hung loosely from his narrow shoulders and flapped around his ankles when he walked. He looked like a deflated pumpkin. Ira was nearly bald, although not quite. Unlike my client, Stuart, Ira did not have a perfect bald head. In fact, his was anything but. Misshapen and oddly flat, it was furrowed with deep grooves that ran from the base of his skull to his forehead. What Monica had seen in the man, I didn't know.

I watched from behind the thick Plexiglas window as Ira was led over to a chair opposite me. I noticed the guard did not remove the handcuffs, which were attached to a loose chain at Ira's waist, giving him just enough freedom of movement to pick up the red phone in front of him and bring it to his ear, which he did now. I picked up the phone on my side of the Plexiglass.

"Who the fuck are you?" he asked.

I knew the warden was listening. The warden had agreed to let me speak to Ira, anything to make this problem go away. And Ira, with his hell bent desire to kill his wife, was proving to be a huge problem for the prison.

"My name's Samantha Moon, and I'm a private investigator. I've been hired to protect your ex-wife."

"Protect her from what?"

"You."

I sometimes get psychic hits, and I got one now. I saw waves of darkness radiating from Ira. Wave after black wave. The man felt polluted. I sensed something hovering around him, something alive and something alien. I sensed this thing had its hooks in Ira. What this thing was, I didn't know. After all, it was only an impression I was getting, a feeling. Something I sensed but didn't really see. Anyway, this *something* was black and ancient and full of hate and vitriol, psychically hanging on to Ira's back, digging its supernatural claws deep within the man. I sensed that Ira had let this dark energy into his life through a lifetime of fear and hate and jealousy. And I knew, without a doubt, that whatever this thing was that had its hooks in Ira, it would never, ever let him go without a phenomenal fight. Whatever clung to Ira would cling to him until his death, and perhaps even beyond, a cancer of the worst kind.

These were all psychic hits. Impressions. Gut feelings. I get these often. Sometimes they're important, sometimes they're a waste of time. But I've learned that I should trust such feelings. And I trusted these.

A smirk touched Ira's lips. And something ancient and dark swept just behind his eyes. Whether or not Ira was possessed by something, I couldn't say for sure. But something foul and alive was eating him away from the inside out.

He asked, "So what are you, a bodyguard or something?"

"Or something."

He laughed, but his was a dry, raspy, dead sound. "Okay, fine, whatever. So who hired you?"

"That's none of your business."

He quit smiling and something passed behind his eyes again, a flitting shadow. Whether or not it was really there, I didn't know. And whether or not I was making it up, I didn't know, either. But there was something off about the guy. Something off, and something wrong. The moment passed and he smiled again. Amazingly, he had a hell of a smile. Perfect teeth. Okay, now I could see how he might have been engaging to a young girl fresh out of high school, which was when Monica had first met him.

"So what the fuck do you want?" he asked.

"Gee, you have such a wonderful way with words, Ira," I said. "It's almost poetic. Maybe you should write a book of poetry in prison, rather than obsessing about your ex-wife. Call it, I don't know, *Poetry From the Pen* or, let's see, *Lock-down Limericks*."

"What the fuck are you talking about?"

"I don't know," I said. "It was a poetry/prison riff. Not my best work, but not my worst either."

He looked at his phone as if there was something wrong with it.

"Lady, either tell me what the fuck you want or get the fuck out of here."

"Okay, now there's a slap in the face for you," I said. "Dismissed by a scumbag who has nothing better to do than to play with his willy."

"Fuck off, bitch."

And as he moved to stand, I said, "Leave Monica alone, Ira."

A long shot, of course, since I suspected Ira Lang spent most of his waking hours obsessing over his wife's frustrating lack of dying. And playing with his willy.

He sat back down slowly. As he did so, he adjusted his grip on the phone, wrapping his surprisingly long fingers tightly around the receiver. His movements were all slow and deliberate, as if he had practiced them beforehand. He now placed the phone carefully against his ear and looked at me for a long, long time. I think I was supposed to be afraid. I think I was supposed to shrink away in fear. Perhaps he thought I would swallow nervously and look away. I didn't swallow, and I didn't look away. I also had the distinct feeling he was memorizing every square inch of my face.

"You want me to leave my wife alone?" he said evenly into the phone. He didn't take his eyes off me.

"Your *ex*-wife, and yes."

"Why would I do that?"

"Because I said so."

He stared at me blankly, and then laughed. A single burst of sound into the phone. He laughed again, longer this time.

"You're funny."

"When I want to be."

"You've got balls coming in here," he said. "I'll give you that much."

"The world's worst compliment to a woman."

"What?"

"Never mind. So will you leave her alone?"

He stared at me some more. I heard guards talking to each other out in the hallway. Ira and I were alone in the visiting room, since it was after hours and I had been given special access. A clock ticked behind me. Somewhere I thought I heard someone scream, but that could have just been my imagination. Or my hypersensitive hearing.

Ira cocked his head a little, and then said, "It's too late."

"Too late for what?"

"Never mind that. The bitch shouldn't have left me. I told her to never leave me."

"Gee, you're such a sweetheart, Ira. How could anyone ever leave you?"

He barely heard me. Or heard what he wanted to hear. "Exactly. I gave her everything. The ungrateful bitch never had to work a day in her life."

"People leave each other every day, Ira. It happens."

"Not to me it don't."

Ira had gotten himself worked up. I knew this because the skin along his slightly misshapen forehead had flushed a little, and he was holding the phone so tight that his knuckles looked like some weird prehistoric spine running along the back of the receiver.

Breathing harder, he said, "I will do everything within my power to make sure the bitch dies. No one leaves me. Ever."

I realized this was going nowhere fast. I honestly hadn't expected anything different, but it had been worth a shot.

"I beg to differ," I said, gathering my stuff together.

"You beg to differ what?"

"Monica very much left you, just as I'm doing now."

"I'm going to remember you, cunt."

"Lucky me."

I was about to hang up when he added, perhaps fatally, "And not just you, Samantha Moon, private investigator and bodyguard. Everyone you know and love. You have kids?"

I heard the sound of boots moving along the hallway outside. Apparently, someone listening to us had heard enough. I took in some air and closed my eyes and did all I could to control myself.

But dumbass wasn't done. He went on, saying, "I see I hit a nerve. So Samantha Moon *is* a mom."

"Did you just threaten my kids?"

"You catch on quick."

I opened my eyes and saw red. In fact, I couldn't really see at all. All I could see was a blurred image of the man behind the bulletproof glass. And I heard pounding. Loud pounding. In my skull.

The sun, I knew, had set thirty or forty minutes ago. I was at full strength. I sat forward in my chair and leaned close to the thick Plexiglas that separated us. I motioned with my index finger for Ira Lane to come closer, too. He grinned, cocky and confident, and as he leaned forward, something very dark and very twisted danced disturbingly just behind his dead eyes.

His face was inches from mine when he said, "Is there something you want to tell me, you stupid bitch? I bet you're wishing right about now you never fucked with—"

I punched the bulletproof glass as hard as I could. My hand burst through in a shower of glass and polycarbonate and whatever the hell else these things are made out of.

Bulletproof but not vampire-proof.

Ira screamed and would have fallen backward if I hadn't grabbed him by the collar through the fist-sized hole in the thick glass. In one motion, I yanked the motherfucker out of his chair and over the counter and slammed him into the clear glass barrier. His nose broke instantly, spraying blood over the glass, and two or three of his front upper teeth had broken back into his mouth. His lips were split clean through.

He flailed at my hand, struggling to free himself, but I wasn't done with him.

Not by a long shot.

Still holding him by the collar, as his warm blood spilled over the back of my hand, I proceeded to slam his face again and again into the glass, breaking more teeth, breaking his face, his skull, his cheekbones, anything and everything, and I kept smashing him into the now blood-smeared glass until I was finally tackled from behind.

26.

I nearly killed a man tonight.

Tell me about it.

And so I wrote it up for Fang, telling him everything from my first impressions of Ira Lang, to the bastard being hauled off on a stretcher. It took three huge blocks of text to get the whole story written, and when I had posted the final segment,

Fang answered nearly instantly. How he could read so fast, I had no clue.

Were there any cameras in the visiting room? he asked.

No.

So there is no visual record of what you did?

Not that I'm aware of.

Don't most prisons have surveillance cameras in the visiting rooms?

Not all of them. It's up to the discretion of the warden.

So no one saw your little, ah, outburst?

No.

When you broke the bullet-resistant glass, did you leave behind any of your own blood?

That was a good question. I had cut my arm while reaching through the shattered glass. However, I hadn't bled at all, as far as I was aware. I explained that to Fang.

So you don't bleed?

Maybe, I wrote. *But apparently not from cuts along my forearm.*

Did the medical staff look at you?

They tried to, but I had wrapped my sweater around my arm, and since there wasn't any blood, they assumed, perhaps, I wasn't in need of any medical attention.

Was he in need of dire medical attention?

According to the warden, with whom I had had a long meeting after the incident, the prison doctors had determined that I had broken Ira's jaw, nose, right orbital ridge, his sinus cavity, and broken out seven teeth. He was going to need countless stitches in his mouth and hours of surgery. I related all this to Fang.

There was a long pause. I looked over at my hotel bed where Monica lay sleeping contentedly on her side. It had, of course, been a long and emotional night for her. She had visited her abusive and murderous ex-husband's prison. She had waited for me anxiously while the warden pieced together what had happened. She had been given snippets of news from the prison staff, and, she told me later, could hardly believe what she was hearing—that I had put the son-of-a-bitch in the hospital . . . even more than that, I had nearly killed him. Later that night, she sat staring at me during the entire ride home from the prison. At one point she reached out and held my hand tightly. She didn't ask me how I punched through the glass. Or how I had the strength to grab a grown man and bash his face repeatedly against the glass. She simply held my hand and stared at me, and I held hers for as long as I could before I became self-conscious of my cold flesh and gently released my grip. I saw that she was crying, but she didn't make a federal case of it. What those tears were for, I didn't know, but I suspected this had been a hell of an emotional night for her. I didn't tell her the bastard had threatened my kids. She had enough to deal with.

So what did the warden say? asked Fang.

He asked me why I didn't kill the bastard?

Was he joking?

I don't think so.

And what did you say?

I told him he should have given me another few seconds.

Jesus. What else did he ask?

He asked me how did I punch through bulletproof glass?

And what did you say?

That I was a vampire, and that if he asked me any more questions, I was going to suck his blooood. (Insert cheesy Bela Lugosi impression.)

Not funny, Moon Dance. You have put yourself at grave risk. There's going to be legal implications to this. He can press charges. There's going to be an investigation.

Maybe, I wrote.

What do you mean, maybe?

The warden heard Ira Lang threaten me.

Still, it's only a threat.

A threat from a known murderer. A threat from a man who has also been known to do anything he could to carry out such threats.

So his threat is much more than a threat.

Yes, I wrote.

So if Ira Lang did press charges, a DA may likely decide not to prosecute.

Right.

So what did you really say when he asked how you punched through the glass?

I reminded him of all those stories of mother's lifting cars off their injured children and such.

He bought that?

Probably not. He was in a state of shock himself. Everyone was.

So is that the end of the case? asked Fang.

No. Ira Lang made it perfectly clear that he wouldn't rest until his ex-wife was dead.

I could almost see Fang nodding, as he wrote: *Not to mention he could still try to carry out that threat on you and your kids.*

Exactly, I wrote.

So what's the plan? asked Fang.

If he won't rest until he's carried out violent crimes against his wife, or even me and my kids, then I think there's only one answer.

Don't tell me.

I went on anyway: *Perhaps I should hasten his rest.*

27.

The backyard to my old house abuts a Pep Boys.

When I say *old house*, I mean my house of just over a month ago, where I had lived with my kids and husband. A house, by some weird turn of events, I had been kicked out of, even though my husband had been the one caught cheating.

Since our house sits in a cul-de-sac, we have an exceptionally large and weirdly-shaped backyard. In fact, our backyard is bigger than most little league baseball fields, which was always fun for the kids and great for parties.

On the other side of our backyard fence was the parking lot to Pep Boys, with its massive, glowing sign of Manny, Moe, and Jack in all of their homoerotic glory. I hated that sign, and thank God they shut the damn thing off at closing time.

It was well after closing time and the lights were off. *Thank God.* Manny, Moe, and Jack were sleeping. Probably spooning. My ex-partner Chad was happily watching over a sleeping Monica—at least, I hoped he let her sleep. No doubt he was watching her in more ways than one. Let's just hope he didn't creep her out too much. Chad was a great guy, even if a little love-starved.

We're all a little love-starved, I thought.

I was sitting on our backyard fence, my feet dangling down,

looking out across the vast sweep of our backyard, toward where I knew my children were sleeping.

Or where they *should have* been sleeping. A flickering glow in Tammy's room meant that she was up well past her bedtime since this was a school night. Her laughter occasionally pierced the air. At least, pierced it to my ears. Actually, I could tell she was trying to laugh quietly, perhaps laughing into a pillow, but occasional bursts of laughter erupted from her.

Most remarkable, and surreal, was that my daughter was laughing at Jay Leno. I could hear his nasally laugh and wildly ranging voice—which went from high to low in the span of a few words—even from here.

Jay Leno? Seriously?

And since when did my ten-year-old daughter watch Jay Leno? And since when was Jay Leno ever laugh-out-loud funny? Perhaps a mild chuckle here and there, sure. But *ha-ha* funny?

At the far end of the house I could hear Danny's light snoring. His snoring never bothered me, since I was a rather deep sleeper. Supernaturally deep, some might say. Anyway, mixed with his snoring was something else. Another sound. Not quite snoring. No, a sort of *wheezing* sound, as if someone was having trouble breathing through one nostril. Along with the wheezing was an occasional murmur. A *female* murmur.

My heart sank. Jesus, his new girlfriend was sleeping with him, in our bed. The fucker. Probably sleeping naked together, their limbs intertwined, touching each other intimately, lovingly. All night long.

Just a month earlier I had been sleeping in that same bed, although Danny had long ago stopped sleeping naked and had made it a point not to touch me.

The fucker.

I stared at my old bedroom window at the end of the house for a long, long time, and then I forced myself to find another sound, and soon I found it. The sound of light snoring. A boy's snore. Little Anthony was sleeping contentedly, and I found myself smiling through the tears on my face.

A small wind made its way through the Pep Boys parking lot, bringing with it the smell of old car oil, new car oil, and every other kind of oil. Living here, you get used to the smell of car oil.

I folded my hands in my lap and lowered my head and listened to the wind and my son's snoring and my daughter's innocent laughter, and I sat like that until her laughter turned into the heavy breathing of deep sleep.

I pulled out my cell phone and sent a text message: *I'm sad.*

The reply from Kingsley Fulcrum came a minute later: *Then come over.*

Okay, I wrote, and did exactly that.

28.

I drove east on Bastanchury, winding my way through streets lined with big homes and big front yards, the best north Orange County has to offer.

It was past midnight, and the sky was clear. The six stars that somehow made their way through Southern California's smog shined weakly and pathetically. The brightest one might have been Mars, or at least that's what a date once told me in college.

Probably just trying to impress me to get into my pants.

Speaking of impressing me, Kingsley Fulcrum was an honest-to-God werewolf. Or, at least, that's what he tells me.

Maybe he just wants to get into my pants, as well.

Granted, I've seen the evidence of his lycanthropy in the form of excessive hair the night *after* one of his transformations, and so I tend to believe the big oaf. But Kingsley is a good wolfie. Apparently, with each full moon, he preferred to transform in what he calls a *panic room* in the basement of his house.

Probably a good thing for the residents of posh Orange County. After all, can't have a big, bad werewolf picking off the surgically-enhanced *Desperate Housewives of Orange County* one at a time like so many slow-moving, top-heavy gazelle. Would probably hurt the ratings.

Or drastically help them; at least, until the show ran out of stars.

Stars? I thought.

Now don't be catty.

Bastanchury was always a pleasant drive, made more pleasant these days because it led to a big, beefy werewolf. I hung a left onto a long, curving, crushed seashell drive, past shrubbery that really needed to be trimmed back; that is, unless Kingsley was purposely going for the creepy feeling they invoked. Or maybe he just didn't want to make his home too inviting. I voted for both.

Soon I pulled up to a rambling estate home that sat on the far edge of north Orange County. The house was a massive Colonial revival, with flanker structures on either end, and more rooms than Kingsley knew what to do with.

I stopped in the driveway near the portico, in a pool of yellow porchlight. My minivan seemed inadequate and out-of-place parked before such an edifice. Hell, I seemed inadequate and out-of-place.

The doorbell gonged loud enough to vibrate the cement porch beneath my feet, and was answered a moment later by a very unusual-looking man. His name was Franklin and he was Kingsley's butler. Yes, *butler*. Yeah, I know, I thought those went the way of *Gone with the Wind*, too, but apparently the super affluent still had them.

Must be nice.

But in the case of Franklin, maybe not so much. There was something very off about the man. For one thing, his left ear was vastly bigger than the right. And it wasn't that it was bigger, it seemed to not, well, belong on his body at all. As if, and this is clearly a crazy thought, it had actually belonged on another person's body altogether. Perhaps strangest of all was the nasty scar that ran from under his neck all the way to the back of his head. The scar, I was sure, wrapped completely around his neck.

My instincts were telling me something very, very strange was going on here, so strange that I didn't want to believe them.

He was tall and broad shouldered, and there seemed to be great strength contained within his very formal butler attire. He looked down at me from a hawkish nose, nodded once, and asked me to follow him to the conservatory. I spared him another "Clue" game joke. This time. Next time, he may not be so lucky. Also, he spoke in what I assumed was an English accent, although it could have been Australian. I could never get the two straight. But my money was on English.

I followed his oddly loping gait to the conservatory. No, I wasn't greeted by Mrs. Plum wielding a candlestick (whatever the hell that is). Instead, I was greeted by a great beast of a man who sprung from his oversized chair with a glass of white wine in hand. How he didn't spill his wine, I didn't know. As he bounded over, exuberant as a puppy, I was half expecting him to jump up on me and lick my face clean. Good thing he didn't, since he would have crushed me. Instead, he set the wine down on an elegant couch table and gave me a crushing bear hug. I think a bone or two popped along my spine. He then led me over to the sofa where a glass of wine was already waiting for me. Along the way, he snatched his own glass.

Franklin waited discreetly near the doorway until Kingsley dismissed him. The gaunt man nodded, a gesture that was meant to be somewhat dignified; instead, it came across as sort of herky-jerky, as if the man didn't have complete control of his head.

No surprise there, I thought.

When the butler was gone, I turned to Kingsley and said, "Are you ever going to tell me Franklin's story?"

The attorney was gazing at me with heavy-lidded eyes. The air around him was suddenly charged. No, *super*charged. His brown eyes crackled with yellow fire, and he looked, for all intents and purposes, like a creature stalking me from the deep woods.

"Maybe someday," he said. His voice was thick and sort of husky.

"Was he in an accident?" I asked, suddenly a little uncomfortable. I quickly reached for the wine and sipped it, keenly aware that Kingsley was staring at me intensely.

"I'm sure parts of him were in an accident," said Kingsley. He had reached out and lifted some of my hair off my shoulder and was now stroking it delicately between his oversized thumb and forefinger.

I drank more wine, suddenly wishing like hell that I could get a serious buzz going.

"*Parts* of him?" I asked, suddenly more nervous than I had been in quite some time. "What does that mean?"

"It means . . . I will tell you later."

"Promise?"

"I promise."

He had slid closer to me, looming over me. I could feel his hot breath on my bare arm. I could feel his eyes on me. Crackling sexual energy radiated from him. I seemed to be caught up by it, sucked into it.

This wasn't meant to be a booty call. In fact, over the past month I had barely even kissed Kingsley. But now I felt myself curious about something more. Excited by the thought of something more. *Terrified* about something more.

But. . . .

"I don't think I'm ready," I said, not wanting to meet his eyes. I loved those big brown eyes.

"You're trembling," he said.

"And you're breathing on me."

I saw him smile out of the corner of my eyes. He was still playing with my hair.

"How long has it been since you've had a man touch you?"

"A man? What's that? I've heard about those curious creatures."

He grinned some more. "How long has it been since you have made love, Samantha?"

"That's a little personal, isn't it?"

He laughed loudly, a sound that erupted from him with such force that I jumped. "And sharing our supernatural secrets *isn't* personal?"

"Don't use your attorney double-speak with me, Kingsley Fulcrum. I'm just not comfortable talking about it."

"Then I retract my question. I was out of line."

But he didn't stop touching my hair. Didn't stop staring at me, but I sensed that some of his supercharged energy, which had been erupting like solar flares from the sun, had died down a little. Also, his breathing wasn't so ragged, either.

I set my wine down and curled up next to him, holding his waist tightly. Kingsley reached down, wrapped a heavy arm around me and softly kissed the top of my head.

Twenty minutes later, when I felt comfortable and safe, I said, "Six years."

"Six years what?" he said groggily. I think he had been dozing lightly on the couch.

"It's been six years," I said again.

He didn't say anything at first, but I heard his heartbeat quicken. Finally, he whispered, "Too long."

I nodded and took in air I really didn't need.

Kingsley moved me aside gently and stood. His knees popped. He offered me his hand. "Come," he said. "I'm exhausted. Let's talk in bed."

"Bed?"

"Yes."

I protested some more—or tried to—but he had already snatched my hand and was pulling me through his opulent home and up his staircase, and to his bedroom and bed.

The horny bastard.

29.

We were in bed.

I was still wearing my jeans and tee shirt. Kingsley was in a pair of black workout shorts and nothing else. We were both on top of the covers. Kingsley had his hands folded behind his head and was staring up at the ceiling. I was on my side, propping my head up with my hand, watching him. In the night, I could see him clearly. He was a little static-y; meaning, there were some limits to my night vision. Light particles flitted through the air like snow flakes caught in a car's headlights. I was used to the light particles. I barely saw them anymore.

Kingsley was a beast of a man. His body was thick and powerful and nothing like the men you see grace most muscle magazines. There wasn't a lot of definition. Meaning, he was just pure muscular mass. Maybe a few pounds overweight, but he wore the weight well. No, he wore it *perfectly*. In fact, I was certain his hulking frame would have looked emaciated if he was at his ideal weight. Tufts of hair ran down the center of his chest and spread over his flat-enough belly. I never much liked hair on men, but with Kingsley it came with the territory.

"So is that a line you use for all the girls you have over here?" I asked.

"What line?"

"'I'm getting tired, talk to me in bed.' That line."

"No," he said. "But it's a good line, apparently. I'll have to remember it."

I slapped his chest. I could have been slapping a side of beef. "Asshole."

"So, has it really been six years, Samantha?"

"Yes."

"Your choice or Danny's choice?"

"His choice, but then again, that part of me sort of shut down and never came back, either. But if he had wanted to make love to me, I would have done anything for him. What was mine, was his."

"But he didn't pursue it."

"Nope."

"Did he ever touch you again?"

"Not like that." I told Kingsley that sometimes Danny and I would get close. Sometimes we would kiss passionately. Sometimes we would be on the verge of making love, and then he would just pull back and shudder. Once or twice he vomited.

"Vomited?"

"Yes," I said. "Not something a wife wants to see after kissing her husband."

"I'm sorry."

"Me, too."

We sat quietly some more. Kingsley's eyes were open. He continued looking up at the ceiling, or at nothing. His chest reminded me of a powerful, idling truck engine.

"So, have you lost all interest in sex?"

"Well, I don't consider myself sexual," I said. "I consider myself, in fact, a monster. Monsters don't have sex."

"When was the last time you orgasmed?"

It was late. We were alone in bed. We were talking softly to each other. My innate need for privacy cringed at the question, but we were adults here, and it was a legitimate, if not too-personal question. I didn't have to answer it, but I did.

"See my comment above."

"Six years?"

I nodded. Kingsley, I knew, could see me in the dark. No doubt he saw my gesture, or sensed it.

"Hell of a long time," he said. "Do you miss it?"

"I don't think about it. Quite honestly, having orgasms is pretty far down there on my list of things to worry about. Besides, I don't think I can anymore."

"Why do you say that? Have you tried?"

I knew my face was red. A crimson-faced vampire. Go figure. But what can I say? I never talk about my sex life. Not even with my sister, who was one of the very few who knew my supersecret identity.

"No," I said. "I haven't tried."

"You haven't *wanted to* or haven't *tried*?"

"Both. I haven't wanted to even try."

"Because you feel you are a monster. And monsters don't have sex, or orgasms, or real lives of any type."

I said nothing. What was there to say? That part of me was dead, I was sure of it.

Kingsley rolled over on his side and faced me. "You have been punishing yourself a long time, Samantha, for something that wasn't your fault."

"I'm not punishing myself," I said. "I'm dealing with it the best I know how. Besides, I don't feel sexy. I feel cold and gross, and what man would ever want to touch me?"

Kingsley suddenly put his hand on my hip as if to answer my question. His hand nearly covered my entire left hip. Jesus, he was a big boy. And then he did something that even I wasn't expecting. He gently nudged me to my back and as I fell backward, he slipped his hand between my thighs and opened my legs. His hand, through my jeans, felt remarkably hot.

I reached down and stopped him. "I'm not ready for sex," I said. "I may *never* be ready for sex."

"Who said I wanted to have sex with you?" he said, winking at me.

"Then what are you doing?"

"Just seeing how dead that part of you really is." He ran his warm palm up the inside of my thigh, over my jeans.

"I think you should stop."

"You *think*?" he said quietly, perhaps even huskily.

His hand continued up my inner thigh and I heard myself gasp. The moment I gasped Kingsley smiled again. The light particles around him were zigzagging like crazy. Like moths on crack.

"Please," I said.

"Please what?"

And then his hand lightly touched me between my legs and I reached down and grabbed his hand. I made a half-hearted effort to push it away, but his hand wouldn't move. Still, I didn't release his hand even as his thick middle finger gently stroked the fabric of my jeans. I wasn't sure if he knew what he was stroking, but the big son-of-a-bitch had found the right spot.

Lucky guess.

I gasped again and made another effort to push his hand away, but this seemed to only inspire him to work his middle finger faster.

"You deserve happiness, Samantha Moon. You are not a monster. You are a sexy woman who has been dealt a very strange hand. But I have a surprise for you."

"What?" I heard myself ask. My hands were still on his hands. It had been so long since anyone had touched me down there. So long. Hell, I had forgotten what to do with my own hands.

"That part of you *didn't* die. In fact . . ." And now his one hand was expertly undoing my jeans, button by button, as if he had done this hundreds of times before, which he might very well have had.

Now he slipped his hands inside my jeans, and his strong, curious fingers found their way under my panties, and now they were moving down with a mind of their own, gently parting me open.

His middle finger touched me almost hesitantly, perhaps testing my readiness. Jesus, I was ready.

And then two things happened simultaneously.

Kingsley lowered his mouth to mine, kissing me harder than I have ever been kissed in my life, and his thick middle finger slipped deep inside me.

30.

I had an orgasm last night, I wrote.

Good for you, Moon Dance.

My first in six years.

Must have been a hell of an orgasm.

I cried, I wrote. *I didn't think I would ever have another one.*

I am happy for you, Moon Dance. But why would you think you couldn't have one?

Because I hadn't had one in six years.

Did you try to have one?

No, not really. Danny wouldn't touch me any more, and I lost all desire to touch myself. It's hard to feel sexy or sexual when your husband finds you repulsive.

And so you touched yourself last night?

My fingers hovered over the keyboard. I knew what I was about to write next would hurt Fang. *No,* I wrote. *I was with the werewolf.*

There was a long pause. My IM box remained static, with no indication that Fang was even typing. Finally, an icon appeared in the box showing that he was busy typing. A second later his response appeared on screen.

I am happy for you, Moon Dance. He's a lucky man.

Several weeks ago, after years of corresponding via chatrooms, Fang had expressed his love for me . . . even though we had yet to meet in person or even talk on the phone, for that matter. I wasn't sure what to think about that. I had never met anyone off the internet, let alone dated from the internet. Besides, Fang was my friend, wasn't he? He knew all the gory—and I do mean gory—details about me.

I'm sorry if that hurt your feelings, Fang.

I'm okay. Really, I am.

Well, you're a big man.

You have no idea.

Are you flirting with me, Fang?

Me? Never!

I'm not so sure about that.

There was a short pause. *I would never flirt with another man's woman.*

I snorted, although he couldn't see me snort. *And who says I'm another man's woman?*

I assumed. . . .

You assumed incorrectly. I am still not there yet. Still not ready. I paused in my typing, thought about my words, then added: *I'm not even sure I'm close.*

Do you still think of yourself as your ex-husband's wife?

Maybe a little. I still feel connected to him. Maybe it's the kids that make me feel connected to him.

Even though he has rejected you in every way?

Well, it's only been a few months, you know. I guess I still need time to heal.

We were silent some more. Lately, I had been thinking of taking up smoking. I hadn't yet, but what the hell? It's not like I was going to ever die of lung cancer, right? Anyway, right about now I could picture myself sucking on the end of a cig just to do something with my hands. I wondered how my body would react to the nicotine.

Well, there was only one way to find out.

Fang was writing something to me, and so I waited. As I waited I looked over at Monica, who was lying on her side and reading a novel. A vampire novel, no less. Maybe I should read one of those. Maybe I could learn a thing or two.

Fang deleted his message and started over. What he deleted, I will never know. A moment later, his message appeared: *Promise me one thing, Moon Dance.*

Okay, I'll try.

Before you commit to the werewolf—or any man, for that matter—please promise me that you will meet me first.

But I'm not committing to anyone, Fang.

Just promise.

Okay, I will consider it. But I have to admit, I'm confused. I thought we were friends.

For a friendship to work, both people have to want the same thing. Both people have to want to be friends.

I wrote, *And if one of the friends suddenly wants something more than friendship?*

It changes things, he wrote.

I don't want things to change, Fang. I like talking to you. You are my outlet. You are my friend and my therapist and my confidant.

I want to be more, Moon Dance.

We were both silent for a long time. The hotel made typical hotel noises: a door slamming somewhere, the ding of the elevator around the corner, the endless drone of hundreds of air conditioners working hard against the warm Orange County night. On the bed nearby, Monica licked her fingers and turned the page. As she did so, her shoulder flexed a little. A narrow cord stood out on her neck. I found myself absently staring at it. Even from here, I could see it pulsating.

You there, Moon Dance?

Yes.

I want to meet you in two weeks.

I sat up suddenly. My heart, nearly useless in my chest, slammed hard once or twice against my ribs. My mouth instantly went dry. *Two weeks??* I reached for a nearby bottle of water and sipped from it, staring at Fang's words. Finally, I answered him.

Okay, I wrote. *Two weeks.*

31.

We were at our favorite bar in Fullerton, called Hero's.

I was with my sister, Mary Lou, and my client, Monica. The three of us were sitting on vinyl stools in front of a long, brass-topped bar. Our favorite mixologist was tending bar, a young guy of about thirty. The fact that he was also kind of cute contributed to the "favorite" part.

We were all sipping white wine. My sister Mary Lou was probably doing a little more than just sipping, since she was already on her third glass. It was Friday evening and the bar was hopping. This was also Casual Friday, apparently, and so Mary Lou, who worked for a small insurance agency in Placentia, was wearing jeans and a bright yellow tee shirt. For the uninitiated, Casual Friday is a sort of mini-national holiday for office workers everywhere. Occurring only four times a month, Casual Friday is commemorated by the wearing of jeans, tee shirts and sneakers, and the consumption of store-bought donuts and bagels. Homemade brownies are also acceptable. From what I understand, the day usually begins with a general air of optimism and hope, and deteriorates rapidly into a serious need to drink something strong and hard. I often reminded my older sister that every day was Casual Friday for me. And I did so now.

"Are you *trying* to depress me?" she said.

"Not clinically," I said. "But a tear or two is always nice. Besides, I have to gloat about something. There's not much else to gloat about these days."

Mary Lou didn't like her job. Unfortunately, she never did anything about it, other than bitch. My philosophy is this: Life is too short to work another minute at a job you don't love. Unless, of course, you're a vampire. And then that philosophy goes out the window.

Anyway, with my client sitting with us, my sister and I kept our conversation to mundane topics. Just three fairly cute girls, sitting in a bar, wrapped in secrets and pain and heartache.

Good times.

Mary Lou knocked back drink number three and waved the bartender over. He caught her eye, nodded, and reached under the counter for the bottle of wine. As he did so, I caught my sister adjusting her bra.

"Why are you adjusting your bra?" I asked.

"I'm not adjusting my bra," she said. "I'm adjusting my boobs."

"Happily married women don't adjust their boobs in front of cute bartenders."

"Happily married women have boobs, too," she said.

"They also have husbands."

"He's coming over—shh, quiet!"

Indeed, he was, grinning at us easily. He had short brown hair. Big brown eyes. Dimples in his cheeks and chin. He wore a combination of metal and leather bracelets, which jangled as he filled Mary Lou's glass with more wine. His sleeves were rolled up to his elbows, revealing tattoos that went down to his wrists and beyond. Some of the tats crawled along the back of his hands. His ears were pierced with silver studs, and he wore a leather strap around his neck, anchored by two huge shark teeth.

"Just a little more," said Mary Lou, slapping his hand lightly. "Pretty please."

Oh, brother, I thought, and caught Monica's eye. She smiled at me and sipped her wine, enjoying my sister's retarded attempt at flirtation. Myself, I wasn't enjoying it so much.

"If I give you more, young lady, then I have to give everyone else more," he said. "And if I give everyone else more, then my boss will fire me."

"Oh, poo. You're no fun."

He winked at me and left.

So far, Monica had remained silent and inexpressive. I sensed that her personality had been beaten out of her by her ex-husband. Sure, she had opened up to me, but not so much with other people. With that said, I suspected she didn't like my sister, either. The excessive drinking might have had something to do with it. Also, when someone laughed particularly loud, or brushed up against her, she jumped. And so she stayed close to me, like a trained puppy, never more than a foot or so away from my elbow. She felt safe with me. She *should* feel safe with me. Hell, I felt safe with me.

While we drank and talked, I stayed alert for any suspicious activity. Her ex-husband, prior to his unfortunate run-in with the bulletproof glass, had indicated that he had succeeded in hiring someone to carry out his threat on her.

Monica touched my forearm and leaned over and whispered into my ear. "I need to use the restroom."

I patted her hand. "Okay." I turned to Mary Lou. "We're going to the restroom."

Mary Lou nodded and kept her eyes on the bartender. Monica and I left and I held her hand as I threaded our way through the crowded bar. She kept about as close to me as she possibly could. Inside the surprisingly uncrowded bathroom, I waited outside the stall for her to finish her business. As I waited, I had a very bad feeling I couldn't shake. I looked over my shoulder, but we were alone. I frowned.

Shortly, we were working our way back through the bar to where we found an ashen-faced Mary Lou staring at us. We took our seats on the stools next to her, and as I sat, Mary Lou leaned over and whispered in my ear: "There was a man here."

"Who?"

She shook her head. My sister looked completely shaken. "I don't know. He came up next to me and ordered a drink."

"So?"

"He looked right at me and smiled . . . the most horrible smile I have ever seen."

"You're not drunk, are you?"

"No, dammit." She kept shaking her head. "He looked . . . wrong. Off. Evil. He looked like what I would imagine a killer would look like."

"A killer?"

"A hired killer."

"Is he here now?"

"No, he ordered a Red Bull, paid cash, and left. Right before you two came back. He wanted me to see him. He wanted you to know he's watching."

"And you're not drunk."

"Goddammit, no."

My first instinct was to run out after the guy. Maybe that's what he wanted me to do. Maybe. The sun was still an hour or so from setting. I wasn't at my strongest, and I wasn't going to leave Monica.

"Okay," I said to Mary Lou. "Hang on."

I motioned for the bartender. He saw me immediately and, even though he was talking to someone else, said something to them, laughed, and came right over. He looked curiously at my mostly full drink.

"You need something else?" he asked.

I nodded. "The guy who ordered the Red Bull a minute ago. Have you ever seen him in here before?"

He shook his head. "No. Why?"

"How tall would you say he was?"

He shrugged. "Six foot maybe. Why?"

"How old would you say he was?"

He shrugged again. "Hard to say. Forty, fifty. Is everything okay?"

"We'll see," I said. "Can you tell me any more about him?" I wanted a description of the guy from someone who wasn't nearly three sheets to the wind.

The bartender studied me with his big brown eyes. His shark teeth glistened whitely at his throat. He had been working here for a few months, but he had never really spoken. Still, I often caught him catching my eye. I think he thought I was cute. Go figure. Finally, he said, "White guy. Thin. Black hair. Black eyes. Probably brown eyes, but they looked black in here."

"Anything else about him?" I asked.

"He was wearing a sign around his neck that said, 'I am exhibiting suspicious behavior.' Does that help?"

"I don't tip you to be funny," I said.

"The humor is free."

I looked away from him, scanning the room. I didn't sense any immediate danger. The sensing of danger is tricky business for me. Lots of things set off my warning bells. If the man honestly didn't intend any sort of physical violence at this moment, I probably wouldn't have picked up on anything. Now, had he been charging us with a pocket knife at this very moment, my spidey-senses would have sprung to life.

I turned back to the bartender, who was watching me curiously. "So that's all you remember?"

He grinned easily. "Hey, he just ordered a Red Bull to go. I think I did pretty good remembering what I remembered."

"Bravo. You get a biscuit."

"So what's this all about anyway?"

"Official undercover chick business," I said.

He nodded. "I see. Well, be safe under those covers, young lady," he said, and then moved quickly away to get another drink order filled.

I turned to Monica; she was staring at me, having heard everything of course. "Is he a bad man?" she asked.

"I don't know," I said.

"Does he want to kill me, too?"

"I don't know," I said, frowning. "But no one is going to kill you or hurt you or anything. I promise."

She smiled, or tried to, and gripped my arm even tighter.

32.

I called right at 7:00 p.m.

Danny picked up and told me to hold on. No other pleasantries were said. There were never any pleasantries said. While I waited and while I listened to him breathing steadily on his end, I thought of us standing together in the shade of the Fullerton Arboretum. It had been a small wedding. Just forty or so family and friends. It had been a beautiful, sunny day. Danny had looked so handsome and awkward in his suit. He kept folding his hands over and over at his waist, trying to look dignified standing in front of everyone, but mostly looking nervous as hell. I had watched him the entire way as walked down the aisle with my father. Danny had watched me, too, and the closer I got the more his nerves abated. He quit fumbling with his hands. He then smiled at me brighter than he had ever smiled at me before or after.

I heard something akin to a hand covering the phone, heard muffled voices, then more scraping sounds and Danny spoke into the phone. "You've got eight minutes."

"Eight!?"

A second later, a squeaky little voice burst from the line.

"Mom!"

"Hi, baby!"

"Don't call me baby, mom. I'm not a baby."

"I'm sorry, Mr. Man."

"I'm not a man, either."

"Then what are you?"

"I'm a boy."

"You're my big boy."

He liked that. I could almost see him jumping up and down on the other end of the line, pressing the phone into his ear with both hands, the way he usually does.

"Daddy says you can't come see us tomorrow. That you are too busy to see us."

"That's not true—"

"Yes, it is true, Sam," said Danny's voice. He had, of course, been listening in from the other phone, as he always does. "You're busy with work and you can't see them."

I took in a lot of air, held it. Let it out slowly.

"I'm sorry, angel," I said to my boy. "I'm going to be busy tomorrow."

"But we never get to see you—"

"That's enough, Anthony. Get your sister on the line."

A moment later, I heard Tammy say, "Give me that, jerk," followed by Anthony bursting into tears. Sounds of running feet and crying faded quickly into the distance, followed by a door slamming. He was probably crying now into his pillow.

"Hi, mommy," she said.

I was too broken up to speak at first. "Is Anthony okay?" I asked, controlling my tears.

"He's just being a baby."

"No, he's just being a little boy."

"Whatever," she said.

"Don't 'whatever' me, young lady."

She said nothing. I heard the pop of chewing gum. I also heard Danny making tiny shuffling movements on his end of the line. No doubt looking at his stopwatch. Yes, stopwatch.

"What did you guys do today?" I asked.

"Nothing," she said.

"How was school?"

"Boring."

"Did you do your homework?"

"Maybe."

"Is that a yes or a no, young lady?"

"It's a *maybe*."

I knew Danny was on the other phone, listening, hearing his daughter disrespect her mother, and not giving a damn. I let the homework go. She was right, after all. I presently had no say in whether or not the homework got done, nor did I have any way of enforcing any house rules. I knew it. She knew it. I also suspected she was deliberately hurting me, since my unexplained absence was hurting her.

"I miss you," I said. "More than you know."

"You have a funny way of showing it, mom."

"I'll figure out a way of seeing you guys more soon. I promise."

"Whoopee."

"That was rude," I said.

"So?"

"Don't be rude to your mother."

"Whatever."

I took a deep breath. I knew my time was running out fast. I suspected Danny sometimes cut our conversations short. Either that, or time disappeared when I spoke to my kids. Even when they were being impossible.

I said, "I promise, I'll see you as soon as I can."

"Tomorrow?" she asked, and I heard the faint hope in her

voice. She was still trying for badass pissy, but the little girl who missed her mother was still in there.

"Not tomorrow, angel," I said, my voice breaking up. "But soon."

She was about to say something, probably something mean or rude or both. But something else came out entirely. A small, hiccuppy gasp. She was crying.

"I love you," I said. "I love you more than you could possibly know."

"I love you, too, mommy," and then she really started crying, and I was crying, and Danny stepped in.

"Time," he said.

"Goodbye, angel," I said quickly. "I love you!"

She was about to say something when the line went dead.

33.

Monica and I were sitting in my minivan down the street from my house. Very far down the street. In fact, we were at the *opposite end* of the street. Still, from here I could see my house—yes, *my* house. In particular, I could see anyone coming or going, especially Danny and his lame new Mustang.

Mustang? Weren't those for college girls?

Also from here, I could see the Pep Boys sign rising above the house. Looming, might be a better word. The lights in the sign were currently out. The boys were asleep. Allegedly.

The night was young and some in the neighborhood were still out and about: pushing baby strollers, walking dogs, jogging, or, in one case, power walking.

My windows were heavily tinted for two reasons: The first was because I happened to be fairly sensitive to the sun. Go figure. The second was because I often used my nondescript minivan for surveillance. And when I was doing a lengthy surveillance, I would actually pull down a dark curtain from behind the front seat and hunker down in the back of the van, looking out through the many blackened windows. I even had a port-a-potty for long surveillances.

Tonight I didn't expect to need my port-a-potty. Tonight I expected the action to begin fairly quick. Call it a hunch.

"So is this a real stakeout?" asked Monica. She was sitting cross-legged in the passenger seat. She could have been a teenager sitting there next to me.

"Real enough," I said.

"And that's your old house up there?"

"Yes."

"So are we stalking your ex-husband?"

"I'm a licensed private investigator," I said. "I'm licensed to stalk."

"Really?"

"In most cases."

"What about this case?"

"In this case," I said. "We're stalking the hell out of him."

She giggled. If Danny spotted me following him, he could report me to the California Bureau of Investigative Services, where I would probably be heavily fined and face jail time, probably a year. The CBIS frowned upon investigators abusing their privileges.

Which was why I was parked *way down* the street. Back when I had first caught Danny cheating on me, I had been reckless and he had spotted me.

This time, I intended to play it safe.

"So what's it like having kids?" asked Monica. She was chewing some gum, occasionally popping bubbles inside her mouth, the way kids used to do it back when I was in high school. I never did figure out how they did that, or how she was doing it now, and with that thought, something fairly exciting occurred to me.

Hey, I can chew gum!

At least gum that had no sugars in it at all. I asked Monica for a piece and she reached into her little purse and produced a rectangular square. It was cinnamon and sugar free. I had no clue what it would do to me, but I was eager to find out.

God, I'm pathetic.

I unwrapped the gum hastily and tossed the discarded paper in my ash tray. Saliva filled my mouth as the sharp bite of cinnamon tore through even my dulled taste buds. Cautiously, I swallowed my own saliva, now filled with cinnamon flavor.

I kept an eye on my dashboard clock. I would know in less than two minutes if my body would reject even this small amount of flavoring.

And while I waited, I chewed and chewed, savoring the flavor, savoring the smooth texture of the gum on my tongue and in my mouth. And, like riding a bike, I produced my first bubble in six years. It popped loudly and Monica giggled. And just as I was scraping the gum off my nose and chin, something in my stomach lurched.

But that's all it did.

Lurched.

Nothing came up. No extreme pain. Nothing more than that initial, slightly painful gurgle. I grinned and continued happily chewing the gum.

So there you have it. Vampires can chew gum. Wrigley should consider a new slogan: "So good, even a vampire won't projectile vomit."

I asked Monica for the brand name of the gum, and she fished the package out again and told me. I grinned. Hell, I was going to buy stock in the company.

"Look," said Monica pointing through the windshield excitedly. "Someone's leaving your house."

I took my binoculars out and adjusted them on the medium-sized figure. It was Danny, and he was dressed to kill.

34.

In his girly Mustang, he exited the driveway, drove briefly towards us, and then hung a left down a side road inside the housing track. I started the van and pulled slowly away from the curb. Like a good girl, Monica checked her seat belt. She was grinning from ear to ear. I'll admit, P.I. work can be fun.

Twenty seconds later, I made a right onto the same road Danny had made a left onto. As I did so I caught a glimpse of him making a left out of the track, and onto Commonwealth Avenue.

It was just past ten and I wondered who was watching the kids. Until I realized it was, of course, his slutty, ho-bag secretary.

I gripped the steering wheel a little tighter.

You probably don't want to piss-off a vampire. Just sayin'.

Anyway, I hung a left on Commonwealth, and easily picked up the shape of the Mustang's taillights about a half mile down the road. One thing about my current condition, my eyesight was eagle-like. And it only got better when I was in my, well, eagle-like form. Or bat-like. Or whatever the hell I transformed into.

While tailing someone, I could hang back farther than most investigators could. Still, it was a fine balance of staying far enough back to not get spotted, but not so far that I hit a red light and lost him altogether. I should probably have rented a car for tonight, but it was too late now.

Live and learn.

Next to me, rocking slightly in her seat, Monica was chewing her nails nervously. From my peripheral vision, her mannerisms and sitting position suggested she was no older than ten years old. About the age of my daughter.

My cell rang.

Shit. I dreaded looking down. Was it Danny? Had he spotted me already? Impossible.

It continued ringing and finally I reached for it in the center console, where it had been charging. I looked at the faceplate. It was Kinglsey.

I unhooked the phone from the charging wire.

"Arooo!" I sang, "Werewolves of London. . . ."

"Not funny," he said, his deep voice rumbling through my ear piece. "And please not over the phone."

"Big Brother and all that," I said.

"Something like that."

"You sound like you're in a pissy mood," I said.

"I am." He paused on the other end. Up ahead, Danny took a right onto Harbor Boulevard. He didn't use his blinker. I should make a citizen's arrest. Kingsley went on, "You nearly killed my client the other day."

I turned onto Harbor as well. I wasn't sure I heard Kingsley right. "Your client? What do you mean?"

"Ira Lang."

I nearly dropped the phone. "Excuse me?"

"Ira Lang is my client, Samantha. And he's been my client for the past few years, since his first arrest. Now he's in the hospital, with a face full of metal pins and screws and staples."

I looked over at Monica, who was still peering ahead, rocking slightly. From this angle, I could see where her left eye drooped badly, the result of her husband's attack with a hammer, the attack which had resulted in Ira's first arrest.

Kingsley's words had sucked the oxygen from my lungs. I found myself driving on automatic, vaguely aware that I was still following the Mustang far ahead. Danny was slowing for a red light. There were three cars between us, and he was still a quarter mile down the road.

"This is a problem," I said.

"Damn straight, Sam. My client's going to press charges."

"I'm not worried about that," I said. "Let's talk later, Kingsley. This isn't a good time."

"Swing by my place when you get a chance."

"Okay," I said, and hung up.

Monica was watching me curiously. She, like most people, was far more psychic than she realized. She had picked up something in my voice, something in my mannerisms. She knew something was wrong.

Hell, yeah, something was wrong. The guy I was seeing—the guy who had touched me more intimately than any man had touched me in a long, long time—had gotten her ex-husband out of jail on a technicality.

Who then went on to bludgeon her father to death.

Sweet Jesus.

Monica was still watching me. I looked over at her and gave her the brightest smile I could muster. It seemed to work. She smiled back at me sweetly, reminding me of a child all over again, a child eager for good news.

I reached out and held her hand; she held mine in return, tightly. I continued following Danny at a distance, and holding Monica's hand.

35.

We were sitting outside a strip club. A filthy, disgusting, vomitous, vile strip club.

We had followed Danny down the 57 Freeway, and then east along the 91 Freeway. He had gotten off in the city of Colton, a tough little area in Riverside County. We were about 60 miles east of Orange County. Here, they did not make reality shows about super-enhanced married women. Here, there was crime and gangs and a sense that something, somewhere had gone very wrong with this city. So wrong that it was beyond hope to fix.

Danny had worked his shiny Mustang along the dark and dirty streets, far removed from our cute little neighborhood, and had ended up at a small strip joint at the far edge of the city.

By the time we had pulled up to the club, Danny was already inside. I circled the packed parking lot, found his car, and then parked as far away from it as I could, all while keeping an eye on the club's front door.

We parked and cracked our windows. Music thumped through the club's open door. Two rather large black men stood on either side of the door. In a raised truck about five cars away, I was pretty sure two people were having sex. Already I felt I needed to shower.

Monica had seemingly shrunk in on herself. She pulled her feet up on the passenger seat and wrapped her arms tightly around her knees.

I was, admittedly, confused as hell. I had never known Danny to be the type to go to strip clubs. Of course, I had never known Danny to be a cheater and a liar and royal piece of shit, either, until recently.

I was tempted to look inside the club, but I wasn't going to bring Monica with me, and I sure as hell wasn't leaving her alone.

And so we sat, staring at the entrance to the strip club. Amazingly, I still felt a pang of jealousy that Danny would find pleasure in looking at other women. That is, until I reminded myself that he had been sleeping with another woman for the past few months.

I felt sick. I felt disgusted. I felt a massive wave of revulsion.

Monica was rocking now. The thumping music and the trashy cars and the trashy guys were all too much for her. She reminded me of a child sitting in her bedroom and listening to her parents fighting downstairs. Listening and rocking and suffering.

I waited another half hour, watching Monica, watching the door, watching the waves of men coming and going. Danny remained inside.

I was having a hard time believing Danny had come all this way to a strip club. There were clubs a lot closer than this. Not as sleazy, certainly, but a lot closer. So why had Danny driven nearly an hour to go to this shit hole? I didn't know, but I was going to find out.

I started the car and left.

Monica rocked in her seat nearly the entire way home.

36.

I comforted Monica with hugs and hot tea.

When she seemed stable again, I called my ex-partner. He was more than up to the challenge of watching over Monica again. In fact, I suspected he might have been waiting eagerly by his phone, since he had snatched it up on the first ring.

Thirty minutes later, with Monica in good (if not adoring) hands, I made my way over to Kingsley's massive estate. Franklin the Butler did not seem pleased to see me this late, and I once again followed his slightly off-kilter, loping gait. This time to the kitchen, where I found Kingsley sitting at a round corner table, working on a double-stuffed ham sandwich. Sitting across from him was a glass of red wine. Mine, I assumed, although I rarely drank red wine since it gave me stomach cramps. Too many impurities.

Kingsley thanked the butler, who expressed his love of servitude with words dripping with sarcasm, and disappeared down a side hallway. To where, I had no clue. No doubt a servant's quarter.

Or perhaps a stone slab with straps and thick cables attached to some sort of medieval antennae on the roof.

Or not.

As I stepped into the kitchen, Kingsley set aside the heavy-looking sandwich and got up and gave me a hug and a light kiss on the lips. The light kiss was my idea. I turned my head, since I wasn't in much of a kissing mood. Kingsley indicated the chair across from him, and as I sat, I realized the glass wasn't full of wine, it was full of something else.

It was full of blood.

Saliva burst instantly from under my tongue. I might have even licked my lips. *Might have.*

Kingsley was watching me. "You don't have fangs."

"What an odd thing to say to a girl," I said, keeping my eyes on the hemoglobin-filled goblet. Say that three times in a row.

"I noticed it the other night, in bed, when we were kissing. Your teeth are normal."

"Gee, thanks."

"But I thought vampires had fangs," he pushed.

"And I thought vampires existed only in teen romance novels."

He chuckled lightly and let it go. I noticed the blood in the goblet was beginning to congeal a little along the surface, sticking to the inside of the thick glass. It was just blood. Disgusting blood. But it was the only thing I could consume comfortably. It was the only thing that gave me nourishment. And now, over the course of six years, blood had become my comfort food. Hell, it had become my only food, my everything. My stomach was doing back flips.

God, I was such a fucking ghoul.

"Drink, honey," he said. As he spoke, he used some strange German accent. Oh?

"Whose blood is it?" I asked.

"Does it matter?" His voice was back to normal.

He was right, of course. I had discovered that the source of the blood mattered not at all. Human, animal, warm, cold. It all had the same effect on me: It nourished me deeply.

I picked up the glass and drank deeply. The blood was warm. It was fresh, too. Something had recently died. Blood has a unique texture and I have grown to both love and loathe it. Good blood, fresh blood, is heavenly. The blood I normally drank, blood provided to me from a local butchery, was filled with all sorts of disgusting "extras," which I constantly found myself spitting out.

Yum.

My account with the butchery was more or less a secret account. The butchery was in Chino Hills, and six years ago, I had convinced the owner I was a vet assistant and that I was involved with animal blood research. He hadn't asked questions, and I hadn't provided any more info other than that. The blood arrived monthly and I paid the exorbitant bill. Meals on wheels.

With that said, this blood was flawless, minus one or two coagulated lumps. I drank from the goblet steadily, briefly unable to pull away from it. Salty and metallic, it coated the inside of my mouth, filling the spaces between my teeth. I didn't need to come up for air because I really didn't need to breathe.

I drank steadily, greedily, happily.

When the goblet had been half-drained, I forced myself to set it down in front of me, and burped.

"Hungry?" asked Kingsley.

"Usually," I said.

"So how often do you eat?" asked Kingsley, and I silently thanked him for not using the word "feed." The word rubbed me the wrong way. Animals *feed*. Monsters *feed*. Ladies with degrees in criminal justice, who had two wonderful children and a successful private eye firm didn't *feed*. We drank, even if our food was liquified.

A smoothie from hell.

"I'm hungry every night," I said, shrugging. "Like most people."

"Most people eat during the day."

"You know what I mean," I said, picking up the glass again. "Asshole."

He grinned. "Do you eat every day?"

"No."

"Why not?"

"Because the packets of animal blood disgust me."

"I've seen your packets," he said, shuddering. "Revolting." He looked at me some more, his sandwich looking minuscule in his oversized hands. "So, then, is it safe to say that you go as long as you can without eating?"

"Yes."

"And how long can you go without eating?"

"Three or four days."

"And then you have to eat."

I nodded, tilting the glass up to my lips, reveling in the purity of the blood, letting it coat my tongue, the roof of my mouth.

"Do you ever worry that you will go too long between meals, and find yourself so hungry that you might do something stupid?"

"Like kill someone?" I asked.

"That would be something stupid, yes."

"I'm not worried," I said. "Not really. I'm generally always close to a source of blood. When I'm hungry enough, I just pop open a packet."

"There might come a day when you don't have such a ready source of blood."

"Maybe," I said. "But I'll cross that bridge when I come to it."

And with that, I finished the glass of blood. I brought it over to the sink and immediately washed it out. When I wasn't hungry, the sight of blood made me want to vomit.

About that time, Kingsley stuffed the rest of his sandwich in his mouth, chewed a half dozen times—surely not enough to fully masticate such a large section of sandwich—and then swallowed it down like a whooping crane, tossing back his head.

We both sat back, looking at each other.

"We have a problem," I said.

Kingsley nodded. "Is it that I'm too sexy?"

I didn't feel like smiling. I felt like clawing his eyes out, if you wanted to know the truth. "You got Ira Lang out of jail the first time around," I said.

"Sure," said Kingsley, shrugging. "And he didn't even have to pay me."

"What do you mean?"

"I was his court-appointed attorney."

"But I thought you were one of the most expensive defense attorneys around."

"I am. But sometimes when there are emergencies or the other attorneys are swamped, a judge will ask me to take over a case."

"So you took over the case."

He winked. "Of course. You don't say no to a judge."

"But Ira tried to kill his wife," I said. "And not just *tried*. The piece of shit did everything within his power to kill her."

"Right. And I got him out of jail," said Kingsley evenly. "It's what I do best."

I searched for words, fought to control myself.

As I did so, Kingsley continued, "Look, Sam. Don't take this so personally, okay? If it wasn't me getting him out of jail, any other defense attorney worth his salt would have done the same. Ira had no previous record. He was a first time offender. He was ordered to stay away from his wife—"

"And I am sure you are proud of yourself for getting him out."

"I did my job well."

"And how did you feel when you heard the news that he had gone after her again, but this time killing her father, who fought to protect her?"

"It was unfortunate."

"And you couldn't have seen that coming?"

"I saw it coming."

"But you did nothing to stop it."

"It's not my job to stop it, Sam. It was my job to get him out of jail."

"You're an animal," I said.

He folded his arms over his great chest. His black tee shirt was stretched to the max over his biceps and shoulders and pectorals and even his slightly-too-big gut. His deep voice remained calm; he never once took his eyes off me.

He said, "You are emotional because you have grown close to the victim."

"I am emotional because I let an animal put his hands on me."

"I seem to recall that you liked my hands on you."

I stood abruptly. "I can't talk to you right now."

He stood, too, and grabbed hold of both my shoulders. He towered over me. His shaggy black hair hung down over his face. He smelled of pastrami and good cologne. He had put the cologne on for me, I realized. He had wanted more tonight, perhaps to sleep with me. I shuddered at the thought.

"Don't go," he said. "I'm not the enemy."

"No," I said. "But you might as well be."

He tightened his grip on my shoulders, but with one swipe of my hand, I easily knocked them off. Shaking, I turned and walked out of the kitchen.

"Don't go," he said after me.

I didn't look back.

37.

I sat on the same thick tree branch and watched the crime lord's regal estate. Just a giant black raptor with a love for cute shoes.

The massive island home was ablaze with lights as Jerry Blum did his personal best to accelerate global warming. Activity had picked up since the last time I was here a few days ago. Now there were more guys with big guns, more beautiful women, and more cars coming and going. The cars looked armor plated. Once, a man and a woman strolled beneath the very tree I was perched in. The man lit a cigarette. The woman was wearing a blouse cut so low that I could see straight down it to her belly button. Probably a good thing neither of them thought to look up.

As I watched them, sitting motionless and squatting on the thick branch, I wondered if I emitted an odor of some sort. I had read years ago that Bigfoot sightings were often preceded first by a horrific stench. Well, I had showered just a few hours earlier, thank you very much. Granted, I had showered as a *human*. Either way, neither crinkled their noses and looked at each other and asked, "Do you smell a giant vampire bat?"

Again, probably a good thing.

The man finished his cigarette and mentioned something about being off in a few hours and why didn't she come up to his room then? She said sure.

He nodded and flicked his cigarette away, and Mr. Romantic and Slutty McSlutbag drifted off over the grounds, to disappear in the controlled mayhem of the estate house. Something seemed to be up, but I didn't know what. I caught snatches of conversation, but couldn't piece anything together. Once I saw Jerry Blum himself, surrounded by a large entourage of men. Big men. Dark-haired men. They moved purposely through the house, and I watched them going from window to window, until they slipped deeper into the house and out of view.

Jerry was going to be hard to get alone. But I was a patient hulking monster.

As the wind picked up and the tree swayed slightly, I adjusted my clawed feet, stretched my wings a little, and hunkered down for the night.

38.

I turned off Carbon Canyon Road, which wound through the Chino foothills, and onto a barely noticeable service road.

Stuart Young, my beautifully bald client who was sitting in the passenger seat next to me, looked over at me nervously. I grinned and winked at him.

"Um, you sure you know where you're going?" he asked.

"No clue," I said.

"Of course not," he said good-naturedly. "Why should you? We're only driving through the deep dark forest in the dark of night."

"Fun, isn't it?"

I doubted we would get lost since there was only about a quarter mile of wilderness between the road and the grass-covered hill before us. Even a soccer mom could get her bearings here. We had been driving down the twisty Carbon Canyon Road, a road some think of as a sort of shortcut from Orange County to Riverside County, but, if you ask me, it's just a more scenic way to fight even more dense traffic.

The van probably wasn't made for dirt roads, but it handled this one well enough. We bounced and scraped through shrubbery until we came across a metal gate that consisted of two horizontal poles.

"It looks locked," said Stuart.

"Hang on," I said.

I put the van in park and hopped out, brushing aside a thorn covered branch with my bare hand. A thorn or two snagged my skin and drew blood. By the time I reached the gate, my hand was already healed.

Cool beans.

A thick chain was wrapped around a rusted pole driven deep into the ground. The chain was padlocked with a heavy-duty lock. I often wondered who carried keys to these random city and county locks. Somewhere out there was a guy standing in front of some obscure park gate with a big wad of keys and going crazy.

This lock was a big one, and heavy, too. As I picked it up, the chain clanked around it. I turned my back to Stuart. I hooked my finger inside the lock's rusted loop and with one quick yank, I snapped the lock open.

"We're in luck," I yelled, letting the lock drop. "It's open."

We were now in a clearing at the edge of a ravine, where a small river flowed twenty feet below. The gurgling sound of it was pleasant. The chirping of the birds was even more pleasant. Darkness was settling over what passed as woods in Southern California, which amounted to a small grove of scraggly elderberry trees, deformed evergreens, beavertail cactus, thick clumps of sagebrush and gooseberry, and other stuff that wasn't taught in my junior college environmental biology course.

We were in a sort of clearing, surrounded by a wall of trees. My sixth sense told me that this place had been used before, for something else, for something physically painful, but I didn't know what. My sixth sense was sketchy at best. Still, I heard the crack of something breaking, perhaps bone, and I heard the crash of a car. I walked over to the edge of the ravine and looked down. Sure enough, deep within the soft soil around the lip, I saw deep tire tracks. Someone, at some time, had taken a nosedive off the edge here and down into the river below.

I turned and faced Stuart. "This is where I will bring him."

Stuart had walked to the center of the clearing, and was taking in the area, perhaps envisioning himself fighting a crime lord to the death in this very spot. Like gladiators in an arena.

"It's a good place," he said, nodding. He looked slightly sick.

A blue jay shot through the clearing, flashing through the shadows and half light, disappearing in the branch high overhead, reminding me of the old George Harrison song, "Blue Jay Way," about fogs and L.A. and friends who had lost their way.

I stood in the clearing with a man who had lost his way, too, his life completely derailed by pain and grief and the burning need for revenge. He stared up into the darkening sky, which filled the scattered spaces above the tangle of trees. His bald head gleamed dully in the muted light.

We all lose our way, I thought. *Some of us just for longer than others.*

Perhaps even for all eternity.

"A part of me doesn't believe you can get him here," said Stuart, still looking up, his voice carrying up to the highest, twisted branches.

I said nothing.

"But another part of me believes you can. It's a small part, granted, but it believes that you can somehow, someway, deliver Orange County's biggest son-of-a-bitch to me."

I was quiet, leaning my hip on the fender of the minivan, my hands folded under my chest. A small, hot wind blew through the clearing.

"So then I ask myself, 'What will you do if he does show up? What will you do if Samantha Moon really can deliver him?'" He lowered his head and looked over at me, his face partially hidden in shadows. I could mostly see through shadows, but I doubted he could. I'm sure to him I was nothing more than a silhouette. A cute silhouette, granted. "But that's the easy part, Sam. If you deliver him to me, I will hurt him. I will do everything within my power to make him feel the pain he has made me feel. But first I will play my wife's last message to him. I want him to hear her voice. I want my wife's voice to be the last thing that son-of-a-bitch hears."

A single prop airplane flew low overhead, its engine droning steadily and peacefully. A bug alighted on my arm. A mosquito. Now there's irony for you. I flicked it off before I inadvertently created a mutant strain of immortal mosquitoes, impervious to bug spray or squishing.

Stuart went on. "But I'm going to give him a fighting chance, more than he gave my wife, the fucking coward. I'm not sure what sort of fighting chance I will give him, but I will think of something."

We were quiet. The woods itself weren't so quiet. Tree branches swished in the hot wind, and birds twittered and sung and squawked. A quiet hum of life and energy seemed to emanate from everywhere, a gentle combination of every little thing moving and breathing and existing. Sometimes a leaf crunched. Sometimes something fast and little scurried up a trunk. A bird or two flashed overhead, through the tangle of branches. Insects buzzed in and out of the faint, slanting half-light.

Stuart was looking down. A bug had alighted on his bald head, threatening its perfection. He casually reached up and slapped his head, then wiped his palm. Whew! Disaster averted. Stuart, I saw, was crying gently, nearly imperceptively.

I waited by the van. He cried some more, then nodded and wiped his eyes. His whole bald head was gleaming red.

"Let's do this," he said, nodding some more.

"You don't have to do this," I said.

"No, this is the best answer. This is the *only* answer, Sam. I want justice, but the courts won't give it to me."

"Jerry Blum is a professional killer. He's going to know how to fight. And he's going to kill you the first chance he gets."

"I have been taking boxing lessons these past few weeks, since our last talk."

"Boxing lessons where?" I asked.

"A little Irish guy. Says he knows you. Says you're a freak of nature."

"Jacky's always exaggerating," I said.

"Says you knocked out a top-ranked Marine boxer."

"The top-ranked Marine boxer had it coming to him."

Stuart looked at me. The red blotches that had covered his head were dissipating. He looked so gentle and kind and little. I couldn't imagine him taking on a crime lord single-handedly. "You are a fascinating woman, Ms. Moon."

"So they say," I said, and decided to change the subject, especially since the subject was me. "Stuart, there's a very real chance you aren't walking out of this grove alive in a few days."

That seemed to hit him. He thought about it. "Well, this is a good place to die, then, isn't it?"

"You don't have to die, Stuart," I said.

"No," he said. "I suppose I could always just shoot him before he knows what hits him. Or have a whole array of weapons at my disposal."

I said nothing. I was liking this plan less and less.

"But he killed my wife, Sam. He put fear in her. He put terror in her. He made the woman I love feel *terror*. Think about that. He made the woman I loved, the woman I had committed my life to, the woman I was going to start a family with, die in a fiery crash. I hate him. I hate him more than you could ever know. Yes, I suppose I should just step out of the shadows with a gun. I suppose I should just level it at him, and blow his fucking brains out. Maybe I still will. I don't know. But I want to beat him, Sam. With my fists. I want to hear his nose break. I want to see his blood flow. I want to punch him harder than I have ever punched anything in my life. I want to see the terror in *his eyes* when he realizes he will never get up again, that he will die in that moment."

"And when you kill him?" I asked. "What then?"

Stuart turned to me and looked perplexed by the question. He hadn't, of course, thought much beyond this. A red welt was blistering on the side of his head, where the mosquito had gotten to him a fraction before he had gotten to the mosquito. The blood-sucking little bastard.

"I don't know, Sam. I don't know." He paused, then looked me directly in the eye. "Will you still help me?"

I was never much for vigilante justice. I had taken an oath years ago to uphold the law. This was very much outside the law. This was also crazy.

These are crazy times, I thought.

"Yes," I said. "Of course."

"Thank you, Sam."

And when he said those words, a dull tingling sensation rippled through me, and something very strange happened to the air around Stuart. A very faint, darkish halo briefly surrounded his body. The black halo flared once, twice, and then disappeared.

39.

There was a knock on my hotel door.

Monica, who had been lying on her side and reading, snapped her head around and looked at me.

I stepped away from my laptop and moved over to the bedside table. I quietly pulled open the top drawer and removed my small handgun from its shoulder holster. Then I slipped quietly over and stood to one side of the door. Never directly in front.

"Who's there?" I asked.

"Detective Sherbet."

I grinned. I was quite fond of the detective, who was an aging homicide investigator here in Fullerton. Several weeks back, Sherbet had helped me solve Kingsley's attempted murder case. And spending long nights sitting together in the rain on stakeouts had gotten us close. But not so close that I had revealed to him my super-secret identity.

I unlocked and opened the door to find the big detective standing there holding a greasy bag of donuts. He was also breathing loudly through his open mouth, and I realized just the effort of walking down the hallway had been a bit much for the old guy. The donuts didn't help.

"Got a minute?" he asked.

"Do I have a choice?" I asked.

"Not really."

"In that case, come in, detective."

He came in, nodded at me, spotted Monica on the bed, and went straight over to her. He took both her hands in his one free hand. The other, of course, was holding the donuts. Monica sat up immediately when she saw him, and now she looked a bit like a teenage girl talking to her grandfather.

"Hello, Monica," he said warmly. "Are you keeping Samantha out of trouble?"

She smiled—or tried to smile—and then she burst into tears. Detective Sherbet calmly set the greasy bag on the night table, then sat next to her and put an arm around her. He made small, comforting noises to her, and they sat like this for a few minutes.

Sherbet squeezed her shoulders one more time, patted her hands, and then stood. He grabbed the bag of donuts and led me out onto the balcony. He closed the sliding glass door behind me. He then sat on one of the dusty, cushioned chairs, calmly opened the oily bag, peered inside, and selected a bright pink donut.

"I thought you didn't like the color pink," I said. "Or, for that matter, pink anything."

"I'm coming around," he said, and held up the effeminate-looking donut.

"Speaking of pink," I said. "How's your son?"

Sherbet paused mid-chew, breathing loudly through his nose. He finished the bite and looked at me sideways. "That was a low blow, Ms. Moon."

"You know I adore your son."

"I do, too," he said. "The kid's fine. I caught him trying on his mother's pantyhose the other day. Pantyhose."

"What did you do?" I asked, suppressing a giggle.

"Honestly? I went into my bedroom, shut the door, and sat in the dark for an hour or two."

"So you took it well."

"About as well as any dad would."

"You love him, though."

Sherbet reached inside the bag again. "In a weird way, I think I love him more."

"Oh?"

He pulled out an apple fritter. Remnants of the pink frosting donut were smeared on the fritter. Sherbet licked the remnants off.

He said, "The kid's going to have it tough in school, and everywhere else, for that matter. He's going to need someone strong by his side."

I patted his roundish knee, hidden beneath slacks that were stretched tight. I think Sherbet had gained 10 or 15 pounds since I'd last seen him. He didn't sound very healthy, either. As he ate the donut, I reached over and gently took the greasy bag from him. He watched in mild shock as I held my hand over the balcony railing.

"Sam, don't," he said.

"You're gaining weight, detective. And you sound like you need a respirator. These things aren't helping."

"You sound like my wife."

"You should listen to her."

I let the bag go. Five seconds later, I heard it splat nine floors below.

Sherbet winced. "I should give you a ticket for littering."

"Then give me a ticket."

He went to work on the rest of the fritter. "My hands are too sticky to write. Besides, I've got some news for you."

"Go ahead."

"We got a call from a guest staying here at the hotel."

Sherbet licked his fingers. I waited.

"She reported that a strange man had been watching the hotel for a few days now. So we sent one of our guys around and talked to him. The guy's story didn't sound kosher, and so we picked him up for questioning."

"And did he answer your questions?"

"Not at first, but, believe it or not, I can play bad cop pretty damn well."

"Bad cop? You? Never!"

Sherbet grinned. There was pink frosting in his cop mustache. I should have told him there was pink frosting in his cop mustache, but he looked so damn cute that I decided not to. "So I shake this guy down and he finally tells me his story."

"He's a hired killer," I said.

"You know the story?"

"I can guess some of it."

"So what else can you guess, Sam?"

"He was hired by Ira Lang."

Sherbet raised his thick finger and shot me. The finger glistened stickily. "Bingo."

40.

Detective Sherbet sat back and folded his hairy arms over his roundish stomach. I mostly wasn't attracted to roundish stomachs and hairy arms—or, for that matter, hairy anything. But on Sherbet, the longish arm hair and extra stomach padding seemed right. On him, oddly, both were attractive. If he had been single and I had been another twenty years older, there was a very good chance I would have had the hots for him.

He seemed to be noticing me looking at his stomach and unconsciously adjusted his shirt over it, not realizing that his padded stomach was adding to his manliness. At least for me. I can't vouch for every woman.

I suspected I had daddy issues, whatever that meant.

"He also said something else," said Sherbet. As he spoke, he looked through the sliding glass door at Monica, who was sitting on the edge of the bed and wringing her hands and rocking slightly. I couldn't be sure, but I think she was mumbling something, or singing something. The woman was tormented beyond words, and my heart went out to her.

I looked back at Sherbet, "What else?"

"He told me that Ira Lang would never give up trying to kill her, that Lang had approached many, many people in prison, and that just because we caught him once, didn't mean we were going to catch the next killer that Ira hired, or the next, or the next."

"He's going to keep coming after her," I said. "Forever, until one or the other dies."

"Which, for him, is sooner rather than later, since he's on Death Row."

"Still a few years away, though."

"Or longer," said Sherbet. "Unless, of course, you visit him again, in which case he might not survive the meeting."

"He threatened the kids."

"You are a mama grizzly."

"I'm a mama something."

Sherbet looked at me, seemed about to say something, paused, then seemed to go a different direction. "Anyway, he's out of the hospital and back on Death Row."

"Where he belongs."

"I couldn't agree more."

We were silent. Sherbet's overtaxed digestive system moaned pitifully as it went to work on the greasy donuts.

"Which reminds me," said Sherbet, reaching down and

opening his briefcase. He extracted a smallish electronic gizmo thingy. "I want to show you something."

"Your new DVD player?" I asked.

He grinned. "Sort of. It's a loaner from the department."

I watched with mild amusement as his sausage-like fingers tried to manipulate the small piece of electronic gadgetry. He picked it up and examined it from every angle.

"Everything's so damned small," he grumbled.

"Let me have a look, detective," I said. He gratefully handed it to me. I took it from him, and flipped a switch on the side and the player whirred to life.

"Should I press 'play'?" I asked.

"Yes," he said.

I set the player on the table between us and pressed "play," and a moment later I saw a sickening scene. It was footage from a security camera, looking down on two people conversing in a jail visiting room. Both were on the phone, speaking to each other through a thick, bulletproof glass window.

Sherbet was watching me closely as the video played on the little screen. I hate being watched closely. My first instinct was to turn the damn thing off and fling it over the balcony railing like I had with the donuts.

My next instinct was to make a joke or two about the video, perhaps something about the camera adding ten pounds. But there was no joking my way out of this.

I had been wrong: there *was* a camera in the jail's visiting room, perhaps hidden.

Besides, I felt too sick to joke, so instead I watched the tape with horror and curiosity. After all, it was a rare day that I actually got to see myself.

Of course, I had worn a lot of make-up that night, knowing there would security cameras everywhere, and wanting to make sure I didn't show up as partially invisible. In fact, anytime I was anywhere that had heightened video security, I made it a point to wear extra make-up.

Anyway, the video was grainy at best. No sound, either. On the tiny screen, I watched as I sat forward in the chair, speaking deliberately to Ira. Ira was leaning some of his weight on his elbows and didn't seem to blink. Ever. I hadn't noticed that before. Then again, that could have been a result of this grainy image. The camera had been filming from above, in the upper corner of the visitor's side of the room.

From this angle, I could see some of my profile, and I watched myself, fascinated, despite my mounting dread over what was about to come.

In the video, I looked leaner than I had ever looked in my life. A good thing, I guess. I also looked strong, vibrant. I didn't look like the stereotypical sickly vampire. But I knew that wasn't always the case. This was early evening. I always looked better in the early evening. Or so I was told.

And, if I do say so myself, I looked striking. Not beautiful. But striking.

As the video played out, I must have said something with some finality because I ducked my head slightly and reached for my purse. As I did so, Ira said something to me, and I immediately sat back down again. I leaned closer to the window. Ira did, too, grinning stupidly from behind the protective glass.

Now my face looked terrible. I suddenly didn't look like me. Truth be known, I didn't recognize the woman in the video clip at all. She seemed strange, otherworldly. Her mannerisms seemed a little off, too. She moved very little, if at all. Every movement controlled, planned, or rehearsed. In fact, the woman in the video seemed content sitting perfectly still.

But now I wasn't sitting still. Now I was motioning with my finger for Ira to come ever closer. And he did.

One moment I was sitting there, and the next I was reaching through the destroyed glass, grabbing Ira, slamming his face over and over into the glass. What I saw didn't make sense, either. A smallish woman reaching through the glass, manhandling a grown man, a convict, a killer. Slamming him repeatedly against the glass as if he were a rag doll.

None of it made sense; it defied explanation.

It defied *normal* explanation.

A moment later the guards burst into the room. The final clip was an image I had not seen since I was struggling under a sea of guards. It was an image of Ira's face, partially pulled through the glass, his skin having been peeled away from his forehead like a sardine can. Also, the glass was cutting deeply into his throat, and he was jerking violently, gagging on his own blood, which flowed freely down the glass, spilling over both sides of the counter, dripping, dripping. He would have surely died within minutes if he had not been given emergency help.

Sherbet reached over and easily turned off the player and sat back, watching me some more. He said, "The guards reported that you were nearly impossible to tackle to the ground. That it took three of them to do so, and even then you wouldn't go down easily."

I said nothing. For some reason, I was remembering what I had looked like in the security video. My passive expression. My inert features.

Sherbet went on, "As you can see in the video, you punched through the glass so fast that there was little or no indication that you moved at all. One moment you're sitting there, and the next you are reaching through the glass. We were certain the digital video had skipped a few seconds ahead, but the timer on it never missed a beat. One second you are sitting there. Two-tenths of a second later you are reaching through the glass. Two-tenths of a second, faster than a blink of an eye. And during those two-tenths, you are seen flinching only slightly. The broken glass itself can be seen hurling through the air at the same time you are holding Ira by the neck." Sherbet shook his head. "It defies all explanation. It defies natural law."

Beyond my hotel balcony, the sky was alive with streaking particles of light, flashing faintly in every direction. Thank God I can mostly ignore these flashing lights, or I would go crazy. Vampirism and OCD do not mix.

Sherbet looked at me. "Do you have anything to say about this, Samantha?"

I continued looking up at the night sky, at the dancing lights. No jokes, no nothing. I needed this to go away. "Obviously there was something wrong with the video, Detective."

He nodded his head as if he had expected that answer. "And the fact that you broke through the security glass?"

"The glass was already broken."

"We can't see any breaks in the image."

"You yourself said the image is not the clearest."

He nodded again. Now he turned his head and looked in the

same direction I was looking. I doubted he could see the zigzagging lights.

I asked, "Why were you shown the video?"

Sherbet chuckled lightly. "Are you kidding, Sam? The video has made its way through our entire department. Hell, half the police in the state have seen it by now. You're lucky it's not on BoobTube."

"YouTube," I said, and thought I was going to vomit. So much for keeping things on the down-low.

Sherbet went on, "You can imagine my surprise when I discovered the freak in the video was, in fact, you."

"Probably so surprised that you nearly dropped your donut," I said.

"I'm never that surprised."

"So why are you here?" I asked.

"Just chatting with an old friend."

"I'm not so old," I said.

He nodded as if that somehow answered a question he had. Now we were both silent. Inside the hotel, Monica had turned on the TV—a comedy show judging by the sudden bursts of laughter. Monica giggled innocently.

"I'm your friend, Sam."

"I know."

"Anything you tell me will remain between us."

"Anything?"

"Anything."

"That's good to know," I said.

"I worry about you, Sam."

The surprising tenderness in his gravelly voice touched me deeply, and I found words temporarily impossible to form. I nodded. My vision blurred into tears.

"If you ever want to talk," he said. "If you ever need a friend. If you ever need help of any kind, I'm always here for you. Always."

And now I was weeping.

He reached over and hugged me tight, pulling me into him, and I smelled his aftershave and the donut grease and the smallest hint of body odor. The body odor went with the manliness. After all, this was the end of a long day of crime fighting. A man *should* have a hint of body odor at the end of a long day.

His hairy arms smothered me completely and for a few seconds, a few rare seconds, I felt safe and comfortable and cared for.

Then he pulled away and carefully packed up his mini-DVD player in his scuffed briefcase. He then gave me the softest jab you could ever imagine on my chin, smiled sadly at me, and left me on the balcony.

Inside the hotel room, through the sliding glass door, I watched as he quietly spoke to Monica. As he did so, he held both of her hands in one of his. He said something else, jerked his head in my direction, and she nodded. He was reassuring her, I knew. Letting her know she was in good hands.

When the door shut behind him, Monica came out and sat beside me. She reached over and took my hand, and we sat like that for a few minutes.

Finally, I said, "They caught a guy hanging around downstairs."

"The guy Ira hired to hurt me." Her voice sounded so tiny and lost and confused. Her simple, sweet, innocent brain was trying to wrap itself around why a man she had loved at one time would actually hire another man to hurt her. To kill her.

And as we sat out there together, as we held hands and watched the quarter moon climb slowly into the hazy night sky, I suddenly knew what I had to do.

41.

I was flying. I was free. Life was good.

The moon, still about a week from being full, shone high and bright. Any thoughts of the moon automatically conjured images of Kingsley. And any thoughts of Kingsley automatically conjured images of the beast he was, or claimed to be. Admittedly, I had never actually seen Kingsley transform into a werewolf, and a part of me still wanted to believe that, in fact, he *wasn't* a werewolf, that this was all one crazy hoax. Or that he was delusional.

I mean, come on, an honest-to-God werewolf? Really?

This, of course, coming from a creature flying slowly over Orange County.

Actually, a part of me—a big part—still hoped that I was in

the middle of one long, horrific nightmare, and that I would wake up at any moment, in bed, gasping, relieved beyond words that this had all been one bad dream.

I'm ready to wake up, I thought. *Please.*

I banked to port and caught a high-altitude wind. I flapped my wings easily, smoothly, comfortably, sailing along in the heavens like an escaped Macy's Thanksgiving Day Parade float from hell.

Still, just because one monster (me) existed, that didn't necessarily mean all *other* monsters existed.

Or did it? Maybe there was some truth to everything that goes bump-in-the-night. If so, where did it end? Were there fairies? Angels? Aliens? Demons? Keebler elves? And weren't elves, in fact, fairies? Or was it the other way around?

I didn't know.

More than likely Kingsley was exactly what he claimed to be: a werewolf. I had seen the excessive hair on his forearms a few times now. I had also seen him survive five bullet shots to the head. Not to mention, he didn't even bat an eye when he found out that I was, in fact, a vampire.

Still, that didn't a werewolf make.

The moon burned silver above me. I wondered if I could fly all the way to the moon. I wondered if I could fly to other worlds, too.

Maybe someday I will fly to the moon.

Dance on the moon.

I hadn't spoken to Kingsley in a few nights now, not since I had discovered that he was, in fact, responsible for getting Ira out of jail. Jesus, how do you respect a man who does that for a living?

An icy wind blasted me, but I held my course. I flapped steadily, powerfully into the night.

Granted, not all of Kinglsey's clients were killers. Some were innocent. Some he legitimately helped. Others, not so much. Others were evil and wretched and should stay in jail. Kingsley knew damn well that he was releasing animals back into society, that he was putting killers back onto the streets.

But I had known this about Kingsley already, hadn't I? It hadn't really bothered me until now. *Until it hit close to home.*

So why should I hold it against him now? Kingsley had done nothing wrong. Hell, he was just doing his job. Like he said, if it hadn't been him, it would have been another defense attorney getting Ira out of jail.

So perhaps I should be angry at the system, not Kingsley.

Perhaps.

Below me was my destination. It was a massive multi-storied structure in Chino, California. It lay sprawled before me in a hodgepodge of auxiliary wings and isolated buildings. My target was one of those isolated buildings, located on the north side of the prison.

The Death Row Compound.

It was a large, grim, three-story structure that housed hundreds of condemned inmates. A lethal, electrified fence encircled the compound. Guard towers were everywhere.

I circled the bleak structure once, twice, getting a feel for the place. I circled again a third time, and as I did so, I felt a pull for a particular area. I focused on that area as I circled the structure again.

The pull grew stronger.

I rarely used my new-found psychic ability in this way. In the past, I just sifted through various hits as they came, rarely directing my heightened senses.

Now I directed them.

I was searching for one inmate in particular. One inmate currently housed in Death Row. One inmate whose time had come.

As I circled the structure a fifth time, I felt a very strong pull toward a corner wall on the second floor.

There he is, I thought.

I knew it. I felt it. I believed it.

But what if I was wrong?

I let the question die in me unanswered; I didn't have the luxury of being wrong.

As I circled back from my fifth fly-by, I tucked in my leathery wings and dove down, fast, the wind howling over my flattened ears.

42.

As I rapidly approached the building, I was suddenly filled with doubt. Was I doing the right thing? Should I veer off now and forget this whole crazy, horrific, stomach-turning plan? Was I even heading toward the right section of prison?

I shook my head and blasted aside the self-doubt.

The decisions had been made hours ago, and I knew, in my heart, they were the right ones.

Now, of course, it only remained to be seen if I was heading towards the correct section of prison wall.

We'll see, I thought.

I flew faster. The west side of the wall grew rapidly before me. I adjusted my wings slightly, a flick here, a dip there, and angled toward a particular spot on the second floor, near the corner of the building.

It just feels right.

I picked up more speed. The massive, oppressive structure grew rapidly in front of me. Behind those walls were the worst of the worst. Killers, cutthroats, and the not very kind. Wind thundered over me, screeching across my ears.

There was a final moment when I could have chosen to veer away, and avoid the building altogether.

I didn't veer away.

Six years ago, I was busting loan swindlers and thieves and low lives. Now I was hurling my nightmarish bat-like body at a maximum security prison.

Would this kill me? I didn't know, but I was about to find out.

My last thought before I struck the wall were: *I love you Tammy and Anthony . . . if I don't make it, I'll see you on the other side.*

The gray wall appeared directly before me. I could see the fine details of thick cinder blocks and heavy bricks. I lowered my head and turned my body slightly and struck the building with such force that I suspected the whole damn building shuddered.

• • •

I sat up in a pile of rubble.

My thick wings were draped around me like a heavy, dusty blanket. Chunks of wall continued to fall and clatter behind me. I should have been dead many times over. I should have been flattened outside on the wall itself. I should have been many things . . . but here I sat, in a prison cell, surrounded by massive chunks of cement, bent rebar, and bricks that looked better suited for a medieval dungeon.

As I sat up, and as the dust still settled around me, I closed my eyes and saw the single flame in my forethoughts. I next saw the woman in the flame, standing there impatiently, and quickly I felt the familiar *rush* towards her. . . .

And when I opened my eyes, there I was. My old self again—completely naked in a maximum secure prison in a cell on Death Row.

Outside, through the massive hole in the prison wall, I heard dozens of men shouting and a cacophony of running feet. A moment later, a siren wailed, so loud that it hurt even my ears.

I stood slowly. Dust and debris slid off my flesh.

Had I guessed right? Was this the right cell? Had my sixth sense led me to the man I wanted?

My eyes needed no time to adjust to the darkness.

There, huddled at the far end of the single cot, was Ira Lang, staring at me with wild, disbelieving eyes. *Believe it, buddy boy.* Ira was a royal mess. His face and forehead were nearly covered in bandages, and if it weren't for his signature bald head, with its deep grooves and odd lumps, I might have wondered if I had the right room. His face, what little of it I could see puffing out between the bandages, was horribly swollen and disfigured. A multitude of pins and bolts and screws were holding the whole thing together.

What a waste, I thought, *of all that work.*

There was no way of knowing what Ira was thinking. Hell, what could he be thinking? One moment he was lying in bed, no doubt plotting his ex-wife's death, or perhaps sleeping, and dreaming of her death, and the next a massive hole appears in his jail cell, filled by a hulking, nightmarish creature. A creature who then turned into a woman. A woman he loathed.

I didn't know what he thought, nor did I care.

I brushed off some dirt and smaller chunks of concrete from my shoulder and shook out cement dust from my hair. A small, grayish cloud briefly hovered around me, and then drifted to the floor.

People were shouting within the prison itself, their voices echoing along what I assumed was a long hallway just beyond. Lights were still out. No one could see me. No one, but Ira.

Now he was blinking at me hard. He then sat forward a little, straining to see through the dark and dust. He breathed raspily through his misshapen and swollen mouth.

Footsteps pounded from somewhere nearby. Sirens blasted from seemingly everywhere. A spotlight flashed through the opening, catching some of the swirling dust.

Ira's eyes widened some more. "You!" he suddenly hissed. His swollen lips never moved, and the sound itself seemed to come from somewhere in his throat. "How the fuck did you get in here?"

I said nothing. There was nothing to say. Things were about to end badly for Ira and there was no reason to joke or elaborate or waste time.

I stood there, waiting, naked as the day I was born. I was certain most of my body was silhouetted by the lights coming in through the large opening in the wall behind me. How much Ira could see of me, I didn't know, nor did I care.

I don't think he cared either.

He reached underneath his flimsy bed mattress, and then hurled himself at me. As he did so, I spotted something flashing in his hands. Growling with what could have been demonic rage, he drove the metal object—which turned out to be a sharpened spoon wired to a wooden stick—as hard as he could at my chest. Whether or not the shank qualified as a stake, I didn't know, nor did I want to find out. I caught his slashing wrist as he slammed into me hard. I stumbled back a foot or two and nearly tripped on a block of cement, but mostly I held my ground. Ira brought his knee up hard into my stomach. Air burst from my lungs. He redoubled his effort with the shank, and I might have squeezed his wrist a little too hard, because I felt bones crunching. As Ira screamed, I spun him around and reached up with one hand and grabbed his already broken jaw and turned his head as hard and fast as I could. I nearly ripped his head off. His neck broke instantly, sickeningly, the vertebrae tearing through his skin and his orange prison jumpsuit like jagged shards of broken glass. Ira shuddered violently, and then went limp. His head fell grotesquely to one side.

More sirens. More running feet. Now lights were turning on in the prison itself.

They were coming for me. At any moment, someone was going to burst into this cell. I had to leave now. But I didn't. Not yet. Instead, I found myself staring down at Ira's broken neck. I wanted to drink from him so bad that I was willing to risk getting caught. I was willing to give it all up for one drink of fresh blood.

More footsteps. Just outside of the door.

I tore my gaze away, gasping, and dropped Ira's lifeless body to the debris-strewn floor. I moved quickly over to the hole in the wall, took a deep breath, and jumped.

43.

Separating Chino and Orange is Chino State Park, which really isn't much of a park. Mostly it's a long stretch of barren hills. The hills are full of coyotes, rabbits, and the occasional mountain lion. And tonight, at least, one giant vampire bat.

I alighted on the roundish summit of the highest hill. From here I could see the lights of North Orange County twinkling beautifully. I folded my wings in and hunkered down on the lip of a rocky overhang.

The wind was strong up here, buffeting me steadily, slapping my wings gently against my side. Something small scurried in the grass nearby. That something popped its little head up and looked at me. A squirrel. It studied me for a moment, cocking its head, and then scurried off in a blink.

Well, excuse me.

The cool night wind carried with it the heady scent of juniper and sage, and I sat silently on that ledge and stared down into

Orange County and remembered the feeling of the man's neck breaking in my hands.

Grass rustled in the wind. My wings continued flapping. Grains of sand sprinkled against my thick hide. A hazy gauze of clouds crawled in front of the moon, nudged along by the high winds.

In my mind's eye, I summoned the leaping flame, summoned the woman within. I opened my eyes a few seconds later and found myself squatting over the ledge, my long dark hair whipping in the wind, my elbows tucked against my sides.

I buried my face in my hands and wanted to cry, but I couldn't cry. I couldn't cry because something had changed within me tonight, something so damn frightening I could barely acknowledge it.

But I had to acknowledge it.

Tonight, as I had held Ira's broken body close to me, I had loved every minute of it. Every fucking second of it. It had been such a thrill killing him.

Fuck.

Double fuck.

The scariest part of tonight was that his killing had felt incomplete. Foreplay, without the pay-off. I had wanted to drink from that broken neck. Desperately. Passionately. Endlessly. Draining every drop of blood.

Sweet Jesus, help me.

I reached down and picked up a handful of cool desert sand. I let the fine granules sift through my fingers and catch on the wind, to be carried off to distant lands and far shores, even if those distant lands were just Orange County and those far shores were heated pools.

I reached up with both hands and covered my head and closed my eyes and listened to the wind and the critters and the swishing grass, and stayed liked that for a long, long time. . . .

44.

I killed a man tonight.

There was a long pause, then Fang wrote: *Are you sure you want to tell me about this here?*

Big Brother?

Big something. You've stirred things up enough that someone, somewhere, might be watching and listening.

I doubt it, I wrote.

Your sixth sense?

Something like that.

You don't feel like anyone's watching?

No, I wrote. *Not yet. Maybe someday I will have to be more careful.*

But not now?

No.

Can we be careful for my benefit? he wrote.

Sure. We can pretend I killed a man tonight.

That's better. Pretend is better. Why did you pretend to kill him?

Because he was a bad man.

You can't kill all the bad men, Moon Dance. What did he do that was so bad?

I told Fang about it, writing up the case quickly, hitting just the high notes. Two seconds after I hit "Send," Fang was already writing me back.

Someone had to die, Moon Dance. Better him than your client.

We were both silent for a long, long time. I tried to imagine what Fang was doing at this moment. Probably sitting back and studying my words. Probably drinking from a bottle of beer, although he had never mentioned if he drank beer or not. *Call it a hunch.* I imagined Fang taking a long pull on his beer, maybe crossing one leg over the other, maybe reaching down and scratching his crotch, as guys are wont to do.

He wrote, *Does your client know about the killing?*

Not yet.

Where is she now?

With me in bed, sleeping.

You sleep together?

Get your mind out of the gutter. This is the first time she has slept so deeply since I have been protecting her.

People are more psychic than they realize. Perhaps a part of her knows she is finally safe.

But I had to kill a man to keep her safe.

Better him than her.

Tonight I had bought a pack of cigarettes. I opened the package and tapped one out and lit it with a lighter. The tip flared and the acrid smell of burning paper and tobacco reached my nose nearly instantly. I loved the initial scent of a freshly lit cigarette, even if I wasn't smoking it. I looked down at the burning cancer stick. It was my first cigarette since before I was pregnant. I had given up smokes completely, being a good preggo. I had thought I had given them up for good, but with the fear of cancer removed, well, what the hell? Why not? I just wouldn't smoke them around my kids. Or if I was about to kiss a man.

I've never killed before, I wrote.

How do you feel?

I sucked on the cigarette and thought about that. *I feel nothing.*

No guilt?

No. Not right now, but it might hit me later.

How did you feel when you were killing him?

Why do you ask?

It is commonly believed that vampires enjoy the kill, that vampires sort of get-off on taking another's life.

I took another hit, inhaling deeply, and came clean. *I enjoyed it so fucking much that it scares the shit out of me.*

Because you might want to do it again?

Exactly.

Did you feed from him?

No. I didn't have time. But I think I would have. I paused, then added: *And now tonight feels incomplete.*

Because you didn't feed?

Right.

You hunted your prey . . . and then lost him to the hyenas.

I shuddered at the imagery. *Something like that.*

Can you control yourself, Moon Dance?

I nodded, even though he couldn't see me nod. *Yes, the feeling passed as soon as I left the cell.*

A good thing it passed.

I nodded again. I knew what Fang meant. If the hunger hadn't passed, if it still gripped me, there was a very good chance that something else—or someone else—would be very dead tonight.

Do you think of me differently, Fang?

Do you think of yourself differently?

I finished the cigarette, stubbed it out in the glass ashtray on the night stand next to me. *I've never killed before. Anyone or anything. I always had that to fall back on. Now I don't.*

Now you're a killer.

Yes.

You killed a bad man who, if given a chance, would have hurt or killed your client.

Yes.

So, in effect, you acted in self-defense of your client.

You could say that.

You had asked him politely to leave her alone, and what did he do?

He threatened me and my children.

So, in effect, you also protected your children.

I'm not sure how serious his threats were.

The man was on Death Row, Moon Dance.

But I still killed him in cold blood, Fang.

That is something you will have to live with, Moon Dance. Can you live with it?

I guess I have to.

An eternity is a long time to carry guilt, Moon Dance.

Our fingers were both silent. I contemplated another cigarette, then decided against it. Now Fang was busy writing something, and so I waited for his response. A minute later, it came.

You did what you had to do. You acted in the best interest of yourself, your kids and your client. You rid the world of an animal who made it his life's goal to destroy other people's lives. You ask me, you had a pretty good night's work.

We were silent for a long time. I gazed out the sliding glass window at the rising moon. I turned back to my laptop.

Get some sleep, Fang.

You know I'm a night owl, Moon Dance.

Yeah, I know.

See you in a week?

My heart pounded once, twice in my chest.

Yes, in a week.

I can't wait, Moon Dance.

I bit my lip. *Neither can I.*

45.

I was boxing with Jacky.

It was late afternoon and I was tired and my hands kept dropping. Jacky hated when my hands dropped and he let me know it. I was working on a punching bag while he stood behind it, absorbing my blows. Each punch seemed to knock the little Irishman off balance a little more. I had learned not to hit the bag with all my strength, or even half my strength, as such blows would send the little man rebounding off the bag as if it had been an electrified fence.

Even in the late afternoon, with the sun not fully set and my strength nowhere near where it could be, my punches had a lot of pop behind them.

I'm such a freak.

And as Jacky worked me in three minute drills—equivalent to boxing rounds—I was pouring sweat. I sometimes wondered what my sweat would look like under a microscope. Was it the same as anyone else's sweat? Was my DNA vastly different? Would a lab technician, studying my little squigglies under the lens, shit his pants if he saw what I was really made up of?

And what was I made up of? *Who knows.*

Still, it gave me an idea. A very interesting idea. Hmm. . . .

"Hands up, wee girl. Hands—"

I hit the bag hard, so hard that it rebounded back into Jacky's face and caused him, I think, to bite his lip. Oops. He cursed and held on tight, but at least he shut the hell up about my damn hands.

Easy girl. He's just doing his job.

I was in a mood. A foul mood. I needed to punch something and punch it hard, but I didn't want to hurt Jacky. A conundrum, for sure.

And as I wrapped up the fourteenth round, finishing in a flurry of punches that made Jacky, no doubt, regret taking me on as a client, Detective Sherbet stepped into the gym. The heavy-set detective looked around, blinking hard, eyes adjusting to the gloom, spotted me, and then motioned for me to come over. I told Jacky I would be back, and the little Irishman, wiping the blood from his lip, seemed only too relieved to be rid of me for a few minutes.

I grabbed a towel and soon the detective and I were sitting on a bench in the far corner of the gym. I was sweating profusely and continuously drying myself. Sherbet was wearing slacks and a nice shirt. There was a fresh jelly stain near one of the buttons. The buttons were doing all they could to contain his girth.

"You sweat a lot for a girl," he said.

"I've heard that before."

Sherbet grinned. "It's not necessarily a bad thing."

"I've heard that before, too. So how did you find me, Detective?"

"I happen to be an ace investigator. That, and Monica told me."

I nodded. "And to what do I owe the honor?"

Sherbet was looking at me closely, and perhaps a little oddly. If I had to put a name to it, I would say he was looking at me *suspiciously*.

He said, "Ira Lang is dead."

"What a shame."

"You don't seem surprised."

"I'm too tired to seem surprised," I said. "There's a reason for all this sweat, you know."

"Don't you care how he died?"

"No."

"His neck was broken."

I made a noncommittal sound. Sherbet interlaced his fingers and formed a sort of human cup with the palms of his hands. He tapped the tips of his thumbs together. Nearby, somebody was kicking a heavy bag with a lot of power.

"It happened last night, in his cell."

I kept saying nothing. Sweat continued to drip, and I continued to mop my brow. I didn't look at Sherbet.

The detective said, "There was an explosion of some type, which blasted a hole into his cell. Crazy, I know, but someone broke into his cell."

"You're not making sense, Detective."

"None of it makes sense, Sam. Whatever broke into his cell appears to have killed him, as well. Nearly ripped his head clean off."

I listened to a woman *hi-yah-ing!* with her trainer, grunting the word with each kick or punch. I wanted to *hi-yah* her face.

"Prison officials don't know what to make of it. The explosion rocked the whole building. Everyone felt it, even those a few buildings away felt it. But there was no evidence of an explosion. It was as if a massive cannonball had been launched at the wall."

"Detective, if I didn't know better, I would say you've been sneaking in some of the hard stuff during your lunch breaks."

He mostly ignored me, although he might have cracked a smile. "They're keeping it out of the press. They have to. Something like this can't get out. Besides, what do they report?"

"So Ira is really dead?"

"Yes."

"And this story of yours is real?"

"So far, it's not much of a story. The warden and his men have no clue what happened."

"And there were no witnesses?"

"Oh, there was a witness."

"What did he see?"

"A guard working the tower heard the explosion. Everyone did. He started looking for the source and found the gaping hole in the Death Row wing. A moment later, he sees what he claims is a naked woman jump from the opening." I burst out laughing, but Sherbet ignored me and continued on. "The guard had been in the process of reporting the hole to the warden when the woman jumped out of Ira's cell. The guard was a fraction of a second too late getting back to his light. The woman disappeared and the last he reports is something quite large and black flew directly over the tower. The woman was never found."

"Was she seen on video?"

"The video they have shows the wall caving in from an unknown impact. An invisible impact. Nothing else can be seen. Nothing inside, since the angle was wrong. And not the woman or whatever the guard had seen flying overhead."

"Did he say what the woman looked like?" I asked.

"He did. Slender. Long black hair. Pale skin. Did a swan dive out of the hole in the wall."

"Any DNA evidence left behind at the scene?"

"None so far, but they're working on it."

I nodded. "And how do you know all of this?"

"Warden is a friend of mine. Ira was my business. And I'm an acquaintance of yours, a woman who had physically assaulted Ira just a week and a half earlier."

"I'm just an acquaintance? I'm hurt."

Sherbet had been watching me closely during this whole exchange. I had been watching two women sparring in the center ring. Both women looked like they would have trouble punching through a wet paper towel. One of them actually turned and ran, squealing.

"There was something else on the video."

Uh, oh. "Please tell me you didn't bring another portable DVD player," I said.

Sherbet chuckled. "No. I learned my lesson with that damned thing. I'll summarize for you. Just after the explosion, the video captured something else. Granted, the camera was only partially facing the wall—and at this time, the spotlight wasn't yet on the hole in the wall—but we can see what appears to be broken bricks and rocks rising in the air and falling on their own."

"Maybe the prison is haunted," I said.

"If I had to guess, I would say it looked like someone—or something—was getting up from the floor. And the chunks of wall were falling away from the body."

"An *invisible* body," I reminded him.

That stopped him. He ducked his head and rubbed his face and groaned a little. He turned and looked at me a moment later, and the poor guy looked truly tortured. The confident detective was gone, replaced by a man who was truly searching for answers.

"What do you make of all that, Sam?" he asked.

"I think someone invisible might have killed Ira," I said.

"Maybe. Is there anything else you would like to add?"

"It's a wild story, Detective," I said, standing. "You boys might want to keep it to yourselves. You wouldn't want the rest of the world thinking that invisible assassins are killing prisoners at Chino State Prison."

I hated lying to the detective, but I had been lying for so long now about my condition it truly came as second nature for me. Still, I hated to see the confused anguish on his face.

Sherbet nodded and looked at his empty hands. I think he was wishing a big fat donut was in one of those hands. Or both hands. The detective nodded some more, this time to himself, I think, and then stood. As he stood, his knees popped so loudly that a girl walking by snapped her head around and looked at us.

The detective looked down at me and said, "I still have questions for you, Sam."

"And I'm still here, Detective."

He nodded and left, limping slightly.

46.

Monica and I were in my hotel room, sitting crossed-legged in the center of the bed, holding hands. I had just told her that her husband of thirteen years, a husband who had twice tried to kill her and who, in fact, succeeded in killing her father, was dead. I left out the facts of his death. I told her only that her ex-husband had died suddenly.

Very suddenly, I thought.

Amazingly, Monica broke down. She cried hard for a long, long time. Sometimes I wondered if she even knew *why* she was crying. I suspected that emotions—many different emotions—were sweeping through her, purging her, one set of emotions blending into another, causing more and more tears, until at last she had cried herself out, and now we sat holding hands in the center of the bed.

"So there's no one trying to hurt me anymore?" she finally asked.

"No one's trying to hurt you," I promised. In fact, Detective Sherbet had just sent me a very choppy and error-filled text message (I could just see his thick sausage fingers hunting and pecking over his cell's tiny keyboard) that he had had a heart-to-heart with the accused hitman. The hitman, currently awaiting arraignment for conspiracy to attempt murder, understood that his employer—in this case Ira Lang—was dead.

The hotel was oddly quiet, even to my ears. No elevator sounds. No creaking. No laughing. And no squeaking bed springs.

After a moment, Monica said, "I can't believe he's dead."

I remembered the way Ira's head had dropped to the side, held in place by only the skin of his neck. I had no problem believing he was dead.

"So I guess you're done protecting me?" she added.

"Yes," I said. "But I'm not done being your friend. If you ever need anything, call me. If you're ever afraid, call me. If you ever need help in any way, call me. If you ever want to go dancing, call me."

She laughed, but mostly she cried some more and now she leaned into me and hugged me, and when she pulled away, she looked at me closely.

"Your hands are always cold," she said, her tiny voice barely above a whisper.

"Yes. I'm always cold."

"Always?"

I thought about that. Yeah, I was usually cold, except when I was flush with blood, especially fresh blood. I kept that part to myself.

"Is that part of your sickness?" she asked.

"Yes."

"I'm so sorry you're sick, Samantha."

"So am I."

She held my hands even tighter in a show of solidarity. And like a small child who's always looking to make things better, she swung my hands out a little. "Did you really mean the part about dancing?"

"Sure," I said. "I haven't been dancing in a long time."

"I'm a good dancer," she said.

"I bet you are."

There was a knock on the door, and I got up and checked the peephole and let Chad in. He came bearing flowers and wearing nice cologne. I mentioned something about the flowers being for me and he said in my dreams. My ex-partner was in love, but certainly not with me. I looked over at Monica who brightened immediately at the sight of Chad, or perhaps the flowers. Whether or not she was in love, I didn't know, but, I think, she was in a better place to explore such feelings. In the least, she was now free to love.

Chad pulled me aside and we briefly discussed Ira's crazy death. He wanted to know if I had any additional information and I told him I didn't. We both agreed Ira's death was crazy as hell and both wondered what had happened. We concluded that we may never know, and it was doubtful the prison was coming clean with all the facts. We both concluded that there was some sort of cover-up going on. The cover-up idea was mine, admittedly.

Chad looked at me, but I could tell he was itching to get back to Monica, who was currently inhaling every flower in the bouquet. Chad said, "She'll be safe with me. Always."

"That's good."

"I won't let anyone ever hurt her."

"You are a good man."

"I love her."

"I'm glad to hear it."

"Do you think she loves me?"

"I don't know," I said. "But I think the two of you are off to a great start."

He nodded enthusiastically. "Yeah, I do too."

The two of them left, together, arm-in-arm, and I suddenly found myself alone in my hotel room for the first time in a few weeks. I went out to my balcony and lit a cigarette and stared silently up at the pale, nearly full moon.

My thoughts were all over the place. I was hungry. Starving, in fact. I hadn't eaten in days. I thought of the chilled packets of blood in my hotel refrigerator and made a face, nearly gagging at the thought.

My scattered thoughts eventually settled on Stuart, my bald client. And I kept thinking about him even as my forgotten cigarette finally burned itself out.

47.

I was taking a hot shower.

No doubt it was too hot for most people, but it was just right for me. In fact, if I didn't know better, I would say that I could almost smell my own cooking flesh. Anyway, such hot showers were some of the few times that I could actually feel real heat radiating from my body. The heat would last all of twenty minutes after stepping out of the shower, granted, but beggars couldn't be choosers.

I did my best thinking in the shower, and I was thinking my ass off now. Danny had two things on me: First, he had a vial of blood he had supposedly drawn while I was sleeping (the piece of shit), and, second, he had pictures of me *not* showing up in a mirror, or on the film itself.

Allegedly.

Both items were currently with an attorney friend of his—*allegedly*—who kept them God-knows-where. How much his attorney friend knew about me and my condition, I didn't know, but I doubted Danny told him very much, if anything. Danny was good at keeping secrets. Anyway, according to my ex-husband, his attorney friend had been given strict instructions to make public the files should Danny meet an unfortunate end.

Briefly distracted by picturing Danny's unfortunate end, I allowed the image to play out for exactly six seconds before I forced myself back to reality. However much I hated my ex, he was still the father of my children.

For that, he has been given asylum.

For now.

Anyway, Danny had also threatened to go public with his evidence should I fight him on anything. And so I didn't fight him on anything. And so I accepted his harsh terms, his mental anguish.

I took it, and I took it, and took it.

I was sick of taking it.

So what could I do about it? I thought about that, turning my body in the shower, letting the spray hit me between my shoulder blades. Danny's evidence was centered around my blood. Danny assumed, wrongly or not, that my blood would be different, and that I could be proven to be a monster. He also had the pictures. I wasn't worried about those. Hell, anyone could manipulate such pictures nowadays, and I doubted anyone would take them seriously. Danny would look like a complete idiot waving those pictures around and would be laughed out of a job.

So I could dismiss the pictures.

But could I dismiss the blood? I didn't think so. At least, not yet. The blood worried me. I needed more information. And as the superheated spray worked its way over me, I thought about what I had to do.

A few minutes later, dried and dressed, I grabbed my car keys and headed for the elevator.

It was time for a Wal-Mart run.

Two hours later, I was back in my bathroom, this time pouring the contents of a plastic bottle of organic juice down the toilet. Wasteful, I know, but what the hell was I going to do with it? Anyway, I flushed the whole shebang down the pooper, as Anthony would call it, and spent the next few minutes thoroughly cleaning out the container in the bathroom sink. I used my hair dryer to carefully dry the plastic without melting it.

Once done, I carefully cleaned my right index fingernail, running hot water over it and using some hand soap. I next swabbed some rubbing alcohol on my forearm, blew the spot dry, and then carefully pressed my right fingernail into the skin of my arm. I didn't bother to look for a vein. A phlebotomist would have been horrified. Which, by the way, would be a good job for a vampire.

Except you would probably be fired for drinking on the job.

I laughed nervously at my own lame joke while I continued to work my nail deeper into my flesh. A knife would have been good, except I didn't have one handy. Besides, my nail worked just fine.

The first thick drop of blood appeared around my naturally sharpened nail. I kept pushing and slicing, and soon I opened up what I thought was a sizable incision.

Blood flowed. Languidly, granted, but flowed nonetheless. I

positioned the empty juice bottle beneath the cut and caught the first drop of blood as it dripped free. The red stuff flowed free for precisely ten seconds before the wound completely healed. No scar, nothing. Just a dried trail of vampire blood.

I repeated the cutting process, caught the fresh flow of blood, and did this eight more times before I was certain I had enough hemoglobin. Eight cuts, no marks. My arm completely healed.

Yeah, I'm a freak.

I swirled the contents of my blood in the container. A smoothie fit for Satan himself, minus the wheat grass and bee pollen, of course. As I swirled the contents, I thought hard about what I was doing. I even paced the small area in the bathroom and rubbed my neck and debated internally, and in the end, I packed the sealed juice bottle full of my dark plasma into a small Styrofoam container.

I had a friend at the FBI crime lab in D.C. A good friend. I was going to have to trust him, especially if my blood came back . . . *irregular*. And if it didn't come back irregular? Well, I had nothing to worry about, then, did I?

I'll cross that bridge when I get there.

Most important, I needed answers, and this was the best way I knew of to get them.

I next checked on the packets of Blue Ice that I had stashed in my mini-fridge's mini-freezer an hour or so earlier. The packets were hard as a rock. Good. I placed one under the bottle of blood, one each on either side, and finally one on top. I closed the Styrofoam container, taped it shut, and placed the whole thing in a small cardboard box. I next went online and found the lab's address in D.C. Once done, I placed an order for UPS to swing by the hotel tomorrow morning for a same-day delivery. The same-day delivery was going to cost me $114. I shot off an email to my friend in D.C., telling him to expect a super-sensitive package from yours truly. I ended my email with a smiley face, because I like smiley faces.

When that was taken care of, I switched outfits. I stepped out of my sweats and tee shirt and into something decidedly more slutty. Interestingly, the slutty outfit was something I had borrowed from my sister and never worn.

Anyway, I was now showing more cleavage and shoulder and

back, and when I was certain I looked like a skank whore, I grabbed my freshly packed box of blood and my car keys and headed out.

No Wal-Mart run his time.

At the front desk, I dropped off my package and filled in the front desk clerk—whose eyes had bugged out of his head and onto my boobs—to expect UPS tomorrow morning. He nodded distractedly. I wonder what he was distracted about? I made him repeat what I said twice before I headed out.

It was kind of fun being slutty. I think every woman should dress like a slut once in a while. It was very liberating.

Now, acting like a slut was something else entirely.

Maybe that would be liberating, too.

Giggling, I gunned my minivan and headed off to Colton. I had a stripper job to apply for, after all.

48.

I parked in the far corner of the dirt parking lot, near where a van was currently a-rocking. I considered a-knocking, just because I hate being told what to do, but ultimately I decided against it, since I really didn't want to know what was going on in there.

And besides, I had a job interview.

Of sorts.

Feeling ridiculous and self-conscious, I strode across the parking lot and up to the front entrance. I didn't see Danny's car, which was a damn good thing.

The bouncer was big and black and scary as hell, even to me. Suddenly insanely self-conscious, I reminded myself that my body still looked like a twenty-eight-year old.

"Excuse me," I said.

"Yeah?" He barely looked at me.

"I hear you're hiring."

He jerked a thumb behind him, toward the inside of the club. "Talk to Rick."

I winked and stepped past him and as I did so, his hand dropped down and grabbed my ass. I convulsed slightly and continued on into the dark club. I entered a small hallway, with an opening at the far end. I passed through the opening and was met by thumping music, losers, and boobs. To my left was the raised stage, which was brightly lit with hundreds of little white light bulbs. The stage was made of dark wood and was heavily scuffed. A single brass pole rose up from the center of the stage, and a single white stripper was currently cavorting around said brass pole. At the moment, just her breasts were out. Her breasts were nothing to write home about, if you ask me. They were fake and probably three or four years past their expiration date. *Don't be catty.* Glitter sparkled between her breasts and over the upper half of her chest. I wondered if any of the men cared about the sparkles. I wondered if any of the men even saw the sparkles.

The place was only half full. Men in varying degrees of drunkenness and physical deterioration sat around the raised stage. Most were drinking beer. Some were drinking shots of the hard stuff. All were staring at the woman with her glittering breasts.

I stood where I was and took in the scene. So why did Danny keep coming here? So what's the draw? Glittering fake breasts?

Maybe. Men have fought for far less.

I continued scanning, realizing I was going to need another hot shower tonight. Smoke filled the air, even though it was illegal to smoke in such establishments. I continued scanning. No one acknowledged me. No one cared that I was standing there at the entrance. A man to my left was currently getting what I assumed was a lap dance, although it looked like a lot of hard grinding. We called that dry humping in my day.

My stomach turned.

Other strippers were making their rounds, running their hands over customer's shoulders and through their hair, offering them some sort of service or another. The men smiled and politely deferred. Many wanted to touch the women, and seemed to forcibly control themselves. Touching the women, I was certain, was highly illegal in such an environment. And, of course, this strip joint was a model in adhering to local laws. *Minus the smoking and the dry humping.* One man actually took a stripper up on her offer, and she promptly led him by the hand into a back room. Another very large man stood outside the door to this room. I shuddered to think what was going on in that back room.

Oh, don't be such a prude, I thought. *It's just sex and lots of it.*

I went over to the bar. A Hispanic bartender was talking to a customer with a thick neck. The bartender didn't look at me. I finally got his attention and told him I wanted to speak to Rick.

The bartender motioned with his jaw, and the customer with the thick neck apparently wasn't a customer at all. The man turned slowly and looked at me. "Waddya want?"

"Are you Rick?"

"Sure."

"I'm looking for a job."

Rick looked me over and somehow held back his excitement. "We ain't hiring, sorry, toots."

Toots? Feeling oddly rejected, I took a gamble. "Danny told me to talk to you about a job."

"Danny, huh?"

"Yeah."

Rick took in a lot of air, which somehow made his thick neck swell out even more. He studied me some more, lingering on my chest. I took in some air and puffed it out a little. Finally, he said, "Come back tonight at eleven when Danny gets here. Then we can all talk to him. But the last I heard, we ain't hiring."

I took another shot in the dark. "But Danny said he was the owner and what he says goes."

"Look, whatever. Come back tonight and we can all have a pow wow." His gaze lingered on me some more. "Let's see your tits and see what we're working with."

I sucked in some air despite myself. I've been undercover before, but not like this. "You can see them tonight, with Danny."

He shrugged and said, "Whatever," and turned back to the bartender, and as I left, I realized that any feelings I had had for Danny, any lingering connection to the man that I had felt, had completely dried up and disappeared in that moment.

49.

I was sitting at a Denny's in the city of Corona, drinking a glass of iced water. There was a hot cup of black coffee sitting in front of me, too, but I didn't touch the black coffee. The coffee was there for show, and just to be ordering something.

I idly wondered how many vampires hung out at Denny's. Maybe none. Maybe most vampires were out running through graveyards or having blood orgies, or whatever the hell else real vampires do.

The waitress came by and glanced at my full cup of coffee and asked if I needed anything else. I smiled and said no. She smiled and dropped off the check and left. I smiled just for the hell of it.

I had a notebook in front of me, open to a blank page. I was loosely holding a pen near the top of the blank page. As I sat there, I remembered the grounding steps from last time, and performed them now. In my mind's eye, I saw myself securely tethered to the earth with glowing silver cords. Then I took in some air and held it for a few minutes and then let it out slowly.

A now familiar tingling appeared in my arm. The pen jerked in my hands. It jerked again, and now the tip was moving, writing. Three words appeared.

Good evening, Samantha.

I stared at them, knowing I should probably be freaked out, but I wasn't. Whatever the hell was going on, I didn't know, but I was game to go along for the ride.

I spoke by subvocalizing the words, that is, speaking them with barely a whisper, just loud enough for me to hear, and hopefully loud enough for my new friend to hear. But, of course, not so loud that I would get thrown out of Denny's.

"Good evening, Sephora," I said. "How are you?"

I'm well. And I can hear you just fine.

I smiled. "I'm sorry I haven't gotten back to you earlier."

There is no reason to feel sorry, Samantha. Remember, I'm always here.

"Yes, you said that. And where is here?"

Where do you think it is?

"Heaven?"

Close. Let's call it the "spirit world."

"And what's that like, the spirit world?"

Oh, you know it well.

"I do?"

Indeed, a very significant part of you still resides in the spirit world.

"You totally lost me."

You are much more than your physical body, Samantha. Do you understand the concept of a soul?

"Yes. I just don't know if I believe in the concept of a soul."

I understand. You live in this physical world of time and space. There isn't, admittedly, a lot of evidence of a soul. Then again, there isn't a lot of evidence for vampires, either. But both exist.

I nodded and sipped my ice water. The coffee had quit letting off steam. Quickly, when no one was looking, I poured a little out onto the table and then mopped it up with my napkin. Now the coffee at least appeared to have been sipped. I wrapped another napkin around the sopping wet napkin. The things I do to appear normal. Sigh.

"So some things are taken on faith, is that what you're saying?"

Something like that, Samantha.

"You can call me Sam."

I'll do that . . . Sam.

"So what did you mean that a significant part of me still resides in the spirit world?"

The easiest way to describe this, Sam, is to say that not all of your soul is focused in your current physical body. Some of your soul—a large portion of your soul, in fact—still resides in the spirit world.

"And what's it doing in the spirit world?"

Watching you, closely.

"This is a lot to take," I said. "And weird."

I understand. So take things slowly. There's time. There's no rush.

"And who are you, exactly?"

Just a friend, Sam.

"A good friend?"

The best.

"Okay, that makes me feel better," I said, and as I said those words quietly, I felt a slight shiver course along the entire length of my body. Oddly, it was a comforting sensation. There was a good chance I might have just been hugged.

I'm glad you feel better, Sam.

"I want to ask you more about me, about what I have become, but maybe that can wait until another night."

I'm always here, Sam.

And just like that, the electrified sensation left my body. I closed the notebook, put the pen back in my purse (along with the sopping napkin, which I had wrapped another napkin around), and paid my bill and left.

50.

The more I thought about delivering Orange County's most notorious crime boss into the hands of the mild-mannered Stuart Young, the more I realized I had given my perfectly bald client a death sentence.

And so I spent a lot of that night thinking about what I could do about this dilemma. I thought long and hard, and somewhere near the break of dawn, I came up with an idea.

I spent all the next evening researching the plane crash; in particular, the victims on board. Because this was a military crash and because most of the victims were key witnesses to an important trial, getting the names wasn't easy. I used every available contact I had in the federal government until finally a list was provided to me.

And once I had the list I went to work.

Two days later, on the night of the full moon, with Kingsley howling away deep inside his safe room—I hoped—I alighted on Jerry Blum's wonderfully ornate alabaster balcony.

I tucked in my massive, leathery wings, focused my thoughts on the woman in the dancing flame, opened my eyes, and found myself standing naked on his stone balcony.

Naked but not without a plan.

My talons might be hideous and scary as hell, but they were good at carrying smaller objects. And one of them, this time, had been my daughter's extra backpack. The backpack was full of, let's just say, crime fighting gear.

Below me, I heard the muted sounds of men talking quietly among themselves. So far, I hadn't been seen. The sliding glass door in front of me was wide open. Apparently, Jerry Blum never expected a giant vampire bat to alight on his balcony. From within the room, I heard the sounds of muffled snoring.

I stepped into his darkened bedroom. My eyes did not need adjusting. His spacious room was electrified with shining filaments of zigzagging light. Ghost light. Vampire light. There was a lone figure sleeping in a massive four poster bed. White gossamer sheets hung from the bed's cross beams. Very *un*crime lord-like.

The figure sleeping in the center of the bed was snoring softly, peacefully, contentedly. There was no evidence that this son-of-a-bitch stayed awake over the crimes against humanity he had committed.

There was a white cotton robe hanging over the wooden sleigh bed footboard. I slipped it on and assessed the situation. I was certain there were guards somewhere nearby, although none seemed directly outside the door. I didn't hear them, nor was my sixth sense jangling. My sixth sense was telling me that, for now, I was safe.

Carrying the backpack, I went over to the side of the bed and looked down at the man who had presumably killed Stuart's wife, a man who was powerful enough to bring down a government-owned airplane. There was a reason why I didn't confront him directly and openly. He would have gone after me and everything I loved, too. I had to hunt him from afar.

I had another reason for being here. Before I condemned the man to death, I had to know if I had the right man. Sure, Jerry Blum was a bastard. But was he the bastard I wanted?

Well, let's find out.

"Wake up, asshole," I said.

Jerry Blum's eyes popped open instantly. His hand snaked beneath his pillow, a practiced motion. He was fast, but I was faster. In a blink, his arm was pinned up over his head, driven into the mattress by my own hand, and I found myself leaning over him, staring down into his startled face. It was a face I had seen often: in the news, in books, and even in magazines. He was a celebrity crime lord, if ever there was one. Celebrity or not, he was a son-of-a-bitch. He was also quite handsome. Blum was in his late fifties, but he could have passed for his early forties. There was some gray at his temples, and there were fine lines that creased from the corners of his eyes and reached down to the corners of his mouth. These were not laugh lines. Worry lines, no doubt. Jerry Blum was not a big man, but I could feel his muscular body beneath me. Shockingly, amazingly, I found myself slightly turned on by the position I found myself in: pinning down a handsome devil in his bed in the middle of the night.

I shook off the feeling as soon as it registered.

He quit struggling, perhaps realizing it was doing him no good, and we stared at each other for a heartbeat or two. Ambient light made its way in through the open French doors. Laughter reached us from somewhere on his grounds, but not very close. A girl giggled. An airplane droned high overhead.

Jerry Blum had thin lips. Too thin for me. He breathed easily, his nostrils flaring slightly. He smelled of good cologne and something else. Lavender. But the scent wasn't coming from him. It was coming from his bed; in fact, it was coming from his pillow. I knew something about aromatherapy. One sprinkled lavender on one's pillow to ensure a good night's sleep. No doubt Mr. Blum had been plagued by a lifetime of nightmares. Or not.

"Who the fuck are you?" he finally said.

"Your worst nightmare," I said, and somehow managed to keep a straight face.

"Yeah, well, you look like a whore."

He next tried to throw me off. *Tried* being the operative word here. He grunted and grimaced and bucked, but I didn't go anywhere. Finally, he lay back, gasping, face contorted slightly in pain. I think he might have pulled something.

"You're a very bad man, Mr. Blum."

"And you're a dead woman."

"You're closer than you think," I said.

He opened his mouth to yell or scream and I used my other hand to slap his face hard. It was a nice slap, harder than I intended, but I didn't care. His eyes literally crossed, then settled back into place. A moment later, he was staring up at me in a daze.

"No yelling or screaming," I said.

Blood trickled from the corner of his mouth. My stomach lurched. I purposely had not eaten tonight.

"Did Danny Boy send you up?"

"No."

"So you ain't no whore?"

"That's a double negative, Mr. Blum."

"What the fuck is going on?"

I found myself staring down at the fine trickle of blood that glistened at the corner of his mouth. Blood was food for me, sure, but it was also something else. The right blood—fresh blood—satisfied more than hunger.

I said, "Do you want the bad news, Jerry, or the really bad news?"

He fought me again, this time harder than before, doing his damnedest to buck me off him. But I didn't move, and he quickly tired of this game, gasping. And that's when I punched him. Hard. It was a straight jab into his left eye. I put a lot of strength behind the punch. I wanted it to hurt. The sound of bone hitting bone was sickening, and the punch drove his head deep into the pillow, where the goose down bloomed around him like a white flower, no doubt dousing him in peaceful lavender.

A very small voice protested what I was doing, as it had been doing all night long. It reminded me that I was a mother, a sister, a friend, an ex-federal agent, an ex-wife, a woman with a conscience and a heart. It reminded me that I was not a killer or a murderer.

And as Jerry Blum shook his head, as a deep cut along the edge of his orbital ridge dripped blood into the corner of his left eye, I listened to that voice. I listened to its arguments and I listened to its reasoning, and I decided, in the end, that Jerry Blum had to die.

But not yet. First, I needed information. First, I had to know.

I said, "You sabotaged an airplane carrying a half dozen government witnesses. The airplane crashed killing everyone on board."

"I don't know what you're talking about."

I punched him again, harder than before, driving his head deeper into the pillow.

"Fuck," he said. Blood was now staining his pillowcase, no doubt adding a nice coppery smell to the lavender.

I didn't come here to beat up Jerry Blum. I didn't come here

to intimidate him. I came here to get a confession from him. And what happened after that, well, I was going to play that by ear.

"Tell me about the plane, Jerry," I said.

"Do you have any idea who I am?"

"You're Jerry Blum. Orange County's biggest crime lord. You are untouchable. Your enemies shudder in your presence. You've destroyed lives and businesses and spread fear far and wide. Did I miss anything?"

"Yeah, I'm rich. I can triple whoever's paying."

"Paying me to do what?"

"To kill me."

"They didn't pay me to kill you, Mr. Blum. I tossed that in as a freebie. Pro bono, so to speak."

He lay back in his bed, bleeding. His nose was perfect, probably surgically altered. His teeth were perfect, probably dentally enhanced. He let out a long breath. His breath was tinged with the scent of blood. In fact, blood wafted up from him everywhere. He wasn't bleeding a lot, granted, but a little bit of blood registered deeply with me.

I'm a shark, I thought, *smelling blood in the water dozens of miles away.*

"Tell me about the plane," I said. The blood, quite honestly, was driving me fucking crazy.

"Go to hell, cunt."

"Tell me about the plane, Jerry."

He threw his face at me, lips pulled back, cords standing out on his neck. His eyes veritably bulged from their sockets. He fought and fought and screeched in frustration and anger and pain, and when he spoke spittle shot from his mouth in a steady stream. "Of course I killed them, you fucking freaky bitch! Just like I'm going to kill you. You can't stop me, no one can stop me. I'm invincible. I kill who I want, when I want, and how I want. You understand, you crazy bitch? You understand? You're a dead woman. Dead! And so is your client and anyone else you fucking know! And that's after I fuck you every which way, you fucking whore! How dare you come into my house, how dare you come in here and—"

And that's as far as he got.

"Enough," I said.

I flipped Jerry Blum over and pulled his hands behind his back. I reached into my bag of tricks and pulled out a pair of handcuffs. I cuffed the bastard and then pulled a black, breathable hood over his face. I cinched it tight. He fought me like a demon on crack, bucking and twisting, but it did him no good.

When I was finished, I hauled him to his feet and threw him over my shoulder. I carried him to his beautiful alabaster balcony, where I set him down, along with my backpack, and ditched the robe. I closed my eyes and saw the flame and the hulking winged creature. When I opened my eyes again, I was easily five feet taller than I had been just seconds before. Jerry was still pinned beneath me, this time beneath one of my massive talons.

My hands in this form are quite dextrous; unfortunately, they're also attached to my wings, just like a bat. Still, I used my hands to drape the backpack over one of my talons. Once done, I gripped Jerry Blum by his shoulders. No doubt my claws hurt like hell.

I flapped my wings hard, causing a thunderous downdraft that whipped Jerry's hair crazily. He screamed and fought me some more, but had no clue what was happening to him. And as I got a little air under me, I adjusted my grip on the crime lord, using both talons now. I flapped my wings harder and now I was rising up into the night sky, Blum dangling beneath me like a kangaroo rat.

51.

We were in the predetermined clearing in Carbon Canyon. One of us unwillingly.

Still wearing the black hood, Jerry Blum was handcuffed to a tree branch, his hands high above him. He had cussed and hollered the entire twenty-minute flight here. I flew on, ignoring him, catching a high altitude current that made flapping my wings a breeze. Once we had arrived in the clearing, I had transformed again and slipped into a little black dress that I had included in my bag of tricks. Blum was full of questions and vitriol and hate. I ignored all of his questions as I cuffed him to the tree branch.

Now from my bag of tricks, I removed my cell phone. I selected eleven recipients and sent out a single text message. I next made a call to my client, Stuart Young. In so many words, I told Stuart that the eagle had landed. I had our man. Stuart had paused, swallowed hard, and said he would be here as soon as possible.

I left Jerry Blum alone, secured to the tree. Jerry Blum, as far as I was concerned, had dug his own grave. From my backpack, I fished out a pack of cigarettes and fired one up and inhaled deeply. I had stepped out of the clearing and into a thicket of twisted trees. As I exhaled, I looked up at the full moon, now just a silver mosaic through the tangle of branches. My thoughts were empty. My heart was empty. I felt empty and cold. I listened to the sounds the forest made, and the sounds of my own distant beating heart. I finished the cigarette and immediately lit another just to be doing something. Jerry Blum bellowed angrily from the clearing behind me, but I ignored him. *He dug his own grave.* I finished the second cigarette but decided against a third. I finally leaned a shoulder against a dusty tree trunk and closed my eyes and stayed in that position until I heard the crunch of tires from somewhere nearby.

I met Stuart on the dirt road, about a hundred yards away from the clearing. Stuart did not look good. He looked sick and scared and probably had to go to the bathroom.

"I have to go to the bathroom," he said.

I nodded and he dashed off. A moment later, he came back, zipping up. He said, "So he's really here?"

I nodded, watching him. "Yes."

"I want to see him."

I nodded again and led Stuart through the forest and into the clearing, which was dappled in bright moonlight. Jerry Blum heard us coming and raised his head.

Seeing a man chained to a tree was no doubt unnerving to Stuart. He immediately stopped in his tracks. "Oh, my God."

Blum shouted, "Who's there, goddammit?"

I ignored Blum. Instead, I took Stuart's hand and walked him over to the shackled crime lord. I removed the hood and Blum shook his head and squinted. I handed Stuart a flashlight from the backpack and he clicked it on and shined it straight into Blum's face, who turned away, blinking hard and spitting mad.

"Goddammit! Who the fuck are you two? What the fuck is going on? How the fuck did I get here?"

"Shut the fuck up, Jerry," I said.

"Fuck you, cunt." He spit at me, tried to kick me. He succeeded in only losing his footing and hanging briefly by the cuffs.

Stuart said nothing. He simply stared in open-mouthed wonder at the man hanging from the tree. Still open-mouthed, Stuart then turned to me.

"You really did it," he said.

I said nothing. I was watching Stuart. My client still did not look good. He looked, in fact, a little hysterical. I covered Jerry's head again and led Stuart away. Blum screamed and repeatedly threw his body against the tree trunk. Stuart looked back but I pulled him along through the high grass to the far end of the clearing. Once there, we stopped.

"And no one knows he's here?"

"No one who matters."

Stuart nodded. His wild eyes were looking increasingly erratic.

"Are you okay?" I asked Stuart.

"I don't know if I can do this, Sam."

"I understand."

Stuart was shaking. He ran a hand over his bald head. "I hate him so much, so fucking much. I still can't believe he's here. How did you do it?"

I shook my head; Stuart nodded. The wind picked up considerably, swishing the branches along the edge of the clearing and slapping the tall grass around our ankles.

And through the wind, I heard many more vehicles driving up along the dirt road. One after another. Stuart didn't hear them. Stuart was lost in his own thoughts. Stuart also didn't have my hearing.

"You don't have to do this," I said.

Stuart nodded. Tears were in his eyes.

"I hate him so fucking much."

We were silent some more. The wind continued to pick up, moaning through the trees. I heard footsteps coming. Many footsteps.

I said, "What if I told you that you didn't have to do this alone, Stuart?"

"What do you mean?"

"What if I told you that Jerry Blum had wronged many people the day he killed your wife? What if I told you that many, many people share your desire for revenge."

"I don't understand."

I waved my hand and in that moment ten figures stepped out of the woods. Ten solemn, white-faced figures. I recognized the faces, all of whom I had met in the past few days. All of whom I had easily convinced to be here tonight. Not one needed prodding. All had jumped at the opportunity.

"Jerry Blum is a bad man, Stuart. He would have hurt you tonight. He would have killed you."

"Who are they?"

"People like you, Stuart, all victims of Jerry Blum."

"What's going to happen tonight?"

"I don't know," I said. "I'm leaving that to all of you."

Stuart looked at me with impossibly wide eyes. He then looked at the others, most of whom nodded at him. They were all here. Mothers, wives, husbands, and children. All had lost loved ones in the crash.

I squeezed Stuart's hand and then left him there with the others. I went over to Jerry Blum and uncuffed him. I took his blindfold off and led him over to the center of the clearing.

"Who the fuck are those assholes?" said Jerry. He only fought me a little.

I didn't answer him. Instead, I turned and walked away, leaving Jerry alone in the light of the full moon. Off to the side of the clearing, I quickly slipped out of the dress and shoved my cell and cuffs and keys inside the backpack.

I had just transformed when I heard the first gunshot. And as I leaped high into the air and flapped my wings hard and flew away from the isolated canyon, I heard shot after shot after shot.

• • •

I asked Stuart a few days later what had happened on the night of the full moon, but he wouldn't give me an answer. And neither would the others.

I had been wrong about Jerry Blum. He didn't dig his own grave. I very much suspected the others had done it for him, leaving Orange County's notorious crime lord buried deep in that forgotten clearing.

52.

I don't get exhausted, but I get mentally fatigued, and tonight had stretched me thin. I was looking forward to coming home to my empty hotel room, closing the curtains tight, and sleeping the day away, dead to the world.

But as I unlocked the door to my room with the keycard and stepped inside, I was immediately met by two things: the first was a fresh breeze that was blowing in through my wide open balcony door, and the second was a nearly overwhelmingly foul stench.

Last time I had been surprised in such a fashion, a vampire hunter had been waiting for me. And what was waiting for me now, stunned even me.

Alert for silver-tipped arrows or silver ninja stars or silver anything else hurling at me, I cautiously entered my hotel room.

I moved cautiously down the very small hallway. To my left was a closet. The door was partially open. I knew immediately there was no one inside. No, whoever was in my suite was in my living room or sleeping area.

The lights were out. Squiggly, rapidly-moving prisms of light shot wildly through the air. These super-charged particles of light illuminated my way, as they always did.

I took another step into my suite.

I was approaching the end of the short hallway. Around the corner to the right would be my bed and the desk. Around the corner to my left were sitting chairs and a round table. Presently, from my position, I could not see very far around either corner.

Directly before me, at the far end of my suite, I could see the sliding glass door. Or what had once been the sliding glass door, as most of the glass was presently scattered across the carpet. The heavy curtains shifted in the breeze, swaying slightly.

I took another step.

My sixth sense was buzzing. The fine hairs on my neck were standing on end. The foul stench grew stronger. Something rancid was in my hotel room.

No, something *dead* was in my room.

I took another step. I was now at the end of the hallway. To my right, I could see the foot of the bed. To my left, was a section of the round table. The stench, I was certain, was coming from my right, on the side where my bed and desk were located.

I paused, listening.

Someone was breathing around the corner. Deep breaths, ragged breaths. My heart thumped fast and hard. I suddenly wished I had a weapon.

You are a weapon, I reminded myself.

I continued listening to the breathing. A slow sound. A deep sound. A rumbling sound. Something big was in my living room. Either that or someone parked a Dodge Charger on my bed.

I stepped around the corner.

The thing standing in the corner of my room was horrific and nightmarish, and if I wasn't so terrified, I would have turned and ran or peed myself. Instead, I stopped and stared and still might have peed myself a little.

The thing was watching me closely, almost curiously, its head slightly angled, its pointed ears erect and alert. Its lower face—or muzzle—projected out slightly, but not quite as long as a traditional dog, or wolf. More like a pug.

Standing there in the corner of my room, the thing looked like a long-forgotten Hollywood movie prop.

Except this movie prop was breathing deeply and growling just under its breath. A low growl. A warning growl. The same kind of growl a guard dog would give. Except this growl was terrifyingly deep.

Blood was dripping from its face. Blood, and something else. Something blackish. Something putrid. I suddenly had a very strong sense that it had dug up a body and feasted on it. In fact, I was certain of this. How I was certain of it, I didn't know. Maybe my sixth sense was evolving into something more.

Or maybe because this thing smells like the walking dead.

I made sure my back was to the open glass door. I wasn't sure what I would do if the thing attacked, but having a readily available escape route seemed like a damned good idea. And if I had to take flight, well, I could kiss these clothes goodbye. They would burst from my body in an instant.

A part of me felt like this was a dream. Hell, *a lot* of me felt like this was a dream.

We continued staring at each other. I continued wanting to pee. The creature continued breathing deeply, throatily. I could have been standing next to a tiger cage.

And that's when the beast took a step toward me.

Every instinct told me to run—and to keep running until I had put hundreds of miles between me and this *thing*. But I didn't run. Something kept me in that room. That something was curiosity.

Curiosity killed the cat. Or, in this case, the vampire.

It took another step toward me. A very long step. One that spanned nearly the entire length of my bed. As it walked, it sort of tucked in its shaggy elbows.

The thing, I was certain, was a werewolf. And that werewolf, I was certain, was Kingsley.

When I transformed, I was all there; meaning, I was still me, and I could control all of my actions and emotions. I doubted Kingsley would have chosen to dig up a grave and feast upon a corpse, if that was, in fact, what he had done. So that alone suggested Kingsley was not all here. Meaning, something else was controlling this beast. But enough of Kingsley was in there to find his way to my hotel room tonight.

What happened to the panic room? And where was Franklin the Butler who, I knew, looked after Kingsley during these monthly transformations?

You ask a lot of questions, vampire.

The words appeared in my thoughts, directly inside my skull, as if someone had whispered them straight into my ear cavity. I didn't jump, but I did step back.

"Who said that?"

As I spoke, the creature cocked its head to one side, its pointed ears, moving independently of each other, shot forward. Cute on a dog, not so cute on a hulking, nightmarish creature.

Who do you think said it, vampire?

The creature stepped forward. Its movements were graceful and surprisingly economical. It only moved when it had to. Nothing wasted.

"Kingsley?" I asked.

Kingsley's not home.

"Then who is this?"

The werewolf stepped closer still, and the wave of revulsion that emanated from it nearly made me retch.

I reminded myself that I was a terrifying creature of the night, able to strike fear in the hearts of even the most hardened criminals.

You look afraid, vampire, said the voice in my head.

Up close, the creature looked even more hideous. And up close, it smelled even worse.

"Who are you?" I asked again. My voice shook.

Does it matter?

"Yes. I want to know where my friend is."

Oh, he's in here, vampire.

"Where is here?"

In the background, vampire. Watching us.

Moonlight reflected off the creature's thick brow and slightly protruding muzzle. Long, white teeth gleamed over black gums. A low, steady, rumble came from its throat and chest. The creature seemed incapable of remaining silent. A low growl seemed to continuously emanate from it. I fought a nearly overwhelming desire to step back. But I didn't.

You are brave, vampire.

"And you smell like shit."

The werewolf tilted its head. One of its ears revolved out to the side, hearing something that was beyond even my own keen hearing.

Kingsley has been wanting to see you, vampire. Very badly. But he has refused to do so out of pride. But I thought I would take it upon myself to visit you tonight. I thought it was time to make your acquaintance. There are, after all, so few of us.

"Us?"

The undead.

"Fine, so you've met me. Now who the fuck are you?"

The werewolf growled a deeper growl, a sound which seemed to resonate from deep within its massive chest.

I am called Maltheus.

I did my best to wrap my brain around what I was hearing. "You are a separate entity that lives within Kingsley?"

Not always within, no. But I do visit him once a month. He's such a gracious host.

I sensed sarcasm. "And what, exactly, are you?"

I am many things, vampire.

"How is it that you can take possession of Kingsley? How is that you can turn into this *thing?*"

This thing, as you call it, is my physical incarnation. And I took possession of my dear fellow Kingsley because he allowed me inside him.

"He *wanted* to be bitten by a werewolf?"

No. He wanted death. He wanted revenge. He was full of hate and despair and emptiness. The voice paused; the werewolf stared down at me, breathing heavily through a partially open mouth. Its lips were pure black. *I exist to fill that emptiness.*

"I don't understand."

You will someday, vampire. And we will meet again. Of that, you can be sure.

In a blink of an eye, moving faster than any creature that size had a right to move, the werewolf turned its massive shoulders and dashed through the shattered door and leaped off the stucco balcony.

I ran over to the edge and watched as it dropped nine stories, landing softly and gracefully. It didn't throw back its head and let loose with an ear-splitting howl, nor did it dash off into the night on all four legs.

No, it simply sniffed the air, scratched behind its ear, and walked calmly away.

53.

It was late and my IM chat window was open. So far, there was no sign of Fang.

I had spent the past three hours cleaning my room, picking up glass and scrubbing clean the blood and other bodily fluids that had been dripping from Kingsley. With the place clean, now all I had to do was come up with a convincing story about the broken glass. I decided on going the drunken, divorced mother route. I had been drinking on the balcony, when I stumbled through the glass door. Could happen to anyone.

Now, with my hotel suite smelling like coconut butter and rotted corpse, I was sitting in front of my computer, waiting for Fang to log on.

I buzzed him again.

And again.

Twenty minutes later, I saw what I wanted to see: A flashing pencil had appeared in the message box. Fang was writing me a message. I felt overjoyed and relieved. I had come to rely on Fang more than he realized.

More than *I* realized.

A moment later, his words appeared: *You are persistent tonight, Moon Dance.*

I have news.

Of that, I have no doubt.

Were you asleep?

I might have been dozing, but I always have time for you, Moon Dance.

My heart swelled. *Thank you, Fang.*

He typed a smiley face and then asked: *So what's your news?*

I saw a werewolf tonight.

Your old client and new lover?

I hesitated. *Yes.*

Tell me about it.

And so I did. I relayed everything that had happened and what was said to the best of my ability. As I typed, Fang waited patiently. Then again, he might have fallen back to sleep.

Nope. I had barely sent my message, when his response appeared nearly instantly.

I'm not surprised. It is commonly believed that werewolves feast on corpses.

Well, if he thinks he's ever going to kiss me with those ghoulish lips again, he's got another think coming.

Isn't that a bit like the teapot calling the kettle black?

I don't eat corpses, Fang.

Point taken. So you say this entity claimed to be living inside your friend?

Yes, I wrote.

Fang paused, then wrote: *There are some who believe that werewolves and other such creatures of the night are, in fact, the physical manifestations of highly evolved dark masters.*

I'm not sure I'm following.

These beings, these powerful entities, are forbidden to incarnate on earth. But they have found, let's call them, loopholes.

And one such loophole is to incarnate once a month, as werewolves.

Exactly. But they don't consider themselves wolves. You are, in fact, looking at the physical expression of the darkest of evils.

I shuddered.

And how do they find . . . a host?

No doubt the usual ways. Being bitten by such a being would be one way. But generally, and I think your ex-client is proof of this, they attach themselves to a willing host.

I'm lost, I wrote. *As usual.*

I have no doubt that your ex-client, the attorney, did not pointedly ask to be a werewolf. But he projected weakness, anguish, pain, despair. Such extreme emotions attract the attention of these highly evolved dark masters. It was just a matter of time until a werewolf-like creature found its way to your friend. Either that, or death.

So they saw my friend as a good host.

You could say that.

So, in effect, he is possessed.

Exactly. But he's possessed by something very dark, and very, very evil.

The sun will be up soon, I wrote.

Spoken like a true vampire. So are we still on for Sunday night?

That was two days from now. My heart slammed in my chest. *Yes.*

Where would you like to meet, Moon Dance?

You are in Southern California? I asked.

Yes.

Are you familiar with Orange County?

Yes.

Do you know where the Downtown Grill is in Fullerton?

There was a pause. *Yes.*

Okay, I will see you there at midnight.

The vampire's hour. So midnight it is, Moon Dance.

Goodnight, Fang.

You mean good morning.

Ha-ha.

Sweet dreams, Moon Dance. See you soon.

54.

I got up earlier than normal to take care of the sliding glass door with hotel management.

Groggy, weak, and feeling less than human, I walked the short, stocky and highly disapproving woman through my fictional drunken escapade last night, which culminated in me supposedly crashing through the glass door. She clucked her tongue numerous times, and in the end, after taking a few photographs of the damages, she seemed to buy my story. An hour or so later, a work crew stopped by and replaced the glass.

As they worked, I wondered if it was finally time for me to find my own place. Of course, I already had my own place. It was the house Danny and I had purchased together. The house he was currently using to fuck his secretary in.

I had been at the Embassy Suites for two months now. Surely, it was time for a change. And with that thought in mind, as I sat in the center of my bed while the work crew positioned the big piece of glass in the balcony doorway, I realized what I *hadn't* seen in the seedy strip club in Colton.

Heart pounding, I fired up my laptop. I jacked into the hotel wireless service and did a quick search for the club. As I expected, there was no mention of it. No mention of it, in fact, anywhere.

As the work crew finished, one of them suggested that next time I fall *away* from the glass door when I was shit-faced drunk. I told him I would keep his suggestion in mind (asshole), and when they were gone, so was I.

Covered in sunscreen and heavy clothing, sporting my cool sunhat and shades, I grabbed my keys and hit the road.

Along the way to the Riverside County Courthouse, my cell phone rang. It was Kingsley. I picked up immediately.

"Hey," he said.

"Hey."

"I'm sorry about last night," he said.

"Last night was a little terrifying. At least I no longer doubt that you really are a . . . you know what."

Kingsley hated for us to talk about our super-secret identities on the phone. He actually laughed. "This coming from a . . . you know what."

"We all have our hang ups."

He was silent as I drove along the congested freeway. Mercifully, the sun was behind me.

Finally, Kingsley said, "Am I to understand you took care of my client the other night?"

"You are to understand anything you want."

I could almost see him nod. "I should be very pissed off at you for that."

"You should thank me. I lessened your workload."

"That was very reckless, Sam."

"These are reckless times."

He was silent some more. I suspected he was in his massive office, surrounded by piles of files.

"So what do we do, Sam?"

"About what?"

"About us."

"I don't know," I said.

"I like you. A lot."

"I'm a very likable person," I said.

He chuckled. "Sometimes. But now you're being distant and cold."

"I feel distant and cold, so no surprise there."

"It's because of what I do," he said.

"I hate what you do."

"Sometimes I help people, Sam. Not everyone belongs in prison."

"And not everyone should be freed on a technicality."

"We can argue this forever," he said.

"And forever is a very long time for . . . us."

He chuckled lightly again. "Can I see you tomorrow night?"

"Tomorrow night I have plans."

He made a noise on the phone. I know he wanted to ask who my plans were with but he held back. "I see. Perhaps next week?"

"Perhaps," I said.

"I'll call you later."

I said okay and we hung up.

My cell rang again. I checked the number and ID on the faceplate. The number came up "Restricted." It was either a creditor or one of my pals with law enforcement. My finances had gotten a little out of hand these past few months. My hotel room hadn't been cheap and Danny wasn't helping me. I took my chances and clicked on.

"I don't have any money," I said.

"Hello? Sam, it's Mel."

Oops. It was my DNA biologist friend from the FBI Crime Lab. Definitely not a creditor, although he did accept deposits in blood. My heart immediately slammed hard against the inside of my ribs. His call could only mean one thing.

"What's shaking, Mel?"

"I have the results to your blood work up, Sam."

I took a deep breath, held it, and then said, "Okay. Lay them on me."

55.

Danny's firm took up the entire second floor of the office building. The building itself wasn't much to write home about. Squarish and ugly and immediately forgotten. A couple of years ago, I had jokingly referred to the building as "Ambulance Chaser Headquarters," and Danny had refused to speak to me for two days.

The big baby.

With the sun still a few hours from setting and myself not at my strongest, I climbed the exterior stairs and pushed through the smoky glass doors. Four leather chairs sat empty to one side of the door. A thick, square mohair carpet spanned the length of the office. A bubbling fountain gurgled in the corner to my left, projecting an aura of zen-like calm in these troubled, accident-prone times. On the walls were the paintings I had picked out with Danny at a swap meet years ago. Big, fake, cheap stuff.

And directly in front of me, sitting behind a kidney-shaped desk, with her shiny, tan legs crossed and absently texting on her cell phone, was my ex-husband's new secretary. The woman he had cheated on me with. The woman he was currently fucking. The woman he entertained at our house, in our bedroom, in our bed. The woman he had introduced to our children.

She had known that he was married. No doubt he had made me out to be a monster. No doubt he had painted a picture of an unfit mother. Unfit or not, she had chosen to cheat with a married man. My married man.

She set her phone aside, uncrossed her thin legs, and gave me a big smile. She was about to ask if she could help me, but then stopped short. Her mouth sort of hung open and her eyes narrowed. She was an ugly woman, I thought. I had no clue what Danny saw in her. Face too thin, skin too tan, boobs too fake. On second thought, I saw exactly what Danny saw in her. She was the opposite of me.

She jumped up and moved quickly around her desk, blocking my path. She crossed her arms under her fake breasts. Her nails were red and long. She looked like a whore.

"What the fuck are you doing here?" she said.

I smiled and, without breaking stride, punched her straight in the face. She flew backward, bounced off the desk, spun around and landed on her face. On her nose, in fact. She moaned. I wasn't at full strength and I certainly didn't hit her as hard as I could, but she would remember me.

Danny appeared from his office door, open-mouthed. He looked at me and then at his secretary on the mohair rug. "Sam, what the fuck is going on?"

And as he stepped out of the office, I punched him hard in his stomach. He *oofed* nicely and doubled over. I grabbed him by the collar and threw him back into his office and shut the door behind me.

56.

I pushed him down into one of his leather client chairs and sat on the edge of his executive desk, which was big enough to land an F-17 on.

Danny still hadn't gotten his breath back entirely. His face was purplish and contorted, and he was staring at me with frightened, angry eyes.

I kicked my legs pleasantly and whistled absently, waiting for his lungs to kick start again. Finally his short rasping breaths turned into longer rasping breaths. And when they did, words vomited from his mouth. "What the fuck are . . . who the hell do you . . . you have royally fucked yourself . . . how dare you attack. . . ."

"Are you quite done, asshole?"

He sat up straighter, took in a long, agonized breath. "I demand to know what's going on."

"Well, since you asked so nicely."

I grinned and continued swinging my legs. I shouldn't have been enjoying this so much, but I was.

He looked at me with very confused, very dark eyes. Danny was not a big guy. Just a few inches shy of six foot, he was also too skinny for me, but I never told him that. I had always liked my men a little beefier, which is why Kingsley had been so damn intoxicating.

He said, "Do you have any idea the shit you just landed yourself in, Sam?"

"About as much shit as you landed in, dickhead."

His eyes narrowed. "What the hell does that mean?"

There was a low moan from outside the closed door, followed by some sobbing. His secretary lying there on the carpet, crying, probably wasn't good for business.

"You're the owner of The Kittycat," I said. "Perhaps the world's sleaziest strip club. In fact, you're the sole owner of it."

The color drained from his already pale face. He tried to sit up. I told him to stay where he was and he did so.

"I don't know what you're talking about, Sam."

"Of course you don't. Deny everything, right? It's the losers' motto."

"Sam, you're talking nonsense."

"Am I? All I have to do is make one call to any number of my friends in law enforcement, and they will come down hard on The Kittycat."

"Just wait a second, Sam. Whether or not I own the business is beside the point. It's hardly a crime to run a strip club."

I crossed my arms under my chest. My own natural bosom didn't push up unnaturally through the top of my own blouse and I was proud of that.

"It's a crime, Danny, when said business—in particular, a *strip club*—operates without a license."

"Shit."

I grinned and sat back. I swung my legs some more. Seeing Danny squirm had just become my favorite new hobby.

"I'm in the process of getting a license—"

"*In the process of* and *having one* are two different things, Danny. And you know that. But you couldn't wait, could you? You just had to open the doors to that shithole of sleaze."

He said nothing. I could see his pressed shirt pulsating slightly over his hammering heart. His mind was spinning in ten different directions. But there was no getting out of this one. Not for him.

"What the fuck happened to you, Danny?" I asked. "How does a respectable family man end up owning that dungeon of filth?"

"I don't have to answer you."

"Hey, I'm not the cops, Danny boy. There are no Miranda rights and I'm not wired. This is just between you and me."

"Well, you don't know what the fuck you're talking about. Now, can I check on Sugar?"

I laughed into my hand. "Sugar?"

"Not now, Sam—"

"Her name is Sugar? Honest to God? Is she also one of your filthy strippers, Danny? Sucking up to the boss in more ways than one?"

"Okay, you caught me. So sue me for looking outside of our shitty marriage for something more. So sue me for jumping on a chance to own something that's going to make me a lot of money."

"You're pathetic."

"And you're a living nightmare. What the fuck do you want, Sam?"

I studied him long and hard. Sugar had quit sobbing from the other side of the door. Sugar wasn't happy.

I said, "I want the house and I want the kids."

He laughed. "No way. There is absolutely no fucking way I'm letting you around our kids unsupervised."

"I don't think you understand the quagmire of shit you find yourself in, Danny. If I say the word, the hammer comes down on your disgusting enterprise. You're looking at an ungodly amount of fines, not to mention automatic disbarment. Oh, yeah, and the world will see you as the slimeball you've turned out to be. And I can't wait to see what your mother thinks about all of this, too." I paused, shaking my head. "No one stops to consider their mothers. It's a pity."

"You forget, Sam. If you say anything, I will expose you for the monster you really are."

I slipped off the desk and approached him slowly. I squatted down between his legs, resting my elbows on his knees. He was in a very, very vulnerable position.

"Expose me for what, Danny? Having a rare skin condition?"

"I've got a vial of your blood, Sam. It's in a safe deposit box. If anything happens to me, my attorney has been notified to have that blood immediately tested. Your secret will be out. You will be exposed to the light for the freak that you are."

"Perhaps you should have already tested the blood, Danny."

"What does that mean?"

I stood again and removed a folded piece of paper from my back pocket. Earlier, I had stopped at a Kinko's and printed out Mel's emailed test results.

"What's this?"

"My blood test results."

"What the fuck are you talking about?"

"I had my blood tested, Danny. A variety of tests, too. The technician was asked to look for any irregularities. Look at the results yourself."

He quickly read through the report. Attorneys, if anything, were great scanners.

"As you can see," I said. "It says *no irregularities found*. My blood is normal, Danny. *Normal*. In every way. So have it tested. Do what you want with it. But I'm taking back my house, and I'm taking back my kids, and you damn well better believe that no sleazeball porn king who brings whores home to my kids will ever—*ever*—be welcomed into my house again. You have until eight p.m. tonight to move your ass out, and anything you leave behind will be trashed. Do you understand?"

He looked at the paper some more, then looked directly across at me, since I was once again squatting down at eye level. "So you won't report me?" he said.

"You disgust me."

And I leveled a punch directly into his groin. As he rolled out of the chair, gasping, I walked out of his office and didn't even look down at his bleeding whore.

57.

It was 8:30 p.m. and Danny had just left.

I gave him the extra thirty minutes out of the goodness of my cold heart, since, after all, he had been working so hard to get his shit moved out. The kids were off eating pizza with Mary Lou, my sister. They would come home to find their daddy gone. Traumatic for them, I know, but they would adjust. They had to adjust.

Before Danny drove off, with his Cadillac Escalade filled with all his crap, he informed me that he had talked Sugar out of pressing charges, mostly by offering her a massive raise. I reminded Danny that I wanted a massive raise, too, in the form of a butt-load of alimony and child support.

As he sat behind the wheel, looking utterly exhausted, he leveled a glare at me that was supposed to make me curl into the fetal position. I didn't curl.

"This isn't over, Sam."

"I certainly hope not," I said. "I'm having too much fun."

He shook his head and drove off. I watched him make a left turn and disappear out of sight, and I realized I didn't even care where he ended up.

Smell you later, asshole.

I flipped the phone open and called my sister. "Bring them home," I said.

We were all eating hot fudge sundaes that were oozing with whipped cream and chocolate syrup. And, yes, some of us were only *pretending* to eat. So far, my kids had not caught on that I could not eat like them. Mostly, they just saw mommy not eating at all, and when I did, the spitting-it-back-into-a-cup routine worked wonders.

Even with all the spitting, some of the ice cream and fudge made it down my esophagus, which caused some seriously uncomfortable cramps. After a few minutes of pretending to eat my ice cream, I finally ditched the bowl and emptied the cup-o'-spit down the garbage disposal. Mostly, no one noticed me, and I just sat there, glowing, watching my kids eat ice cream and laugh with their aunt . . . in the comfort of my own home with Danny not watching over me.

The kids had asked repeatedly where their dad was, and I told them that it was mommy's turn to have the house, and that daddy was going to stay with a friend of his for a while, and that everything was going to be okay.

Tammy later came over and held my hand for nearly the entire night. She told me again and again how sorry she was for yelling at me on the phone. I told her again and again that it didn't matter and that I loved her with all my heart.

When we were done with the ice cream, I grabbed a clean comforter from the hall closet and we all snuggled together on the living room couch and watched an illegal copy of *Toy Story* 3 that Mary Lou had purchased at a liquor store. I told her I couldn't condone such illicit behavior and vowed to purchase a real copy when the movie hit the DVD stands. Mary Lou stuck her tongue out at me.

About halfway through the movie, Anthony giggled. I knew that giggle.

"Oh, no you didn't!" I cried out.

He laughed harder and lifted up the comforter. "Dutch oven!" he shouted and a wave of stink hit us.

We all piled out of the living room, laughing and tumbling over ourselves.

And later, after the room had cleared and after we had finished the movie, while Mary Lou was twisting Tammy's long hair into a braid and while Anthony was showering, I found myself crying tears of joy.

58.

It was the next night and I was getting ready for my big date. I didn't often get nervous these days, but I was nervous as hell now. And while I got ready, my AOL account twirped. It was Fang.

See you in one hour, Moon Dance?

You bet.

Are you nervous? he asked.

More than you know.

Don't worry. I don't bite.

I would have laughed if my stomach wasn't doing somersaults. I took a deep, shuddering breath. I really didn't need such deep breaths, but they did help to calm me.

How do I find you? I wrote when I had calmed myself down enough to focus on the keyboard.

Look for the man with a twinkle in his eye.

Smartass.

Trust me, Moon Dance, there will be no mistaking me tonight.

What's your name? I wrote. *I mean, your real name?*

I will tell you my name tonight, Moon Dance. Deal?

Okay, deal. I have to get ready.

See you in fifty-six minutes.

So we're really doing this?

Yes, wrote Fang. *We're really doing this.*

I shut down my laptop and went back to work on my hair. My hands, I noticed, were shaking.

I was driving down Chapman Avenue when my cell rang. I looked at the faceplate. Another restricted number. At this late hour, it could only be a cop. I even had a sneaking suspicion who it was. I clicked on.

"It wasn't me, officer, I swear. Please don't use the rubber hose again."

"We don't use rubber hoses any more," said Sherbet.

"So what do you use?"

"Proper interrogation techniques."

"And if that doesn't work?"

"We dig out the rubber hoses." He paused. "Do you have a couple of minutes?"

"Anything for you, detective."

"I'll remember that. Anyway, we had numerous eyewitness reports of something running through the streets of Fullerton a couple of nights ago, and I want your opinion."

"And because I have a rare skin disease and I'm forced to stay out of the light of day, that makes me an expert in all things that go bump-in-the-night?"

"Something like that."

"Was this *something* about nine feet tall and covered in fur?"

"How did you know?"

"Was there also a grave defiled?"

"Yes, over on Beacon Street, but—"

"Just a lucky guess, Detective."

"Don't give me that bullshit, Sam. What the hell is going on in my city?"

"You would never believe it, Detective."

"Try me."

"Soon. I promise."

He was silent on his end of the phone. Finally, he said, "How soon?"

"Soon."

He sighed. "I can be your best friend, Sam. Or your worst enemy. I have a city to protect."

"We will talk soon, Detective. I promise."

He didn't like it, but accepted it.

"Get some sleep, Detective."

"With a nine-foot creature running around? Hardly."

"You're safe," I said. "At least until the next full moon."

"You're shitting me."

"We'll talk later, Detective."

And we clicked off just as I pulled into the Downtown Bar & Grill parking lot.

59.

I was in the same parking lot where a young lady had been killed not too long ago in connection with a case of mine. A case that had involved Kingsley.

The parking lot was mostly empty. It was late Sunday night, so no surprise there. I was in a spot that afforded me a perfect view of the parking lot's entrance.

I'm really doing this, I thought.

I was a few minutes early. To my right was an alley that ran behind the restaurant. The alley was clean and dimly lit and led to the back entrances to the stores that ran along Harbor Boulevard. Potted plants were arranged outside the bar's back door, and a nearby fire escape appeared freshly painted. The alley itself was composed of cobblestones, like something you would see in an English village. I remembered the way the girl's blood had soaked between the stones, zigzagging rapidly away from her dying body.

The moon was bright, but not full. Clouds were scattered thinly across the glowing sky. Glowing, at least, to my eyes. A small wind made its way through my partially opened driver's side window. I couldn't keep my hands from shaking, and so

I kept them there on the steering wheel, gripping tightly, my knuckles glowing white.

A car turned slowly into the parking lot, making a left from Chapman Avenue. Its headlights bounced as the vehicle angled up the slight driveway and into the parking lot.

I'm really doing this.

I hadn't expected to be this nervous. Fang knew everything about me. He knew my dirtiest secrets. So what did I know about him? I knew he was a lady's man. I knew he had a massive fascination for vampires. I knew he was mortal.

And that was it.

In a way, I loved Fang. He was always, always there for me. In my darkest hours, he consoled me. He lifted me up and reminded me that I was not a monster. I shared with him my heart, and in return he accepted it with tenderness and compassion. He was the perfect man. The perfect confidant.

I didn't want to lose what I had with Fang.

The car continued moving through the parking lot. I could hear its tires crunching. The car, I soon saw, was an old muscle car. A beautiful thing. Not quite cherry, but obviously well taken care of. It gave off a throaty growl, not unlike the growl of the werewolf the other night.

I didn't want to lose Fang. I love what we have. Our connection was so rare, so helpful, so loving, so sweet, so important to me.

I can't lose that.

I wrapped my hands around my keys, which were still hanging in the ignition.

This was a bad idea. I should never have agreed to this.

"What am I doing?" I whispered, feeling real panic, perhaps the first panic I had felt in a long time. Far worse panic than when a nine-foot-tall werewolf approached me in my hotel room.

And what if Fang isn't who he says he is? What if he's someone completely different? Someone untrustworthy?

What if I have to silence him?

I started rocking in the driver's seat. The throaty growl of a muscle car reverberated through the empty lot, bouncing off the surrounding dark buildings. The car pulled slowly into a parking space two rows in front of me.

We were now facing each other. The windshield was tinted enough for me to have a hard time seeing inside. Still, I could see a single figure. A man.

The driver turned the car off and the parking lot fell silent again. A moment later, the muscle car's headlights flashed twice.

My heart slammed inside me. My right hand was still holding the keys. I could start the car now and get the hell out of here and forget this night ever happened, and Fang and I could go back to what we had.

I could. But I didn't.

I reached down and flashed my headlights twice in return. A moment later, the muscle car's driver's side door opened. A booted foot stepped out.

Close to hyperventilating, I went to open my door but stopped short. Shit, I had forgotten about my seat belt. I hastily unfastened it and opened the door.

I'm really doing this.

As I stepped out of my van completely, the person oppsite me did the same. The night air was cool. Sounds from the nearby bar reached us. Laughter. Music. The low murmur of a handful of conversations going on at once.

I stepped around to the front of my minivan, and the figure in front me did the same. He leaned a hip casually against the front fender. When I saw him, I stopped and gasped and covered my mouth with both hands.

Fang grinned at me. "Hello, Moon Dance."

[CONTINUED IN BOOK 3]

BOOK 3

American Vampire

Vampire for Hire #3

DEDICATION

*To all of you who dream of change.
May you take those first, tentative steps towards creating the life you've always wanted. Follow your heart always, my friends, and may you make this world a better place.*

ACKNOWLEDGMENTS

A big thank you to Sandy Johnston (again!), Eve Paludan and Elaine Babich, always my first readers. All writers should be so lucky.

"How do we seem to you? Do you think us beautiful, magical, our white skin, our fierce eyes? Drink, you ask me! Have you any idea of the thing you will become?"

—*Interview with a Vampire*

"We're all kept alive by magic, Sookie. My magic's just a little different from yours, that's all."

—*True Blood*

American Vampire

1.

The night was cool.

The waning moon hovered just above the old downtown buildings, its silver light suffusing with the yellow of the parking lot lights. Both sets of lights served to illuminate the tall man standing in front of me. Not that I needed much light to see him in the dark, thanks to the phosphorescent streaks of incandescence that seemed visible only to me. And perhaps others like me.

A small wind rattled a tree next to me. The tree had thick, waxy leaves that reflected the surrounding light. The tree didn't seem native to Southern California. Trees in Southern California tended to be stunted and pathetic-looking. A plastic grocery bag scuttled halfheartedly across the parking lot, passing between Fang and me. We both ignored it.

"Aren't you going to say something?" he asked, grinning easily. There was humor in his deep voice, but there was also something else. Doubt. Just a shred of it. But it was there, underlying his humor. And I knew the reason for his doubt, for I shared it, too. Fang wasn't at all certain this meeting was a good idea, either. And I suspected why.

He has a secret, too. A big secret.

How I knew this, I wasn't sure. A psychic hit, perhaps. But I was suddenly certain that Fang stood to lose much by this meeting; after all, his past—whatever it was—would not remain hidden, not with me in the picture.

We all have our secrets.

I finally moved my hands away from my mouth and took in a lot of air. I don't generally need a lot of air; in fact, I'm fairly certain I don't need *any* air at all. But breathing deep helped calm my nerves, and since my lungs still worked, I figured I might as well use them every now and again.

I also found myself scanning the parking lot, wondering if I had somehow walked into an elaborate prank . . . or something far worse. A trap perhaps. But I sensed no danger here and I sensed no malice from Fang. Granted, my sixth sense wasn't foolproof, but in situations like this, well, it certainly would have been triggered. Especially since my extrasensory perception seemed to be getting stronger and stronger of late.

"Don't look so concerned, Moon Dance," Fang said. He eased himself off the fender of his car and faced me. "We're alone."

I still hadn't spoken. Music pumped from the bar nearby and I might have heard the sharp crack of a pool ball striking another pool ball. Either that, or someone had just broken a kneecap. There was a slight hint of beer on the wind . . . and vomit. The two often went hand in hand, especially at this late hour and especially in a back alley parking lot.

I stopped scanning the surrounding area and focused on the man before me. Now with my shock abating, the investigator in me was surfacing. The man, I was certain, had stalked me. In fact, I was sure of it. That raised all sorts of alarm bells within me, although I should have known it would happen sooner or later. Fang was, admittedly, a vampire aficionado. I should have known he would have used all the clues I had laid out before him over the years to eventually find me.

Perhaps you wanted to be found, Sam.

Perhaps.

Granted, a part of me had hoped Fang would be Kingsley, but Kingsley was a very different kind of creature of the night. In the end, I knew that Fang could not have been Kingsley.

But I never expected the man standing before me now.

Finally, I spoke. "They let you off work early." Now I, too, stepped away from my van.

"Yeah, well, I told them it was an emergency," said Fang easily.

He moved away from his car and stepped over the crumbling concrete parking curb with its exposed, rusted rebars.

"And this is an emergency?" I asked.

His face lit up. "Of the highest order, Moon Dance."

Now he was coming toward me, moving across the empty parking lot. On his chest, the two great shark teeth swung and bounced from the leather strap. Only I was beginning to think they *weren't* shark teeth.

Fang. His name is Fang for a reason.

More deep breaths. I was tempted to step away from my van, but I couldn't make my legs work. In fact, they suddenly felt gelatinous and heavy and not really my own.

I put my hand on the van's warm hood, stabilizing myself.

Fang was a tall man, and his long strides quickly ate up the asphalt between us. When he was just a few arms lengths away, he stopped, chest heaving.

"I don't know your name," I said, suddenly self-conscious. His eyes rapidly roamed over me, taking me in. But I was used to him looking at me, wasn't I? After all, I had often caught him looking at me.

"You never asked for my name," he said.

"Married women don't ask bartenders for their names," I said.

"You're not married now."

"Technically I'm separated. The divorce paperwork is being drawn up now by my attorney."

"You're doing an awful lot of talking," said the Hero's bartender, smiling at me again. His white teeth shone brightly, and so did the monstrously long teeth dangling from his neck. "And not enough asking."

"Fine," I said, feeling my heart calming down. This was Fang, after all, my best friend, my confidant, the man I had opened my life up to . . . all my secrets, all my fears. Everything. "What's your name?"

"You can call me Eli Roberts," he said. "But my given name is," he paused. "Aaron Parker."

I blinked, and might have gasped, too.

Aaron Parker. I knew the name, of course. Anyone in law enforcement would know the name. I looked at the man in front of me again . . . looked at the fangs hanging from the leather strap. Indeed, those *weren't* shark teeth.

"You're the American Vampire," I said.

He smiled and laughed lightly. "Could you say that a little louder, Moon Dance?"

2.

The Downtown Bar & Grill was a new restaurant in a very old building. The walls were brick and the black lacquer bar counter was epic. It stretched from nearly end to end and I could only imagine how many drinks had been served on its polished, scarred surface.

Aaron Parker, aka Fang, found us a table in the darkest corner of the deepest part of the lounge. Music thumped from nearby speakers. There wouldn't be a soul on earth who could overhear us. A waitress materialized out of the darkness like a ghost and took our orders. Aaron ordered for us. White wine for me. Jack and Coke for him.

"You remembered what I drink," I said. I found myself feeling wary and highly exposed and vulnerable. I also found myself fighting a very strong desire to run. But to run was to leave a lot of questions unanswered.

To run was to screw everything up, and I didn't want to screw everything up.

Aaron sat forward and studied me intently. I don't like to be studied intently. He knew that, didn't he? Interestingly, his look was the same look he'd given me many times at Hero's, a bar I had frequented with my sister. Silly me, I had thought his probing glance had been an interest of a different sort. Now I knew differently. He had been stalking me. He had known who I was all along.

I instinctively looked away, feeling a bit like a freak at a carnival: *"Come one, come all—see the real-life bloodsucker!"*

Now that he was sitting across from me and not endlessly serving customers, I had a chance to really study him. I had always found him attractive. I'm sure he knew that. And my sister had an unhealthy crush on him that her husband really should probably be concerned about. Aaron Parker was tall. Perhaps one of the tallest men I had ever seen. I suspected he was an athlete and I resisted the urge to ask him if he played basketball. Aaron had full lips. The kind most women drool over. He had sad, puppy dog eyes, as brown and bright as polished cherry wood. But it was his mouth that I found the most curious. He didn't seem to know what to do with those beautiful lips of his. Sometimes he pulled them back as if snarling. And sometimes the upper seemed to drape over his lower lip. Often they moved and shifted and I kept having the impression he was about to say something, but words rarely followed the movement. It was the oddest twitch I had ever seen.

Finally, his moving lips formed words. When he spoke, he did so softly. If not for my better-than-average hearing, I might have missed what he said: "I remember everything you tell me, Samantha."

"Except I never told you my name."

Now he looked away, suddenly embarrassed. He should be embarrassed. He had stalked the shit out of me. "Yes, I've known your name for some time."

"It's not nice to stalk people," I said. "Especially someone who can kill you and deposit your body somewhere over shark-infested waters where it will never be seen again."

Aaron's eyes flashed briefly with amusement. "It was a chance I had to take."

Our drinks came. It was late Sunday night and the bar crowd was thinning. No doubt only the hardcore drinkers were left . . . and a creature or two of the night. As we sat in the bar, toasting to good health and long life (which put a smile on my face), I was suddenly certain Aaron and I were being watched. I glanced over his shoulder, searching for the source, but there was only an empty stairway leading up to God knew what. Still, the electrified field that only I seemed to see, a field that consisted of glowing streaks of light that helped me see on the darkest of nights, seemed to be buzzing with more than usual activity. Light streaks zipped about as if energized by something unseen.

Something's coming, I suddenly thought. What that I was, I didn't know.

I turned back to Fang. "So how did you find me?" I asked, although I had already intuited the answer. Obviously, I had given the man enough clues about my life—in particular, the cases I had worked on—for him to find me. Quite simply, he had put two and two together. Even if *two and two* had come over the course of years.

He confirmed my hunch, and explained. To his credit, he looked a bit sheepish. Anyway, it had been one of my bigger cases four months ago that had gotten some national attention, a case that involved a runaway girl and a murderous dad. Despite my best efforts to remain anonymous, my name had appeared once or twice in the newspaper. I had, of course, mentioned to Fang that I was working on an important missing person case. By this point, I had already inadvertently dropped enough clues over the years to direct him to the general region where I lived. And once he knew the general region, well, it had just been a matter of scanning the local headlines for any news about a runaway.

I said, "So everything I ever told you. . . ."

"I made notes," he said. "I saved our messages. I pored over them later, searching for hidden clues about you. About how to find you. In the beginning, you gave me very little to work with. But you loosened up over the years."

I wasn't sure how I felt about that. There was a creep factor here that was hard to ignore. But I also understood human nature. Or, at least, tried my damned best to. Yes, of course he had been curious about me. Who wouldn't have been? I was a woman who was professing to be much more than a woman. And, admittedly, I had certainly been curious to find him, too, but I had never acted on it. I was a married woman at the time, working hard to keep things happy and seemingly normal.

Too hard.

A marriage shouldn't have to be so much work. Love shouldn't crush your soul. A relationship should add to your life, not take away from it. Something I'm only now beginning to understand.

But it was hard to remain mad at Fang . . . or Aaron. There was a gentleness to him that I never saw coming. His instant messages to me had exuded confidence. But I wasn't seeing the confidence here. No, I was seeing a man, perhaps in his late twenties or early thirties, who had anything but confidence. I was missing something here, and I wasn't sure what it was.

I looked again at the teeth dangling from his neck. They were long and thick—but not quite as thick as shark teeth. They looked like dog canines. Big dog canines. I looked again at his twitching mouth, and saw him curl his upper lip down as if to. . . .

As if to cover two massively prominent canines. Two unnaturally long canines.

"Those teeth," I said, motioning to his chest. "Are yours."

"Why, Moon Dance," he said, and I sensed his old charm. "You are quite the detective."

3.

I knew the story of the American Vampire, of course.

In essence, a young man with two extraordinarily long canine teeth had sucked his girlfriend dry. His trial had been as sensational as they get, and who could forget the images of the young man opening his mouth and exposing those two insanely long canines for all the world to see.

And here he was. In the flesh. Sitting across from me. A young man who had been tried and convicted of murder. A young man who had been deemed criminally insane. And there were very few who would argue that point.

And he's Fang, I thought. This is crazy.

If I looked hard enough I could see the similarities, but the truth was, he looked nothing like the tormented young man whose image had been broadcast across the airwaves and newsrooms and the early internet. Now his thick beard would make him nearly impossible to place, and I was almost certain he had had some nose work done. And as I looked again, I could see he was wearing brown contact lenses. Almost certainly his eyes had been blue originally. But the biggest difference was his great height. He had not been quite this tall when he was eighteen years old. Then again, it was hard to know for sure, since he had often sat petulantly next to his attorneys. Still, I would guess he had grown another five inches . . . perhaps enough to completely throw authorities off his trail.

He was, after all, an escaped convict—and allegedly responsible for two more deaths. A guard at the prison for the criminally insane and the owner of a creepy museum in Hollywood who had purchased Aaron's teeth for a morally questionable display.

A sick display. There had been outrage, of course.

But the outrage turned moot when the owner was found dead some months later, and the teeth had been stolen.

The same teeth that now dangled from Fang's neck.

The same fangs.

"You are a killer," I said.

"As are you, Samantha," he said, sitting back and sipping casually on a drink that smelled strong enough to preserve a warthog. "We are both victims of circumstance. Never forget that."

His faux brown eyes continued scanning my face. I could see the wonder in them; I could sense his awe. His thoughts were alive to me, nearly registering in my mind as my own. After all, I had a deep connection to Fang, deeper than I had ever thought possible with another human being, and although the man in front of me was largely a stranger, now that we had met in the flesh, our connection seemed only to intensify.

He closed his eyes and took in some air. "I can feel you, Moon Dance."

I blinked. "Feel me how?"

"In my head. You're there. In my thoughts. Just off to the side. Listening. Picking up words here and there."

He cocked his head slightly to one side, like a dog listening to something on the wind. Now it was my turn to study his face. The man was gorgeous. Of that, there was no doubt. After all, there was a reason why my sister turned into a gibbering idiot every time he served us a drink. His brown hair was jauntily disheveled, or perhaps messily windblown. Mostly, it was his lips that commanded my attention. So full, especially the lower one. There was a spot of liquid on the bottom one and all I could think of doing was tasting that spot. Just that one, sexy spot.

His eyelids quivered, when I saw a brief flash of white, and realized his eyes had rolled up into his head. "Yes, there you are, Moon Dance."

I said nothing. Music continued pumping through the bar. A very old drunk man got up from his stool and started slow dancing with himself. He spun himself once, twice, and I thought he might even dip himself, but luckily he bumped into the bar and grabbed hold of it. No one seemed to notice him but me.

And seemingly inside my skull, I heard a very faint, yet very distinct whisper: *Hello, Moon Dance.*

Fang opened his eyes and smiled at me.

"Okay," I said. "That's never happened before."

4.

"It is common knowledge that vampires can control others with their minds," said Fang.

"But I'm not trying to control you," I said.

"Yet," he said. "But if I find myself suddenly giving you a pedicure, I might suspect otherwise." He winked.

I lifted my hand. "Trust me, there isn't a file strong enough for these nails."

"Let me see your nails, Moon Dance."

"No."

"Please."

I sighed and held out my hands. He took them gently and did not flinch at the extreme cold of my flesh like most do. Indeed, shivering and smiling, he seemed to revel in the iciness. He next tapped the tip of my index finger. I felt like a horse being sold at auction. "You could disembowel a rhino with these things."

"Or a bartender who lets my secret out."

He grinned again. "I didn't realize how feisty you were, Moon Dance."

"We never had this much at stake, Fang."

"We both hold equally damaging secrets. I, too, am trusting you to keep my secret safe."

"You're a convicted murder and an escaped prisoner."

"And you're a blood-sucking fiend."

I studied him. The corner of his mouth lifted in a small smile, along with some of his beard. "Fair enough," I said, sitting back. "So what's this mind control business you're talking about?"

He finished his drink and waved the waitress over. I had barely touched my own wine. When she was gone, he sat forward, resting his weight on his sharp elbows. "You have already mentioned your sixth sense, Moon Dance. You have even mentioned that you felt it is getting stronger."

I nodded; it was.

He went on, "Well, your sixth sense is a little more far-reaching than you have thought; at least, that is my understanding."

"How far-reaching?"

"Telepathy. Hypnosis. Mediumship."

"One at a time," I said. "Hypnosis?"

"You've seen *Dracula*, right?"

"Maybe."

"Did you read the book?"

"No."

"A vampire who's never read *Dracula?*"

"I've been busy raising kids and trying to keep a husband happy. At least I'm batting .500."

He smiled sadly. "I'm sorry he hurt you, Moon Dance."

"So am I."

"Want to change the subject?"

I nodded.

"Back to mind control. Dracula, you see, has the ability to induce hypnosis with just his gaze. You might want to look into it."

I shook my head at his silly pun. "Fine. What about mediumship?"

"That's speaking to the dead, either to those who have passed on or still linger."

"Linger?"

"Ghosts, Moon Dance. You should be able to see ghosts."

I scanned our surroundings. The electrified air, usually so alive with light filaments, seemed particularly erratic in here. To my eyes, the streaking lights zigzagged even more crazily, sometimes coalescing into bigger shapes. As I scanned the air around us, Fang continued speaking.

"You are a supernatural being, Moon Dance. A supernatural being in the world of mortals. You should be seeing things I could never, ever imagine."

The squiggly lights in the bar flashed and zigzagged like

thousands upon thousands of electrified fireflies. I watched as they whipped crazily around a nearby stairway, a stairway that led up into the black depths. The flashing lights began gathering together, collecting other squiggly lights. I had seen such things before but had dismissed them. They were just strange lights, right? Nothing more.

"Creatures of the night seem to attract each other, Samantha, whether they know it or not . . . or whether they want it or not. It is not a coincidence that the werewolf came into your life. Soon, I expect others like yourself to make appearances."

"Like myself?"

"Vampires, Moon Dance. You cannot be an island for long. Not in this world of fantastical creatures."

I continued studying the glowing object at the foot of the stairway. More light gathered around it. Now, if I looked hard enough, I could see shoulders, hips, and a head forming. Even what appeared to be longish hair. And then, amazingly, the light creature turned toward me. I couldn't see its features, but I sensed its great pain. And then, buried deep in my mind's eye, I saw a flash of a knife's blade, heard a strangled cry, then weeping, and then . . . nothing.

"I see a ghost," I said. "There by the stairway."

I saw Aaron turn out of the corner of my eye. "I don't see anything, Moon Dance. But I'm not surprised. This is supposedly one of the most haunted buildings in Fullerton."

And just like that the vaguely humanoid column of light dispersed, scattering into a thousand glowing, fluorescent shards of energy.

Son of a biscuit, I thought, reciting my son's favorite expression.

After a moment, Aaron Parker looked back at me. "So does it feel strange finally meeting me, Moon Dance?"

"Yes and no. A part of me wants to run back to my computer and continue this conversation there. I felt safe there. I felt open. I felt free to be me."

"You don't feel free now?"

"I don't know how I feel, to be honest."

"Do I feel a bit like a stranger?" he asked.

I nodded and I felt the tears come to my eyes. "Yes."

"A stranger who knows your deepest and darkest secrets."

I nodded, suddenly finding it hard to speak.

He said, "Do you regret meeting me, Moon Dance?"

I sat motionless for a long time before I reached out and took his warm hands in my mine. As I did so, he curled his long fingers around mine. "I don't know," I whispered, and it was perhaps the hardest three words I have ever spoken.

He continued holding my hands. Now he rubbed his thumb along my knuckles. His thumb was rough, calloused. He was a grease monkey, no doubt. Tending bar at night, fixing up his classic muscle car during the day.

Fang tilted his head slightly. "Grease monkey is not a politically correct term, Moon Dance. We prefer to be called lubed primates."

I snorted. "Sounds like a bad porno."

"There are no bad pornos, Moon Dance."

"Eww, and you just read my thoughts."

"Yes," he said. "I heard a few snatches here and there."

"So how is it that you can read my thoughts?"

"I don't have all the answers, Moon Dance."

"Well, give it your best shot, big guy."

He stared at me long and hard. As he did so, his tongue slid along his lower lip and seemed to be searching for something that was not there. I sensed his great sadness for what was lost. I suspected I knew the source of his sadness.

Finally, he said, "We are connected, Moon Dance. Or, more accurately, you have allowed me access into your mind."

"So I can turn it off?" I asked.

"I don't see why not," he said. "And you're right, Sam, I do miss them every day. More than you know."

His teeth, of course.

5.

Instead of going home, I went to a place I was familiar with: The Embassy Suites in Brea. My home over the past month.

I parked the minivan in my old spot, and shortly said hello to Justin who was working the front desk. He smiled and nodded and seemed to have forgotten that I had checked out a week earlier. Of course, just last week, when I had busted my husband for running an illegal strip club in Colton, I had dressed the part of a stripper. I might be little, but I'm a curvy thing, and Justin the night clerk hasn't looked at me the same since.

I felt his eyes on me all the way to the bank of elevators. At the ninth floor, I found a locked service door I had seen many times in the past. A service door I had taken note of. Why? Because the plaque on it read: Roof Access. Maintenance Personnel Only.

I glanced up and down the hall, took hold of the locked doorknob, and turned steadily until the inner mechanisms shattered in my hand. The knob broke off.

God, I'm a freak.

I pushed the door open, and, after wiping the knob with the hem of my shirt, tossed it in the corner of the stairwell. Next I stepped over a low gate and quickly headed up a metal flight of stairs, taking them two at a time and noticing how strong my legs felt. The door at the top of the landing was locked as well. But not for long.

As pieces of the broken door knob fell away at my feet, I stepped out onto the roof.

Immediately, wind buffeted me. The waning moon was higher now and shone through a thin layer of pathetic-looking stratus clouds. Mostly, though, the sky was clear, and I could even see a star or two.

At the service door, I quickly removed my clothing and naked as the day I was born, moved across the dusty roof, avoiding, of all things, a broken beer bottle.

Hell of a party up here.

Now standing at the roof's edge, I stared down at the city of Brea, which shone before me like a brilliant constellation, providing me a view that the heavens could not. At least, not the heavens here in Southern California. Thousands of lights winked and sparkled. Some were brighter than others—street lamps, perhaps. Others were barely discernible—bathroom nightlights and perhaps the glows of Kindles and Nooks.

Whatever those were.

The wind pulled at the edge of the building. It rocked my naked body. But I had no fear of falling. My hair whipped around my head like so many serpents. Medusa would have been proud. Or envious. I breathed slowly, deeply, each intake spiced with exhaust and tar and the sage from the nearby foothills.

The world lay at my feet. The normal world. Where people prayed to God and Jesus, where people worried about their kids' health and Charlie Sheen's career, where life went on steadily and predictably.

Life hadn't gone so predictably for me. Life had hung a hard right turn at "predictable" and detoured through a forbidden forest where the Headless Horseman was real, where werewolves existed, where a mother of two could be changed forever into something nightmarish.

I took in more air and lifted my face toward the heavens. The day's latent heat rose up from the roof's surface, warming my eternally cold buns. I heard honking and tires squealing. The crash of a fender-bender.

Oops.

I heard a baby crying from the hotel below and the steady hum of a hundred or so air conditioners powering through the warm night. The building beneath me seemed alive, vibrating and swaying slightly. Or perhaps that was just my imagination.

I stood there for a heartbeat longer.

And then spread my arms wide and jumped.

6.

The drop down from this hotel was always a little dicey, although jumping from the roof gave me some extra wiggle room. But not much.

I arched up and out over the roof . . . and seemed to pause briefly at the apex of the arch. From here I had a glimpse of an ambulance flashing down Birch Street, heading away from me. But there was no sound. No sirens. No honking. Nothing. Time and sound always seemed to subside in these moments.

These wonderful, exhilarating moments.

Now I tilted forward, arms outstretched. A falling, inverted cross.

I picked up speed.

Hair whipping behind me like a failed parachute. Wind thundering over me. The hotel rushing past me.

Someone was standing at the hotel balcony, smoking a cigarette. He never saw me. Or maybe I didn't register in his conscious brain. Maybe tonight he would dream about a curvy, black-haired woman plummeting past his balcony, arms outstretched, and naked as all get out.

I was rapidly running out of floors.

A single flame appeared in my thoughts. The flame burned bright, seemingly in the center of my forehead, no doubt in the region the New Age gurus call the Third Eye. In the center of the flame was a winged creature that would have given anyone nightmares.

Except that winged creature was me.

It was my monster familiar. It was my monster alter-ego. It was one hell of a wicked-cool-looking creature.

And it was me.

It waited in the flame, its wings tucked in, elongated head cocked slightly to one side. It always waited for me, ready at my beck and call. My own personal flying demon.

Except *I* was that flying demon.

As the floors swept past me and the concrete sidewalk rapidly approached, I felt myself being pulled to that creature, drawn to it powerfully, supernaturally, miraculously.

The metamorphosis happened in an instant.

The flame disappeared in an explosion of light and when I opened my eyes again, a pair of massive leathery wings—which attached to my wrists and ran down below my knees—snapped taut, slowing my decent. The gravitational force on my wings was incredible, but this new body of mine was more than up to the task. My arms held strong.

I adjusted my arms and angled forward, sweeping nine or ten feet over the ground and just missing a handicap parking sign. It rattled angrily in my wake.

Now I flapped my wings. Yeah, I know. A crazy statement. But these are crazy times.

At least, for me.

I flapped my wings and quickly gained altitude. I found the effort of flying easy. My shoulders were powerful. The thickly membraned wings caught the wind and forced it down and behind me. The sound of my beating wings thundered everywhere at once. Anyone nearby would have heard me. They would have looked up . . . and seen something they wouldn't soon forget.

My body was aerodynamic and pierced the wind effortlessly.

I continued rising above the glittering city of Brea. Yeah, it was cold up here, but I was perfectly adapted for that, too. Thick skinned. Insulated. Perfectly adapted or perfectly created?

I didn't know which. And I didn't care.

I rose higher and higher. The thrill of weightlessness was so exhilarating that it drove all thought from my mind. Wind whispered over me, seemed to part for me, opened for me new sights few people would ever see or experience.

And still I climbed.

The temperature dropped exponentially. I plunged into a roiling cumulus cloud and the world briefly disappeared. I was surrounded by ice crystals which was at once serene and mildly disorienting. I shook my great head where the crystals had collected. They broke free and fell away.

The cloud opened and soon I was flying parallel with it, rising and falling with its amorphous contours, like a fighter plane over a desert floor. The movements of my wings were minute, so minute I wasn't consciously aware of making them. The moon shone over my shoulder, reflecting brightly off the cloud's pale surface. My shadow kept pace, rising and falling. A monster's moon shadow. Wings outstretched, flapping almost lazily, I was a massive creature.

The sky above me was clear, filled with millions upon millions of glittering stars. I focused on one such star and flew toward it. What would happen if I just kept on flying? No doubt the deep vacuum of space would wreak havoc on my flying. With no air, I would float aimlessly and endlessly.

I shuddered at the thought.

The cloud dispersed and a great sweeping hillside appeared beneath me, dotted with brightly lit homes. I thought of Fang. The man was a killer, of that there was no doubt. He was also a fugitive. Once, long ago, I had made an oath to uphold the law and bring such fugitives to justice.

But that was then. . . .

. . . and this was now. Now, I had some dirty secrets of my own, didn't I? Now I had taken one life and was responsible for a second.

Victims of circumstance, Fang had said. I agreed to an extent. Victims were not given a free pass to hurt others.

I flapped my wings languidly, riding along a powerful jet stream, which propelled me forward powerfully, effortlessly. Fang, aka Aaron Parker, aka Eli Roberts (his assumed name) was a beautiful man. There was a reason my sister seriously had the hots for him.

I nearly laughed at the thought that this flying creature could have a sister. And then I almost laughed at the thought that this flying creature could laugh.

Life is weird.

The clouds below opened and I saw a small plane flying beneath me, buzzing laboriously even as I flew effortlessly and silently. Its lights flashed, in accordance with aviation law. There were no laws for giant flying monsters. I was beyond law. I could give a damn about laws, anyway.

To an extent.

I still had a life to live and children to raise and food to put on the table. By necessity, I had to play by the rules of man.

Yes, Fang was a beautiful man. He was also my closest friend. But everything had changed, hadn't it? He was no longer my anonymous friend who I could open up to about everything. He had a face. A history. A *troubled* history.

He was also, of course, a world-class stalker.

And a killer.

Shit.

Below, I spotted the Hollywood sign, the word so tiny that by all rights I shouldn't have been able to read them. But I could. Giant vampire bats had eagle-like vision.

I dipped a wing and turned to starboard slowly, a great arching turn that took a full minute. The sky was my playground. The clouds my jungle gym.

I completed my turn and innately headed home, following an

inner guidance system that was so inherent that I didn't doubt it or question it.

It's good to be me sometimes.

I headed back to the Embassy Suites.

7.

I was answering emails on my laptop and watching Judge Judy emasculate this deadbeat dad when my cell phone rang. I picked it up from the coffee table and looked at the faceplate: *Caller Unknown.*

I almost didn't pick up. By nature, I don't like *Caller Unknown* calls. What are people hiding?

The phone rang a second time. And as it did so, an electrical sensation crackled along the length of my spine. As if a ghost had run an ethereal finger down the center of my back.

I shivered. I knew to pay attention to such sensations. Such sensations were strong indications that something important was going on.

The phone rang a third time. Yes, I use old school rings, even for my cell phone. Phones are supposed to *ring*, dammit. Not sing Christina Aguilera's failed national anthem attempt.

Now Judge Judy was really laying into this asshole again. Reminding him he was the child's father. That he had responsibilities. She also let him know what she thought of him. Trust me, she didn't think very highly. I loved every second of it.

The phone rang a fourth time. My phone will ring five times before it goes to voicemail. The buzzing along my spine continued to crackle. The fine hair on my forearms was also standing on end.

Something's wrong, I thought.

My email was unfinished. Judge Judy continued her verbal berating. I looked at the time on my phone. I had to pick up my kids in a few minutes. Normally, I would have let the call go to my voicemail.

Normally.

"Answer the phone."

The words came from behind me. Except behind me was a

wall. I jumped off the couch, screaming and gasping. The voice was soft and whispery and it scared the shit out of me.

I answered the phone, still scanning the room, still scared shitless. Who had spoken to me?

"Hello," I said, feeling my heart beating somewhere near my throat. I was alone in the house. I was sure of it. I would have heard someone enter. I would have *sensed* someone entering.

There was no response from the other end of the line. I headed for the hallway. Scanned it. No one was here. Now from the line I could hear faint breathing. And as I searched the bedrooms and bathroom, I said hello again. And when I got to my own bedroom, a voice finally answered.

And it was the tiniest voice I had ever heard.

"Hi." A girl's voice. Maybe five. Maybe less.

I paused, doing a quick mental rundown of all my nieces and nephews. Although I was not as close to some of my sisters and brothers as I wanted to be, I rarely received a call from any of their children. Still, I could not think of a niece this young.

"Well, hello," I said. "And who is this?" I asked, my own voice rising a friendly octave or two. I glanced in my room. My house was completely empty.

So who had spoken to me?

I didn't know. But I let it go and wrote it off to stress. After all, these past few weeks had not been without their trials. And last night. . . .

Yes, last night.

Last night still had me reeling. Had it really happened? Had I really met Fang?

I had. Oh, yes, I had.

The little voice spoke again over the phone. "I'm Maddie."

"Hi Maddie," I said, switching my focus from the strange voice to the little girl. Just about all the hair on my body was standing on end.

Something's wrong, I thought.

"Where's your mommy, Maddie?" Near my bed, my alarm clock registered exactly 3:00 p.m. I had to leave now to pick up my kids. I had been missing my kids all day; or, rather, ever since I got up a few hours ago. I had an overwhelming need to see them, to hold them, to pull them in close and keep them safe. The feeling seemed particularly poignant and slightly irrational. But now I wondered if something else was going on. I wondered if my sixth sense had picked up on this call long before it had come.

"My mommy got kilt."

Kilt?

My heart stopped. *Killed.* A strong and now not-so-irrational panic had completely replaced any subtle sixth sense I was feeling. A mommy instinct was kicking in, and it was kicking in hard.

"Where are you, Maddie?"

"A bad man's house."

"Maddie, baby, where's your dad?"

"I don't have a daddy."

"Who's the bad man, Maddie?"

And now the little girl lowered her voice to a soft whisper and it broke my heart. "He's very very bad," she said. "And he hurted me."

I was standing, pacing. Tears appeared in my eyes. Sweet Jesus. What the hell was going on?

"Maddie, please, honey . . . where are you?"

"I don't know." More whispering. "It's dark. And cold."

I covered my face. This was real. And my alarm system was ringing off the hook. This was real. This wasn't a prank.

Get information. Get all the information you can.

"Maddie, honey, what's the name of the bad man?"

"He kilt my mom. He shot her. He shot her dead."

"Baby, where are you?"

"I scared."

"Everything's going to be okay, Maddie. Please, honey, do you have any idea where—"

And now the little girl must have pressed her mouth hard into the phone, because her next whispered words were barely discernible. "He's coming!" I heard shuffling, and now I heard her whimpering. "He's coming. I scared. I so scared."

"Maddie—"

And then the line went dead.

8.

I stared at my phone, completely rattled. I heard again and again the little girl's tiny voice: *"I scared. I so scared."*

The iPhone soon drifted to sleeper mode, then powered down. I inhaled deeply. There were tears on my cheeks. I relaxed my grip on the phone. Any harder and it would have broken. The call had gone straight to my heart. It would have gone straight to the heart of any mother. Hell, it would have gone straight to the heart of anyone with an ounce of humanity.

I wiped the tears from my eyes and cheeks.

Someone killed her mother. And now someone was keeping her in a dark and cold place. A bad man who was hurting her.

I inhaled. I was rattled, totally shaken. The call had caught me completely off guard. Hell, it would have caught anyone off guard. I found myself, perhaps for the first time in a long, long time, completely unsure of what to do next.

I heard the fear in her voice. I heard again and again her childish attempt to keep her voice quiet.

Who was she? Who was her mother?

And, perhaps the biggest question of all: How had little Maddie gotten my number?

I didn't know. But I was going to find out.

Knowing I was incurring the wrath of my kids' principal, a man who already didn't look very kindly on me, I briefly put off picking them up and called my ex-partner, Chad Helling. One time, not so long ago, I was a federal agent. Now, because of circumstances very much out of my control, I had gone private.

Chad picked up on the fourth ring. I said, "I'm only a four-ring gal now, huh?"

"Be glad I answered on the fourth ring, Sam. I happen to be a very busy federal investigator."

"Uh huh, and whatcha doing now?"

"Waiting in line at Starbucks."

"And it took you four rings to pick up?"

"It took me four rings to hang up on my mom and take your call."

"You hung up on your mom to take my call?"

"Yes. So this better be good."

I told him about the phone conversation with little Maddie, reciting it nearly word for word since it would be forever seared into my memory.

Chad was silent, digesting this. Finally, he said, "Brave little girl. And savvy."

"Brave and savvy aren't going to be enough," I said. "She's with a monster."

He took in some air, inhaling sharply. "I can look into recent murders. See if anything involves an abducted child, too."

"The mother was murdered recently. There's a good chance she hasn't been found. And may never be found."

"An abduction, then."

"Yes, look for a missing mother and child. There won't be a murder reported. At least not yet."

"And you know this how?"

"Call it a hunch."

"Fine." He paused. "Any chance the child was playing a prank on you?"

"Not a chance in hell."

"Don't hold back, Sam. Tell me what you really think."

"Smart ass."

He said, "My question is: How did Maddie find your number?"

I had been thinking that, too. I bit my lip, and looked at my watch. Shit. I was already seriously late. "Hard to know, but my guess is that the number was already programmed into the phone."

"Her mother's phone? Or the killer's?"

"The million-dollar question," I said.

"Maybe Maddie hit redial. Who was your last call?"

I could have smacked my forehead. I told Chad to hang on as I quickly scrolled through the iPhone.

"A creditor," I said.

"Keep scrolling."

I did. "Nothing unusual. Nothing out of the ordinary."

"Keep looking," said Chad. "Perhaps a past client."

"Nothing," I said. "But I'll go through it again when I'm not in a hurry."

"When you're not in a hurry? Hey, I was the one jonesing for coffee."

"Just please find out what you can," I said. "And tell your mother sorry."

He said he would and before he clicked off I heard him ordering an iced venti vanilla latte . . . and my mouth watered.

God, I missed coffee.

Still shaken, I quickly scrambled around my house, grabbing my sunhat and my purse. I had already slathered my cheeks and hands with a heavy application of the market's strongest sunblock, although that did little to stop the searing pain as I now dashed out of the house and crossed the small patch of grass that separated my house and the garage. Oh, how I envied those with connecting garages!

I was gasping by the time I reached the minivan. There had to be an easier way to get my kids. Maybe there was, but for now, no one was picking my kids up but me.

When my hot, irritated, inflamed skin had calmed down, I started the minivan, turned on the AC, and headed out to my kids' school.

9.

My kids were being pills.

Anthony had gotten into a fight . . . with a girl, no less. The girl, apparently, had seriously kicked his ass (and is it wrong that I secretly found this funny?), and as we drove to Burger King, his older sister, Tammy, wouldn't let him forget it. It took the threat of a week's grounding to finally get her to ease up.

I think my boxing trainer, Jacky, might be getting a new client this summer. Someone needed to teach the boy how to fight, and obviously it wasn't going to be his worthless dad. Granted, I wasn't advocating fighting, especially fighting girls, but who wants to hear about their boy getting their ass kicked at school?

"But Mom," said Tammy. "She *sat* on him."

I stifled a giggle behind my hand. Anthony, who was sitting next to me and sporting a swollen lip, looked at me sideways. When I gained some semblance of control over myself, I said,

"Then maybe you should protect your little brother and not let girls sit on him."

"Who do you think pulled her off him, Mom?" said Tammy. "I wasn't going to let that cow sit on my brother. Well, not for very long, anyway."

She giggled again, and I did my damndest not to join her.

We pulled up to Burger King and I put in our orders. I repeated Anthony's plain hamburger order twice, knowing he wouldn't touch anything with ketchup or mustard or anything else on it. With our food bagged, we headed home, and while the kids ate and did their homework, I took a hot shower. The shower was intended to clean off the copious amounts of sunscreen, but it also served another purpose.

I craved heat. My body had no natural warmth. I lived with an eternal chill, and so I craved blessed warmth. Showers were certainly nice, but, admittedly, nothing beat the warmth of a man lying next to me, a warmth I rarely felt since my own ex-husband had basically shunned me.

Of course, I had recently experienced such warmth. In fact, just over a week ago, in the arms of another man. A former client of mine. A man with his own dark secrets and a body that radiated heat unlike anything I had ever experienced.

A shiver went through me. A very pleasurable shiver, especially as I recalled Kingsley's skillet-sized hands on my body. His touch, his expert touch, had sent shockwaves through me in more ways than one.

But as I stood there in the shower, as the water did its damned best to penetrate my eternal cold, I thought of another man.

Aaron Parker. Aka Fang.

The heat had worked deep into my skin, and as I stood there under the powerful spray, I reached behind me and turned the temperature even higher. Anyone else would have yelped. Anyone else would have leaped from the shower as surely as if being dropped into a boiling cauldron.

But I only moaned with pleasure.

After having drinks with Aaron, he had walked me back to my van where we had stood together awkwardly. He wanted to kiss me. He wanted to do a lot more to me, too. His thoughts were as clear as a bell, although anyone with a half a brain could have read his body language. I reminded him that I had a lot to digest. I reminded him that he had been aware of me for a lot longer than I had been aware of him. This needed to sink in. I had to sort through my feelings and emotions. . . .

And that's when he kissed me.

He kissed me long and hard and although I had nearly pushed him back—hell, he was lucky he didn't go flying into the trunk of a nearby tree—I decided I liked his kiss. There had been a crazy hunger to him.

Or maybe he was just crazy.

His lips covered mine and I knew he wanted to bite me, or at least use his teeth. To nibble, to bite. To draw blood. When he got too aggressive, I pulled back. He apologized, and then went back to chewing on my lower face.

Never had I been kissed like that before.

Never. And never did I expect to be kissed like that again.

The shower spray felt so damn good. Too good. I could stand in it all night. I could probably do other things in there all night, too. After all, I had recently discovered that I could experience something very pleasurable. Something I had thought was lost to me.

That thought alone sent a shiver through me.

I pushed it away and turned off the shower. There was work to be done. There was a little girl scared and alone and living with a monster.

And with images of Fang whispering goodbye in my ear, I got dressed and headed for my office at the back of the house.

10.

I was scouring over internet leads, scanning heartbreaking article after heartbreaking article, when my cell phone rang. It was Chad.

"Hey, Sunshine," he said.

"It never gets old, does it?"

Chad was, of course, poking fun at my "condition." A condition called *xeroderma pigmentosum*, which was what most of the world thought I had. Believe it or not, I didn't run around telling people I was a vampire.

"Probably not ever," he said. "Besides, I'm your ex-partner. I can get away with goofing on you. Kind of like an older brother."

"A stupid-face older brother."

"Clever Sam. Anyway, I have news on Maddie."

I sat up. "Talk to me."

"Three months ago a mother and daughter went missing. Lauren and Madison Monk."

I exhaled and squeezed the phone tighter. "Go on."

"The mother was a known user and prostitute and probably not a very good mother, either. The daughter was born into a mess. The mother would often disappear with boyfriends and drug dealers, bringing her daughter along with her. Some seedy shit going on here, Sam. No one reported them missing for many weeks, and she spent so much time with so many different shady characters, that it's nearly impossible to pinpoint where she was staying or who had seen her last."

"Someone knows," I said.

"Sure, but we're talking about the lowest of the lowlifes, Sam. Folks who break laws every hour on the hour. No one is talking."

"Who's working the case?"

"Fullerton Police Missing Persons Unit."

"The name of the officer?"

He told me and I wrote it down. When finished, I said, "I think the missing person has turned into a murder and kidnapping."

"You'll hear no argument from me, Sam."

"Thank you, Chad."

"We're working on something big over here, but I'll help you when I can."

"I know; thank you. How's Monica?" I asked, referring to my client of just a few weeks ago. Chad, who had taken over partial bodyguard duties for me, had been smitten by her instantly.

"Beautiful as ever; I love her."

"Just don't smother her, for Christ's sake. Give her space."

"I'll give her whatever she wants."

"Oh, brother."

We hung up and I considered my options. Without the case

file, there was really nothing I could do tonight. Tomorrow I would check in with the Fullerton PD. For now, though, I quickly scanned my files and notes, doing a global search for the name Lauren Monk. Nothing came up. That didn't mean I hadn't come across her at some point, just that the name hadn't made it to any of my files or notes. Of course, that's if I had ever worked with her or come into contact with her in the first place.

Well, she had my number somehow.

Or, at least, *someone* had it.

I was sitting back and thinking about little Maddie and her little voice when I sensed a presence behind me. I turned and found Anthony standing there and looking miserable. "What's wrong, booger butt," I asked, waving him over.

"I don't feel good, Mommy."

"Hey, you're already suspended for a day, honey. You don't have to fake being sick." But I knew he wasn't faking it. My boy looked miserable and I could feel the palpable waves of heat coming off his body.

"But I'm not faking it, Mommy. I swear."

I put a hand on his forehead. The kid was burning up. He flinched at my icy touch. No surprise there. The dichotomy between hot and cold was probably startling.

He climbed up onto my lap and nuzzled his burning face into my neck, and as he did so, alarm bells went off inside me. They rang loud and clear.

Something was very wrong.

11.

I lay by Anthony's side for many hours, lightly running my fingers through his fine hair, periodically checking his fever with my palm. His cheek was clammy and frighteningly hot. His breathing was even, although I detected a slight rattle in his chest. Every now and then from his sleep he would cough wetly.

Something's wrong.

Or maybe I'm just worrying too much. He's just sick. A fever. Perhaps the flu.

The electrified air around my son was agitated, the glowing

streaks buzzing like so many bees around a hive. I held my son closer and listened to his heartbeat; it beat strong and steady. I monitored his breathing, too, and was certain that, as the hours passed, his breathing was growing more ragged.

Hours later, I kissed him on his forehead and headed out into the living room. Tammy was snoring lightly with the TV playing quietly. An infomercial selling an electric wheelchair was on. The old guy cruising on it never looked happier. I doubted it.

I clicked off the TV and bent down. She was ten years old and weighed nearly as much as I did, that didn't stop me from scooping her up easily and cradling her in my arms like a baby. Her body was warm, but not alarmingly so. Unlike Anthony. I held her close to me and buried my nose in her hair, inhaling deeply. She smelled of strawberries. Again, unlike Anthony, who had smelled of sweat.

I stood there briefly in the living room, holding my daughter effortlessly while she mewed slightly in her sleep.

Somewhere out there was a little girl named Maddie who would never feel her mother nuzzle against her again. A little girl who knew only fear and perhaps pain. A little girl with the tiniest voice I had ever heard.

With my face still mostly buried in my daughter's hair, I carried her into her bedroom and eased her carefully down into bed. I pulled the covers up over her and kissed her warm forehead, and then wiped a tear off her cheek.

It had, of course, been my tear.

12.

You there, Fang?

It was late. Or early. Take your pick. Creatures of the night often get this distinction wrong. Anyway, I knew I would be waking Fang up, but I needed to talk.

I waited in front of my laptop for a few minutes with no response. I checked the time. Nearly 4:30 in the morning. Fang had worked tonight, I knew, which meant he would have gotten off at two-ish.

You're sleeping, I'm sure, I wrote in the IM screen. Years ago,

Fang and I had met online in a community vampire room. I had been curious and lonely. Fang had not only landed a friend, but the real deal. A true bloodsucker.

Fang had entered my life when I needed him the most. Funny how life is like that. He was my outlet. My source of information, too, since he was knowledgeable in all things vampiric. We had bonded in ways I never thought possible, and I had revealed my deepest secrets. Fang knew everything.

And now I knew a lot more about him, too.

Fang was a killer. By my count, he had murdered three people. How many more after his jailbreak, I didn't know. I hoped none.

He had stalked me these past few years. Writing down clues. Saving our IM entries. That meant he had confession after confession of my vampirism on record. Stored somewhere. I trusted Fang, but I wasn't sure what to think about this. He was certainly in a position to blackmail me, if he so chose, but I knew he wouldn't. I knew, and yes, *sensed*, that his interest in me stemmed from two sources: his love for vampires . . . and his love for me.

A strange day today, I wrote. *I thought of you often, I'll admit. And the most prevalent thought was: I kissed Fang! Do you mind if I still call you Fang? I kind of like it when you call me Moon Dance. Coming from you. it just feels right. It feels secretive, too, like spies, and these are our code names. I like that. I think everyone in life should have a code name. I won't mention your real name here, but I definitely don't see you as an Eli, either. You are Fang to me. Always Fang.*

I paused and reached for a pack of cigarettes sitting next to my computer. Recently I'd discovered that I could smoke. I don't recommend this to anyone but vampires, since smokes can't kill us. There are precious few things that I can ingest into my body without cramping up in pain, and smoking is one of them.

I'll take what I can get.

I lit up and exhaled a long plume of roiling gray smoke. The smoke cloud hovered briefly in front of me, then dissipated, and with the cigarette hanging from the corner of my mouth, I continued typing:

I'm not sure about the kiss. I'm not sure about anything, really. You know that I'm kind of involved with the attorney. He and I had a moment last week that I will never forget, although I won't go into it in any detail here. Let's just say it's hard for a woman to forget an experience like that (sorry if that hurts your feelings). But it's also hard for me to forget our kiss last night. So, tell me, what was it like to kiss a vampire? I'm sure my lips were cold. I'm sure my breath was cold, too. Isn't that a turn-off?

I was babbling, I knew, but these were thoughts that had been plaguing through my mind for years, and since my relationship with Fang had gone to another level, a physical level, I could ask him these questions.

I continued: *It was a turn-off for my husband. Once he vomited. No joke. He tried to lie about it, but I heard him retch and could smell the vomit on his breath. It's always nice when your husband vomits when making love to you. That was early on in my vampirism, of course. He never touched me again. Well, not in an intimate way. I never touched me, either. Transference, I believe the psychologists call it. I was unlovable in his eyes and so therefore I was unlovable in my own eyes. Yes, I know, I put too much weight into what he thought, but what was I supposed to do? I didn't know what was happening to me. Everything was all so new. His love meant everything to me. I needed it so bad and he wasn't there for me.*

I stopped writing and sat back. Ashes from my cigarette dropped onto my blouse. I always forgot to tap off the ashes. Smoking was still new to me. I wasn't sure how much I liked it, but it was at least nice to do something with my hands.

I guess I'm here to tell you that I don't want to lose what we have, Fang. But I'm not saying no to anything more, either. I guess I'm just not in any place to make decisions right now . . . and now my poor son is sick, and every alarm bell I have is ringing loudly. Something is wrong with him, Fang. But maybe that's just me worrying. Just a mom worrying.

I dashed out the last of the cigarette and looked at the blocks of words that filled the IM screen. Fang would have some reading to do once he wakes up.

The sun was coming. I could feel it. A deep tiredness was setting in and I stumbled to my room where my shades were always drawn tight, and collapsed in sleep.

The sleep of the dead. Or undead.

13.

I need an alarm clock—a very *loud* alarm clock—if I want to awaken any time before sunset. Left to my own devices, I awaken naturally just moments before the sun actually sets.

It's a nice system . . . unless you have kids.

It's very rare that I awaken on my own. But I did so now, and I awakened to find my son sleeping next to me. It was noonish. He had come in here on his own, to sleep next to his mommy. I wrapped my arms around his burning body and pulled him in close, feeling his forehead and was profoundly relieved that he didn't seem as hot.

Then again, I was barely cognizant. I was hardly in a place to make any sort of expert mommy inspections. Still, he seemed cooler and he was sleeping contently next to me.

As I fell back into my dreamless sleep, I probably should have realized my son barely stirred, if at all.

My alarm went off at 2:00 p.m., my normal time to get up and get ready to pick up my kids.

As consciousness grudgingly returned, I listened to my son's even breathing next to me. Even, yet shallow. I turned on my side and touched his cheek. Shit. He was burning up again. Not quite as hot as last night, but my little boy was clearly sick.

I lay there for as long as I dared, alternately running my fingers through his hair and lightly touching his cheeks. He had my dark hair and Danny's broad-cheekboned looks. He had my long eyelashes, of which his sister was eternally jealous.

Finally I slipped out of bed and checked my email. Nothing of importance, although it did appear that I had been handpicked to help a wealthy and desperate gentleman from Nigeria transfer his funds to the United States. His plan was genius: He would send me a whopper of a check, and I would send him a much smaller check in return. And get this: I get to keep the difference. Boy, what could go wrong with *that* idea?

I then spotted something blinking in the lower right-hand corner of my screen. An instant message from Fang. I *squee'd* and eagerly clicked on it. I might have gasped, too, and my heart definitely slammed hard against my third or fourth rib bone. Funny, I never reacted like this to Fang before.

His message was simple and to the point and it brought a big smile to my face:

I dreamed about you, Moon Dance. I always dream about you.

Smiling like a goofball, I quickly threw on a pair of jeans and a long-sleeved shirt. These days, I had quite the array of long-sleeved shirts. My day shirts, as I thought of them. My night attire was cuter. But my daytime wardrobe was all about survival . . . and staying out of the sun as much as possible.

Anyway, I slathered my hands and cheeks and neck with my heavy-duty sunblock, grabbed one of my many sunhats, carefully scooped my son up off my bed, and headed out the front door.

I dashed across the front yard, which never felt hotter. I threw open the garage door with a quick flick of my hand and plunged into the merciful shadows. Once there, I gasped and caught my breath.

My son barely stirred. He murmured "Mommy" and continued sleeping. I next buckled him into the back seat and wadded up the van's emergency blanket for a pillow.

And with the window shades pulled down, I backed up into the sunlight, and a few minutes later I was picking up my daughter. A few minutes after that I was at the Urgent Care, with my son in my arms.

14.

It was four hours later and I was sitting in Detective Sherbet's office. Mary Lou, my sister, was watching the kids; in particular, keeping an eye on Anthony.

"Is everything okay?" asked Sherbet. He was sitting behind his desk and watching me curiously. He always watched me curiously.

I wanted to make a joke about how odd it was seeing Sherbet without a donut in his hand, but I just wasn't up to it. Instead, I said, "My son's sick."

Sherbet sat forward. He was a father who loved his own son. A son who was as effeminate as Sherbet was masculine. And Sherbet was as masculine as they come. Thick hair covered his forearms and the back of his hands. The hair was mostly gray. His belly pushed hard against his white dress shirt, putting a lot of pressure on the center buttons. In fact, the third button from the bottom was slightly frayed.

It's gonna blow, I thought.

The arm hair and rotund belly looked oddly appealing on Sherbet. Really, he was a man who had no business being thin. His body frame was built to hold the extra weight, and he did so in a sexy way. I always figured that if I was twenty years older I would have a serious crush on the man. I must not be the only one, since his own wife had to be pretty young to have a child still in elementary school. A child who, according to Sherbet, was on the fast track to homosexuality. A child who was forcing my detective friend to open his heart and mind in ways he never had before.

"So what do the doctors say?" he asked.

I shrugged. "Apparently the flu's going around. They told me not to worry."

"You're not doing a very good job of it, kiddo."

I shrugged. "Mostly, I'm worried your button is gonna blow and take out my eye."

He looked down at his belly. And now that I looked again, I was certain I could see the faint outline of a jelly stain. A jelly donut stain.

He nodded. "Okay, I get it. You don't want to talk about it."

"Not really," I said.

"And to deflect talk about your son, you choose instead to talk about my belly."

"It's quite a belly."

"I like my belly."

"I never said it was a bad belly."

He drummed his thick fingers on the wide desk. His fingernails were perfectly squared and seemed almost as thick as my own supernaturally thick nails.

"Can we stop talking about my belly?" he asked. "Besides, I don't think cops are supposed to say *belly*."

"And yet you've now said it four times."

He shook his head. "Don't worry about your boy, Sam. He'll be fine."

I nodded and wished I could believe him. Sherbet asked why I was here, and warned me from saying anything about his belly. I told him about Maddie and what my ex-partner had turned up. Sherbet listened quietly, and when I was finished he reached over and typed something on his keyboard. By typing, I mean he hunted and pecked slowly with his big sausage-like fingers.

"Hanner's working the case," he said.

"May I speak with him?"

"Her. Rachel Hanner. Hang on."

He got up from behind his desk, and as he did so, one of his knees popped so loudly that I nearly took cover. Sherbet looked slightly embarrassed. "Don't say a word," he cautioned.

"Wouldn't dream of it," I smirked.

He returned a moment later with a young woman with perfect milky skin. She was also damn pretty, and I fought an overwhelming desire to hate her. She nodded at me pleasantly but didn't shake my hand.

Bitch, although I was secretly relieved. Shaking hands always followed a small bit of stress for me.

Sherbet asked her to sit and she did so next to me. Sherbet next asked me to retell my story and I did so, reciting it nearly word for word. These days, my memory seemed sharper and sharper. I had no idea what to attribute that to, but I wasn't complaining.

When I was finished, Hanner nodded once and turned and looked at me. Her movements were economical and precise. She seemed like a well-oiled—and quite beautiful—machine. Her blond hair was pulled back tightly, revealing a smooth sweep of forehead. Her eyes were impossibly big, and most guys probably would have had the hots for her if she didn't project such a fiercely calm and professional presence.

"I can't imagine that a child knows how to block caller ID," she said when I was finished. Her voice had a hint of an accent. Or maybe, for once, I was simply hearing perfectly enunciated English.

"Which is why I figured the phone had the block already programmed in."

She nodded. "A reasonable assumption. Is your business number a toll free number, Samantha?"

"At the time of the call, no."

"But you have it now?"

"Better. Just before coming here I added another feature to my phone, called Trap Call."

"I'm not following," said Sherbet.

No surprise there. Sherbet was an old-school homicide detective and probably not up to date on some of the modern tracing technology. Conversely, private investigators were almost always up on such new gadgets. New gadgets gave us an edge over our competitors. Including the police. Of course, having a freaky sixth sense was a hell of an advantage, too. He said, "And what does that do?"

"It's a call forwarding service," I said, "When a blocked call comes through, I forward it to Trap Call and their toll-free line. The caller's ID shows up on their end, and Trap Call relays the information to me. Within seconds."

Sherbet looked at Hanner. "This make sense to you?"

"Perfectly."

"Good enough. So we wait for the next call, then?" he said.

I nodded. "If it comes. Until then, I would like to assist you on this case."

"Do you have a paying client?" asked Sherbet.

"No."

Sherbet looked at Hanner. "Could you use the help?"

"More than you know," she answered.

He looked back at me. "You can help. Unofficially, of course."

"Of course."

Sherbet asked Hanner to leave the case file with him and she obliged. She smiled at me, nodded at Sherbet, and left.

The detective touched the file on his desk, and said, "I'm going to get some coffee. Maybe a donut. Okay, definitely a donut. I'll be gone for about ten minutes. You are not to look at this official police file, and you are most definitely not to copy them on the convenient copy machine in the corner of my office."

"Yes, sir."

He set the file down in front of me, and when he left to get his coffee and donut, I quickly made a copy of the file. I slipped my copy in my purse and returned the original to its folder.

When Sherbet returned with his coffee and a fresh jelly stain, he calmly picked up the file and dropped it in the "Out" box at the corner of his desk.

"I trust you didn't look at the file," he said.

"Wouldn't dream of it, sir."

"So what's your first step?" he asked.

"First, I'm going to read a file I most certainly didn't copy. And second, then I'm going to do what I do best."

"Drive to soccer games in your minivan?"

"Hey, I only do that twice a week."

"Go on."

I said, "I'm going to relentlessly look for this little girl until I find her, using whatever means I have at my disposal."

"All of them legal, of course."

"Of course," I said.

Sherbet sipped his coffee, and promptly splashed some down his shirt. He briefly glanced at it but he really didn't seem to care, truth be known. Okay, now *that* is manly.

He said, "And don't think I haven't forgotten about our little talk, Samantha."

Sherbet was referring to the recent supernatural activity happening in his town. Minor stuff, really. Just a werewolf sighting or two. Maybe a grave robbery. Maybe.

"I haven't, Detective. It's just that now isn't a good time."

He was nodding. "When your son's better and you have a little time, we're going to talk."

"Of course," I said, and got up. "I can find my way out."

I left him staring after me, with his coffee and jelly donut stains.

15.

I called my sister Mary Lou, and she told me that Anthony was sleeping peacefully. I breathed a sigh of relief.

"I think I just heard you breathe an actual sigh of relief," said Mary Lou.

"Wouldn't you?"

"He's going to be fine, Sam. You worry too much."

"It's my job to worry too much," I said.

"And it's my job to call you on it."

I asked her to watch him a little longer and she said she was planning on staying the night. Her own children were at home with their dad, which made me briefly envious. Hey, I'm only human.

I think.

Having Danny around had made my job infinitely easier. That is, until he started coming home later and later—and reeking of perfume. Then my life wasn't easier. Then it had been a living hell.

I thanked her and clicked off and checked the time on my dash. It was going to be a tight squeeze but I should make it to my meeting on time.

I took Chapman Avenue to the 57 Freeway. From there, I joined a sea of other cars and headed south. Luckily, this sea was moving at a decent clip, and soon I was going east on the 22, where I exited at Main Street. From there, I headed south, passing one of Orange County's greatest edifices: The Main Place Mall, whose postmodern glass-and-metal facade sparkled in the last light of the day like a giant beacon to desperate housewives with too much money and a penchant for giant-sized cinnamon rolls.

Somehow, I managed to resist the urge to spend thirty minutes looking for parking and pay twice the going rate for anything. Of course, I was dead broke and I doubted Cinnabons served chilled hemoglobin.

The broke part was why I was taking this meeting.

A few blocks later, I turned into the Wharton Museum

parking lot. As I did so, the sun finally set behind a horizon cluttered with apartment buildings and old homes. I stepped out of my minivan and inhaled the warm dusk air and felt more alive than I ever did when I was human.

God, I felt so strong. So powerful.

I swept through a long, arched tunnel full of hanging vines, past the sitting area of an outdoor cafe, nodded at a large tour group leaving the museum, and stepped inside Orange County's only significant cultural museum.

At the front desk, a young docent smiled brightly at me. "I'm sorry, ma'am, but we're closed." She seemed profoundly relieved that they were closed. Perhaps today had been a particularly difficult day at the museum. I suspected I knew why. In fact, I knew the reason why.

I told her who I was and why I was here. Somehow, she managed to contain her excitement. She made a call, nodded, and a moment later led me down a hallway lined with offices and cubicles. Or perhaps these weren't offices and cubicles. Maybe this was some weird, hip, modernistic "Cubicles as Art" exhibit.

Or not.

I was led to the last office on the left, where a tall woman with a vigorous handshake greeted me and showed me to a guest chair in front of her desk.

I sat and she sat, and after a short exchange of pleasantries, she got right to the point. "As you know, Ms. Moon, we had a robbery here last night."

"Yes, you mentioned that over the phone. I'm sorry to hear it."

Her name was Ms. Dickens. Yes, that's how she introduced herself to me on the phone and even now in person. So, on that note, I introduced myself as Ms. Moon, and she seemed perfectly at ease with that. I wasn't at ease with it. I mean, c'mon.

Anyway, *Ms.* Dickens wore a very old-fashioned business suit and seemed about twenty years older than I suspected she really was. She was a seventy-year-old woman trapped in a fifty-year-old's body.

She said, "I assure you, so am I. The police have been called, of course. And as far as they can tell it was an inside job. The police, however, don't seem to grasp the nature of the crime or the importance of the stolen artifact. I fear that our case will be forgotten by the overworked Santa Ana Police Department."

I made sympathetic noises. Truth was, overworked police departments are what keep many private eyes in business. Had police departments been adequately staffed, I would have been relegated to doing background searches and cheating spouse cases. Background cases were fine, and were easy money, but I avoided cheating spouse cases at all costs. I hated hearing the rotten cheating stories, and I hated being involved in the painful drama.

Not to mention, I tended to want to strangle all the cheating men. I wonder why?

Not to mention, I was a trained federal agent. I was above cheating spouse cases . . . unless, of course, I needed money.

Anyway, I asked what had been stolen, since Ms. Dickens had been vague on the phone. "A single item," she answered. "A crystal egg sculpture from the Harold Van Pelt collection."

Harold Van Pelt, apparently, was a world-class gem photographer. But what wasn't so well-known was that he had become, over the course of 35 years, a master gemstone carver. Apparently, he had perfected the art of taking a solid block of quartz and turning it into hollowed vases or, in this case, a hollowed egg. The Wharton was the first museum to showcase his work.

"The quartz is cut so paper thin and polished so perfectly that it is as clear as glass. How he does it, I have no clue."

"Well, like they always say, just carve away anything that doesn't look like a crystal egg, right?"

She stared at me. "I'm sure there's more to it than that, Ms. Moon." I was fairly certain that if she had a ruler, she would have rapped my knuckles with it.

"Why do the police think this was an inside job?" I asked.

"They haven't said."

"Which makes sense," I said. "If it was an inside job."

Ms. Dickens tilted her head to one side. "Are you implying that I'm a suspect, Ms. Moon?"

"Oh, it's much too soon for me to imply that," I said, smiling brightly.

Not to mention I wasn't getting a negative feel from Ms. Dickens; meaning, she checked out clean to my sixth sense. That is, if it was to be relied upon.

Brightly or not, Ms. Dickens didn't like the direction this conversation was going. I didn't, either, for that matter. I needed the job and I needed her retainer check. Badly. The last thing I needed to do was offend the lady. There was always time to offend her later.

The curator unpursed her lips. She was, after all, a reasonable woman. Or so I hoped. She said, "If this was an inside job, then I suppose everyone here is indeed a potential suspect. Me included."

"Some people are less suspect than others," I added.

"You have a job to do," she said, which was encouraging. "And part of that job is getting answers. I get it."

"Thank you," I said.

"Well, you certainly seem capable, Ms. Moon. I called your references. In particular, your boss at HUD. Earl, I believe his name was. Anyway, he assured me you are very professional and reliable. I think he used the word *spunky*."

I had worked at HUD for a number of years before my attack rendered me into something . . . very different. After the attack, I had been forced to quit my job and work the night shift as a private eye. The transition from a federal investigator to a private investigator had been an easy one, although I missed the camaraderie of a partner and the massive resources of the federal government. Luckily, or perhaps, smartly, I retained my friendships with most people in the agency, and often they gave me access to their super-cool computers.

"Earl always thought highly of me," I said.

"He also said you were forced to quit suddenly because of a rare skin disease." She tilted her head down, studying me over her bifocals. "Could you expand on that?"

"It's a rare disease that I have under control. Mostly, I have to stay out of the sun and away from McDonald's heating lamps."

"I see some of that spunkiness coming through."

"You caught me."

"Will your condition affect your performance?"

"No, ma'am, although I tend to work nights, as we've already discussed over the phone."

"Working nights is fine with us. We don't need any more distractions during the day. And besides, the theft occurred at night, too. Maybe there's something to that."

"Maybe," I said. *Sheesh, everyone's a detective.* "Is there a special crew that works the night shift?"

"Security crew, yes. I will introduce you to some of them shortly." Ms. Dickens paused and held my gaze. "I need to underline the importance of this investigation, Ms. Moon. We are a respectable, although small, cultural museum. We've had everything from rare Egyptian treasures to paintings by van Gogh. A theft like this could shatter our international image and keep the popular exhibits away. Ms. Moon, the Wharton Museum is slowly making a name for itself as a world class cultural museum. We need all the help we can get, and we will pay big if you can recover the crystal egg."

We discussed exactly how big, and it was all I could do to keep my mouth from dropping open. We next discussed a retainer fee, and she paid it without blinking, writing me a company check. The retainer fee would pay my mortgage for the next three months, and maybe a car payment or two.

Things were looking up.

She gave me a quick tour, and then we shook hands and I left the way I had come, passing more live exhibits of mankind in his natural working habitat.

Or perhaps they were just offices and cubicles.

16.

I called Mary Lou and got the rundown.

Anthony was awake and seemed to be holding steady. No real progress, but no relapse either. Still, my gut churned. When I thought about my son, I saw something dark around him. The brightness and vitality that surrounded him was gone.

I desperately feared what that darkness could mean.

To get my thoughts off my son, I headed over to Zov's Bistro in Costa Mesa, where I ordered a rare steak and a glass of white wine. The upscale Mediterranean restaurant was the epitome of hip, and I even noticed Orange County's bestselling writer sitting just a few tables down. He looked serious. Maybe he was plotting his next thriller. I wondered if he could sense that a real live vampire was sitting just a few tables away.

While I waited, I plunged into Maddie's police file, reading every note and witness statement.

I knew I should be with my son, and I would be soon, but for now there was a little girl missing, and she had made it very personal by calling me.

By calling me, even accidentally, she had assured herself of one thing: a private investigating psychic vampire mommy who was going to find her.

No matter what.

My food arrived quickly. The nice thing about ordering steaks rare is that they don't take long to cook. And as I read from the folder, I discreetly used a spoon to slurp the blood that had pooled around the meat. I also cut the meat up without actually eating it. I scattered the chunks around my plate, hiding some under my salad. I felt like a kid hiding her food.

The blood was wonderful and satisfied some of my craving, although I would need more later. And when I had drained the meat dry, I moved on to the glass of white wine. When the wine was done, I was done reading the police report, too.

Granted, there wasn't much to go on, but I had a few leads. I paid my bill, glanced a final time at the writer—who was now openly staring at me—and left Zov's Bistro.

I had a girl to find.

17.

I was driving down the 57 Freeway when my cell rang. I glanced down at it. Kingsley Fulcrum, a one-time client of mine who had turned into something more than a client.

A few weeks ago we had been intimate, an experience that had rocked my world, and shortly after that I was reminded of what a scumbag he could be. Kingsley was a defense attorney. A very high-profile and rich defense attorney. He got paid the big bucks to get people out of jail. As far as I could tell, the man had no moral compass. Killer or not, if the price was right, he would do his damnedest to get you to walk.

Did I still care for the big lug? Yeah, I did. Did the thought of him in bed turn me on more than I cared to admit? Sweet Jesus, it did. Did the fact that he had shown up in my hotel room a week or so ago as a fully morphed werewolf, dripping blood and reeking of death, scare the shit out of me? Hell, yeah.

I clicked on, resisting the urge to sing "Werewolves of London" yet again. When your boy is sick and you're looking for a kidnapped girl, well, your humor is the first to go.

"What, no 'Werewolves of London'? No 'Arooo'? You're losing your touch, Sam."

"It's not a good time, Kingsley."

"So serious. Okay, have it your way. Where will you be in about an hour?"

"My best guess? In the face of some crackhead punk."

"A shakedown. Sounds exciting. Tell me about it."

I did. I also told him about my son.

"Yeah, you've had a rough few days. How's your son now?"

"Sleeping last I heard."

"But you're still worried."

"More than you know." I paused, gathered my wits, and plunged on. "I see death around him, Kingsley."

"Death?"

"A blackness. A coldness. A sort of dark halo that surrounds his body. I'm totally freaked out."

Kingsley was silent for a heartbeat or two. "He'll be fine, Sam."

But I heard it in his voice. I heard the doubt.

"You don't believe that," I said. Tears suddenly blurred my eyes. I was having a hard time keeping the van in the center of the lane. "And don't deny it."

"Sam, I don't know anything, okay? I'm not psychic. My kind are not traditionally psychic."

"But my kind is?"

"Often. And you seem to be growing more psychic by the day."

"What do you know of the black halo? Tell me. Please."

"I know very little, Sam."

A nearly overwhelming sense of panic gripped me. "But you know it's not good."

"I know nothing, Sam. Look, now is not a good time to talk about this. You're driving. You're helping this little girl. Let's meet for drinks later this week, okay?"

"Okay," I said.

"Good. And Sam?"

"Yes?"

"I care about you deeply. Your family, too. Everything will be okay. I promise."

I broke down, crying hard, and clicked off.

18.

I pulled up to a squalid house in Buena Park, about a mile north of Knott's Berry Farm. I sat in my minivan for a few minutes and took in the scene. Apartments across the street. A gang of Hispanic males a block away to the west. They were smoking and drinking and listening to music. The music pumped from a four-door sedan whose front end was hydraulically propped up off the ground two or three feet. The car looked ridiculous and cool at the same time. I wasn't sure which. The gang ignored my van, which was probably a good idea. The last time I had a run-in with a Latino gang someone had died.

And gotten himself drained of blood, too.

The moon was obscured by a gauzy veil of clouds. The street had a mean feel to it. The area itself seemed malevolent, and I suspected this awareness was a result of my increased psychic abilities. I sensed death on this street. I sensed stabbings and robberies and harassment and fear. I sensed drug deals and drug deals gone bad. I sensed a ramshackle attempt at organized crime. I sensed killers and victims. It was all here, infusing the air and the earth, the trees and the buildings. A calling card of hate for anyone sensitive enough to feel it. And I was sensitive enough. Perhaps too sensitive. The feeling was overwhelming. Energy crackled crazily through the air, too—and now that I knew what to look for, I saw many vague spirits walking among the living. Murder victims mostly. But some were lost souls, whose lives were taken by drug abuse or physical abuse.

It was into this environment of loss and despair and suffering that I stepped out of my minivan.

A low iron fence surrounded the property. The gate was topped with rusted iron spikes. The spikes were mostly rounded and probably wouldn't do much damage unless someone fell from a great height. The front gate was not locked and swung open on rusted hinges. As I moved across the front yard, I felt eyes on me from across the street. I had attracted the attention of the neighbors in the apartment building. No doubt watching from one of the windows.

I stepped up onto the cement porch, which was cracked and flaked with peeling paint. I paused a moment, getting a feel for the house. Someone was inside, I knew that much. I could hear a TV on somewhere. The house itself was drenched in so much tragedy that it was a beehive of bad vibes, depression and anything else negative.

More than anything, the house was the last known residence of Lauren Monk and her daughter Maddie. I shook my head. What a place to raise a little girl.

Granted, I doubted there was much "raising" going on here. *Existing* was more like it.

I knocked on the door loudly. The door was made of metal and seemed better suited in a parking garage stairwell. There were dents in the door, about waist high. Someone had tried to kick it in at some point. Maybe many points. I looked around the metal frame. As far as I could tell, they weren't successful. The door and frame had held firm.

The TV continued to blare. A distant siren wailed behind me. Down the street someone laughed and others followed suit. I knocked again, and again.

No response.

I stepped back, lifted my foot, and kicked the door in.

19.

The door swung violently back, slamming hard into the wall behind it, so hard that the doorknob punctured the drywall. It stayed open like that as I stepped in. Unless someone was brandishing a stake or silver-tipped arrows, I wasn't too concerned about what was waiting for me on the other side. Sure, a bullet to the chest probably would hurt like hell, and no doubt ruin my blouse, but gone were the days where I worried much about my own physical safety.

I found myself standing in a living room. Or a toxic bio-hazard. Take your pick. The long clump of trash to my right was probably a couch. The rectangular clump in front of it was probably a coffee table. Everything from shopping bags to clothing to pizza boxes were everywhere. Including used heroin needles. Everywhere. Hundreds of them.

I stepped over broken glass and empty beer cans and a McDonald's Happy Meal. I moved through the living room and into a kitchen that hadn't been used as a kitchen in some time.

Instead, it was being used as a meth lab.

There were bottles and jars with rubber tubing. There were stripped-down lithium batteries piled on tables. Paint thinner and starter fluid containers lined the floors. Empty packets of cold tablets, no doubt containing pseudoephedrine, were piled on the tables and counters. Also on the tables were jars containing clear liquid with red and white bottom layers. Ether and ammonia wafted from them. Propane tanks were everywhere. Okay, the propane tanks made me a little nervous.

There was a strong smell of something else. And it was coming from the next room. I knew that smell. Any cop or agent would know that smell.

I moved through the kitchen and down a short hallway. I had sensed someone else in the house, but what I had not sensed was whether or not that someone was alive or dead.

At the far end of the hallway, in a room to the right, a TV was on and a man wearing boxer shorts was lying face down in a pool of blood. In death, he had made an unholy mess of himself, but that did not stop me from checking him out.

I rolled him over. Blood stained the mattress. Probably all the way through and to the bed springs below. I counted five shots to the chest. I wrinkled my nose, although wrinkling did little against what was wafting up from him.

I did a quick examination. White male in his early fifties. Dead for less than 24 hours, give or take a half a day. Heavy set. No indication of a fight. The body already in full rigor mortis. Face bright crimson where the blood had settled like oil at the bottom of an oil pan.

I eased him back down.

Years ago such a scene might have turned my stomach. I might have picked a quiet spot behind the house to vomit, careful not to disrupt a crime scene. Now, not so much. I had seen many dead bodies in my time, certainly, but there was something else going on. Something that worried me. I should care more about death, about the loss of life. But I didn't.

Death no longer bothered me. Didn't faze me. I felt no emotion or concern or anything.

It was just death.

The natural order of things.

I wasn't always this way, but something had changed inside of me, and I think I knew what that something was.

I was becoming less human . . . and that scared the shit out of me.

I spent the next twenty minutes carefully picking through the house, looking for any clues that might help me find little Maddie, but nothing stood out. No Rolodexes filled with the names of drug kingpins. No computers or laptops. No cell phones. Nothing that seemed to indicate that a little girl had ever lived here.

Nothing, that is, except for the Happy Meal box.

I pulled out my cell phone and called Detective Sherbet.

20.

I spent the next two hours with Detective Sherbet and Detective Hanner. I gave them my statement, stood back and watched the preliminary crime scene investigation, and when all the fuss was over, I headed over to Hero's in Fullerton, where Fang worked.

As I walked up to Hero's single door, a door which always somehow seemed to be slightly cracked open, I ran a hand through my thick hair and fought a sudden wave of nerves. I adjusted and readjusted my light leather jacket.

It was just after 1:00 a.m. when I stepped inside the bar. Hero's is filled with a lot of wooden beams and colums. The floor creaks when you walk across it, and more often than not, you will find a pool of spilled beer somewhere nearby, reflecting the muted track lighting above.

Aaron Parker, aka Eli something or other, aka the American Vampire, aka Fang, was tending bar alone tonight. He was chatting with two guys in flannel shirts when he looked up and caught my eye. He smiled broadly. It was the same look he had always given me since being hired here months ago.

Since stalking me and taking this job.

I must have mentioned in one of my IMs to him that my sister frequented Hero's. Initially, I had thought I would be more careful than that, but I had let my guard down with Fang. And he had not only found out who I was, but had gotten a job at the very bar I frequented with my sister.

Creepy. And well, sweet, too.

Aaron Parker was clearly a nut. That much was certain. He was also a killer. But, more than anything, he was Fang. My Fang.

Maybe we're all nuts.

I saw now the hint of longing in his eyes. Saw the deep concern for me. Perhaps it was love. I had never noticed it before. Or, if I did, I hadn't given it much attention. I had been a married woman until recently. Besides, maybe I thought he had been hamming it up for an extra big tip.

But I saw him differently now. In a new light, so to speak. The attention, the intent behind his gaze . . . all of it was for me.

I took in a small, sharp breath.

He smiled and unconsciously pulled back his upper lip. In that moment, in this lighting, I had a brief flashback to the disturbed teenage boy who seemed to relish pulling back his upper lip in the courtroom, the boy whose fanged smile had made front page headlines across the country.

That boy was a man now. And although he had some plastic surgery, appeared to have grown a foot or more, and was sporting a beard, there was enough similarity to give me pause.

He's a killer, I thought. *A murderer.*

The tormented young man had grown into something beautiful, but that made him no less tormented or sick. I had not known Fang to be sick. Obsessive, certainly. But his advice had always been spot on, and his caring for me had been genuine. Or, at least, *seemed* genuine.

And his smile—that sexy, slightly awkward smile—seemed genuine, too. I walked up to the bar just as he reached for a bottle of white wine.

"Hello Sam," he said easily. The massive teeth that dangled from the leather strap around his neck clanked together with the sound of two thick beer mugs toasting. Clearly the rest of the world thought these were shark teeth. Or perhaps some other creature. Barracuda? Sasquatch?

"Hello Eli," I said, using his official name, although I sat at the far end of the mostly empty bar.

"We are so formal tonight," he said.

"*We* are still in shock from last night."

"We are?"

"Oh yes," I said.

"You never expected me to be so dashingly handsome, perhaps?"

"I didn't expect you to be a renowned fugitive."

He calmly cleaned a shot glass, as if he was just another bartender. "And does that bother you?"

"That you're a wanted man? That I'm cavorting with a known criminal?"

"Cavorting?"

"It's a word," I said.

He grinned easily and leaned across the counter, putting

most of his weight on his palms. His two teeth hung freely from his neck like pale corpses twisting in the wind. "It's kind of a sexy word."

I looked away. I would have blushed if I could have. "I think you're taking it out of context."

"I prefer my context."

"Are you quite done?" I said. "I thought we were just friends."

"Just friends? After that kiss last night?"

"That kiss was your idea."

"I seem to recall you enthusiastically participating."

"Can we change the subject?" I said.

He grinned broadly. "Sure. Whatever would you like to talk about, my lady?"

I shrugged and sipped the white wine. Wine has no effect on me, but it's one of the few things, outside of hemoglobin, that I can drink like a regular person. Red wine not so much. Red wines contain tannins that upset my stomach. For someone who is supposedly immortal, my digestive system is hypersensitive.

I said, "I just want to talk to a friend."

"You know I'm your friend, Moon Dance."

"I like when you call me Moon Dance."

"I know. I read your epic IMs this morning when I woke up. Truth be known, I like it when you call me Fang, too."

"Fang and Moon Dance," I said, shaking my head. "We're weird."

"More than anyone could possibly know." He glanced around his mostly empty bar as any good bartender would, saw that his few patrons were content, and looked back at me. "Sorry I missed your IMs last night. I crashed as soon as I got home."

"No worries. It was late."

"It's difficult to keep up with your schedule, you know."

I laughed and set down the worthless wine. Who was I kidding? I wasn't normal. Why was I so concerned about looking normal?

Fang reached out and touched the back of my hand. His warm touch sent a shockwave of shivers up my arms and down my back. "You know," he said, "there is a way that you and I could have the same schedule."

"Oh?" I said, curious. "Would I need to get a second job here as a barback?"

"That's not what I meant, Moon Dance."

He continued touching me. His thumb lightly stroked the back of my hand. His fingers slipped under and caressed my palm. I shivered. Fang wasn't looking at me. I sensed his hesitation, and I sensed his insane desire.

Now Fang turned to me and our eyes met and I found myself looking deep into another person's soul for the first time in my life. Everything opened up to me. All his secrets. All his desires. All his wants and needs and hopes and dreams. And cravings. I gasped.

Fang gave me a lopsided smile.

"Yes, Moon Dance," he said. "Make me a vampire."

21.

It had been a long night.

When I got home, I discovered that everyone was sleeping in my bed, including little Anthony. I stood in the doorway of my bedroom, taking the scene in: Tammy on her back and snoring lightly. My sister in the middle and lying on her side with her palm resting lightly on Anthony's back.

A beautiful blue glow surrounded my daughter. The blue glow was interlaced with swatches of gold. The aura around my sister was a powerful orange, a contented color, a peaceful color.

There was no color around my son. There was only a deep blackness. It was as if he didn't exist at all. The light energy around him seemed to enter that black field and disappear. Like a black hole.

I rubbed my eyes and fought my tears. I slipped into some sweats and a tank top and slid into bed next to Anthony. I, too, rested my palm on his back.

His burning back.

I lay like that for a long time, waiting for the sun to rise, and when it did, I was out to the world.

Some hours later, I was awakened by my ringing cell phone.

Generally, my ringing cell phone doesn't awaken me. But in the darkness of my deep sleep, a sleep where I seriously suspected I lay in a state of suspended animation somewhere between life and death—I had heard a shouting. Someone, somewhere had shouted my name.

It had been shocking enough to awaken me from my coma-like sleep.

Half-dead, I snatched the ringing phone off the nightstand and flipped it open, barely aware that it had said "Caller Unknown" on the faceplate. My son, I saw, was lying next to me . . . in a pool of sweat.

"Hello?" I said, instinctively reaching for my son and feeling his forehead. Burning up. My heart skip-hopped in my chest. Panic raced through me.

"Hi," said a tiny and familiar voice.

But I was too distracted with my son for the voice to fully register. Two seconds later, the voice sank in, and I snapped my head around as if someone had spoken next to me, rather than through my phone line.

"Maddie!" I gasped, practically squealing.

"Hi," she said again. Her voice, if anything, sounded even smaller and fainter. I had an image of her covering her mouth as she spoke. This image came to me with crystal clarity and I suspected it was a psychic hit. Takes awhile to believe such hits are accurate . . . until you see enough evidence. I've seen the evidence now.

At that moment, a text message appeared on my phone. The call tracing had worked. A phone number was waiting for me. Maddie's number.

"Maddie," I gasped, trying to control myself. "Please, honey, can you tell me the name of the person you're with?"

"He's the bad man."

"Do you know his name, angel?"

I saw her shaking her head in my mind's eye. She didn't answer me, but I knew her answer: No, she didn't know.

"Honey, what does he look like?"

"He shot my mommy. He kilt her dead."

"I know, baby. Please can you tell me what he looks like?"

"Old."

Old to a five-year-old could be anything from nineteen to ninety. "Does he have gray hair?"

"None."

"No hair?"

"No hair," she said. "He eats too much."

"Good, honey. Good. Is he fat? Does he have a big belly?"

I sensed her nodding but she didn't answer. I also sensed that she didn't completely understand that I couldn't see her nod, that she thought she had answered my question. I had a fabulous connection with this little girl. Almost an immediate one, perhaps born of desperation. I had an idea.

"Honey," I said, "close your eyes."

"But why?"

"Please, just close your eyes."

There was a sound from somewhere and in my mind's eye I saw the little girl's head jerk up. Someone was coming.

"Please, honey, just close your eyes."

"The bad man is coming."

"Close them for one second."

"He's going to hurted me again."

"Please honey. Please. Do it for me. One time."

And she did. I knew she did, because I was instantly given a deeper access to her mind and memories and I saw an image of a room. A nice room. No, a beautiful room. A house? Condo? Apartment? I was having a hard time placing the interior. Whatever it was, it was epic. Where the hell was she? I didn't know. Through her window I saw something glittering brightly on the hillside. A desert hillside.

I saw something else. A black man. A bald black with an enormous stomach. He was standing over her and doing things that would be the death of him.

"He's coming!" she whispered over the phone, snapping me out of my reverie and out of her own memories.

"Okay, angel. Okay. Thank you, baby." I was crying now, but she would never know it. "Be strong, Maddie, for me, okay?"

"I scared."

"Be strong, angel. I'm coming for you soon. I swear."

"Okay," she said, "I strong."

I sensed a great presence near her, coming from somewhere

behind her, and now her fear knew no end. As if my own, I felt her heart race faster than I had ever felt a heart race before.

"Go!" I said. "Go!"

Next I heard a scraping sound, perhaps her hand moving over the mouthpiece, and what she said next broke me into a million little pieces. She whispered: "I love you."

And then she hung up.

22.

I was at the Urgent Care again.

It was late afternoon and I was determined to get my son some help. No, I'd be damned if I wasn't going to get him some help. The gut-wrenching call from Maddie had sent me into a panicked frenzy with my own son.

As soon as I hung up with her, as soon as I stopped hearing her precocious little voice telling me she loved me, I traced the call. Nothing was coming up. I called my ex-partner, Chad, and he ran the number through the Agency's database. The news was grim: The phone number belonged to an unregistered, throw-away cell phone.

Shit.

Next, I threw on my clothes and sunscreen, picked up my boy, and hit the road. He barely stirred in my arms or in the van.

It was still hours before I had to pick up Tammy. In the waiting room, with Anthony in my arms, I texted Danny and caught him up to date on the situation, asking him to pick Tammy up for me. His reply was immediate and curt: "Meetings all day; update me on Anthony ASAP."

Yes, he actually used a semi-colon. The piece of shit had enough time to find the semi-colon button but not enough time to help me.

My reply was equally curt: "Thanks for the help, asshole;;;;;"

Yes, complete with five semi-colons in a row.

Childish, certainly, but I didn't care. I needed help. I didn't need semi-colons.

The asshole.

I replayed Maddie's words again and again. As I did so, I

rocked my son in my arms. It was mid-day and I felt weak and agitated and vulnerable. But even at my weakest, I was still stronger than I had any right to be.

The black man was bald. He was in his fifties. I saw him from Maddie's perspective, from her eyes. He was a big man. Often sweating. Odor wafted from his body.

I blocked some of the other images I had seen. I didn't need to dwell on those. Those images would tear my heart out.

I locked them away as best as I could.

But not his face. No. I would never forget his face.

I'm coming for you, asshole, I thought.

I had a strong connection to Maddie. Perhaps it was a connection out of necessity. Amazingly, her phone call had roused me from the deepest of sleeps. Trust me, no easy feat. That connection, I was certain, would lead me to her. Eventually.

Sooner rather than later.

My son stirred in my arms, moaning slightly, and then nuzzled deeper into the crook of my neck.

Where was that fucking doctor?

I haven't been sick in six years, except if you count the overwhelming fatigue I feel before the sun goes down. Vampire Fatigue Syndrome. Whatever. Anyway, I suspected I would never get sick again. I couldn't say the same for my kids.

Anthony wriggled in my arms and leaned back. He turned his sweating face toward me, opened his eyes. "Mommy?" he croaked.

The instant he said the word I heard another little voice in my head say something similar: "He kilt my mommy dead."

"Hey, baby," I said. I did my best to ignore the black halo around his angelic face.

"Where are we?"

"At the doctor's, honey."

He nodded. "I don't feel very good."

"I know, baby doll."

He continued staring at me even while I looked ahead and tried to be strong. He was so hot. I started rocking him slightly. I could feel the tears on my cheeks.

"Mommy?"

"Yes, sweetie?"

"I'm gonna die."

I stopped rocking and snapped my head down. "Why would you say that?"

"I dream that I go to heaven. I always dream it now. And he's waiting for me."

I think my heart stopped. "Who's waiting for you?"

Anthony actually smiled and reached up and touched my face. "You know, Mommy."

I was crying now. Openly crying and I couldn't stop myself. No, I didn't know who. God? Jesus? Krishna? Who was waiting for my son? *What was happening?*

"Don't cry, Mommy," he said. "He told me to be brave. He told me to be brave for you." He touched my cheek gently and I realized he was wiping away my tears. "I'm being brave for you, Mommy."

I pulled him into me and rocked faster and faster, and as I rocked, words tumbled out of me uncontrollably: "You're not dying. You're not dying. *You're not dying. . . .*"

23.

The visit to the Urgent Care turned into something more than a visit. My son's fever was climbing. The doctor there examined my son's stomach and thyroid glands. He didn't like what he was seeing. I didn't either. My son had a rash on his belly that I had missed and his thyroid was swollen many millimeters. Blood samples were taken. My son never blinked when he was pricked with the many needles.

I impassively watched his blood being drawn.

The doctor left and I sat holding my son, who seemed to doze off and on. I rocked him gently and discovered I was humming a song to myself. I fought to remain calm but I couldn't. My lower jaw was shaking nearly uncontrollably. I had never felt so damned cold in my life, even while I held my burning son.

I rocked and hummed and prayed. The tears came without saying.

An hour later, my son woke up laughing. Startled, I asked him what he was laughing about, and he told me that Jesus had told him a funny joke. He giggled again and went back to sleep.

I continued rocking.

The doctor came back. He had arranged for a bed at St. Jude Children's Research Hospital in Orange, which is where I found myself an hour later.

The doctor who met me at the hospital smiled warmly and held my cold hands with a look of utter fascination. What he made of my cold hands, I didn't know or care. He did not ask me about them, which was a relief.

He was the pediatric infectious disease specialist and just hearing those words alone nearly sent me into hysterics. He did his best to calm me down, emphasizing that many more tests still needed to be done, but as of right now it was too soon to tell what was going on with my son.

For now, they were waiting for the blood test results, which they would have in a few hours. Once the blood tests were in, he would know which tests were needed next.

One step at a time. Detective work, really. Looking for clues, following up on hunches. Following the evidence.

Now I was alone with my son while he slept fitfully, looking so damn tiny in his bed. Just a small mound of dark hair and chubby red cheeks.

Hard as it was to do, I briefly left his side to go outside and make all the phone calls and text messages I needed to make. My sister assured me she would pick up my daughter. My ex-husband never called back. Neither did Kingsley.

Back in my son's room, I sat on the edge of his bed and held his left hand. The curtains were drawn and the lights were low. We had a room to ourselves, which was just as well, because I couldn't stop crying. The black halo that surrounded his body seemed to have grown a few millimeters as well. I didn't know much about the spirit world, but I was certain that I knew what I was seeing.

His soul was leaving.

Or perhaps it was already gone.

No, I thought. I refused to believe that.

He was just sick. Very sick. I am looking at the aura of a sick boy, that is all. A very sick boy. *My* sick boy.

Shit.

The light particles that flitted through the room, swirling and flashing and illuminating the air, disappeared completely into his aura. My hand, which glowed silverish to my own eyes, seemed to disappear into the blackness, as well. It was as if I had plunged my hand into freshly turned soil.

Graveyard soil.

I sat like that until the blood tests came back, miserable and borderline hysterical. The doctor returned and talked about normocytic anemia and thrombocytosis and blood count. He discussed something called an erythrocyte sedimentation rate and C-reactive protein levels being elevated. None of it sounded good to me. As he spoke, the doctor bit his lip a lot and looked grave and I sensed from him extreme concern and even alarm.

He next ordered liver function tests, an electrocardiogram, an echocardiogram, an ultrasound and a urinalysis.

And while they poked and prodded my son, my ex-husband Danny appeared in the doorway of the hospital room.

24.

He blinked, taking in the scene.

It was quite a scene. Three nurses and two doctors, all swarming around my son, who appeared to doze in and out of sleep. Or in and out of consciousness.

In our separation, Danny had proven to be particularly vindictive and mean-spirited. Unless, of course, you saw things from his point of view. Admittedly, very few people on the face of this earth would ever find themselves in his peculiar position. His once mostly happy household had been turned upside down. His wife of five years (which was how long we had been married prior to my attack) was suddenly not the person he had wed . . . and for the next six years Danny didn't handle things very well.

Yes, eleven years of marriage down the drain.

Would it have taken a special man to be strong and stay by my side? Certainly. It also would have taken true love, too. That was, perhaps, the hardest realization of all. That my husband didn't love me enough to be there for me.

So, yes, if you saw things from his point of view then perhaps some of his actions began to make sense.

Some.

The cheating part was unforgivable. Call me what you want, but I didn't deserve that. Next, he had fought for sole custody of the children. He believed I could hurt them. That if I was desperate enough, or hungry enough, I might feed on my own children. Insanity, of course. If I was desperate enough or hungry enough, my neighbor's yipping chihuahua would suddenly go missing.

Fighting for the well-being of our children was admirable enough on Danny's part, although there was no basis for it. I had never once exhibited any lack of control. My children received nothing but love from me. I suspected he was doing it out of spite. To purposefully hurt me.

Danny wasn't a bad father. Sure, he worked too much and often missed out on anything that had to do with school and sports, but he made up for it the best way he could. Often he read to them at night. As I worked in my office, I would listen to him patiently explain the meanings of words and help his son and daughter pronounce them. Often I would hear little Anthony giggle at *Curious George* or Tammy beg him to read one more page of *Twilight*. (Ironic, I know.) He spoke gently to each of them, sometimes so quietly that I never knew what he told them. I always wondered what they talked about, but I never wanted to ask. It seemed so personal. Just a son and a father, or a daughter and her father, exchanging sweet moments meant only for each other.

We'd gotten along like this for many years, living in quiet desperation, our kids content enough, but our marriage collapsing. I would have continued living like that forever. I was a monster and Danny seemed to at least accept me.

But it all came to a crashing end months ago when I had caught him cheating.

Danny still stood in the doorway, unsure what to do. His tie was still pushed up against his Adam's apple, and he looked pale and worried. He was still wearing his nice Italian suit. Danny rarely wore his nice suits, so he must have been in court today. An injury attorney, Danny hated going to court. Injury attorneys prefer to settle over the phone. They like easy, cut-and-dried cases. Anyway, if he had been in court, that might explain why he had been so short over the phone.

He finally spotted me in the far corner of the room, where I had sat while the doctors and nurses swarmed over my son. A few long strides later and he was sitting in the spare seat next to me, where he surprised the hell out of me by leaning over and giving me a small hug. I didn't hug him back.

"How is he, Sam?"

I started to tell him what I knew, but only about six coherent words came out. I broke down completely, sobbing hard into my hands, and I was slightly less surprised when Danny reached over again and pulled me into his shoulder.

25.

We were sitting side by side at the foot of my son's hospital bed. It was after hours, although "after hours" didn't mean much in a children's hospital intensive-care unit, since parents or guardians are usually permitted to stay with their children overnight.

We had been sitting there quietly for some time before I realized Danny had been holding my hand. I gently pulled it away, shocked and surprised all over again. Danny hadn't held my hand in six years. And if he did happen to touch me, it was always immediately followed by a visible shudder.

He wasn't shuddering now. Why, I don't know, and I certainly didn't care. Danny was the least of my concerns.

Anthony was breathing lightly on his own. Occasionally his aura would flash yellow, but mostly it was a deep black. Interestingly, bigger flashes of light seemed to hover over his body, and then scuttle away again like frightened fish. I sensed these could be other entities. But I wasn't sure. How could I be sure? I didn't know what the hell was going on with myself half the time.

Another curious glob of light came over him, hovering briefly over his head, and then seemed to dart around my son almost hectically.

No, not hectically.

Playfully.

It was the spirit of a child, I realized. And I was suddenly certain this child had died in this hospital. A ghost child. Trying to play with my son.

I took in a lot of air but the sound was strangled and Danny glanced sharply over at me. He didn't seem to know what to do with his hand now that I had removed mine from his.

"What?" he asked.

"Nothing," I said. I had long ago learned not to share my supernatural experiences with Danny. Such experiences served only to freak him out and distance him even further. Now, I just didn't care to share anything with him.

As I watched the amorphous light zigzag over my son's inert body, I thought of another child. A girl who was being held prisoner by God knows who. A girl who was alone and scared and probably hurt.

I looked at Danny. "Will you stay with Anthony?"

My ex-husband blinked, and then his eyes narrowed. "Of course. Are you going somewhere?"

"Yes."

"I want to talk to you about something, Sam," he said, and I heard, amazingly, desperation and a hint of something else in his voice. What that hint was, I refused to believe.

"Can it wait?"

He almost reached out for my hand again, but stopped. I noticed a subtle ripple of revulsion pass through him, but he fought through it. "Yes, it can. When will you be back?"

I stood and grabbed my purse. I looked at my sleeping son. I looked at the impenetrable black halo that surrounded him. I decided against sharing any information with Danny, especially about the black halo. I also didn't want to talk about the phone call with little Maddie. Danny had lost his intimacy privilege long ago, and was nowhere near my inner circle.

I said, "I might be out all night."

He nodded. "It's okay. I'll be here. You have work to do. Anthony isn't going anywhere. Are you working a case?"

"Yes."

"An important case?"

"Very."

He nodded again. "I'll be here all night. I took half the day off tomorrow, too." He motioned to the nearby, partially open window which showed a sliver of silver-tipped clouds in the night sky. "Probably wouldn't be a good idea to have you sleeping here in the morning, right? Might raise a few suspicions."

I fought through my own shock and surprise of Danny showing an ounce of consideration. I said, "I'll try to make it back as soon as I can. Call me if anything comes up."

He nodded, and almost reached for me. I shrank back.

"Where are you going?" he asked.

"Out," I said, and left.

26.

McDonald's was hopping.

The smell of French fries hung heavy in the air. I hadn't eaten a French fry in over a half a decade. I wondered if they still tasted perfect. A creepy, life-sized, cardboard clown grinned at me from a far corner. Outside, shoeless children swarmed over the mother of all jungle gyms. A half-masticated chicken nugget sat under a nearby plastic booth.

And hanging from the ceiling above the counter was a video surveillance camera.

Bingo.

According to my Google map search, this was the closest McDonald's to Maddie's last known address—the same address where I had found the working meth lab and the not-so-working dead man.

I headed over to the counter, where a teenage Hispanic girl smiled at me blankly from behind a cash register. Instead of ordering, I asked to see the McManager.

Now I was sitting in the McDonald's manager's office. It wasn't much of an office. It was just a desk at one end of a narrow room. At the other end was the employee's time clock and the drive-thru window.

"We have to make this quick," he said. He was a very short,

oddly shaped man with a bad limp. So bad, in fact, that I think his right leg might have been a prosthetic.

"Or the clown gets pissed," I said.

He grinned. "Something like that."

He didn't bother introducing himself. I guess when you're wearing name tags, introducing yourself is redundant. Anyway, according to his shiny black and silver tag, his name was Bill, and he was the general manager.

He listened to my story attentively. As he listened, he leaned a little to the right. He seemed to be mildly in pain. I would be, too, if I was sitting on half an ass. I concluded my story with my request to view the surveillance video.

"And you're working with the police?"

I gave him Detective Hanner's card. "Call her if you'd like."

He took it from me, studied it. "I'll do that. But I'll have to get approval from my district manager before I release the surveillance video."

"Of course."

"It's not that I don't want to help you."

"I understand."

"We just have procedure."

"Of course you do."

"Aw, fuck it. There's a missing girl. Hang on, and I'll get you set up in here. I'm not exactly sure how to run some of these electronic gizmos, though."

"I'm pretty handy with electronic gizmos."

"Of course you are. A regular James Bond."

"Minus the babes and the goofy English accent."

He grinned again. "Hang on."

He got up and limped out of the office. As I waited for him to return, I thought of my son and the black aura, and a crushing despair unlike anything I had ever felt took hold of me right there. All thought escaped me. Rational thought, that is. I had an image of myself grabbing him and jumping through the hospital window. Of me running off into the night with my son in my arms. Where I would go, I didn't know, but I had an image of us together, somewhere, alone, while I willed him to perfect health. The image was strong. The image was real, and I wondered if it was perhaps precognitive.

Could I now see into the future?

I didn't know, but more than likely it was just an image of a helpless mother doing something, anything, to help her sick son.

Bill came back with a remote control and a small three-ring binder. He sat back at his desk, easing himself down slowly. As he did so, gasping and wincing, a wrecked motorcycle briefly flashed before me. I saw it steaming and twisted on the asphalt.

"You were in a motorcycle accident," I said suddenly and without thinking.

Bill snapped his head up. He had been flipping through the binder. Now his hand paused in mid-flip. His eyes narrowed. "How did you know?"

I could have pointed to the Harley-Davidson picture frame or the Harley-Davidson coffee mug, both of which were sitting on his desk. I could have told him that it had been a lucky conjecture. But I didn't. I was too mentally exhausted for lies and half-truths.

"I had a vision of you crashing. I saw the twisted wreck of your bike. I saw the twisted wreck of your leg."

He continued looking at me, and then finally nodded. "Yeah, I crashed it. Took a right turn too wide. Head on into a minivan. To this day I have no clue why I'm alive."

"You still ride, though," I said.

He nodded. "It's the only thing that keeps me sane. How did you know?"

"Lucky guess."

"You're a freaky lady."

"You have no idea."

"And this little girl," he said.

"She was here." I said. "I know it."

"There's a lot of tape here. I was just looking through the instructions on how to—"

"Video surveillance 101," I said. "I can manage."

He pushed the folder over to me. "Here's the passwords to access the program. It's all stored on remote hard drives, but we can access it from here, and elsewhere, too. We have a lot of shit that goes down in our parking lots. Cops are always here checking out our video feeds."

"Thank you," I said. "I'll be fine."

"Do you know what day she was here?"

"No clue."

"Do you know what the girl looks like?"

"No clue."

"Do you know what the bad guys look like?"

"I have an idea," I said, thinking of the big black man in Maddie's memory. "I do have a picture of the mother."

"It's a start," he said.

The strong smell of French fries seemed to eddy in his back office. I said, "You ever get sick of the smell of French fries?"

"Honestly?" he said. "It turns my stomach."

27.

The surveillance program was one I was familiar with. The images recorded were stored on a Cisco Video Surveillance Storage System, which permitted the authorized user, yours truly, to access any point in time over the past five years.

So where to begin? Admittedly, using my apparently increasing psychic powers could help here, but I wasn't sure how to harness such extrasensory perceptions to an actual date. Maybe someday I would get to the point where if I sat quietly enough, an actual date would just appear in my thoughts. I wasn't quite there yet, and I somehow doubted my gifts could be *that* accurate.

So I went about this as any investigator would. Deduction, deduction, deduction.

According to official accounts, Madison and her mother had gone missing about three months ago. According to Bill, the "My Little Pony" Happy Meal theme had concluded nearly four months ago. Those timelines nearly coincided.

I removed the police file from my handbag, opened it, and looked again at the only picture of Maddie's mother on record. The woman was probably twenty-two but she looked fifty. She also looked like a typical user: skeletal, pallid, lost. Meth eats away at the brain like a tapeworm from undercooked pork, and the results are typically the same: extreme paranoia, loss of motor control, and a disinterest in anything that isn't meth. Even your kids. The woman in the picture—a mug shot taken of her years before—wouldn't have cared about her daughter's health. Or anyone's health. She cared only for getting high and it had gotten her killed. And put her daughter in harm's way.

I decided I would start four months ago and work my way forward.

And that's exactly what I did for the next five hours. Going through day after day, studying the faces of anyone who was towing a child with them. The camera was a good one, and it was set up behind the counter, looking over the employee's shoulder. There were only three active cash registers and the wide-lensed camera was able to capture the faces of any and everyone who walked up to the counter. Little kids tended to disappear *below* the counter, but I generally had a good view of any kids approaching the registers. Not that it mattered since I had no clue what Maddie looked like anyway.

I'll know her when I see her, I thought. Or so I hoped.

As I went through the days and fast-forwarded only to promising targets, I thought about my son, Danny, Fang, and Kingsley.

The men in my life.

My thoughts lingered on Kingsley and something pulled at me. Something important. What was it? I wasn't sure. Something he had said perhaps. Something that had been important, or could be important. Whatever it was, it got my heart racing.

I would think about it later, whatever it was.

Days and weeks passed. I paused often and studied faces. There were a few possibilities that made me sit up and take notice. But upon further view, the woman/child or man/child didn't add up. The girl was too perky. The mother was too happy. The father seemed particularly loving. None of this added up, at least not to me.

I continued forward. Hours sped by. Whole families appeared in the frame. I wasn't looking for whole families. I was looking for a lonely girl and someone else. Someone that made sense.

And then I found them.

The girl was dirty, dressed in a stained dress that had a torn Strawberry Shortcake patch over her chest. She trailed behind a woman who seemed confused by the McDonald's order board. Who gets confused over a McDonald's order board? It's the most famous menu in the world. She frowned and bit her lip and seemed to talk to herself. The woman herself was dressed in torn denim shorts. One leg was torn higher than the other. A white pocket hung free, squared off with a package of cigarettes. Not once did the mother look back for her little girl, who stayed behind her, swaying gently to unheard music. The girl hooked one of her tiny fingers in her mouth and waited for her mother. She could have just turned and walked out of the restaurant and her mother would never have known, and perhaps never have cared. The little girl kept swaying. She was barefoot. Her feet were dirty. So were her ankles. The mother had been wearing flip flops, but now I couldn't see the mother's feet, since they were below the counter. The girl was far back, easily in the camera frame. I stared at the girl, fascinated, my eyes glued to the monitor in front of me. In my thoughts, I could hear the girl talking. *This* little girl.

"He kilt my mother. He shot her dead."

"Maddie," I whispered.

And as the mother fumbled her way through the order, the worker placed an open Happy Meal on the counter, and as Lauren dug into her pocket, presumably for money, someone else came into the McDonald's. A man. A big black man wearing a long trenchcoat. Maddie saw him and shrank away immediately. The man said something sharply and the mother nodded. She, too, shrank away.

The man jerked his head and little Maddie followed him deeper into McDonald's, where she disappeared out of the camera frame.

I watched Lauren count out her money, then wait for her change, and finally hurry deeper into the restaurant. Thirty-three minutes later, the happy family left together, with Maddie trailing behind, forgotten, her finger hooked in her mouth.

Holding her Happy Meal box.

28.

The surveillance software has a nice feature that allows you to freeze a face and zero in on it, which I did for Maddie, her mother, and the man.

Now I was sitting outside a Starbucks on a cool night with Detective Hanner of the Fullerton Police Missing Persons Unit. Neither of us was drinking a coffee, which was a damn shame. Detective Hanner was studying the photos and making small, disapproving noises. I wondered if she knew she was making those sounds. Then again, my hearing tends to be exceptional these days, so perhaps I was never meant to hear her small, disapproving noises.

She looked up from the pictures.

"Good work," she said.

"I sometimes get it right."

"Detective Sherbet said that if anyone was likely to turn something up, it would be you."

"Detective Sherbet says the nicest things."

Hanner shook her head. "Actually, rarely. He likes you."

"The feeling is mutual."

She tapped the photo of the black man in a trench coat. Her fingernail was long. And sharp. I might have gasped a little. "He was with them around the time of their disappearance," Hanner said. "He's a person of interest."

"He's got my interest," I said.

"This photo will be everywhere as soon as I get back to the station. We'll catch this bastard."

"If you don't mind, I would still like to help."

"Hey, Maddie picked you. Maybe there's something bigger at work here. Of course I want your help. After I drop by the station, I'm heading out to work three more missing persons cases. One of them is an old lady from a nearby nursing home. My second call about her in two weeks. Found her last time partying with some local crackheads, high as a kite, dancing the Charleston naked."

I snorted. "Now that's getting high old school."

"If you saw the place she lived, you probably wouldn't blame her. Creepy as hell. An old folks home for retired witches and wizards, if you ask me. A sort of Hogwarts for old farts."

"Here in this city?" I asked.

She looked at me for a heartbeat or two before smiling. "You would be surprised what's in this city."

I found her oddly closed off, as if there was some sort of

shield around her. Her aura, I noticed, was an even blue. The same color as Kingsley's. It also hovered only a few inches from her skin, same as with Kingsley.

"I like you," she added. "We should get a drink some time, and talk." She winked, and as she did so, her pupils shrank noticeably. "You know . . . girl talk."

"Sure," I said.

"Good." She got up and threw her handbag over one shoulder. She reached out for my hand. "Let me know what you find, and thanks again."

As always, I hesitated before shaking any hand. But hers I was almost eager to shake. I did so now, taking her small hand in my own, and I was not very surprised to discover it was ice cold.

She stared at me intently, just a few feet away. The hair at the back of my neck was standing on end. And then she winked at me, turned, and strode off through the parking lot.

She moved gracefully and effortlessly, and I watched her until she got into her dark Mercury Sable and drove out of the parking lot, and as she did so, I was certain I had just met my first vampire.

29.

I sent Danny a text asking for an update, and he responded almost instantly: Anthony was in stable condition and sleeping soundly. I texted Danny back and reminded him that his cell phone was supposed to be turned off.

He wrote back: *Yes, Mommy.* And added a happy face.

Danny was being oddly playful and, well, *nice*. Maybe it had to do with his son being seriously ill. I didn't know, but I found it creepy as hell. Any feelings I had had for Danny were long gone.

And what did he want to talk about? I didn't know.

I sat in my minivan for a few minutes, wondering what I should do next. The museum could wait. The girl needed my help, except I didn't have much to go on. I removed my copy of the picture of the big black man, and I suddenly knew what I needed most.

Manpower.

His business card was still in the van's center console. I turned the interior light on, even though I really didn't need it.

His card was simple but compelling. On the right side were written the words: Jim Knighthorse, Private Investigator. On the other side, filling the entire left half of the card, was his picture. He was smiling. A sort of crooked half-smile that showed a lot of teeth. The smile was arrogant. The smile was casual. The light in his eyes was filled with good humor, as if he alone was in on a joke.

I had met the tall man a few weeks earlier. At the time, he had radiated a quiet strength and a lot of cockiness. Both were good qualities when it came to investigations. In fact, I would argue that both were *ideal* in a good investigator. But more than anything, I had sensed a sort of old-school chivalry in him, that he was a man who protected those who couldn't protect themselves.

I needed this man.

I made the call and, despite the fact that I sensed I had interrupted him from something important, he immediately agreed to meet me.

"I had a strange feeling we would meet again," he said, as he approached my van.

Correction: *swaggered* to my van. Even though he limped noticeably.

"Maybe you're psychic," I said.

"I'm a lot of things," he said, grinning easily, "but being psychic isn't one of them."

By a *lot of things*, I knew he meant *a lot of good things*. I shook my head. The guy was too much. But he was hard not to love.

I was standing outside my minivan, itself parked outside a Norm's in Santa Ana. When you work the night shift like me, you're fully aware of each and every all-night restaurant, even if, like me, you can't actually partake from them, outside of water and cheap wine.

Knighthorse glanced over at the dimly lit Norm's. "You would make a cheap date."

"What can I say, I'm a simple woman."

He glanced at me sideways. "I somehow doubt that. Anyone

who hangs out with Orange County's most famous defense attorney has a few surprises up her sleeve."

He was, of course, talking about Kingsley, whom I was with when I first met Knighthorse on the beach a few weeks ago. "Okay, maybe one or two," I said.

He folded his arms over his chest and leaned a hip against the van's front fender. Although it was chilly out, he was wearing only a black tee shirt and blue jeans.

I'm a woman. I'm recently divorced. Outside of an orgasm a few weeks ago, I hadn't had any sex in six years. The orgasm, I think, opened the floodgates.

So I'll admit it. I found myself staring at his biceps. Just his biceps, I swear. The way they reflected the yellowish parking lot lights. The way the thick veins protruded nearly an inch off his muscles. The way the muscle itself seemed to undulate even with the slightest of movements. I have keen eyesight, and I used every bit of it as I studied his biceps.

He looked down at his shirt. "Is there something on me? It's jelly, isn't it? I just ate a jelly donut and I felt some of it drop, I just didn't know where."

"It's not jelly. Sorry, I just have a lot on my mind."

He quit inspecting his shirt and went back to leaning a hip against my fender.

"So tell me more about the little girl."

I did, recalling everything I could. I handed him a photocopy of the trio at McDonald's. He studied it closely. Holding it up to the parking lot lights. Myself, I could see it perfectly, but he didn't need to know that.

"We'll need to canvass the area," he said.

"That's what I figured."

"A guy like this, some lowlife drug-dealing asshole, is probably on the move, especially if he just killed the mother."

"We're making a lot of leaps here," I said. "The guy could be innocent. Maybe he's an old friend."

Knighthorse shook his head and came over to me. He smelled of raspberry donuts and Old Spice. God, I love a man who wears Old Spice. The jelly donuts, not so much. He held up the picture of the black man and pointed.

"Look here," he said. "He's wearing a trench coat for a reason."

"Covering a gun?"

"Why else? It's 80 degrees here 300 days of the year. But look . . ." Knighthorse shuffled through the three photos I had given him. "There. Look."

I saw it. It was a slight bulge at the man's hip. "A gun," I said.

"Of course."

"And we're not racially stereotyping him?" I said. "Because he's black?"

Knighthorse looked down at me, and all the swagger and cockiness was gone, and I saw the real investigator in him, the man who took his job deadly serious. "What does your gut say about him?"

"That he's our guy. That he killed Maddie's mom, or at least knows the person who did. That he presently has Maddie somewhere, perhaps hurting her, perhaps killing her."

Knighthorse's jaw rippled. I think his teeth actually ground together. "Yeah, that's what my gut says, too. And race has nothing to do with that."

"What are the chances he's a drug dealer?"

"About the same chance that I'm tall and roguishly good-looking."

I shook my head. The guy was too much. I said, "So, if he supplies drugs to the neighborhood. . . ."

"Few will talk," he said.

"That, and they're probably scared of him."

"Someone will talk," said Knighthorse.

"And if he did kill Maddie's mother, then he's laying low."

Knighthorse winked. "We're gonna need more manpower."

30.

There were four of us now.

We were all sitting in the McDonald's in Buena Park, the same McDonald's where, for all I knew, Maddie's mother was last seen alive.

I was drinking a cup of water. Knighthorse had just polished off three Big Macs and a large vanilla shake. Now he was munching on a bag of fries the size of my purse. The fries smelled so damn good that I nearly reached over for one. I resisted. Fries and my undead stomach do not mix.

The thirty-something man sitting next to Knighthorse was about a foot shorter. He was also a specialist in finding the missing, particularly children. His name was Spinoza, and he was a private investigator out of Los Angeles and a friend of Knighthorse. Spinoza, who was oddly shy for a private eye, was shrouded in a heavy layer of darkness. His aura itself seemed weighed down by something.

Guilt, I suddenly thought. Something is eating away at him. Tearing him apart. And just as I thought that, a brief image appeared in my thoughts, so horrific and heartbreaking that I nearly broke down myself. It was snapshot of him holding a burned body. A tiny burned body.

It was his son, and now I understood the waves of guilt.

The image was of a car accident. Like with the McDonald's manager, I saw a burned-out vehicle, but this time I received another sensory hit: The smell of alcohol, along with the smell of burned flesh.

Sweet Jesus.

His palpable waves of guilt nearly overwhelmed me in my current, fragile state, and I was beginning to see the downside of this ESP business.

I need to learn how to shut this shit off, I thought.

Spinoza was friendly enough and had smiled and shaken my hand, but he easily lapsed into a dark silence that made it nearly impossible to warm up to the man.

Sitting next to him was another investigator—yet another specialist in finding the missing. His name was Aaron King and he was older than the hills. He was also damn good-looking and frustratingly familiar-looking.

And the psychic hit I got from him was an unusual one: *Mr. Aaron King has a secret. A big secret.*

He caught me looking at him and and gave me a beautiful smile, complete with twinkling eyes. I found my heart beating a little faster.

Aaron King and Spinoza (I never did catch his first name) passed on eating and instead sipped from oversized drinks. Men and their oversized drinks. Sheesh. They examined the photos while I recounted the events of the last few days, beginning with the first phone call from Maddie, my discussion with Chad, my conversation with Detective Hanner, Maddie's second call, the meth lab and dead body, the Happy Meal, and the video surveillance.

"All this from a wrong number," said Aaron. God, I loved the lilt to his voice. A hint of an accent. Melodious. A beautiful and agonizingly familiar voice.

"Probably not a wrong number," said Spinoza. The man spoke as if it were a great effort. As if it took all his energy and strength to form the words. If ever there was a man who needed a hug, it was him.

Knighthorse nodded. "Your number was programmed into the phone. No way a kid that young finds you in the phone book."

"Could be our guy's phone," said Spinoza.

Knighthorse looked at me. "Any reason why a six-foot-five black thug would have your number programmed in his phone?"

"Maybe he's looking for a good time?" I said.

Knighthorse grinned, and so did Spinoza. I think. Aaron King chuckled lightly.

"Maybe it wasn't his phone," offered Spinoza.

"Her mother's?" said King.

I nodded. "Maybe her mother gave it to her before her death."

Spinoza said, "Maybe she suspected something bad might happen. If so, she wanted her daughter to have it in case of an emergency."

"And she pre-programmed it with Samantha's info?" said Aaron King. "Why not the police?"

"Or maybe she took it off her mother's dead body," said Knighthorse, and the expression that briefly crossed his face was one of profound pain. Knighthorse, I realized, knew something about dead mothers. His own dead mother.

Jesus, we're all a mess, I thought.

"And you don't recognize the woman?" King asked me.

"No. And her name doesn't show up in any of my case files."

"Did you check all your case files?" asked King.

"All my files are in a database."

Knighthorse and King whistled. "Maybe I should get me one of those," said the old guy, winking at me in such a way that my stomach literally did a somersault.

Spinoza plowed forward. "Still, that doesn't mean the mother, what's her name—"

"Lauren," I said.

"That doesn't mean Lauren didn't look you up prior to being killed. Maybe she knew something was wrong."

"Or something was about to go wrong," said King.

"Right," said Knighthorse. "She looks you up in the Yellow Pages, punches you in her phone for a later call."

"But never makes the call," I said.

"Right."

"Maybe the mother tried calling you, Samantha," said Spinoza. "Perhaps you were her last call."

"Except you were too damn busy with your database to pick up," said King. He winked at me, and I elbowed the old guy in the ribs. He chuckled again.

"If so," said Knighthorse, "then perhaps you were the last call she ever made. And if the call came through as blocked, which can be done automatically, then you would have no record of the call."

"It's a theory," I said.

Knighthorse said, "And then all the daughter had to do was hit redial."

"And she would call me," I said.

"Bingo."

We let that theory digest for a few seconds. Then Spinoza sat his oversized drink down. No doubt his normal-sized bladder was bursting at the seams. "So let's hit it," he said.

And we did. But first he went to the bathroom.

31.

Private investigators seem to hold a certain allure for many people. I get that. TV has certainly made the work appear glamorous; after all, there's something exciting about being a lone wolf (no pun intended), working when you want, living on the edge of society, and catching the bad guys. The adventure. The excitement. The mystery.

Sorry folks, but fifty percent of P.I. work is following cheating spouses and doing background checks. And even then, the background work is getting sparser and sparser, thanks to so many new internet sites that do the work for us.

But, yeah, every now and then we do get a juicy case. And it can be fun. Especially when you do help those in need.

More often than not, P.I. work takes great patience, especially when you're watching a subject at home for days on end. Or when you're beating down doors looking for leads.

Like we were doing now.

Canvassing a targeted area will eventually turn up something. With enough people pounding doors and stopping people on the streets, someone, somewhere will recognize the man in the picture.

Canvassing is painstaking and frustrating at best, hopeless and infuriating at worst. And just when you think you couldn't knock on another door, or stop another stranger on the street, someone starts talking, and that someone will tell you exactly what you need to know.

Ideally.

So the four of us hit the pavement and, using a street map, centered our efforts on four different quadrants surrounding the meth house. I had the northeast section, which included a lot of rundown apartments, rundown homes, and a handful of motels. The guys didn't like me running off on my own but I reminded them that I was a highly trained federal agent. They didn't like it, and made me promise to keep my cell phone and pepper spray handy. I didn't have any pepper spray, but the old man Aaron gave me his.

I checked with Danny once, confirmed that Anthony was still sleeping, checked with my sister, confirmed Tammy was safe and sound at their home, and then hit the pavement.

And hit it hard.

We did this for four hours.

I questioned dozens and dozens, if not hundreds of people. I sensed that many of the young men recognized the man in the picture. None of them were talking. I would make them talk if I had to. I remembered where all of them lived.

Sometimes I don't play by the rules. Sometimes I make up the rules. Someone was going to talk, whether they wanted to or not.

A few of these men let it be known that they didn't appreciate me walking around and asking a lot of questions. One of these men might have threatened me. One of these men might have soon thereafter suffered a broken finger.

Might have.

I handed out all the fliers I had, each one with my cell phone number on the bottom and a promise that the call would remain confidential. And at the end of the night, with no one talking and the neighborhood shutting down, the four of us reconvened at the McDonald's. We discussed our options. We all felt we had hit the area pretty hard. Most of us felt someone knew something but wasn't talking. We all agreed that unless someone started talking soon, we would have to take drastic measures. None of us talked about what those drastic measures were. I suspected each of us had our own definitions.

Knighthorse and Spinoza would both be back tomorrow morning. I would be back in the evening. Aaron King had a lead or two he wanted to follow up tonight. He insisted on following up alone, stating he would use his old Southern charm to get the information he needed. He even winked. Hell, I was charmed ten times over.

As I stepped into my minivan, Knighthorse pulled up beside me in his classic Mustang. He cranked down his window and said he'd heard from someone on the street that a mean, dark-haired lady had broken some gangbanger's finger. His eyes narrowed. "That wouldn't have been you, would it?" he asked.

"Everything but the mean part. It's not nice to threaten a lady."

He threw back his head and laughed. "I knew you were a badass."

"Badder than most."

"Hey, that's my line," he said, winking. He rolled up his window and peeled out of the parking lot.

Spinoza followed behind in his nondescript Toyota Camry, a car much better suited for investigations than Knighthorse's eye-catching classic Mustang. He nodded at me and told me we would find her. I thanked the deeply troubled man for his help, and secretly hoped he would find himself.

As I started up my minivan—a vehicle even better suited for long surveillances—Aaron King sidled up to the window. His eyes twinkled. As if he was in on a private joke. Or if he knew a secret. I rolled down my window.

"We'll find that girl," he said. "I have a daughter. I can't stand the thought of a little girl alone and scared and possibly abused."

"I have a daughter, too," I said. "And a son."

But that was all I could get out. My voice caught in my throat.

Aaron King angled his beautiful face down into my window. "Is there something wrong, lil' darling?" he asked.

"No, I—" But my voice did it again. Or, rather, my throat did. It shut tight, and all I could do was shake my head.

But there was something so tender, so serene, so warm about Aaron King. I felt myself opening up to him, responding to him. Connecting with him.

I tried again. "My son . . ." But, dammit, that was all I could say. Even those words came out in a strangled choke.

Aaron reached through the driver's side window and gently touched my chin. "Hey, even highly trained federal agents cry," he said.

And I did. Hard. Much harder than I thought I would around a stranger. Aaron King let me cry. The hand he used to touch my cheek now reached around and patted my head and shoulders gently. He was a loving grandfather. A man with a big, beautiful heart.

And when I was all cried out, he rested his forehead against the upper window frame. "I'm sorry you're sad, lil' lady. But everything's going to be all right."

Some of the McDonald's yellowish parking lot light caught his eyes, and when he smiled again—a smile that was so bright that it lifted my spirits immediately—I got the mother of all psychic hits. So powerful . . . and so mind blowing. So much so that I was certain I had made it up.

No way, I thought.

But the hit persisted. His name wasn't Aaron King. At least, not the name the world knew him by.

Unbelievable.

"I'll call you tomorrow, Samantha Moon. And you can tell me about your son then."

I nodded, too dumbfounded to speak.

He winked at me. "Go take care of your son." And then he reached through the window and gave my chin a small boxing jab, smiled at me again, and walked back to his own car.

A Cadillac.

Might as well have been a *pink* Cadillac.

32.

Still reeling from my encounter with Aaron King, whose real name, of course, *wasn't* Aaron King, I found myself at the Wharton Museum.

Danny had promised to call me immediately if anything came up, and since I hadn't received a call, I might as well keep working, right? And with Aaron still working the case in Buena Park, I thought it was best to tackle some of my paying work.

I might be undead. I might drink blood. And I might be one hell of a freaky chick, but I still needed to feed my kids and pay my bills.

Still in my van, I removed my secret stash of foundation make-up, which I often applied heavily to my face and the back of my hands. I may not show up in mirrors or on surveillance video—weird as hell, I know—but the make-up still did. And after a long night of pounding doors and breaking fingers, well, I wasn't sure how much of my make-up was still in place.

I had already been introduced to the head night security guard, whose name was Eddie. Eddie was a heavy-set Hispanic guy who seemed as cool as cool gets, and oozed a smooth confidence. The way he carried himself, you would have thought he looked a little more like George Clooney and a lot less like Chris Farley.

Then again, I always did think Chris Farley was a cutie.

We were in Eddie's office, which was just inside the main doors of the museum. His office looked a little like Mission Control, minus all the nerds in white short-sleeved, button-down dress shirts. There were ten monitors placed in and around his desk, all providing live feeds from within the museum. While we sat, he cycled through some exterior cameras and some back-room cameras. All in all, there were over twenty cameras situated throughout the small museum.

Eddie leaned back in his swivel chair, a chair that looked abused and ready to give out. I was sitting in a metal foldout chair he had grabbed from a storage closet behind him. The cold metal was almost as cold as my own flesh.

Eddie, to his credit, rarely took his eyes off the monitors. There was a Starbucks coffee sitting next to a keyboard. The keyboard had old coffee stains on it. I wondered how many keyboards Eddie had fried spilling his coffees.

"Would you mind telling me about the night the crystal sculpture was stolen?" I asked.

He shrugged defensively. "Like any other night."

I waited. Eddie stared at the monitors. Apparently that's all I was getting.

I said, "So nothing out of the ordinary?"

"Nothing other than our back-room cameras suddenly stopped working."

"Did the theft take place in the back room?"

"Wow, you're good," he said, still not looking at me. "It's no wonder they hired you."

I ignored the remark. "How long were the cameras not working?"

"Twenty-one minutes."

"Did you catch this immediately?"

He shook his head. "Both pictures were frozen in place. How they did it, we have no clue. But the image looked fine, until I noticed the timer had stopped."

"And how long until you noticed that?"

"Thirty, forty minutes."

"Long enough for the egg to be stolen."

"Yes."

"Could have happened to anyone," I said.

He squinted at me, trying to decide if I was being as big of an asshole as he was, and finally decided that I wasn't. He relaxed a little. "I guess so, yes."

"Where in the back room did the theft occur?"

He pointed to one of the images on the screen. "There. The shipping and receiving room. We had just received the collection from the artist himself."

"And does the artist know of the theft?"

"Not yet, as far as I'm aware."

"When is the exhibit set to debut?"

"One week."

"And the cameras caught nothing?"

"Not a thing."

"Was anything else stolen?"

"Just the crystal egg."

I knew the museum had insurance to cover such a loss, but there was no insurance to cover one's reputation. From what I understood, the theft would be a black eye that the museum could ill afford.

I said, "Other than security guards, does anyone else work the night shift?"

"No, although sometimes the docents and museum staff put in late hours, especially when a new exhibit is about to open."

"Were any of the museum staff working the night the sculpture was stolen?"

"Yes, but they had left hours before."

"How many security guards typically work the night shift?"

"We have four working after hours. Ten when the museum is open. We only have three working tonight."

"Why's that?"

Now Eddie looked pissed. "No clue. Thad never showed."

"What's Thad's full name?"

"Thad Perry."

"Was Thad working on the night in question?"

"No."

"Has he ever not shown up before?"

"Never."

"So you would call this unusual behavior?"

"Extremely."

"May I have a list of the names and numbers to all four security guards working that night?"

Eddie nodded once and slowly eased forward. He tapped a

few keys at his keyboard, somehow avoiding knocking his coffee over in the process. This time. He wrote down four names and four phone numbers on a mini-sized pad of legal paper. He handed me the paper. His name was on the list.

"At the time of the theft, where were you?"

Eddie looked at me long and hard. I wasn't getting a guilty hit from Eddie. But I was getting a hostile one. He said, "I was here, manning the desk."

"The whole night?"

"Yes," he said, "the whole night."

"What about bathroom breaks?"

He jabbed a thumb behind him toward the small storage room. A storage room that, I saw, doubled as a small bathroom. "I take my potty breaks in there."

"Who on this list is working tonight?"

"Just Joey."

"I'd like to talk to Joey."

"Of course."

"Were any other private investigators hired to work the case?" I asked.

He nodded. "You and two other private dicks."

He grinned and flicked his gaze toward my crotch. He enjoyed being crude in my presence. I wondered if he would enjoy being dropped into a Jacuzzi from a fourth story balcony.

Crudeness aside, it made sense to hire more than one detective. People did it all the time. When a customer found a human finger in a bowl of Wendy's chili, Wendy's hired over ten private eyes to break the case, which one of them finally did. The finger belonged to one of the customer's friends, a finger he had lost in an industrial accident. The friends then cooked up a scheme, no pun intended, and it might have worked if not for the tenacity of one detective, and the foresight of Wendy's to hire a slew of them.

"Has anyone made any headway?" I asked.

He flicked his gaze at me sideways. Cool as cool gets. "The egg is still missing, if that answers your question."

"Oh, most definitely. I'd like to see the back room now."

He reached inside his desk and handed me a generic security badge. "It's a temporary badge. Swipe it, then key in '0000.' And I'll send Joey over, too."

He showed me on the monitors where to find the back room. I thanked him for his time. Eddie nodded once.

Too cool to nod twice.

33.

I could almost feel Eddie watching me as I worked my way through the museum, past exhibits called Native American Art and Ancient Art of China. I wondered what my butt looked like on camera. Probably cute. Maybe a little bubbly, since my daughter called me bubble butt sometimes.

I made my way through the Spirits and Headhunters collection, stopping briefly to ogle at a half dozen shrunken heads.

Real, honest-to-God shrunken heads.

And they call me a monster.

I moved through another room, and entered the Mayan exhibit, complete with a stone sarcophagus and beautifully adorned stelae covered in hieroglyphs. The room was particularly alive with zigzagging light . . . and much bigger balls of light. I knew now what these bigger balls of light were.

Spirits.

The balls seemed to orient on me. Sometimes they grew bigger and sometimes smaller. Sometimes they hovered just above the floor or shot up to the far corners of the room. One or two of them followed behind me.

They were silent, almost curious.

But they could see me. I felt it. I sensed it. Eyes were on me. Unseen eyes. And it wasn't Eddie ogling me from the Command Center.

And if the ghosts could see me, what else could they see?

Perhaps a crime?

I thought about that as I found the back door. I swiped the security card and entered the cryptic "0000" code and found myself in a spacious room. Spacious and dark.

I was about to flip on a light switch when one of the balls of light that had been following me slipped under the closed door and hovered before me.

I was standing off to the side of the door, partially facing a vast room with shelves and storage everywhere. I knew that most museums only displayed a small fraction of their exhibits, and that most pieces were in special storage within the museum, usually in basements. The Wharton, it appeared, didn't have a basement, and allotted this vast room for storage.

The room was pitch black, but that didn't stop me from seeing deep within it, and what I could see were various glass-walled bays that were probably temperature controlled. The bays contained what appeared to be rolling racks of paintings. No doubt very expensive paintings.

The ball of light crackled with energy. Yes, I could almost hear it now, a steady hum, too low for most people to hear. The hair on my arms was standing on end and I realized that the ball of light was trying to draw energy from me.

So how much energy did an ice-cold vampire have?

I didn't know, but the ball of light began taking on shape and as it did so, my mouth dropped open. And the more it took on shape, the more my mouth dropped open.

It seemed to pull in the surrounding particles of light, gathering them together the way cotton candy collects around a twirling stick.

The particles of light blended with the ball of light, which began to take on shape. A human shape. And when my mouth had dropped fully open, the vague figure of a tall, thin man stood fully before me.

And, if I wasn't mistaken, he bowed slightly.

34.

I almost bowed back, but stopped myself.

The hair along my arms was standing on end, and I saw why. A part of his crackling, frenetic, human-like essence had reached out to me. It reminded me of a white blood cell attacking a virus. I wasn't sure what was happening, until it hit me: He was drawing energy from me.

Amazing.

He wasn't a composed whole. A few times some of the light energy that composed his body seemed to disperse and scatter like frightened fish, only to reform again into the tall, thin man standing before me.

The entity tilted his head slightly to one side, and as he did so, a brief image flashed into my thoughts. The image was of a kindly old man and his wife. They were standing in front of a small building, smiling happily. I had, of course, seen pictures of this same building, especially during the past few days. It was the original 7,000-square-foot site of the Wharton Museum. In the picture was the same old couple, smiling happily.

The Whartons.

Next, a single word appeared in my thoughts. Honestly, I didn't know if I thought it or heard it. Either way, it appeared just inside my eardrum:

Come.

With that, the entity that I now thought of as Mr. Wharton drifted away. As he drifted away, he lost some of his shape and looked, more than anything, like a floating, glowing amoeba.

He wanted me to follow him. That much I was certain of.

I obliged, following the amorphous ball of energy deeper into the back room, past rows and shelves of Native American art, African art, and Chinese art. In fact, dozens and dozens of rows. The majority of the shelves were filled with wooden and clay sculptures, weapons that still looked like they could seriously do some harm, and what had to be priceless jewelry. The jewelry was behind glass cases, as were some of the more delicate pieces. Not surprisingly, Mr. Wharton seemed to know his way.

We passed the small shipping and receiving room, which was lined with metal tables and boxes of all shapes and sizes. Some looked like they were going, and no doubt some still needed to be received. What was in those boxes was anyone's guess.

He led me deeper. Or, rather, the glowing ball of light led me deeper, as it had now lost all human shape. It was dimmer back here, and there was only a single security camera a few rows down. Eddie would have a hard time seeing me. No doubt he was wondering what the hell I was doing back here. I was wondering, too.

Mr. Wharton hung a left. And by hanging a left, I mean the ball of light that was the ghostly imprint of Mr. Wharton, went *through* some shelves and entered a side corridor. I hung the left the old-fashioned way.

He continued on, and so did I.

The camera, I saw, did not reach down this side corridor, which meant that Mr. Wharton and I were alone. And at the far end of the corridor was a massive storage freezer that looked vaguely like a coffin.

I wasn't sure what the museum would need such a storage freezer for, until I remembered the shrunken heads outside. No doubt the museum kept anything biological in cold storage. At least, that's what I would do if I had a collection of shrunken heads.

Crackling and spitting energy and doing his best impression of a human torch, Mr. Wharton materialized again. He stood next to the freezer.

As I approached, Mr. Wharton actually stepped aside to give me access.

Ghostly etiquette. Nice.

I reached down and slowly opened the lid. Cool air rushed out, and the stench of frozen meat. And when the swirling mist had subsided, a very dead face was looking up at me from the depths of the freezer. Wearing a museum guard uniform. I think I had just found Thad, the missing guard.

Two dead bodies in two days.

I was on a roll.

35.

It was late, and I was sitting in Kingsley's spacious living room. I had spent the last few hours talking to various Santa Ana homicide detectives. When they were done asking questions and satisfied with my answers, I texted Kingsley and he invited me over.

Franklin, Kingsley's butler, was noisily preparing our drinks in the kitchen. The kitchen was down the hall and around a corner and through a swinging door. Something banged loudly, or possibly even broke.

"I think Franklin is letting it be known that he doesn't appreciate my late-night sojourns," I said.

"Luckily, Franklin doesn't have much say in the matter," said Kingsley. "How's your son doing?"

"Not good."

"I'm sorry, Sam."

I nodded and fought through the tears. It was amazing how quickly tears came these days.

The big defense attorney, who had been lounging in a chair-and-a-half across from me, sat forward. The chair-and-a-half was barely big enough to contain him. Kingsley, I could tell, wanted to reach out for me, but stopped himself. Our relationship had cooled noticeably a few weeks ago when I had discovered he'd worked the system to free a suspected killer. A killer who had killed again . . . the father of my client.

I had serious issues with that. I knew that Kingsley was doing his job. I get it. But it didn't mean I had to respect it or like it.

To Kingsley's credit he hadn't pushed the issue with me. Mostly, he had sat back and waited for me to work through my issues. And to my own credit, I knew enough not to make a rash decision. Too many people act too quickly, end relationships too quickly. Better to be clear about what you want.

I wasn't clear yet; I was still conflicted.

But now wasn't the time for that. I had had a long day and an even longer night, and now all I wanted was a warm hug, a warm smile, and a warm body.

It was no surprise that Kingsley came immediately to mind, although I had flirted with the idea of contacting Fang. The idea didn't stick. Fang was a whole new jigsaw puzzle of confusion that I needed to piece together, and I just wasn't up to it, not now. Not with everything else going on. Kingsley, although a bastard, was familiar and loveable and warm as hell.

The banging in the kitchen stopped, and a few moments later Franklin appeared in the living room with a tray of drinks. He set a goblet in front of each of us and stood back. Franklin wasn't happy. He was also a piece of work. Literally. The man, I was certain, had been pieced together from many different men. Where Kingsley met him, I didn't know. Why such a creature served as a werewolf's butler, I couldn't imagine. But there was a hell of a story here, somewhere. Kingsley had promised he would tell me the butler's tale. Someday. And if and when I was done being pissed at Kingsley, maybe I would finally hear it.

"Is that all?" asked the butler. His slightly melodic accent was nearly impossible to place. It could have been British, but it wasn't any British accent I had ever heard. The words *Old English* came to mind, too. As in old, *old* English. This, I'm certain, was a psychic hit, but I could have been wrong. Just how old Franklin was remained to be seen.

"Thank you, Franklin. That will be all," said Kingsley, waving him off.

The butler nodded. "If you and the lady need anything else, please do not hesitate to rouse me from a deep and satisfying sleep."

"We won't, Franklin. Now, off you go!"

Franklin bowed and turned and loped off, his legs seemingly not quite working together. Almost as if they had been two different legs from two different bodies. A theory that I was beginning to accept.

Kingsley reached for his wine. "Drink up, dear."

I reached for my own drink, but it wasn't wine. It was chilled hemoglobin, and if I didn't hurry and drink, the surface layer would coagulate.

I picked the cold glass up with both hands and brought it to my nose, inhaling deeply the strong coppery scent. Metallic, rich, alive. I brought the goblet to my lips and that first dribble of blood sent a shiver through me that was akin to a smoker's high.

It had taken me a long, long time to actually acquire a taste for blood. To actually enjoy it. But it depended on the blood. The finer the plasma, the more I enjoyed it. The purer the hemoglobin, the better the experience. The more pleasurable the experience. The more beneficial, too. Fine blood gave me extra energy, added strength, and a better life experience.

But my blood of choice—or of necessity—comes from a butchery in nearby Norco, where I had a running account with them. Once a week they delivered the stuff to my door, no questions asked, although they believed it was for scientific purposes. The blood was often filled with fur and skin and other floaties that I couldn't quite place. Didn't *want* to place. It was utterly disgusting, but it nourished me and no doubt kept me alive.

This blood was different. This blood was heavenly. This blood, I was certain, was from a human. There were no impurities in it. It was silky smooth and fresh and filled with a life force that absolutely electrified me.

"Thirsty?" asked Kingsley.

I opened my eyes. I found myself staring into the empty goblet, whose interior was coated now with a thin film of blood.

"Very," I said. "Would you think less of me if I licked the inside?"

"Waste not, want not, I say."

I ran my tongue inside, licking hungrily, and only then did I realize how ghoulish I looked. "Did that look as ghoulish as I think it did?" I asked.

He grinned. "Worse."

"Great." But that didn't stop me from using my index finger to swipe at the last few drops of blood.

Kingsley watched me with a bemused expression. He was wearing a robe and not much else. His legs were hairy as hell, but also roped with muscle. His toes, I saw, were extraordinarily long. And hairy, too. He wiggled them at me when he saw me looking at them. They looked like ten frightened mice.

"I'm getting more and more used to drinking blood," I said.

"It was bound to happen."

"I mean, I'll always hate the animal blood, but this human blood was nearly orgasmic."

"Do you feel stronger?"

"In every way, but it's late, or early, and I feel myself getting tired."

"No worries. The blood will more than sustain you for a few days. Much more so than that polluted pig and cow crap you drink."

I had experienced this before. Human blood revitalized me unlike anything else. So much so that I realized that I was *meant* to drink human blood. I was meant—designed—to kill humans.

"So whose blood is this?" I asked.

"Do you really want to know?"

"No. Yes. Shit."

Kingsley got up, and as he did so, he flashed me the goods. Whether he meant to or not, I don't know . . . but holy sweet

Jesus. Did I really just see that? My God, how did he walk around with that thing?

Kingsley, defense attorney, werewolf—and now, apparently, *pervert*—sat next to me and gave no indication that he had just given me the mother of all peep shows.

"I'm going to let you in on a little secret," he said, and knocked back the rest of his wine like it was booze-flavored Kool-Aid.

"It's not a secret," I said. "And it ain't little."

"Excuse me?"

"Never mind."

But I caught the smallest of shit-eating grins on his face.

"Go on," I said, shaking my head. "And this time try to keep the robe closed."

"I do my best to keep it closed."

I patted his meaty knee. "Well, do better, big boy. Now, what is it that's such a big secret?"

He sat back, but this time he kept the robe closed well enough. "The blood is from a donor, Sam."

"A donor?"

He nodded.

"A willing donor?" I prodded.

"Willing enough," he said.

"I don't like the sound of that."

"It's not as bad as it seems."

"But it's still bad?"

"Gruesome, perhaps. Macabre."

"Perhaps you should just tell me what you know."

"There's a world of vampires out there, Sam, that you haven't been introduced to yet. At least, I don't think you have."

I thought back to Detective Hanner. Whether or not she was a vampire, I didn't know, and I most certainly hadn't been officially introduced to other vampires.

The defense attorney went on. "You're not the only one of your kind, Sam, and the vampire who attacked you wasn't the last."

Knowing this set off alarm bells within me. I didn't like knowing there were others like me, truth be known. I knew *me*. And I trusted me. I didn't trust others. "How many more are there?" I asked.

"Not many; in fact, very few."

"Are we talking thousands?"

"Hundreds, perhaps. Scattered around the world."

And yet there were two in Fullerton, I mused, but didn't say anything. The one who had attacked me (and was subsequently killed by a vampire hunter a few months back . . . the same hunter who later came looking for me), and now perhaps Detective Hanner. If you add me into the mix, that's three in Orange County alone. Hell, three in Fullerton alone.

Kingsley went on: "There's a larger than normal grouping of vamps here in Southern California; particularly Los Angeles."

"I might have met one."

"Who?"

I hesitated, wondering if I might be giving away Detective Hanner's secret. After all, I wasn't sure if there couldn't be some weird, age-old vampire/werewolf feud going on. (And if there was, why hadn't I gotten the memo?)

Kingsley reached over and laid his warm hand on my knee. I inwardly sighed. I craved warmth. And other than the snuggling hugs of my kids, the warmth from a man was the next best.

He said, "Don't worry, Sam. Many of the local vampires are friends of mine."

"Friends?"

"Close acquaintances. We sort of naturally gravitate to each other."

"And there's no, like, war or something going on?"

He chuckled. "War?"

"You know, like in *Twilight* or *Underworld*."

He squeezed my knee a little. "And what would we be fighting over?"

"Dominion over the earth? The blood of humanity?"

"There are others who control the earth, Sam, and they are very human. And, hell, even I'm afraid of them."

I told him about the Fullerton detective. As I did, Kingsley nodded and smiled. "An old friend."

"How old?"

"Older than you and I combined. Anyway, Hanner, like other immortals, has taken precautions to discreetly blend in with society."

"So they don't run around killing people."

"Not as often as you would think."

I said, "And that's where the donors come in."

"Right."

"And who are these donors?" I asked.

"Selected humans."

"And how are they selected?"

"Most are lovers. Some are enemies. And a few are simply unfortunate enough to have crossed paths with a hungry vampire."

"Do these donors know they are donating to real vampires?"

"My guess would be yes and no. Perhaps a few of the more trusted ones do."

"And the others?"

"The others are, I imagine, giving their blood most unwillingly."

"Then why call them 'donors'?"

"It sounds better, don't you think?"

I turned the empty goblet in my hand. What little of the red stuff remained had long since dried. I suddenly felt sick to my stomach. So whose blood had this belonged to? I may never know.

A sudden wave of weakness hit me. The sun was coming. "I need a place to crash," I said.

"Mi bed es su bed."

"That's some of the worst Spanish I've ever heard."

He squeezed my knee harder. "I'm getting up now anyway. You can have the bed to yourself."

My heart sank a little.

"Is something wrong, Sam?"

I still hadn't forgiven Kingsley, but I did miss his touch. "Would you . . ." I paused, then tried again. "Would you lay with me until I fall asleep?"

He smiled brightly. "Would be my pleasure. And I'll wake Franklin up and have him vampire-treat the windows with some blankets or something."

"Oh, great," I said, as the first wave of exhaustion hit me. "Give him even more reason to hate me."

36.

Although I generally need to crank my alarm clock as loud as it gets to rouse me from my sleep, I found myself emerging from the blackest of depths at the sound of my cell phone ringing.

By the fourth ring, I was almost alive again.

By the fifth, I had fumbled for it on Kingsley's nightstand. I had a brief glimpse of the time: 10:18 a.m. I also had a brief glimpse of the caller: Aaron King, the old L.A. detective with the killer smile.

I answered the phone. At least, I think I answered the phone. I touched a button on the cell and hoped for the best.

"Hello?"

"Did you just say 'hello'?" said Aaron King.

"I think so, yes."

"You sound like a dying frog."

"You're closer than you think."

"I've got news," he said.

"Don't tell me you've been working all night."

"There's no rest for the wicked. Besides, I don't sleep well these days."

I sat up a little straighter. Kingsley, I saw, was long gone. The shades in the room had been drawn tight. A blanket, a bed comforter perhaps, had also been hung over a small window above the bed. And it had been hung neatly, too. Franklin might not like me very much, but he did good work.

I said, "What's your news?"

"I just got a call from a kid in Buena Park. He recognized our guy on the flyer. Apparently, Lauren and Maddie's friend is a big-time drug runner and all-around scary man."

"You should see me trembling. What else does our contact know?"

"The guy's name is Carl Luck. Known drug dealer and pornographer."

"Mommy would be proud."

"Last our contact heard, Mr. Luck lives in Simi Valley."

"The porn capital of the world."

"You say that like it's a bad thing."

"Eww," I said. "Is that all?"

"Nope. It gets better."

"I love better."

"Apparently Carl Luck drinks and gambles at an Indian casino near Simi, called Moon Feathers."

"A fitting name."

"I thought so," he said. "Anyway, I did a background check on Carl Luck."

"And?"

"And nothing."

I thought about that. "Maybe that's not his real name."

"Maybe it's his gambling *nom de plume*."

"Better than calling yourself Carl Loser."

I could almost see King grin on his end of the line.

"Anyway, his name doesn't matter," I said. "He could call himself Pepé Le Pew for all I care. Just as long as he shows up at Moon Feathers."

"Don't forget the part about him being a bad man. Remember, there's a very good chance that he killed Maddie's mother. And don't give me that shit about you being a highly trained federal agent."

"I'm a highly trained federal agent, I'll be fine."

"Shit." He paused, then added. "I want to come with you. Maybe bring the boys as backups."

I shook my head even though Aaron couldn't see me shaking my head. "No. I want to go alone. I'll be fine. Promise."

He didn't like it, and I didn't blame him. I wouldn't have liked it either. The truth was, the boys just might get in the way. He said, "I'll keep my phone handy. Call me if you need anything."

"I will."

"Promise me."

"Scout's honor."

He laughed harder. "Okay, a federal agent I believe, but I *know* you weren't a Boy Scout."

We fell into silence and I felt that there was something heavy on Aaron's heart. I waited for him. Twenty seconds later he spoke, and I sensed it was after much deliberation. "I saw you looking at me last night."

I waited, sensing where this would go.

"I know that look," he said.

"And what look is that?"

"Recognition," he said simply.

Just outside the bedroom, I heard the sounds of someone cleaning: items on a table being moved and then being replaced again. I knew Kingsley didn't use a house cleaner. It was just Franklin. The idea of catching the gangly, patchwork man using a feather duster almost made me laugh.

"What do you mean?" I asked, although I was certain I knew perfectly well what he meant.

"You know who I am."

"Oh?"

"Don't play coy with me, kiddo. I saw the look in your eyes last night. How did you know?"

Now I heard Franklin humming to himself. Humming and dusting. A man composed of perhaps a dozen different men. I had Frankenstein outside my door, and Elvis on the phone.

My life is weird.

"I know things," I said.

"How?"

"Some call it a gift. I don't know what to call it."

"Are we talking ESP or something?"

"Yeah, something like that."

"So then there's no secrets from you."

"Often, no, although I can't always control the psychic hits I get," I said.

I could almost see him nodding to himself at the other end of the line. He said, "I know a thing or two about secrets, lil' lady, especially after keeping such a big one for so long."

"I bet," I said, although I didn't like where this was going.

He paused, then said, "And you have a big one yourself."

"No comment," I said.

He chuckled lightly into the mouthpiece. "Call me if you need any help. Psychic or not, I don't like the idea of you heading out to that casino alone."

"I can take care of myself."

"Maybe," he said, and now he didn't bother to disguise his voice. A harmonious and deep Southern twang came through, edged with age, but as familiar as apple pie. He said, "Either way, lil' mama, let's get a coffee some time and talk about secrets."

"Sounds like a plan," I said, and shivered. I felt like a teenager at her first concert. An Elvis concert, no less.

He chuckled lightly and hung up.

37.

It was early afternoon, and I was sitting next to my son's bed. The blinds were drawn tight, but I was still feeling weak and miserable and utterly exhausted.

I shouldn't be awake. I should be asleep in the dark.

Of course, whether or not I actually sleep is still an unanswered question. A few years ago, just after my attack and back when Danny was still making an effort to be a supportive husband, we had done an experiment. He had watched me closely while I slept. His conclusion (and he had looked seriously rattled when he had reported this), was that I didn't appear to be moving or breathing or even alive. That I had looked like a corpse in a morgue.

Hell, that might have been when I started losing him.

Speaking of Danny, he had waited here until my arrival, and had then given me a long and creepy hug that had included a little pelvic thrust that made me want to vomit.

I mean, what the hell was that? Our son is lying in a hospital bed and he's coming on to me?

It had taken all my willpower not to drive my knee up into said groin. He then patted my shoulder, gave me a pathetic puppy dog look with a crooked grin, and then quickly departed. After all, he had ambulances to chase.

I shuddered again.

Some errant sunlight from an opening in the window splashed across the far wall, and just looking at it seemed to have an ill effect on me. Sunlight, quite simply, drained me. It also physically hurt like hell, which led me to believe that if I were exposed to it long enough, without protection, I had every reason to believe I would die a very painful and miserable death.

So much for being immortal.

My son had yet to stir. Nurses had come and gone. All of whom smiled sadly at me, although most tried to lift my spirits. For a boy to lie unconscious this long, for a boy to be this sick, for a boy to have doctors this concerned, well, things did not look good for a loving mama, and they knew it.

Still, they smiled and said kind things, and I nodded and accepted their words, and when they were gone, I wept.

I was not weeping when Detective Sherbet stepped into the room. The big guy came bearing gifts, and the sight of him daintily holding the string of a helium-filled balloon in one hand and clutching a fistful of flowers in the other was enough to make my heart smile. He stood there blinking, eyes adjusting to the gloom.

And while he blinked and adjusted, I eased off the bed and crossed the room and threw my arms around the detective in a move that I think surprised him.

"Excuse me, ma'am, but am I in the right place?" he asked.

"Most definitely," I said. I was still hugging him. God, he was so warm . . . and thick around the middle. Just the way I liked it.

"You do realize that you are still hugging me," he said, but I felt him switch the balloon over and then use his free hand to pat me gently on the head.

I couldn't speak. Instead, a big choking sob burst out of me and I hugged him harder than I had hugged anyone before, and my tears quickly stained his shirt.

38.

Hidden in the crook of his arm, previously unnoticed, had been a big, greasy bag of donuts.

We were now sitting across from each other at the foot of my son's bed. The smell of the greasy donuts was both delicious and nauseating. Sherbet was currently working on a maple old-fashioned. Some of the frosting broke off and had sprinkled down his shirt and over his thick thighs. He ignored the frosting crumbs. I thought they looked delicious.

"I'd offer you one," he said. "Except I know you'll say no."

"Thanks anyway, but I'm not hungry."

"Gee, how did I know you were going to say that?" he asked between bites.

"Because anyone who cared an ounce about their bodies wouldn't put that crap in them." Which was a lie. I loved donuts. I just couldn't eat them . . . or anything, for that matter.

"Except for those whose bodies are indestructible," said Sherbet off-handedly.

My heart slammed hard against my ribs. *Sweet, Jesus, what did Sherbet know?*

He stopped chewing and looked at me curiously. "You look like you just saw a ghost. Relax, my doctor tells me my heart has no business being as strong as it is."

I breathed again. *Good Lord.*

I said, "And so you figure you might as well push your heart to the limit?"

"Not really," he said, sucking on his fingers. "I just like donuts."

I shook my head while he dug into the bag, coming up with something pink and sprinkled. He said, "I've grown rather fond of these donuts."

"And how's your son, by the way?" I asked.

Sherbet looked at me from over the donut. "I bring out a pink donut and it immediately reminds you of my son?"

"Yes and no."

He chomped into it. Pink frosting coated his thick, cop mustache. "He's fine, of course. I love him terribly, but there's something definitely wrong."

"Wrong how?"

"I keep catching him in his mother's clothing, especially her shoes."

"Is it that you catch him, or he likes to wear them?"

"Both, I think. Makes me want to cry."

We were silent, and as the wall clock behind me ticked so loudly that I could practically hear the inner gears grinding together, Sherbet figured out what an ass he was being.

"Look, I'm sorry," he said. "You've got your little one here fighting for his life and I'm bitching because mine likes to dress up like Nanny McPhee."

I nodded, said nothing.

Sherbet reached out and placed his warm hand over my own.

He took mine tightly and didn't flinch from the cold. I think he was getting used to my icy hands.

"Let's change the subject, okay?" he suggested.

I nodded again and looked away. I wasn't going to cry. I was tired of crying.

He said, "The guy you found dead in the meth house was murdered."

"I'm shocked and outraged," I said. I was neither, of course. Drug hits were common and quickly forgotten by the police.

"Execution style, too."

"Do we care enough about him to know his name?" I asked.

"No," said Sherbet. "We don't. He was a known user and dealer. Too many suspects, too little time. The place was Grand Central Station for meth and blow . . . and other things as well."

"Prostitutes," I said.

"And various child abuses that we need not get into here."

"Let's call it for what it is, detective. Child slavery and prostitution."

The detective looked sick. I felt sick, too. He nodded gravely and dropped the unfinished donut in his bag. It's hard to have an appetite for pink donuts when the talk turns to child abuse.

He said, "From what we understand, the children are used as . . . payments, of one sort or another."

I nodded, and felt bile rise in the back of my throat.

Sherbet continued, "Maddie's mother was no doubt caught up in it. And now she's dead, apparently."

"And little Maddie is alone," I said.

Sherbet nodded and we were silent. He turned to me. "You making any headway on the case?"

"Some," I said. I decided not to mention Aaron's hot lead in Simi Valley. Mostly because I didn't trust the police enough at this point to get Maddie out alive, wherever she was. I trusted Sherbet, certainly, but he was only one man, and Simi Valley was not his beat, not by a long shot.

"Let me know if you need some help," he said.

"You bet."

Sherbet was openly staring at me.

"What?" I said.

"I was just thinking."

"Don't hurt yourself, Detective."

He ignored me. "It's funny how suspects keep ending up dead on cases you investigate."

"Whatever do you mean, Detective?"

"You were working an angle on the Jerry Blum case last month."

"You know this how?"

"I have friends in the FBI, too, Sam."

"Good for you."

"You were making inquiries for your client. A Stuart something-or-other."

"Stuart Young."

"Whatever. Anyway, Jerry Blum has been missing for a month."

"Maybe he's on the lam."

"Or maybe he's dead," said Sherbet.

I shrugged.

"Well, let's try to keep the body count down this time, Sam."

"People die," I said. "Especially bad people."

"I'll pretend I didn't hear that."

My son made a small sound and turned over in his sleep. As he turned, the black shadow that surrounded him turned with him. My heart sank further.

Sherbet patted me on the shoulder and stood. He looked down at me long and hard, and then left.

39.

You there, Moon Dance?

It was Fang via a text message. With our super-secret identities now revealed, we had graduated from anonymous IM messages to exchanging our cell numbers and texting like real people. Or, at least, like teenagers.

I was still sitting next to my son. It was coming on noon and I was weak and sad and tired.

Hi, Fang. :(

There was a slight delay, perhaps a minute. Texting wasn't as fast as IMing.

Why are you sad, Moon Dance?

It's my son.

You mentioned he was sick. Is he not better?

Worse, I wrote, paused, and then added: *He's dying.*

That was all I could write. And even writing those two words was nearly impossible. The words seemed so unlikely, implausible, unreal. More so than my own vampirism. How could my healthy, happy, quirky little boy be dying?

Outside the room, a doctor rushed quickly by. I heard shouting from somewhere. Two orderlies quickly followed behind. Doctors risked their lives more than people realized.

You would never say that lightly, wrote Fang. *So it must be true.*

I spent the next few minutes catching him up to date on my son's health and the black halo surrounding his body.

There was a long period of silence from my phone, which I had set to vibrate. I adjusted my weight on my hip and reached out and stroked my son's face. He was burning up.

The phone vibrated. *Do the doctor's know what's wrong with him?*

They're saying it could be Kawasaki Disease.

Hold on.

And I knew Fang was looking up the disease. I ran my fingers through my son's hair for the next five minutes. My phone buzzed again.

There's only a 2% mortality rate, Fang wrote.

2% is enough, I wrote.

I'm sorry, Moon Dance. I wish there was something I could do.

I was about to write to him, when another message appeared from Fang. It was simple and to the point:

Actually, Moon Dance, I think I know of a way to save your son. Don't go anywhere! I'm calling you.

40.

I was outside of St. Jude's, huddled under the eve of the main entrance, as deep in the shadows as I could be. Still, I could literally feel my skin burning.

I could give a damn about my skin.

Fang answered my call immediately. "Hello, Moon Dance."

I found myself pacing, turning small circles in front of the hospital entrance. The automatic door kept sliding open. The information nurse working the front desk gave me a nasty look. I ignored her.

"Talk to me, Fang."

"I'm talking," he said, and I could hear the excitement in his voice. "There is a way to save your son."

"What way?"

And the moment I asked the question, I knew the answer. Fang and I were deeply connected and I either picked up on his thoughts or intuited his meaning. I think I gasped and nearly choked.

"No," I said. "No fucking way. I'm not doing it."

"You read my mind, Moon Dance."

"Of course I read your fucking mind. I have to sit."

There was an alabaster bench just inside the shade that I would risk, and as I sat, I regretted doing so almost immediately. I could practically smell my burning skin, despite my long sleeves and heavy sunscreen.

I ignored the pain and buried my face in my hands. People were looking at me, sure, but a grieving mother outside of a children's hospital wasn't anything new.

But a grieving mother contemplating giving her son eternal life was another matter altogether.

I said, "I can't do it, Fang. I could never do that to him. How could you even suggest that?"

"You didn't let me finish. Or, for that matter, speak, since you read my thoughts."

Yes, I knew there was more. I knew he was eager to continue with this, but my own wildly spinning emotions prevented me from picking up on his additional thoughts. In fact, they still did.

"Go ahead," I said.

"The medallion, Moon Dance."

And that's all he needed to say; in an instant I knew what he meant and what he was getting at.

The medallion, or amulet. Or whatever it was. Worn by my attacker six years ago, and hand-delivered to me by the vampire hunter who killed him.

The medallion, that, according to Kingsley, could *reverse* vampirism.

Fang was speaking, but I was having a hell of a time focusing. He said, "Heal him with vampirism, Moon Dance, and then return him to mortality with the medallion."

"But how?" I said. "How does it work?"

"I don't know . . . but someone out there does."

"I gotta go," I said suddenly, and clicked off.

41.

Kingsley Fulcrum had a new secretary. No surprise there since I had watched the last one die a few months ago, shot to death by none other than Detective Sherbet. And, since killing together has a way of bonding people, perhaps that's why the good detective and I got along so swimmingly.

It was a working theory.

This new secretary wasn't as sexy as the last. Which was probably a good thing. Maybe after a century or more, the big bad wolf was finally learning to keep it in his pants, or tucked away in his fur.

Anyway, this slightly older and plainer secretary (although still cute in her ruffled cardigan sweater) told me that Kingsley was with a client. Kingsley's clients were often murderers with a lot of money.

I could give a fuck about his clients.

As I marched past her and down a hallway, I heard her rapidly punching buttons on the intercom. She must have successfully buzzed Kingsley, because as I threw open his door he was just reaching for the phone with what appeared to be a look of irritation. The mighty attorney didn't like to be disturbed, apparently. The look of irritation quickly turned to one of dumbfounded shock when he saw me.

The big guy cleaned up well. He was looking absolutely debonair in a black Armani suit, a pair of over-the-top and beyond stylish Berluti shoes, and hair so slicked back that a girl might break a nail scratching behind his ears.

Unless that girl, of course, was a vampire.

"Sam," he said, standing slowly from behind his desk. "This isn't a good time."

His client turned to me. Another man dressed in a nice suit. A man who looked bored and rich and entitled. Okay, it's hard to look entitled, but that was the feeling I was getting from him. I also got a very strong hit that he was a murderer. A cold-blooded murderer. I got another hit . . . he had strangled his own wife in her sleep. I heard her last strangled gasps as I stood there in the doorway and he sat there looking bored.

Sweet Jesus my hits were getting stronger and stronger.

I walked over to the guy and pulled him out of his chair. He didn't go willingly. He tried to push my hands away but couldn't. As I pulled him out of his chair, Kingsley ran from around his desk, his Armani suit *swooshing*.

"Hey!" shouted the guy as I held him in front of me.

Kingsley shouted something similar.

The guy tried again to shove me away, but I wasn't going anywhere. I had him by the collar of his nice suit. And now that he was on his feet, I slammed his face hard onto the table.

"You killed her, you worthless piece of shit. You strangled her in her sleep, you fucking coward, and then you lit a Cuban cigar after a job well done. An *illegal* Cuban cigar."

He struggled to get up, but I held him down on the table and all the anger and frustration and pain and confusion and despair I had felt over the past few days came flooding out of me. I lifted his face and slammed it again into the table. Blood immediately pooled around his eye socket. I had split the skin along his upper orbital ridge. Poor baby.

"I will personally see to it that you rot in hell, you fucking—"

And that's when Kingsley pulled me off the man. Kicking and screaming, I didn't go willingly. But Kingsley happened to be one hell of a strong guy.

42.

"What the hell was that, Sam?"

I was sitting in an empty side office. Apparently, Kingsley Fulcrum made so much blood money representing rich, murderous scumbags that he could afford to have empty offices.

"What was what?" I asked. I was still fuming, and I was having a hard time looking Kingsley in the eye. The big son-of-a-bitch was really bothering me these days. I had come here for a completely different reason, but I had let my emotions get the better of me.

Hey, I'm only human.

Or something.

"Playing Whack-A-Mole with my client's head, Sam. That's what."

"Whack-A-Mole?" I asked, and I started laughing, nearly hysterically, and then I was crying, definitely hysterically, harder than I had in quite a long time. Kingsley stood apart from me, watching me, and then he came over and gave me a big hug, wrapping those huge arms around me, patting my back and rubbing my shoulders, and telling me everything would be okay.

I was calmer. We were back in Kingsley's office, minus the murderous scumbag, who had apparently left holding a bag of ice to his face. Someone had cleaned the blood off the table, although I could still smell the sharp hemoglobin radiating off the freshly polished wood surface. Must be the vampire in me.

My stomach growled, and I hated myself for that.

"You can't keep killing my clients, Sam," said Kingsley. His right butt cheek was sitting on the corner of his desk. I was sitting in one of his client chairs. Everywhere around me were depictions of moons: moon photographs, paperweights, lamps. Even a moon screen saver. The moon bookends, each by itself a half moon, seemed to be the newest edition to his office.

Yeah, the man had a moon obsession, which stands to reason. His obsession was also how he had found me in the phone book so many months ago. Under "Moon," of course.

"Well, your clients are scumbags," I said.

"Be that as it may, they deserve a fair trial."

"Whatever helps you sleep at night, big guy."

"Why are you here, Sam?"

I stared at him . . . no doubt icily. He calmly returned my gaze. We did this for about ten seconds before I finally lowered my eyes and looked away. "I'm sorry," I said. "That wasn't cool. I guess I'm desperate."

"A desperate vampire is a sight to see."

"A desperate mother is worse."

He nodded and eased off the corner of his desk. He sat next to me and adjusted the drape of his pants. Kingsley, as always, smelled of fine cologne and that special something else. Something wild. He waited. As he waited, I gathered my thoughts.

Finally, I said, "The medallion that's in my possession . . ."

He looked at me sideways, turning his head just a fraction of an inch. "What about it?"

"Is it really true that it can reverse vampirism?"

Although I wasn't looking at him, I knew he had narrowed his eyes. Kingsley was nearly impossible for me to read psychically. I wondered if it was like that for all other immortals, too.

He said, "That's the legend about it."

"What else do you know about it?"

"I know that a lot of people are looking for it."

"People? Or vampires?"

"Vampires are people, too," he said, grinning easily. And then he grew serious. "Why, Sam?"

The smell of blood wafting up from the desk was diminishing. The growling in my stomach subsided accordingly. I told Kingsley about my plan, minus any references to Fang. There was no need to make the big werewolf jealous. Fang might be a freaky dude, but he was no physical match for Kingsley. At least, not presently.

Make me into a vampire, Moon Dance.

Yeah, I still haven't forgotten those words.

Anyway, I laid the plan out to Kingsley, and as I did so, he leaned a meaty elbow against the chair's arm and took me in, watching me closely as I spoke. And as I spoke, I couldn't help but notice that the slight amber in his eyes caught some of the office lighting and reflected it back to me twofold. Tenfold. He could look so wild sometimes.

When I was done talking, Kingsley's reply was instant and heartbreaking: "I don't like it, Sam."

"What's not to like?" I said, jumping up. I paced behind him. "I save my son and later, I return him to being human. It's perfect."

He was shaking his head, and the amber glow was gone from his eyes, replaced with something close to alarm. And also something else. Concern. "Unless it doesn't work, Sam."

"But why wouldn't it work?" I heard the desperation in my voice, which had risen an octave or two. I spun on Kingsley, standing before him.

"Because it's just a story, Sam. A legend."

"All legends have some basis of truth. Look at us. And quit looking at me that way."

"What way?"

"Like I've lost my mind."

He stood suddenly and towered over me. "I don't think you've lost your mind, but I think you're desperate, and dangerous, and if you would for one second listen to yourself you would see how scary you sound."

I looked up at him as he looked down at me. He was breathing hard, and I could hear his heart thumping through his wide chest. "Who do I need to talk to?" I asked. "Who would know more about the medallion?"

He looked at me long and hard. "Sam, please."

"I'm going to do whatever it takes to save my son, goddammit."

"Even if it means turning him into a monster, Sam? Even if it means draining the blood from his body? And what if you can't turn him back? What then, Sam?"

I heard footsteps just outside Kingsley's office door. His new secretary was there. How much she'd heard, I didn't know, but I suspected his doors were quite thick. If anything, she was concerned for her boss's welfare.

I said nothing. How could anyone answer that question? Hell, has that question ever been posed before? Ever? In the history of mankind?

Kingsley continued, "I'll tell you what would happen if you

can't change him back, Sam. Your son will be undead, like you. He will feed on blood, like you. He will be a monster."

"Like me?"

"For all eternity, Sam. Your boy. Your little boy. Don't do this to him, Sam. You can't take this chance."

I held his gaze long and hard. "Who do I talk to, Kingsley?"

He took in a lot of air, crossed his arms, and looked away. "Let me ask around, Sam."

I nodded and felt a combination of joy and dread, fear and hope. "Thank you," I said.

But he didn't answer me or look at me, and shortly after that I left his office.

43.

I had just slipped into my car after practically sprinting across the baking asphalt when my phone rang. Gasping and in real pain, I looked at the faceplate:

Caller Unknown.

Heart thumping and still reeling from my singed skin, I clicked on the phone.

"Hello," I said. My face and hands were on fire, despite the copious amounts of sunscreen—and a sunhat that was wide enough to shade a small Balkan country.

"Hi," said the tiny voice, a voice that was somehow even tinier than I remembered.

"Maddie!"

"You know my name."

"Of course I know your name, honey." But as much as I wanted to comfort her and reassure her, I needed information. "Maddie, honey, how many people live with you?"

"Two grownup men now."

"Are they black or white?"

"Bofth. The white man is new. He's really mean."

Maddie had a slight lisp and it was the most precious sound I had ever heard. I absently started my car and turned my air conditioner full blast on me, while huddling as far away from any sunlight as I could. My van's side windows were equipped with pull-down shades, which I rarely, if ever, pulled up. The windshield sunshade was still in place, blocking most of the sun, although laser-like beams still found their way through here and there.

So there was a black guy and a white guy. The white guy, I knew, could have been Hispanic or even Asian. Maddie was only five. I doubted she saw race and color like an older child would. Or as an adult would.

Sherbet had confirmed the worst, that some kind of child swapping was going on. Children for drugs. Children for money. Children for sex. A slave trade where lives meant little, and no doubt most kids disappeared or ended up dead. Along with the mothers.

"Maddie, honey, are you in a house?"

"A house?"

"Or is it an apartment?"

"Peoples live here. We take the vader."

The vader? My head was swimming. Jesus, I had had my questions rehearsed for when and if I heard from Maddie again, but now all my questions had gone out the window.

Think. Focus.

"Honey, what can you see from the window? Can you see anything?"

There was a slight pause. I heard her pushing aside what sounded like blinds. "I see a big house."

"Where?"

"It's high on top of the biggest mountain I've ever seen!"

My heart started hammering. I knew Simi Valley. The federal agency I had worked for, HUD, used a facility outside of the city to hold seminars and training. The facility was away from prying eyes, up against the base of a majestic, sweeping mountain range. Or, perhaps, a very big hill. Certainly big enough to call a mountain if you were a small girl from the streets of Buena Park.

And at the top of the hill, majestically overlooking the city, was a museum. Not quite a mansion, but it looked like one from a distance.

The Ronald Reagan Museum.

The Moon Feather Indian casino, if I recalled correctly, wasn't too far away from our training facility, either.

She's in Simi Valley. I knew it. I felt it in every fiber of my being.

I also sensed something else. Or, rather *someone* else. And from somewhere over the phone line, I heard what sounded like a door slam followed by a man's yell. The yell sounded drunken and angry.

"I have to go," said Maddie, whispering into the mouthpiece. Her whisper sounded nearly as loud as her little voice.

The line dropped before I could say goodbye.

44.

I was back at the hospital, sitting in a chair at the foot of my son's bed. He was sleeping quietly. Too quietly. I would have thought he was dead if not for the hospital equipment that chirped out a heartbeat.

The dark halo around him was bigger than ever. My son, to my eyes, seemed lost in a cloud of black smoke.

Sitting on my lap was a clipboard with a mostly blank sheet of paper I had found in the backseat of my car. The paper had my daughter's name on it and the beginning of an assignment. I wondered idly if she had ever finished the assignment.

I held in my hand a Pilot Gel Ink Rolling Ball pen, which I preferred to use when I did my automatic writing sessions.

Automatic writing is still new to me. In fact, I'd only done it a couple of times, and both times I was certain I was going crazy.

In essence, as it was initially explained to me by Fang (and verified by a little online research) the process of automatic writing is a way to communicate with the spirit world. In particular, with highly evolved enlightened beings who know what the hell they're talking about.

At least, that was the idea.

Who or what came through in these sessions was certainly open to debate. And, yes, there was a part of me that seriously suspected I was moving my own hand, and giving myself the answers I wanted to hear.

Just a part of me.

The other part of me, perhaps the part that was still human, believed that I was getting messages from beyond. By spirit guides, or spiritual beings.

Or, for all I knew, Jim Morrison, unless he was alive, too, and working as a bounty hunter in Hawaii.

I went through the various steps of centering myself, imagining silver cords attaching themselves to my ankles and lower spine and reaching down through the many hospital floors, the building's foundation, through the very ground itself, down through Hell and a lost world of dinosaurs, and all the way to the center of the earth, where I mentally tied them tightly around three massive boulders.

Now firmly anchored, I closed my eyes and attempted to empty my mind by focusing on the physical act of breathing, drawing air in through my nose and out my mouth, even if it was air I didn't need. Except I kept thinking about my son, lying there just a few feet away, fighting for his life.

Focus, Sam.

I closed my eyes and, as I breathed, I pictured the stale, medicinal hospital air flowing over my lips and down deep into my lungs. I breathed in, holding the air, and then exhaled it.

I did this over and over, breathing and picturing, and any time I thought of my son, I gently released the thought.

In and out, in and out.

Breathe, breathe.

My hand twitched.

I kept reminding myself to breathe, and as I breathed I imagined the air currents tinged with gold, and the golden air flowing into my mouth and filling me with golden light.

My hand twitched again, followed by a full-blown spasm.

The pen gripped in my fingers moved back and forth.

It's coming, I thought. Whatever it is.

Keep breathing. Breathing. In and out. Golden light.

Jesus, my hand is moving.

Don't think about it. Good, good.

But now I couldn't deny that something seemed to have settled in me. I actually felt another presence. A warm and loving presence.

And then my hand moved again, and again, and I realized it was writing. I looked down at my clipboard as two words appeared:

Hello, Samantha.

45.

"Hello," I said quietly, feeling slightly silly, but also feeling like something very important, and very exciting, was happening. "Um, how are you?" I added lamely.

My hand twitched again and again, and it kept on twitching until it wrote out a reply. I could only watch in stunned silence. My hand, in these moments, did not feel like my own.

I'm doing very well, it wrote. *It's a great day to be alive, is it not?*

I thought of my son, and a great pain filled my heart. I had come here to ask about Anthony, but suddenly I wasn't sure I really wanted to hear the answers.

My son was showing signs of stabilizing. This should be good news, but it wasn't. Not to me. I knew better. His black halo was growing. How do you convince a doctor that you need a second or third opinion when the patient seems to be responding to treatment?

Responding for now. I knew that would all change.

I had called children's hospital after children's hospital, burning up my phone, demanding to speak to other infectious disease specialists. Few would speak to me, and those who did were generally guarded. I begged them to come see my boy, that I felt something was very, very wrong, and they reassured me that my son's doctor was one of the best in the business.

One specialist in Chicago told me he would look into it, and later called to tell me that he was flying in to see my son. I thanked him profusely, crying nearly hysterically, but in my heart of hearts, I knew he would fail.

Modern medicine would fail. I needed a miracle. And thanks to Fang, I had an idea what that miracle might entail.

For now, though, I simply said, "Am I really alive?" My voice was barely above a whisper. "There are some who believe that beings such as myself are dead."

More twitching and tingling. More writing. *Do you feel dead, Samantha?*

"No, but I feel very . . . different."

Twitch, write. *You should feel different. We are all different.*

"But am I dead?" I asked. "And please don't say: 'Do you feel dead?'"

Your body went through a massive transformation, or metamorphosis, Samantha, but it did not die.

"Then why don't I breathe? Why can't I eat?"

That's one of the metamorphoses of which I speak. Or write. Your body, quite literally, is not the same, and thus does not have the same requirements.

"Like food or air."

Exactly. Yes.

"But I still need blood."

Of course. This is your new body's requirement.

"And so my new body is a killer, if it must feast on blood."

Does all blood need to come from that which is dead?

"No," I said, and my voice trailed off. I thought about something Kingsley had said earlier, about blood donors. Those who donated willingly . . . and those who most certainly did not. Blood debt perhaps.

Yes, Samantha, you are a far more powerful being than you were before, but what you make of your new physical form is up to you.

"I could choose to kill. Or not to kill."

Exactly. Yes. Just like everyone else.

"So I have a new body . . . but I still have the same moral code."

You are still you, sweet child, no matter what shape you take.

"Don't call me sweet child. It makes me want to cry."

Why?

"Because it sounds like you care about me. That you love me. But I don't know who you are or what you are."

Understood. But remember, all you have to do is ask.

"I have asked, but you've avoided the question."

I did not avoid. I simply gave you the answer you were ready for. Are you ready for the answer now?

I thought about that. I looked at my son sleeping on his back. My God, had the black halo actually grown in just a few minutes?

"Yes," I said.

We are many, Samantha. There are many of us here who have taken an active interest in you.

"So you are not Sephora?" A sense of alarm rang through me. Who was I talking to? Sephora had been the loving being I had spoken to in my last sessions.

She is here, of course, overseeing this dialogue. She is your personal guide, after all, who has been with you for all eternity.

"And who are you?"

With her blessing, I have come through.

"I don't understand."

I am a specialist in the arcane, Samantha.

"Arcane?"

In immortality. In the magicks of your realm, so to speak. Some would call them dark magicks, but they would be mistaken.

"Who are you?"

My hand paused, then wrote: *I am called by many names, through many lives, but I'm most commonly called Saint Germain.*

I'd heard of the name, of course. Saint Germain had been a European mystic. An alchemist of the highest order. He supposedly lived for centuries. And, from most accounts, never died. They say he ascended; that is, turned to light. A heavenly being who was just as comfortable in the spirit world as the physical world, often alternating between the two. And helping those in need. Immortal indeed.

And no, Samantha, I'm not a vampire, either.

"Then what are you?"

A seeker of truth.

"And did you find the truth?"

I found what I was looking for, yes. But there are always bigger questions, with bigger answers.

"So you eternally seek answers."

Forever and ever.

"So why are you here with me now?"

You have called out for answers, Samantha Moon. I'm here to help you find them.

"But why you?"

Why not?

"Fine," I said and rubbed my head. I looked at my sick boy. "I want to talk about my son."

What would you like to know?

"Is he . . . is he going to die?"

There was a slight pause and the tingly sensation briefly abated, but then it returned. I realized that maybe I didn't want to know the answer. My hand moved across the page, and the gel ink flowed freely.

Your son has his own path, Samantha.

"What does that mean?"

We all follow our own paths, generally agreed on and known before our births.

"Who agrees on this?"

You. And many others.

"Which others?"

Those who care deeply about you. And those who care deeply about your son.

"And what's his path?" My voice was shaking now.

You know his path, Sam. You have foreseen it.

"Just tell me."

There was a short, agonizing pause, and then: *Your son's path will come to an end in this physical plane soon, as it has been decided upon, as he has decided, as well.*

"He's only a little boy, goddammit. What the hell does he know about anything?"

A little boy now, in the flesh, certainly. But a very wise old soul eternally.

I covered my eyes with my free hand. Tears poured between my fingers. It was all I could do to not throw the clipboard across the room.

"Why, why would he decide to end his life now? Who would decide such a thing? Why take him from me?"

There are many, many reasons, Sam. And most of those involve the growth of his own soul, and the growth of the souls around him. Adapting to loss is a big step toward growth.

"It's a horrible, cruel step toward growth. How could you take my boy?"

I'm not taking him, Sam. No one can take. Leaving this world is his choice and his choice alone.

"But he's just a boy. He doesn't know what he's doing, and don't give me that crap that he's an old soul. He's not. He's just a little boy. A little, sick boy."

A little, sick boy with a highly evolved soul, Samantha. He understands his purpose here at the soul level, even if not at the physical level.

"Fuck you."

I'm sorry, Samantha.

I wept hard for a few minutes, barely able to control myself. Finally, when I could speak again, I said, "Are you there?"

Always.

"I have a question."

We are here for answers.

"Okay. Okay." I took a deep breath, and plunged forward. "Is there anyway that I can save him?"

He does not need to be saved, Sam.

"Please."

We all have free will, Sam. You can do anything you want.

"So there is a way to save him?"

Of course there is. The body can heal itself immediately if it so chooses. What your doctors call miracles.

"The doctors are going down the wrong path," I said. "They think they're helping."

The doctors have diagnosed your son correctly, Samantha. There is nothing left for them to do. Although considerable, they have exhausted their collective expertise.

"But I know of another way."

I know, Sam. There are often many ways. The key is finding the one that feels the best.

"So my way is such a path."

Of course. But ask yourself: does it feel right?

"It feels right to me," I said quickly, although doubt ate at me.

Then so be it.

I took a deep breath. "Well, you haven't told me not to do it."

I would never tell you not to do anything, Samantha. This is called a free-will universe for a reason.

"But would you caution against it?"

I would caution against doing anything that doesn't feel right, Samantha. Always ask yourself if the choices you are making feel right, and act according to your feelings. Then you will know you are on the right path. Always.

"But how do I know how I feel if I'm truly confused?"

You always know, Sam. Always.

46.

I was driving.

My mind was still reeling from the phone call with Maddie. My mind was still reeling from my conversation with Kingsley. Reeling from my conversation with Saint Germain. Reeling from the possibility that my son could be saved. Possibly.

I was doing a lot of reeling and no doubt a lot of erratic driving, too. I forced myself to calm down. To focus.

It was early afternoon. My sister and daughter were with Anthony. I had work to do, and this was my time to do it, even if I was a royal mess.

I could head out to Simi Valley now, but I suspected I would be waiting a long, long time in the casino before anyone of note showed up. It was better to wait, and head out there later.

For now, I knew where to go. And it just so happened to be right around the corner, too.

I parked at the Wharton Museum and dashed across the parking lot, past the rich and not-so-famous dining at the Wharton outdoor cafe, and ducked into the main building, gasping for breath I didn't need, and feeling as if I had just run across hot coals.

"You okay?" asked the security guard at the door.

"I'm fine," I lied. Actually, I felt like shit.

He asked if I wanted some help and I waved him off and did my best to walk with some dignity toward the side offices, all too aware of a slight burning smell wafting up from my skin.

I've never felt sexier.

A few minutes later I was seated across from a shell-shocked Ms. Dickens. The old lady didn't look well, and I didn't blame her. A lot of bad luck had come her way. Granted, not as bad as the night guard I had found stuffed in an oversized Igloo.

"I guess the cat's out of the bag," she said. She was holding her forehead in her hands.

I nodded.

"No more hiding the fact that the sculpture was stolen."

"Sometimes there's more important things than stolen sculptures," I said. "Like dead people."

She looked up at me briefly, parting her hands slightly to do so. Her blank stare told me that perhaps she didn't subscribe to my philosophy. A stolen crystal egg, apparently, meant more to her than human life.

"Yes," she said, reluctantly agreeing. "I suppose so."

After a few more minutes of our strained silence, I asked her if I was still on the job. After all, part of my job description had been to help find the missing art piece before the official opening this weekend.

"Yes, of course," she snapped. "We still need to find it. We will just have to deal with the backlash of the theft and death. We've overcome tragedy before, and we will overcome this, too. The Wharton will be world famous someday. World famous. Mark my words."

I nearly stood up and cheered.

Now that we'd established that I still had a job, I thanked her for her time and left her at her desk, where she didn't move or acknowledge my departure.

The police had come and gone in the wee hours of the morning. With their initial investigation completed, the museum had opened on time and business was as usual. To a degree. The place was mostly empty; I felt as if I had it all to myself.

I headed deeper into the museum, looking for Mr. Wharton himself.

The resident ghost.

47.

I used my temporary security pass to enter the back room and although it was still daytime, you would never know it in here. The place was dark and ominous, and knowing there was a ghost creeping around here made the fine hair at the back of my neck stand on end.

There were two security cameras back here, both placed in such a way that they could see anyone coming and going. The cameras could also see down the main aisle that led between all the side aisles.

Except the cameras hadn't been working for 20 minutes. Long enough for someone to come in and get out with a prized sculpture worth hundreds of thousands of dollars, or whatever he could get for it on eBay. Long enough to kill a guard and stuff him in a freezer.

As I stood there taking in the back room, I heard shuffling down a side aisle. A ghost? A murderer? Neither. A few seconds later, a young girl emerged. She looked thoroughly freaked out. I didn't blame her. A theft, a murder, a ghost, and a vampire. Had I been anyone but me, I might have been freaked, too.

She saw me and gasped, clutching her throat. I smiled apologetically and she relaxed a little. She was holding a box of something. Small museum pieces, although I couldn't see what. She moved quickly past me with a forced smile, and left by the same door I had just stepped through.

Crime scenes can take hours or weeks to clear. The fact that the Santa Ana Police Department had cleared this one in a matter of hours was telling: It meant there was little, if any, evidence. The crime scene itself had been trampled to hell. If there had been evidence, it was probably gone.

With very few clues to collect, and with little hope of collecting anything of value, the museum had been given the green light to open for business with no apparent disruptions. That didn't mean the Santa Ana PD wouldn't take the murder case any less seriously. It just meant they had little to work with.

Although not on public display, many of the artifacts back here were still highly valuable and some were one-of-a-kind. The muted, indirect lighting was no doubt UV and IR free so as not to cause any damage to the highly sensitive paintings and sculptures and various rare artifacts.

The lighting could be adjusted, I could see. The young lady had had it as high as it would go. Again, I didn't blame her. I reached over and turned it down low. No doubt Eddie—if Eddie was indeed watching me back in the control room—wondered why the hell I had done that. I wondered if he would believe me if I told him that it was to better see the ghost of Mr. Wharton.

Now with the room mostly in deep shadows, my senses sprang to life. Granted, it was still daytime, and I wouldn't be fully alive and alert until the sun set, but the cool darkness in the back room was the next best thing and I was feeling a little better.

I headed deeper into the room. The air around me was electrified. Little squigglies of light danced before my eyes. These supercharged particles emanated a glow that only I could see and it gave the room added light. At least for me.

All of my senses told me that I was alone in the back room. I walked slowly down the center aisle. I felt my mind reaching out before me, searching for something both physical and non-physical.

I was getting a lot of feedback. I sensed strange energy around a lot of the artifacts, for instance. Some of these relics had been acquired over the years—not necessarily by the museum, but by others—through force or coercion. These artifacts had a lot of negative energy around them, a darkness that surrounded them. Cursed, perhaps. Other artifacts and pieces of art had a lot of bright energy buzzing around them, light particles that swarmed like bees around a beehive, and I realized these were aspects of the owners' souls still attached to the artifacts. Perhaps forever attached.

Owner and art forever linked.

These were strange concepts that I was only now beginning to understand through my own strange second sight.

I soon found myself standing in the very aisle where the freezer box was located. There was still yellow police "caution tape" around it. Although the police had gathered all the evidence they could early this morning, they could—and probably would—come back for a follow-up investigation, with the hope of acquiring additional evidence. Of course, the tape itself meant little to someone determined to tamper with the evidence. I wasn't going to tamper with the evidence.

Instead, I just stood there, getting a feel for the place. A man had died here not too long ago and I idly wondered where his spirit had gone. Was he still here, roaming the museum with Mr. Wharton?

I didn't know, but there was some strange energy around the

ice box, and it very well could have been his spirit, but the energy was scattered and without much shape. I suspected the murdered security guard had gone on to wherever most spirits go on to.

It was then that I knew I was being watched, and not just by Eddie in the control room. Something had appeared behind me. Something that caused the hair on my neck to stand up.

I turned and was not very surprised to see a figure taking shape behind me. A human-shaped nexus gathered the surrounding light particles the way a black hole attracts all the heavenly bodies around it. Unlike a black hole, these light particles didn't disappear into a dimension occupied by only Charlie Sheen and Mel Gibson. These light particles formed a shape I readily recognized.

Mr. Bernard Wharton.

And when the last of the particles morphed into the shape of a fedora sitting slightly askew on its head, the entity before me nodded. I did the only thing I could think of and nodded back. In the control room, Eddie was getting quite a show. What Eddie made of the show, I didn't know or care.

And because I knew there wasn't any sound being recorded, I felt free to speak. "You know who killed the guard, don't you, Mr. Wharton?"

The figure before me didn't react at first, but then finally nodded, almost reluctantly.

I was about to ask the rather pointed question of *who* had killed the guard, but now the ghost was moving, flitting down the hallway and into another, darker room. I assumed I was meant to follow him and so I did—into the same dark room.

I didn't bother with the lights. I could see that we were in the shipping and receiving room. I knew this because there was a huge plastic bag filled with Styrofoam popcorn hovering over one of the tables, the *shipping* table, I presumed. There were computers, and crates and other random knickknacks. The room obviously doubled as a sort of storage room, too, with brooms and mops and cleaning supplies propped near the door.

Mr. Wharton led me deeper into the room to a work station off in the far corner. Random boxes were piled here, most of them opened and discarded. There were also packing supplies here and other boxes that appeared ready to be shipped.

He floated over to one of the boxes. I followed behind and looked down. The box was packed and taped, but the recipient hadn't yet been filled out. Correction, there was a single letter on the box, an "M," followed by a squiggly line, as if the writer had lost heart.

Or been scared to death.

Mr. Wharton stood next to me. Some of his crackling energy reached out to me, attaching itself to me, and as it did so, something very strange started to happen.

Flashing images appeared in my thoughts. Images I had never seen before. Images that weren't mine. Memories that weren't mine.

They were *his* images. *His* memories. Mr. Wharton's.

I saw a flash of a security guard wearing gloves and working on an electrical panel. Perhaps the panel that powered the security cameras. I recognized the guard easily enough, especially since I had found him dead in the cold storage box.

The next flash. Now the guard was standing over this very box, writing something, when his head suddenly snapped around, eyes thoroughly spooked.

The next image was the same guard heading through the back room. He was following me, but he wasn't really following me. He was following Mr. Wharton. And for good reason.

Every now and then Mr. Wharton would knock something over, and each sound would cause the guard to jump . . . and consequently to investigate further. Deeper into the bowels of the back room.

Toward, I saw, the cold storage freezer.

Something else fell over—a marble Buddha, I think—and the guard nearly jumped out of his skin. But he continued on, doggedly, perhaps driven by fascination, or perhaps driven by the sick realization that tonight wasn't going according to plan. That someone was watching him. That someone knew what he was up to. Perhaps at any other time he would have turned away in fear. But not tonight. No, tonight—or rather, the night in question—he continued forward, inevitably, toward Mr. Wharton and the ice box.

Thad the security guard paused when he heard another noise. A noise that came from the ice box itself. A thumping, knocking sound. I even had a brief, flashing image of Mr. Wharton reaching down *through* the box and rapping something inside.

Thad the security guard whined a little. He was also making small, gasping sounds.

From a perspective of somewhere near the ice box, I watched—or, more accurately, Mr. Wharton watched—as the terrified man reached down and slowly opened the ice chest.

I could see that Thad didn't really want to open it, that he was scared shitless. But he seemed somehow *compelled* to open it. Like a man possessed. Which got me thinking.

Either way, as the lid came up, all hell broke loose.

The images jumped crazily. No, it wasn't the image that jumped crazily. It was Mr. Wharton moving rapidly. One moment he was down by the ice chest, and the next he was hovering somewhere above the security guard. The ice box was open. Frost and mist issued out, swirling around the man.

Mr. Wharton's attention shifted, and since I was seeing this through his eyes, his memory, my attention shifted, too.

To a shelf above the refrigerated box.

On the shelf, marked very neatly, were rows of stone tools and weapons; in particular, stone hatchets.

An arm reached up for the hatchet, and I was startled to see that it was Mr. Wharton's arm. A very real-looking arm. But not entirely real. Although solid-looking, I could still see through it.

Ectoplasm. A ghost body.

Now that very real-looking arm, draped in a slightly dusty reddish dinner jacket, removed the hatchet from the shelf. No doubt this was a Native American hatchet, or another tribal weapon from somewhere around the world. My knowledge of such artifacts was slim to none.

But one thing was obvious: it was heavy-looking, and it was topped by a razor-sharp flint head. A weapon used, no doubt, in battle or for skinning animals.

Or, in this case, for murder.

Thad must have heard something. As he turned to look, crying out, the hatchet flashed down and buried itself deep into his forehead. Thad jerked and nearly bit off his tongue. His left eye popped clean out of his head, to dangle by its neon-red optical nerves. I next watched in sick fascination as Mr. Wharton worked the hatchet free from the dead man's skull. When he did, Thad the security guard toppled into the freezer.

The ghost of Mr. Wharton calmly shut the lid, returned the bloody hatchet to its proper place, and promptly disappeared.

48.

I was at Hero's, where only one person knew my name, and that was just the way I liked it.

I had already picked up Tammy from school and dropped her off at my sister's. Danny, remarkably, was with Anthony at the hospital. My sister had asked if I would be there as well, and I said I would as soon as I could. She didn't like it but knew that only something very, very important would keep me away from my son.

Now, it was almost five and it had been a helluva day. Soon I would be heading out to Simi Valley, but first I needed to speak with Fang, my rock. And since our relationship had graduated to the physical level, I paid him a visit before heading out. The bar was mostly empty and we could speak freely enough. I caught him up to date on the past few days' activities.

"So the crystal egg was in the box," said Fang. He wasn't polishing the stereotypical glass; instead, he was cutting lime wedges.

"Yup."

"Any idea where he was going to send it?"

"Hard to say with only an 'M' in the address. Could have been his grandma. A P.O. box anywhere. And before you ask, his name was Thad."

"Thad?"

"Yup."

"Is that a real name?"

"As real as Fang."

He grinned. "Pretty clever idea just shipping that sucker out right under their noses."

"Would have worked, too, if Mr. Wharton hadn't cleaved his skull nearly in two."

"With a five-hundred-year-old war ax. Very fitting, being that this was his museum and all."

"And that he protects to this day," I said.

Fang leaned across the bar. As he did so, his two canine teeth clacked together like two marbles. He said, "So did you unpack the box right there?"

"No. I left it for Ms. Dickens. She opened it with a few other staff members standing nearby . . . and when she did, well, she nearly wept."

"A murder is one thing, but the theft of a piece of art is another."

"It is to a small museum trying to make a name for itself."

"Our world is weird," said Fang.

"Tell me about it."

His eyes crinkled a little. Maybe he got some squirted lime juice in them. "How did you explain that you knew the egg was in the box?"

"I told her I had a hunch."

"Your hunches are pretty damn good."

"Better than most," I said.

He nodded. "So the ghost of Mr. Wharton killed the security guard."

"He wasn't going to let anyone steal from his museum."

"Death by ghost," said Fang.

"Our world is weird," I said, and both Fang and I smiled at each other.

"So, it will go down as an unsolved crime?"

"No doubt," I said.

"Would be hard to arrest Mr. Wharton," he said, laughing lightly. He added, "Can a ghost still go to hell for killing?"

"You'd have to ask God."

He grinned again, and his eyes did this sort of sparkly thing that made my heart beat a little faster. Knowing my thoughts, he smiled brightly.

"Oh, give it a rest," I said. "You have a nice smile, so what?"

"Whatever you say, Moon Dance." He reached out and took my hands. "Have you thought about my request?"

"Not really, no. Too much on my mind."

He nodded. "I understand. Things have been crazy."

He squeezed my hands a little tighter. His hands were soft in spots, but rough in others. They were the hands of a man who poured drinks for a living, but worked on muscle cars when he could. They were also the hands of a man who had killed three people.

"I regret the killings," said Fang, squeezing my hands a little tighter and reading my thoughts. "I'm not a killer, Sam."

"Then why do you want to be a vampire?"

"Because I want to be with you," he said, bringing my knuckles to his lips and kissing them lightly. "Forever."

49.

The traffic out to Simi Valley was so bad that I was tempted to just pull over and take flight.

I resisted and two hours later, after winding my way through the foothills that connect Northridge to Simi Valley, I headed down a long incline toward the glittering lights that porn built.

Porn Valley. Or, as some people call it, Sili*cone* Valley.

As a one-time federal agent, I knew that nearly 90% of all legally produced pornographic films made in the United States were produced in studios based in the San Fernando Valley, of which Simi Valley was the heart.

The key phrase here was "legally produced." Other porn was produced here, as well. Some not so legal.

This, of course, was what made me nervous.

My cell rang. It was Danny. Oh, joy. Then again, he might have news about my son. Ever the cautious driver, I hooked my Bluetooth around my ear and clicked on.

"Hey, Sam," he said. His voice sounded strained. Something was either obstructing his throat or he had been crying. Or was still crying.

Shit. "Hey."

"He's dying, isn't he?" But Danny didn't really get the words out. Not really. Instead, a choked, strangled sound came out, and it was a horrible sound to hear. "Please, tell me the truth, Sam. Please. I'm so scared."

I closed my eyes. His pain went straight to my heart. I debated how much to tell him, until I realized he had a right to know.

"Yes, he is," I said.

Danny wept harder than I had ever heard him weep, harder than I had ever heard any man weep, and we cried together on the phone for many, many miles.

A trail of red brake lights snaked ahead of me as far as the eye could see. Although an hour outside of L.A., traffic in Southern California knew no city boundaries.

When I had hung up with Danny, I was an emotional wreck. Still driving, I did my best to compose myself, wiping the tears from my cheeks. Say what you want about the guy, the man loved his kids.

Traffic picked up, and as I worked my way into Simi Valley, one building clearly shone brighter than all others, up on a large hill—or a mountain, as one little girl put it—the Ronald Reagan Museum.

Below it, near the base and about three miles south of me, glittering in a far different way, was a massive casino. The Juarez Indian Tribe, on land reserved for them, had built one of the most popular casinos in Southern California, and even from here, as I made my way off the freeway, the casino lights flashed and strobed and practically jiggled—anything to lure dollars away from wallets.

A few minutes later, with the half moon hanging high in the sky, I pulled up to the casino and stepped out of my minivan. I scanned the fifteen-story facade of the hotel. Some of the windows were bright, but most were dark.

Maddie's words came flooding back to me. Perhaps they had been unlocked because I was staring up at the massive hotel, or perhaps I had gotten a psychic hit. Sometimes I didn't know. Hey, I'm still figuring this stuff out as I go.

Either way, I heard her words again: "We take the vader up."

The vader.

The elevator.

Maddie was here, in this hotel. Somewhere.

I was sure of it.

50.

I was dressed to kill. Or at least to seriously maim someone. I was wearing a tight black dress, fully aware of my rounded hips and thighs on the one hand, but not giving a shit on the other. It had been a while since I had worn this black dress and I had forgotten how much skin it showed.

How much *pale* skin, that is.

I'm a jeans-and-tee-shirt kind of gal, but sometimes you have to look the part. And what was the part I was looking? I didn't know, but dressing as a slutty whore in a casino in Porn Valley seemed the best way to blend in.

The black man in the photographs was named Carl Luck. A known drug dealer and pornographer. And, apparently, murderer and kidnapper.

Allegedly, of course.

I parked my minivan in the back of the crowded parking lot. After huffing it across the vast lot, I strode past an epic water fountain with a stone eagle feather motif. I walked under a glittering eagle feather arch, and across an eagle feather tiled mosaic near the entry way.

I sensed a pattern here.

Inside, the Moon Feather Casino was epic. I felt lost just standing there at the entrance. Where to start? I had no clue. I had Carl Luck's face seared, as they say, on the back of my retina. I would know the guy anywhere. Now it was just a matter of finding him without attracting attention to myself, or getting myself kicked out by the tribal police.

If I were a regular, where would I go in a casino?

I had no clue. I would have thought the bar, except the whole damn place was one big, honking bar. Waitresses criss-crossed everywhere, each carrying trays of colorful drinks. The waitresses were all middle-aged and tired-looking. They wore shiny leotards that showed a lot of stockinged legs. An eagle tail feather hung behind them, seemingly flapping as they walked.

Oh, brother.

Ignoring the occasionally discreet and mostly not-so-discreet stares of men old enough to be my grandfather, I made a circuit of the casino. At least, I think I did. Quite frankly, I had no clue where I ended up. It all looked the same. Exits everywhere. Restaurants everywhere. Hallways to exotic-sounding clubs. And the games. My God, the games. Rows upon rows of video poker and slot machines, with every conceivable theme. There were elaborate and colorful ancient Egyptian-themed slots: "Play with the Pharaohs!" Rows of ancient Mayan slot machines with pictures of treasures and stepped pyramids. An ancient Troy slot machine with a flashing Trojan horse, but instead of men pouring out of its underbelly, golden coins poured free. Hell, I could receive a thumbnail history lesson all while losing my money. If anything, the casino was a "Who's Who" of the ancient world.

And as I walked past a row of Easter Island slot machines, complete with megalithic-shaped heads, I decided to wait it out at what appeared to be the casino's central bar.

I ordered a house white wine and noted idly that the bartender wasn't anywhere near as cute as Fang. And as I sat there, drinking it sporadically and watching the crowd, I realized that this was a little like looking for a needle in a haystack.

That is, if the needle was a child-trafficking killer.

So I decided to pull out the big guns.

51.

I closed my eyes and did my best to clear my thoughts.

It's hard to clear your thoughts with the sounds of a casino assaulting your ears. Maybe that's the casino's secret plan. Assault the senses. Overstimulate them, confuse them, and thus lead you down dark roads where pulling out gobs of money and shoving them into a machine for "credits" suddenly seems like a damn good idea.

Or maybe the machines were just fucking annoying.

Anyway, I closed my eyes and cleared my thoughts and ignored the guy who had just sat next to me, reeking of alcohol and cigarettes. I tried to hone in on my guy.

I let a single name ease into my thoughts:

Carl Luck.

I let his image slide in next. The picture of him exiting McDonald's, with little Maddie and her mom, Lauren, in tow. In the picture he's looking down, perhaps at Maddie. But it's a good shot of his face. His strong cheek bones. His flat forehead. The tight position of his eyes in relation to his nose. All of this was permanently emblazoned in my thoughts.

Next, I did something that was new even to me, and it just sort of happened on its own. In my mind's eye, I saw my thoughts rippling away from me, further and further out like a widening gyre. And as my mind reached out, it seemed to touch down on everyone around me, searching.

Searching.

It kept reaching out, kept searching—

"Excuse me, baby?"

My probing thoughts came racing back, nearly slamming physically back into me. Jolting me. I gasped. It took me a moment to orient myself, and when I did, my smiling drunk neighbor's face was about three inches from my own. Three purple, wormy veins snaked just under the skin of his bulbous nose.

"What?" I asked, confused. I was still coming back. Back into my body. I had been out there somehow. Out in the casino. Somehow out of my body.

Sweet Jesus.

"Hey, baby, *you* were the one talking to *me*."

"I wasn't talking to you."

"Sure, baby. You kept saying something about luck. And, since I'm the only lucky bastard sitting next to you, I figured you were talking to me."

"I wasn't talking to you, sorry."

He put a firm hand on my bare thigh. "Of course you were, angel. Tonight's my lucky night."

He was a big guy. Granted, when you're five foot three, even sixth graders look big. But this guy was closing in on three hundred, and nearly had me by three times my own weight. I've got nothing against big guys. Actually, I find them adorable. But not drunk guys who lay their drunken fat hands on my thighs.

I put my hand on his and he smiled. This was encouraging for him. And, apparently, some drunken guy green light. He immediately tried to move his hand up the inside of my thigh. Except his hand didn't move. I calmly lifted it off my thigh and started squeezing.

"Hey!"

"Go away."

"My hand!"

"Go far away."

I let go and he tumbled backward off the stool, his feet flying up. He landed with a squishy thud. Keys and a cell phone toppled out of his pockets. Along with a condom. Eww. The not-quite-as-good-looking-as-Fang bartender rushed over to us, but I only shrugged and made a drinking motion. The guy got to his feet, gathered his stuff, and hurried away from me without looking back.

The bartender lingered briefly, certain that something strange had gone on, but then moved further down the bar to take an order, glancing at me a final time.

Way to stay inconspicuous, Sam. Easy, girl.

With the excitement over and alone once again, I closed my eyes and went through the previous steps and cast my thoughts outward.

And they continued outward until they reached the far end of the casino. I went through a double door and into an exclusive poker room. And sitting near the poker table was a dead ringer for public enemy #1, Mr. Carl Luck.

Whose luck might have just run out.

Hey, I had to say it.

As an experiment, I cast my thoughts even further out, up through the hotel, floor after floor, but there seemed to be a limit to this. The further I got, the more scattered my thoughts were.

I retracted them, this time not so violently, and opened my eyes. When I had steadied myself, I plunked down a $10 bill, got up, and headed for the far side of the casino.

To the poker room.

52.

Feeling as if I had done this before, I wove my way past roulette tables and blackjack tables, and past tables of made-up games I had never heard before. Games like Flash Poker and Three-Card Texas Slam.

Okay, now they're just making stuff up.

As I walked, I was aware that a lot of flesh was showing and a part of me didn't entirely mind. A steady diet of blood, staying out of the sun, and my own nighttime jogs had done wonders for my body. The ultimate Atkins Diet. I was still naturally curvy, but a petite curvy. Petite and now roped with muscle.

Some men looked. Some women did, too. I wasn't the sexiest or prettiest woman here, not by a long shot, but I suspected I projected a certain presence. What that presence was, I didn't know. Confidence? Blood lust?

Soon, I reached the far corner of the casino, where I wasn't too surprised to see the same double doors there. There were two guys—both Native American—standing just outside the open doors, and I suspected they would have stopped most people. But I put on my best "don't fuck with me" look and they simply blinked and smiled and let me through.

And as I swept through, I wondered: Had they let me in because of my "don't fuck with me look" or something else?

What that something was, I didn't know. But the words "mind control" came to mind.

Too weird.

I surveyed the room. Definitely high rollers. Seven men were seated around the table, no women. Two of the men were wearing Arab *keffiyehs*. Another was wearing a white cowboy hat, and the remaining four were a mix of ethnicities. All were dressed immaculately. None noticed me. All were intent on the dealer who was currently shuffling. A few more security types stood around the room, all of them Native American. The casino's own security, no doubt. There were a handful of plush chairs surrounding the main poker table, and these were filled with babes. Various hookers, no doubt. And at a private bar on the far side of the room sat Carl Luck, wearing shades and drinking a draft beer. He was watching the game intently.

My heart slammed against a rib or two. My first instinct was to fly across the room and slam his face into the bar, and keep slamming it until he told me where Maddie was.

Calm down. Deep breaths.

Instead, I crossed the big room as calmly as I could and found a stool next to Carl Luck.

He was a big man. Not as big as some of the other men in my life, but he was certainly up there. Other than glancing at me from over his shades, Carl did little to acknowledge me. The thick black man smelled of nice cologne. His shiny, mottled boots were ostrich skin. His maroon leather jacket fit him perfectly. If I had to guess, I would say Carl Luck had recently come into a lot of money. The man in the picture at McDonald's had been nowhere near as slick.

"Who's winning?" I asked innocently.

Carl slowly turned his shiny head. Nothing else moved. He was leaning one elbow on the counter. His elbow looked exceptionally sharp. His eyes were hidden behind the cool shades.

"Captain Jack's up," he said. His deep-throated voice was as smooth as smooth gets. He sounded like a radio talk show host. The kind women swoon for.

"Always better to be up than down, I say." Except I didn't know what the hell I was talking about.

Carl looked at me but said nothing, although I could hear his nasally breathing from here. One of his nostrils was backed up.

Gee, I wonder why.

"Who's Captain Jack?" I asked.

"Cowboy hat."

"Of course. Should have figured that one out."

Carl turned back to the game. Once again, only his head moved. Nothing else. Correction. His jaw tightened a little. I was making him nervous.

He's wondering who the hell I am.

Good question. This was an exclusive, high-stakes room that I really had no business being in—and no real reason for being here.

Other than to find Maddie.

Someone from the table whooped loudly. Captain Jack. He yanked off his hat and waved it like a cowboy riding a bucking bronco. A whole mass of chips just got pushed his way. He whooped again.

Next to me, Carl grinned slightly.

He's with Captain Jack, I thought.

One white and one black, said little Maddie.

"Do you play?" I asked.

"Hell no."

"Why not?"

"It's a two hundred and fifty thou buy-in."

"More than my house."

"More than most houses."

"I bet they fly these guys in," I said. "I heard some hotels do that."

"Shit. They roll out the red carpet for these brothers. Fly them in, bring them women, and anything else they want."

"What else could they want?"

"Anything."

I nodded. Carl was tense. Very tense. The cords along his neck were throbbing. His hands opened and closed. Waves of apprehension emanated from him.

I said, "Free hotel room. Free everything, I bet."

"Yeah, something like that," he said. He turned his back to me.

So Carl and Captain Jack were staying here. And now Carl was shutting down and I didn't want to push it.

"Well, the nickel slot machines are calling my name," I said.

But Carl didn't acknowledge me as I left, although I could feel his eyes on me as I crossed the room and exited through the double doors.

53.

I leaned a shoulder against a smooth wall and exhaled a billowing plume of gray smoke. I was standing just inside a narrow hallway that led to the casino's bathrooms and public phones. From here, I had a good view of the double doors of the exclusive parlor.

I inhaled deeply, filling my lungs to the maximum. Smoking did nothing for me. No smoker's high. Nothing. No nicotine addiction. Nothing. For me, smoking was a purely voluntary act. It was one of the few things that I could do without a violent reaction. So I did it because I could.

The good thing about casinos is that you can smoke in them. The good thing about being a vampire is that you don't get lung cancer.

At least, that's what they tell me. And by *they*, I mean Fang. The man was my sole source for all things vampiric.

I found myself grinning thinking about the Toothless Wonder. Toothless because his canines had been removed. His dogteeth, as they are sometimes called.

His *vampire* teeth.

Interesting thing about that, since my own teeth had never once changed size or shape in the six years since I'd been unwillingly recruited into the creature of the night club. Admittedly, it made sense that longer canine teeth would aid a vampire. Of course, so would a hypodermic needle. Longer teeth aided creatures who hunted with their mouth, those who didn't have the benefit of hands or weapons. Longer teeth latched onto prey, held it down. Longer teeth aided in tearing into the flesh.

I couldn't eat flesh. I needed only a steady flow of blood to be sustained. I didn't need to kill other creatures, either.

A voluntary source would be adequate.

A donor.

These thoughts were new to me. They were revolutionary. They made me look at myself differently.

I didn't have to kill.

I only had to drink.

Of course, I received my supply of blood from a local butchery, so I didn't kill. But the blood was also disgusting and mixed with hundreds of other creatures, some of which might very well be diseased or sick.

All mixed in a big bloody soup for yours truly to enjoy night after night.

But it didn't have to be that way, did it? All I needed was a steady source.

I thought of Fang. I also thought of his request.

Make me a vampire.

I inhaled again, squinting through the smoke even though it didn't really hurt my eyes. The room beyond the double doors was still quiet. A few people passed in and out, but not Carl Luck or Captain Jack.

Jesus, had Fang proposed to me tonight? I mean, he had taken my hand and said he wanted to be with me for all eternity.

A proposal if I'd ever heard one.

Wow.

I dashed out my cigarette in a glass ashtray around the corner, then went back to my post just inside the hallway. I would think about Fang's proposal later. At the moment, Fang's proposal was way down on my list.

High on my list was the grim realization that I was certain—dead certain—that I was going to kill two men tonight.

Thirty minutes later, a group of wealthy men emerged from the parlor room. Only one looked particularly cheerful, a tall man wearing a *keffiyeh*. Captain Jack, who followed behind, looked like he was in a sour mood.

Carl Luck slapped him on his back reassuringly, and the two men headed off toward a bank of elevators.

Vaders.

54.

Fifteen minutes later, I took the elevator up to the upper suites.

The luxury suites. The high rollers' suites. Suites where the big boys stayed with their big bucks. Suites that were spacious enough that you probably couldn't hear someone scream. Especially a little girl.

I set my jaw as the elevator doors opened. My purse was still over my shoulder. Cool air met me in the spacious hallway. I could turn right or left. I automatically turned right, feeling my way.

The hallway was lined with polished tables and flowers. I doubted the other floors had polished tables and flowers. The doors here were recessed deep in the walls and inlaid with brass relief designs. The designs were, you guessed it, eagle feathers. The doors, I saw, were also designed for security. Although the reliefs were in brass, the doors themselves were made of steel.

I continued down the hall, guided entirely by my sixth sense. As I made a right turn, a small buzzing began just inside my eardrum. And the further I walked down the hallway, the louder the buzzing became.

I found myself staring at one recessed doorway in particular. It was on my left and it looked like all the others.

Except it didn't *feel* like all the others. I was drawn to it, and even as I was drawn to it, my innate warning system—the buzzing in my ears—grew louder and louder.

There's danger here.

The gilded door gleamed dully in the muted lights. I was alone in the hallway. I couldn't hear a sound, and my hearing was damn good.

Still, my head buzzed; my skin prickled.

Behind this door was a terrified little girl—the same little girl who had been calling me these past few days.

The steel door might as well have been a vault door. The hotel gave its exalted guests a lot of security and privacy.

Too much privacy.

The door would have multiple locks, including a deadbolt and no doubt another one elsewhere. Maybe near the floor or ceiling. This wasn't your standard hotel door. Up here, on this floor, nothing was standard.

Sometimes I wondered how strong I really was. It's not an easy thing to test, unless you want to draw attention to yourself. A few years back, while out jogging, I paused next to an old Volkswagen Beetle. On a whim, I reached down, felt underneath, and then lifted it three feet off the ground.

A few weeks ago I had punched through a bulletproof prison glass and nearly killed a man.

A steel, ornamental, security door seemed forbidding in and of itself. I could have knocked, sure. I could have called the police and pleaded my case. With luck, an emergency search warrant might be issued.

Think again, Sam. This is reservation land. Things are done differently here.

How differently, I didn't know, but I suspected the hotel would think twice, or maybe even three or four times, before upsetting a guest who plunks down $250K on a card game . . . and then loses.

Yes, I could have done a lot of things differently at this moment, but none of them felt right.

None, that is, except this.

I raised my foot, leaned back, and drove the heel of my foot as hard as I could into the door. Obliterating my expensive high heel, and obliterating the door hinges, too.

The steel slab fell inward, landing with a thunderous crash.

55.

I instinctively stood to one side of the doorway. The metallic echo of the falling door continued to reverberate throughout the suite.

Hell of an entrance.

But there was no one directly in front of me, and as I slipped inside, kicking off my worthless high heels, the alarm in my head continued to buzz, stronger than ever.

Something was very, very wrong. More wrong than I had previously imagined. What it was, I didn't know. Yet.

Maybe I should have called the police. Or at least had a gun.

The suite was opulent. Sickeningly so. No doubt it cost thousands a night, although a guy like Captain Jack probably had it comped.

I'd never had anything comped in my life.

The balcony doors were wide open. Even from the doorway, I had a majestic view of the sweeping southern hillside . . . and the Ronald Reagan Library.

I had the right place.

Where the door had fallen, it had shattered about a dozen expensive Italian marble slabs. I stepped over the fallen door, crunched over the broken tile, and slipped deeper into the room.

The suite was designed with two main wings that branched off from the main living room. The hallway to my left led to the back rooms, and a shorter hallway to the right led off to a kitchen space and a billiard room and bar. The bar was big enough to liquor up the entire casino.

So far, I hadn't seen anyone. Or heard anyone.

But they were here.

I knew it.

Standing just outside the hallway to the bedroom wing, I closed my eyes and searched for them. Or at least tried to. My senses were chaotic, unclear. I needed a clear head to focus, and focusing now was nearly impossible.

They're in the bedrooms. One of the bedrooms.

I turned down the hallway wing, padding softly over the smooth tiles with my bare feet. There were four doors along this hallway, two on each side. This luxury suite was bigger than three of my houses put together.

They knew I was here. They had to have known. No way that fallen door went undetected. The alarm inside my head continued to sound, a buzzing that surrounded my head like so many wasps.

The doors into the bedrooms were all double doors. Three of the four double doors stood open. The doors at the far end of the hallway were the only ones closed.

They're in there. Doing whatever it is that they're doing.

I felt sick, but I continued forward. I paused at each open door, but the rooms, although packed with luggage, were empty.

Now standing at the far door at the far end of the hallway, I heard a little voice whimpering.

Ah, fuck.

I tried the handle. It was unlocked.

I inhaled deeply, took hold of the handle, and threw the door open.

I thought I was ready for anything.

But I wasn't ready for this.

56.

The first thing I saw was a table. A medical table of some type. It was sitting in the center of the spacious room.

The next thing I saw was a little girl on the table.

Maddie.

Oh, sweet Jesus.

She was dead, or close to it.

Red tubes ran from her arms to plastic bags full of blood. Her blood. She was wrapped in a white robe covered with droplets of blood. Her blood. Her eyes were closed and now I could just make out her little chest rising and falling slowly. A single light shone down on her.

What the fuck was going on?

My first instinct was to run to her. But I resisted. My agency training superseded my natural instinct.

She's breathing; she's not dead; stay still.

I knew I wasn't alone. Other than Maddie, I knew someone else was in the room.

Perhaps more than one.

Psychic hits are great. But they only get you so far.

At the open doorway, I paused, listening. I heard nothing. No, wait. I heard breathing from deeper inside the room. Nasally breathing.

Mr. Carl Luck.

So where was Captain Jack?

He's in here, too. The sick bastard is in here, too. Siphoning Maddie's blood.

For what?

The answer was all too obvious.

He's a vampire.

"You got that right, little lady."

I couldn't pinpoint the location of the voice, but it seemed to come from somewhere above. I was also all too aware that the speaker had read my thoughts.

"Right again, little lady. Now don't be shy, step on in here. We don't bite." The voice chuckled.

My head was buzzing. Danger was everywhere. Perhaps at every turn. I looked down the hall. There was nothing. The danger was all in this room.

I had seen only one other vampire in my life, and that was just the other day. The vampire who had attacked me years ago had done so in a blur.

For the first time in a long, long time, I didn't know what to do.

Meanwhile, there was a little girl bleeding to death.

I hadn't used a gun in a long time, but I wished I had one now. Carl I wasn't worried about. Captain Jack was another story. Captain Jack was the enigma. The kink in the chain.

Maddie made a small, mewing sound. I saw something forming around her. A black halo.

Shit.

I considered dashing in and grabbing her, but I knew a recently fed vampire like Captain Jack would be powerful. Not to mention I knew instinctively that Carl Luck was armed . . . and not with just a traditional weapon, either.

It was the reason my alarm was sounding off so loudly.

He had silver bullets in his gun. I was sure of it.

The moment I thought that, the Southern voice laughed heartily from somewhere in the room.

The black halo around Maddie continued growing.

I didn't know what to do.

It was an ambush, that much was for sure.

And that's when I heard a noise from behind me. When I turned to look, I saw a sight that was both welcomed and very, very surreal.

It was Aaron King, the old detective from Los Angeles, slipping into the hallway behind me. He raised a finger to his lips to shush me. I nodded.

Maddie needed to be saved.

Now.

I dashed into the room, trusting my instincts, trusting Aaron King, and praying like hell we all made it through this alive.

57.

I had a hard time zeroing in on the vampire, but I knew, could *feel*, exactly where Carl Luck was in the room.

The heavy-set drug dealer—and apparent *blood* dealer—was crouching in the far corner of the huge bedroom, taking aim. I twisted my body just as a shot rang out. The bullet grazed my shoulder, searing it, and impacted the wall behind me.

I crouched and ran forward, sprinting as fast as I could. The room blurred past me.

Another shot rang out. But I was going too fast to turn or duck or do anything. A wicked pain kicked me in the stomach. But I didn't stop running, and now I was leaping.

Carl Luck screamed and shrank back, and I drove my flattened hand, with its sharp, pointed nails, straight through his throat. Through skin and Adam's apple, and through his spine, as well, severing it.

He jerked hard and instantly shit his pants.

Blood spurted everywhere as I pulled my hand free. I was already spinning, searching for the vampire, but there was no one there.

The pain in my stomach flared mightily, and I nearly doubled over. I gasped, fought to stay on my feet. It had been a silver bullet, I was sure of it. The pain . . . nearly unbearable. The searing pain . . . so similar to the crossbow bolt of a few months ago. Had the bullet gone all the way through? I didn't know.

Something flashed overhead. A white blur.

I looked up, raising my hand, just as something dropped down from above. A wide fist, like a hammer, that drove my head straight down into the floor.

The force of the blow was unlike anything I had ever felt before. How it didn't kill me, I don't know.

I lay there, gasping, struggling for breath, bleeding on the floor from my stomach, shoulder, and mouth. My nose was broken, I was sure of it. Perhaps my jaw, too. The force of the punch had driven my face into the tiles, cracking the tiles. Blood flowed freely, filling the cracks like little crimson tributaries.

Someone grabbed my hair, lifted me up. My jaw hung slack. Yeah, it was broken. Shattered, perhaps.

"So who do we have here?" I heard a voice ask from somewhere seemingly far away. It was the same voice I had heard earlier from the hallway. The same Southern drawl.

He continued lifting until I was facing him. It was Captain Jack, of course, only this time he wasn't wearing his huge cowboy hat. No doubt he had lost his hat as he ambushed me from above.

"Can't talk, huh? Cat got your tongue?" And he slapped me hard across the face. My disjointed jaw swung around like a swing in a storm, nearly hitting the back of my neck. The only thing keeping it in place was the bone and tendons and skin.

Now he gripped me by the throat and lifted. My jaw hung on his hand, bleeding down his arm. "Hmm. I've never seen you before. You must be a newbie. Only a newbie would break in on someone feeding." He pulled me a little closer to his face. My eyes were so blurred I could barely make out the big Texan. "I don't like newbies. Newbies don't get it. Newbies try to change everything. I don't like change."

I couldn't talk, but I could think.

You're killing the little girl.

"Oh, you mean my food source? I suppose so, but food sources know no ages, Newbie, although little girls and boys tend to have a richer, purer blood, which is what I prefer."

You're a fucking animal.

"You don't know me well enough to call me names, little lady. Killing our own kind is looked down upon, but I think I'll make an exception here. I have a feeling you might make my life difficult if I let you out of here alive."

Now his hand tightened, crushing my throat. I saw his other hand reaching inside his coat pocket. I knew his thoughts. Hell, I was inside his twisted head.

He was reaching for a silver dagger.

I quit flailing and grabbed his hand at my throat with both of my own. I didn't know who the fuck this asshole was, but I knew I wasn't dead yet.

And with all the strength I had, I broke his wrist.

He screamed and dropped me. I landed on my feet and squared off.

"You bitch!"

But I was moving, using all my training and instincts, focusing my fear and hate and anger. I wasn't a slouch. I knew what I was doing. I hit him hard, repeatedly, driving my punches into the face. Who he was, I didn't care. How strong he was, I didn't know. How much damage I was doing, I couldn't tell.

Out of the corner of my eye, I saw Aaron King standing in the doorway, his own jaw hanging down, holding a stun gun. I motioned for him to get the girl, projecting my thoughts to him as strongly as I could. He looked briefly confused and then moved to Maddie.

My brief pause was all Captain Jack needed. He leveled a

devastating punch into my right eye. So hard that I heard my cheekbone shatter.

I stumbled backwards and as I did so, I saw something silver slash before me. His dagger. Amazingly, as it came down on me, all I could think of was my kids. I saw their faces. Their beautiful faces. The dagger sliced down, no doubt heading for my heart. Whether or not that would kill me, I didn't know, but I suspected it would. I suspected Captain Jack knew exactly what he was doing.

Except I've been trained in knife fighting. Trained by the best. I did the one thing we were taught to do when there was no real hope of avoiding a plunging knife.

Use my arm as a shield.

And, as I did just that, I heard my old instructor's voice: "Better to cut your arm than to die."

The knife slashed down as my arm came up. . . .

58.

The narrow blade plunged through my arm.

This was shaping up to be a hell of a shitty day. I couldn't even scream. I grunted while my lower jaw flapped.

But, believe it or not, I knew what I was doing. I turned my arm, and the blade came out of his hand. I backed away, stumbling, steam hissing from my forearm where the silver dagger's handle protruded from it.

Gasping and choking on my own blood, I pulled the blade free.

And that's when something snaked across the bedroom, something crackling and alive.

Aaron King's stun gun.

It did little damage to the big Texan in front of me, but the vampire did turn and grab at the wires, and when he did so, I leaped forward, and drove the silver dagger deep into him.

Deep into his heart.

I shrank away as the Texan went into wild convulsions. I had seen death before, but never quite like this. He didn't want to die. That much was clear. His body fought it, clawing at his bloody chest, which hissed steam. He turned to me more than once as if to ask: What the hell have you done? He even lunged at me one more time but didn't get very far.

He collapsed on the tiled floor, back arched, steam rising, holding his chest, gasping like a fish out of water. He did that for an unbelievable amount of time before he finally quit moving.

"I've seen some weird shit in my time," said Aaron King next to me. "But this takes the cake."

We were in the living room. Little Maddie was wrapped in blankets and resting in one corner of the voluminous couch. Aaron was sitting next to me, holding my hand, and holding my jaw in place, too.

"You can't talk, I know, but what happened back there . . ." he started shaking his head, his face paler than any vampire's. "What the hell *did* happen back there?"

I could have reached out with my mind, but I didn't. The old guy seemed to have had enough of a shock. I was just too exhausted to speak, even telepathically.

The bullet had traveled through my stomach and out my lower back, leaving a hell of a messy hole. Still, the exposure to silver was doing a number on me, leaving me exhausted and nearly unconscious.

"Your poor jaw, lil' darlin'. Your poor arm. Sweet Jesus, what the hell went on back there?" He started shaking his head again, and then I saw there were tears in his eyes. "And what were they doing to this little one? They were taking her blood, weren't they? Is she sick?"

I tried shaking my head. He understood my minute impulse. "No, of course she ain't sick. They're sick. Good Lord, what were they doing to her?"

I tried shaking my head again.

Aaron King said, "Maybe I should quit asking so many questions."

I tried to smile. The old man held my jaw and my arms and did his best to comfort me.

"The paramedics are coming. Tribal police will be here soon, too. We have a hell of a mess on our hands. I don't know where to start explaining or what to say." He looked at me kindly, but I saw the confusion in his eyes. And fear. "You were shot in the stomach, stabbed in the arm. But your wounds have stopped bleeding . . ."

He let his voice trail off and the old guy just kept holding me and patting me and keeping my poor, broken jaw in place, and we sat like that until the police swarmed into the room. . . .

It was late.

I was loaded in the back of an ambulance. It was also coming on morning, which was perhaps an hour or so away. We had spent the night being quizzed from every conceivable angle. Mercifully, Detective Hanner from the Fullerton Police Department had appeared. And once she arrived, things started settling down.

Now Aaron King and I were left alone, and that's when he told me that he had decided to come check things out for himself. He didn't like the idea of me being alone. A few routine questions at the front desk—and no doubt full use of his Southern charm—had led him to connect Carl Luck with the oil-rich Texan. A few more inquiries later and he was on his way up to the suite . . . when he'd discovered the shattered door.

I nodded and whispered a thank you. Amazingly, I felt my jaw healing. It had also settled back into place; that is, roughly where it should be. Maybe I would forever have an overbite. As Aaron King sat there in the back of the ambulance, holding my hand, Detective Hanner opened the back door. She asked if she could have a moment alone with me, and the old investigator nodded. She told him he was no longer needed and he squeezed my hand lightly and said he would check up on me in a few days.

I nodded and wanted to thank him and I think he knew how grateful I was to him. Aaron King, who wasn't really Aaron King, nodded to Detective Hanner and left.

Hanner looked at me, then jabbed a thumb in King's direction. "Was that who I think it was?"

I nodded again, and she shook her head and slipped inside the ambulance and shut the door behind her.

"We need to talk," she said.

59.

"Well, I need to talk," she corrected. "I assume your jaw has not healed yet."

I shook my head gingerly.

She leaned over and examined me carefully. "Yeah, that's bad. Give it a day or so and you should be fine. At least, well enough to talk." She lowered her voice further. "Kingsley asked me to talk to you."

She laughed lightly, as I'm sure my eyes just about popped out of my head.

"Yes, I've known Mr. Fulcrum for a long, long time. Probably longer than you've been alive." She sat on the edge of my gurney, resting her hands in her lap, and only occasionally looked me directly in the eyes. And when she did, those few times that our eyes actually met, I had the disconcerting feeling that I was looking at something very alien. Her eyes were a little too wide. Too searching. Too penetrating. And wild. So damn wild.

She's not human, I thought, and then wondered if she could hear my thoughts, too. Maybe that's why she rarely looked me in the eye. Maybe she knew the effect her eyes had.

Jesus, did I look like that, too?

But Detective Hanner did not give me any indication that she had heard my thoughts. Or maybe I was getting better at shielding them. I didn't know. There was still so much to learn.

"Kingsley told me that you might have the medallion. He was sketchy on this, as he knows its importance and value. And he is right in not being too forthcoming about this. People will kill for that medallion. Vampires especially. You see, not all of us desire our current state. Some of us wish to be human again."

Her eyes flashed over mine briefly, and her pupils were nothing more than tiny black pinpricks. Her eyes continued over my face and settled on my jaw.

"He thought he could trust me, and that I might help you."

She looked at me again, and I suddenly realized how vulnerable I was in this position. Her pupils flared briefly, and she nodded. "He's right, of course. You can trust me." She looked at my arm, cocking her head to one side. "But you shouldn't take my word for it. There's many like us who aren't honorable. There are many like us who are like him—" and here she nodded to another ambulance where I knew lay two bodies, Carl Luck and Captain Jack— "Yes, there are many who rape and pillage and act like asses. Just like humans, I suppose.

"But you can trust me, even if you don't yet." She rested her hand lightly on my leg and hers was an oddly comforting touch. I say oddly because I could feel the cold radiating through the blanket. "Long ago, I had a child once, too. He died of old age, and I watched him die from a distance, never getting close enough for him to recognize me. He, of course, thought his mother had died in a fire, as I had planned. You see, he was getting too old, and his mother was staying so young. It was the hardest decision I ever had to make." She smiled weakly at me. "But I watched him from afar, helping him when he needed it. I suspect he thought he had a guardian angel. But little did he know it was just me." She smiled again. "Lord help anyone who crossed him."

She laughed lightly and so did I. Mostly, though, I was entranced by her. Enchanted, even. *She's like me,* I kept thinking. *She's like me. And I'm not alone.*

"We do not have much time, Samantha. I will take care of things on this end. Some killings are not as heavily investigated as others. Some people need to be convinced of this. I suspect, by the time everyone leaves here tonight, they will be convinced that this had been a drug deal gone bad. Very, very bad.

"Oh, and the body of Captain Jack? Not to worry. He will decompose like anyone else. As far as the authorities are concerned, he is just another dead man. And not the creature he had been."

She looked at me again, and her alien eyes briefly locked onto mine. "I have already convinced them to let you go. In fact, many of the police have no idea why you are here." She smiled slyly. "Yes, I have been a vampire for a long, long time. I know things. You and I need to talk."

I nodded. Yes, we very much needed to talk.

And now she reached out and took my hand and the cold that permeated from her was shocking. I did my best not to gasp. "But first, you must take care of your little one. Do what you need to do, Samantha Moon, and I will help you find the answers you seek. Answers about the medallion . . ." Her voice trailed off. "But know this: There are no guarantees. Few know anything about this medallion. And those who do may not talk. Those who do, may, in fact, be dead."

I nodded and felt the tears come to me. So many tears these past few days. Detective Hanner squeezed my hand a little tighter. Two ice cold hands.

"I don't envy you, Samantha. I don't know you, of course. But I don't envy you. You have a decision to make. Perhaps the most difficult decision I can imagine."

Detective Hanner released my hand and came over to my side and hugged me deeply, careful of my jaw. As she held me, I wept into her shoulder.

60.

I was flying over the Pacific Ocean.

It was the next night. I had spent the day by my son's side, holding his hands, even as the doctors had raced in and out of the hospital. Some screamed at me to get out of the way. One even shoved me out of the way. They fought for his life. They fought hard to save him.

I watched from his bedside as the doctors used all their skill and medicines and machines. One doctor told me to expect the worst. To start making preparations. I told him to go to hell.

My son, for now, was still hanging on. Still alive.

For now.

The ocean was black and infinite. Crazy, glowing lights zig-zagged beneath the surface, some bigger than others, and I knew this was life. Ocean life. Some of the bigger shapes didn't zig or zag so much as lumber slowly through the ocean, sometimes surfacing and blowing out great sprays of water that refracted the moonlight.

I flapped my massive wings languidly, riding the tides of night. Cold wind blew over my perfectly aerodynamic body.

It had been a hell of a day. The black halo around my son was so dense. Nearly syrupy. He had only hours to live, I knew it. Danny was by his side. And so was my sister and my daughter. Sherbet had stopped by, and so had Fang and Kingsley. Mercifully at separate times. Aaron King, Knighthorse, and Spinoza all stopped by, too, each bringing flowers. Aaron King checked my jaw, saw me talking, and just shook his head in wonder. Knighthorse and Spinoza were both irked that they had not been invited to the big showdown at the casino, until I reminded them I was a highly trained federal agent who could take care of herself.

The air was cold. Perhaps even freezing, but I felt perfectly comfortable. The moon was only half full overhead.

Had it really been only two weeks ago that the hulking monster that was Kingsley had appeared in my hotel suite?

I had checked on Maddie, too. The little girl was going to make it. She had needed a full blood transfusion. The black halo around her little body had all but disappeared.

The specialist from Chicago had arrived, too, along with another colleague of his. The agreement was unilateral: My son had a particularly aggressive form of Kawasaki disease. Already three doses of intravenous immunoglobulin had been administered to Anthony. Most children respond within 24 hours to the first dose. My son showed no signs of responding. They next tried salicylate therapy and corticosteroids. Neither worked. Finally, they tried cyclophosphamide and plasma exchange, experimental treatments with variable outcomes. Nothing worked.

I listened to the doctors conferring with each other from across the room. They didn't know that I could hear them, of course. One doctor mentioned that there was nothing left to try. The other doctor nodded grimly. The first doctor came over to me and gave me the bad news. My son was not responding to any treatments, he said. I asked what that meant, and he looked at me sadly, and said sometimes children pull through. He didn't sound very hopeful.

Sometimes they pull through, he said, but I heard him think: *and sometimes they die, too.*

The wind seemed to pick up from behind me, and I soared effortlessly. Below me, the pod of whales seemed to be keeping pace, their glowing bodies surfacing and spraying. I quickly swept past them.

I thought of the water. The dark water. The world seemed to slow down under water. Sound became muted, and light diffused.

I looked down again . . . stopped flapping, then tucked my wings in and dove.

I closed my eyes as I broke the surface.

My aerodynamic body cut easily through the water, and I shot down into the dark depths. But the water, much like the air, wasn't truly dark. Sparks of light zipped through it. Bright filaments that lit my way.

I flapped my wings and discovered to my great surprise and pleasure that I easily moved through the water, my wings expelling it behind me powerfully, moving me quickly along. Like a manta ray. I was a giant, bat-shaped manta ray.

I flapped my wings slowly but powerfully. Water surged past me, but did not hurt my eyes. This creature that I had become was amazingly adaptive and resilient.

I was amazingly adaptive and resilient.

But not my son. No, my son was dying, and he would be dead within hours. I knew it. The doctors knew it. Everyone knew it. You did not need to be a doctor or a psychic to see the encroachment of death.

I could stop his death. I could give him eternal life, in fact. I could have my baby boy by my side forever. Detective Hanner had told me how to do it. The process of transformation. Of turning mortal into immortal.

It was a crazy idea. A reckless idea.

But I could save him—and then later return his mortality to him with the medallion.

Maybe. Except no one seemed to know for sure.

I continued flapping, my heart heavy. A creature sidled up next to me. A dolphin. No, two dolphins. They kept pace with me, thrusting with their powerful tails. I knew very little about dolphins but if I had to guess, they looked perplexed as hell. I didn't blame them. No doubt they had never seen the likes of me. A moment later, they peeled away, their auras leaving behind brightly phosphorescent vapor trails.

My son was going to die within hours. Maybe sooner.

This much was true.

I could save him. Giving him eternal life.

And I possessed a legendary medallion that could give him back his mortality. A loophole in death.

Not too many people had that option.

Not too many mothers. Desperate mothers.

I heard Kingsley's words again. *And what if you can't change him back, Sam?*

Anthony would be immortal. At age seven. Doomed to walk the earth forever. At age seven. To drink blood for all eternity.

At age seven.

It was one thing to consider turning the handsome, love-struck Fang into my immortal lover, someone who wanted to fill my nights with pleasure and companionship, perhaps for the rest of my existence, which could be thousands of years, but who knew? It was quite another thing to doom Anthony, my precious, precious child, to that same fate—he would always be seven years old, and a vampire. I could not even imagine how to explain it all to him if the medallion did not work.

My heart gave a tremendous heave.

I didn't know what to do. Who could possibly know what to do?

Time was running out.

My son was dying.

I tipped one of my wings and veered back toward the direction I had come.

My mind raced as I flapped hard, surging through the water, scattering tiny silver fish before me.

And then I came to a decision.

God, help me, I came to a decision.

I flapped my wings as hard as I could and burst free from the ocean and shot up into the night sky.

[CONTINUED IN BOOK 4]

BOOK 4

Moon Child

Vampire for Hire #4

DEDICATION

To Tatinha, with love and many beijos.

ACKNOWLEDGMENTS

A big thank you to Sandy Johnston, Eve Paludan, and Elaine Babich. My crew.

"To be immortal is commonplace; except for man, all creatures are immortal, for they are ignorant of death; what is divine, terrible, incomprehensible, is to know that one is immortal."

—*Jorge Luis Borges*

"The only thing wrong with immortality is that it tends to go on forever."

—*Herb Caen*

Moon Child

1.

The ocean swept beneath me.

The waxing moon reflected off the ripping currents, keeping pace with my swiftly racing body. White caps appeared and disappeared and once I caught the spraying plume of a grey whale surfacing.

Some mothers would fault me for leaving my son's side, I knew this. Some would even fault me for saving the life of a little girl while my son is sick in the hospital, that I should be by my son's side at all times, no matter what. I get it. No doubt some would feel that I should be beating down doors looking for a cure, not resting until my son is healthy again. I get that, too.

Below me, a seagull raced just above the surface, briefly keeping pace with me, until I pulled away. I dropped my right wing, angling to starboard. The beaches appeared, and soon the exorbitantly expensive homes. A party was raging in the back of one of them. I passed in front of the moon, and I spied one or two of the party-goers looking up, pointing.

But I'm not like most mothers. In fact, I would even hazard to guess there are very few of us, indeed. I could *see* my son's imminent death. I could *see* the doctors failing. I could *see* it, feel it, *hear* it.

And not only that, I knew the hour of his death, and it was approaching.

Fast.

The beachfront homes gave way to marshy lands which gave way to beautiful condos and hillside homes. I swept over UCI and into a low-lying cloud which scattered before me, dispersed by my powerfully beating wings.

I had a decision to make. I had the biggest decision of my life to make. So I had to think. I had to get away, even for just a few minutes to sort through it. I had to know that what I was about to do, *or not do*, was the right decision.

Until I realized there was only one answer.

I was a mother first. Always first, and if I had a chance to save my son, you better damn well believe I was going to save him.

I flapped harder, powering through the cloud and out into the open air. My innate sense of navigation kicked in and I was locked on to St. Jude's Hospital in Orange.

2.

It was late when I swept into the parking lot.

I circled just above the glow of halogen lighting, making sure the parking lot was indeed empty, before dropping down next to my minivan.

To think that this hulking, winged creature owned a five-year-old minivan with license plates that were about to expire was laughable. No, it was incomprehensible.

I wasn't worried about security cameras. They would capture nothing . . . except maybe a car door opening and closing . . . followed later by a spunky, thirty-seven year old mother who may or may not fully appear in the image, depending on whether I wore make-up. Without make-up, the camera would capture only the curvy outline of empty clothing.

Of course, knowing that I did not appear on camera prompted me to remember to wear make-up, including a light coating on my arms and backs of my hands. Still, no doubt there were hundreds of surveillance videos out there of an unseen woman. Want to know how to find vampires? Check surveillance video.

For now, though, I alighted near the van's cargo door, which itself faced a listless magnolia tree. The tree was surrounded by some low bushes and curved pipes that I assumed had something to with the hospital's plumbing. But what the hell did I know?

The area wasn't quite big enough to accommodate a hulking, mythical monster, and I ended up trampling some of the bushes, breaking a branch and denting one of the pipes.

Life goes on.

In my mind's eye, I saw the woman in the flame, watching me calmly, waiting. I focused on her, and she seemed to move toward me, or I to her. I was never sure which. The feeling that came next was difficult to describe, since there really was no feeling. As if awakening from a short nap, I gasped lightly, and raised my head. I was on one knee, which was digging into a small spider plant that had seen better days. I fluffed up the little plant and stood. Next, I reached under my fender and found the small hide-a-key that I kept there.

Shh. Don't tell anyone.

I unlocked the minivan and slipped inside. My clothing was still there, and a few minutes later, after a quick dusting of foundation, I emerged from the minivan, purse in hand. The transformation from giant monster bat into a concerned mommy was now complete.

My life is weird.

I checked the time on my cell. It was just after 2:00 a.m. I would say the *vampire's hour*, but the truth is, any time between sundown to sunup are the *vampire's hours*.

My daughter Tammy was staying with my sister, and no doubt they had all gone home by now. After all, Anthony appeared, to all those concerned, to be fairly stable. It was only me and my heightened extrasensory perception that suspected that not all was as it seemed.

Indeed, I knew my son had only hours to live. If that.

I had taken some of that time to come to a decision.

And I had made my decision.

With the waxing moon overhead shining its silent strength, a strength I seemed to somehow draw from, I turned and headed for the hospital, knowing the staff there would allow me in to be with my sick son.

A sick son, I thought determinedly, *who would be sick no more.*

3.

"Hello, Samantha," said Rob, the front desk security guard. Rob was a big guy who probably took steroids. You know there's trouble when the night shift at a children's hospital knows you by name.

I said "hi" and he smiled at me kindly and let me through.

At the far end of the center hallway was a bank of elevators. As I headed toward it, I heard a vacuum running down a side hallway. I glanced casually at the cleaning crew working away . . . and saw something else.

Crackling, staticky balls of light hovered around the cleaning crew. Many such balls of light. I knew what these were now. They were spirits in their purest forms. Some called them orbs, and sometimes they showed up on photographs. Many non-believers assumed such orbs were dust on the lens. But the camera could never fully capture what I could see. To my eyes, the balls of light were alive with energy, endlessly forming and reforming, gathering smaller particles of energy around them like mini-black holes in outer space. But there was nothing black about these. Indeed, they were often whitish or golden, and sometimes they appeared red. And sometimes they were more than balls. Much more. Sometimes they were fully formed humans.

As I swept past the hallway, a cleaning lady looked up at me. I smiled and turned my head just as one of the whitish electrified balls seemed to orient on me. Soon it was behind me, keeping pace with me.

I just hate being followed by ghosts.

And as the elevator doors closed in front of me and I selected the third-floor button, the ball of white light slipped through the elevator's seam and joined me for a ride up.

It hovered just in front of me, spitting fire like a mini sun.

It moved to the right and then to the left, and then it hovered about a foot in front of my face.

The elevator slowly rose one floor.

"It's not polite to stare," I said.

The ball of light flared briefly, clearly agitated. It then shot over to the far corner of the elevator and stayed there for the rest of the ride up.

The doors dinged open and I stepped out onto my son's floor.

Alone.

Danny was there, sleeping.

He was sitting in one of the wooden chairs at the foot of the bed. His head had flopped back and he was snoring loudly up at the heavens. Probably irritating the hell out of God. One thing I didn't miss from living with the man was all his damn snoring.

Well, that and the cheating.

My son wasn't snoring. He was sleeping lightly. A black cloud hung over him, a black cloud that only I, and perhaps others like me, could see.

And it wasn't so much as hovering as surrounding him completely, wrapping around his small frame entirely. A blanket, perhaps. A thick, evil blanket that seemed intent on obliterating the bright light that was my son.

The lights were off, although I could see clearly enough. The energy that fills the spaces between the spaces gives off an effervescent light. These were individual filaments, no bigger than a spark. By themselves, the light didn't amount to much. But taken as a whole, and the night was illuminated nicely.

For me, at least, and others like me.

The frenetic streaks of energy often concentrated around the living, and they now buzzed around my ex-husband, flitting about him like living things, adding to his own brilliant aura, which was presently a soft red with streaks of blue. I have come to know that streaks of blue indicated a state of deep sleep. The red was worry or strong concern. So, even in sleep, he was worried.

Worried for our boy.

Danny was a bastard, of that there was no doubt. He had proven to be particularly nasty and sleazy and underhanded. He was also confused and weak, and neither of those qualities were what I needed in a man. I needed a rock. I needed strength. I needed confidence and sympathy.

Not all relationships are meant to last forever, I had read once. And forever is a very long time for a vampire.

I stepped through the room and over to Danny's side. His snoring paused briefly and he shivered inexorably, as if a cold wind had drifted over him.

Or a cold soon-to-be ex-wife.

I touched his shoulder and he shivered again, and I saw the fine hair along his neck stand on end. Was he reacting to my coldness or to supernaturalism? I didn't know, but probably both. Probably some psychic part of him was aware that a predator had just sidled up next to him. Maybe this psychic alarm system was even now doing its best to awaken him, to warn him that here be monsters.

But Danny kept on snoring, although goose bumps now cropped up along his forearm.

I shook him gently and his snore turned into a sharp snort and I briefly worried that he would swallow his tongue. Then next he did what any woman would want to see.

His eyes opened, focused on me, and he screamed bloody murder.

And he kept on screaming even as he leaped backward falling over his chair, which clattered loudly to the floor. He landed on his back with an *umph*, as air burst from his lungs. He kept on trying to scream, but only a wheezing rasp came from his empty lungs. He scuttled backwards like a clawed thing at the bottom of the ocean.

I stood there staring down at him, shaking my head sadly, knowing that he had attracted nurses from here to Nantucket.

"Are you quite done?" I said, standing over him and shaking my head at the pathetic excuse for a man.

He clutched his chest and stared at me briefly, and then he seemed to remember where he was. But he was still having trouble breathing, and that was scaring him, too.

"Just calm down," I said, kneeling next to him and taking his hand. "Calm down, you big oaf, and relax. I'm not going to eat you. Yet."

I patted his hand as he continued clutching his chest. And then his lungs kicked into gear and he took a deep breath, sucking in half the oxygen in the room.

"Sorry," he said weakly, as running footsteps sounded in the hallway. "You scared me."

"Ya think?"

I stood and pulled him up with me. Perhaps a little too roughly. He flew up to his feet and seemed surprised as hell to find himself standing.

He looked around, mouth open. "Jesus, Sam. You never cease to amaze me."

Just then a nurse rounded the doorway, hitting the lights. She looked first at Anthony in his bed, and then at us. She saw the toppled chair and our proximity.

"It's okay," I said. "I just startled Danny."

"I was sleeping," he said, lamely. He shot me a glance. "You know, nightmares."

The nurse studied us some more, then came over to Anthony's side and checked him out. Satisfied, she left, although she looked back one more time as she exited.

Danny studied me for a moment or two and seemed like he wanted to say something. His hair was mussed and there might have been a welt developing on the side of his head. Whatever he wanted to say, I really didn't want to hear it. Instead, I looked over at Anthony, who had stirred a little during the commotion. He almost appeared to be watching us, except his eyes were still closed.

"How is he?" I asked.

"The same, I think. He woke up about an hour ago and asked where he was. I told him he was still in the hospital and that he would be going home soon." Danny looked away. "And . . . he shook his head and said he was sorry and that he loved me." Danny fought to control himself. "I asked him what he was sorry about . . . and he said for . . . being a bad boy and for . . . leaving us. He said he has to go but that everything will be okay."

"He said that?"

Danny covered his face and nodded, words briefly escaping him. After a few deep breaths, he tried again. "Jesus, Sam, what the hell is he talking about?"

"He was probably just dreaming."

"But he was *awake*. He was looking *right at me*. And he didn't look sick, either. He looked . . . peaceful. Good God, he was even *smiling*."

"Calm down, Danny—"

"But what's happening, Sam? Is he dying? Does he know that he's going to die or something?"

"Don't talk like that."

Now Danny was shaking. Violently. He was going into shock, or something close to shock. No doubt a thousand different emotions and chemicals had been released into his bloodstream. I reached for his shaking hands and this time he only slightly recoiled.

"I can't lose him, Sam. I can't. I don't know what I'll do without him. He's my baby boy. My little partner. He's everything to me, Sam. Everything. I'll quit my job to spend more time with him. I'll do anything to have him back. Anything. Jesus, we can't lose him."

His words continued on, but they had turned hysterical and incomprehensible. Before I realized what I was doing, I pulled the big oaf into me and hugged him tight.

But I did not share his tears. Not this time.

Unlike him, I knew there was hope.

When Danny had cried himself out, holding onto me a bit longer than I was comfortable, I showed him to the door and told him to go home and get some rest and that everything was going to be okay.

He paused only briefly at the doorway, checked his pockets automatically for his cell, wallet, and keys, then nodded once and slipped out of the doorway, wiping his eyes.

I briefly watched him go, then I turned back to my sick son.

Who would be sick no more.

4.

I stood by his side.

Opposite his bed, rain began pattering against the hospital window, lightly at first and then stronger.

Something wants my attention, I thought.

I ignored the rain, even as a strong gust of wind now shook the window, which was hidden behind the closed blinds. I ignored the rain and the wind and reached down and stroked my son's hair. My narrow fingers slipped through his hot tangled locks. He was too hot. He was too sick. He wasn't going to make it. I knew it all the way to the very depths of my being. His vitals hadn't registered anything yet, but they would.

Soon.

I continued stroking his hair. He seemed to be getting hotter by the second. He also shifted toward my touch, moving toward me imperceptibly, making a small, mewing sound.

The rain picked up, drumming now on the window.

My heart was racing, and for me that's saying something. I continued standing by his side, knowing that this was my one chance to turn away. To not do this thing. I had been advised that he had fulfilled his life's mission, and that it was time for him to move on. I had been advised by a very powerful entity that my son was meant to die. That it had been ordained so, or some such bullshit.

Well, fuck that.

I was his mother. I carried him in me for nine months, I stayed up with him countless nights, bathed him, fed him, and worried about him daily. I loved him so much that it hurt. I loved him so much that I would kill for him. I loved him so much that. . . .

I would give my life, my soul, my eternity for him.

I was his mother, and I was ordaining—declaring, dammit—that he would live. And Lord help anyone who tried to stop me.

I knew I could be damning him forever. I knew this, understood this, but I also knew there was a glimmer of hope. The medallion. Reputed to reverse vampirism. I had always figured I would seek its answers for myself.

But not anymore.

Now I would seek its answers for him. At all costs. I would devote my life to finding a way to turn him mortal again, to give him back his normal life.

And in the meantime, how would I explain to him what I had done to him? I didn't know, but I would think of something.

Later.

For now, though, time was wasting. My son was growing dangerously hot. I reached down and touched his narrow shoulder.

"Anthony," I whispered, leaning down, speaking directly into his ear. "Wake up, baby. Mommy's here . . . and everything's going to be okay."

5.

It took a few more tries to awaken him, but I finally succeeded.

He emerged slowly from wherever he'd been. I suspected that place was the blackest of depths. Then again, perhaps not. Perhaps he'd been in heaven. Perhaps he'd been playing on streets paved with gold. Or, more likely, playing Xbox with Jesus.

Only to return here, with me, sick as hell in a hospital and ready to die. Perhaps had I let him be, he wouldn't have suffered. Perhaps he would have slipped out of this world and into the next with ease and little pain.

Perhaps.

He awakened slowly. As he did, a part of me screamed to let him sleep. If a nurse came in now, she would have been mortified.

What am I doing?

"Mommy?" He squirmed under my arm.

"Hi, baby."

"What's happening, Mommy?"

I'm saving your life, I thought. *I'm saving it the only way I know how.*

"How would you like to feel a little better, baby?" I whispered, and it was all I could do to keep my voice steady, to keep it from cracking with fear and uncertainty.

Anthony turned his sweating face toward me; his eyes focused on me for the first time. As they did so, I was surprised by their strength and ferocity. Despite the darkness, he seemed to look deeply into me.

It was hard to imagine that this strong-looking boy was dying, but the black halo hadn't retreated; indeed, it was thicker than ever, and I saw his impending death as surely as I was seeing him now.

"They're waiting for me, Mommy."

I started shaking my head. "No, don't say that."

"It's okay, Mommy. I'll always be with you. Forever and ever."

"No, baby, please don't say that."

"I'm supposed to go soon, Mommy. They're waiting for me."

I was still shaking my head, crying, whimpering, rocking, holding him tightly. Too tightly. "Stop talking like that, baby. We're going to get you better. I have some medicine for you."

His eyes narrowed, studying me in the darkness. He then turned his head and looked to the right. I looked, too, and saw something I wasn't prepared to see. The light energy near the window seemed somehow brighter, more frenetic, more alive. Something was there, something had materialized, but I couldn't see what. At least, not clearly. Whatever it was, it wasn't a human spirit, that much I knew. It was somehow brighter and it radiated a warmth that I could feel from across the room.

"He wants me to tell you something, Mommy."

I was crying now. I couldn't stop my emotions. I wanted to be strong for my son, but I couldn't. I just couldn't. This was too much for me.

"Who, honey?"

"The man in the light."

I tried to speak but I couldn't. Sobs burst from my throat. Finally, I said, "What . . . what does he want to say?"

But I knew what he was going to say, didn't I? That my son was only here on earth for a brief time. That he was meant to pass on at a young age, a death that was meant to help others grow. That he was here to fulfill some cosmic karma bullshit. I didn't want to hear it. What mother wanted to hear that?

My son was quiet for a moment, cocking his head slightly, listening. Then he smiled broadly. "He says that he loves you, Mommy. That he has loved you from the beginning of time, and will always love you. Forever and ever." He paused, smiling at me serenely, and now I saw now a golden light around his face. The light shone through even the blanketing darkness. My son looked beautiful, angelic. He cocked his head again, and listened some more. "He wants me to be strong for you." My son's face turned somber, and now he was nodding . . . a very sad and solemn nod. "He says you are making the best choice you can. He wants you not to be so hard on yourself."

"I don't," I gasped, my words strangled, "I don't understand what's happening."

My son reached out, took my hand. I could barely see him through the blur of tears. He said, "Mommy, sometimes it's okay not to understand."

The words came from my little boy, but they were not his own. They were from someone older and wiser, and I felt again that I was speaking directly to his soul.

"But I don't want to lose you, baby. I can't bear the thought. I couldn't live. I wouldn't know how to live. But I can help you. I know how to help you. You can stay here with me. Is that what you want, honey?"

He squeezed my hand, and now he stroked my hair gently, his little fingers running through my matted locks before they gently turned my face toward him. "Of course, Mommy."

I sensed that he was making a great sacrifice. I sensed that he was postponing heaven to be here with me now.

"He's telling me there are many paths a life can take, Mommy. There are many alternate routes to the main road—" Hearing my little boy say *alternate* was just surreal—"We are going to head down an alternate route, a longer route. But we'll still get there, Mommy, eventually."

My son paused, looking over at the warm source of light. He squeezed my hand.

"He's going now, Mommy. He wants you to know there are no wrong choices. Do what you have to do to be happy."

Now the light near the window began to fade, and as it did so, my son turned somber. A moment later, his eyes shut tightly.

"Anthony!" I cried, suddenly terrified. But he was still breathing. Barely.

"Mommy?" His voice sounded weak, tiny. It wasn't the same voice I had just heard.

What the hell was going on?

"It's me, honey," I said, sounding weak myself.

"I feel sick, Mommy." He was hotter than ever.

"I know, baby," I said, as I pushed up the sleeve of my sweatshirt. "I know, and I have some medicine for you."

I brought my exposed wrist to my mouth, paused briefly, and then bit down.

6.

The hospital was nearly silent. The hum of machines. Light murmurings. Beeping somewhere. Actually, lots of beeping.

But now another sound filled the air. This one had been barely distinguishable at first, but now it was growing louder. And not just louder. More frequent, too.

It was the sound of drinking, slurping, swallowing.

At first, I had let the blood from my wrist drip freely into his mouth, although a lot of it didn't actually make it into his mouth. Some of it had spilled down his chin, and I had acted quickly with tissues from his bedside table to catch the stray droplets before they stained his sheets and gown, and led to unwanted questions.

But as more blood passed through his mostly closed lips, he began to react. First, his tongue appeared, swiping at the blood. Then his lips parted.

And then he swallowed.

He made a noise then, a strangled gasping noise, and as he did so, I saw something remarkable. A soft white light issued from his mouth, briefly hovered before the bed, and then faded away.

And just as it faded away, my son reached up and gripped my wrist with surprising strength, and held onto it tightly as he drank from my wound.

And he drank and drank.

My blood. My tainted blood. I'm horrible. I'm a horrible mother. I'm a ghoul. I should be locked away. But you're saving him, dammit. You're giving him a chance to fight another day.

I was a wreck. My mind was a wreck. My heart was a wreck.

As my son suckled from my wrist—reminding me briefly of the babe who had suckled at my breast so long ago—something else amazing happened, something that made me realize there was no turning back.

The black halo began to recede . . . to be slowly replaced by a faint silver shimmering, emanating perhaps an inch or two from his body. My son's beautiful natural golden and red aura was nowhere to be seen.

It's happening, I thought.

And still my son drank from my wrist. I could feel the blood being drawn from my arm, sucked into his ravenous mouth. The instructions had been quite clear: You will know he's had enough when you begin to feel weak, as weak as you do in the presence of the sun. The instructions had come from a fellow creature of the night. A much older creature of the night. It was, she said, a fine balance of giving him enough but also not depleting myself.

In the hallway, I heard footsteps. In fact, two sets of footsteps.

They're coming.

And still my son drank, biting down onto my wrist hungrily, drinking great gulps of blood from my open wound.

The footsteps were just outside the doorway. I could hear urgent talking now.

The weakness hit me with a shudder. I gasped and yanked my arm away, tearing some of the flesh. My son's drinking had kept the wound open, kept it from healing supernaturally, as it was inclined to do.

But now as I pulled it free, I could already feel it closing, healing. I grabbed tissue from the bedside table next to me, and had just wiped my son's lips and chin when the lights flicked on.

Doctors and nurses rushed in, and as I stepped aside, I discreetly wiped the blood from my wrist and pocketed the crimson-stained tissues.

The cause for the alarm had been simple enough.

My son's heartbeat had rapidly decreased, so much so that the heart monitors had alerted the nursing staff.

I stood back, watching the nurses and doctors swarm over my son, and as they swarmed over him, my son sat motionless. Fully alert and awake.

Watching me.

7.

While the doctors fussed with my son, I stepped out of the room and headed quickly for the elevators.

My hands shook the entire way down, even when I held them tightly together. As I stepped past the receptionist and security guards, I found myself cursing God, the Universe, and everything in-between for putting me in such a shitty situation. The security guard said something to me, but I couldn't hear him. I hid my face and walked quickly out into the night. Certainly, this hadn't been the first time he'd seen an upset mother.

Outside, I took in a lot of air, filling my dead lungs, walking in tight circles, running my hands through my hair. I was a wreck. The tears flowed.

What had I done? What had I done to my baby boy?

You saved him, I thought. *You saved him, dammit.*

I fished out my cell phone from my handbag and called my rock, the man I had leaned on for so long, the man who had been just a name until recently. Now he was a name and a face . . . and teeth.

"It's late, Moon Dance," he said, his voice groggy. He yawned loudly, smacking his lips a little. It was only recently that my relationship with Fang had graduated from instant messaging to phone conversations and even personal meetings. Even so, I was still getting used to the gentle sound of Fang's voice. A mellow tenor, so different than Kingsley's deep baritone. "How's your son?" he asked.

I told him much better. Much, much better, and he snapped awake instantly. I filled him in on my night, a night that had taken me from the depths of the Pacific Ocean, to my son's side, and feeding him from my bleeding wrist.

Fang said nothing at first. As he digested this information, I realized that just by hearing his soothing voice I had calmed down enough to stop my hands from shaking. As I waited for Fang to speak, I saw a man standing in a nearby pool of light, smoking and looking up towards the heavens. The gleam of tears on his cheeks was evident. A children's hospital in the dead of night is not a good place for a parent to be.

Finally, Fang said, "So, you really did it?"

"I had to."

"I'm not judging, Moon Dance. Actually, I think you made the right choice. A brave choice."

"Then why do I feel so horrible?"

"Because it's the unknown. Because it just happened. You saved your son, honey. He's alive because of you. Because of his mommy."

But I couldn't escape the feeling of being selfish, that I had exposed my son to something dark and horrible just to keep him alive, just to keep me from dealing with a lifetime of heartbreak.

"You're not being selfish, Sam," said Fang, using my real name, which he rarely did. He also read my thoughts, which was of no surprise since he and I had developed an unusual psychic connection over the years. And meeting him recently for the first time had only enhanced that connection. "It's your job to look out for your son. It's your job to keep him safe from harm."

"But look what I've done to him."

"Only temporarily, Sam. Remember the medallion."

"But what if it doesn't work?"

"But what if it does?" he countered.

"You're ever the optimist."

"My friend is a gloomy vampire. Someone has to be the optimist in this relationship."

"But what about the psychological harm? I mean, even if I can turn him back, will he ever have a normal life again?"

The man smoking nearby snubbed out his cigarette. He glanced at me once and I saw the darkness around his heart. I didn't know what that meant, but I suspected its implication: Someone close to him was going to die. I tried to smile and he tried to smile, but in the end, we only stared at each other with empty eyes as he slipped back into the hospital.

Fang was thinking hard on his end. He was always thinking hard for me. Always helping. Always working through my problems with me.

"It's because I'm a helluva guy," he said, picking up on my thoughts.

"And because you're obsessed with vampires."

"Well, someone has to be. Now, speaking of vampires . . . six years ago, after your attack, when did you first realize that you were something, ah, something different?"

"When did I first realize that I was a vampire?"

"Yes."

"Weeks later. But I knew something was vastly wrong only a few days later."

"But did you suspect you were a vampire?"

"No. Not at first. I just knew something was wrong."

"When did you crave blood?"

"A few days later."

"How many days later?"

I thought back to my time in the hospital, and then to my first few days at home. "Four days. But I thought I was low on iron or something."

I had an image of my son drinking blood and it was almost too much to bear. I started pacing again and hating myself all over again.

"Calm down, Moon Dance," said Fang, despite the fact that I hadn't said anything, so pure was our mental connection. "The way I see it, you have four days to find him a cure."

I stopped pacing; he was right.

He went on. "You have four days before your son realizes that something is wrong, that he's something different."

"Four days," I said. Relief flooded me. My God, he was right. I had four days to find a cure.

"Four days, Sam, to unlock the secret to the medallion."

"I gotta go," I said. "Love ya."

The words caught him by surprise, as they did me.

"Love ya, too," he said after a short pause, and clicked off.

8.

I checked on my son.

According to the doctor on staff—a young guy who could not have looked more bewildered—Anthony's fever was dropping at an astonishing rate, even though the fever hadn't appeared to break; as in, my son hadn't yet broken out in a sweat.

More astonishing, at least to the doctors, were his eyes. Red, swollen eyes were a hallmark of Kawasaki disease. Anthony's eyes, however, had shown marked improvement. In fact, there was no indication of redness and the swelling was nearly gone. Same with his tongue. "Strawberry tongue" was common with children with Kawasaki disease. His tongue was a normal, healthy pink. Same with his hands and feet, which had earlier developed severe erythema of the palms and soles, now appeared normal and healthy.

The doctor just stood there by my son's side, blinking and stammering and smiling. He was certain he was witnessing a miracle. He had—just a very different kind of miracle.

When the doctor left to order some blood work, I sat by my son's side, holding his warm hands. He continued staring at me quietly, and I was having a hard time looking him in the eye. Did he know what I had done? I didn't think so, but I suspected he knew on a very deep level. The soul level, perhaps. His outer level, the physical level, was still confused and wondering.

Finally, he spoke, and my son's little voice sounded strong. He told me he felt weird and sick to his stomach. I remember feeling sick to my stomach, too. Years ago, I had been attacked in the woods while jogging, an attack that had changed my life forever.

Why? I asked myself again. *Why attack me? For what purpose? What good was a vampire mama?*

For now, though, I comforted my son as best as I could. I asked him if he was hungry and he shook his head emphatically, his black locks whipping back and forth about his forehead. I really needed to get him a haircut.

I told him to rest. He nodded and I hugged him tightly and did my best to ignore the guilt that gripped my heart. Six years ago, after my attack, I had slept often throughout those first four days. Perhaps the length of time necessary for the body to fully assimilate the vampire blood, for the transformation to be complete. I didn't know.

Anthony would be sleeping often for the next four days, and for that I was thankful. After all, I was going to be busy looking for answers. And since his health was now assured, I felt free to leave his side.

I gave him a kiss on his cooling forehead just as he was drifting off to sleep. I got up from his side and closed the curtains tight, and slipped out of the room and out of the hospital and headed for my minivan.

I checked my watch as I stepped in. Two hours before sunlight.

As I started my vehicle, I made a call to the only other vampire in the world that I knew.

9.

I was at Detective Hanner's home in Fullerton.

The home was located in the hills above the city, and as we sat together on her second-story deck, she pointed out the rooftop of another home, barely distinguishable among a copse of thick trees. According to Hanner, the old man there was a Kabbalistic grandmaster, and was considered by many to be immortal himself.

"Then again," said Detective Hanner, crossing her bare legs and flashing me a grin, "neighbors do tend to talk."

"What, exactly, is a Kabbalistic grandmaster?"

"One who has mastered the nuances of the Kabbalah, the esoteric Jewish doctrine that facilitates a deeper connection with the great unknown, helps one gain a profound understanding of other realities, and illuminates the meaning of life." Hanner turned her face toward me and I was struck again by the wildness of her eyes. They belonged to something untamed and free and hungry, a puma hunting at night, a tiger hunting in the jungles, a lion tracking its prey across the Serengeti. She grinned fiercely and added, "Or something like that."

We next discussed the subject of the medallion. Wrong or not, I trusted my new friend, and so I told her about it, and about what I needed: answers to unlocking its secret.

"Where did you get the medallion, Sam?"

"From the vampire who attacked me."

"Amazing. Others have been looking for it for a very long time. Others like us."

"There are that many who seek to end their lives?" I asked, confused.

She shrugged. "Or there are others who seek to end the lives of other immortals."

"I don't understand," I said.

"There are some immortals who are so old, so powerful, that they cannot be killed by any means, Sam."

"And the medallion could kill them?"

"Perhaps. That's the theory at least."

I shook my head, amazed all over again. "I just want my son returned to me."

Pain flashed briefly over her face, and although her thoughts were impenetrable to me and her aura was non-existent, I was still a mother and an investigator and I could read her like a book. She was thinking of the loss of her own son who had died years ago.

Tears filled her eyes and, perhaps embarrassed, she changed the subject. "You must be famished," she said, standing.

I was. I hadn't eaten tonight and it was hitting me hard. Not to mention I had given copious amounts of my own blood to my son.

Hanner disappeared into her impressive home, and while I waited the electrified particles of light in the sky seemed agitated and frenzied, but that could have been my imagination. Or a reflection of my own inner struggles. I was having a hard time holding onto a thought for long, before it slipped away into the ether, to be quickly replaced by an equally chaotic thought.

She mercifully appeared a few minutes later, holding two full wine goblets that were filled with anything but wine. She handed one to me, which I eagerly accepted.

The glass was warm. "Fresh blood," I said.

"Of course."

"But where?"

"I have an arrangement with a mortal, Sam. A few mortals, in fact. Most of us do. It makes our lives easier."

I nodded but was soon drinking hungrily. Hell, I nearly bit through the glass. As I drank I was aware of Hanner watching me from over her own glass, her eyes as wild as I had ever seen them. I could only imagine what my own looked like.

Like an animal. A hungry animal.

I didn't savor the blood. In fact, I barely tasted it, so quickly did it pass over my lips and down my throat and into my stomach, where it interacted on some supernatural level with my own supernatural body.

When you don't need to come up for air, one can quickly down a glass of blood, and shortly it was finished but I was hesitant to return it. After all, there was still some blood pooling in the bottom and coating the inside of the glass.

"Thank you," I said, then motioned to the empty glass. "And thank . . . whoever provided this."

"Oh, I will." And she said that with such enthusiasm I briefly wondered what *other* kind of arrangement she had with her donors.

The hemoglobin had an immediate effect, no doubt due to its freshness. Rarely had I drank blood so fresh and pure. Even the stuff provided by Kingsley had no doubt been days or weeks old, and stored in his refrigerator.

This was different. This was straight from the source, and it was so damn good. Unable to control myself, I tilted the bloody goblet up and waited for the last few drops to crawl down, where I eagerly lapped them up. Once done, I used the edge of my index finger to scrape the inside of the glass clean.

"I'm a ghoul," I said, embarrassed.

"No different than licking brownie batter from a whisk. At least, that's what I tell myself."

"I'll tell myself that, too, but I think I'll pretend it's chocolate chip cookie dough."

She smiled and sipped her own drink much more lady-like than I had. I set my glass down and secretly wished for another.

Such a ghoul.

Hanner said, "You should consider getting your own donor, Samantha. They are terribly important. I cannot imagine what you have been feeding on these past few years."

"You don't want to know."

"No, I suppose I don't."

We were silent some more and I finally set aside the glass, which had now been completely scraped clean. I found myself idly sucking under my nail.

"You are in an interesting situation, Sam."

"I don't know if I would use the word *interesting*," I said. "*Frightening*, perhaps."

"You misunderstand," said Hanner, and not for the first time I detected an odd lilt to her voice. "I mean, you have been given an interesting choice regarding your son."

"You mean I *had* been given," I said. "I already made my choice, remember, and now I must turn him back before it's too late, before he realizes what his mother has done to him."

"You misunderstand again, so let me explain clearly: Sam, you have a chance to be with your son . . . forever."

Her words didn't immediately sink in, but when they did, when the full realization of them hit, I was left speechless and my mouth hanging open.

"Eternity is a long, long time, Sam. Too long to be alone. Now, you will never have to be alone. Ever . . ." Her voice trailed off and she looked away and somewhere in the far distance a coyote howled. At least, I think it was a coyote.

10.

I parked my minivan in front of a high, wrought-iron fence, where I sat and studied the grounds beyond. Even to my eyes, which could penetrate the darkest of nights, I couldn't see much. A long winding road that led away from the fence plunged into some deep, dark woods.

Well, as deep and dark as they got in the hills above Fullerton.

I understood Detective Hanner's heartache. I understood how much she missed her own son, but I wasn't about to sentence my own son to a lifetime of blood-drinking adolescence. Not if I could help it.

According to Detective Hanner and her neighbors, the old man's property was not only protected by a high fence but also by dark magicks. I asked her what, exactly, she meant by *dark magicks*, and she shrugged and said she was only reporting what she'd heard from her neighbors. Hanner added that she wouldn't put anything past the creepy old man who may or may not be immortal.

What the hell kind of neighborhood was this?

Except this really didn't feel like a neighborhood. Not anymore. Not out here in the dark and surrounded by trees and high fences and apparently black magicks. In fact, I felt like I was in a fairy tale. A Brothers Grimm fairytale, as twisted and dark as they come. And there was no prince waiting for me at the end of this cobblestone drive. No, only an ancient master of the black arts, who may or may not be a vampire. Who may or may not be undead.

I debated turning back, but instead I got out of the minivan and approached the gate. I could have scaled the fence easy enough, but the "protected by dark magicks" part had me a little nervous. And curious.

So what would happen if I broke in? Would a wart appear on my nose? Would a she-devil manifest in a swirl of black smoke to drag me down to hell? Would Lady Gaga apparate and give me a make-over? I shuddered. I didn't know, but now was not the time to find out.

So I did it by the book, and pushed the red intercom button above a cobwebbed touchpad. I had no sooner released my finger when I got a prompt reply.

"State your name," crackled a strongly-accented voice through a speaker.

"Samantha Moon."

The speaker crackled again. "Please turn around."

"Excuse me?"

"Turn please."

I did, turning slowly, knowing there was a camera somewhere and wondering how well my make-up was holding up.

"The left side of your neck, just below your jawline, is missing."

"Excuse me?"

"It shows up as . . . empty on my monitors. Are you a vampire, Samantha Moon?"

I touched the area in question, and sure enough, I had missed a spot there. Damn. "Now, what kind of question is that to ask—"

"Are you a vampire or not?"

"Perhaps we can discuss this inside, where we can have a little more pri—"

"You are alone in the woods, dear girl. Let me assure you. Again, I ask: Are you a vampire or not?"

I rarely, if ever, go around blurting my super-secret identity. The man in the house, whoever he was, was obviously privy to the ways of the undead. How much so, I didn't know. But I needed help for my son and I needed it ASAP.

"Yes," I said. "I guess you could say I'm a vampire, although I really don't think of myself as—"

"State your reason for being here, vampire. And hurry please, you are cutting into my morning rituals."

Morning rituals? I didn't like the sound of that. I suddenly had an image of a bloody forest animal staked within a pentagram, but this wasn't a psychic hit. Just my overactive imagination. In fact, as I thought about it, I wasn't getting any psychic hits from the old man. Whoever he was, he was good at concealing his thoughts.

I said, "I'm here because I need help with my son."

"What kind of help?"

"Can we please talk inside?"

There was a long pause, and then the speaker went dead and the iron gate swung open on silent hinges. I got back into the minivan and drove through. As I did so, the iron gate shut immediately behind me.

I was a vampire, dammit. I shouldn't be afraid.

But I was.

11.

There's a reason why they don't make roads out of cobblestones anymore.

Teeth rattling and brain turning nearly to mush, I soon pulled around a massive fountain that featured three rather robust mermaids, each more endowed than the next. Men and their damned mermaids, I thought. As I turned off the minivan, I actually paused to wonder if mermaids were, in fact, true.

Hell, why not?

The house was huge, complete with massive columns and a wide portico, all befitting a man who may or may not be a human. My sixth sense was telling me to be wary. It wasn't exactly ringing off the hook, but it was letting me know that there was danger here, perhaps not necessarily of the physical kind, but . . . something.

I stepped out of the minivan and into the cool night air. Crickets chirped nearby and the waxing moon shown through some of the taller, ornamental evergreens that marched around the property.

The house was a massive Colonial mansion, befitting America's forefathers. Our very rich forefathers. I followed a cement path through what appeared to be crushed seashells, and then stepped up on a cement veranda, and found myself before two massive double doors. My internal warning system continued beeping steady, neither increasing or decreasing. Nothing would harm me here, I was sure, but I was being warned to stay alert and cautious.

No problem with that.

I pressed a doorbell button inlaid within an ornate brass fixture that seemed about right for a house this gaudy. A gong resonated from seemingly everywhere, followed shortly by footsteps on a wooden floor. Soon, the right door swung open and I was greeted by a wide-shouldered man with a red nose, holding a tissue. He studied me briefly, eying me along his red nose, which could have used another wipe or two, but that was probably just the mother in me. He was balding and what few stray hairs he had were wildly askew. Was he the butler? I didn't know, but I suspected so. My only experience with butlers was with Franklin, Kingsley's wildly disproportionate butler.

Finally, he nodded and wiped his nose—thank God—and said, "This way, madam."

And like Franklin, he didn't sound very happy about being roused to service in the middle of the night. But like a trooper he led me down hallways and around corners, past marble sculptures and fine works of art. The deeper we got, the more I realized that something was off. Something was different. Very different.

It was the energy in the house. It was moving slowly, spiraling oddly. Normally, energy zigzagged randomly, illuminating my night world nicely. But this energy spiraled in seemingly slow motion, as if the very house itself had slipped out of the normal flow of time. And the particles themselves blazed in multiple colors of oranges and blues and violets.

What the hell?

I stopped and stared, feeling like a teenager at her first laser light show, minus the funny mushrooms.

"This way," said the butler, and I followed him deeper into the house.

12.

The man looked like a gnome or something out of Xanth.

But it was hard to tell, since he was sitting cross-legged on a cushioned mat in the center of an empty room. I saw that a similar cushion had been placed before him. Was that for me?

He was wearing a white robe and a peaceful expression. He wasn't a vampire, I knew, because I could see his aura around him, and I was getting minor psychic hits, too, which is not the case when I'm in the presence of Detective Hanner. And it hadn't been the case when I had faced off with Captain Jack, whose mind had been completely closed to me.

But that wasn't the case here.

As I stood in the doorway, I began picking up on some fairly random thoughts. Almost as if someone were switching the channels to a radio. But no, not quite. These thoughts were on a loop, repeating over and over.

What the hell was going on? I focused on the words, trying to make sense of them, but couldn't:

"Tread carefully," came one repeated phrase. "The Great Cosmic Law is unerring," came another, and "Life is a continuous circle," and, "You cannot give without receiving, and cannot receive without giving." And still more, "Thine evil returns to thee, with still more of its kind," "Here be monsters," and others that were far stranger and completely incoherent. At least, incoherent to me, such as: "Thus humidity or water is the body, the vehicle and tool, but the spirit or fire is the operator, the universal agent and fabricator of all natural things."

They were esoteric sayings, surely. Spiritual sayings. The kind of sayings that might randomly flit through a highly-evolved mind. Or one who practiced the Kabbalah.

But the words, repeated over and over, created a sort of buzz. A white noise that was almost deafening, to the point where I was having a hard time thinking, or hearing my own thoughts.

"Please sit down, young lady," said the little man, motioning to the cushion before him. I noticed he didn't open his eyes. "At least, I assume you're young. With vampires, you just never know."

The air in the room was filled with more of the swirling, colorful particles; somehow, these particles were moving even slower in this room.

"I'm fine right here," I said.

He nodded. "Forgive the voices you might be hearing; that is, if you can hear them. Not all creatures of the night possess this skill."

"What . . . what are the voices?" I asked.

He cracked a smile, although he still hadn't opened his eyes. "Ah, you can hear them. Very interesting. Yes, the voices are my defense."

"I don't understand."

"You see, it is impossible to close off your thoughts to a vampire, especially a powerful vampire, but one can provide a sort of 'white noise.' Clutter, if you will."

I nodded as if I understood—which, disturbingly, I think I did.

The old man continued, "Of course, I cannot penetrate your thoughts; at least, not yet. Not until we've developed a deeper bond or relationship, and I don't see that happening unless you have an unflagging desire to become chums with a very old man."

I smiled despite the strangeness of the situation.

"How old?" I asked.

"Old enough not to answer that question. Anyway, I will not bother to ask how you came to find me, as I'm generally always found by your kind. Indeed, the how is not important. It is the why that I'm after. *Why* are you here?"

"I need help with my son."

He smiled again. "A vampire with children?"

"Yes."

"Tragic," he said, making small noises and shaking his head.

"Why?"

"Because you will inevitably outlive your son, only to spend an eternity being barren."

"Barren?"

"Vampirism is the ultimate contraceptive."

I hadn't thought about having more kids. I hadn't realized that I would never, ever have children again. My heart sank. No wonder Hanner was so distraught.

"Ah, I see that this is news to you," he said, and still he had not opened his eyes.

I nodded. "Yes."

"You can see, then, the tragedy. There is but one way to overcome this, of course."

I suddenly knew the way, because despite his looping gibberish that filled my thoughts, I had caught a quick glance into his mind.

"Yes," I said. "The medallion."

His eyes shot open.

13.

He said nothing at first, but I saw the suspicion on his face, especially in his strange eyes, eyes that seemed devoid of color. I knew he was wondering if I had read his thoughts, or if I had simply made a supposition based on his last statement.

"What about the medallion, my dear?" he asked. He closed his eyes again, and it was just as well since his colorless irises were creepy as hell.

I told him about my son, opening up to the strange man and telling him secrets that I told few mortals. He might hold the answers to my son's return to mortality, and that was enough to keep me talking, to keep me babbling until I finally caught him up to date.

As I spoke, he sat quietly, no doubt watching me in ways that I couldn't quite fathom. When I was finished, he said, "You have spared your son from death. Is that not the goal of most parents?"

"The goal of most parents is *not* to turn their children into blood-sucking fiends."

He nodded. "So you've turned your son, and now you wish to turn him back?"

"Yes."

"You are playing God, Samantha. Granting immortality and then taking it away."

"I'm using the tools I've been given to save my son. No more, no less."

He nodded. "The medallion. Is it in your possession?"

"It is somewhere safe."

"And you seek to unlock its secret?"

"I seek to give my son a normal life."

"Normal lives are overrated."

The energy in the room had shifted a little. It was moving a fraction faster. I think my own anger and frustration was charging the room. The old man continued sitting still, while his looping white noise continued filling my brain. What kind of secrets was he keeping from me? Perhaps it was better that I didn't know.

"I do not have strength to argue the point," he said. "Keeping you out of my thoughts is highly taxing. Tell me, what exactly can I do for you?"

"I need help in unlocking the medallion."

"And reversing your son's vampirism?"

"Yes."

He sat quietly. He was tiring. The whispery phrases that cluttered my thoughts seemed to be faltering, skipping words here and there. His defense was breaking down, and I idly wondered what mysteries might be lurking in his brain.

"There is a way, of course," he said. "There's always a way. But for my services I always requirement payment."

My eyes narrowed. Any woman's eyes would narrow when she hears a creepy old man utter the words: *I require payment*.

"What kind of payment?" I asked warily.

"Life, of course."

"What does that mean?"

"It means that for my service I require life, usually in the form of years removed from yours and added to mine."

So he was a vampire, after all. Or a type of vampire. One that sucked life, not blood, no doubt through the use of arcane magicks.

He went on, "But you have no years to remove, my dear, being immortal. To remove years implies that one's life has an ending point." He opened his eyes and looked directly at me. "You, lass, will live forever, if you are lucky."

Indeed. For creatures who are immortal, we tend to die easily enough if we find ourselves on the wrong end of a silver dagger.

My eyes narrowed. "So what are you getting at?"

"Your son's life, of course, Samantha. For my help, I require three years from your son's life, that is, of course, if you are successful in your bid to return him to his mortality."

"How will this be done?"

"Delicately, my dear. Your son will not be harmed."

I felt sick all over again. Jesus, what had I gotten Anthony involved with? "He will lose three years of his life?"

He opened his eyes again and now that his psychic shell was cracking, I saw something monstrous about the man. A darkness appeared around him, swirled briefly, and then disappeared again. The man was possessed by something dark. Of that I was sure. Something that required the years of the living to sustain it.

"Or your son can live forever," he said. "The choice is yours, my dear."

The air in the room had grown agitated. The calm, beautiful lights had been replaced by crazed, dancing butterflies of all colors.

"And what are you offering me in return? Do you know how to unlock the medallion?"

"I know of one who does. An alchemist older than even me."

"So you are not a vampire?"

He grinned wickedly. "No. At least, not the blood-sucking kind."

"And that's all you're offering me? The name of an alchemist for three years of my son's life?"

"Yes."

"And what, exactly, does that mean? Three years of his life?"

"Your son's life, should he become mortal again, will be cut short by three years. Years which will then be transferred to me."

"You're sick."

"No," he breathed. "I'm *alive*, as I plan on being for many years to come."

He explained further: My son's life would not necessarily end tragically. It would simply end as it was meant to end, only three years earlier.

Lord help me.

"Where do I find this guy?"

"I know not, my dear. In fact, no one knows. And those who have seen him claim that *he* has found *them*."

Great. I closed my eyes and took in a lot of air, and held it for seemingly an eternity. "One year," I finally said.

"Three!" he hissed angrily.

Sweet Jesus. I was bargaining with my son's life. His years. "One," I said. "Only one."

"Two," he screeched. "Two! And no less!"

"Okay," I said weakly. "Two."

He clapped his hands thunderously. "Then it is done!"

14.

Before crawling into bed, I called the hospital. According to the doctor on staff, Anthony was sleeping quietly and showing signs of marked improvement. I could hear the relief in his voice.

I thanked him for everything and hung up. My daughter, I knew, was with my sister. I was alone and exhausted. My body was shutting down. I sent texts to Danny and my sister, too weak to call. I told them the good news, that Anthony was miraculously recovering. I didn't explain the miraculous part. I hoped I would never have to, either. I told my sister to tell Tammy that I loved her, then set my alarm for noon. I had just slipped into bed when I felt the sun rise, felt it in every fiber of my being.

Oh, what a night.

And just before blackness overcame me, I thought of the name I had been given.

Archibald Maximus.

I awoke sluggishly, reluctantly, painfully.

During the day, I felt mortal. During the day, I felt less than human. I dragged my tired ass out of bed, hopped in the shower, where I stood under the scalding hot spray until I used up all the hot water. In the bathroom mirror, other than a few beads of water that seemed to be floating in mid-air, I saw nothing. Neither follicle nor fingernail.

Nothing.

How is that possible? What the hell is happening?

My son would see nothing, too. Forever nothing, unless I found him a cure. And with that thought, as I gazed at nothing in the mirror, I realized that I would forever be undead.

Forever.

Jesus.

Recently, I had held out hope that I might someday use the medallion for myself, the thought never occurring to me that I would need it for my son instead.

An eternity on this earth.

Alone.

I continued standing before the empty mirror, dripping on the bathroom floor. I looked down at the puddle forming below me . . . there was no reflection there either.

I don't exist, I thought.

Panic gripped me. It had been quite a while since I had had a full-blown panic attack, but I was close to having one now. I circled the bathroom, slipping in the puddle once. There was no image pacing alongside of me in the bathroom mirror. Nothing.

Not seeing yourself in a mirror, or window, or fucking puddle has a way of playing on one's nerves. And my nerves were shot.

Completely fucking shot.

I circled, breathing deeply, trying to calm myself, until I realized that breathing deeply didn't calm me. Breathing deeply didn't do *shit*.

I broke out in a sweat.

Maybe I really don't exist. It's a fear I've had over the years. A fear that I was still back in the hospital, recovering from my attacks so many years ago. In a coma. Or worse. Maybe I was dead. Maybe all of this is happening in my dead mind. Was that even possible?

I continued sweating, continued pacing in the bathroom. I looked to my right, in the mirror. Nothing except a ghostly, wet outline of a curvy woman.

That's just not right. That's just fucked up. I mean, who can't see themselves in mirrors?

Vampires can't, Sam. Vampires.

Calm down. Relax. You're okay. You're here. You're really here.

Naked and still dripping, I found myself in my living room, at my house phone. I called the only number I trusted to call. My sister Mary Lou answered immediately.

"Hi, love!" she said excitedly. "I've been waiting for you to wake up. Such great news about Anthony!"

I agreed and her excitement buoyed me, but I was far from better. I was far from thinking reasonably. A great panic had taken hold and I was a woman drowning in her own fear.

"Mary Lou," I said, and her name caught in my throat.

"Sam? Is everything okay?"

"Mary Lou, I don't understand."

"Understand what?"

I tried again, my mind racing, my heart beating faster than it had in quite some time. "Mary Lou, is this really happening?"

"What do you mean, Sam?"

I started crying, so hard that I could barely hold the phone. I was losing it. You would, too. Anyone would. Trust me, there's only so much a person can take. "Am I really here, Mary Lou . . . please . . . I need to know. Is this real? Is this really happening to me?"

"Is this about Anthony? But he's okay, Sam. He's—"

"No. It's not about Anthony. Please, Louie. Please."

"What do you need, Sam? What is it?"

"I don't understand what's happened to me, Louie."

"Oh, honey . . . sweetie . . ."

I wept harder than I had wept in a long, long time. I sank to my knees. It took a full minute before I could speak again. "Is this all a dream, Louie?"

"It's not a dream, honey. This is real. Everything's real."

I thought of the empty mirror and shook my head even though my sister couldn't see me shaking my head.

"No, it can't be. It's impossible."

"Honey, listen to me. Something very bad happened to you, but you're going to be okay. I promise. And now Anthony's going to be okay, too."

I thought of Anthony and what I had done to him, and found myself sobbing nearly hysterically. The last words I heard from my sister was that she was coming right over.

15.

My sister is one of the few people on earth who know about my "condition."

I have other family members, of course. A sister in San Francisco, a brother in New York, and my parents in the high desert, but I was not close to them. My sister, Mary Lou, and I had always been more like twins, even though she was six years older than me. Back when I was attacked and left for dead—or, more accurately, left for *eternity*—it had been Mary Lou who was by my side. In fact, I didn't even receive a phone call from my brother until three days later.

It's hard to forget something like that.

Mary Lou and I will probably never live very far apart. She is my rock. Men come and go, friends come and go, but my sister will always be there for me.

That I would someday outlive her is a very real possibility. That I would watch my sister steadily grow old and wither is a very real possibility. Somehow, this was less difficult to accept than watching my own kids grow into old age.

Of course, if I failed to unlock the secrets of the medallion, I wouldn't have to worry about this with Anthony.

Panic gripped me.

Calm down, Samantha. Be calm. You're of no use to anyone if you're panicking.

As I waited for my sister, sitting there with my back against the living room wall, sitting between an end table and a bookcase, I realized that I didn't know what the hell I was doing. What if unlocking the medallion somehow hurt Anthony? What if the process of returning him to his mortality was painful? What if something went wrong?

Oh, Jesus . . . what have I done?

"You saved him," I whispered to myself, hugging my knees

and rocking. "You saved him. That's what you did. Now just fix it, Sam. *Fix it*."

A car pulled up outside and soon I heard feet rapidly approaching. My sister was using her own key to unlock the door and soon she was inside and in the living room and on the ground next to me, holding me closely, and crying with me.

God, I loved my sister.

But she had no idea why I was crying, and I would not tell her, not ever. Not if I didn't have to.

"C'mon," she said, hauling me to my feet. "Let's go see Anthony."

"Where's Tammy?"

"Rick's watching her and the kids."

"Rick's a good man."

"The best. Now, let's get you dressed . . ."

16.

At the hospital, we found Anthony asleep. No surprise there, since it was the middle of the day.

With guilt nearly overwhelming me, I listened to the doctor express his concerned over my son's slower than normal heartbeat, a condition he called *bradycardia*, which apparently could lead to a cardiac arrest. My sister looked increasingly concerned about this news, but I held my poise. The slowing of my son's heart rate was to be expected, after all. Expected by me, at least. Hell, my own heart barely beat a few times a minute.

Other than the decreasing heartbeat, everything looked good and, according to the doctor, if my son kept up this healing pace, he might even be released in a few days.

Good news, surely, for any mother. Mary Lou hugged me tightly and I felt her tears on my face. She pulled away and wiped her eyes and was unaware of a very different expression on my face.

I could not predict how I looked, but I suspected it was a look of desperation. After all, I had three and a half days by my reckoning to unlock the secret to the medallion.

Or my son would forever stay a vampire.

At age seven.

Sweet Jesus.

I asked Mary Lou if she would stay with Anthony for a few hours while I took care of some business. She said of course, and as she pulled up a chair, she took out a black and narrow device that looked suspiciously like one of those Kindle thingies.

She powered it on, settled in, and I headed out.

Maybe I should get one of those someday.

17.

In my minivan, with my specialized window shades drawn tight, I Googled *Archibald Maximus* on my iPhone, a device that was quickly becoming the private investigator's greatest tool.

Nothing of note.

I tried the name without the quotes, including other possible related keywords:

Archibald Maximus, vampire. Although a ton of sites popped up, very few were even close to what I was looking for. And the few that were turned out to be either porn or dead ends.

Archibald Maximus, medallion. Same thing. Nothing.

Archibald Maximus, alchemist. Nothing.

Archibald Maximus, wizard. Nothing. Wait! Something. No, never mind. Just another porn site.

I really hadn't expected an obscure alchemist to have a web page or even a Twitter account, although that would have certainly made my job easier.

I next tried the name in my various industry databases, sites that only private investigators have access to. Nothing. Not even an unlikely hit. Whoever Archibald Maximus was, he didn't own property, have a criminal record in the United States, nor had he applied for credit.

I next called my ex-partner at HUD, Chad Helling. He answered on the second ring, which made me feel good.

"Good morning, Sunshine."

"Never gets old does it?" I was referring to his nickname for me. *Sunshine.* In Chad Helling's simple world, the nickname was supposed to be ironic. And funny.

"Not yet," he said, chuckling.

"You need to get a life."

"I'm working on it," he said. "I'm going to ask her, Sam."

"Ask her what? And who?"

"Monica. I'm going to ask her to marry me."

I shook my head. The poor dope. "Isn't it a little too soon?"

"For love? Never!"

Oh, brother. "Listen, Romeo, I've got a job for you."

"Paying work?"

"Sure," I said. "A coffee and a scone."

"The coffee I'll take. I'm still not sure what the hell a scone is."

I gave him the name and asked him to use the agency's database.

"Archibald Maximus?" he asked, confirming.

"Yes."

"What is he, a wrestler or something?"

"Maybe."

"Really?"

"No."

Chad grumbled something about doing my work for me and told me he would get back to me as soon as he had something.

I was still in the hospital parking lot, parked under a pathetic-looking tree, whose branches only provided me with partial shade. The minivan was heating up and by all rights I should crack the windows and let in some fresh air. Except, I didn't need fresh air, and so I didn't bother. Cracked windows let in sunlight, and sunlight was far more detrimental to me than stale air. Also, there wasn't a car on earth that could heat up hot enough to remove the eternal cold from my bones. In fact, I craved the heat, and so I sat in the minivan, baking, breathing stale air, and thinking hard.

I had only one answer.

I reached into my purse and removed the small legal pad I now kept tucked in a side pocket. I also removed a favorite pen with flowing, liquid black ink. I love flowing, liquid black ink.

As a small wind rushed over the van, swishing the tree above and scattering a few precious leaves from its sparse branches, I spent the next few minutes going through a meditation exercise that both grounded me to the earth and opened me to the spirit world.

Once grounded and open, I sat quietly with pen in hand, waiting. Shorty, I felt the familiar tingle in my right arm. The tingle turned into something more than a tingle. In fact, it turned into an electrical impulse and my right arm involuntarily spasmed. It spasmed again and again, lightly, and soon the pen in my hand was moving, seemingly on its own. Writing. Two words appeared on the mini-sheet of legal paper before me.

Hello, Samantha.

"Hello," I said within the empty minivan, feeling slightly silly.

In the past, two different entities had come through in this form of communication, what many call "automatic writing." I asked now who I was speaking with. My hand twitched once, twice, and the name *Sephora* appeared before me. Sephora, I knew, was my personal spirit guide.

Whatever the hell that was.

"I might have done a bad thing," I said.

My hand jerked and spasmed and more words appeared on the notepad on my lap.

You are only as bad as you feel, Samantha.

"Well, I feel like shit and I'm scared to death."

My hand flinched rapidly.

Did you act out of love or fear when you saved your son?

I thought hard about that. Sweat was now breaking out on my brow. It took a lot for sweat to break out on my brow. The car was heating up rapidly. "I acted out of instinct," I said. "For me, it was the only answer. I had a means to save my son, and I took it. Some would call that love, others would call it selfishness."

The electrical impulse crackled through my arm.

What would you call it, Samantha?

"Love. It has to be. I love my kids more than anything."

Then so be it.

Interestingly, had I not possessed the medallion, I don't think I would have done it. In fact, I *know* I wouldn't have done it. I would not have sentenced my son to . . . *this* . . . if there was no way to turn him back.

"Does my son know what's happened to him?" I asked.

Your son sleeps deeply while the change comes over him. In the physical, outer world, no. But, yes, his greater self, his soul self, knows exactly what you have done.

"Does he forgive me?"

My child, he loves you with all his heart. He understands this was a difficult decision for you, and that you made the best choice you could.

I stared down at the words on the pad, wondering again if I was making them up or if they were really flowing through me from the spirit world.

"You make it seem like there's two of him," I said.

There is his higher, spiritual self, Samantha, and his lower, physical self. The higher self resides in the spirit world, and the lower self in the physical world, your world.

I thought about that, then got to why I was here. "I have a name of a man who might be able to help me," I said.

There was no response. No weird electrical impulse. My arm rested lightly on the center console.

"Is there a way you can help me find him?"

Precious child, there is always a way. To find what is missing, lost or hidden, requires great faith, patience, and perseverance.

I waited, but apparently that's all I was going to be given.

"Is that it?" I asked.

It is enough, Samantha.

I slammed the pen down and tore out the sheet of paper. A few seconds later, the paper was nothing more than confetti. I knew I was acting like a baby. Losing control was exactly what I *shouldn't* be doing. But I didn't need riddles and spiritual platitudes. I needed Archibald Maximus.

And I needed him now.

18.

The only other vampire I knew—outside of my newly anointed son—had led me to the world's creepiest man, which cost my son two years of his life. As shitty as that sounded, a name had been gleaned, which was more than I started with.

The only other immortal that I knew was Kingsley Fulcrum,

a beast of a man in more ways than one. He had an office a block or two from the hospital, across the street from the opulent Main Place Mall, which I was driving past now. The mall gleamed and sparkled and apparently emitted a siren call to Orange County housewives everywhere.

I somehow managed to ignore the call, and soon I was turning into the parking lot of Kingsley's plush, red-brick office building, which brought to mind the last time I was here.

Last week, I had stormed into Kingsley's office, scaring off a wife killer that Kingsley had been set to represent. Exactly. I'd never been more proud. Anyway, the last I heard Kingsley had dropped the piece of shit. Unfortunately for the killer, I had gotten a very strong psychic hit from him. I knew, without a doubt, that he had killed his wife. Now he was on my radar, and I intended to follow through with my threat to make sure that he spent a lifetime in prison.

But that was for another time. For now, I had a son to save.

From what? I asked myself. *From an eternity of life? From an eternity of not experiencing death?*

No, I answered. *From an eternity of childhood. From an eternity of consuming blood. From an eternity of questioning his sanity.*

It was mid-day and I was at my weakest and frailest. I also felt vulnerable and clumsy. As I stood there on the bottom floor, inside the glass doors, blinking and waiting for my eyes to adjust to the gloom within, I realized something else. I had condemned my son to a lifetime of shunning the sun.

My son would never again go to the beach, never again go on a field trip with his class, never again play Frisbee in the park. Granted, he never played Frisbee in the park, anyway, but that possibility had been removed.

For now, I thought. *Only for now. There is an answer. There has to be an answer.*

I moved heavily through the building, all too aware that my legs felt unusually heavy, that each step was an effort, that I did not belong with the day dwellers.

A tall man wearing an outdated blue blazer smiled at me sadly as I boarded the elevator. He asked what floor and I noticed we were going to the same floor, Kingsley's floor. As we rode up together, I touched my brow and winced. Despite my wide-brimmed hat, some of the sun had made it through. There might have been a small area near my hairline where I had missed some sunblock because the skin there was burning. I ignored the pain, knowing it would go away in a few hours.

We rode the elevator in silence. I was aware of the man in the old business suit watching me. I hated to be watched and self-consciously moved away, ducking my head, wishing like hell he would look away, but too weak to do anything other than shrink away like a frightened puppy.

"Pardon me," he said in a thick French accent, leaning in front of me and pushing the button to the floor just beneath Kingsley's offices. "Wrong floor."

The elevator doors opened immediately, and he stepped out. As he did so, he turned and looked at me again. He was a tall man wearing a bow tie. I hadn't noticed the bow tie before. His age was indeterminate, anything from 48 to 78. Then he did something that shocked the hell out of me.

He smiled.

The elevator doors closed and I headed up to see Kingsley.

19.

Like I said, the last time I was here, I stormed Kingsley's office like a mad woman.

Or a desperate mom.

This time I waited patiently in the lobby while Kingsley finished up with a client. Oh, I was still desperate. I was still driven. It's just that I had eased up on the panic button. A few days ago, when I had stormed in here, my son was close to death. Now he was very much alive, although I was faced with a whole new dilemma.

Had I been anything less than what I am now, my son, I knew, would be dead. He would have fulfilled his life mission, a mission that included checking out early, apparently, and the rest of us would have been left to pick up the pieces of our own lives, if that was even possible.

There were a lot of unanswered questions. The use of the medallion was so vague, so strange, and just so damn weird.

That I was pinning my son's eternity on a golden coin hanging from a leather strap was mind-boggling and disturbing, at best.

And what was I working so hard for? To ensure that my son *would* someday die? Where things stood, he would survive and keep surviving forever. Wasn't that a *good* thing? And how did I know that he would stop growing? Maybe he would continue to grow. Maybe he would reach adulthood. Maybe he would thank me every day for the rest of his life, for all eternity, for sparing him from death, and for giving him great physical gifts, too. Knowing my son, in the least, he would thank me for getting him out of school.

This line of thinking had me confused. Jesus, maybe I should let him be. Maybe with proper guidance, I could walk him through the eternal experience, help him, teach him, guide him. Something no one had done for me. Maybe he would indeed grow into his adult body.

Maybe.

Or maybe not.

I didn't know; I knew so little.

Shit.

A few minutes later, Kingsley's office door opened and out came a familiar client. The same client I had seen just days earlier. The same client who had prompted a powerful vision of him strangling his wife to death in her sleep. The same coward. The same piece of shit. The same asshole I had threatened to bring down.

It was no threat.

And here he was. Coming out of Kingsley's office.

Again.

We locked eyes and I think we both gasped. My stomach heaved at the sight of the bastard. He made a small, whimpering sound and took a step back . . . into Kingsley, who was standing behind him. Kingsley looked surprised, too. He also looked a little sheepish and embarrassed. I was too stunned to speak.

Kingsley quickly stepped between us, and actually escorted the bastard out of his office. A moment later, my werewolf friend returned, all six foot, six inches of him, and gestured toward his office.

"Let's talk," he said.

Numb and sick, I silently stood and headed through his open door.

He followed behind, shutting the door.

"Have a seat," he said.

20.

I did as I was told, still too stunned to speak.

Kingsley moved around his office with an ease and speed uncommon for a man his size. He sat in his executive chair and studied me for a long moment before speaking. I could not look into his eyes.

"Well, I suppose I should thank you for not playing Whack-A-Mole with my client's head," he finally said, and I could hear the gentle humor in his voice. He was referring to an inadvertent joke he'd made the other day.

I didn't smile. Not now.

He took in a lot of air. Unlike me, Kingsley seemed to need normal amounts of oxygen. I know this because I had listened to him snore once or twice. *Listened*, of course, was putting it mildly. *Experienced*, perhaps? His snoring was unlike anything I had ever heard before. It sounded like the bombing of a small village.

He filled his massive chest to capacity, which put a lot of pressure on his nice dress shirt, especially the buttons. I was prepared to duck should buttons start flying like so many bullets from a Gatling gun.

He studied me like that for a moment, his chest filled, button threads hanging on for dear life, and then finally expelled. He leaned back and crossed his legs, adjusting the drape of his hem.

"Don't judge me, Sam," he said. I noticed he looked away when he spoke.

"Who's judging?" I said. "I'm just admiring the fine handiwork of your shirt."

"Every man deserves a fair trial, Sam."

"And every defense attorney deserves a hefty payday."

"This has nothing to do with money, Sam."

"Say that to your mansion in Yorba Linda."

"My home is the result of a lot of hard work."

"And a lot of freed killers."

Perhaps in frustration, he closed both hands into boulder-like fists, and as he did so, his knuckles cracked mightily. Jesus, he was an intimidating son-of-a-bitch, but I was not easily intimidated.

"What do you want, Sam?" he asked.

I found myself wanting to lash out, too. I found myself wanting to storm out and flip him the bird. How . . . how could a man represent such scum? And how could I ever respect such a man?

The answer was easy: I couldn't.

I continued saying nothing. I just sat there, battling my emotions, knowing that Kingsley might be the only person I knew who could help me find Archibald Maximus, but hating that I needed his help.

And in my silence, Kingsley must have spotted something. His thick eyebrows knitted and he sat forward a little. "Unbelievable," he said.

"What?"

"You did it, didn't you?"

"Did what?" But I knew what he was talking about. Kingsley was closed to me, as were all immortals, apparently, but we both were experts in reading body language.

"You turned him, Sam, didn't you?"

"I saved him."

He looked away, shaking his great head. "And *you* have the nerve to come in here and accuse *me* of being selfish. You, who condemned your own son to an eternity of childhood."

"What was I supposed to do, goddammit? Watch him die?"

"There's a natural order to things, Sam."

"And we're not natural?"

"No, we're not."

"And part of that natural order is to let my son die?"

He said nothing, but I saw his brain working. The great attorney was looking for a counter-argument, but I would be damned if I was going to listen to an argument *for* my son's death.

"Look," I said. "I don't know much about much, but I know one thing: I'm a mother first. I am a mother and that is my baby in the hospital. He was sick and I had an answer. It might not have been the best answer, and I sure as hell don't expect to win any 'Mother of the Year' awards. I also don't understand what the hell happened to me, or what the hell even happened to you. I have no clue the power and magicks behind what keeps us alive. But if this fucking curse, this disease, that I live with every day can somehow save my son, somehow keep my life from spinning completely and totally out of fucking control, you damn well better believe I'm going to utilize it, because it sure as hell has taken a lot from me, Kingsley."

He was nodding. "Okay, now that you've justified turning your son into a blood-sucking fiend, what are you going to do now?"

"I'm going to find someone who can help me."

"Help you how? With the medallion?"

"Yes. I have a name."

"Where did you get the name?"

"It doesn't matter," I said, and debated storming out of the office. Instead, I kept my ego in check for my son. "Have you ever heard of someone named Archibald Maximus?"

There was no recognition on his face. "No," he said. "You don't forget a name like that."

"Do you know anyone who could help me?"

"I pointed you to the only person I knew who could help you," he said.

That had been Detective Hanner. I sensed Kingsley's hesitation. Did he know someone else? I sensed that he might, but he didn't say anything else. Instead, he was now looking at me like I was the biggest piece of shit he'd ever seen. Probably with the same expression I had been wearing just a few minutes earlier.

"I don't know who else to turn to," I said, biting the bullet. "I know you don't agree with what I've done. Quite frankly, I don't agree with a lot of what you've done, either. But let's put aside our differences for now, okay? I made the best choice I could. I did what I thought was right. There's a chance, a very small chance, that I can return my son to mortality without any lasting repercussion or effects. But if I hadn't done what I did, there was a hundred percent chance that I was going to lose my son. I gave him a chance at life, Kingsley. Was it selfish for me to keep my little boy alive and expose him to something he never asked for? Yes, it was. I agree. I'm horrible. But my son is alive, and there is a chance to return things to normal. Normal is all I'm asking for, Kingsley. Please help me."

He looked at me for a long moment, and the fact that he had to decide whether or not to help me, crushed my heart almost completely. I didn't want a man who had to decide whether or not to help me, even if he didn't agree with my choices.

Finally, he sighed and nodded, and said, "I'll see what I can do, Sam. But I make no promises."

I smiled even as my heart broke. "Thank you, Kingsley."

As I left his office, Kingsley wouldn't look at me. I said goodbye and he merely nodded. If I was a betting woman, I would bet that our relationship was over.

Forever.

21.

I was driving north on the 57 Freeway.

I checked with my sister and my son was still sleeping contentedly. The doctors seemed pleased that he was stable, but there was still mild concern, most notably that his body temperature had now dropped to 97 degrees, one degree lower than normal.

This didn't worry me. My son was going to make it, and the doctors were going to have a conundrum on their hands, much as they had with me, in a different hospital, over six years ago.

My sister asked what I was up to, and I told her that it was a very important case, a matter of life and death. She understood, but just barely. Her husband, who was watching Tammy and her kids, would be picking her up soon. I made it a point to be there when the sun set.

After all, tonight would be my son's first night as . . . something far different than he was before.

I exited on Orangethorpe and worked my way over to Hero's in Fullerton. I checked the time. Fang should just be showing up to work. I was right.

As I dashed in from the blistering heat, gasping and clutching my chest, I saw the tall bartender doing something very unbartender-like. He was texting. Just as I stepped into the bar, my cell phone chimed.

I paused just inside the doorway and fished out the cell. It was a text, of course, from Fang. It read: *Good afternoon, Moon Dance, how are you?*

I wrote: *I could say I'm fine, but that would be a lie. By the way, the guy at the end of the bar needs another beer, so quit texting and start working.*

I hit send and waited.

Fang had just spotted the guy at the end of the bar, who had just motioned him over, when his cell phone vibrated. Fang paused and read the screen, and I watched with some satisfaction from the doorway as his mouth dropped open. Then he started looking around until he spotted me. I waved, and he shook his head.

"I was beginning to think you were everywhere, Moon Dance," he said.

"Is that a bad thing?"

He winked. "Not for me. Hold on." He drew the guy a draft of beer and came back. "I think our connection is growing stronger."

"How so?" I asked.

"I was texting you as you came in."

"Could have been a coincidence, and is texting even a word?"

"If not, it should be," he said. "Anyway, there are no coincidences, Moon Dance."

I grabbed a stool at the far end of the bar. Privacy, for me, is always good. I said, "That would sound deep if it wasn't bullshit."

"Bullshit, huh? Then how do you explain that for the past half hour I've been feeling increasingly . . . troubled."

"Maybe you had some bad Chinese."

"Not bad Chinese, Sam. And how would you explain that I've felt incredible *grief* coming from you. Wave after wave of it. I sensed that something profound had ended."

I thought of my relationship with Kingsley. "Ended?"

He shook his head. "Crazy, I know. But, to me, I felt a finality to something, as if something emotional and tragic had ended. Of course, I assumed it was something to do with your son."

Jesus, my connection with Fang is growing. "My son is fine," I said.

He narrowed his eyes. "How fine?"

I nodded, confirming his suspicions.

His jaw dropped. "You really did it?"

I nodded again.

"And how is he?"

"He's fine. He's great, in fact."

Fang leaned on his elbows. The grisly teeth around his neck—definitely *not* shark teeth—clacked together with the sound of knuckles striking knuckles.

"But you're not fine," he said.

"My job's not over."

He nodded. "The medallion."

I caught him up to date, noting the striking difference between the way he handled the news and the way Kingsley had. There was no judgment in Fang's voice. There was only concern for me and my son.

He said, "And so the ending I felt was the end of your relationship with Kingsley."

"Maybe," I said.

"I'm sorry."

"No, you're not. I'm sure you're glad he's out of the picture."

Aaron Parker, aka Fang, shook his head. "I would not be much of a friend if I wished for you to experience pain on any level."

Now I was shaking my head. "Not as much pain as you might think. Kingsley is an amazing man, as you well know, and he was there for me when I needed him the most, but . . . it was bad timing. I was just dealing with the end of my marriage. I wasn't ready to start a new relationship."

"And he wanted to start one?"

"He wanted something, more than what I could give him. But it's not that."

"It's ideological," said Fang, picking up on my thoughts. In fact, I could even *feel* him in my thoughts.

"We're just too different," I said. "Apples and oranges."

"Vampires and werewolves."

I smiled at that. Fang smiled, too, and I sensed his strong need to reach out and touch me, but he held back. One relationship had ended. Now was not the time to push for another. Perhaps not for a long, long time.

"It takes all my willpower, Sam," he said, tracing his finger along the scarred bar top in front of my hand, "to *not* touch you."

"I just need a friend," I said.

"I know," he said. "And you have one. Always."

22.

I was on my second glass of wine, even if the first one did little more than upset my stomach. I haven't had a good buzz in half a decade, and I suspected my days of being buzzed were long gone.

Being buzzed was overrated, I thought. Now, flying high over Orange County was a different story.

There are some benefits to being a creature of the night.

Fang and I got back to the subject of my son. He said, "I'm still fairly involved in the vampire online community. I'll ask around about our friend Archibald Maximus."

"You're still hanging out in chat rooms?"

"Often."

"They seem so . . . five years ago."

"Don't knock them, young lady. It's where I met you, after all."

Years ago, confused and lost, I had joined a vampire IM chat group hoping to learn anything I could about the undead. I hadn't expected to learn much of anything, let alone create such a deep and lasting friendship.

I said, "Well, I don't have a lot of hope."

"We'll see what turns up. Remember, you never know who might be popping into some of those chat rooms."

"Like me," I said.

"Right, like you. Sometimes I come across the real deal."

"How do you know they're the real deal?" I asked, suddenly feeling a pang of jealousy for reasons I couldn't quite understand but wasn't in the mood to probe very deeply.

"Oh, you know. I've made it my life's ambition to find vampires."

"And to be one."

Fang glanced at me sharply. Last week, the handsome freak asked me to turn him into a vampire, so that we could live together, or some cheesy crap like that. Not that I didn't believe him, but I was suspecting he would do anything—anything—to be a vampire. Fang's story was . . . interesting, to say the least. Interesting and disturbing. Born with a rare defect, his canine teeth had grown in exceptionally long, so long that he had lived with the "vampire" stigma during his entire adolescence and most of his teen years. Childish insults, mostly, but with such ferocity and frequency that he came to believe he was vampire.

In an act of passion and violence, his teenage girlfriend had ended up dead and Fang had gone on to have one of the most memorable trials to date. O.J. Simpson with teeth, as some called it.

Later, Fang would escape a high-security insane asylum . . . and kill one guard in the process. His whereabouts were presently unknown to law enforcement, a secret he had entrusted to me, much as I had entrusted one to him.

We all have our secrets.

Fang, or Aaron Parker, had never lost his passion for vampires, even when his two massive canine teeth had been gruesomely removed in the insane asylum—teeth that now hung around his neck to this day. Six years of online chatting and one bang-up job of stalking on his part later, and here we were. Friends with issues. Friends with secrets. But most important . . . friends.

His request had caught me off guard, and I would consider it later, but for now I could only think about my son. He understood this, of course, which wasn't hard to do since he was powerfully and psychically connected to me.

He grinned at that last line of thought. "I can think of no other person I would rather be powerfully and psychically attached to, Moon Dance," he said, using my old chat room username.

"You've been reading my thoughts," I said.

"It's not like I can help it," said Fang. "So, from what I gather, you don't find me such a bad guy."

"No," I said. "But you have your issues. Scary issues."

"I could say the same thing about you."

"Touché," I said, although I thought his comparison wasn't quite fair. I had never asked for any of this.

"And neither had I," said Fang, picking up on my thoughts.

"Victims of circumstance, you had said."

"Something like that," said Fang. "We are what we are."

"Fine," I said. "But be discreet with your inquiries."

"Of course," he said.

I thought of my son. I didn't have to check my watch to know that the sun would be setting in a few hours. I seemed chrono-kinetically attuned to the sun. Soon, Anthony would be waking up after sleeping through his first day. I wanted to be there for him.

"Chrono-kinetically?" said Fang, picking up my thoughts.

"It works," I said.

He grinned. "Hey, it just occurred to me that you might want to take a look at Cal State Fullerton's library."

"Why?"

"Apparently they've got quite an occult department there. You know, books. Real books. With paper and dust and ink. A guy was just in here going on and on about their extensive collection."

"What guy?"

"Young guy."

"Maybe," I said, standing, leaving my wine half-finished. Always the pessimist these days.

"Where to now?" he asked.

I thought about it. I had a few hours before Anthony awakened. I said, "I need to beat the shit out of something."

23.

I was at my gym with my trainer.

By "gym" I meant my boxing studio. By "trainer" I meant the little old Irish guy named Jacky who talked like a leprechaun.

"Hands up, lass. Up, up!"

"Go to hell," I grunted, as I lifted my heavy hands. Vampire or not, I was nearly mortal during the day, and my hands felt like lead, especially after going through a few rounds on the heavy bag.

But even though sunset was still under two hours away, I had more than enough strength to hit the bag hard enough to rock the little trainer. He grunted through the shockwaves, screaming at me to keep my hands up even as he struggled to hold onto the bag.

"End round!" he shouted, just as I leveled another hard roundhouse. Unfortunately, the Irishman had let his guard down just enough. The punch, although mostly absorbed by the heavy bag, sent him staggering backwards.

"You okay, Jacky?" I cried out, moving over to him and catching him just as he stumbled over my gym bag.

As I held him up, the Irishman looked at me with eyes slightly crossed, sweat pouring down his face. A second later his eyes uncrossed and he stared at me. "Jesus, you're a freak."

"I've heard that before. From you, in fact."

But he was still staring at me. "And how did you get over here so fast?"

"What can I say? Cat-like reflexes."

"Freak-like reflexes," he said in his Irish trill. "I need a break, Sam."

He took his break, and in his office, through his partially open door, I saw him down a few cups of water and what looked like pain medication. He came back, cracked his neck, grabbed the heavy bag from behind, and said, "Round four. Let's do this."

And we did this, with Jacky grunting and taking the brunt of the impacts and screaming at me to keep my hands up. I cursed and punched and did my best to keep my hands up, and all the while I felt the sun slipping slowly toward the horizon.

24.

A quick shower and a few miles later and I was at the Cal State Fullerton library, which was bigger than I remembered.

I had graduated here in my early twenties with a degree in criminal justice. That degree led to a job interview with the Department of Housing and Urban Development, where I was eventually hired as a federal agent. A great job, and one I regretted leaving, but it's hard to work the day shift when you're a creature of the night.

The Cal State Fullerton library was epic. Granted, I've never been to other university libraries but I would be hard-pressed to believe any of them could be as big as this one. There were five floors of books, with rows upon rows of aisles that seemed endless. Cubicles everywhere, filled with students connected to iPods, iPhones, and iEverything else. The juxtaposition of dusty library with modern technology was striking. Two worlds colliding.

At the information desk, I found a terminal and punched in the name "Archibald Maximus." Or tried to. Typing with these sharp nails was a bitch. A few tries later and I hit "enter" with little hope.

I wasn't surprised. As expected, nothing came up.

I thought about what Fang had said about the university having a considerable occult section and decided to ask someone about it.

That someone turned out to be a flirty young man with a killer smile. He was standing behind a long, curved desk, stacking books.

"Where might I find your occult section?" I asked.

He blinked. "The Occult Reading Room?" Some of the flirt left him. Just some.

I nodded encouragingly, and his grin returned and I could see his mind trying to find some angle to use for a come-on line. He found none, and seemed disappointed with himself. That is, if his long sigh was any indication.

"Third floor," he said. "And you're in luck. The room's only open two hours a day and you have about twenty minutes."

"Lucky me," I said, turning. "Thank you."

"I can show it to you, if you like—"

"No, thanks, cutie. I'll manage."

He smiled and nearly said something else but I had already turned away, heading quickly to the bank of elevators, where one opened immediately. As the doors were closing, I caught sight of something so disturbing that I immediately tried to punch the door open. Too late, they closed and I was heading up.

A tall man had been moving purposely toward me. A tall man wearing a bow tie.

25.

The elevator doors opened on the third floor.

I half expected to see the same man in the bow tie appear, but, as far as I could tell, I was alone on the third floor. And if anything, the floor appeared even bigger and more spacious than the ground floor. Row after row of endless shelving that stretched as far as the eye could see, all lit gloomily by halogen lighting that dully reflected off the scuffed acrylic flooring.

Cryptic signs with seemingly random words and numbers pointed in various directions, apparently of use to only those who spoke Librarian.

Since I hadn't yet seen a sign that said "Occult Reading Room" and my time was rapidly running out, I decided to try something new in my bag of tricks: remote viewing.

Or, in my case, *nearby* viewing.

I closed my eyes and quieted my mind and thought about what I wanted. The Occult Reading Room. Interestingly, the young kid downstairs came into view . . . followed immediately by the man in the bow tie. I blinked, refocused, and another image came to mind, swimming up from the black depths like a creature from the deep. Except this was an image of a doorway, and it was to my right and up another hallway.

My consciousness returned quickly; my eyes snapped open.

Whoa.

I hung a right and followed a row of books to the south wall. Once there, I headed north and soon came across the very same doorway I had just seen in my mind's eye.

Unbelievable.

The sign above said "Occult Reading Room," and as I stepped through the open door, I was distinctly aware of the faint sound of an elevator door opening.

26.

The Occult Reading Room was surprisingly bright.

A young man with bright blue eyes and a short beard that came to a point was manning the front desk. He looked up from the pages of an old book that looked like it belonged on the set of a Harry Potter film. I glanced down at the open page and saw various diagrams and words that I was certain were not in English. Then again, I was never very adept at reading upside down.

"I'm looking for information about a man."

He pointed to a card catalog on a nearby wall. "We're still in the process of computerizing the card catalog, but everything we have is in there."

"Sure, um . . ."

He smiled warmly. "You have no clue how to use a card catalog."

"I haven't used one since high school, and even then I didn't know what I was doing. Mostly I just needed a place to hide my gum."

He shook his head. "You're not chewing any gum now, are you?"

"No."

He grinned. "Then come on."

At the card catalog, he patiently showed me how to search under "subject." I thanked him and he had just returned to his epic tome, when I heard footsteps approaching in the outer hallway.

From my position at the card catalog I had a view of the entrance into the Occult Reading Room. No one was there. Indeed, the footsteps seemed to be receding now, perhaps heading down a side aisle.

I debated following, but remembered the reading room would be closing in just a few minutes.

The creep in the bow tie had me on edge. Had he been the same tall man I had seen in Kingsley's building? I didn't know, but I could count on one hand the number of men I had seen wearing bow ties this last year. Hell, in the last five years.

And now I had seen two in one day.

Coincidence? I think not.

And, yes, I thought back to Fang's words: *"There are no coincidences, Moon Dance."*

Although my sixth sense was always a little sketchy during the day, I wasn't picking up on any danger. Still, I stepped briefly outside and scanned the hallway. No one there.

Back at the card catalog, I found the drawer labeled "Ma-Mi," and started flipping through the ancient cards, my sharp nails and heightened dexterity making it easy to whip through them rapidly.

My blurred fingers stopped on a name that I wasn't entirely prepared to see. In fact, I had already given up the search as a lost cause. But there, on the yellowed piece of paper, were the words: *Archibald Maximus: My Life as a Mystic, Alchemist and Philosopher.*

"Unbelievable," I whispered.

Dazed, I jotted down the Dewey Decimal Numbers and proceeded to hunt through the reading room. The energy in the Occult Reading Room, I noticed, was off. I wasn't sure why, truth be known, but I wondered if it had something to do with the room's darker contents. Indeed, as I read some of the spines of the books, I could see why:

A Compleat History of Magick, Amulets and Superstitions.

Vampires: Alive and Well and Living Among Us.

Magick in Theory and Practice.

Curse Tablets and Binding Spells.

Lycans: Our Wolf Brothers.

Additionally, there were countless books on alchemy, magic, demonology, divination, Satanism, freemasonry, Middle Eastern magical grimoires. Books on East Asian magical practices, Tibetan secret practices, books on the Tarot and raising the dead. Some of the books looked ancient, so old that I was afraid to touch them. Many of them were surrounded by a darkness visible to my eyes, similar to the darkness that had surrounded my son. Sometimes I heard whispering as I went down the aisles, as if I were not alone.

One book in particular radiated a blackness so dark that I gave it a wide berth. Even still, as I stepped past it, I heard whispering in my ear, "Sister, come to us . . ."

Sweet Jesus.

Shaking, I finally reached the aisle I wanted. Ignoring the slithering, psychic chattering that now seemed to come from everywhere, I quickly ran my pointed nail along the books' spines, praying like hell that the book I needed would be there.

Not this row. I scanned the next one and the next.

And there it was. I literally breathed a sigh of relief.

I carefully removed the narrow volume. The book was clearly ancient, bound in leather and written in what appeared to be vellum, sheep skin. The title was clear enough and written in modern English, which surprised me since the book was obviously bound centuries earlier.

But I didn't have time to think about it.

The young man behind the desk was now carefully stacking his books. As he turned away from me, I quickly slipped the narrow volume down the front of my jeans.

I made haste, exiting via a different route, ignoring the beseeching cries from some of the darker books. At the desk, the young man smiled and asked if I had found what I was looking for.

I said maybe, smiled, and exited the Occult Reading Room, noting for the first time that the aura around him was violet and utterly beautiful.

On the way out of the library, walking a little funny, I didn't see the man with the bow tie.

27.

I was sitting by my son's side.

The sun was setting and I was feeling excited and nervous and guilty as hell. I thought back to my first few nights as a vampire, and I was certain that I wasn't aware that a drastic change had occurred. Not yet. It would take a few days.

Indeed, I just remember sleeping and healing, and it wasn't until a few days later, at home, that the cravings began. Cravings for the red stuff.

I looked down at my son. In a matter of days or hours or minutes—or perhaps it had already happened, he would go from being a sweet little boy, to an immortal with a hunger for blood and a penchant for turning into a little vampire bat. No doubt, a cute little vampire bat.

And be with you forever.

I heard the words again. And again. And again.

I suddenly had an image of me fighting traffic for an eternity, listening to infomercials for an eternity. An eternity of bad hair days, of showering and putting on deodorant. An eternity of drinking blood.

Mostly, though, an eternity alone.

I never feared death. Death was the natural order of things and I was always certain that there was something waiting for us beyond. If so, then why fear death?

But I would never discover what lay beyond, would I? I would never see the face of God. I would never sit across from Jesus or Buddha or Krishna. Instead, I would only sit across from a TV, or whatever passed for a TV in the far future, watching yet another infomercial for yet another magic dishrag.

The medallion had been my answer, of course. It had been my way out of the immortality game. The immortality prison. My chance to escape an eternity of doldrums.

But not anymore.

The sun was setting. I knew this because I could feel some of the weight on my shoulders diminishing. Also, there was a small tingling that was beginning to creep up along my spine. A sort of awakening perhaps. An awakening to all that I could be. I ached for the sun to set. Longed for it to do so.

Hurry, dammit.

Next to me, my son stirred.

"Mommy?"

"Hi baby," I said.

"Mommy, I had a bad dream."

I had no doubt. "I know, honey. I know."

28.

I stayed my son's side for many hours.

My ex-husband sent me a text, asking how our son was doing. I told him he was improving, and Danny sent a happy face and an "XO." As in hugs and kisses.

I didn't reply. Receiving X's and O's from Danny felt all kinds of weird. We were long, long past the days of X's and O's.

Now we were just "ex's." Period.

My son's illness had somehow brought me closer to Danny—or, more accurately, brought him closer to me. Except, I didn't want him closer. Not anymore. I forgave, but I didn't forget. How could I forget getting banned from my own kids? How could I forget the blackmail and the heartlessness? How could I forget the blatant cheating?

I couldn't. Not ever.

In fact, I went back into the message and erased his "XO," shuddering as I did so.

Anthony slipped in and out of consciousness. Doctors and nurses came and went, as well, drawing blood, checking his vitals, seemingly impressed by his progress. Everything, that is, except his lowering body temperature.

Anthony described one of his dreams to me, and as he spoke, my heart broke. He described a dark room. In the room was something calling to him, asking him to come closer. He didn't want to get closer. He wanted to turn and run but he was trapped. In fact, there was no door in the room. No door and no light, but something was in there with him, asking him again to come closer. Afraid and crying and screaming my name, he finally turned and faced what was calling to him.

Except he couldn't see it. The voice told him he was a good boy and to step just a little bit closer. He did so. The voice had told him: *Good good, that's a good boy, now come closer still.* And he did so. One tentative step at a time, and each time he drew closer to the voice, he was praised. And when he was certain he was standing in front of whatever was calling to him, hands seized him, squeezing him, hurting him, and, while he told me this story, he burst into tears and so did I.

Nurses came running. I assured them that everything was okay. And when we were alone, I hugged my son tight and he lapsed into a deep sleep.

As he slept, I cracked the ancient book open with excitement and trepidation. I had no clue what it contained, and I had waited until this moment to scan the contents. The title had given me hope that the book would be written in English, but a part of me still feared that it was in Latin, Greek, or even Hebrew.

Dust sifted down from the cover, catching some of the light from the lamp near my son's bed. Outside the door, two nurses hurried past. Someone was weeping not too far away. The weeping could have been a mother.

There was a title page . . . in English, thank God. According to the title page the book had been published . . . this couldn't be right. What the hell was going on? Had Fang set me up? Was this some kind of sick joke?

Hands shaking, I read the copyright date, and unlike most books that gave copyright years, this one gave an exact date.

Today's date.

I stared at it long and hard.

Surely someone was playing a joke on me, and the only person who knew I was at the library was Fang, and that was impossible since I was privy to most of Fang's thoughts—

There was, of course, another who knew I was in the library.

The tall man with the bow tie. He knew I was there. Or, at least, had followed me there. Had he planted the book? And then inserted the corresponding card into the card catalog system?

So weird.

There was only one thing left to do . . . I turned to the first page and started reading.

29.

It was full dark by the time I pulled out of the hospital.

Danny had come by bearing gifts. He brought Anthony a milkshake from McDonald's and me a bottled water. Danny, of course, knew of my dietary restrictions. He was in a good mood and I didn't appreciate the overly familiar hug he gave me. Also, with Anthony's marked improvements, he was being transferred from the intensive care unit to the immediate care unit, where his team of doctors could still keep an eye on him while he continued to recover.

I didn't know much about anything but *immediate care* sounded a whole hell of a lot better than *intensive care*.

By my reckoning, I had only three days to find an answer for Anthony before my son realized what his mommy had done to him. With father and son chumming it up, I gave Anthony a kiss, nodded at a beaming Danny, and left the hospital with my book.

Now driving, I couldn't help but feel so damn alive and strong. So unstoppable. It was all I could do to sit still in the driver's seat. There was so much energy surging through me that I could have burst into flames. I wanted to fly. I wanted to take flight. To where, I didn't know. Just somewhere. Anywhere. I wanted to be free and feel the wind on my face and watch the earth sweep far below me.

Soon, I thought. *Soon . . .*

Twenty minutes later, I was back at Hero's in Fullerton. After all, Fang had directed me to the university library, which had led me to this strange book, and I needed to know what the hell was going on.

The bar was hopping. I spotted Fang working like a madman behind the bar. He seemed to be making two or three drinks at once. He might be a wanted man, but he was also a helluva bartender. I was tempted to march over to him and demand to know what he knew about the book, but now wasn't a good time.

I could wait for the crowd to die down or for him to catch his breath. Because he had a lot of explaining to do.

He caught my eye through the sea of people, and I think that was a testament more to our psychic connection than dumb luck. I was a small girl, and the chances of him seeing me through the crowd and dim light were slim to none.

And yet there he was, pausing, staring, smiling.

Hello, Moon Dance.

The words appeared in my thoughts as surely as if he had been standing next to me. I nearly jumped and he laughed lightly from across the room.

I didn't mean to startle you, Moon Dance.

Vampires don't get startled. We get even.

He chuckled again. *So what brings you back? Do you have news about your son?*

Yes, and we need to talk.

Can you give me a few minutes? There are a lot of people who need to get drunk tonight.

Inelegantly put.

I do try. Let's talk in a bit, okay?

But we're not talking, we're thinking. We're freaks.

No, you're the freak.

Fine, I thought. *Think at you soon.*

And from across the bar he winked and got back to work. I stepped outside and looked up at the waxing moon. I reached into my jeans pocket and pulled out a stick of sugar-free gum. Recently, I had discovered that I could chew gum without any ill side effects—other than the occasional minor stomachache—and you can damn well better believe I was going to chew all the gum I could.

I marveled at the juicy fruit flavor as my taste buds sprang into action.

I could also smoke without any adverse side effects, like pesky lung cancer. I did that often, too, but tonight the gum chewing was enough.

A glance at the moon invariably conjured thoughts of Kingsley Fulcrum and his own freaky condition. Was this really the last I had seen of the big lug? It felt final. It felt empty.

And yet . . .

I cared for the big oaf. But maybe it was just a classic example of rebound love. He was the first man I had grown close to after the dissolution of my marriage. All my emotions—and maybe even a small amount of love—had been erroneously dumped onto him.

Confusing him and me.

I had just blown the mother of all bubbles when Fang appeared in the doorway. The bubble burst.

"So let's talk," he said. "I only have a few minutes. And you've got gum in your hair."

30.

We were in my minivan as I caught Fang up on my trip to the college, about twice seeing the gaunt man with the bow tie, and about removing the book from the library—

"You mean you stole it?"

"Big picture, Fang."

"Right."

I next told him about the copyright date, and his eyes narrowed in what I took to be disbelief, and so I reached into the glove compartment to show him the book . . . but it was gone.

I frantically riffled through the overstuffed glove compartment, pulling out a clump of napkins, insurance papers, bills I still needed to pay, some of Anthony's drawings, and . . . nothing.

"It was here, in the glove box. I just put it in here an hour ago." Stunned, I now looked through the backseat and on the floor between Fang's feet. Had someone broken in and stolen just the book? Did I ever even have the book? Was I losing my friggin' mind? "I don't understand what's happening."

"I don't either, Moon Dance. Tell me more about the book."

"You wouldn't believe me if I told you."

"Try me."

I sat back in my seat, completely shaken. Maybe I shouldn't have been so worked up, especially considering the contents of the book. It was, after all, not so much a book, but a personal message to me. And so I told Fang about it, about how the author appeared to be speaking directly to me. About the advice it contained.

"It was all very spiritual stuff," I said. "It seemed to apply to me directly."

Fang was looking at me through narrowed eyes again. Dubiously, as some would call it. "How so?"

I shrugged. "A lot of advice about staying in the 'light,' about not giving into my 'dark nature.' That those who have been granted premature power have a special challenge in keeping that power in check, to use it for good."

"He's talking about you being a vampire?"

"Not in so many words. The book was very vague about what kind of powers, but it seemed to be directed to anyone who had found themselves in my position. But it could have just as easily been written for a—"

"Werewolf."

"Sure. Or anyone else who suddenly finds themselves in a position of power or authority."

"Wild. But why do you think it was written for you?"

"Hard to pinpoint. It just felt directed at me. It gave a lot of advice, too, too much to talk about now in your ten-minute break."

"And it was copyrighted today?"

I nodded. "Fang, you said that a young guy came in and told you about the Occult Reading Room."

"Right."

"Tell me more about him."

"Like I said, he was a young guy. He came in and soon we were talking about Cal State Fullerton's baseball team. They're in the finals again this year—how their program can consistently put together some of the best teams in college—"

"Focus, Fang."

"Yes, right. He finished his beer and mentioned he had to get back to work in the Occult Reading Room at Cal State's library."

"He said it like that? Not, 'I have to get back to work'?"

"Yeah, you're right. At the time, I thought it been a little specific, but I blew it off because he had my interest."

I knew about Fang's interest in the occult. His knowledge of the arcane had come in handy more than once.

He went on, "So, he told me more about the collection; in particular, its thoroughness on nearly all esoteric subjects."

"And he wasn't wearing a bow tie?"

Fang smiled. "Hardly. He couldn't have been more than twenty-five."

"Blue eyes and a pointy beard."

"That's him."

I was thinking about that when my cell rang. I fished it off my van's charger. Danny. "I have to take this," I said to Fang.

"No prob," he said, and leaned over and kissed me on the cheek. "I have to scoot anyway. Love ya."

And before I realized what I was saying, I said, "Love ya, too."

When he was gone, I answered the phone, and Danny didn't waste any time getting to the point. "What the fuck did you do to our boy, you goddamned monster?!"

31.

"Calm down, Danny."

"Don't tell me to calm you down, you goddamn freak! You changed him, Sam. *You fucking changed him.* That's why he's so cold. That's why his body temperature is dropping."

"And that's why he's alive, Danny."

"Fuck you, Sam. This is too much. This is just too fucking much. Unbelievable. I hate you, Sam. I hate you more than I've ever hated you."

He went on like this for a few more minutes. I tried to speak, but couldn't get a word in edgewise. Finally, when he took a breath, I said, "He was dying, Danny. He was dying. Do you understand? He would be dead now."

"You don't know that. How could you know that? You didn't give him a chance. He could have pulled through."

"No, he wouldn't have. I saw his death, Danny. I saw it as plain as day."

"Better he dies a human than be a freak like you."

"You don't mean that—"

"Go to hell, you bitch. I will never forgive you for this or forget this, and I am going to make it my life's fucking mission to drag you down to hell where you belong."

He clicked off, no doubt angrily, just as I received another call. It was from a restricted line. Restricted lines often meant one of two things: telemarketers or cops. In this case, it was the cops. In particular, Detective Sherbet.

"Samantha," he said simply.

"Detective."

"We have a situation here at the hospital. I need to see you ASAP."

"What's wrong? Is it my son?" My voice instantly went from calm to nearly hysterical.

"Your son is fine, Sam. No, this is something else, and we need to see you ASAP."

32.

I was sitting with Detective Sherbet in the hospital break room, or one of its break rooms, after a very tense ride from Hero's. My frantic mind had imagined every conceivable, horrific scenario, each one worse than the other.

But never had I imagined this.

The hospital was in complete anarchy. Police everywhere. A mother weeping uncontrollably. Nurses frightened. Doctors frightened. Hell, everyone looked frightened. A very grave Sherbet had shut the break room door behind him and sat across from me.

Detective Sherbet and I had become close over these past few months. Not so close that I had disclosed to him my super-secret identity, but pretty damn close. Sherbet, no idiot, was aware that some really freaky shit was going down in his city. He knew I was connected to it, and in fact, might be the freakiest of them all. To his credit, he had yet to confront me about who—or what—I might know. Rather, he'd been approaching this from the outside, nibbling away at the edges. Perhaps his approach was a good one: absorbing small details at a time.

Sherbet was a big man, but not as big as Kingsley or my new

detective friend out of Huntington Beach. If anything, he looked like a panda bear: salt-and-pepper hair, way too round around the middle, serious yet playful. And, if necessary, tough as hell.

"We have a child missing," he said simply. We were sitting at a round and heavily scarred table. His belly, I noted, actually rested on the edge of the table.

My own stomach sank. "What do you mean?"

"A patient, a child, was kidnapped not too long ago by an unknown male."

My heart froze. "When?"

"Just over thirty minutes ago. Kidnapped here, from the hospital."

"Oh my God."

"The hospital is on lockdown. No one in or out. Absolute insanity." As he spoke, Sherbet was watching me closely. The muscles along his hairy forearms moved just under his thin skin, as he clenched and unclenched his fists. "The city of Orange isn't my beat, but the guys here are good friends of mine. When a child goes missing all available hands come running. When I first heard the report, I thought of your son here."

"But he's okay." I knew this because I had already checked on him.

He nodded. "Sam, the boy was kidnapped from your son's old room."

"I don't understand."

"Your son, from what I understand, was recently moved from ICU to immediate care." I wasn't following but he continued on. "Another boy took your son's room. Within thirty minutes, he was gone."

"Oh, my God."

Through the closed doors, I could hear someone barking an order. A child was crying somewhere. In fact, many children were crying.

Sweet Jesus. What was going on?

Sherbet went on, "The parents were down in the cafeteria getting some coffee and preparing for another all-nighter when they got the news."

"Were there any witnesses?" My voice sounded hollow and distant.

"Oh, yeah. A man comes in claiming to be an uncle. Charming, smooth as hell, apparently. Says everything right. Front desk lets the bastard right in. Same with the nurses up here. Against protocol left and right. Heads will roll. Yet these same people don't remember letting the guy in. I don't understand any of it."

"They don't remember letting him, but they let him in?"

"Something like that."

"As in no memory of doing it?"

"Right." Sherbet frowned at me. The muscles of his forearm continued to undulate.

"What happened next?"

"You'll never believe it."

"Try me," I said.

"Better I show you."

He led me out of the break room and over to the room I was so familiar with, the same room my son had occupied for the past few days. Except now there was something vastly different about the room.

The entire window was missing.

33.

Sherbet said, "A minute or two after stepping into the room, the nurses heard what sounded like an explosion. When they rushed in to investigate, the boy was gone and the window was broken."

I was speechless. Beyond speechless. I couldn't formulate words. All I wanted to do was run to my son again and check on him, to hold him close and protect him forever.

What the hell was happening?

"For the love of God, Sam, what's going on?"

"I don't know, Detective, I swear—" I stopped when a disturbing image came to mind. "What did the man look like?"

"Tall. Caucasian. Dressed in slacks and a blazer. A blue blazer—Sam, what's wrong?"

"Just go on," I said. I had braced myself against the wall. Although I had little use for my lungs, they suddenly felt constricted, as if an anaconda had curled around my chest and was squeezing, squeezing. "Was he wearing anything else?"

Detective Sherbet was watching me closely.

"A bow tie," he said.

"Oh, shit."

"What do you know, Sam? Dammit, what the hell's going on here?"

"He was following me today."

"Who was following you today?"

"The man with the bow tie."

Sherbet blinked. "If he was following you, then why in the devil would he kidnap the boy?"

"The man was after Anthony, I think."

"Sweet Jesus, Sam."

"And got the wrong boy. He was just a few minutes too late."

"Why would he want your son?"

"He's trying to get to me."

"Who's trying to get to you?"

"I don't know."

"Who is he?"

"I don't know."

"Why does he want you?"

That I did know. Or, at least, I suspected I knew. "I have something he wants."

"Who is he, Sam? And dammit, don't tell me you don't know. You know something. I can feel it. You're holding back and now is not the time to hold back. There's a sick little boy out there who needs immediate medical attention, who's terrified and possibly hurt."

Sherbet had a son of his own, about the same age as Anthony, in fact. I thought about how Sherbet had been such a good friend to me. I also thought about how he was so close to the truth. To my secret. I looked into his eyes now. His desperate and wild eyes. I thought about the little missing boy—a missing boy that was supposed to have been Anthony. My heart broke for him and his family, and I realized that my secret could be a secret no more. At least not with Detective Sherbet.

"Can we talk somewhere more private?"

"No, Sam. We talk here."

"Please, Detective."

He didn't like it. "Fine," he said. "We'll talk in my squad car."

34.

His squad car was an unmarked Ford Crown Victoria, and he was parked in a handicapped spot directly in front of the hospital. The car was immaculate, as I suspected it would be. Not even a wadded-up bag of donuts, which I half expected to find.

As he slid in, he clicked the doors locked. "It's just me and you, kiddo," he said. "Now talk."

"I have an artifact," I started. "A very valuable artifact for some people. I suspect that whoever took the boy wants this artifact. No doubt he thought he was taking my son."

"Ransom," said Sherbet. He hadn't taken his eyes off me.

"That's what I'm thinking."

"And the man in the bow tie?"

"I have no idea who he is."

"But he was following you?"

I nodded. "Yeah, I think so."

Sherbet absorbed these strange details silently, his fine investigative mind sorting them out mentally, labeling them and filing them in his mental file folders. "What's the artifact, Samantha?"

Sherbet was staring at me. I could hear his heart beating steadily, strongly. Sherbet smelled of aftershave and potatoes.

I took a deep breath, held it, and looked my friend in the eye. Sherbet returned my stare, his eyes wide and hungry, searching for information.

"Please, Samantha," he said. "Talk to me."

I continued staring at him, and finally came to a decision. I said, "I'm not what you think I am, Detective."

"What the devil does that mean, Sam?"

"When I was attacked six years ago, I was changed forever."

"No shit, Sam. An attack like that would change any—"

"That's not what I meant, Detective. It changed me in a physical sense. In an eternal sense, too."

"Eternal? What the devil are you talking—wait. Good God, you're not telling you're one of those were-thingies?"

I smiled despite the seriousness of the situation. "No, Detective. I'm a vampire."

35.

"A vampire?" he said.

"Yes."

"And you're serious?"

"As a corpse."

"I don't know whether to laugh or be afraid."

"You can laugh, if you want. Lord knows I've done it a few times. Of course, my laughter usually turns into tears. But you certainly don't need to be afraid, Detective."

Yet another police car pulled up to the hospital. A young officer dashed out and headed for the hospital's main doors. Through it all, Sherbet hadn't taken his eyes off me. I didn't blame him.

"I have a secret, too," he said finally.

"Oh no," I said. "Please don't tell me you're the Werewolf King or something."

He chuckled lightly. "No, but I would have loved to see the look on your face."

"What's your secret, Detective? Seems like a good night to spill them."

"I've known you were a vampire for some time."

"Really?"

"It's the only thing that made sense. Your strange disease, the dead gang banger drained of blood, the punch through the bulletproof glass, the dead prisoner."

"Why didn't you say anything?"

"Because it was a new theory and I was still debating whether or not I was going insane."

"A question I've asked myself a thousand times."

"I have another secret," he confessed.

"I don't think I can handle any more secrets," I said.

"I've seen *Twilight* five times."

I wasn't sure I'd heard him right. "You saw *what* five times?"

"*Twilight*. My boy loves it. He can't get it enough of it. We've seen the sequels a few times, too. Also, I watched them for, you know, research."

Detective Sherbet loved his boy. Of that there was no doubt. That he had been worried sick that his young son was showing early signs of homosexuality was almost comical. With that said, I had been touched by Sherbet's ability to come to terms with the concept. If anything, he loved his boy even more. Still, the thought of the gruff detective sitting through the various naked torso scenes in *Twilight* and its sequels for "research" would normally have had me laughing so hard that I might have peed. But not tonight.

"Anyway," he said, clearly embarrassed. "You could say I'm something of a vampire expert now."

"I see," I said, and now I did laugh. "I hadn't realized I was sitting next to an expert."

He laughed, too, but then quickly turned somber. "But those are just movies. This is real, isn't it, Sam?"

"I'm afraid so."

"You really are a vampire."

I shrugged, my old defense kicking in. "I don't know what I am, Detective."

"What does that mean?"

"It means I'm the same person I've always been, except sometimes when I'm not. It means that I feel the same that I've always felt, except sometimes when I don't. It means I act the same, think the same, and do the same things I've always done."

"Except when you don't," said Sherbet.

"Yes, exactly. It means I'm still me. I'm still a mom. I'm still a woman. I'm still a sister. And I'm still a friend."

"But you're also something else. Something more."

I nodded. "And sometimes I'm that, too."

We were silent for a minute or two. The detective's heart rate, I noted, had increased significantly. "It happened six years ago, didn't it?"

I nodded.

"It left you . . . the way you are now."

"Yes."

"You never asked for this, did you?"

I shook my head.

"And it's ripped your life apart, hasn't it?"

I nodded and fought the tears. Enough crying. I was sick of

crying, but it felt so damn nice to be understood, especially by a man I respected and admired so much.

"And now you're doing all you can to keep it together."

Shit. The tears started. Damn Detective Sherbet.

He reached over and patted my hand. A grandfatherly gesture. A warm gesture.

"So you believe me?" I asked.

"I believe something. What that is, I don't know. Most of me thinks you're insane, or that I'm insane. Most people would think, in the least, that you're a hazard to your kids."

"Do you think I'm a hazard to my kids?"

"No. I think you're a wonderful mother. I really believe that."

"Thank you," I said, moved all over again.

Sherbet touched the back of my hand again. My instinct was, of course, to retract my hand, but I didn't. Not this time. His fingertips explored my skin, almost like a blind man would the face of his lover. "Your cold skin always confused me. And your skin disease never felt right."

"Because it wasn't."

He nodded. "And Ira Lang . . . sweet Jesus. The visiting room."

Sherbet was referring to the time a month or so ago when I had punched through a bulletproof piece of glass to grab a piece of shit named Ira Lang, and proceeded to let him know what I thought of him threatening me and my kids.

"You killed him, Sam."

I said nothing. I wasn't admitting anything, especially to a homicide investigator.

"You nearly ripped his head off."

I kept saying nothing.

"Of course, I should arrest you. For his murder, and for anyone else who's gone missing or been killed on any of your other cases." He turned his shoulder and propped a meaty elbow up on the seat's head rest. "Just tell me one thing, Sam: Do you kill people for blood?"

"No."

"Do you drink blood?"

His tone was challenging. I felt like a daughter confronted by her father about smoking weed or drinking booze.

"I have to," I said, looking away.

He stared at me so long and hard that I wanted to crawl under a rock.

"Please don't judge me," I finally said. "I never asked for this."

"I'm not judging, Sam. I'm just trying to wrap my brain around all of this. I mean, a part of me suspected something was up, and perhaps even a very small part of me began to believe . . . this. But to hear it now, from a pretty young investigator I've grown to admire, is something else entirely."

"I'll deny everything, Detective. So let's get that clear now."

I wasn't looking at him but I felt him grin. I sensed only confusion and compassion and more confusion from him. And also a steady sense of alarm. But not for his own health or well-being. We still had a missing boy out there, after all.

"And I'll never admit to watching the *Twilight* movies," he said.

"I'll take your secret to my grave," I said.

"I thought vampires were immortal," he said.

"We'll see."

"So what do we do about Eddy?" said Sherbet. "The kidnapped boy?"

"If it's a ransom," I said. "Then I'll be hearing from his abductor."

Sherbet nodded. "Makes sense. And his abductor . . . would he also be a vampire?"

"More than likely," I said.

"And what's this about a relic?"

I reached inside my jeans pocket and removed the medallion. I didn't trust it anywhere except on my person. He turned on the car's interior light, and I showed him the golden disc.

"It's a necklace with ruby roses," he said.

"Your observational skills are second to none, Detective."

"Don't sass me, young lady. What's so special about this?"

"It's reputed to reverse vampirism."

"Ah," he said. "And that's a good thing?"

"For some."

"And you don't want to give it up?"

"I can't," I said. "Under any circumstances."

"Even to save a little boy?"

I put the medallion back in my pocket. Just having it out made me nervous.

"I need it," I said.

He heard the anguish in my voice, and since Sherbet also happened to be a helluva detective, he looked at me sharply. "Your son," he said.

I buried my face in my hands.

"You need it to change your son back, don't you?"

Now I was rocking in my seat and crying, and talking incomprehensibly about saving my son, and doing all I had to do to keep him from dying, and knowing I was a horrible mother, but what else could I do? I loved him so much, and I had a chance to save him, and I had to take it, I had to take it. . . .

And as I babbled nearly incoherently, Detective Sherbet reached out and put his arm around my shoulders and pulled me in close and told me that everything was going to be okay. Somehow, someway, everything was going to be okay. . . .

36.

Mary Lou arrived an hour or so later with Tammy.

They had stopped at McDonald's and had sneaked in a Big Mac for Anthony. I told them Anthony was probably too weak to eat, but boy was I wrong. He devoured the sandwich in a few quick bites and was looking for more. He next pounded his sister's fries, and I waited for what I was sure was coming next:

Upchuck city.

Food, for me, lasts only a few minutes before it comes up violently. But Anthony never did vomit. Instead, he complained slightly of an upset stomach and I realized what was happening. Although only a half inch or so above his skin, his aura was still there. His humanity was still there. For now. Until the change overcame him completely. By contrast, his sister, who was sitting on the edge of his bed and playing "Angry Birds" on my sister's cell phone, shone like a beacon in the night. Pale yellows and reds, streaked with silvers and golds, surrounded her body many feet or more, sometimes flaring like mini-nuclear explosions on the surface of the sun.

But not Anthony. His aura was only a fine dusting of light. Almost an afterthought.

Shit.

His last meal, I thought. *Or close to it.*

I was, admittedly, torn. I knew I had to find Archibald Maximus ASAP, especially since his book had given me an intriguing clue. From what I gathered, he lived in the mountains above San Bernardino, Lake Arrowhead or Big Bear, one of those, both popular ski resorts. With Anthony getting better, and simultaneously losing his mortality, now was as good a time as any to set out for the mountains and Mr. Maximus.

But the missing boy was tearing me to pieces. An innocent family had gotten caught up in my insanity, and now their boy was missing, having been abducted by a true monster.

Who was Bow Tie? A vampire? I had no doubt, unless the medallion could reverse other supernatural curses, which it very well might. That he jumped from a third-floor hospital room, leaving behind no evidence—it turns out he had thrown a chair through the window—could mean anything. I suspected someone like Kingsley could withstand such a fall. After all, I had seen him in his wolf's form leap nine stories without missing a beat. Whether or not Kingsley could perform such an act in his human form, I didn't know. There was so much I didn't know.

There was a family not very far from this room who had been torn to pieces. All because of my actions. I had to do something.

I looked again at the faint aura around my son's body. I still had time. Not much, granted, but at least a day and a half, maybe two.

I stood and paced and my daughter ignored me. That her little brother was suddenly doing much better didn't seem to matter much to her. The faith of children. No doubt she always assumed he would get better.

My sister was watching me with huge eyes. She alternately looked at Anthony and I saw her confusion. She suspected something, too. But not enough to confront me about it, and I couldn't talk to her about it, not now, and not in present company. She was just going to have to keep wondering.

Where would the bastard have gone? Would he be contacting me soon? Had he realized his mistake and simply killed the boy? Would he next be coming after Anthony?

I didn't know, but I didn't have long to wait.

After pacing a few more minutes and wondering also what

Danny was up to, my cell phone rang. Another restricted number.

I answered with a simple hello.

"Miss Moon," said a man with a heavy French accent. "I believe you have something I want."

37.

I stepped out of the room and into the hallway.

"Who is this?"

"Never mind that, Samantha Moon of the Moon Agency. I realize I have made a critical error, but perhaps not all is lost."

He paused and I could have jumped in with another wasted question. Instead, I waited, breathless, realizing without a doubt that a vampire was on the other end of the line.

He spoke again in his heavy French accent. "The real question here, Samantha Moon, is how much compassion you have for your fellow man. Or, in this case, boy."

"Go on," I said.

"Give me the medallion and I give you the boy, alive."

"You're a piece of shit."

"A desperate piece of shit, Samantha Moon. I know what you are, and I know that you know what I am. At least now you do. Who else would want the medallion?" He paused as my mind reeled. He went on: "And perhaps you don't realize that the longer you live, the harder you are to kill. Has this occurred to you?"

"Fuck you."

"I see it hasn't. Well, let me assure you, I am old. Very, very old. And I am desperate to end this existence, Miss Moon. Desperate. I am tired of living, and I cannot die. Not by silver. Not by anything. Do you understand me?"

I said nothing. Thinking was hard. The man's voice was so damn . . . hypnotic. Even for me. I could see why anyone and everyone would have given him what he wanted. It took all my effort to keep my thoughts clear. I felt him pushing in, even from a distance, trying to claim my thoughts.

"Ah, I see you are not new at this, Miss Moon. Not everyone, undead included, can resist me. Very well. Let me assure you that I am tired of living, and I will bring this entire fucking planet to hell with me, if I have to. The boy means nothing to me. Your son means nothing to me. You mean nothing to me. Nothing has any meaning except my own death, my removal from this earth. Do you understand me?"

"Yes," I said, aware that I was indeed speaking on my own free will.

"Nothing can end my life except for one thing, and one thing alone. The medallion. The wonderfully enchanted medallion that I have searched so long for. So very, very long."

"Where are you?"

"I am not far, my dear."

"How do I find you?"

For an answer, I suddenly had an image of a rooftop. But this wasn't just any rooftop. There were stairs leading everywhere. The roof itself had many levels and platforms and turrets. It was the roof to the Mission Inn in Riverside. I would know it anywhere.

"Good, good. You recognize this. Do not speak of it, my dear, or I will kill this little one and fetch another and another and another until you bring to me what I want. Do you understand?"

I thought of my son. I thought of many, many things, all of which I shielded from the bastard who kept probing my thoughts. "I do."

"Then I will see you in two hours."

And the line went dead.

38.

I found Sherbet inside the office of the hospital's public relations administrator. Through the open door, I saw a young couple sitting together. The couple had their backs to me and appeared to be listening to someone in command. No doubt the captain of Orange Police Department's Investigative Division. The woman mostly had her face buried in her hands, while her husband had his arms around her, comforting her. I couldn't see their faces.

Sherbet saw me and stepped outside. He read my expression instantly. The man was damn good.

"Our guy called," he said.

"Yes."

"Where is he?"

I shook my head. "I have to do this alone or he kills the boy."

"No way, Sam. I'm going with you, along with some of my boys."

I shook my head. "He will know, Detective. He'll know and he'll kill the boy."

"How will he know?"

"In ways you won't understand."

He didn't like it. "Maybe he's bluffing."

"He's not."

"How do you know?"

"Call it a hunch."

"Not good enough, Sam."

"Fine," I said. "Because he's a very, very old vampire who cares little for anything, if at all. He will kill the boy and find another."

"We'll catch him."

"And risk the boy's life?"

Sherbet looked away, so frustrated that he growled. He rubbed his bristled face repeatedly. "I don't like it, Sam."

"Who would?"

"So what are you going to do?"

"I'm going to get the boy."

"How?"

"Any way I can."

"Are you going to hand over the medallion?"

"I don't know."

"If you give up the medallion, what happens to your son?"

"I don't want to think about it," I said.

He continued rubbing his face. Nervous energy crackled through him."I don't like it, Sam," he said again.

"Neither do I," I said and turned to leave. "I gotta go."

"Sam," he called after me.

I stopped and looked back. The big detective looked sick with worry. "Please be careful, kid."

"I wouldn't have it any other way."

And I turned and left.

39.

I was tempted to call Fang, but I didn't.

Like the detective, he would want to come, too. Unlike the detective, he didn't know what the hell he was doing, and the last I checked, Fang didn't even have a weapon.

Which was probably a moot point anyway, since according to the vampire, nothing could kill him, silver included. *"And I am desperate to end this existence, Miss Moon. Desperate. I am tired of living, and I cannot die. Not by silver. Not by anything."*

Sweet Jesus.

Of course, that's if he was telling me the truth.

I merged onto the 57 North, slipping into the fast lane, and gave the minivan a lot of gas. I loved my little minivan. Sure, it screamed soccer mom, but it was so handy and smooth and comfortable that I just didn't give a shit what people thought.

Traffic was light and fast, which is the way I liked it. Brake lights, blinker lights, headlights, and street lights all mostly blended together with the zigzagging streaks of energy that filled my vision, the glowing filaments that made it possible for me to see into the night.

I gave the van more gas and thought about the medallion. I wasn't sure what I was going to do. Whoever Bow Tie was, he surely wasn't going to accept anything less than the medallion.

One problem: As noted by Detective Sherbet, I needed it to give my son back his mortality.

My phone rang. Another restricted call. At this point, it could have been anyone, from a vampire kidnapper to Sherbet. It was neither.

"Hey, Sunshine," said Chad Helling, my ex-partner, a man who did not know my super-secret identity . . . only that I had a rare skin disease.

"Hey, Romeo."

"I heard about the shitty business at the hospital. Is your son okay?"

"My son's fine, which is more than I can say for another little boy."

"You need me to come down?" he asked. "Once a partner, always a partner."

"Thanks, Chad, but I'll manage."

"I know you will. You always do." He paused.

"You have news about Archibald Maximus."

"Yes, how did you—never mind. You could always read my mind."

I grinned to myself. He was right, and there was nothing psychic about it. I said, "Once a partner, always a partner."

He chuckled. "Anyway, no luck with Mr. Archibald Maximus, although something strange did turn up."

"How strange?"

"Oh, it's nothing. Never mind."

"Tell me, dammit."

"Easy, girl. Okay, fine. There was an Archibald Maximus who died fifty years ago."

I did find that interesting, but Chad didn't need to know that. "And this helps me how?"

"Well, the strange part is that his family and friends reported seeing him on two other occasions."

"After his death?"

"Right."

"And how do you know this?"

"The wife filed a report. She wanted his body exhumed."

"Did they?"

"No."

I chewed on this. But Chad didn't need to know I was chewing on this. Instead, I said, "Well, thanks for wasting the last three minutes of my life."

"Anytime. Be safe, Sunshine."

"Jerk."

And he clicked off, laughing.

The 57 North merged into the 91 East. I was soon shooting past the 80 mph mark—and still there were drivers riding my ass. You can never go fast enough in Southern California.

I was cruising at 85 mph and had just settled in for the hour-long drive to Riverside when my cell phone chirped. A text message. I rummaged through my purse, swerving slightly into the next lane, until I found the iPhone. A text from Fang.

Something's wrong, he wrote. *I can feel it. What's going on? Where are you going?*

Jesus, our connection was growing stronger. I wasn't sure how I felt about that, but maybe there was something greater at work here than I thought. Maybe Fang was destined to be something more. Much more. I didn't know, but I certainly couldn't think about it now.

I rapidly typed out my reply: *Just getting ice cream with Tammy. On our way to Cold Stone now.*

Bullshit, Sam. Why do I feel a tremendous sense of . . . dread.

Maybe you had some bad Chinese.

A car horn blasted next to me, and I straightened out my minivan. Apparently I had given the guy next to me a fright. I waved an apology and he waved back with his middle finger.

Enough with the bad Chinese, Sam. Please. What's going on? I'm worried sick over here.

It's better if you don't know, Fang. I'm sorry.

Let me help you. Please. I've never felt this way before.

Welcome to my world, I thought. Instead, I wrote: *I'm sorry, Fang. I'll call later. Love you.*

Love you? Now what the hell had gotten into me?

40.

The Mission Inn is a national treasure.

And it's found right here in downtown Riverside, a city that isn't much of a national treasure. For me, Riverside conjures images of heat and gangs and neighborhoods that aren't so nice. A false image, surely, as its downtown is actually quite nice, and boasts some cool bars and nice restaurants. But, most importantly, it boasts the Mission Inn, getaway to presidents and celebrities alike, where thousands have been married and many tens of thousands have passed through.

After negotiating through some heavy downtown traffic, in

which I passed exactly three prostitutes and a guy dressed like Lady Gaga, and parked in a small parking lot across the street from the inn. There I sat quietly, closed my eyes, and tried to get a feel for the place. Eyes closed, I sensed lots of movement, lots of happy people, lots of great moments. The Mission Inn is a special place.

I next tried to get a sense of any danger, of what I might be up against, but the place was just too big for me to get a feel for it. Either that, or my thoughts were too scattered to focus correctly. Then again, I still didn't entirely know what I was doing.

Next I focused on the roof, rising as surely as if I was physically floating above the edifice. The suites up here were nicer, more expensive. The roof area, which sported many walkways and ramps that led to various floors and balconies, looked like something out of a medieval fairy tale. A handful of couples were sitting together on their balconies, enjoying the night, smoking, drinking, kissing, writhing.

Uh oh.

Above it all was one of the inn's three majestic domes, this one a mosaic jewel that crowned this section of the inn, and as it came into view in my mind, I gasped.

There was a darkness within. It surrounded the dome as surely as the dark halo had surrounded my son. I tried to dip into the dome, but I couldn't. Somehow, I was blocked. More, I didn't *want* to go inside. The dome repelled me, horrified me.

He's in there, I thought.

And that's when my cell phone rang. Restricted call, of course. It was him, I knew it. How an ancient vampire knew how to restrict his calls, I hadn't a clue.

I clicked on and he spoke immediately: "You're here," he said. "I can feel another."

"What does that mean?"

"It means I can feel another of our kind, Miss Moon."

"I'm nothing like you."

He laughed sharply, so sharply that my ear hurt. "Oh, we are very much alike, my dear."

"You're in the dome," I said.

"Yes," he said, and sounded impressed. "With the other bats."

"Is the boy with you?"

"You mean that sickly little thing? Sure, he's here somewhere, but he's not long for this world. I should probably just help him along."

"You touch him, and you'll never get the medallion."

"Oh, relax, my dear. I'm won't touch him . . . yet. I'll see if you'll play by my rules first. If so, he may be spared. If not, there's going to be blood tonight."

"Enough with the threats, asshole. I have the medallion."

He veritably hissed with pleasure. "Good, good! Then I expect to see you soon," and he clicked off.

41.

The massive hotel stretched from city block to city block, surrounded by a low, medieval-style brick wall.

An array of lights lit the hotel, and the building's sheer complexity of style was enough to nearly overwhelm the senses, everything from Spanish Gothic, Mission Revival, Moorish Revival, Renaissance Revival, and Mediterranean Revival. I know something about architecture. If I hadn't been an investigator, I would have been an architect. And the inn was a wonder to behold.

I was in a parking lot on Orange Street, along the southeast side of the building. There was a side opening here that I was familiar with, one that led to a small bar that Danny and I had frequented many times, where we drank wine and beer and ate lightly breaded chicken strips and listened to a talented cellist and talked about our days.

Those days were long gone.

Years ago, before I met Danny, my first visit to the hotel had been a laughable one. I was running late to my then-boyfriend's cousin's wedding. I was in college and working two jobs and I had barely gotten off in time to rush out from Orange County on a Saturday evening. Running in high heels and clutching my dress, I dashed into the first chapel I saw. The wedding was about to start. Feeling self-conscious, I sat in the back row and looked wildly for my boyfriend, assuming he was sitting somewhere in the front. I felt like shit that I had come so late that I couldn't find him, but at least I made it, right? I had never met his cousins, and I didn't know anyone in his family, and so I sat in the back alone, going through the motions of a very Catholic wedding, kneeling and crossing and saying prayers with everyone else.

After the longish wedding, when everyone poured out into the courtyard, I was caught up by a group of women who forced me up a spiraled staircase for pictures. As I continued to scan the milling crowd below for my boyfriend, I paused every so often for the photographer. We took a God-awful amount of pictures, and when I was finally released, I happened to see another chapel on the far side of the courtyard. Another wedding had taken place, and was just now finishing.

And there, exiting through the doors, was my boyfriend.

Exactly. I had gone to the wrong wedding. That's me, Samantha Moon, the original wedding crasher. To this day, I'm certain the bride is wondering who that cute, dark-haired girl was in all her photos.

Back when I could take photos, of course.

Needless to say, that night only went from bad to worse, and my boyfriend and I broke up in an epic fight. I met Danny shortly thereafter and the rest, as they say, is history.

Good times, I thought, as I stepped across the street and headed under the veranda and into the gloomy bar where the cello player had long since disappeared. Now, no one played, and that was a damn shame.

I moved through the lobby and front desks, and through what appeared to be yet another lobby lined with presidential portraits. I assumed these were all the presidents who had stayed here. The hotel felt damn old and I sensed many, many lingering spirits. Hell, if I was a spirit, I would linger here, too. A ghost could do worse than haunt the Mission Inn.

Now with the hair on my neck standing on end, I turned and saw where one spirit was semi-manifesting. Staticky energy formed into the shape of what appeared to be a teenage boy. He was watching me casually from one of the spiraling staircases that led up to the more expensive suites. As I watched him, he took on more shape and made a partial appearance, the crackling energy briefly replaced by a wispy cloud of ectoplasm. Had someone chosen now to take a picture of the staircase, they would have captured an honest-to-God ghost. Anyway, his eyes widened with some surprise when he no doubt realized that I was watching him in return. He came to life, so to speak, and drifted immediately over to me, where he stood in front of me, smiling. Was that a wink?

I could be wrong, but I think he was flirting with me.

Next, the strong impression of a name appeared in my thoughts. "Your name is . . . Leland?" I asked.

He nodded vigorously, and now other spirits seemed to take note. They were manifesting around us rapidly, like human-shaped sparklers. Some fully formed, although most crackled and spat crackling energy, only vaguely humanoid. Most were dressed in older-style clothing. Some of the men even wore hats.

"Now look what you started, Leland," I whispered to the teen boy.

He frowned, and then shooed the other spirits away, moving quickly to each. The others departed, some clearly irritated, others fading into nothing or zipping away like blazing comets through the hotel. As they did so, I caught a very real little girl watching us from across the room. She was standing next to her mother, her index finger hooked into her mouth. Her wide eyes followed some of the fleeing spirits. Kids can see far more than we realize.

The teen ghost faded in and out of clarity, sometimes reverting to nothing more than a crackling human torch, and other times to a dapper young man who could have hailed from the 1920s. Once, he even made a gesture to dance, holding out his hand as one would lead a woman to the dance floor, and only then did I notice the ambient music playing over the hotel's speakers. A sort of jazzy/classical rag-time, of the type my grandmother would listen to. Had the classical music drawn him downstairs, I wondered, reminding him of his days when he was alive?

I was about to say goodbye and turn away when I noticed something about his face. There was something that looked like blood coating his lower jaw and staining the front of his shirt. I next had the strong hit of a single word: *tuberculosis*.

So Leland had died here at the hotel, long ago, and has been hanging around ever since, his chin and shirt forever stained with the ghostly hint of perhaps his last coughing fit.

"I have to go," I whispered to him, "but thank you for the offer to dance."

As I turned to leave, I realized I had no clue how to actually get up to the dome. I turned back to the young man, and somehow, someway, he was able to read my thoughts, because he was nodding excitedly and motioning for me to follow him. He held out his hand and, feeling rather silly, I reached out and took it—or simulated taking it—knowing full well I looked silly as hell to just about everyone else. Everyone, that is, but the little girl.

He led me quickly through the massive hotel.

42.

We went through some doors—well, he went through them, I had to open them—and once in the outside courtyard, moved quickly past an elegant restaurant that I had always wanted to try. Back in the day, Danny and I were too poor to dine elegantly. Drinks and chicken tenders were about all we could afford.

Anyway, the teen boy led me along the main artery that led down the center of the hotel, past beautiful planters and water fountains and the pool. We plunged under Mediterranean Revival-style archways lit with hanging lanterns, and dashed quickly over Spanish tile that looked both ancient and impenetrable. We passed couples holding hands or sitting contentedly on ornate benches. We passed more crackling spirits, all of which seemed to have somewhere to go.

Now above us, shining like a mother ship descending from the heavens, was the jaw-droppingly beautiful north tower dome. I only had a glimpse of it before the ghost teen disappeared through a closed door. A closed *locked* door.

A very bloody and sheepish face appeared a moment later in the center of the door. Leland smiled and the ancient blood on his lower jaw almost seemed to sparkle.

"Through here?" I asked.

He nodded vigorously. I tried the handle. Locked.

"I don't suppose you can unlock it from the inside, could you?"

He nodded again and disappeared back through the door. I next heard some very odd, lightly scraping sounds from the other side, and shortly his gruesomely handsome face reappeared. He shook his head sadly.

I looked from side to side, and didn't see anyone paying particular attention to us. I then took hold of the doorknob and applied a smidgen of pressure.

The lock shattered and the handle broke off in my hand. Pieces of metal fell everywhere, inside and outside the door.

Lord, I'm a freak.

The shattering lock would surely have attracted some attention, and so I ignored the stares and pushed the door open like I belonged there. I kicked the broken knob inside.

Leland took my hand again, which felt a bit like plunging my hand in a picnic cooler, and led me up a very narrow spiral staircase that was clearly not meant for hotel guests, judging by how rickety and unstable it was. Who used this staircase and why, I didn't know, but it felt unsafe as hell.

I heard the sounds of pots and pans banging, the sizzle of something or other, and someone shouting an order in Spanish. We were behind the kitchen, perhaps in a forgotten storage room, along a forgotten staircase. I suspected this old hotel, with its many additions, had many such forgotten rooms and staircases.

Sometimes our hands broke contact, but the teen boy would always reach back for me. Sometimes I could see the concern on his face, but mostly I saw his excitement. And with each step we took, my inner warning system sounded louder and louder. Perhaps the loudest I had ever heard it sound. So loud now that even the ghost boy turned and looked at me.

Jesus, had he heard my own alarm system?

There was just so much to learn about the spirit world, a world that had unexpectedly opened up to me these past few months.

Now we were at another door. This was unlocked and soon we were standing in a very long and creepy hallway. The hallway had been used for storage. Now, I suspected, it was long since forgotten. Old sinks and clawed bathtubs and disgusting toilets that turned my stomach.

He led me deeper. I noted Leland didn't kick up any dust, whereas I left behind great swirling plumes of the stuff.

We hung a right and soon came upon another narrow flight of wrought-iron stairs. The boy floated up them effortlessly, whereas, I climbed up them as quietly as possible. I felt for the medallion in my pocket, suddenly wishing I had left it in the van, after all.

Lord, if I lost this . . .

The few breaths I took echoed loudly around me, filling the small space. The ladder seemed like it might creak, but mercifully, it didn't. I followed the boy up, sometimes looking through a pair of ghostly buns.

We reached the upper landing and stood before another door and I had a sense that we were very high up. As high as the mosaic dome, no doubt.

"In here?" I asked.

Leland nodded. He had now made a full appearance, and I could see all the fine details of his handsome young face, a face that was now creased with concern.

Who knew ghosts could crease?

When I reached for the door knob, he seized my wrist with hands solid enough to pull my own away. Crazy goose bumps appeared instantly up and down my arm. He shook his head vigorously.

"It'll be okay," I said quietly. "Thank you for your help."

"Please," Leland said, speaking for the first time, his voice a grating whisper. "There's a very bad man inside."

I smiled and reached out and touched his face. A shiver went through me again.

"I'm pretty bad myself," I said, and opened the door.

43.

The door opened loudly enough to wake the dead.

Hell, maybe it did.

Although I doubted I would ever sneak up on the vampire, any hope of doing that went out the window.

Or through the squeaky door.

The ghost teen stayed behind, clearly worried, and anything that worried a ghost should seriously worry me, too, I figured.

Except, I rarely backed down from a fight, even back in the days when I was very mortal. Bullies and assholes never scared me, and this French vampire piece-of-a-bitch was clearly both.

A narrow catwalk encircled the entire area, branching off in both directions. Above me was the inverted arch, sealing off the night sky. A small pinprick of moonlight made its way through a window. An open window, actually, and I suddenly realized how the vampire had been coming and going.

Below, the floor dropped down about twenty feet, to what appeared to be more storage. With the dome arching two stories above, there was, in total, about forty to fifty feet of open space here. Big enough for one's voice to echo, and certainly big enough for a giant vampire bat to take flight.

As my eyes fully accustomed to the big, open space, I heard the sound of breathing. Short, frightened gasps. Coming from seemingly everywhere at once.

There, on the far side of the catwalk. A small figure was curled in the fetal position, shivering violently. He was still wearing his thin hospital down, which was next to useless. Fury raged through me. The boy needed immediate medical attention. The heartless piece of shit. I couldn't imagine the horror this little one had endured.

The catwalk was even more wobbly than the last staircase. As I stepped onto it, the boy's head rolled in my direction. My instincts were to run to him. Hell, anyone's instincts would have been to run to him. Running to him would have entailed racing along the metal catwalk, which curved around the inside of the circular dome and hugged the gently sloping wall.

But I forced myself to stop. To think. To wait. Hard as it was. As nearly impossible as it was. I would be of no use to the boy if I died.

Although I couldn't sense him, I knew the vampire was here. He had to be here. The only beacon of light energy that I could see formed around the boy. The vampire, like other immortals I had seen, was immune to my detection.

But he was here. Somewhere. Watching me.

The hair on the back of my neck stood on end, and that was

a completely human response to the feeling of being watched. I listened for breathing—other breathing—but heard nothing.

Wait, a flutter from above.

I looked up sharply. The tiny silhouette of a bat crossing in front of the window in the upper dome.

I remembered his words: *I'm here with the other bats.*

I turned right onto the catwalk, although I could have just as easily gone left, since the boy was directly opposite me. As I walked, I held onto the rusted guardrail, all too aware that the mesh flooring beneath me felt unsafe at best.

My footfalls echoed metallically. The whole damn catwalk seemed to sway. I scanned above and around, searching for a winged creature or the tall man with the bow tie.

I considered the possibility that I was dealing with a very powerful vampire. How long had this vampire been alive? Hundreds of years? Thousands? In that time period, what dark secrets had he uncovered? Invisibility, perhaps?

I had no clue, but I hoped like hell I didn't bump into him unexpectedly. That would just suck.

Something scuttled from above, too heavy for a bat. I snapped my head up.

Nothing there, other than beams and rafters and larger, seemingly random planks of wood. No vampire bat. Although the hiding spots were few and far between, he'd certainly had enough time to pick a good one.

He was watching me now. From somewhere. Of that, I had no doubt.

I was halfway to the boy, who was now trying to sit up. He couldn't see me in the dark, but he could certainly hear me coming. Hell, the dead could hear me coming, with all this rattling.

"It's going to be okay, Eddy," I said, although I was still thirty feet away. "I'll get you home soon."

"Oh, it's most assuredly *not* going to be okay," said a voice with a French accent above.

I looked up again, and this time, crawling down through the hole in the dome like a four-legged insect, was a man.

44.

As I watched him crawl through the hole, briefly blotting out the night sky, an uncontrollable shiver raced through me. He looked so inhuman, so unnatural, so alien.

I picked up my pace, moving rapidly now along the narrow catwalk, my weight causing the whole damn thing to shudder.

"Mommy?" cried the little boy.

"It's okay, baby," I said, moving faster still. The old catwalk wasn't designed for running. I could see the screws in the walls giving way, dust sifting down everywhere.

Sweet Jesus.

The man scuttled down along the inside of the dome, defying gravity, defying logic, defying sanity. I actually paused, watching him moving rapidly over beams and I-beams, around planks and fasteners, down the smooth inside paneling with no obvious handholds.

And all of this he did upside down. He should have fallen a hundred times over.

The angle he took was a good one, because now it put him directly between me and the boy. Within moments, the man in the bow tie flipped down and dropped smoothly to his feet. He turned to face me, straightening his dinner jacket and adjusting his bow tie.

"A pleasure to finally meet you, Samantha Moon," he said, his voice so heavily accented that he was difficult to understand. "I believe you have something I want."

The little boy had found his way to his knees, where he now sat on the mesh flooring. He turned his head this way and that, trying to see us, which I doubted he could. The interior of the dome was pitch black.

I had no intention of leaving here without the boy—and without my medallion. Yes, I wanted my cake and I wanted to eat it, too. I realized I needed more time. I needed to know what I was up against.

"What's your name?" I asked.

"Now," he said in his heavy French accent, "is that really important?"

Behind the gaunt figure, I saw for the first time the outline of a narrow door, maybe just a few feet from the little boy. Where the door led off to, I hadn't a clue. For all I knew it was a storage closet.

I said, "Then I guess you wouldn't mind if I call you Shithead."

He cocked his head slightly and his lips might have formed a smile. He was taller than me by a lot. Tall and thin and ghastly, the quintessential vampire. He advanced toward me, which was a good thing, I realized. Anything to get him away from the boy.

I held my ground.

The far less selfish thing for me to do was hand over the medallion and save the sick boy. But what about my son? How could I at least not first pursue another alternative?

Yes, I wanted my cake and to eat it, too.

It was then that I felt a heavy presence surround me, a sticky, sickly, foreign presence. It pushed on me, prodding me, trying to gain entrance. And just as suddenly the presence retreated.

"You are a strong one, *mademoiselle*," he said, frowning, clearly not happy. "Stronger than most. Too strong for even me to gain access."

"Lucky me," I said.

Whether or not the vampire could feel the ghost behind me, I didn't know, but I sure as hell could. Leland was clearly agitated, watching all of this from the shadows of the door, and I had an idea, recalling how the teen ghost had nearly manifested a physical hand for me to grab.

Leland, sweetie, I thought. *I need your help.*

Although behind me, I saw in my mind's eye the young man suddenly perk up, his countenance brightening. He didn't speak, but I had his attention.

When one is open to such communication, words and thoughts tend to be the same, and so I focused my thoughts on the door behind the boy.

Where does this lead to, Leland?

An image was returned to me, one of a long and narrow hallway, similar to the one that had granted us access to within the dome. Leland had recognized the door.

Good, I thought. *Thank you.*

As quickly as I could, I explained what I needed. He nodded

eagerly and disappeared. To where he went, I hadn't a clue. Would he help me? I didn't know that, either. I was noticing that ghosts, although quite social, weren't the best communicators.

I turned my attention back to the tall man who was watching me curiously. "I have lived a long, long time, Miss Moon," he said. "I'm tired of these old bones. I'm tired of this world, of this race. I'm tired of feeding . . . constantly feeding. Mostly I'm tired of the loneliness. The eternal loneliness. You will feel it someday, Miss Moon, if you haven't already."

His words were oddly hypnotic, captivating me in ways that I hadn't experienced before. I suspected this creature before me had mastered various levels of hypnotism or persuasion, or whatever the hell he was doing with his haunting voice.

I shook my head, cleared my thoughts, and imagined a sort of psychic barrier between me and this son-of-a-bitch. Except I didn't need a barrier. I needed ear plugs.

"I choose a French accent because I have lived most often in Paris, and this accent suits me. I enjoy hearing it. But I could just as easily switch to Baroque or German or ancient languages of which you would have no comprehension. This will be you someday, Miss Moon. When all those you love are long gone, when you find yourself alone yet again, speaking dead languages, and seeking new lands, new faces, new loves, new hunting grounds. And when even these places have been used up, you will set out again. And again. Forever seeking. But never finding."

"Are you quite done, Shithead?"

He paused and smiled. "You are a rare treat. I do not want to kill you, but I will. Please give me the medallion, then take the boy and be gone."

"Maybe," I said.

He cocked his head, and was about to speak when we both heard it. The squeak of a door being opened, perhaps for the first time in decades.

Bow Tie looked back just in time to see a brightly energetic being appear in the doorway.

Leland, and he had fully manifested. He was reaching for Eddy, having solidified enough to take the boy's hand.

Bow Tie growled furiously and lunged backwards.

I didn't growl, but I lunged, too.

45.

I had a small advantage since I was already facing forward.

I quickly covered the ground between us, and before Bow Tie could pick up any real speed, I hurled myself onto his back.

I had a brief glimpse of Leland, now fully manifested, gripping Eddy's hand, before the vampire and I toppled over the railing and fell briefly through space . . .

Unfortunately, the gangly bastard landed on me. I slammed my head hard, stars bursting behind my eyelids. The pain was severe but only fleeting. Already, my head was clearing, and as I looked up, past the vampire on top of me, I could see the ghost teen slipping back through the side door, gently pulling the little boy with him.

With any luck, the boy would never know that an honest-to-God ghost was leading him through the dark hallway.

Bow Tie looked wildly up, too, just as Leland and the boy spirited away through the narrow door. He made a move to get up, but I moved, too. I bucked my legs hard and sent the asshole flying over me, where he crashed hard, knocking over all sorts of shit that I couldn't see from my present position.

I stood and turned.

"Leave him alone," I said. "It's between you and me now."

The vampire, who had briefly disappeared behind some toppled night tables and desks, now stood, easily rising to his feet. His arm, I saw, was badly dislocated at the elbow. He winced slightly as he held it out, and what he did next didn't surprise me, although it caused the bile to rise up in the back of my mouth.

He gripped his forearm below the elbow and twisted and wrenched until his arm was back in place. All of this was accompanied by horrific sounds of bone grating against bone, of tendons grinding. He briefly made a face, but was soon opening and closing his hand. He next flexed his arm and seemed pleased with the results.

He looked at me.

"You are strong, little one. Stronger than most. You are a very unusual creature. Who made you?"

"Made me?"

"Who ended your mortal life, dear? And gave you immortality?"

"Let's not worry about that."

He stepped over the desk in one big stride, his long legs making the move seemingly effortless. As he did so, something else fell and settled behind him, kicking up even more dust, all of which plumed around like a personal thunderstorm. He stepped out of the dust and faced me.

"Yes, Kingsley said you would be a feisty one, but he never told me just how powerful you were."

My jaw dropped. "Kingsley?"

"Oh? You didn't realize that he's a good friend of mine? Or, rather, a client of mine." He cocked his head, clearly enjoying the obvious shock on my face. "Why, who do you think told me about the medallion, my dear?"

Now my jaw dropped open, and I felt as if someone had sucker punched me. Bow Tie began circling me, not approaching me directly, but in a circuitous route, as if sizing me up. There wasn't much to size up, trust me.

"And who do you think supplies him with his blood for his many . . . guests."

"Many guests?"

"Oh, I assume he has many guests. After all, I keep the red stuff coming fairly regularly."

I thought of the blood I had drank just a few weeks ago. It had come from *him*. This bastard. And where had Bow Tie gotten it? No doubt a most unwilling donor.

I felt sick. I felt betrayed. I felt pissed.

"Oh, don't be too hard on the big oaf," said Bow Tie. "I can be very persuasive when I want to be. You see, not everyone can resist me as you did. Not even Kingsley. Unfortunately for him, and you, he let it slip that something of great importance had turned up. And all it took were a few suggestions, a few tonal changes in my voice, and soon he was telling me everything I needed to know. I doubted the big bad wolf had any clue just how desperately I've been looking for your medallion. I knew it was in the area, and I had even narrowed down the city. Clues, rumors, whispers. All of which I paid attention to."

Some of my anger toward Kingsley had abated. But still. Why

had Kingsley even mentioned the medallion, or even hinted at it? Big oaf indeed. And how could Kingsley befriend such a fucking piece of shit like Bow Tie?

And what most pissed me off was this: who was Kingsley sharing the blood with, if not me? At last count, I had only had two glasses of the "red stuff."

Big picture, Sam, I thought. *Deal with Kingsley later.*

As we circled, I reached down and felt for the medallion . . . only to discover my jeans had torn during the fall from the catwalk.

Oh, shit!

Panic ripped through me until I felt the familiar bulge of the disc. Not risking my torn pocket, I extracted the medallion, and as I did so, Bow Tie nearly dove at me. But he kept his composure. Instead, a strange light flared in his eyes. I certainly had his entire attention. The exhaustion I had seen earlier was gone, replaced now with desperation.

I did the only thing I could think of to keep the medallion safe.

I slipped the leather strap over my head, dropping the medallion down inside my blouse—and that's when it happened.

Boy, did it happen.

46.

"No!" shouted the vampire, his voice echoing everywhere.

To my utter shock, the medallion began burning my chest, so much so that I yelped. Steam was coming off my flesh, rising up from my blouse.

"You stupid girl!" he spat angrily. "You stupid, stupid girl. Do you realize what you've done?"

I looked up, confused as hell and wincing. The burning was not pleasant.

Bow Tie stepped closer. "You've sealed the medallion to yourself forever."

"I don't understand—"

"Of course not, because you're a stupid girl."

Pain or not, the guy was pissing me off. "Say that again, asshole, and see what happens."

But he was right. I reached down and immediately winced. My skin was tender, but already it was healing, and forming *over* the medallion. Amazingly, horrifyingly, the golden disk was now embedded *into* my chest.

Oh, no. No, no, no!

Bow Tie was shaking his head. "You and the medallion are one, forever, *mademoiselle*. Perhaps good for you, but not for me. And certainly not for your little one, whom you had hoped to save from an eternity of . . . this. There's no way to remove it." He paused and cocked his head. "Well, there is *one* way."

He pulled out a small pistol from inside his coat pocket. He pointed it at me haphazardly. "It's true. I cannot die from silver. Not anymore. Not ever." He leveled the weapon at me. "But you are not so fortunate, my dear. Five silver bullets. Only one needs to find your heart."

Not everyone is a great shot, even vampire assholes. The agency teaches you to be a moving target, which is always harder to hit than a stationary one.

I dove right, rolling just as the first shot was fired. The sound was so damn loud and echoing that it appeared he fired dozens of time.

I rolled again and had a brief glimpse of the vampire calmly taking aim. It's a surreal experience having someone take aim at you with a gun. To want to hurt you, to kill you.

All the talk of immortality was out the window. With a simple silver bullet, my six-year immortal run would be over.

They say your life flashes before your eyes, but mine didn't. Not then. I only thought of Tammy and Anthony. That's it. No more. I didn't think of Fang or my sister or even Kingsley. I thought only of my children and what would happen to them without their freaky mother.

I rolled again when he fired. This time I felt an impact in my right shoulder. I cried out, clutching my shoulder, incapable of rolling or even really moving.

"Hurts, doesn't it?" said the vampire. "We are elemental creatures, finely attuned to the days and nights. We crave the metals in blood: zinc, iron, copper, magnesium. Is it no surprise, then, that another metal, silver, can destroy us? Well, some of us."

He seemed to smile, but it was hard to tell. Tears had burst from my eyes. The pain was intense. Too intense. I could barely focus or function.

He leveled the gun again, and I could not imagine more pain. I could not imagine another impact. I couldn't handle it. It would be too much. Way too much.

I turned away, my reflexes still amazingly sharp.

The bullet went through my neck. The shock sent me into a spasm. I went from clutching my shoulder to clutching my neck. The bullet had exited the side of my neck, exploding out, leaving a massive crater behind. Blood pumped over my hands, down over my shirt, down into my windpipe and lungs. I choked and gagged and flopped on the ground, drowning in my own blood.

Except I didn't need air to breathe, and so I wasn't really drowning.

I backed away, clutching my throat, blood gushing everywhere. The wounds were capable of closing. I tried to cough but couldn't. I felt like I was drowning, but I wasn't.

Bow Tie stepped closer and took careful aim.

Somewhere inside me, I had kept count of the bullets. Three shots. Two left. So far I was alive. So far he had missed my heart.

He stepped closer and took dead aim.

"Missed again," he said. "But not this time. I hope to see you in the next life."

I tried to move, but I slipped on my own blood, I fell to my back, still clutching my bleeding throat. All thoughts of my kids were gone. I only saw darkness. I only saw the bastard standing over me, taking careful aim at my chest.

And that's when I saw something else. Something else moving rapidly, leaping down from the catwalk above and covering the space between us in a blink of an eye. Something impossibly big, impossibly powerful.

Impossibly, it was Kingsley.

47.

A shot was fired, but it went wild.

It went wild because the great dark creature who had bounded over the railing and landed on the floor twenty feet below had slammed hard into the vampire. The force of the collision was enough to send the tall vampire hurtling off to one side, crashing beyond my field of blurred vision.

The gunshot had surely been as loud and echoing as the others had been, but to me it sounded distant and faint. I was seriously losing it and losing it fast.

I had a ground's-eye view of what happened next, although the images were sometimes too fast for even me to fully grasp.

The dark shadow was indeed Kingsley. He was in human form, which was no surprise since this was not a night of a full moon. But there was something about him. Something that was hard for my fading mind to grasp. But he seemed bigger, impossibly fast, and so damn . . . inhuman.

I tried to sit up, but I couldn't. Instead, I rolled my head toward the action, and as I did so, I felt the gristle and bone in my neck crunch. More blood pumped free and I choked all over again. And as I choked, a presence hovered over me. A handsome, smiling, angelic face. A face with a bloody lower jaw.

Leland was here and he was kneeling next to me, trying his best to hold my head in his transparent arms that faded in and out of solidity.

From this position, I watched with horrific fascination as a battle waged. The vampire was fast. Perhaps too fast for Kingsley. But every now and then the big guy would catch the fast-moving blood sucker with a powerful blow. To my horror, I saw that Kingsley's face was bloodied already. The faster-moving vampire had already landed blow after blow.

Leland crouched next to me, still clutching my bleeding face, watching the scene as well. I briefly wondered where Eddy was but knew he had to be safe somewhere.

Kingsley hadn't transformed, but he had taken on the mannerisms of a cornered wolf. He often crouched, his back hunched. Deep-throated growls reverberated continuously, some louder than others, all ferocious-sounding.

As the action moved across the floor of the dome, I turned my head to follow it, or tried to. Mostly I moved my eyes, all too aware that a deep darkness was encroaching from my peripheral vision. Two silver bullets had hit me. One of them, I was certain, was still lodged in my shoulder. The other, I was equally certain, had gone straight through my neck, exploding out its side.

That's going to leave a mark.

Vampire and werewolf were a blur. Fists flying. Blood flying. Shredded clothing flying. At one point, Kingsley grabbed hold of the Frenchman, and pummeled him mercilessly with fists that looked, from my perspective, as big as anvils. Bone crunched against bone.

One moment Kingsley was pummeling the son-of-a-bitch, and the next the French bastard was gone, having squirmed his way free, moving quickly.

Now the two men faced off. Kingsley, I saw, was badly beaten up, his clothing completely shredded. For all of Kingsley's might, he couldn't keep up with the speed of the Frenchman.

"Until we meet again," said the Frenchman, and in a blink, his clothing, including that damn bow tie, burst from his body. Before us was a massive winged creature. Next to me, Leland squeaked loud enough to be heard in the physical world and huddled next to me, afraid even in death. Kingsley stood unmovingly before the winged creature, taking great, heaving breaths.

A moment later, the creature's monstrous wings flapped once, twice, and then he was airborne. A few flaps later and he had burst through the top of the dome, raining wood and brick around us. Kingsley immediately shielded me, protecting me with his thick body. As he did so, blood from his wounded face dripped over me.

He looked down at me with wide, amber eyes. "I'm so sorry, Samantha. I'm so very sorry."

And that's when I blacked out.

48.

I saw the yellow light first.

Two glowing disks that hovered in front of me. One of the lights was picking at me, digging into my shoulder, causing me excruciating pain. It was the pain that had forced me back to consciousness.

I opened my eyes slowly and saw two faces hanging over me. One of them belonged to Detective Hanner, my female vampire friend, and the other was an unknown man. The unknown man was finishing up working on my shoulder. He picked up a metal dish and held it up, rattling it. Hanner peered inside. "Good work, doc."

He said, "I would normally be stitching her up but, as you can see, her wound is already healing."

"Again, thank you, doctor. Speak to no one as you leave."

"Of course." He nodded, grabbed a small handbag, and left through the back door of an ambulance.

"This is beginning to be a habit," said Hanner. She was, of course, referring to one of our last meetings when she and I had ended up in an ambulance outside of an Indian casino in Simi Valley. "And don't try to speak, Sam. Doctor Hector tells me that your throat is shredded to hell. Even for us that will take a few hours to heal. Oh, and don't worry. He's on our payroll, so to speak. So your secret is safe with him."

Full comprehension of where I was or what was going on hadn't fully settled in. I heard voices everywhere. Shouting. One woman crying. A man crying, too. Sirens.

"You see, there are a few carefully selected mortals out there who work with us. The good doctor is one such man."

Why he would help, I had no idea, but I couldn't think about that now. She saw my eyes shift towards the sound of nearby crying.

"Yes, we're still at the Mission Inn. The boy you saved is with his parents, and we can only thank you. You are proving to be quite the superhero, Samantha." She leaned over and inspected my throat. "Nasty business, made worse because it was a silver bullet. But it will heal soon enough."

I heard more sirens, some nearby, and she saw the alarm in my eyes. "Not to worry, Sam. We're already forgotten by the Riverside Police. I have a few talents of my own, and one of them is, let's just say, *persuasion*. As far as the police are concerned, we're just another ambulance waiting to help."

I soon recognized another voice from outside, coming closer.

Hanner reached over and patted my knee. "I imagine you're

going to want to speak with Kingsley." She smiled warmly and touched the back of my hand. "Well, you know what I mean."

As she left, Kingsley Fulcrum and his massive bulk eased into the ambulance.

49.

"Doctor Hector tells me you can't speak, maybe that's just as well," said Kingsley. He had eased down at the foot of the gurney. I think my end of the metal bed had risen an inch or two.

Kingsley was hunched into a sort of cannonball, his meaty knees up around his chest. He looked uncomfortable and didn't seem to know what to do with his thick arms. He was dressed in another shirt, clearly one that wasn't his own, since that had been bloodied and shredded. His own wounds had long since healed.

He reached out and touched my right ankle which was poking out of the thick blanket covering me. I flinched and withdrew it. He nodded to himself. "I deserved that. I deserve, in fact, for you to never talk to me again. I should consider myself lucky that I have you here, alone, in this small place, so that you are more or less forced to hear my apology."

I was still in some pain, as the effects of the silver bullet still lingered. Perhaps there were trace elements of silver still lodged in my muscle tissue? Lord, I hoped not. Or, more than likely, my actual muscles and tendons and flesh supernaturally mending themselves.

Lord, I'm such a freak.

Kingsley's longish hair spilled over his collar. Known as a maverick lawyer, Mr. Fulcrum propagated the image by keeping his hair long and thick and lustrous. Then again, maybe his flowing locks were a result of his own particular wolfish condition. Now, for the first time in a long time, Kingsley looked at me so tenderly that my heart heaved.

"You took a helluva beating tonight, kid. I'm sorry you had to go through that alone. I should have been there earlier to help." He made a move to pat my ankle again, but stopped himself. This time I wasn't so sure I would have moved my leg. "You deserved better. You deserved a friend who supported you through thick and thin, good and bad. Who am I to tell you how to run your life, how to deal with your dying boy? Who am I to play God from afar? You made the best choice you could, and I should have been there to support you. My God, I'm an ass, and I almost lost you forever because of it. Look at you, babe. You can't even talk. Your poor throat. And you did this all to help another boy, risking life and limb and the very medallion you need to help your son, and I couldn't even be there for you."

Now I did something that surprised even me. I leaned forward and took his warm hand. It took both of mine to comfortably hold one of his, and we gripped each other like this for a few minutes.

I wanted to tell him that he did come, that he did help me, that he did save my ass, but I couldn't speak, nor could I penetrate Kingsley's thoughts. An immortal, he was closed to me.

He chuckled lightly, running his thick thumb over the back of my hand. "I bet you're wondering how I came to be there on time. Well, the *on time* part was dumb luck. The being here part, not so much. I realized I had made an egregious error when I had mentioned the medallion to Dominique." He caught my raised eyebrows. "Oh, you didn't know his name?"

Ah, so the bastard had a name. Dominique. I was certain I hadn't seen the last of him.

Kingsley continued, "I can't be certain, but I think Dominique has been around long enough to read the minds of fellow immortals. But that's no excuse. I've been around long enough to learn how to guard myself from such an attack. I suspected he scanned my thoughts and knew that you and that damn medallion were heavy on my thoughts. He then mentioned something about it and I felt oddly . . . *compelled* to tell him what I knew. He's a bastard. A sneaky bastard, but what do you expect from a blood dealer? Still, I should have been more guarded in his presence."

Kingsley looked away and I wanted to desperately ask him about the blood. Who else was he sharing it with? Another woman? Should I even care if it was another woman? Kingsley had been famous as a womanizer. Did his harem of women also include vampires? It seemed so unlikely. But my thoughts were cut short when Kingsley went on.

"I knew he was staying at the Mission Inn. In fact, he's been here for quite some time. After I blurted out the info on the medallion, I was on edge, nervous. I should have warned you. Instead, I lashed out at you, perhaps more angry at myself for not keeping your potentially dangerous artifact a secret. And when I heard about the kidnapping at the hospital, it seemed fairly obvious to me what had happened, and I headed out to the Mission Inn immediately. I have fairly good instincts, too, and, as you might imagine, a helluva sniffer."

I laughed lightly, which tore at my throat. I reached for it immediately, wincing.

"Easy," he said. "No more laughing, young lady. Anyway, I'm quite familiar with your scent and I was soon on the trail."

What every woman wants to hear, I thought.

I think he read my expression. "Oh, nothing bad, of course. Your scent is all your own, and the way my own supernatural hard-wiring works, I can distinguish individual scents from thousands, even millions, of other scents. Call it my gift. Hey, you turn into a giant vampire bat and I can smell feet."

I slapped his hand and stifled my laughter. He squeezed my hand tenderly and looked at me so deeply that I felt a stirring deep in my heart. Love?

Damn him.

"Anyway, I was soon following a winding pair of stairs when I came across a rather strange young man. Poor guy looked like he'd been through hell, face bloodied and all. He immediately led the way down a side hallway, up another flights of stairs, and that's when I heard the gunshots. I came running, fast. Where the young man went off to, or who he was, I haven't a clue—"

Leland had, of course, been there by my side, comforting me the best way he knew how. A sweet guardian angel with a crush.

Kingsley went on, "And before I knew it, I was on top of Dominique and I think you know the rest. The boy, Eddy, I believe, is safely with his family and apparently unhurt. Interestingly, he too spoke of a young man leading him out to safety. I suspect it was the same young man who had helped me. Do you know him, Sam?"

I simply nodded.

"Well, he's an unsung hero and there are a lot of people who want to thank him. The police are looking, of course, for the man who kidnapped Eddy, but for the most part, the police are unaware of your involvement, Sam. Thanks in part to Detective Hanner. She can put quite a spell on people. She even went back and cleaned up your blood. Mine, too."

He continued stroking my hand, and as he did so, I saw the tears forming in his eyes. The moment his tears formed, my own came running free, too.

Damn him.

"I don't expect you to forgive me, Sam, for being a holier-than-thou ass, but if you can find it in your heart to give me one more chance, I promise I will do my best to never hurt you again. You see . . ." And now he covered my two hands with both of his, and never have I felt so protected. "I think I'm falling for you, Sam, and I don't want to screw it up any worse than I already have."

His words caught me by surprise. Mostly, because they echoed my own thoughts.

"Take care of yourself, kiddo, and take care of your little one, too. You're a good mother, and I respect you more than you can possibly know."

He leaned over the gurney and kissed me lightly on my lips, then turned away and headed out, pushing through the ambulance's door.

50.

I awoke by my son's side in the early afternoon.

With Dominique still out there, it was hard to truly feel at peace, although I suspected any attack now would be on me personally, and not my son, since the medallion was still sealed to my chest.

Where Dominique had gone, I hadn't a clue. But I would be ever vigilant for him and perhaps others like him, especially since he had proven to be such a bastard.

I soon got the news I was dying for. The doctors were releasing

Anthony later today. For now, two policeman had guard duty just outside his door. The hospital, apparently, was taking all necessary security precautions, especially since little Eddy's abductor had not been found.

I absently felt for the medallion that had melded into my flesh. I hated the irony. I possessed the very artifact that would have returned Anthony's mortality, an artifact that, apparently, was sealed to me forever.

Or so said the vampire, Dominique. I wanted a second opinion. In the least, I still wanted to find Archibald Maximus, whoever the hell he was.

My cell rang. I glanced at the faceplate. Restricted call. It was Detective Sherbet. I was sure of it.

I clicked on briefly and told him to call me back in five minutes since I was at the hospital. He called me back in four, just as I was exiting through the sliding glass doors.

"You did good, kid," he said.

"Thank you," I whispered. I still had not gotten the full use of my voice back. Not to mention that my shoulder still hurt.

"Interestingly, no one mentioned you in any reports. Only a young man who saved the day."

"God bless him."

"Apparently the little boy had been held captive, albeit briefly, within one of the domes. They found damage to the ceiling and what appeared to be an epic fight. You wouldn't happen to know anything about this, would you, Sam?"

"Do you really want to know?"

"I want to know everything, dammit."

"I've told you more than I should have."

"That's not good enough. Not in this case."

"Soon, Detective. I've had a rough night."

"I bet. You vampires are weird. Take care of yourself, Samantha, and expect a visit from me soon."

"Looking forward to it."

"Don't sass me," he said, chuckling, and hung up.

I was about to head inside when I got another call. This one was a local Orange County number. It was probably work related but I wasn't interested. I was about to hang up when I got an overwhelming sense that I should definitely pick up.

Damn psychic ability.

I clicked on, immediately regretting it because my sunscreen wasn't applied as thick as it should have been. Already I was feeling the first wave of some serious pain.

"Samantha Moon?" asked a pleasant young man.

"You got her," I said.

"You removed a book from our library the other day and we would like it returned."

"Who is this?"

"I'm with the university."

I frowned. "How did you know about the book? How did you know it was me?"

But he ignored my question and asked cheerily: "We would like our book back, Miss Moon."

I forgot about the heat, about the searing pain. "I don't have it anymore."

"I see," said the voice, somehow even more cheerily. "Then there will be a fine. We will need that taken care of immediately."

"A fine? How much?"

"I think you know the price, Miss Moon." And the moment he said that, the medallion in my chest pulsed with heat of its own. "I will be expecting you soon."

And he hung up.

51.

I was back at the university library, and this time I was certain a bastard in a bow tie wasn't following me.

Anthony wouldn't be released for another few hours and Tammy was with Mary Lou. Feeling an odd sense that I was either stepping into a trap, or into something extraordinary, I moved through the busy ground floor, and on an impulse I stopped at the main desk.

"Who works in the Occult Reading Room?" I asked the flirty young clerk.

"In the Occult Reading Room? No one. It's a self-service reading room. But I could help you if you—"

"Thank you," I said, and turned away. I headed over to the bank of elevators. In a daze, admittedly.

At the third floor, which was as empty as the first time I had been here, with my curiosity and wariness growing exponentially, I made my way down an empty aisle, stepping lightly over the dull acrylic flooring. With each step, my shoulder ached. My throat was still raw and red and for now I kept a scarf around it. The air conditioner hummed from seemingly everywhere.

At the end of the aisle I came to the far wall. Ahead of me was the opening to the Occult Reading Room. Would the same young man be there? The young man with the bright eyes and the slightly pointed beard, a young man I hadn't thought much about the first time I had seen him, but who was now very much the object of my attention.

Prepared for just about anything, I moved forward, all too aware that the medallion on my chest was growing warmer and warmer.

The same young man was there, and he was once again sitting behind what I had assumed was an employee desk, but was, in fact, just an oversized reading desk.

I sat cautiously opposite him, noting that my own inner alarm system was as quiet as could be. In fact, I even felt oddly at peace, perhaps for the first time in a long, long time.

"You don't really work here," I said, as I sat my purse on the floor next to me.

"Not officially," he said, dipping his head slightly, apologetically.

He couldn't have been more than twenty-five, perhaps even as young as twenty. He looked like a student, surely. Other than the bright twinkle in his eye and his pointy beard, he looked unremarkable.

"Who are you?" I asked.

"Archibald Maximus, of course," he said. "You can just call me Max, though."

I stared at him a long time. His aura was violet. A beautiful violet unlike anything I had ever seen. "How old are you, Max?"

He gave me a half smile. "Does it matter?"

"I guess not," I said. I liked the way Max looked at me. He

didn't stare rudely. In fact, he seemed to find great pleasure in looking at me, as if he were soaking me up, remembering my every detail. Normally, I don't like to draw attention to myself and I like to be ignored. But sometimes I make exceptions. "You're not a student here, are you?"

He smiled warmly. "No."

"And you're not twenty-something, either?"

"Let's just say no."

We looked at each other some more. I noticed now how perfectly groomed his beard was. I also noticed that his blue eyes were not really blue . . . holy hell, were they violet?

"I . . . I don't have your book," I said.

"I know."

"I don't know what happened to it."

"That's okay."

"Do I still owe a fine?"

His lips broke into a wide smile, his cheeks rising high enough that the fine point of his beard wasn't so fine.

"I don't think the library would appreciate me taking fines for books that don't officially exist."

"I don't understand."

"It's okay if you don't understand. There's lots I don't understand, too. That's half the fun: finding answers." He leaned forward a little and his gaze locked onto the area just beneath my throat, an area that was now throbbing with real warmth.

"Ah, I see you're wearing the medallion. Or, more accurately, it's wearing you."

Which should have been a highly unlikely statement, since the medallion was currently concealed beneath my shirt.

"I . . . was protecting it. I had no idea it would . . ."

"Attach itself to you?"

"Yes."

"Would you like for me to remove it?"

"Yes. But I had heard—"

"The seal was permanent?"

"Yes."

"Normally, yes. But I'm fairly familiar with it. Would you mind?" he asked.

I shook my head and he got up from behind the desk and stepped around to me.

"Just try to relax," he said.

He put his hands on my shoulders, which sent a shiver of warm energy through me, charging me from the inside. Next he moved his fingers around my throat and slipped them down inside my shirt.

I gasped and felt a different kind of thrill.

His searching hands found the medallion, where he rested the flat of his palms over it. There was no pain, just a sense of . . . release.

A moment later he removed his hands, and held up the gleaming medallion. He grinned.

I was relieved beyond words. There was hope again. There was hope my son could live a normal life.

"Now, Sam, what would you like to do with this?"

But I was having difficulty speaking. I was so afraid to have hope, so afraid to believe. I tried speaking again: "I had heard that the medallion . . ." but I couldn't get the words out.

"You had heard that it could reverse vampirism?"

"Yes," I said, but I was terrified to hear his answer. Oh, sweet Jesus. What if he couldn't do it? Or what if he said no? What would I do then?

"Yes," he said, smiling. "The medallion can do this. Or, rather, the magic encoded within it can."

"And you . . . you can decode this?"

He nodded. "I can, Sam. And before you ask, yes, I will help your little one."

Relief flooded me. So much so that I couldn't stop shaking. He reached out and took my hand.

"You've had a rough few days, haven't you?"

I could only nod as the shaking, the relief, overcame me.

"You're never alone, Sam. Ever. As hard as life might seem, there's always hope. There's always a way, and there's always love. Always."

I waited before I was certain I could speak, then asked, "How did you know I was looking for you?"

"How do you know *I* wasn't looking for *you*?" he asked, eyes twinkling. He saw my confusion and smiled sweetly. "Very few call my name, Sam, but when they do, I listen."

I couldn't speak. I could only nod my thanks.

He said, "Now give me a few minutes. Feel free to peruse the books, but stay away from the ones that call out to you. They're trouble."

I told him I would be careful, and he slipped away into a side room and closed the door. A few minutes later, he returned holding a small glass container with a cork cap, filled with amber liquid.

"Have your son drink this tonight. He will sleep soundly for twenty-four hours, and will awaken with little memory of the past few days."

"And he will be . . . human?"

"As human as ever."

"And the medallion?" I asked.

He motioned to the amber liquid. "The medallion is no more."

I raised the glass container, mystified. "It's in here?"

He winked. "Distilled through, let's just say, highly-advanced alchemical means. And Samantha?"

"Yes?"

"There's only enough for one."

"Somehow I knew that."

"Remember, Samantha, there's always an answer. Somewhere. You just have to look."

I hugged the young man as hard as I could, and thanked him. When I finally pulled away, I saw that my own tears had stained his white shirt.

"I'm always here, Samantha, if you ever need anything."

"Here in the Occult Reading Room?"

He grinned and winked. "There's a lot to read. Oh, I have one question: How did you come upon my name?"

I told him about the creepy old gnome who lived in Fullerton. As I spoke, Max pulled on his pointed beard.

"And he bargained for your son's life?" he asked.

"I'm horrible, I know. I was desperate."

"Not to fear, Sam. One cannot bargain with another's life. Ever."

I looked at him sharply. "What do you mean?"

"I mean, your son is safe."

"And the creepy old gnome?"

"The creepy old gnome will never bother you again."

I hugged him for a second time. Somehow, even tighter.

52.

It was a week later.

Summer was in full bloom and I was working a few cases. I had two cheating spouse cases and an undercover assignment working for a shipping company to find the reason for their occasional missing shipments. Two nights ago, I had gone on a date with Kingsley, to the musical premier of *Annie* in Los Angeles. He had kissed me goodnight and bowed slightly, and I was reminded all over again of his grace and charm and just how old he really was. Yes, we still had our issues, but to his credit he had dropped his loser client once and for all.

Fang was there, too. Always texting, IMing, and emailing. During one of our exchanges, I told him that Kingsley and I were going to explore a relationship together, but I always wanted Fang as my friend.

He had paused for a few minutes before answering. When he did, he said that, of course, we would always be friends and that he was happy for me. To his credit, he appeared to be happy for me, but I could feel his hurt. We were, after all, still deeply connected.

Danny had visited the kids once, and although he seemed pleased that his son was alive and well and not a freak, as he liked to call me, I could see that his old suspicion was back. The fear was back. The hate was back.

Admittedly, I almost preferred Danny like this. I could handle his hate and suspicion. His flirting this past week had just been damn creepy.

Now it was a Saturday evening and I would work the night shift later. It was dinner time, and I called the kids in from the backyard where they were playing on a Slip N' Slide. Both were as red as tomatoes from their sun block having long since worn off, and never had I been more happy to see a sunburn on my son. Anthony was showing no ill effects from either the vampirism or the Kawasaki disease, either.

My son was back, alive and healthy. Had I altered his soul's journey? Maybe. Had I played with his karma? No doubt.

But he was back. Oh, yes, he was back.

Dripping and arguing, they came running inside, snatching hot dogs and chips. A few minutes later, Mary Lou and her family arrived. My sister gave me a big hug and Anthony an even bigger hug.

We all settled in with hot dogs and chips—or water, in my case—and put in a movie. About halfway through the movie a strong and foul smell permeated my living room, and that's when the looks started.

"Mommy did it!" Anthony cried out, giggling.

"That's it," I said, grabbing him and throwing him over my legs, exposing his bony butt to the air. I was soon playing butt bongos off his little tush while he squealed with laughter. Soon Tammy joined in and so did my sister. There might have been some tickling thrown in for good measure.

It was later, at night, when I was putting Anthony to sleep when he looked up at me and said, "Thank you, Mommy."

"For what?"

"For what you did."

"What did I do?"

"You know, Mommy," he said, and reached up and hugged me tighter than he had ever hugged me before.

[THE END]

BOOK 4.5

Christmas Moon

Vampire for Hire #4.5

DEDICATION

To H.T. Night, for all his invaluable help.
Merry Christmas, little brother.

Christmas Moon

1.

I was cleaning house in the dark and watching Judge Judy rip some cheating ex-husband a new one, when my doorbell rang. Enjoying this more than I probably should have, I hurried over to the door and opened it.

My appointment—and potential new client—was right on time. His name was Charlie Anderson, and he was a tall fellow with a short, gray beard, bad teeth, nervous eyes, and a peaceful aura. In fact, the aura that surrounded him was so serene that I did a double take.

I showed him to my back office where he took a seat in one of the four client chairs. I moved around my desk and sat in my leather chair, which made rude noises. I might have blushed if I could have.

I picked up my liquid gel pen and opened my pad of paper to a blank page. I said, "You mentioned in your email something about needing help finding something that was lost."

"Stolen, actually."

I clicked open my pen. "And what was that?"

"A safe," he said.

I think I blinked. "A safe?"

"Yes. A safe. It was stolen from me, and I need your help to find it."

He explained. The safe had been handed down through his family for many generations. It had never been opened, and no one knew what was inside. Charlie's father, now deceased, had left the safe to him nearly twenty years ago. Recently, a gang of hoodlums had moved into Charlie's neighborhood, and soon after, some of Charlie's things had gone missing. A gas can, loose change from the ashtray in his car. If he was a betting man—and Charlie assured me he wasn't—he would bet that these punks had stolen his safe.

I made notes. Charlie spoke haltingly, often circling back and repeating what he'd just said. Charlie was a shy man and he wasn't used to being the center of attention. He was even shy about being the center of attention of a smallish woman in her small back office.

"When was the safe stolen?"

"Two days ago."

"Where was it stolen from?"

"My home. A mobile home. A trailer, really."

I nodded. I wasn't sure I knew what the difference was, but kept that to myself. "And where did you keep the safe in your trailer?"

"I kept it behind the furnace."

"Behind?"

"The furnace is non-functional."

"I see."

"If you remove the blower, there's a space to hide stuff."

I nodded, impressed. "Seems like a good hiding spot to me."

"I thought so, too."

"Any chance it could have been stolen a while back, and you only recently noticed?"

He shrugged. In fact, he often shrugged, sometimes for no apparent reason. Shrugging seemed to be a sort of nervous tic for Charlie. He said, "A week ago, maybe."

"Were you alone when you checked the safe?"

"Yes."

I studied my notes . . . tapping my pen against the pad. My house was quiet, as it should be. The kids were at school. As they should be. I looked at the time on my computer screen. I had to pick them up in about twenty minutes.

At about this time of the day, my brain is foggy at best. So foggy that sometimes the most obvious question eludes me. I blinked, focused my thoughts, and ignored the nearly overwhelming desire to crawl back into bed . . . and shut out the world.

At least until the sunset. Then, I was a new woman.

Or a new *something*.

I kept tapping the tip of the pen against the pad of paper until the question finally came to me. Finally, it did. "Why would the thieves know to look behind the furnace? Seems a highly unlikely place for any thief to ever look."

He shrugged.

I said, "Shrugging doesn't help me, Mr. Anderson."

"Well, I don't know why they would look there."

"Fair enough. Did you ever tell anyone about the safe?"

"No."

"Did anyone ever see you, ah, looking at the safe?"

"I live alone. It's just me."

"Any family members know about the safe?"

"Maybe a few do, but I don't keep in touch with them."

"Do you have any children?"

"Yes."

Bingo. "Where do your kids live?"

"The Philippines, presently. I'm a retired Navy vet. My ex-wife is from the Philippines. The kids stay with her most of the time."

"But some of the time they stay with you?"

"Yes?"

"How long ago has it been since they were last with you?"

"A month ago."

More notes, more thinking. I put the pen aside. I had asked just about everything my dull brain could think of. Besides, I had to start wrapping this up.

"I can help you," I said. "But under one condition."

"What's that?"

"I get half of whatever's in the safe."

"What about the retainer fee?"

"I'll waive the fee."

"And if you don't find the safe?"

"You owe me nothing," I said.

He looked at me for a good twenty seconds before he started nodding. "I've always wondered what the hell was in that thing."

"So, do we have a deal then, Mr. Anderson?"

"We have a deal," he said.

2.

I picked up the kids from school and, as promised, we made a dollar store run. Once there, I gave the kids each a hand basket and told them to have it.

They had at it, tearing through the store like game show contestants. Tammy crammed some packages of red velvet bows in her hand basket and moved onto the jingle bells, shaking them vigorously. I chuckled as I watched little Anthony grab some scented Christmas candles. The candles filled up at least half his hand basket. Now, what did an eight-year-old need with Christmas candles? Nothing. He simply grabbed them because it was the first of the Christmas items he'd seen. I was fairly certain that he would later regret his choice.

As the kids attacked the many holiday rows, I smiled to myself and strolled casually through the mostly-clean store, trying like hell to ignore the way my legs shook, or the way my skin still burned from the five-second sprint from the minivan to the store.

Sadly, even with the winter-shortened days, we were still about two hours from sunset.

Two hours.

That thought alone almost depressed me.

Since my transmutation seven years ago, I'm supernaturally aware of the location of the sun in the sky. I can be in any building at any time and tell you exactly where the sun is, either above or below the Earth. Even now I could feel it directly above me, angling just over my right shoulder, heading west.

I powered through the shakiness and heaviness, and worked my way down an aisle of discounted hardback novels. I paused and flipped through a historical mystery novel, read a random paragraph, liked it, and dropped it into my own hand basket. For a buck, I'll try anything. Hell, the Kindle app on my iPhone was filled with free ebooks and 99-cent ebooks that I had snagged in a buying frenzy a few days ago. Now, all I needed to do was to find the time to read them. I'm sure the one about the vampire mom—written, of all people, by a guy with a beard—should give me a good laugh.

I continued down the aisle. I didn't often shop at the dollar store, but when I did, I made the most of it. And the kids, I knew, had been waiting all week for this trip.

It was, after all, a Christmas tradition with us. Each year about this time, the kids were given an empty basket and told to fill them with Christmas decorations. At a dollar a pop, no one was going to break the bank, and once home, together we hung or displayed the decorations. Usually with cookies baking in the oven. Of course, this was the first year we were doing it without Danny, but so far, neither of the kids had mentioned the exclusion of their father, and I sure as hell wasn't going to say anything.

Seven months ago, just after a rare disease nearly cost my son his life, I had filed for divorce. Just last month, the divorce had been finalized. I was technically single, although my relationship with Kingsley Fulcrum had taken on legs. Or teeth. We had grown closer and more comfortable with each other, and for that I was grateful to him.

The famed defense attorney—never known for his moral compass, nor morals of any type—had suddenly developed a conscience. Now, he was a little more selective with his defense cases, a little more discerning. He winnowed out the obvious slimeballs. Of late, he seemed to choose his clients with some care.

He did this, I knew, for me.

After all, I had found it nearly impossible to get too close to a man who actively defended murderers and cutthroats, rapists, and all-around jerk-offs. He got it. If he wanted me in the picture, he was going to have to change.

And he did.

Yeah, I'm still amazed and a little in shock.

But we were taking things slowly. I had to move slowly. Anything faster, and I would have seriously freaked out. So I only saw the big lug a few times a week, sometimes only once a week. He never stayed over . . . and only rarely did I stay over at his palatial estate. Half the time, he took me out. The other half, I cooked for him. It took me months before I formally introduced my kids to him. And even then, I only did so as my "friend."

I knew the friend comment hurt him, but he went with it. Anthony, I knew, had never seen a man this big in his life, and Kingsley was immediately the designated jungle gym. I couldn't help but laugh every time Kingsley showed up, especially in his two-thousand-dollar Armani suits, only to watch Anthony climb all over him.

I chuckled at the recent image of Kingsley sighing resignedly as Anthony used the defense attorney's massive bicep as a pull-up bar. To Kingsley's credit, he always let Anthony play, and never once did he mention his clothes. I figured that someday he would wise up and show up in jeans and a tee shirt.

We'll see.

I had just spotted an end-cap stacked with organic soup. Granted, I couldn't eat organic soup, but my kids could. And at a dollar a pop, I eagerly started scooping them up.

As I did so, I sensed someone behind me and paused and turned.

And gasped.

Okay, a small gasp. After all, I wasn't expecting to see such a beautiful man there, leaning casually against a shelf full of cheap spatulas, and smiling warmly at me. His eyes even twinkled, and I couldn't help but notice the soft, silvery aura that surrounded him. Never before had I seen a silver aura, and never an aura so alive and vibrant.

Who the hell was this guy?

I didn't know, but one thing was for sure: I was especially not expecting him to say my name, but that's exactly what he did.

He crossed his arms over his massive chest, and said, "Hello, Samantha. How are you?"

This time, I definitely gasped.

3.

A peaceful calm radiated from the tall man.

His silver aura shimmered around him like a halo. His warm smile put me immediately at ease. My inner alarm system, too, since it was as silent as could be. He wore a red cashmere turtleneck sweater, very Christmas-y looking, with relaxed fit jeans and hiking shoes. His shoes looked new. His fingers, which curled around his biceps, were long and whitish, capped by pinkish, thick nails.

"Do I know you?" I asked.

"Not directly," he said.

"Indirectly?"

"You could say that."

I wracked my brain. Had he been a client? A high school boyfriend? A friend of a high school boyfriend? Was he the boy I kissed behind the backstop in the fourth grade? Or the boy I kissed at the bus stop? Other than realizing that I showed a predisposition for love triangles at an early age, my mind remained maddeningly blank, although something nagged at me distantly.

"You got me," I said. "How do you know me?"

He continued leaning against the shelf, watching me. "Through my work."

"Your work?"

He nodded. "Yes."

"And what kind of work is that?"

"I'm a . . . bodyguard of sorts."

Technically, so was I. As a licensed private investigator in the State of California, I could legally work as a bodyguard, too. Granted, at five-foot three inches tall, I couldn't cover much of anyone's body. Still, I bring other . . . skill sets to the table.

Despite sensing no danger, my guard was up. I instinctively looked over at my kids, who were presently fighting over a huge Styrofoam candy cane, apparently the only one in the store. The candy cane promptly snapped in half like a wish bone. Anthony let out a wail. Tammy gave him her broken piece and slinked away. I would deal with her later. The kids, at least, were fine.

"I'm sorry," I said to him, "but I don't remember you."

"I wouldn't expect you to."

He spoke calmly, assuredly, with no judgment in his voice. If anything, there was a hint of humor. He watched me closely, his blazing eyes almost never leaving me. Whoever he was, I had his full attention. I nearly just wished him a merry Christmas and turned and left, but something made me stick around.

"So, what's your name?" I asked.

"Ishmael."

I almost made a *Moby Dick* joke, but held back. Truth be known, I was a little freaked out that this guy knew me, and I hadn't a clue who he was.

"Where do you know me from, Ishmael? And give it to me straight. No more double speak."

"I'm afraid you wouldn't remember me, Samantha. But I can say this: You know my client."

Ishmael was an unusual-looking man. He seemed both comfortably relaxed and oddly uncomfortable. He often didn't know what to do with his hands, which sometimes hung straight down, or crossed over his chest. He radiated serenity, but every now and then, perplexingly, a black streak of darkness, like a worm, would weave through his beautiful, silver aura. Amazingly, my inner alarm system remained silent.

"And who's your client?" I asked.

He continued to watch me. Now, he held his hands together loosely at his waist. I think the guy would have been better off utilizing his pants pockets. Another streak of blackness flashed through his aura, so fast that I nearly didn't see it. Then another.

He smiled at me in a way that few men have ever smiled at me: knowingly, lovingly, comfortably, happily, sexily.

Finally, he said, "The client, Sam, was you."

4.

We had spent the evening baking cookies and generally making a mess of the kitchen. Flour, cinnamon, sprinkles, and sugar dusted the floor, our three sets of footprints overlapping on the tile, like some mad Family Circus diagram. But what's Christmas for, if not to bake with children?

Then we all cuddled up on the couch. I had put in the *Groundhog Day* DVD and we watched it with a fresh batch of cookies and milk. Of course, I only pretended to eat my cookies, which I promptly spit back into my milk. Ah, but those few seconds of sugary delight were heaven . . . but I would pay a price for it. . . . Anything not blood, no matter how minute, would cause me severe cramping and the dry heaves later.

When the kids were in bed and I had gotten caught up on my office paperwork and billing, I grabbed my laptop and curled up on one corner of the living room couch.

You there, Fang?

No doubt, other creatures of the night were out running around . . . doing whatever it was that creatures of the night do. I knew what I did. I worked. And besides, tonight was a school night. And, despite being a professional private investigator who works the late shift, I couldn't leave my kids alone at night unless I could find a sitter.

That was why being married had been so convenient. Danny, my ex-husband, would watch the kids while I worked late. That is, until he started staying late himself, for reasons that weren't so admirable.

I drummed my fingers along the laptop case, waiting for Fang to reply. At the far end of the hallway, I could hear Anthony snoring lightly, even through his closed door. Along with my condition came an increased perception of many of my senses. Hearing and sight were two of them. I could hear and see things that I had no business hearing and seeing. The sense of taste and touch, not so much, which was just as well. I couldn't eat food anyway, and I certainly didn't need inadvertent orgasms every time someone touched my shoulder. The jury was still out on my sense of smell, although it might have increased a little. Not necessarily a good thing with a gaseous eight-year-old around. Anyway, I had always had a good sniffer, so it was kind of hard to tell for sure.

Ah . . . there he was. The little pencil icon appeared in the chatbox window, indicating that Fang was typing a response.

Good evening, Moon Dance. Or, more accurately, good middle-of-the-night.

Good middle-of-the-night to you, too.

He typed a smiley face, followed by: *So, to what do I owe the pleasure of your company, Moon Dance?*

Fang was my online confidant. He was also a convicted murderer and escaped convict with serious psychological issues. But that's another story for another time. Over the years, though, he had proven to be loyal, knowledgeable, and extremely helpful. After six years of anonymously chatting, Fang and I had finally met for the first time six months ago. The meeting had been interesting, and there had been some physical chemistry.

But then came "The Request."

Again, six months ago, back when my son was losing his battle with the extremely rare Kawasaki disease, Fang had asked me to turn him into a vampire.

Now, that's a helluva request, even among close friends. At the time I was dealing with too much and had told him so. He understood. His timing was off. He got it. We hadn't discussed his request for a while now, but it was always out there, simmering, seething just below the current of all our conversations. We both knew it was out there. We both knew I would get around to it when the time was right.

And what would be my answer? I didn't know. Not yet. The question, for now, was bigger than I was. I need time to wrap my brain around it. To let it simmer. Percolate. Brew.

But someday, perhaps someday soon, I would give him my answer.

I wrote: *I have a question.*

You usually do, Fang replied.

What do you know of silver auras?

They're common, although they're usually associated with other colors, why?

I saw a silver aura today, but a bright one. Perhaps the brightest I'd ever seen. A radiant, glorious silver.

No other colors?

I shook my head, even though he couldn't see me shaking my head. *Just silver,* I typed.

Hang on.

There was a long pause, and I suspected Fang was either thinking or Googling or consulting what I knew to be a vast, private occult library. I knew something of occult libraries . . . having met a curious young curator of such a library, six months ago.

I waited. My house was mostly silently, other than Anthony's light snoring. Was it normal for an eight-year-old to snore? I wondered if I should have that checked. These days, after the ordeal with Kawasaki disease, I was constantly on guard with Anthony's health.

Fang came back, typing: *Please describe him to me, Moon Dance.*

Tallish, I wrote. *Well-built. Narrow waist. Broad shoulders. Smiled a lot.*

What did he say to you?

I thought about that. *Said he knew me, and had known me from way back, that he worked with me . . . or implied that he had worked with me. He knew my name.*

But did you recognize him?

No.

What about your inner alarm system? Did he trigger it? Were you on guard?

Quite the opposite, I wrote. *If anything, I felt at peace.*

There was a long delay, then finally, Fang's words appeared in the IM chat box:

Unless I'm mistaken, Moon Dance, I believe you just met your guardian angel.

5.

Charlie lived in a single-wide trailer.

Although the trailer looked old, it appeared well-enough maintained. As I approached the door in the late evening, I realized that I had never been inside a single-wide trailer.

Somehow, I controlled my excitement.

The exterior was composed of metal siding, and there was a lot of junk piled around the house. Controlled junk, as it was mostly on old tables and shelving. Lawn mower parts, fan belts, engine parts, and just about everything else that belonged in a garage, except the mobile home didn't have a garage.

The front door was, in fact, a sliding glass door. Charlie, apparently, used the mobile home's rear door as his front door. A quick glance around the home explained why: The front door had no steps leading up to it.

Leading up to the sliding glass door was a small wooden deck, which I used now. I peered inside. It was the living room, and where the exterior had controlled mayhem, the interior was a straight-up mess. Charlie Anderson, it appeared, was a hoarder. The shelving theme from outside was extended to the inside. Shelves lined the walls, packed with plastic containers, themselves filled with computer parts, cables, and other electronic doodads. Interestingly, not a single book lined his book shelves. The floor was stacked with newspapers and speakers and car radios and old computer towers in various stages of disarray. Boxes were piled everywhere. And not neatly. Dog toys and old bones littered the floor. A huge TV sat in the far corner of the room, draped in a blanket, while a much smaller TV sat next to it, currently showing something science-fictiony. Zombies or robots, or both.

I was just about to knock on the glass door when a fat little white terrier sprang from the couch and charged me, barking furiously. All teeth and chub. But at the door, it suddenly pulled up, stopped barking, and looked at me curiously. I looked back at it. It cocked its head to one side. I didn't cock my head.

Then it whimpered and dashed off.

As it did so, I heard more movement . . . the sound of someone getting out of a recliner, followed by Charlie Anderson's happy-go-lucky, round face.

He let me in, asking if I'd found the place okay. I assured him I had. Once inside, I could fully appreciate just how much crap Charlie had. And yet . . . I had a sneaking suspicion that Charlie knew exactly where all his junk was.

"Nice place you have here." I was speaking facetiously, and a little in awe, too.

But Charlie took it as a real compliment, bless his heart.

"Thanks, but it's just home. I used to worry about cleaning and stuff like that, but I figured what's the point? My friends call me a hoarder, but I just like junk. I think there's a difference."

"Sure," I said.

He looked at me eagerly. "So, you agree there's a difference?"

I could tell he wanted me to agree, to confirm that he didn't have a hoarding problem, that he was just another guy with thousands of glass jars stacked on a long shelf over his kitchen table. The jars, as far as I could tell, were filled with every conceivable nut and bolt known to man. Thank God they weren't filled with human hearts. I leaned over. The jar cloest to me was filled with—and I had to do a double take here—*bent* nails.

"Yes," I said. "There's a huge difference."

Charlie exhaled, relieved. I think we might have just bonded a little. "I think so, too," he said, nodding enthusiastically. "Would you like a Diet Pepsi?"

"I'm okay."

"Water?"

"I'm fine. Maybe you can show me where you kept the safe, Charlie?"

"Oh, yes. Right this way."

He led me through his many stacks of random junk. We even stepped around an old car fender. A fender. Seriously? Lying next to the fender was the upper half of a desk, the half with the doors that no one ever uses. There was no sign of the lower half anywhere. Just the upper. Seriously?

But there was more. So much more.

The junk seemed eternal. I already felt lost, consumed. How anyone could live like this, I didn't know. The junk almost seemed to take on a life of its own, as if it was the real inhabitant of the house, and we were the strangers, the trespassers. Indeed, I could even see the chaotic energy, bright and pulsating, swirling throughout the house. Crazy, frenetic energy that seemed trapped and still-connected to the many inanimate objects.

Energy, I knew, could attach to an object, especially an object of great importance, and so, really, I wasn't too surprised to see the spirit of the old woman hanging around an even older-looking piano. Granted, the piano itself was mostly covered in junk, but the old woman didn't seem to care much about that.

"Where did you get this piano?" I asked.

As I spoke, the old woman, who had mostly been ignoring us, turned and looked at me with some interest.

Charlie, who was about to lead the way down a narrow hallway, paused, and looked back. "My neighbor was throwing it out."

"Why?"

"He was moving. I guess it belonged to his mother, who was a music teacher, I think. She died a few years back. I shored up my floor with some extra jacks underneath and pushed it through the sliding glass door. It wasn't easy, but I got it in here."

"Do you play?" I asked.

"No."

"Have you ever, ah, heard it play before?"

"What do you mean?"

"I mean, have you ever heard it play on its own?"

He looked at me, seemed to think about, or, more accurately, decide how much he wanted to tell me, then finally nodded. "Yeah, sometimes. Just a few notes. I figure it's mice."

"Do you believe in ghosts?" I asked. As I did so, the old lady drifted up from the piano seat where she'd been sitting along with some stacks of automobile manuals.

"Why do you ask?"

The woman approached me carefully. She was composed of a thousands, if not millions of staticky, supernatural filaments of super-bright light. Sometimes the filaments dispersed a little. When they did, she grew less distinct. Sometimes they came together tightly, and when they did, she took on more form, more details. As she approached, I could see where light pulsated brightly at the side of her head, and knew that she had died of a brain aneurysm. She reached out a hand, which looked so bright and detailed that it could have been physical. I reached out my own and took hers, and as I did so, a shiver coursed through me.

In that moment, I had an image of a school, with many dozens of children playing this very piano.

"No reason," I said. "But, wouldn't you think this piano would do some kids some good? Maybe at an elementary school?"

Charlie blinked hard, thought about that. Giving up his junk, I knew, was a torturous act. He shrugged. "Yeah, I suppose."

"Would you do that for me?"

He shrugged again. "Sure. But why?"

The old woman, who was still holding my hand, had covered her face with her other hand. Shivers continued up and down my arm. "Seems the right thing to do, doesn't it?"

Charlie shrugged. "Yeah, I suppose so. I am sort of worried about the floor. Even with the extra jacks underneath. I'll do it tomorrow. I can check around with some schools."

"You're a good man, Charlie Brown."

He smiled and turned a little red. I released the old woman's hand, who smiled and drifted back to the piano. As I did so, I had a thought, "When did you acquire the piano?"

"Last week."

"Before or after the theft of the safe?"

"After. Why?"

Ghosts, I knew from firsthand experience, made for excellent witnesses. Unfortunately, the timing didn't line up here. "No reason," I said.

Charlie studied me, shrugged for the millionth time, and led me over to the furnace, which was located about halfway down the hallway. Once there, he removed the metal cover, set it down, and grabbed a flashlight from the nearby bathroom.

"I kept the safe in here," he said, and shined the light at an empty space above the furnace. "I just set it in there."

"It wasn't bolted in?"

"No. It's heavy, but so's the furnace. The safe just sat right where the old blower used to be. The thing broke ages ago. That's it right over there."

He pointed the flashlight over to a dome-shaped, metal-encased fan. Surrounding the fan were a lot of old baggies full of random screws and washers. One of the baggies even had baggies in it. Hoarding at its purest.

"Can you give me a minute alone?" I asked.

"Sure . . . you gonna dust for prints or something?"

"Or something," I said.

He nodded and smiled eagerly, anything to please me. No doubt anything to please anyone. He stepped back through his labyrinthine hallway, contorting his body this way and that, and when he was gone, I went to work.

6.

First, I scanned the hallway.

I noted a window directly opposite the furnace. The window was covered by both blinds and a curtain. Upon closer inspection, I saw that the blind wasn't really made for this window. It was a half inch too narrow . . . perhaps just narrow enough for someone to see through.

I next ran my fingers along the dusty curtain, and what struck me immediately was how thin the material was. Thin and see-through. Individually, the blinds were too narrow and the curtains too thin. But together, they should have done the job of keeping away prying eyes.

I thought about that as I scanned his hallway . . . and spotted the oscillating fan at the end. The fan was turned off, but I had another thought.

I went over to it and turned it on. It faced into what appeared to be Charlie's bedroom. Then it started oscillating, turning briefly toward the hallway. The blast of air from the fan wasn't much. But it was enough. A moment later, the hem of the curtain fluttered up.

I watched three or four revolutions of the fan, and each time, the hem of the curtain fluttered higher and higher. I went back to the window and studied it, and as I studied it, an image began to form in my thoughts.

The image coalesced into that of a young man standing just outside the window. I closed my eyes and the image came into sharper focus. A young man who was watching Charlie. Standing just outside the trailer. Late at night.

Who the person was, I hadn't a clue. Why he happened to be standing just outside the trailer, I didn't know that either. My psychic hits are just that. Hits. Not all-knowing information. Glimpses of information. Snapshots of information. It was up to me to dig deeper, to decipher, to probe, and ultimately to figure out what the hell it all meant.

I went back into the living room, walked around the upper half of a recliner—just the upper half, mind you—and found

Charlie scratching his fat little pooch. The dog saw me, promptly piddled on the carpet, and dashed off into the kitchen. Or what should have been a kitchen. In Charlie's world, it was just another storage room.

"Rocko!" he shouted, but Charlie didn't really sound angry. He sounded shocked, if anything. He immediately produced a rag from somewhere on his person and went to work on the pee stain in the carpet. "I don't know what's gotten into him."

"Maybe he smells my sister's cat on me," I said, since it seemed safer to say than: *It's probably because I'm a blood-sucking fiend, and dogs, for some reason, can sense us.*

"Maybe," said Charlie. "But dogs are going to be dogs, ya know? You can't get mad at them for being dogs."

I smiled at his simple philosophy. I asked, "Do you ever leave Rocko alone?"

"Sometimes, but he likes to ride in the car with me."

"So there are times when your house is completely empty?"

"I suppose so, yeah."

As he cleaned, I asked him how often he checked on the safe. He looked up at me from the floor, a little sweat already appearing on his brow as he worked at the dog pee. "Well, I don't really check it."

"What do you do?"

He looked away, suddenly embarrassed. He stopped scrubbing the floor. His balding head gleamed. "I guess I sometimes look at it."

"Look at it?"

He thought some more. "Well, I guess it reminds me of my dad, you know? And my grandfather. We all had the safe at one time or another. We all talked about it. And sometimes . . ." But Charlie suddenly got choked up and couldn't continue.

So I finished for him. "And sometimes when you looked at it, or when you touched it, you could feel your father and grandfather nearby."

Charlie wiped his eyes and nodded and looked away.

7.

Admittedly, the blood wasn't very Christmas-y.

It was late and I was alone in my office with a packet of the good stuff, freshly delivered today from the slaughterhouse in Norco. As I slit open the top of the plastic bag with a fingernail that was a little too thick and a little too sharp, I reflected on what I knew about blood.

Fresh blood energized me, lifted me, made me feel more than human. With fresh blood flowing through my veins, I felt like I could do anything. And for all I knew, maybe I could.

Acquiring fresh blood is another issue altogether.

I'm not a killer, although I have killed. To drink fresh blood implies two things: it has either been taken . . . or freely given. The freely given part was a concept I was still wrapping my brain around. One of the perks of dating Kingsley these past few months was that he always kept a fresh supply of hemoglobin for me. Where he got it, I may never know, and he wasn't telling. All I knew was that it made me feel like a new woman. Hell, like a new species.

But I will not take blood unwillingly from humans, although I certainly could if I wanted to. I imagined there were others like me out there who took from others when and where they wanted it. I suspected that many of the missing person cases around the world were a result of this, although I could be wrong, since I'm not exactly immersed in the vampire sub-culture. I'm immersed in my kids and school and work, and dealing with an ex-husband who had revamped his efforts to bring me down. How he would do this, I don't know, but if ever there was someone who ran hot and cold, it was Danny.

Bi-polar, as my sister put it.

I studied the semi-clear packet of blood. The packet was no bigger than my hand. I didn't need much blood, and a packet this size would keep me going for three or four days. I didn't need to drink nightly, although I could, if I chose to. As I studied the packet, a thick animal hair rotated slowly within. Shuddering, I fished it out and flicked it in the waste basket.

Blech.

Hating my life, I brought the packet to my mouth, tilted it up, and drank deeply as the thick blood filled my mouth. I ignored the bigger chunks of flesh, and only gagged two times. I kept drinking until the packet was empty, until I'd squeezed out every last drop.

When I did, I shuddered and closed my eyes and willed the blood to stay down. I kept my fist over my mouth and kept shuddering. When I opened my eyes, I saw him standing there, in the far corner of my office, watching me.

The man from the dollar store.

Or, as Fang put it . . . my guardian angel.

8.

I gasped.

I might be a creature of the night, but that doesn't mean I don't get startled. My first instinct was to dash toward the door of my office, which is what I did, blocking the stranger from further access into my house. One moment I was sitting at my desk, downing a packet of cow blood, gagging, and the next, I was standing guard at my office door.

"I didn't mean to startle you, Samantha."

"Of course not, asshole. Which is why you appeared suddenly in my office. You have five seconds before I throw you through that wall."

I was a mixture of rage and confusion. The adrenaline-fueled rage for obvious reasons. The confusion because my inner alarm system had been completely bypassed. What the hell was going on?

I kept an ear out towards my kids, listening hard, but all I could hear was Anthony's light snoring. Tammy wasn't snoring, but I could sense her there in her room, curled up in her bed, one arm tucked under her pillow.

"Your extrasensory skills are progressing rapidly, Samantha."

"What do you mean?" I asked, perplexed, angered, racking my brain for an explanation of how he had appeared so suddenly in my office. I found none.

He watched me from the corner of the room, hands folded in front of him, smiling serenely. His blondish hair seemed to lift and fall on currents of air that I sure as hell didn't feel.

He cocked his head slightly to one side. "Your image of your sleeping daughter, of course. Your psychic hit is completely accurate."

At any other time I might have rushed the guy. At the least, slamming him up against the wall to get some straight answers. But I held back. For now.

"Who the hell are you, goddammit?" I asked.

"God never damns, Samantha."

"You'd better start talking, mister. Or Ishmael. Or whoever the hell you are."

He smiled again, so warmly that at any other time, he might have won me over. Any other time, that is, other than appearing in my office in the dead of night, while seemingly knowing the details of my sleeping daughter.

"Who do you think I am, Samantha?" he asked.

"A dead man, unless you start talking."

His hair, which hung just over his ears, lifted and fell again, and I was beginning to wonder if I was dreaming. The light particles that formed brilliantly around him seemed to disappear into him, which was a first to me.

"You have grown stronger over these past seven years . . . and more violent, too. The violence is part of your nature now, I suppose, but my hope is that you learn to suppress it. Violence has a way of getting out of control, controlling you." He stepped slowly out of the shadows of my office, away from the bookcase, and stepped around my old recliner. When I don't use the office for work, it's my escape from my kids, where I come to read . . . or sometimes just to cry, although no one knows about the crying.

"Who are you?" I asked again.

"I am that which you think I am, Samantha."

"How do you know what I'm thinking?"

He smiled, but did not answer.

I waited. He waited. My conversation with Fang came roaring back. I shook my head in disbelief. Ishmael smiled even broader and held out his hands a little.

"You're my guardian angel?" I said, unable to hide the disbelief from my voice.

He continuing smiling as he stepped around my recliner. "You sound incredulous, Sam. This coming from someone such as yourself."

"Such as myself? And what would that be? Exactly?"

"A vampire, Samantha Moon. At least, that's what this present generation calls your condition. It has, of course, been called many other things, over many centuries. Admittedly, the curse has flared darker and stronger in this generation."

"I don't understand."

"When enough people speak of something, read of something, believe in something, watch something, ingest something . . . this something begins to take on a life of its own. This something is called into existence."

My head was spinning. "Called into existence from where?"

"From the nether-sphere, Sam. From out there. From the great soup of all ideas and thoughts and creative expressions."

He continued toward me and I held up my hand. "I think you should stop right there."

He did stop. Next to one of my client chairs. "I will not hurt you, Sam. It's against my very nature to hurt you. In fact, quite the opposite."

"Opposite?"

He nodded once, sharply. "My nature is to protect you."

"Because you're my guardian angel."

"Yes, Sam. Because I'm your guardian angel."

9.

"Perhaps we can sit and I can explain," he said. "Your children are safe. Perhaps more safe than you know."

I stared at his pleasantly handsome face as he regarded me in turn. His bright green eyes could have been emerald flames, if such things existed. He radiated waves of strength and confidence and . . . love. My mind reeled.

"Okay, let's sit," I said finally.

We did so, he in one of my client chairs, myself behind my

desk. Ishmael was wearing a light-colored sweater and slacks. Both were unremarkable, although both looked good on him. He sat collected and at ease, his hands folded loosely in his lap. He looked at me calmly, staring into my eyes, although sometimes his eyes would shift to take in other aspects of my face. A small part of me wondered what my hair looked like.

"So," I said, "they call you Ishmael."

His eyes, which shone like twin sparks of emerald fire, flashed brightly with mild amusement. "Yes, they do."

I watched with interest as the bright streaks of light that seemingly only I could see, the bright streaks that illuminated the night world for my eyes, flared more brightly the closer they got to him. Flared, and then disappeared into him. As if the being seated across from me was the source of the light.

Or perhaps its destination.

"So, why are you here, Ishmael?"

He sat perfectly still, perfectly composed, perfectly at ease. He nodded once before he spoke. "I'm here, in part, to tell you that my service is no longer needed."

"And what service is that?"

"The protective service."

My cell phone chimed. I had a text message from someone. At this late hour, it was either from Fang or Kingsley. I ignored it. Truth be known, I kept waiting to either wake up or be told that this was all some big practical joke.

In the meantime, I noted that Ishmael's thoughts were closed to me. In my experience, only other immortals were closed to me, as I was to them. And yet, he seemed to have read my mind.

I tried an experiment and thought: *You're in the protective services because you're a guardian angel?*

His bright green eyes, which had been regarding me serenely from across the desk, widened a little. "Yes, Sam. But we don't call ourselves guardian angels."

You can read my thoughts.

He smiled. "Of course."

To date, only Fang had access to my thoughts, and even then his access seemed limited by my willingness to let him in. Kingsley, a fellow freak, did not have access, nor did I have access to his. Same with the few other immortals I had encountered, who were all closed off to me.

"So, there are others like you?" I asked.

"Of course."

"And what do you call yourselves?"

"We are watchers."

I nodded. "And what do you watch?"

"I watch you, Sam."

"Just watch?"

"Watch and protect and guide."

"Then you've done a shitty job of it," I said suddenly, thinking of my attack seven years ago.

Ishmael kept his eyes on me. After a moment, he said, "I was with you, Sam. Always with you."

"Even while that animal attacked me?" I couldn't help the anger in my voice.

Ishmael said nothing at first, although he slowly raised a hand to his face and rubbed his jaw. He continued to stare at me. Even his minor movements were fluid and hypnotic. "Perhaps you wonder why you were not killed that night, Sam."

"Actually, I do."

"Perhaps you should know that your attacker ended many lives, Samantha. He would have ended yours, too. In fact, he was just seconds from doing so."

The so-called watcher lapsed into silence and continued rubbing his jaw. The physical movement seemed to intrigue him, and now he slowly ran his hand over his own soft lips, feeling them, using his fingertips as a painter would a sable-tipped brush. I had the impression Ishmael rarely manifested in the physical.

I was about to speak, but suddenly found speaking difficult. I was back to that moment in the park, experiencing again the ungodly strength of the thing that had attacked me, the blast of pain of being hurled against a tree . . . the fear of being pounced on by something so much stronger than me. Yes, I should have been dead many times over. So, instead of speaking, I thought: *You saved me.*

Ishmael briefly paused in his exploration of his face. "It wasn't your time."

"Then why let me get attacked at all? Why let me get turned into . . . this thing?"

"Fair questions, Sam, but we are not quite the guardian angels as you think of us. Not the static lighted angel on top of your Christmas tree, assembled by small children in an Asian country. Not the Michelangelo-ish ones painted on ceilings of cathedrals or glorified in Christmas carols and hymns galore. Not the ones in old movies on TV, getting our wings every time someone rings a bell. Not those angels. Not."

"Then what the hell are you?"

"Think of us as custodians of destiny."

I blinked, processing that. "You help fulfill destinies?"

He nodded. "I helped you fulfill your destiny, Sam."

"And my destiny was to become a vampire?"

"Your destiny was to become immortal. Vampirism was one way to achieve that."

"So, I chose this life?"

"You did."

"Why?"

"I'm not at liberty to say."

"Why not?"

"You are not ready for the answer."

I fought through my frustration. "Will I ever find the answer?"

"Yes, someday."

I drummed my fingers along my desk, my thick nails clicking loudly. They sounded fiendish, like the claws of something dark and slimy moving quickly over the floor. I said, "So, in effect, the moment I turned into a vampire, the moment I became immortal myself, you were out of a job."

"That's correct, Sam."

"So, what have you been doing these past seven years?"

"Watching you, Sam. Always watching you."

"Why?"

He looked away, and as he did so, he looked very, very human. And even a little uncomfortable. He kept looking away as he spoke. "Because I'm in love with you, Samantha Moon."

10.

You there, Fang?

I'm always here for you, Moon Dance.

Oh, cut the crap. Half the time, you've got a woman over there.

Not as frequently as you think, Moon Dance. And not since we've met.

But that was over six months ago.

It was.

But why?

It seems the right thing to do. Besides, I've lost interest in dating in general.

Since you met me?

That might have something to do with it, Moon Dance. But don't flatter yourself. Perhaps it was time for me to slow down, to take stock of who I am and what I want in life.

You want to be a vampire.

There was a short pause before he wrote: *Among other things.*

I did not have to dip very far into Fang's mind to know he was referring to me. Truth be known, I didn't much enjoy dipping into Fang's mind. His mind was not healthy, although he was doing an admirable job of dealing with his many issues. I found it ironic that the one mind I was most linked to was a deeply troubled one.

I felt him probing my mind in return and let him do it, giving him access of the events of the night before. A moment later, his words appeared in the IM chat box.

You have got to be kidding, Moon Dance.

I'm not.

Now I have to compete with a freakin' angel, too?

Despite myself, I laughed. I wrote: You're not competing with anyone, Fang. I'm with Kingsley. Happily with Kingsley.

Is that what you told Captain Ahab?

Ishmael, I wrote. And yes. After I spent about three minutes getting over my shock . . . and another two minutes convincing myself I wasn't dreaming, I told him I was happily with Kingsley.

And how did he take it?

He laughed and said he was infinitely patient, that we had all eternity.

Since when do angels cavort with vampires?

He calls himself a watcher.

Either way. I don't like it, Moon Dance.

I didn't think you would.

I need to look into this.

I figured you would.

Was he handsome?

I thought about it, still reeling from the encounter, still wondering if this was all some elaborate practical joke, and, as always, still wondering if I was still back at the hospital, lying comatose after my attack seven years ago. For now, though, I recalled Ishmael's emerald eyes and quiet strength . . . and the love that emanated from him seemingly unconditionally.

I thought about it some more, then wrote: *He was radiant.*

Ah, shit.

11.

I was back at Charlie's single-wide mobile home. Or, rather, standing just outside it.

It was evening and the mobile home park was mostly quiet. I could smell fish frying and meats baking. TV sets glowed in many of the mobile homes. Outside the window in question, where the blinds were a little too narrow and the curtains were a little too thin, I paused and took in the scene.

The area between Charlie's home and the home next to his was covered in white gravel and seemed to serve as a small parking lot. There was also a path that led between the two homes. The path seemed to connect one side of the park to the other. The path led just outside the window in question.

Amazingly, there were no flood lights here, and the whole space was blanketed in darkness. It would have been easy enough for someone to pause outside the window and watch Charlie with his safe.

A narrow road curved through the mobile home park, which

cars occasionally sped along, heedless of children, pets, Santa's reindeer, or vampires.

The question was: Who had been watching Charlie?

Still standing next to Charlie's mobile home, listening to a cacophony of "It's a Holly, Jolly Christmas," TV news anchormen, video game explosions and the clanking of dishes, I closed my eyes and expanded my consciousness out through the park. A trick I had learned a few months ago. In my mind's eye, I saw glimpses of men in Christmas tree print boxers, women in tubs of vanilla bubbles, most of them shaving their legs, and even an older couple getting frisky under the covers. I saw teens playing Xbox and even grown men playing Xbox. I saw men and women talking excitedly, passionately, agitatedly. I saw children crying and playing, but mostly crying and being warned that Santa was still making his list of naughty and nice children. I saw sumptuous dinners being eaten in front of TVs tuned into Donna Reed and Jimmy Stewart but rarely at dinner tables. Gather round the TV, all ye faithful.

I also saw four young men sitting together in the living room of one of the nearby double wide mobile homes. The young men were sitting around bags of weed and the occasional bag of crack cocaine. I saw guns in waistbands and a lot of bad attitudes. There was no sign of Christmas in their house, nor Hanukkah, nor Kwanzaa. A dead giveaway, for sure. No holiday cheer or spirit at all. Of any sort.

My consciousness snapped back, leaving me briefly discombobulated. What I hadn't seen was the stolen safe, but I figured the drug dealers' home was as good a place to start as any.

12.

I knocked on the drug dealers' front door.

I listened with a small grin to the frantic sounds of weed and crack being hidden in everything from toilets to cookie jars, to no doubt deep inside boxers and briefs. I heard a chair fall over. I heard someone curse under his breath. I heard the sounds of shushing and the running of footsteps.

I was tempted to yell, "Police" and really listen to the fireworks within. I might even hear a window crash as one of them makes a run for it.

Instead, I waited, rocking gently back and forth, hands behind my back, just a five-foot-three-inch mother of two confronting your neighborhood drug dealers.

My alarm system was jangling, but I mostly ignored it. I knew, after all, what I was walking into.

Finally, I heard footsteps cautiously approach the door.

An acne-covered Caucasian face peered at me through the door's dirty curtain. The face frowned, and then looked almost comically left and right before he partially opened the door.

"Excuse me," I said. "But my car broke down and I was wondering if I could borrow your phone?"

"My phone? Yo, fuck off, bitch. This ain't no Triple Fucking A." And he promptly slammed the door in my face.

Or tried to.

I stuck out my hand, and the door rebounded off it so hard that it slammed back into the drug dealer's face. I followed the swinging door in, pushing harder. The young punk reached for his nose and for something under his shirt. And since I didn't feel like getting shot tonight, I caught his hand in mid-reach, twisted until he dropped to both knees, and grabbed what he'd been reaching for under his shirt.

I came away with a Smith & Wesson revolver.

I swung the gun around and pointed it at the others, who were all reaching inside their own pants. Apparently, this was the official greeting of drug dealers everywhere.

"Hello, boys," I said. "Hands where I can see them."

"Fuck this shit," said a tall black kid who couldn't have been more than eighteen. He pulled up his shirt, revealing the gleaming walnut handle of an expensive revolver, and before his hand got very far beyond that, I fired the weapon. A bullet hole appeared in the kitchen linoleum next to his foot, perhaps just inches away.

He jumped maybe three feet, screaming like a girl. "Holy sweet Jesus! The bitch is crazy!"

I held the gun steady on the trio who were standing around the kitchen table. All three were in their late teens or early twenties. Hardly drug lords.

I said, "Next one who calls me a bitch gets a bullet in their big toe. Got it?"

No one moved or said anything. The guy next to me whimpered a little, and I realized I was still twisting his arm. I let him go and threw him a little at the same time. He skidded across the kitchen floor. Okay, I might have thrown him ***a lot***.

I next had them drop their guns and kick them over to me. Once done, I gathered the weapons and emptied them of their bullets. I dropped the bullets in one of my jacket pockets. Next, I had the four hoodlums sit around the kitchen table like good little boys.

Or bad boys.

They didn't like a woman telling them what to do. Myself, I was getting a kick out of it. When they were all seated and staring at me sullenly, I hopped up on a stool and held the gun casually in front of me. I couldn't help but notice my feet not only didn't reach the floor, they didn't even reach the first rung of the stool. Still, I swung them happily and looked at my four new friends.

"Well," I said, "here we all are."

The oldest of the four, a Hispanic guy with a tattoo on his neck, leaned forward on his elbows. "Fuck you, bi—" But he stopped himself.

"Nice catch," I said. "You just saved yourself a big toe. Merry Christmas from me."

It was all the guy could do to stay seated. I sensed he wanted to rush me. In fact, I was sure of it. Every now and then, he caught the eye of the black guy across from him. Something passed between them. I didn't care what passed between them.

For now, though, he needed more information, like who the hell I was, and so he stayed seated. For now.

"You ain't no cop," he said.

"Nope."

"You with the feds?"

"Used to be."

"Then what the hell are you?"

"That's the million-dollar question."

They all looked at each other. Two of them shrugged. From

the living room, I heard the *Jeopardy* theme song. I was willing to bet that drug dealers the world over had *Jeopardy* playing in the background. Nothing so innocent as four hoodlums watching *Jeopardy* together.

The Caucasian kid who had greeted me at the door had yet to look me in the eye. He stared down at the table. His wrist was raw and red where I had subdued him. He knew the potential of my strength, and kept his eyes off me and his mouth shut. The fourth guy was another black youth, maybe twenty. He had yet to speak, although he found all of this highly amusing. I sensed he was high as a kite. If I was high as a kite, I would find all this amusing, too. I focused on the Hispanic leader and the talkative black guy.

I said, "Somebody stole something that belonged to me, and I want it back." Technically, that was true, since half of whatever was in the safe was now mine.

"We lovers," said the talkative black guy. "Not thieves."

The high-as-a-kite black guy laughed. The Hispanic guy frowned. The sullen white guy kept being sullen.

"Cut the shit," I said. "I know there's drugs here." I pointed to a Pillsbury Doughboy cookie jar with a crack running up along its doughy body. "I know there're drugs in that cookie jar over there. I know there're drugs in the toilet bowl, and I know there're drugs down all your pants."

The high-as-a-kite black guy giggled nearly uncontrollably. The Hispanic leader sat forward. The energy around him crackled and spat. He said, "What the fuck do you want, lady?"

"I want the safe," I said.

"What safe?"

As I said those words, I watched the others in the room. The talkative black guy blinked. The high black guy continued grinning from ear to ear. The sullen white guy sank a little deeper in his chair. Just a little. Perhaps only a fraction. Not to mention his darkish aura grew darker still.

I had my man.

It was at that moment that I saw the old man in the far corner of the living room. Correction, two old men, as another just materialized. And they weren't exactly men.

They were ghosts.

13.

I jumped off the stool.

As I did so, the Hispanic guy made a move to stand. He didn't move very far. A casual backhand across his face sent him spinning sideways to the floor. The others stayed seated, which wasn't a bad idea. I told them not to move and they mostly didn't, although the high-as-a-kite guy continued to fight through a case of the giggles.

I moved past them, slipping the gun inside my waistband. The backhand smack to their leader would keep the trio quiet for a few minutes.

People don't realize that spirits tend to be just about everywhere. I see them appearing and disappearing almost continuously, sometimes randomly. I'll see them briefly materialize by someone's side, squeeze their hand or hug them, and then flit off again. Usually the object of such affection is left shivering pleasantly. No doubt, the unseen encounter suddenly brought an unexpected memory to the recipient.

And some spirits, like the old lady and her piano, attach themselves to objects, seemingly for decades, although I always suspected that only an aspect of their spirit attached. The majority of their spirit was elsewhere, wherever spirits might go.

Then again, I could be wrong.

As I approached the two old men, they turned toward me. Their attention, I saw, had been centered around something in the far corner of the room, something hidden under a blanket. The spirits themselves were formed of bright filaments of light that coalesced to form shapes. In this case, the shapes of two older men.

They didn't speak and their shapes were only vaguely held together, which suggested to me that these were older spirits. Older, as in having died long ago.

Charlie had said that his father had died nearly two decades ago . . . and no doubt his grandfather had died many years before that. His grandfather and father were certainly two spirits who would have been powerfully connected to an object.

The safe.

The corner of this room smelled of smoke, or of something burned, and as I got closer, I saw tools scattered around the living room that didn't belong there. Hammers. Mallets. Crowbars. Even a blowtorch. The corner of the couch was blackened, too, but that's what happens when you use a blowtorch indoors.

I had the attention of both spirits, who watched me closely, silently, as I reached down and pulled back the corner of a stained quilt, revealing a very old-looking and heavy safe, the lock of which had been blackened by the blowtorch.

But the safe was still locked . . . and that's all that mattered.

14.

As tomorrow was Christmas Eve, I thought it a fitting gift when I delivered the safe to Charlie's door.

Orange County doesn't get snow. Hell, we rarely get rain, but as I approached the door, carrying the safe under one arm, a stiff, cool breeze appeared, and that was good enough. Any weather was good enough at this time of the year.

I knocked on his door to the rhythm of "Jingle bells, jingle bells, jingle all the way" and fat little Rocko jumped from the couch, barking his brains out, until he got a look at me, then he hit the brakes, and scuttled off with his tail between his legs. Thank God Kingsley didn't have the same reaction.

I set the safe down on the wooden deck, noting how the wood sagged mightily under the weight of the safe.

Charlie's round face soon appeared and he gave me a big smile. Charlie, I saw, needed some serious dental work. Except he didn't seem to care that he needed dental work, or that his teeth looked like crooked tombstones. Charlie was just happy to be Charlie.

He was about to slide open his door when he glanced down, and his crooked smile seemed to freeze in place. He blinked. Hard.

Then threw open the door.

I shouldn't have been surprised when he gave me the mother of all hugs, but I was.

• • •

We were in his living room.

I had told him that a friend of mine had helped me lug the heavy safe onto his deck, and I made a show of pretending to struggle with the safe as we moved it from the deck to the center of his living room.

Amid leaning towers of Laserjet printer cartridges, 40's science fiction magazines, and enough clipboards to last two lifetimes, we set the heavy safe down.

Earlier in the night, after my discovery of the safe, I gave the boys ten minutes to clear out before I called the police. Most were gone in five. I kept their weapons and ammunition, which I would hand over to Detective Sherbet of the Fullerton Police Department.

For now, though, it was just me, Charlie, and the safe. And inside, something, neither of us knew what.

The safe was clearly old. So old that it looked like it belonged on the back of a Wells Fargo stage coach. Part of the safe's dial still gleamed brightly, although most of it was covered in blackened soot from the blowtorch. The handle was badly dented, no doubt thanks to the various hammers I had seen lying around.

Still, the safe had held fast, and that's all that mattered.

Charlie stared down at it. So did I. My compensation was in that safe, whatever it might be. Could be gold. Could be old war bonds. Could be jewelry, gemstones, or pirate booty, for all I knew.

I had been tempted to see if my own psychic gifts could penetrate the heavy steel safe, but I had resisted.

"I guess this is it, then," said Charlie. He didn't sound very enthusiastic.

"Do you know the combination?"

He pointed to the upper corner of the safe, where, upon closer inspection, I saw a number etched, 14. Two other numbers were etched into other corners, 29 and 63.

I said them out loud and he nodded. "Don't think of them as three numbers, think of them as six numbers. One, four, two, nine, six and three. With that in mind, what are the two lowest numbers?"

I glanced at them again. "One and two."

He nodded. "Good. And the next lowest?"

"Three and four."

"Good, good. And the two highest?"

"Six and nine."

"You got it," he said, giving me a half smile.

"Twelve, thirty-four, and sixty-nine?"

He nodded. "You're the first person I've ever given the key to. Not even to my own son."

"How old's your son?"

"Twenty-one. But it's too soon to give him the key. My father gave it to me on his deathbed."

"I feel honored," I said, and meant it.

We stared at it some more. He made no move to open it, and I certainly wasn't about to. Somewhere down the hall, one of his piles of junk shifted, groaning, as boulders do in the deserts. The piano, I saw, was gone.

The light particles behind Charlie began coagulating and taking on shape, and shortly, two very faint old men appeared behind him. I noticed the hair on Charlie's arm immediately stood on end, as his body registered the spiritual presence of his father and grandfather, even if his mind hadn't. Charlie absently rubbed his arms.

"Well, let's get on with it," he said, and reached down for the safe.

As he did so, I said, "You really don't want to open the safe, do you, Charlie?"

"I do. Really, I do. A deal's a deal, and I want to pay you. Your half."

"But wouldn't you rather pass it along to your own boy?"

"Without you, Ms. Moon, I would have nothing to pass on to my kid. Besides, it's really a silly tradition."

"No, it's not. It's about family."

"We've been keeping this thing going for years and it's impractical at best, like a joke from beyond the grave."

"I think it's an amazing tradition," I said.

He didn't say it, but his body language suggested he thought so, too. He said, "Well, it is kind of fun not knowing what's in this thing. I mean, it could be anything, right? But I suppose it's time to find out once and for all?"

He made a move for the safe again, but he didn't get very far, mostly because I grabbed his wrist. He shivered at my cold touch.

I said, "This isn't right."

"A deal's a deal, Ms. Moon. Besides, I have no other way of repaying you."

I thought about that, then looked around. "Not true. You have enough junk to stock a dozen houses. There's got to be something in here that I want."

"What are you saying, Ms. Moon?"

"I'm saying, let me pick something out of your junk, and the safe is yours. Keep it in your family. Pass it along to your son."

He processed that information, and I saw the relief ripple through him and his shining aura. "Are you sure?"

"As sure as I've ever been."

"But aren't you a little bit curious what's in the safe?"

"More than you know," and as I said those words, I briefly closed my eyes, and expanded my consciousness throughout the room, and as I did so, two things made me gasp.

The first was the contents of the safe, which I saw clearly. The second was what I saw resting inside a wooden box deep under a pile of newspapers.

Charlie was watching me curiously. "Are you okay?"

"Er, yes," I said, then patted him on the shoulder. "I would suggest you find a much better place for your safe."

"I will."

"A very safe place."

"You think the contents are valuable?"

I thought of the two old spirits, Charlie's father and grandfather. I thought of Charlie's own son and the unique bond that kept the generations connected. The safe. I also saw in my mind's eye the tightly rolled vellum document that might just be the rarest of all American documents, a document signed by our founding fathers, centuries ago. A document thought to be lost . . . until now.

Then again, I could be wrong.

Next, I moved through the piles of junk and headed to the far corner of the room. There, I began moving aside old newspapers and magazines, until I finally uncovered an ornately carved box.

I picked it up carefully, my hands trembling.

Slowly, I opened the lid . . .

Unbelievable.

Inside was another golden medallion. This time, the three roses were cut from brilliant amethysts.

Charlie was looking over my shoulder. "Oh, that. I got it at an estate sale a while back. In Fullerton. Get this, some old guy was murdered by some nut with a crossbow. Anyway, it's gold, I think. Probably worth a lot. I've been keeping it for a rainy day." He paused. "Truth be known, it kind of gives me the creeps. You can have it if you want."

I closed the lid and held out my hand. "Merry Christmas."

But Charlie had other designs on me. He wrapped me in a huge, smothering hug. "Merry Christmas, Ms. Moon!"

15.

With the box sitting safely on the seat next to me, I had just pulled out of Charlie's mobile home park when my cell rang. It was Fang.

"Merry Christmas," I said.

"That sounds odd coming from a vampire," said Fang.

"Why, because I'm a creature of the night?"

"Something like that."

"I'll remind you that Santa does his best work at night."

"Santa isn't real."

"I thought the same about vampires," I said. "And someone recently told me that if people believe in something hard enough and long enough, it becomes true."

Fang laughed. "Enough about Santa Claus. I've got news. Your watcher friend is likely a fallen angel."

"He's no demon, Fang."

"Have you ever met a demon, Moon Dance?"

"I don't know," I said, recalling meeting Kingsley in my hotel room when he had fully transformed into a werewolf. The thing living inside him was as close to a demon as I've ever met. "I just know he's not evil."

"At least not yet."

"What, exactly, is a fallen angel?"

"A spiritual being that no longer commits itself to helping others evolve. In fact, quite the opposite."

"A being who helps others devolve?"

"Close. A being who spreads fear. Living in fear, any kind of fear, separates the individual from the Creator."

My head began to throb. Headaches, for me, rarely lasted more than a few minutes. I chewed my lip and drove and didn't like any of this. I said, "And so, what, one day he decides to turn bad?"

"It probably wasn't just one day, Moon Dance. It had probably been a long time coming."

"He said he's no longer bound to me . . ."

"If he was your guardian angel, that makes sense. Why should one immortal protect another?"

"Now that he's not bound to me . . ."

"Right," said Fang, picking up on my thoughts. "Now that he's not bound to you, he's free to approach me. A sort of metaphysical loophole." Fang paused. "I had a thought, Moon Dance, and a not very pleasant one."

"Tell me."

"What if he *allowed* you to be attacked?"

"What do you mean?"

"What if he not only allowed you to be attacked, but he had planned the whole night?"

"But why?" But even as I asked the question, I knew the answer.

Fang voiced it for me. "To turn you, Moon Dance. To turn you into that which he could finally approach. Or that which he could finally love."

I shuddered as I drove on into the night, wending my way now through the streets of Yorba Linda. "But he said my destiny was to become immortal. To become a vampire."

"Perhaps. Or perhaps he wasn't telling you the truth."

"But isn't he, you know, obligated to protect me?"

"I don't know, Moon Dance. We're talking about the spirit world, something I'm not privy to. But I am familiar with the concept of spirit guides and guardian angels. From my understanding, yes, such beings are generally there to guide and protect and nurture. Unless . . ."

"Unless what?" I asked.

"Unless they decide not to."

"A fallen angel," I said.

"Exactly."

16.

Christmas Day, late.

They were all here. Mary Lou, her husband, and three kids. Her three kids were about Tammy's and Anthony's ages, and they mostly all got along. Except when playing video games. Then, all bets were off.

Kingsley was here, too, and he looked absolutely sumptuous in his thick sweater and scarf, which hung loosely over a chest that should be illegal in most states. Kingsley wasn't a slender man. He was thick and hulking and as yummy as they get.

Detective Sherbet and his lovely Hungarian wife swung by to say hello. He also pulled me aside and caught me up on another killing. Turns out the city of Fullerton had a bona fide serial killer. This would be the fifth body in as many months. He wanted me to come by the department tomorrow and compare notes, since I was an official consultant on the case. Sherbet was one of the few people who knew my super-secret identity. He and his wife stayed just long enough to drink some hot cider and eat some Christmas brownies, before moving on to another party.

Danny even stopped by to drop off the kids' presents. As he stood at the front door, peering over me into a home we had once shared together, no doubt taking in the dollar store decorations, the aromas, the laughter, and even the corny Christmas music, he looked positively miserable and envious. I had it on good word that his relationship with his secretary was over. I also had it on good word that she was suing him for sexual harassment. Nice. But don't feel too bad for the guy. Apparently, he was now dating one of his strippers. Yes, my ex-husband, besides being an ambulance chaser, was also part-owner of a strip club in Colton.

Right. I couldn't be more proud.

As we stood awkwardly at the door, I sensed Kingsley watching us from within the living room, his hulking form backlit by the Christmas tree. Danny, it seemed, was waiting for an invitation to come in. This coming from a guy who was actively trying to ruin me. I thanked him for the presents, wished him a merry Christmas and, against my better judgment, gave him a half-hearted offer to come in, which he pounced on. He pushed past me and immediately went over to kitchen table where he began piling snacks on a paper plate.

Watching him, I reminded myself that it was Christmas, a day when even porn kings and slimeballs were given a one-day pardon.

When it came time for dinner, I thought of Fang alone in his little apartment. I had invited him, too, but was secretly relieved when he declined. He and Kingsley in the same room would have made everyone uncomfortable. Yes, Kingsley knew all about Fang. I believe in honesty and openness in a relationship. To a degree. Kingsley didn't need to know about Fang's criminal past.

I kept myself busy serving dinner, so busy that everyone forgot that I hadn't actually eaten. I would eat later tonight, with Kingsley. A rather nontraditional holiday meal, you could say.

With dinner over and dessert being served, I thought it best to step outside and get some fresh air. I excused myself, patting Kingsley's meaty thigh. He was deep in a conversation with, of all people, my ex-husband. Two attorneys talking shop.

Blech.

My house is small, but I have a big yard. I followed a curving, cement path that led from my front door to my garage, a path I had sprinted across many times during the heat of the day, each time gasping for breath and sometimes literally thinking I couldn't take another step. But I did it each and every day to pick up my kids from school.

A small price to pay.

The sun had long ago set. I felt strong and clear-headed. Cars were parked seemingly randomly outside my house. I lived in a narrow cul-de-sac, and parking here was always a challenge. Especially for Kingsley, who was a surprisingly bad parker. Even now, his black Escalade barely touching the curb, with most of the rear end blocking my driveway.

Pathetic. I expected more from an immortal with decades of driving experience.

I slipped my hands into my coat pocket and looked up into the evening sky. This would have been a good night for flying. Clear, cool skies, with Christmas tree lights sparkling far below. In fact, maybe I would try to get up tonight. Maybe fly out to see Kingsley later.

Maybe.

As I stepped out from behind the comically-parked Cadillac, I saw him standing there in the middle of the street, watching me.

Ishmael.

17.

Once again, I gasped.

"I didn't mean to startle you, Samantha."

"You have a way of doing that."

"Sometimes, I forget how easily humans startle. Humans . . . and vampires."

"I'm not human?"

"You haven't been human for many years, Sam."

"I feel human."

"Do you feel human when you're soaring above the earth?"

He stepped closer to me, hands clasped behind his back. To my eyes he seemed a little taller than I remembered.

He nodded. "I am taller, Sam. I am whatever I choose to be."

Glowing particles of light swarmed around him . . . and disappeared into him. He was a being unlike anything I had ever seen. And to be clear, I've seen some weird shit.

But as he drew closer, walking casually with his hands behind his back, his movements so fluid and smooth that he appeared to be walking on air, I saw something else. Intermixed within the light particles were darker particles. The darker particles were still new to me . . . and still alarming. Never had I seen anything so black. Worse, the dark particles seemed to contaminate the light, spreading like a disease.

"A disease?" he said, nodding thoughtfully. "An interesting choice of words, since you yourself often call the darkness living within you a disease."

"There is no darkness in me."

Ishmael threw back his head and laughed, and it was the first time he had expressed real emotion. His first seeming loss of control. Everything prior to that, every move, every word, had seemed almost rehearsed.

"What do you think keeps you alive, Samantha Moon? What do you think you feed each and every time you consume blood? You're feeding the thing that lives within you."

"I am still me."

"Or so you think."

"I want you to leave."

He continued to approach me, continued his slow glide over the street tarmac. "You know so little, my dear. But I can show you so much. I can reveal it all to you. I can help you fight that which lives within you, that which is slowly consuming you."

Now he stood before me and, son of a bitch, he was even taller than just a few seconds before. By at least another six inches. Surely, he was taller now than even Kingsley.

I must be dreaming, I thought.

"You're not dreaming, Sam."

"Get the hell out of my head."

"I'm afraid I can't do that."

"Why?"

He reached out and touched me, running his fingers under my chin, lifting my face up to his. I shivered. His touch was hot. Almost superheated. "I don't want to get out of your head. Your thoughts are the only place I have sanctuary."

"I know what you are, and I'm telling you to leave me alone."

"Oh? And what am I, Sam?"

"A demon."

I could see the heartbreak in his eyes. He thought he could see me, but for the first time I was seeing him. He was lost, just as I felt lost sometimes. He had needs and desires, just as I did, and on this night, in the middle of this street, his eyes told me everything I needed to know. He was in love with me.

Could demons love? I didn't know, but I doubted it.

"Demon is such an ugly word, Sam."

"Then what are you?"

"I said it was ugly, I didn't say it was inaccurate."

I shuddered. The blackness swirled around him like black worms, weaving in and out of the light. "You look different."

"I am different. I gave up much to be with you, Sam."

"And you took much from me."

"I gave you immortality."

"You stole my humanity. You abused your power in the name of love. Or what you think of as love. You have put a curse on me that will never be fully released. You put me in danger and my own children in danger."

He laughed. "Your own immortality saved your boy from an agonizing death."

"If I had known that my immortality would be the only thing that would save my child, yes, I would have begged you to allow me to be attacked. To allow me to become what I am. But you can't claim responsibility for a twist of fate."

Then again, maybe he could. I was in uncharted territory here. How much of the future did Ishmael know? Had he known that my son would acquire a terminal disease? I didn't know. Truth was, I didn't know what watchers were capable of and not capable of. But I knew something about free will, and I suspected Ishmael was pulling my strings like a puppet master. He was a person, a being, who had abused his influence.

"No," he said, reading my thoughts. "A person in love."

"You turned me into a monster," I said.

"Not a monster, Sam. An immortal. And the darkness that lives within you can be controlled. I can show you how. I can show you so many things."

"You *could* show me how? You *could* show me many things? Your love is conditional. Your love is not real. Whatever illusion you have about you and me ends tonight. You were given an amazing gift by the Almighty and you squandered it over illusions of love. You might have been able to read my thoughts, but you lacked something. Subtext. Hearing my thoughts isn't the same as experiencing my heart. Because if you ever had, you would have never done what you did to me on that night seven years ago."

"You have it all wrong, Sam. It was your destiny to become that which you are. I only helped . . . facilitate the process."

"I don't believe you."

"Believe what you will. But we are destined to be together, Samantha Moon. And when you are done playing with your dog, Kingsley, I will return for you."

And what happened next challenged my sanity. The solid man who had been standing before me, faded from view, and the particles of light that had been swarming around him winked out of existence, too.

I was left standing alone in the street.

18.

I was flying over Orange County.

The wind was cold, but my thick hide kept me comfortable. I was above a smattering of clouds, and far below, Christmas lights twinkled endlessly. From up here, it was very obvious that Californians were very much into the Christmas spirit.

I angled a little higher, caught a powerful jetstream, and was hurled along at a glorious rate. My thick, leathery wings were stretched taut, and a part of me wanted to just keep on flying, endlessly, to continuously trail behind the setting sun, to live in perpetual darkness forever.

A guardian angel had professed his love for me. I suspected it was a misguided love. I suspected he was already well on his way to the dark side, that he had only used me to help facilitate the process. Whatever that process was.

And yet . . .

And yet, I felt his love for me. It had been real. I had seen it in his eyes, and heard it in his voice.

You can't fake love.

Or can you?

Yet, he could have gone about it a thousand different ways, a thousand better ways. Any of which would have gotten a better response from me.

We are destined to be together, he had said.

The San Gabriel Mountains appeared in the north, and I followed the contour of the ridge-line, rising and falling with the peaks and valleys, just a few feet above the pines and snow-covered cornices. Yes, even Southern California gets snow, four thousand feet up.

I suspected that Ishmael had to break his connection to me, whatever that connection was. I suspected that, as my watcher, he was bound to me as my guardian.

But once I became immortal, all bets were off.

I angled up, followed a mountainous ridge, and when the ridge dropped away, I kept angling up, flapping my wings harder and harder. Up I went, surging through vaporous clouds, blinded, until finally I broke through.

Above me was the half moon, shining brilliantly. I flew toward it, higher and higher, until ice crystals formed on my wings, until all oxygen disappeared in the air.

And there I hovered, briefly, at the far edges of our atmosphere, pondering destiny, until finally I tucked in my own wings and dove down, speeding through the night, faster than I had ever flown before . . .

After all, Christmas was over and I had a killer to find.

[THE END]

A SHORT STORY

Vampire Dreams

Vampire Dreams

The dream came again.

It was the third dream in as many days. Normally I don't dream. Normally I close my eyes and sink into an eternal darkness, and don't awaken until the persistent blaring of my alarm clock pulls me out of whatever black chasm I had descended into. Sure, I might have major issues, but insomnia isn't one of them.

Except sometimes I do dream. I dreamed of Kingsley and the ruby-rose medallion last year. I've dreamed of Fang before, especially prior to meeting him. Not so much anymore. I suspect having Kingsley in my life has something to do with that.

And now, for the past three days, the dreams with the girl. I have no clue who she is. Young, cute, dressed in a waitress uniform, sitting on a bus bench, just prior to a runaway city bus obliterating her. The same dream. Over and over.

Now, as I sat up in bed, gasping, blinking hard as my alarm blared on the bedside table next to me, I saw her broken body again. Hell, I could even smell her blood.

Jesus.

Waking up in the middle of the day was hard enough. Waking up in the middle of the day to images like that was just plain unfair. So I sat there for a few minutes, rubbing my face, listening to the alarm, seeing her broken body, smelling her spilled blood. And through the pulsating alarm, I could hear her cries . . . until she could cry no more.

Jesus.

I got out of bed. Time to do some chores, then off to pick up the children. In the living room, where the window shades were always drawn tight, I automatically turned on Judge Judy.

I was sitting in my minivan, parked on the side of the road.

Sundown was minutes away, and I was feeling anxious. The way I always felt just before the sun set. Excited. Relieved. Impatient. Desperate. Incomplete.

I forced myself to calm down.

Not an easy thing to do. Not at this hour.

I was on my way to see Detective Sherbet. He had a case for me. A big case. Someone was leaving dead bodies around Fullerton. Bodies drained of blood.

My son was heavy on my heart, but I was able to console myself with the knowledge that he seemed so . . . comfortable with who he was. And why shouldn't he? He was just a growing boy, a boy who happened to be stronger than everyone else at his school. Sure, he might think he was a little freaky. But this was a good freaky, wasn't it?

I nodded and wiped a tear that had somehow found its way to my cheekbone. "Yes," I whispered. "A good freaky."

I was going to have to tell him. I knew that. He had to know.

"He has to know," I said to no one.

I was parked along Harbor Boulevard. Not too far from mine and Kingsley's favorite restaurant . . . and not too far from Hero's, either, where Fang worked. I checked my watch. Yup, he would be working now. Just around the corner. Serving drinks and dreaming of becoming a vampire. Fang, with his freaky teeth hanging from his neck.

Lots of freaky going on here.

I was parked on Amerige Street, facing east.

In front of me, maybe twenty feet away, was Harbor Boulevard, which ran north and south. Diagonal from me, across Harbor, was a familiar bus bench and a u-shaped hedge. It was the same bus bench and hedge I had seen in my dream. I was sure of it.

Seeing it had surprised me, so much so that I stopped my minivan and just stared.

The same bus bench. The same hedge. Minus the dead girl.

I knew Harbor like the back of my hand, but, during the dream, I hadn't been aware that it was *this* bus bench, on *this* section of street.

What the hell was going on?

I didn't know, but I decided to wait out the final few minutes of the day. Hell, I might as well be firing on all cylinders when I met with Sherbet in a few minutes. Didn't hurt to have a clear mind when discussing a serial killer.

So I waited. And I watched.

I knew the sun was inching closer to the horizon without having to look at it. I always knew where the sun was. Always. Just as I knew it was sitting on the far horizon, slipping slowly away.

Too slowly.

I made fists in my lap. Two small, white, knobby fists. I saw the sun in my mind's eye. Orange and burning. So beautiful that it hurt. Halfway above the horizon. Now a quarter. Slipping ever lower.

Hurry, hurry.

I opened my hands, closed them again.

And then it happened. Actually, two things happened simultaneously:

First, the sun dropped below the horizon and relief flooded my system. The night was truly my drug.

Second, I saw her.

The broken girl from my dreams.

Sitting down now on the bus bench.

I drummed my fingers on the steering wheel, thinking.

My position on Amerige afforded a perfect view of the bus bench along Harbor, where cars zipped up and down. A few pedestrians, too. Downtown Fullerton was a happening, vibrant place, filled with banks, coffee shops, and restaurants. The local congressman had an office here, too, which sort of added to the air of coolness.

Except I wasn't thinking about the congressman or the fact that I hadn't had a coffee in nearly seven years.

I was trying to decide what to do.

Unlike someone I know, I never asked to be a vampire. And I never asked to be saddled with the many side effects of vampirism, either. One such side effect was enhanced extrasensory perception. Or ESP. Over the years, this ability, this psychic ability, had grown stronger.

But so far, I had never been able to predict the future. Or even see the future.

Until now.

So, as I sat in my minivan, I was beginning to get a very bad feeling. I suspected things were about to go very, very badly for the young lady sitting on the bus bench.

Unless, of course, I helped.

I drummed my fingers some more, watching the girl through the windshield. She was now leaning back on the bench, looking down at her cell phone. As comfortable as could be. As peaceful as could be. She was cute and petite. Maybe even smaller than me, although I had her by a few pounds. Normally this would be cause for some minor jealousy, but I wasn't feeling any jealously now.

No, I was worried sick.

Interestingly, I have warning bells that alert me to danger . . . but danger only to myself. Not to others. Presently, my inner alarm was quiet as the grave.

Maybe my dream was wrong.

Maybe.

Except everything looked the same. The same girl. Same bus bench. Same street. Same surrounding bushes. The only thing that was missing was the out-of-control bus.

It's coming, I thought. *And it's coming soon.*

The girl on the bench suddenly laughed and appeared to text something rapidly on her phone. It was a similar laugh I had heard in my dream. I had seen all this before. Three different times, in fact.

And it was not going to end well for this young girl.

No, it was going to end very, very badly.

And soon.

Unless I did something about it.

I stepped out of my van.

• • •

The sun had set minutes earlier and I felt like a million bucks. Or, more accurately, I felt like a freaky, nearly invincible, blood-sucking creature of the night who will probably never sniff a million bucks.

Potatoes, po*tat*oes.

I inhaled the evening air—the sunless air—supercharging my undead body. Feeling stronger than I ever had, I beeped my minivan locked out of instinct, shoved the keys in my front pocket, and headed across the street.

Like a good pedestrian, I waited for the light to turn green before I crossed Harbor going east. As I did so, I kept my eyes on the young girl, who was currently digging in her handbag for something. That something turned out to be a black e-book reader. My guess was a Kindle. Then again, I'd only just gotten a Kindle this Christmas, so what the hell did I know?

She turned it on and sat back and crossed her legs. Her left foot kicked up and down. I watched all of this as I continued across the street.

She was still south of me; Amerige Street still separated us.

Now, as I waited for this light to turn green, I watched her suddenly look up and frown. She turned and looked behind her. I looked, too. There was no sign of a bus anywhere. She frowned some more and almost reluctantly went back to her Kindle.

As I waited for the light, frowning myself, I reflected that people were more psychic than they realized. Had she sensed some impending doom? Had her body given her its own warning bell, and she chose to ignore it?

I didn't know, but it was something to think about as my light finally turned green, and I crossed Amerige street, heading south on Harbor.

I suddenly felt foolish.

It was just a dream, after all. Granted, a very freaky dream. But a dream nonetheless. And yet . . .

And yet . . . all the pieces of the puzzle were here. Everything. From the girl, to the bench, to the hedge behind her. Everything except the runaway bus.

And one thing was certain: A bus was coming.

Yes, I felt foolish, but if I've learned anything over these past seven years, it's to expect the unexpected. A prophetic dream seemed strange as hell, sure. But no stranger than drinking blood and changing into a giant vampire bat.

God, I'm such a freak.

So, I moved toward her a little more confidently, even picking up my pace. I passed a few pedestrians, couples mostly, no doubt on their way to one of the many downtown restaurants. No one paid me any mind, and no one paid the girl any mind, either. No one but me.

Your friendly neighborhood vampire.

So how do you warn someone of danger?

I didn't know, but I was going to figure it out. Feeling nervous and more than a little anxious, I sat on the far end of the bus bench. She looked up as I did so, and I smiled. The smile caught her off guard. She gave me a weird half-smile, as if she'd never smiled at a stranger before. Good enough.

I sat straight, knees together, wringing my hands, the very picture of the crazy bus lady.

Maybe I am crazy, I thought.

Maybe. But the dream was real.

I leaned forward a little and looked down Harbor Boulevard. There, about two blocks down, was the bus. The same bus from my dreams. I'm sure of it. Down to the red stripe over the wide grill. Presently, it was unloading some passengers as many more boarded. No doubt making its last stop before it would stop here . . . for her. Or us. I hadn't ridden on a bus in years, and I had no plans to ride this one.

And I had no plans to watch a young girl die today, either.

The bus lurched forward again. The crawling marquee over the windshield proclaimed it was heading toward Fullerton College, which was up the street past us on Chapman.

I swallowed hard, forced myself to calm down. To think.

I was a mom, dammit. I had two kids. I watched *Survivor*. I wasn't a hero. I wasn't something out of a comic book. Sure, I was freaky as hell, but I never asked for any of this.

I rocked a little on the bench as the bus drew ever closer.

So how do you walk up to a complete stranger and tell them

you'd been dreaming of their death? I didn't know, but I was going to have to think of something. And quick.

Think, Sam.

A favorite writer of mine likes to have his characters "cudgel their balky brains." I was beginning to appreciate that phrase. My balky brain needed some cudgeling, some sense knocked into it. Something, anything to kick start it.

Just talk to her, I thought. *Do something.*

"What kind of reader is that?" I asked.

She looked up at me again. This time she wasn't smiling. After all, to smile at the crazy street lady would only encourage her, right?

"Kindle," she said simply, emotionlessly, and went back to reading. She was wearing a Cocoa's uniform: black slacks, red pin-striped, short-sleeved blouse.

"Do you like it?"

"It's okay I guess." She kept her head down.

The bus was a block away. Waiting at a red light, it looked menacing as hell, especially if you imagined it careening out-of-control, bounding up the curb like an enraged beast.

Sweet Jesus.

I swallowed my pride and said, in as non-threatening a voice as I could, "This is going to sound crazy"—words, I'm sure, every person waiting at a bus stop wants to hear—"but I believe your bus is going to . . . be involved in some sort of accident. I'm sorry. I know I sound like a crazy woman, but I really, really think you should listen to me."

Her eyes shot up as the Kindle came down.

"What?"

The bus was a half block away and picking up speed. From here I could see the driver. An older man, both hands securely on the steering wheel, staring intently ahead. The picture of professionalism. There were a few passengers further back, I could see, but it was impossible to tell how many. I could hear the bus's big engine growling, its shocks squeaking as it bounced over the pavement.

When I looked back at the girl, I saw that she was now sitting as far away from me as possible.

I spoke urgently now, admitting to something I rarely admitted to anyone, let alone a stranger. "Look, I see things. I know things. I'm weird like that, I know. But I'm here now to warn you."

"Warn me, why?"

"You're going to die."

She stared at me, long and hard. Sure, I was expecting a reaction, but not the one I received. As she stared at me, and as the bus bore down on us, she burst out laughing. "Who set you up? Dillon? That fucker. Where is he? Is he filming this shit? What are you, like, his mom or something?"

"Or something. Look, I don't know who Dillon is, but—"

The laughter abruptly stopped. She leaned toward me aggressively. "Then what the fuck do you want, lady? Money? I don't have any money. Drugs? I don't have that shit, either."

"All I want is for you to just move. To get up. Stand ten or twenty feet away. Maybe thirty."

"Maybe you should go fuck yourself."

The bus grew louder. It blotted out most of the street. The driver sat high above us. He looked alert and clear-headed. He didn't look like someone who was about to lose control of a massive vehicle that, if out-of-control, might as well be a Sherman tank.

I sat forward, ready to spring into action. Would I be fast enough to save the girl? Should I just grab her now and haul her out off the bench and over the far wall?

I nearly did. In fact, I had just started to rise off the bench when something happened.

That something was the hiss of air brakes.

The bus was stopping.

I didn't relax until the bus had fully stopped in front of us. And when it did, the girl leaped to her feet, throwing her bag over a shoulder. She turned to me as the bus door hissed open. "Nice call, bitch." She stepped inside, looked back at me once, and promptly flipped me the bird.

The bus driver leaned toward me. An elderly man with a red face. "Hey lady, you coming in or what?"

"No, sorry," I said, my voice trailing off. "Wrong bus."

He shrugged, reached for a lever, shut the door. A moment later, the bus was heading north again on Harbor Boulevard, leaving me sitting alone and confused as hell. I didn't know whether or not to feel relieved or irritated.

What the hell had just happened?

I didn't know, but the very bus I had seen smashing into the cement bench and crushing the young girl in the waitress uniform had just passed me by. And just as that thought crossed my mind, just as the bus crossed the next intersection, I looked down at the bench beneath me.

It was wooden.

I snapped my head up, searching desperately ahead. Yes, there was another bus stop two blocks away. A bus stop that was directly in front of a Cocoa's restaurant—

Where a young waitress—wearing the same black slacks and pin-striped blouse—was sitting, on what was surely a *cement* bench. A young girl digging in a handbag and not paying attention to the bus bearing down on her.

I leaped to my feet, sprinted down the sidewalk. I would never get there in time, not even with my freaky enhanced speed. And the bus, if anything, was picking up speed.

All while the girl continued digging in her bag.

Shit.

I ran faster, passing people on the street. Many turned to watch me speed by. Many didn't care or notice.

Someone screamed far ahead. I looked up and saw why. The bus was slewing across the lane, bouncing into the curb. Metal sparked from the rims.

The light on Amerige Street was mercifully green, and I dashed across it, running faster than I ever had before, but knowing I would never make it in time.

And knowing there was only one thing I could . . .

A single flame appeared in my thoughts.

I focused on the flame and ran and dodged signs and people and trees. As the flame grew brighter, I leaped as high as I could, holding my arms out. I convulsed. My clothing burst from my body. And when I opened my eyes again, giant, black, leathery wings stretched out far and wide to either side. Wings that were once my arms. And instead of falling back to the sidewalk, I sailed forward, low to the ground.

Someone screamed behind me. Two, three, four screams.

A tree was fast approaching. I flapped my wings hard, gaining altitude—and just clipped the tree. A car to my left hit its brakes, squealing. Another car hit its brakes. More squealing, but mercifully I didn't hear the sounds of cars crashing.

The building next to me was mostly smoked glass, nearly as dark as my thick hide. I hoped it camouflaged me enough to not cause a major panic.

Below, the bus careened off a small tree, flattening it, scattering leaves and birds everywhere.

I flapped my wings faster, racing forward. Wind thundered over me. One or two people below stopped and pointed at me, but most people were watching the out-of-control bus, oblivious that something giant and horrific was speeding through the night air just a few feet above their heads.

The bus bounced and jolted—and bounded onto the curb like something hungry and destructive. Now I heard screaming from inside the bus. What had happened to the driver?

I didn't know, and I had no time to think about it. I had seen in my dreams what happens to this poor girl, and it's not pretty. And, just like in my dreams, she sat directly in the path of the runaway bus.

I angled my wings and rocketed down. I was still about a half a city block away.

The bus slammed into another tree, plowed through a hedge, obliterated a trash can. Someone in its path dove out of the way, saving themselves.

The girl on the bench still hadn't looked up, was still clueless, was still rocking out to whatever the hell she was listening to.

Someone yelled at her from across the street, waving their arms in vain trying to get her attention.

No luck. Now she suddenly laughed at something. Perhaps a funny lyric in the song. Perhaps recalling a funny conversation she'd had today. Either way, it was the same laugh from my dreams.

I dropped from the sky, talons extended. A bird of prey. A beast of prey. The bus was now half on the curb, half on the street, rumbling inevitably toward the girl.

I sliced through the air. A black streak. A black streak with claws and teeth and wings.

People were screaming. The girl finally looked up.

She screamed too, tried to run.

Too late. The bus was upon her.

Except, I was upon her, too. Or, rather, on top of her. Just as the bus blasted through the cement bench, my clawed talons snatched her from under her arms and around her shoulders.

I beat my wings hard, lifting the girl, who screamed and twisted beneath me. I lifted her higher and higher, all while I heard the destruction below. Concrete and metal colliding. Horns honking. More screaming than I had ever heard in my life.

Soon, we were above the highest building.

Near the corner of the roof, near a door I suspected led to stairs, I set her down.

She was still screaming as she crumpled into a heap. I saw immediately that her clothing was torn where I had grabbed her. Blood oozed from a few wounds as well. Her shoulders, I was certain, were dislocated.

But at least she was alive.

I didn't linger.

I flapped my wings hard and rocketed up into the night sky.

There was much talk about the bus crash.

The driver, an old man who was nearing retirement, had suffered a massive heart attack. He'd fallen over the steering wheel, and it had taken many passengers to finally wrestle him off and gain control of the bus. And despite going up the curb of a busy, downtown sidewalk, no one had been seriously injured.

Much had been made of the creature that had appeared. A creature witnessed by many people. Also, much had been made of the girl who was seen on the park bench in one instant, and then seemingly gone the next. Only to reappear miraculously on a nearby rooftop. Injured but safe.

There was much talk of a guardian angel.

Or a guardian *something*, since those who had seen the creature proclaimed it was no angel.

A demon, if anything.

I knew all of this because Detective Sherbet of the Fullerton Police Department had talked to me about it, confirming that it had been me. Secretly, of course, as he knew most of my secrets. He reminded me that I wasn't a superhero, but he also thanked me.

Most intriguing were the reports of a naked woman seen sneaking through town, only to disappear into a minivan.

And drive off.

I knew that hide-a-key would come in handy.

[THE END]

[OTHER BOOKS BY J.R. RAIN]

The Lost Ark
The Body Departed

THE JIM KNIGHTHORSE SERIES
Dark Horse
The Mummy Case
Hail Mary

ELVIS MYSTERY SERIES
Elvis Has Not Left the Building
You Ain't Nothin' But a Hound Dog (coming soon)

THE SPINOZA SERIES
The Vampire With the Dragon Tattoo
The Vampire Who Played Dead
The Vampire in the Iron Mask (coming soon)

THE GRAIL QUEST TRILOGY
Arthur
Merlin (coming soon)

WITH SCOTT NICHOLSON
Cursed!
Ghost College
The Vampire Club

WITH PIERS ANTHONY
Aladdin Relighted
Aladdin Sins Bad

WITH SCOTT NICHOLSON AND H.T. NIGHT
Bad Blood

SHORT STORIES
The Bleeder and Other Stories
Teeth and Other Stories
Vampire Nights and Other Stories
Vampire Blues: Four Stories
Vampire Rain and Other Stories

SCREENPLAYS
Judas Silver
Lost Eden

SHORT STORY ANTHOLOGIES
Vampires, Zombies and Ghosts, Oh My!

NON-FICTION
The Rain Interviews (2008-2011)

ABOUT THE AUTHOR

J.R. RAIN is an ex-private investigator who now lives in a small house on a small island with his small dog, Sadie, who has more energy than Robin Williams. Please visit him at www.jrrain.com.